A Long Way from Home

Bilingual Press/Editorial Bilingüe

General Editor
    Gary D. Keller

Managing Editor
    Karen S. Van Hooft

Senior Editor
    Mary M. Keller

Assistant Editor
    Linda St. George Thurston

Editorial Board
    Juan Goytisolo
    Francisco Jiménez
    Eduardo Rivera
    Severo Sarduy
    Mario Vargas Llosa

Editorial Consultant
    Juliette L. Spence

Address:
Bilingual Review/Press
Hispanic Research Center
Arizona State University
Tempe, Arizona 85287

(602) 965-3867

A Long Way from Home

Clásicos Chicanos/Chicano Classics 4

Gordon Kahn

Bilingual Press/Editorial Bilingüe
TEMPE, ARIZONA

Library of Congress Cataloging-in-Publication Data

Kahn, Gordon.
  A long way from home.

  (Clásicos chicanos = Chicano classics ; 4)
  I. Title. II. Series: Clásicos chicanos ; 4.
PS3561.A364L66   1989   813'.54   88-34238
ISBN 0-916950-90-5

PRINTED IN THE UNITED STATES OF AMERICA

Cover design by Christopher J. Bidlack

Acknowledgments

This volume is supported by a grant from the National Endowment for the Arts in Washington, D.C., a Federal agency.

About Clásicos Chicanos/Chicano Classics and *A Long Way from Home*

The Clásicos Chicanos/Chicano Classics series is intended to ensure the accessibility over the long term of deserving works of Chicano literature and culture that have become unavailable over the years or that are in imminent danger of becoming inaccessible. While the overwhelming number of such works will be primary texts, that is, works written by Chicanos themselves, occasionally the series will publish a book written by a non-Chicano if it appears to have signal importance for understanding Raza culture or recuperating its intellectual or historical identity. Such is the case of the novel presented here, Gordon Kahn's *A Long Way from Home*.

Each of the volumes published in the series carries with it a scholarly apparatus that includes an extended introduction contextualizing the work historically or otherwise. The series is designed to be a vehicle that will help in the recuperation of Raza literary history, maintain the instruments of our culture in our own hands, and permit the continued experience and enjoyment of our literature by present and future generations of readers and scholars.

The fortunes and tribulations that Gordon Kahn's *A Long Way from Home* has endured are remarkable and unique. The novel itself was written nearly forty years ago, in the early 1950s, by an important and, unfortunately, politically maligned writer who was primarily a journalist and screenwriter and who died in 1962, some twenty-five years before anyone had an inkling that his novel would be published, for the first time ever, by the Bilingual Press.

About three years ago, while exhibiting at the New York Book Fair, I was approached by Gordon's brother Joseph V. Kahn, who ever since Gordon's death in 1962 had zealously and disinterestedly committed himself to his brother's book and to finding a publisher for it. I was touched by Joe's commitment to the manuscript, and when I learned of its nature I was immediately interested in editorially reviewing this sunken treasure and, subsequently, in both bringing it to light and providing it with the historical documentation to enable it to be better appreciated. In this I was helped by both Joe and by Gordon's son Tony Kahn, an accomplished scriptwriter in his own right who is currently at work on a book about his own experience growing up under the Hollywood blacklist and the political persecution of the McCarthy era. Unfortunately, Joe Kahn died before the appearance of this book, credit for the publication of which is primarily his.

A Long Way from Home speaks to us from the same maelstrom out of which emerged another highly important work for the understanding of Chicano intellectual history, the screenplay and subsequent film, *Salt of the Earth*.

Indeed, there is a very direct and tangible connection between the author of the novel and the director of *Salt*, Herbert Biberman. In 1950, Gordon Kahn felt compelled to flee the United States in advance of an impending subpoena which he judged in all probability carried with it the risk of a prison sentence. Prior to that, however, in 1948, with his career as a screenwriter still viable although increasingly shaky, he wrote in collaboration with the "Hollywood Ten" (Alvah Bessie, Herbert Biberman, Lester Cole, Edward Dmytryk, Ring Lardner, Jr., John Howard Lawson, Albert Maltz, Samuel Ornitz, Adrian Scott, and Dalton Trumbo) an important book, *Hollywood on Trial: The Story of the 10 Who Were Indicted*. The book states that it "was written by Gordon Kahn in full collaboration with the ten indicted men. All ten assume responsibility for their statements in this book." Interestingly, the copyright was issued not in the name of Gordon Kahn but Herbert Biberman.

Later, finding himself in exile, Gordon Kahn turned for the first time in his literary career to the genre of the novel. He also turned to subjects close to his heart, ones by which he could express the theme of his own painful exile and disenfranchisement from his civil rights. According to his brother Joe, Gordon said that *A Long Way from Home* was his "version of the Great American Novel . . . and I choose the Chicano as my American."

A Long Way from Home, Salt of the Earth, and Anthony Quinn's autobiography, *The Original Sin: A Self Portrait by Anthony Quinn*, with its details of his activities on behalf of the Raza involved in the "Sleepy Lagoon" case, together with other buried or suppressed works that we need to dredge up, are critical to our understanding of that moment in history which Luis Leal has pointed to as the transition from the "Mexican-American" period to the "Chicano" period. It is with a rare sense of accomplishment that the editors of the Bilingual Press launch this book. These are the moments that make the painstaking, the tedious, and the exacting all worthwhile.

G. D. Keller

Contents

Dedication

On May 13, 1987, Gordon Kahn's youngest brother Joseph died at the age of 73.

Joe was a man of boundless energy and perseverance and the person most responsible for finding a publisher for *A Long Way from Home*.

Gordon had been a professional writer for over forty years, but nothing he wrote gave fuller expression to his deep political convictions than did his only novel, *A Long Way from Home*.

Joe shared many of Gordon's political beliefs. He also shared the feeling that *A Long Way from Home* was probably Gordon's best work. For a quarter of a century, from the time of Gordon's death almost to the time of his own, Joe carried the manuscript of *A Long Way from Home* from one publishing house to another, convinced he would someday find an editor sympathetic to the book's message and willing to assume the commercial risk of publishing the only novel of a deceased author.

In Gary Keller of the Bilingual Press he succeeded.

Gordon never indicated to whom he might dedicate the book if it were published, but his wife and two sons feel that, in acknowledgment of his brother's love and support, Gordon would have been pleased to see *A Long Way from Home* dedicated to Joseph V. Kahn.

Gordon Kahn's *A Long Way from Home:* A Wishful Journey

Santiago Daydí-Tolson

Nearly forty years ago, in 1950, Gordon Kahn, a well-known Hollywood screenwriter, had to flee the United States, driven away by social and political forces that had deprived him of his basic rights as an American citizen. The short trip across the border that led to a five-year exile in Mexico came to represent for him a long journey away from home, a sad estrangement, as well as a search for that ideal place he had always wanted his country to be. A critical and experienced observer of American political trends and a writer of clear ideological convictions, he fictionalized his affective and intellectual trek in the story of a young Mexican American who, like himself, has to leave his country and look for a new home in Mexico. Thus, Gordon Kahn, an immigrant from Central Europe living in Mexico, wrote *A Long Way from Home,* one of the few novels of the 1950s that deals with Mexican-American issues from the perspective of a Mexican-American protagonist.

A novel about the Mexican-American experience written by someone who, not being Mexican American himself, has to interpret from the point of view of an outsider the experiences, mental outlook, and attitudes of the group he wants to portray should raise among Chicano critics a justifiable concern about its pertinence and validity as a Chicano literary text and as a document of a people. To what extent a novel that tries to adopt a cultural stance from a relatively alien perspective could become an integral part of Chicano literary history and, consequently, receive serious critical consideration depends on many factors and should be a matter of thoughtful discussion. Gordon Kahn's novel is a case in point, as it provides an example of a work written from a position of sincere concern and understanding of the issues defining the peculiar situation of Mexican Americans at a particularly difficult time in their history.

Never published before, *A Long Way from Home* stands as a literary document of much interest to writers, readers, and critics of Chicano literature. In spite of being the work of a writer who could hardly be considered a Chicano, the novel conveys a level of understanding and a sense of authenticity which, coupled with a strong affirmation of an ethnic and cultural identity, make it a viable representation of a Mexican-American point of view and give it some level of validity as a Mexican-American text. Because of his sincere interest in the language and culture of Mexico and Mexican Americans, and because of his deeply held political convictions, Gordon Kahn was an excellent witness and a good analyst of the situation confronted by Mexican Americans at a time of an exacerbated sense of patriotism that combined with the anti-Communist sentiment and discriminatory attitudes and actions emerging from the post-war period and the Korean conflict.

Kahn's novel should be of particular interest to present-day Chicanos for several reasons very much related to essential factors in the development of a Chicano literary canon. *A Long Way from Home* purports to describe, analyze, and define a Mexican-American world view in relation to the social, cultural, and political characteristics of both the United States and Mexico. It also provides an ideologically determined view of the Mexican-American situation which, with its rebellious and explicit criticism of the American system and its positive view of old Mexican traditions and values, prefigures the cultural, political, and social developments that would lead a decade later to the growing consciousness of a Chicano culture and to the political developments of the Chicano movement with its creation of the visionary image of Aztlán. The author of *A Long Way from Home* could take such an advanced political position at such an early time because of his own experiences and convictions. He had a cultural and political background that few Mexican Americans could have had in those days.

Born in 1902 in Hungary, Gordon Kahn arrived in the United States with his parents when he was only six years old. Like many other Central European immigrants who grew up on the East Coast in the first decades of this century, he received a good education and developed a great interest in literature and politics. He adopted an intellectually well-informed leftist political philosophy which throughout his life shaped his work as a writer and his actions as a citizen. His critical attitude toward the American social and political circumstances around 1930 are subtly insinuated in his *A Gentleman's Guide to Bars and Beverages,* the ironic and slightly disparaging texts he wrote for a series of Al Hirschfeld's caricatures of New York barmen, derisively conceived and published as a book during Prohibition under the title *Manhattan Oases: New York's 1932 Speak-Easies.*[1]

As an experienced New York City newspaperman in a period of few and elusive writing opportunities on the East Coast, Kahn was lured by the promise of work in the film industry, and, like many others at the time, in 1930 he moved to California. Technological advances had made possible after 1928 the production of films with sound, and the need for scripts with dialogue generated a great demand for writers and scenarists. "With the advent of talkies, anybody who could write dialogue might have the keys to the kingdom."[2] The opportunities available in the movie industry at that time of economic depression were, in effect, unparalleled, and many writers "flocked to Hollywood following the lead of Ben Hecht, who cabled fellow newspaperman Herman Mankiewicz to come and make his fortune easily" (Schwartz,

19). As the historian of *The Hollywood Writers' Wars* comments, "Hollywood in the thirties was a haven for orphan talent" (Schwartz, 18).

For the twenty-eight-year-old Kahn, the move to Hollywood proved to be the right one. Within a year he had coauthored his first story for a movie, and from then on he kept a steady rhythm of work, collaborating as story writer and scenarist in many films. By 1949, almost twenty years after his arrival in Hollywood, his filmography included more than thirty movies.[3] As a professionally active Hollywood writer with clear political ideals, Gordon Kahn could not help but get directly involved in the labor disputes that characterized the movie industry in the 1930s and 1940s. He was one of the original members of the Screen Writers Guild, serving on its board from 1944 to 1946, and for a period ending in 1949 he was the editor of *Screen Writer*, the Guild's magazine. It is not surprising, then, that after the war he found himself caught up in the political and ideological battles that were to radically change Hollywood and the way motion pictures were made in the United States.

The social, economic, and political impact of the movies and the film industry in the United States greatly influenced the professional lives of many in Hollywood. Particularly affected were the writers, whose relationship with studios, producers, and political interests defined a bizarre and preposterous chapter in the history of American motion pictures. It began combatively in 1933 with several writers meeting "at the Hollywood Knickerbocker Hotel to discuss the betterment of conditions under which writers worked in Hollywood" (Schwartz, 15) and closed grimly in the 1950s with a series of hearings by House and Senate committees investigating Communist infiltration in the film industry and with the consequent blacklisting of scores of producers, directors, writers, and actors. Because of his convictions and involvement in labor politics, Gordon Kahn became one of the protagonists in this tragic chapter in the cultural history of the United States.

His participation in the "writers' war" was a natural consequence of his leftist political inclinations. John Bright, one of the writers who participated in the creation of the Screen Writers Guild in 1933, gives a good idea of Kahn's ideological position in his comments on the founders: "There was no real Communist Party in Hollywood at that time, but several of us had working-class backgrounds or left-wing origins we hadn't forgotten. Hell, we'd all come out of the Depression. We were all New Deal progressives" (Schwartz, 15, 18). Their progressive ideals were to cost Kahn and several of his colleagues their jobs as Hollywood writers and their basic rights as American citizens. In the late 1940s they were blacklisted by the studios after having been publicly accused by colleagues and fellow workers of being Communist infiltrators working for the demise of the American system through the popular and effective medium of motion pictures.

The accusations, which were the obvious consequence of a growing racist and xenophobic anti-Communist movement in the United States, came as part of the investigation of Hollywood Communist propaganda started in

1947 by the House Un-American Activities Committee, under the chairmanship of J. Parnell Thomas. Forty-one filmmakers, including producers, directors, and writers, were subpoenaed by the Committee in September of that year. "An indignant and vocal group immediately let it be known that they would not under any circumstances cooperate with the HUAC, which they called an inquisition. They became known as the 'unfriendly nineteen' even before they got to Washington, and were, of course, Thomas' prime suspects."[4] Not surprisingly, Gordon Kahn was among the nineteen singled out by the Committee for their undaunted protest against the unconstitutional investigation of the political ideologies and associations of so many Hollywood talents.

Gordon Kahn attended the public hearings in Washington and followed closely the developments of the investigation. His turn to testify before the Committee never came, but judging from the outcome of the investigation, he would have been cited for contempt of the House, taken to trial, and condemned, as happened with the ten men who, having been called to testify, refused to answer the questions related to their political and labor associations. In his book *Hollywood on Trial* (1948), a testimony to his sincere political convictions and vital dedication to his ideals, the infuriated Kahn gave a detailed account of the investigation and tacitly expressed his willingness to fight back.[5] But the next year, 1949, marked the end of his career as a screenwriter, as shown by the last title in his filmography. By then he was already among the blacklisted writers, producers, actors, and directors who could not find work in Hollywood or anywhere else in the United States.

Accused of being a Communist by a score of writers and actors, Gordon Kahn was repeatedly identified in later investigations as one of the writers whose aim was to infiltrate films with anti-American ideologies.[6] In 1950 things took a turn for the worse. In June,

> within a few weeks, three events expanded the rolls of the proscribed and gave the decade its style and bias. The Supreme Court, under Chief Justice Vinson, refused to review the cases of the Ten. . . . At almost the same instant North Korean troops marched across the 38th Parallel, committing the administration to a more formidable position of anti-Communist militancy. . . . The final event—the publication of a thin white paperback—seemed so trivial that few newspapers bothered to record it. *Red Channels* had, in June, a cheap and irrelevant air. (Kanfer, 99-100)

A few weeks later, in August, the Hollywood Ten were sentenced in Washington.

As the second round of congressional hearings approached, Kahn, fearing another subpoena, decided that he could not stay in the country without risking prison. A practical solution was to leave for Mexico, a country he knew from previous trips. There he and his family could live among a people he had learned to love and understand. It was while living there that he began to work on *A Long Way from Home,* his only novel, a fictionalized document reflecting his times and his views on the social and political issues affecting democratic life in America. Unable to write for the screen, the medium in which he had expressed his ideas for almost twenty years, Kahn chose the narrative form of the novel as the best suited to his talent and to communicating to the general public his understanding of the issues that were at the core of the Hollywood investigations. In *Hollywood on Trial* the professional writer had used his abilities to report directly and with no elaborations on the first round of hearings; in *A Long Way from Home* he tried to dramatize the essence of the problem by means of a story conceived very much like the narrative for a film.

In 1955, unable to sustain a family in Mexico with his writing, Gordon Kahn moved back to the United States and settled far from Hollywood, in New Hampshire. For the last seven years of his life he wrote periodically, under the pseudonym of Hugh G. Foster, for *Holiday* and *Harper's,* and he published two short stories in *Playboy.* One of these stories, "The Doll" (*Playboy,* Sept. 1956, pp. 20, 22), was adapted from a scene in his novel. The selection says very little, if anything, about the main thrust of the novel; it is only a simple anecdote, a well-narrated joke, obviously written for publication in a magazine of entertainment for men. In its superficiality it contrasts starkly with "Taste of Fear," the second of his stories to appear in *Playboy* (Sept. 1959, pp. 40, 42, 108-115). A direct and critical treatment of censorship and political persecution in Hollywood during the early 1950s, this story was praised by readers as an example of excellent writing and suggests a change in the circumstances affecting freedom of speech for writers in the United States. It is not taken from the novel, unlike the previous story, but it shows unmistakably how Kahn was still concerned at the end of the decade with the same issues that had led him to write *A Long Way from Home* while exiled in Mexico.

Gordon Kahn died in 1962; the manuscript of his book, finished and ready for submission, remained unpublished. Today, almost thirty years later, it is finally available as a means to underline an aspect of American history which, despite its great importance to Chicanos and all minorities, remains largely unknown. The novel calls attention to an almost forgotten side of Chicano cultural development, of Chicano letters and politics. *A Long Way from Home* is the product of a deeply personal involvement with the subject, and a testament of sorts. Kahn lived and worked in a region of the country where Mexican Americans were fighting daily for a better life in a society that set them apart, and he was sensitive to those kinds of circumstances. Likewise, his five-year stay in Mexico gave him a good knowledge and understanding of its people, their values and traditions.

In the same Hollywood circles that Kahn frequented when he lived there, another writer who was also an actor was experiencing the difficulties of making a career in movies as a Chicano and as a man opposed to the

injustices committed against his people.[7] In a sense, Anthony Quinn's autobiography, *The Original Sin*, can be seen as a book in many ways related to the
novel written by Kahn. Both works deal with the experiences of a Mexican
American growing up in the years prior to the political gains made by
Chicanos. Although the differences between the two books are too great to
discuss here, the coincidental element of a central character dealing with his
own destiny as a Chicano indicates an essential correspondence that cannot
be overlooked. In the same terms, both books can also be compared to *Pocho*,
the novel that has been identified as the most characteristic manifestation of a
growing Chicano consciousness during this period in history.

In many ways, *A Long Way from Home* compares well with *Pocho*, the
representative Mexican-American novel of the 1950s, if only because of their
similar interest in documenting the socialization process of a young Mexican
American. Both novels take differing views that point to a central and endur-
ing conflict within the Mexican-American political mind. Obviously, they
represent two different cultural perspectives. In one case the narrative con-
forms to the actual point of view of a Mexican American; in the other, it offers
a purely fictionalized point of view which derives from an ideological and
somewhat detached analysis of the Mexican-American situation. Of some
interest is the fact that this analysis was done by an intellectual who, being
himself from an ethnic minority that has suffered greatly because of racial
discrimination, understood quite well the predicaments affecting the social
development of another minority group and could provide a well-informed
perspective.

In *Pocho*, José Antonio Villarreal proposes as a solution for the Mexican-
American identity problem the unconditional acceptance of American society
and a complete adoption of its values, as represented by the protagonist's last
act in the novel—enlisting in the U.S. Navy. In *A Long Way from Home*,
Gordon Kahn postulates, instead, the need for a critical rejection of the
system. Significantly enough, this rebellion is made evident in the protagonist's refusal to be drafted and in his idealistic readoption of traditional
Mexican values in his actual return to the land of his forebears. This return to
the old country, with the full recuperation of the Mexican nationality, is
reinforced in the novel by an action that contrasts absolutely with the initial
draft evasion: Gilberto Reyes' voluntary enlisting in the Mexican Army to
serve not in a war against another country but in the Mexican internal war
against ignorance and underdevelopment. The idealized motive of the return
to the land of origin in search of one's roots acquires political urgency in the
novel, for it is presented as the best solution to the problems of the Mexican-
American minority.

Gilberto's flight from army service runs counter to the general Chicano
feeling of a patriotic sense of duty to the country; his action seems more
appropriate to a later period in the history of United States military involvement in foreign countries. In *Pocho*, the protagonist voluntarily joins the navy
as a means of proving to himself, and to the society that discriminates against

him, that he is a true American; he needs to accept the country as it is. This attitude, which was criticized during the years of the Movimiento, has been seen as representing the submissive position taken by Mexican Americans during the 1950s. Kahn's novel says something totally different. That he could envision a Mexican-American youth *not* joining the army when called by his country in time of war is indicative of his own point of view in relation to the American political scene at the time and also of his views on minority issues.

Kahn writes, then, about social disruption, about a politically based Chicano action against oppression. He chooses to write about his own experience as a minority by switching his point of view from his own mature, well-educated, politically sophisticated self to the naive, youthful character of the Mexican-American teenager who comes to understand things through a brief but significant journey from the United States to the land of his ancestors. The novelist could have chosen as his subject matter his own experience as a fifty-year-old writer, but he preferred the story of someone younger who, to a certain extent, could represent fictionally his own ideals. He must have been aware of the historical significance of Gilberto's ethnic group at that particular moment. Mexican Americans must have represented for him a people who, like his own ancestors, the Central European Jews who arrived in the United States at the turn of the century, were fighting to become part of a newly adopted nation without losing their own cultural values and ethnic identity.

Although Kahn writes his novel as a means of dealing with his personal political defeat and exile, his choice of protagonist and subject indicates his understanding of the problem within a larger framework. On the one hand, he meditates on the political developments that have deprived him, and many of his fellow Americans, of their basic rights as citizens. In the novel he focuses on the same issues that surfaced constantly during the Washington hearings he documented in *Hollywood on Trial*: xenophobia and racism, with special reference to anti-Semitism; political fascism, with its evident manifestations in the ideas of racial superiority, militarism, and anti-Communism; and social injustice as a consequence of conservative political ideas and economic practices. On the other hand, having decided to live in Mexico as an expatriate, he meditates on the differences between the two countries and about the choices left for Mexican Americans, a people he cannot help but compare with his own people.

At a moment when ethnic minorities were seen as aliens in their own country and were accused of being ideological enemies of the American nation, Kahn, the foreign-born son of immigrants, must have felt deeply troubled by doubts about his American identity, and he naturally found himself comparing his own country with others. He could not find much to compare with the old European country of his origin, which he did not know. Both in Mexico and in the Spanish language, Kahn saw an ideal which contrasted with the grim reality of his own country. The trip across the border into Mexico took, in his mind, the form of a journey to a land of origins, a travel in time and space to a world existing on a different level of political development and much nearer to the proverbial natural society of many socialist dreams.

The title of the novel, *A Long Way from Home*, is somehow ambivalent and nostalgic. It points to the spiritual and emotional experience of the immigrant, with its double allegiances to the land of origin and to the adopted country. This dual state of mind must have been of utmost interest to the novelist, who found himself living in Mexico, exiled from his country, and probably troubled by endless considerations about his situation as an American citizen of foreign descent belonging to an ethnic minority. For him, home was the United States, but for his character, it was Mexico, the land of ancient traditions where the American expatriate could find those values lost in post-Second-World-War America.

Kahn's utopian faith in a better world finds in the bildungsroman an appropriate literary form to communicate his own intepretation of the political dream. A well-read and educated writer with an extensive knowledge of European literature, he could learn from the tradition of the bildungsroman the techniques for devising a convincing story that could serve as the basis for proposing a social model. It is probably not coincidental that the other Mexican-American novel of the period also follows the same literary pattern.[8] The first manifestation of a growing sense of identity among Mexican Americans indicates, as in the case of the boy who grows up to be a man, a movement away from dependency and toward growth and development into a mature cultural and social entity.

Although in several aspects Kahn's novel departs from the literary model, *A Long Way from Home* coincides in essence with the basic structural pattern characteristic of the well-established form of the bildungsroman. One of the correspondences that must be taken into consideration in this case is the conceptual and even ideological content of the novel. It is obvious to the reader from the very beginning that the novelist is trying to translate into fictional terms a series of analyses, interpretations, conceptions, and theories about cultural values and characteristics of the United States and Mexico and that these conceptual components are directly related to the protagonist's social and political definition as a mature individual. In contrast to other novels of personal growth, *A Long Way from Home* focuses on the comparison of two societies and presents the protagonist with a choice between two worlds. The main issue in the novel is, precisely, the need for the individual to decide on one type of life or another.

As an immigrant himself, Kahn understands the dilemma presented by the need to choose a land to call one's own. He has a keen interest in the fictional journey back to one's roots and shows a deeply felt pain for what is happening to his country of adoption. The figure of the young Chicano who decides to leave the United States and settle in Mexico becomes a symbol of his own hopes, an ideal image of what could have been. The novel documents the process by which the protagonist becomes aware of his own situation, takes into account all elements affecting his identification with one country or the other, and measures the ethical value of his actions before deciding to stay in Mexico. By deciding to stay and marry one of his own family, he figuratively resumes the lives of his parents, lives that had been left unfinished when they went north looking for a better existence that, unbeknownst to them, was impossible to obtain there. Gilberto recovers what had been lost by learning how to become an individual within Mexican society. And that is, after all, the whole purpose of every bildungsroman—to record the growth of a young person from the immature lack of definition to full social integration as a mature individual.

The journey, in this case the flight from the United States to Mexico, is typical of the genre and it is a very useful pattern for a novel of ideas. The action is basically linear and the plot is limited mostly to a series of encounters between the protagonist and different characters he meets along the way. Actions and dialogues, then, tend to be presented in terms of scenes not necessarily related to each other. The focus is always on the protagonist and his own reactions to the characters he encounters and the different experiences he undergoes. Most characters are developed only as representations of specific human values or defects and they rarely interact with characters other than the protagonist. Following this basic pattern, Kahn organizes his narrative into a simple division by chapters, which are easily defined by each of the significant steps taken by the protagonist in his journey to the final destination.

Within this simple framework, another structural division can be established by recognizing three basic movements within the novel. At the beginning, and to a certain extent as an introduction to the main body of the novel, the narrative appears to deal with a different protagonist, Gilberto's mother. Everything seems to indicate that the novel will address the problems of Mexican Americans living in Los Angeles. But this brief introductory section, which gives a family and social background for understanding Gilberto much as happens in most bildungsromans, is immediately followed by the first encounter among several that constitute the journey of the protagonist, the body of the novel. The figure of the ailing Mexican-American woman with whom the novel opens represents, in her sad and tragic life of defeats, a compassionate and sympathetic portrait which Kahn uses to show the best characteristics of a despised social group.

The third and final section narrates the action that follows the moment when the protagonist reaches the end of his journey. At this point, which coincides with the completion of the socializing process of the maturing individual, the author introduces a new plot involving the interaction of several characters; he also resolves the main motive with a letter from the character who at the beginning of the novel started Gilberto on his trip. This last section serves as a conclusion in that it details the several elements that will define the parameters within which the protagonist will have to build his

life in Mexico. Although the journey actually ends with his finding a home in
the house of Don Solomón, the passage is not complete until Gilberto ascer-
tains—by way of decisive actions—his position in society. That is the last
measure of his success.

In the main body of the novel, Kahn sets himself the task of portraying the
main character and narrating his ideal journey. Very much dependent on a
socialist view of literature, and probably wanting to follow the pattern of a
socialist novel, he selects as his protagonist a figure who embodies the ideal
populist hero, the underdog. Essential to this figure are not only his lowly
social extraction but the ethnicity and moral superiority that distinguish him
from a large sector of society. Thus, the world of his novel is clearly divided
into two opposing grounds. On one side are the few individuals who can
exercise personal choice in matters of political conscience; on the other is
society at large and its fundamentally oppressing forces, represented by the
overreaching arm of the government and by a few characters from the ruling
class or from other groups that in one way or another abuse the lower classes.
It is obvious that for the novelist the superior characters are those who are
being oppressed by the system because of their ideas and, more so, because of
their belonging to groups suspected of social and political subversion.

This sharply divided world exists as much in Mexico as in the United
States. In both cases the powerful forces of oppression are directly related to a
political world view that coincides in many aspects with fascism and to-
talitarianism. In both countries the individuals who cannot accept this inter-
pretation of the world find themselves in danger and have to act as if they
were fugitives in hiding. But still, Mexico is depicted as a much better place to
live, while the United States is pictured as a society controlled by the worst
fears raised by the Cold War and by the abuses of the system. This being the
situation, the novelist conceives a Mexican-American teenager who, in an act
of moral strength, frees himself from the discrimination that American society has tried to impose on him and triumphs, as an individual, over a system
built on subservience and fear. On a deeper level, Gilberto's journey takes
him from a state of dependence on a world of injustice and oppression to one
of personal freedom and a sense of belonging.

This struggle is important to the development of the novel because comparing and selecting, exerting the right to act following a personal set of
values distinctly defined as the right ones, are the essence of the protagonist's
action. Through a learning process that is clearly indicated in the series of
experiences undergone by the protagonist in his journey back to his roots, the
young Mexican American develops the values that dictate his actions. These
are the values that American society has not only lost but is also attacking
and denying in the name of democracy and patriotic ideals. Patriotism, in
effect, accounts for many of the problems that the protagonist has to solve.
For many foreign-born Americans, patriotism became quite a delicate subject during the Cold War years. Chauvinism and racism made several minority groups the center of criticism and attack. Anti-Semitism was directly

related to the subject of national security, patriotism, and national allegiance. Kahn counterattacks in his novel by creating two main Jewish characters—one in the United States, the other in Mexico—who represent the values and qualities of a group that was being unjustly accused of an untold number of offenses.

Both characters play a fundamental role in the protagonist's life. The one in the United States is the doctor who cares for Gilberto's mother; after her death he acts as a father figure and is responsible for Gilberto's decision to go to Mexico in search of his relatives. His interest in the Mexican-American teenager goes beyond a sense of duty or a need to perform a charitable action; the experienced older man sees in the young Mexican American the representative of another group singled out for discrimination because of its distinct ethnic characteristics. He feels a bond between himself and the young boy whose destiny is clearly written in his developing experiences, in his family situation, and in his immediate future as a soldier in a country at war. The Jewish character in Mexico, Don Solomón, also plays the role of a father figure. Thus, both characters are seen in an ideal light; both are created as rich and complex individuals with strongly idealistic views of man and the world.

In comparison to all the other characters in the novel, the two Jewish characters are given special treatment and serve as models of humanity. They are good men, men who have suffered and have developed a strong and just set of values based on a humanist belief in mankind. The young protagonist feels compelled to follow their example, thus confirming the essential truth of their point of view and the basically correct attitude they have taken before the world. The purity of Gilberto's soul, his naiveté, his chivalric attitudes and values are reinforced by those of his two teachers, typical figures taken from the traditional journey motif in the bildungsroman.

The anti-Semitism of the period was in great part based on the idea that Jews, being mostly of Central European extraction, were agents of Russia, or at least supporters of international Communism, and that, consequently, they were plotting the destruction of the American system. That several Jews, among them some Hollywood writers, actually belonged to the Communist Party was a fact that did not help much to improve the appreciation of Jews by the American public. To prove how wrong it was even to suggest that Jews were anti-American, Kahn decided to make his American Jew the descendant of one of the early immigrants who had fought in the war of Independence. Like his ancestors, the doctor had been an officer of the United States Army during the Second World War, but his participation in the Spanish Civil War, another indication of his ideals, did not help him when accused of anti-American activities.

Wars and soldiers were essential to the American concept of patriotism, particularly during a time when the country had become involved in military action in Korea and was still under the spell of the European war and obsessed with anti-Communism. Although nearly every male in American

Jewish families had participated in one war or another while serving his country, all of them had later been discriminated against and denied their most basic rights as individuals. The same treatment was given to Mexican Americans after the Second World War and during the Korean War. The coincidence for Kahn was evident. His concern for the Latino population is clearly expressed in the attitude the doctor takes toward the boy, and it is further developed in the attitude of the Jew in Mexico. Both characters are anti-militarists and are opposed to the war. Anti-militarism constitutes one of the elements determining the quality of a better world. Military men are shown in negative terms, just as they appear in "Taste of Fear," Kahn's short story published in *Playboy* in 1959.

It is indicative of the way Kahn tries to manipulate the different elements in his view of these issues that at the end Gilberto decides to enlist in the Mexican Army. On the one hand, this action proves that the young man is not opposed to serving in the army, per se, but that he is against serving in an army engaged in an unjust war. Almost twenty years before American youth began to react against the war in Vietnam by avoiding the draft, Kahn gave his character the conviction and moral strength to rebel. In addition, his enlisting in the Mexican Army indicates his decision to become Mexican, a clear choice between two worlds, and his desire to get involved in a productive enterprise, the reforestation of the land. The opposing images of an army devoted to actually building the country and an army sent to fight a foreign people in a foreign land are underscored by the ironic detail that what is done in Mexico by soldiers, in the United States is the work of delinquents and prisoners. Gilberto had learned all he knew about trees in the reformatory.

The comparison between Mexico and the United States is a constant factor in the development of the novel. Most of the comparing is done through the mental and emotional processes in the mind of the protagonist, who is constantly weighing his Mexican experiences against his knowledge of the ways and customs of the United States. As such, the comparisons can be seen as a personal search for the essence of reality and as an expression of a peculiarly Mexican-American characteristic. It is obvious, though, that Kahn himself had a personal interest in comparing both worlds; like his protagonist, he found himself in a position of indecisiveness, wishing at the same time the best and the worst for both opposites. In certain respects his country was better than Mexico, in others the Mexican world looked much more alluring. The two Jewish characters figure at both ends of the conflict, stressing the importance of those values that do not change.

To make valid comparisons, Kahn introduces a character who embodies the qualities of the common man, that ideal figure in socialist literature who represents the views of the working classes. In his journey from Los Angeles to Mexico, Gilberto finds in Fred Bishop a solution to the problem of crossing into Mexico without being discovered by the border police. Bishop is an American who lives in the border region and travels constantly between the United States and Mexico. Besides being able to take Gilberto to the other side without raising any suspicions from either the American or the Mexican police, he is in the perfect position to compare both countries. Bishop represents in the novel the center of the conflict, around which the differences and the passage from one world to the other become defined. During the long ride along the border, Bishop has ample opportunity to discuss the differences between the two countries. Kahn devotes several chapters to this trip, allowing Bishop to talk extensively about the subject.

Although Mexico appears in less than bright colors, as Kahn does point to many problems, it is obvious that at another level it takes on an ideal quality related mainly to the character of its people. In recognizing this difference, the author is siding with the minority of the oppressed: the poor, the Indians, the women. A score of incidental characters represents these various groups and conditions. In the United States they are mostly Hispanics living in Los Angeles; in Mexico they include a series of portraits of common people: an old man who sweeps the park in Matamoros, the passengers on the bus, the young man who helps Don Solomón in his store, the young woman with whom Gilberto experiences sex for the first time, several children and passersby. Each of them receives a sympathetic glance from the author through the eyes of the protagonist. Quite the opposite happens when Kahn deals with those characters who represent the common, non-minority American. No one particular figure represents this opposing ideological ground, although several minor characters are depicted with simple brush strokes that provide basic portraits. Several of them are only named or referred to by others. Especially distinctive among those who do have a presence in the action are two Mexican priests; but, then, they only serve the purpose of criticizing the Church's support for those groups Kahn considers anti-democratic.

An example of the kind of story that would not likely have been conceived by a Mexican American in the 1950s, *A Long Way from Home* serves today as a document of a period when Mexican Americans had no voice in American literature. Although this novel is not part of the Chicano literary canon, it should be counted among those works that shed some light on the development of a Chicano consciousness in the 1950s and the resulting political action of the ensuing decades. That the book was not published until now, added to the absence of films dealing with Hispanic minorities, is an indication of the almost total lack of serious reflection by non-Latino artists on a social issue that for years was dismissed as practically non-existent. It is very significant, though, that this novel was written by a non-Mexican American, by someone who because of his own experiences, his knowledge of history, and his political and intellectual formation could see beyond the immediate circumstances.

From the current perspective, *A Long Way from Home* does not offer innovation in terms of structure, plot, and style. Kahn, an able professional writer with an impressive list of works for the movies and for periodical publications of general interest, does not concern himself with experimental narrative writing but with a straightforward communication of his own ideas and point of view. For readers in the 1980s normally accustomed to verbal and stylistic experimentation, particularly among Chicano writers who take new approaches to the literary language, *A Long Way from Home* can best be appreciated by reading it with a clear understanding of its historical value as a document of a period when a group of American writers were truly concerned with the social and political function of literature in modern society. A novel that could not have been published when it was written, *A Long Way from Home* comes to light today as a rarity, as a literary work that helps us understand a little better a moment in the development of the present-day Chicano spirit.

UNIVERSITY OF WISCONSIN–MILWAUKEE

NOTES

[1]The complete title page of this book reads: *Manhattan Oases* by Al Hirschfeld. *New York's 1932 Speak-Easies. With A Gentleman's Guide to Bars and Beverages by Gordon Kahn.* With an Introduction by Heywood Broun. (New York: E.P. Hutton, 1932.)

[2]Nancy Lynn Schwartz, *The Hollywood Writers' Wars* (New York: Alfred A. Knopf, 1982), pp. 18-19.

[3]In her filmography of Kahn, Nancy Lynn Schwartz lists thirty-two titles, including several films for which Kahn provided additional dialogue or narration, as in the case of the 1937 rerelease of *All Quiet on the Western Front* (Schwartz, 309-10). Jay Robert Nash and Stanley Ralph Ross, *The Motion Picture Guide* (Chicago: Cinebooks, Inc., 1987), include only twenty-six titles.

[4]Stefan Kanfer, *A Journal of the Plague Years* (New York: Atheneum, 1973), pp. 40-41.

[5]*Hollywood on Trial: The Story of the 10 Who Were Indicted.* Foreword by Thomas Mann (New York: Boni & Gaer, 1948). A note following the names of the indicted "Hollywood Ten" listed before the title page explains that the book "was written by Gordon Kahn in full collaboration with the ten indicted men."

[6]At least fifteen individuals, among them writers, producers, directors, actors, and editors, named Kahn as a Communist during the congressional investigations of the entertainment field from 1951 to 1956. Robert Vaughn, *Only Victims: A Study of Show Business Blacklisting* (New York: G. P. Putnam's Sons, 1972), pp. 118-215, and Appendix I, pp. 275-292.

[7]In 1944 and 1945 Anthony Quinn worked actively in Hollywood looking for support for the Mexican Americans involved in the "Sleepy Lagoon" case. *The Original Sin: A Self-Portrait by Anthony Quinn* (Boston & Toronto: Little, Brown and Company, 1972), pp. 81-85.

[8]Carl R. Shirley, "*Pocho:* Bildungsroman of a Chicano." *Revista Chicano-Riqueña*, VII, 2 (1979), 63-68.

1

Each time Gilberto looked out of the window behind Elvira's bed, the same thing would happen. The woman, who wore only a pair of loose shorts and a halter with the straps unfastened, would cover her eyes with her forearm and indolently raise one knee.

The other five women in the row of steamer chairs out on the lawn never budged. From where he stood, three of them, in gray bathrobes, looked like wingless moths. The two farthest away were wrapped to their chins in blue surplus U.S. Navy blankets.

"Could it be too cold out there for you?" he asked, without turning from the window. If she answered, he didn't hear. He faced the bed. "Bundled up warm, I should think you'd enjoy it."

"Pretty soon," Elvira said, hurrying to finish in the same breath. "Right now, it's too strong—the sun."

"It's the same with me," sighed Mrs. Neff from the next cot. "Dr. Bergman gave us skin tests and came up with it we're sensitive to certain kinds of rays. Elvira and me." She pronounced it to rhyme with Myra.

"You girls better watch that schoolgirl complexion," Gilberto said. "Keep beautiful." Both women smiled; Mrs. Neff, with clumsy ardor, squirming to erect her breasts under the sheet. Her eyes became excessively bright, and two red patches appeared in the middle of her cheeks where a clown might put them.

He heard the squeak of rubber soles on the linoleum. Miss Horowitz, the four-to-midnight nurse, trying to look stern, tapped her large wrist watch. "Have to call time on you, Buster."

"My half hour up, already?"

"Plus six minutes. And before you leave the grounds, Social Service wants you to check with them—Miss Schwartz."

Elvira raised her arms as Gilberto approached the bed. "Rules!" Miss Horowitz said, sharply. No kissing in this ward. He touched her cheek with his knuckles; her lips brushed his hand as he drew it away.

"Be good, now," he called from the door. "Both of you."

Prone, as she lay, Elvira could see him only from the shoulders up as he stopped to look back. Putting a kiss in the palm of her hand, she thought of it automatically as a glass bead that would roll and stop at his feet.

That notion had been there a long time; it might have originated in a dream. Maybe, if she let herself get drowsy while thinking about it, it might come back to her.

In a flash it was there—and real. Only, it wasn't a clear glass bead; it was a cloudy green marble. He found it himself, crawled in under the bureau after it, and popped it in his moth, cobwebs and all.

He was only seven months old then. And good—? He just never seemed to cry. People used to notice that. Once, on the Eighth Street bus, after riding all the way from Grand to past Rossmore, a woman sitting opposite remarked, "My, he's a cute one—real cute. Not a peep out of him all this time. It must be true what they say, Mexican babies never cry." She wanted to say something to the woman about what difference does a baby's nationality make, but Gilberto gave her a big smile instead.

Elvira was on the brink of sleep. But this wonderful languor was sweeter than sleep—even with the tears. They might stop, if she let her eyelids close of their own weight.

Miss Horowitz spoke very softly. "Honest, if it was up to me, he could stay as long as he wanted. But you know that crab, Bergman—"

"I'm not—"

"Shhh. If he knew how much that half hour takes out of you, he'd cut the visits out altogether."

"No."

"Bergman, I mean. You didn't think I meant—why, you silly bitch, the way that boy loves you—you could see it in his expression—he'd sleep out in the corridor if we'd let him."

Mrs. Neff, turning on her side with a creaking of bed springs, beckoned to the nurse. Miss Horowitz motioned her to be quiet.

"C'mere a minute, Belle," Mrs. Neff urged in a loud whisper.

"Okay. She's asleep. What do you want?"

"Did you notice—in the last year—how he shot up? I mean Elvira's boy. You must've."

"Well?"

"You know what I was thinking?"

The nurse smiled. "I can just about imagine, knowing you."

"No kidding, Belle. I bet he's getting plenty."

"That's strictly none of my business," the nurse answered, starting away, then pausing to add, "or yours, either, at your age."

"Up your bucket!" Mrs. Neff growled. Panting, she pivoted on her elbow. She couldn't tell if Elvira was actually asleep, or merely dozing. She was breathing softly and evenly.

"Elvira, honey, you asleep?"

A thin, one-cornered smile lightened the bony hollows in Elvira's face. But it was not an answer.

"That pischerke!" Mrs. Neff grumbled at the ceiling. "You *heard* what that chippie said to me?"

She was listening to The Band. Chuy Heredia and His Rhumbaleers. Though her own name—*Featuring* ELVIRA REYES, *Latin Song Stylist*—and picture were on the lobby frames, she still couldn't say, "My band." A girl working in the May Co. could say, "My store." But working with a band, it was different. Still, it felt good, and quite natural, when the hairdresser said, "I see where you're opening with your band, Miss Reyes. It says in Variety."

"Yes. Sunday night. At the Trocadero. I hope I'll see you there."

That's what Chuy told her and the boys to do, talk up the opening everywhere they went and spent a dollar. Let the Troc management see they had a following.

"And *what* a following!" Fermín, the bass player, mocked during the last rehearsal. "Lettuce pickers from up in Salinas. Clam diggers from up in Pismo Beach. Braceros off the lima bean farms in Oxnard. That's a *following?*"

Chuy was too keyed-up to let anything bother him. "Tonight's a new chapter. We hit the Sunset Strip, like I predicted, didn't we? And being organized altogether only how long—a year?"

Longer than that. Fifteen months. Practically all of it one-night stands, across and up and down California, Arizona, Texas. Towns with wooden sidewalks, with names so obscure they had to include the county in the address. Inyo, Siskiyou, Jim Hogg, Deaf Smith.

"All borscht under the bridge," Chuy said. "Tonight we kill them."

The boys wore regular tuxedo pants and light-green satin shirts with full sleeves, Cuban style. Chuy Heredia's was salmon color. Elvira's gown was ivory white, backless, but rather high-up in front. That was Chuy's idea. "Not that you don't swing a first-class pair of knockers. You do," he explained. "But the way the experts like them is, you know, under wraps."

One of the boys called out, "That ain't the way you like 'em, Chucho!"

"He's no expert," somebody else cracked.

"Covered up," Chuy repeated, "but fighting to get out. Like this—" Cupping his hands over his chest, he snapped them away. "Uh!"

"It's tremendous," Chuy reported back after taking a look. "Everybody and his brother. Lots of our friends."

"How'll we know 'em with their shoes on?" Fermín gagged.

It was one of those Talent Nights and, regardless of how many people The Band may have drawn, the Troc was jammed. Being a Sunday night, the people looked rested and easy to amuse. Another good sign was the presence of parties with bottles of Scotch, $25, and Champagne, $18 for the cheapest, on the tables. Not many looked like the kind of customers that spend only the miminum.

The show got off to a late start. By 10:45, sitting on the inside half-circle of the revolving platform, everybody in The Band was nerved up. Chuy, worst of all—he kept making fun of the orchestra working out front, Les La Marr, a standard dance combination.

"The poor man's Woody Herman. Ahh, if we couldn't blow better music out of our nose—" The buzzer cut him short. "That's us! Places—"

They heard the faint applause out front for La Marr. The platform
vibrated a little and the M.C., a charm-boy type, went to work. Chuy had
told him that he didn't want any cornball introduction. "My music will do
the talking for me. Just give 'em the facts: Back from a sensational three-state
tour, and pronounce my name right for once. It's Eh-*reh*-dee-ah. Chuy Heredia, Master of Latin Melodies in the Modern Manner."

The first number was "El Manisero," probably the oldest and, according
to some experts, still the best rhumba ever written. Chuy worked from the
original Lecuona Cuban Boys recording and put in a few improvements of his
own, including Fermín in a solo rhumba, balancing a big tray of roasted
peanuts on his head.

It went over all right—as a signature number. At least, the people were
willing to listen to more. The next—the showcase number for Elvira was "El
Caimán."

While the brass section was taking the second chorus, Joe Ramos, clarinet, sitting next to Elvira, touched her elbow. "The money," he said. "Over
there, that party of six. Froolick. Books all the bands for the Corbett Chain.
Nineteen hotels, here to Florida."

For the third time around, Chuy himself tossed down his stick and hit the
bongos. First he was on his knees, then cross-legged on the floor, working the
skins with just the balls of his thumbs. You had to give it to him. He could
take a simple beat and split it in a million pieces.

The finish left the dancers standing in their tracks, straining to feel the
switch to a deep, far-away drumbeat as the platform darkened. Over this,
Elvira, still seated, hummed sixteen bars of the chorus right into the mike so
that it sounded like wind moaning in the swampland. Right there Chuy threw
in everything behind her, full flood amber and blue lights, and it was "El
Caimán" for fair.

> Si El Caimán quieres bailar
> Para lucir con destreza
> Tu habilidad y admirar,
> Lleva el paso con firmeza.
> Y mal no habrás de quedar.

She saw Froolick push back his chair to see past the shoulder of a woman
in his party. He nodded, apparently pleased. She smiled back in professional
acknowledgment.

During the eight-beat rest before the last verse, she took two deep breaths,
counting four for each. The second stung sharply, under the ribs.

> Ausente de mí tú estarás—

Too much strain; too hard, she told herself; or she wouldn't be having this
tearing pain. It was getting worse. Something—it felt like a coke bottle—was
breaking up in her chest; crushing itself into sharp-edged crystals.

Esto así lo asentarás—

Blood began dribbling out of the corners of her mouth in frothy streams. She saw it on her dress. "Y para ti—Oh, Jesus!"

Clearly, she heard people gasping, a platter crash and somebody shout, "Get her off!"

Clamping her lips, she made an effort to swallow. It was useless against a piston coming up freighted. Her hands were pressed tightly against her mouth, but the gush of blood sluiced between the fingers; jets of it broke on the dance floor. Catching the mike stand with both hands, she fell with it. The lights on the bandstand went out.

People were leaving in a swirl of fur wraps. Somebody kept banging on the table with a bottle and shouting, "Waiter! Check here, waiter!"

Elvira looked up from the floor to see who was making all that racket. Froolick. She had a good mind to tell him, "Say! Who do you think *you* are— King Shit? Yelling like that when an artist is trying to perform. You ought to . . ."

The whistling drafts told Elvira she was lying in the tunnel between the kitchen and the back entrance of the night club. These lumpy cylinders under her must be laundry bags stuffed with used linen. They weren't comfortable, but if she didn't lie still, she would have to face Chuy Heredia, and right now, she didn't have the strength for that. Without warning, suddenly, a brusque hand opened the front of her dress. The tape of the brassiere snapped, and a rough, bony cheek lay against her bare skin. "Hey—!"

"I'm a doctor, miss. Lie back the way you were and breathe slowly. Now—"

He was faced away from her. She saw his thin neck and the bald top of his head, surrounded by short, curly brown hair. He was a doctor all right, he smelled like one.

He stood up and handed a coatroom check to the nearest man. "Would you please get my bag and topcoat? Dr. Samuel Eisen. What's the young woman's name?"

Chuy came forward. "Elvira Reyes."

"Married?"

Chuy shrugged, but the doctor kept looking at him, waiting for an answer. "Widow, she told *me*. How bad is she, Doc?"

"We'll know after the X-ray pictures." He knew almost as well now, from the bright red, aerated color of the film that was still on Elvira's hands.

The owner of the night club himself came in with the doctor's bag. "Thanks for being around, Doctor. Your check is taken care of. Shall I ask the lady to wait?"

"Yes, please."

One man spoke as they watched the doctor prepare a hypodermic. "Morphine, Doc?"

"Something to keep her from coughing and bringing on another one of those."

Heredia and two others turned away as the needle was pushed into Elvira's arm. "Any of you men been in the service?" the doctor asked.

Only Vilches, trumpet, answered. "Me. In the Navy."

"The reason I asked is on the off-chance that one of you may have O Type blood."

"Mine is B," said Vilches.

Dr. Eisen took a prescription pad out of his bag and closed it. "I'm going to send her to the emergency hospital on Santa Monica between Orange Grove and the next block." He turned directly to Heredia. "She can go in a taxi, but keep her wrapped up warm." He wrote something on a prescription slip and handed it to Chuy. "Give this to whoever is in charge there. Now, which two men do you want to send first?"

"First? What do you mean, Doc?"

"Blood donors. So, if they're sent back, two more go, and so on, until we get the right blood type."

In a worried quaver, Heredia said, "Don't they have plasma for that?"

"I wouldn't risk it in a massive hemorrhage, no. Whole blood. Well, who are the first two?"

Before anybody moved, Heredia called loudly in Spanish, "Nobody leaves here! All of you stay right where you are!" And in English again, to Dr. Eisen, he said, "Look, Doc, I don't know who called you in, but you're not sending any of my musicians away from their work. I'm under a contract here to play music."

Cooly, and in Spanish almost as good as Heredia's, the doctor said, "You dirty, no-good son of a bitch!" In that language, the word is whore.

"We'll call that contract finished, Chuy," the owner said. "I'll make you out a check for the whole week."

Then Elvira knew it was no longer her band, and it never would be again.

"No llores, chula," the doctor said. "I'll take my wife home and be over to see you right away."

Mrs. Neff stared morosely at the plump, little nurse, who, skillfully, and without waking Elvira, reversed her moist pillow.

"Anything you want, Sophie?"

"When I do, I'll flash my light."

"Still mad at me?"

"Up your keister!"

If Elvira and two other women in the ward weren't asleep, she wouldn't mind some banter with Mrs. Neff. Anyhow, it was coffee-time for her, and, soon, the patients' supper trays would be up.

There were fresh, warm doughnuts from the diet kitchen, as a change from the usual oatmeal cookies. Pearl Gerson, the other nurse on the floor, her senior by six years, made room for her at the desk. "Everything under control in the Junior Miss Department, Belle?"

"The same," Miss Horowitz said and added, as an opening for general gossip about her charges, "except for the sexual appetites I see around."

"They say it's nothing compared to a leprosarium."

"Don't tell me lepers—"

"Hansenians, Belle. Never let a staff member hear you say lepers."

"Thanks for telling me . . . especially that Neff woman."

"Sophie the Slob, we used to call her before you came to work here."

"I mean the way she tried to seduce Elvira's son; that nice, tall boy."

"If he gets tempted," Pearl said, "tell him he could have a better time with a catcher's mitt."

Belle giggled. "But all in all, she's really a good-hearted soul, Mrs. Neff."

"They all are—the bed patients, I mean. It's the ambulant ones, like that goon, Flo Pfeffer, who's always out there sunning herself. How that one loves to heckle people. 'No wonder you look so smug, Miss Gerson,' she says to me. 'You're *mar*-ried. You get serviced regular.' Yeah, regular—New Years and Fourth of July."

"Aw, come on, Pearl, you're making it out worse than it is."

Pearl looked into her cup with a slow, modest grin.

"Now I'm not married," Belle said, "and I do better than that."

"I should hope so."

They sipped their coffee. The floor was quiet and the light board on the wall had been dark for a long time.

"Now—" Belle broke the pause, "if none of them were any more trouble than Elvira Reyes—"

"*That* poor kid! *She* should be giving trouble? She had enough of her own to last—you want to take a look in her S.S. file? Of course we're not supposed to, but Bergman just happened to have it up here open." Her voice dropped. "Lost her cherry when she was twelve—"

"The Mexicans—"

"Hell, no. The truant officer. Caught her singing for nickels in Olvera Street. Married at sixteen—"

2

Elvira had written Bellflower, California, in the space for Place of Birth on the marriage license application.

"County of?" the clerk, looking at it, asked. She shook her head, bewildered. "There may be any number of Bellflowers in the State," the man said.

"It's just a little ways from downtown here." She pointed. "That way."

"L.A., then. Anyway, you'll have to bring your birth certificate." The clerk was ready to hand her application back.

"This?" She handed up the moist square of paper which she had clutched tightly.

The clerk looked at it sourly and handed it back. Jutting his hand out toward Fernando, he called, "Now let's see yours. Fernando Reyes, place of birth, Golden, Colorado. September fourteen, nineteen-o-three. That makes you thirty-one. Both of you get your blood tests?"

"Yes, sir. Here's the paper," Fernando said.

The clerk snapped, "Give it to me when I ask you for it." And he took his time asking. He fumbled with some papers, lit a cigarette, and finally said, "Now. Let's have it."

Two other couples were ahead of them for the civil ceremony, and after it was over, they walked the three blocks to Figueroa and got her things. From there, a taxi to Fernando's room on Bixel. He had barely enough time to carry the stuff up and explain to the landlady who she was before leaving for the barber shop on East Fifth, where he worked.

A little before noon the next day, while she was looking out of the window, two men came into the room. Not only didn't they knock, but she didn't even hear their steps on the landing. Instantly, their eyes were all over the place, from floor to ceiling.

"What do you want here?"

"See if we can find your boyfriend's gun before you tell us." As the man spoke, he showed her a blue and gold badge. She read: Los Angeles Police Dep't.

"He's my husband. I don't know anything about a gun. Where is he?"

They didn't answer until they had stripped the bed, dumped her clothes as well as Fernando's on the floor, and pawed through everything. "City Jail. You can see him at three o'clock, after his nap. Bring him soap, handkerchiefs, toothbrush and a safety razor. No lawyer. He said he doesn't want a lawyer."

She saw Fernando that afternoon, but before he was able to tell her anything, some excitement broke out and all visitors were hustled into the elevators and taken down. Somebody said it was an attempted jail break.

Three days later, she saw him in the courtroom. They were very polite. "Defendant's wife? You can sit right down here, in front." Fernando sat on a bench, inside the railing, between the same two detectives who had come to search the room.

The man—the district attorney, she supposed—who read the charges, spoke rapidly. The judge, at the same time, was reading something else in a blue cover. What she could gather was that "the Defendant" took a car, a Chevrolet, from the parking lot of the finance company by using a duplicate key. A felony. Fernando claimed, according to what the man read, that he had only two more payments of $29 each to make on the car, and he could have sold it for $350.

At about that point, the man stopped reading, and the judge said, impatiently, "Go on, conclude."

"The defendant pleads guilty," the man read, and sat down.

The judge, without looking at Fernando, turned to somebody else and said, "Remand to custody of State Penitentiary. To serve not less than two, and not more than five years."

Fernando asked the two detectives something; they nodded and brought him up to the rail to speak to her.

"When is the baby due?" he asked first.

"Ten days—two weeks."

"What's it going to be, boy or girl?"

"What would you like?"

"Whatever it is. Let me know right away; they'll tell you where. And take good care of yourselves."

As she was leaving, going up the aisle, one of the men in uniform took her arm and said, "Judge wants to talk to you, Mrs. Reyes."

The judge started right in with, "When this man married you, did you know that he had served two prison terms before?"

"No. He didn't tell me." That was a mistake. She realized, too late, that she should have said yes, that she knew.

"I advise you to see a lawyer and get an annulment. You have the grounds."

"I don't want anything like that," she answered.

"I don't mean a divorce. An annulment. It's allowed by your Church."

"I don't want that, either."

"You can marry a decent man."

"No," she persisted.

"That's all, then," said the judge and swung his chair away from her.

Before she left, she asked one of the men how she could drop a line to her husband, and was told, "They'll let you know."

Gilberto was ten days old, and she was five days out of the hospital, when she finally heard. It was a printed slip which gave an ordinary street address for the prison, and said she could send one letter every ten days to F. Reyes, #32-4311. It also gave a date when she could make her first visit; almost a month away. Time enough to save up for the round trip fare.

She sat down and wrote him a long letter, all about the baby and then had to do it all over again because the instruction slip said that letters couldn't be more than a single page.

A few days before the date on which she could make the first visit, she took Gilberto's picture. In one of those booths on Main Street, by putting a quarter in the slot and holding him up in front of the lens, the picture came out in a metal frame. This would make up for all the things she didn't have room to say about the baby.

The night bus would get her up there by seven o'clock. "Free Bus Service for Accredited Visitors to Main Gate. Divine Services in Chapel Open to All."

She was packing when the telegram came; not like an ordinary telegram, but through the mail, with a stamp on it.

> Regret to advise you death of Fernando Reyes #32-4311 this a.m. May 10, cause pneumonia. Unless private arrangements concluded within 24 hours, interment will proceed as authorized by law. W. W. Fraser, Warden.

May 10th. This was the 14th.

Weeks afterward there came an official letter from Sacramento. It was to inform her that she owed the State Treasurer $56.24 "to expenses, burial F. Reyes, #32-4311(D)." She could send the money in the form of "cash or P.O. Money Order (no checks accepted)." Otherwise, she is to fill out, sign and have notarized, the enclosed pauper's oath.

The notary's charge was fifty cents.

Elvira had not looked at the baby picture since the day she was admitted to this place. It was downstairs, in the storage locker, with her other things. Belle Horowitz would bring it up if she asked.

The call button was hanging behind her, at the head of the bed. She took her arm from under the blanket to reach for it, but remembered that raising it always made her cough. Anyway, in a few minutes, they would be coming in with the trays of milk.

Gilberto rarely ever got milk; he didn't seem to care for it. And the lack of it didn't do him any harm. At the Board of Health baby center they would weigh him every two weeks and say he was doing fine, just keep him on his present diet, Mother. That was easy—fried rice with bits of chicken and shrimp from the Chinese restaurant where she worked, on McDougal Alley. He also loved chow mein with strips of pork and egg-flower soup.

A dollar a day, two meals and tips came to about $16 for the week. The charge at the day nursery for Gilberto was $5 for six days. Her room rent was $4.50. That didn't leave too much. But tips were never more than ten cents in a Chinese restaurant that featured a 75-cent lunch.

It went on like that for a couple of years; a little better and a little worse. Gilberto was growing out of his clothes as quickly as she could buy them. It would soon be time to send him to regular kindergarten. She felt she ought to start looking for a place that paid better.

Soon she had to. The waiters' union came in and the Chinese group that owned the restaurant signed up. One of the terms of the contract was that men waiters had to serve the dinners and all customers up to closing time. The girls could join the union, with no initiation fee, but they could only serve lunches, with no reduction in pay. The management couldn't afford that.

Tommy Koy, who managed the place, did a nice thing the last day the girls worked. He sat all four of them down to the $3.50 Special Mandarin Dinner and had the new men wait on them. Each of the girls had a drink of Tiger Bone wine out of a stone bottle. Elvira broke open her two rice cakes and read her fortune. One said: "Wealth attends good character and learning." The other one: "To eye of ant, wasp is fierce dragon."

Tommy took her aside to talk to her. "Try to get some lighter work than waiting tables. And if things don't go so good, you come in here and sit down to a meal anytime. Bring the boy, too." And he gave her a present: a package of real Chinese tea, and, for luck, a little animal carved out of soft stone; pink jade, he said.

She lasted four days as a bus girl in a cafeteria on Hill Street. They didn't even have carts to move the dishes; they had to be lugged on trays. Nor were they thin and light as in the Chinese place.

Somehow, she thought because she had been taking Gilberto to the child care center, her name got on Relief. A woman came to the room, asked some questions and gave her a card good for blue and red food stamps, good at any grocery. She got mostly those things which Gilberto needed, eggs, dry cereals, spaghetti, hamburger, and canned corn.

One time, at the Relief Station, there was a sign up which said: "Positions Open—Knitting Machine Operators (girls) No experience necessary. Call mornings."

Although it was in the afternoon, she went straight to the address on Long Beach Boulevard and was told to come ready to work at 7:45 the following morning.

The hours were from 8 to 12 and from 1 to 5, and the first day the work, pushing a handle back and forth, didn't seem too hard. The factory made rayon stockings. The pay was $22.50 a week.

At the beginning of her second week, she knew she wouldn't last. From eight to eleven she could keep up, but the last hour she had to stop every twelfth stroke until she could get her breath. And it was always then that the foreman stopped by and said, "What's the matter, girlie?"

It was the same after the lunch hour. O.K. up to four o'clock, and then the same breathlessness and pains. At the end of the week, they called her into the office and told her, "Sorry, but we're going to have to let you go. You don't seem to be able to keep up with the rest of us."

Finally, one night, she went to Koy's. She wasn't thinking of the meal; it could be that the union rules had changed and she might be able to go back to work.

You couldn't just sit down and say to the waiter, "I'm waiting for Mr. Koy," so she ordered some fried shrimp, egg foo yong, and a pot of tea. When an hour passed and there was no sign of Tommy, she called the waiter and asked, "What time is Mr. Koy coming on?"

"Tommy Koy? He isn't connected here any more, not for some time. Anything else, miss?"

No, thanks. He gave her the check, $1.45. She had 60 cents in her bag. She counted it over, hoping it was 65, so that if she could find another dollar, she could pay the check and leave the waiter 20 cents. Once a dollar bill had slipped into the lining. It could happen again.

A short, well-dressed Chinese fellow, who sat facing her across the aisle, called his own waiter and sent him over to pick up her check. She pretended to be surprised, but in the end she had to thank him. When he said, "Please, sit down," she couldn't refuse.

He knew Tommy Koy, he said. He gave Elvira his card. Charles Mo, Importer, San Francisco. "What would you like to drink?"

"Thanks just the same, but I rarely—"

"Bourbon and ginger ale; mostly ginger ale, O.K.?"

The first one was that way. The next one was a good deal stronger. "How about one more?"

"No, thanks. I'm a little woozy from the last one."

He asked her, "Were you waiting for someone?"

"Tommy Koy."

"Didn't he tell you he was working in Stockton?"

"No. The last I saw him was here. He said any time—"

He stood up before she finished and pulled out the chair for her, and they walked out together. He held her arm going down the stairs to the street. They crossed the Plaza and went into a building on Aliso Street. It must have been a hotel because he took a key off a board in the lobby.

There was more bourbon in the room, but no ginger ale. There was a glass in her hand, and she was standing in her slip when it occurred to her why he took everything so much for granted: He thought she was one of Tommy Koy's girls.

It was too late, now, to tell him different.

The light stayed on all the time.

It was almost daylight when she left. There was no streetcar in sight. She thought if she ran, fewer people would see her.

Gilberto was asleep just where she left him, in the middle of the Murphy bed. She wanted to kiss him, but couldn't. If he didn't stir and call out, she wouldn't even have to get into the same bed.

As she started to undress, she found a $20 bill in the top of her stocking.

After that, for a long time, it was fives, and sometimes a ten. A few times nothing.

Whenever a man got ideas that it was "for love," she discovered that if she talked about the light-bill, or a payment due on the furniture, she could get odd amounts, depending on the number of one dollar bills he could fumble out of his pocket.

Vermont and Third, she found, was a good place to wait, on the bench "Courtesy of Enna Jettick Shoes" where the automobiles had to pass close to the sidewalk. She would smile at men alone in cars. If they slowed up, looked back and stopped at the opposite corner, she would stroll over.

When they opened the door for her, most of them would say, "How far are you going?"

The best answer was, "How far would you *like* to go?" Quite a number of them, as soon as they realized she meant business, would get flustered, or lose their nerve and pretend that all they stopped for was to give her a lift. Otherwise, if the man had a place, fine; if not, they would turn into a residential street with few lights, and do it right in the car.

The night she really wasn't out to do anything, and waiting for the bus at Beverly and LaBrea, two men in a Buick stopped and motioned her in. They fixed it so that she sat between them in the front seat.

The driver made the proposition. "Aw, come on. You don't want to go downtown yet. Let's stop over at my place and have a little fun. What do you say?"

"The two of you?"

"Just Joe here," the man on her right said. "He goes for the muchachas. But if he needs any help—"

They turned in on June Street and pulled up in front of an apartment house.

"You better take this. I might forget later," the driver told her, as he handed her a folded $5 bill. As soon as she put it in her bag, he laughed, "Okay, sister, *now* we can start for downtown."

That was the second time she saw the blue and gold police badge.

They let her out before ten o'clock the same night. And now, she had a Record—a big, white card, with her picture in one corner and her finger-prints in ten ruled squares. The blanks were filled in on a typewriter, most of them in a kind of criminal shorthand.

Arresting Officer(s): Berkeley, shld. no. 473; deMitrich, shld. no. 296.

Offense: Soliciting purp. of prost.

Previous Conviction(s): No file. *Prev. Arrest(s):* ditto.

Medical Report: Wass. Neg. Kahn, Neg. U'thrtis, trace.

Treatment Given: Sulfa 40 gr. prescr.
Disposition of Case: 30 days, sent. suspnd.

The student nurse, wheeling the empty milk pitchers back from the ward, stopped at the desk. "They all had theirs, except Mis' Reyes. Should she have it? Should I waken her up?"

Miss Horowitz wasn't sure. "What do you think, Pearl?"

"If she's asleep, don't bother her."

"I could swear to both," the student said, "sleeping and also singing. Humming like, but it's a tune."

3

The night she heard "Noche de ronda" for the first time, Elvira Reyes was standing on the corner of Sixth and Alvarado. It had begun to drizzle, and she had about decided to walk over to Seventh and take the street car home, when this Oldsmobile pulled up.

The first thing the driver, a man about 40, said was, "You know, Miss, you're taking a chance riding in this car. It's a Driv-Urself, and they told me the insurance don't cover any riders except on business. But if you want to take the chance, tell me where you want to go."

This was going to be a waste of time, she thought. "Just any place downtown."

"Would we be passing a place called The Goodfellows' Grotto, on the way?"

"If you turn left on the next block and go straight down Main."

"You mind pointing it out to me so's I can make a note of where it is? Customer in San Diego says it's good. He said to get their New York cut steak with French-fried onions."

She wished this dope would stop making her hungry. He kept talking about how a man wants a change from hotel food. He was staying at the Biltmore, incidentally. It was a good place, all right. A woman at a desk on every floor, right by the elevators, to check on everybody. But a man gets tired of the Coffee Shop food; it's so damn—excuse me, Miss—monotonous.

"There's the place. You can park up the street in that lot," she said. "I can walk from here."

While parking, he had been working up to say something to her, and finally, he got it out. "I don't want you to be getting any wrong ideas, Miss, just because of the way we met."

"Don't think about it," she assured him.

"I'm a family man. Got a daughter's a freshman in Penn State," he went on, while she wondered what he was getting at. "I may get this territory permanent, representing Hirsch Mastercraft of Philadelphia, and I don't go around making a habit of luring women."

"I could see that," she said. But what was he getting at? Did he want to keep her, or something?

"I just thought, if you wouldn't mind having dinner with me—that is, unless you got an engagement already—and maybe a show afterwards."

"It's all right for the dinner part."

He acted as if she were doing him a big favor. "I want to introduce myself. Chris, stands for Christian, Shulmeister." He gave her his card to prove it. When she told him her name was Mrs. Reyes, he looked frightened and said, "I'm afraid I made a mistake. I wouldn't have talked to you like this if I knew you were a married woman." He would have run if she hadn't told him she was a widow.

"Oh, I'm sorry," said the man, and looked it, too. "Terribly sorry. How long ago did Mr. Reyes pass away?"

This was fall, 1936. More than four years ago.

When she had cut across the charcoal broiled meat and taken her first bite, she said, "Your friend in San Diego certainly didn't steer you wrong." She didn't mean it as a pun, but Shulmeister got a wonderful laugh out of that remark.

Naturally, he showed his wife's picture, two of his daughter, and one of his house, "owned free and clear," in North Philadelphia. The people he worked for—"Work? That's a joke. The line is going so fast, all the work I have to do is write the orders and make no promises of delivery under sixty days."

Too bad, he said, he wasn't wearing one of the products himself, but he would explain it to her. "Sport jackets, for men. Like every other kind; same cut, same materials. But with this difference: They come with the suede leather patches already sewn in the elbows."

Then, he explained to her where the idea came from. "You know these society horse-people, regardless if they're wealthy, they got a habit of wearing their riding jackets till they fall off in rags; ten, fifteen years, sometimes. Well, when they're out at the elbows, they get their grooms or saddle maker to sew on the patches. Now anybody wearing a twenty-two fifty to thirty-nine ninety-five Hirschcraft, can have the same thing."

The check was big; $4.40 for the steaks, eclairs and coffees. He left 75 cents for the waiter, and before getting up, he wrote the amount down in a notebook.

Leaving the car parked, they walked for an hour up one side of Olvera Street and down the other. He remarked about the things on sale at the stands that they were very poorly made and overpriced.

They stopped at a place selling silver jewelry and the owner said to her in Spanish, "There's ten percent in it for you on whatever he buys."

She answered him in Spanish. "If you want to give me a job selling, that's all right. Otherwise it's none of my business."

Shulmeister was amazed. "Say, I didn't know you talked Mexican. You don't have the slightest accent of a Mexican."

"Spanish," she said. "I was brought up with it."

"You mean it's your *native* language."

"No. That's English."

He didn't quite understand, but he seemed intrigued. Not that he wanted to stay up too late, no later than eleven; and if she didn't mind, he would like to spend a little time in one or two of these little cafes along the street. That is, if the places didn't insist on people having hard liquor. "Got to have a clear head, tomorrow. Seeing people in Laguna Beach and Whittier."

"They usually do," Elvira lied. She hated these two-steps-down joints and the phony Mexican atmosphere they peddled. All the music they ever played was "Allá en el rancho grande" and "Cielito lindo." Strictly for tourists. "I'd just as soon walk."

They came out at the west end of Olvera Street and turned left. A few steps took them in front of the Club Bamba. A blast of music slowed Shulmeister down. He appeared interested. "Bamba, heh? What kind of a place is it? I mean, it isn't one of those real fancy places just stuck down here?"

"Oh, it's nothing like that,"Elvira said. She had never been inside the place, but she felt like going in now.

"There's a show—those pictures in the window. 'Hermanas Ruiz Bailarinas'—what does that mean?"

"The Ruiz Sisters, dancers. They're marvelous."

"Well—if you'd come in with me, Mrs. Reyes; you speaking the language—"

"I hate to refuse you, after you've been so nice. So—all right."

The first thing, even before a waiter came over to take their order, the cigarette girl tried to pin a gardenia on Elvira—for a dollar. She declined it—in Spanish. Shulmeister appreciated that, she could see. There was no cover charge, and only a $1.50 minimum.

"You were right," Shulmeister said. "For a place like this, I'd say it was reasonable." Maybe he'd take a chance on a tequila. He never had any; was it as strong as they say?

"Don't ask me. I'd sooner have an orangeade," Elvira said. After thinking it over, Shulmeister decided he would have an orangeade, too.

There were some wonderful dancers on the floor, most of them people from the neighborhood. They gave the orchestra a mark to shoot at, and so the dancers and the musicians were keeping each other sharp. Shulmeister had never seen dancing like this. "You got to be in the professional ranks to step out there with them," he said.

Elvira kept watching a party of eight, at a large table across the dance floor. Without being able to hear what they said, she knew they were speaking Spanish. The people talked politely, in turn, but always, it seemed, to the same individual, a slight, dark man with a serious face.

The handsome woman who ran the Bamba came up three or four times with somebody to introduce to him. Each time, he stood up, shook hands with the person briefly, and smiled. It was not a happy smile, and he didn't look like a happy man.

Elvira wondered who he could be. Somebody famous, she was sure. If a movie actor, not anybody she recognized; maybe a stage actor.

The music stopped rather abruptly, and many couples were still on the floor when the master of ceremonies came out. He signalled for the spotlight and waited for silence. "Señoras y señores—"

"Is it the show already?" Shulmeister asked.

The M.C. continued in Spanish, "With great pride and pleasure—" and stopped. It was still too noisy.

"He's going to introduce somebody," Elvira said.

"Who?"

"A personality of great distinction," the M.C. went on, "who has honored us with his presence here tonight. A man whom you will all be joyful to meet, and who needs no introduction." Applause began. "I mean, none other than the Irving Berlin of México—the great composer, Agustín Lara!"

Violent applause broke out as the spotlight swung and caught the dark, slender man. There were shouts of "¡Viva, Lara!" and almost everybody in the place stood up. Shulmeister, as well. "I'll stand up for Irving Berlin any time," he said, clapping.

Lara bowed curtly and sat down. This time, the musicians stood up and applauded; the violinists tapping their bows against the backs of their fiddles. Lara nodded, and stepping away from the table, extended his hand to one of the women in his party, leading her out on the floor. He left her by the microphone and the spotlight followed him to the piano. Sitting down, he waved the spotlight away from him, upon the girl at the mike.

Lara touched the piano, and it became so quiet that you could hear the hum in the loudspeaker system.

"Noche de ronda, ¡qué triste pasa! ¡qué triste cruzas, por mi balcón!" the girl sang. But it wasn't the singer, whoever she may have been; it was the song. It was the kind of song you could sing to yourself—and feel, if you were a woman and were ever deep, deep in love. Even if that passed, this song would make you remember it.

Many people shouted for an encore when it was finished. But Lara made only one quick bow and brought the singer back to the table.

Elvira said, "Excuse me," to Shulmeister and left the table. Entering the powder room, she saw a tall, pretty girl leaning on the shoulder of the Negro woman attendant, and sobbing loudly.

That, Elvira remembered, is what she came to do. She closed the door quietly and found an exit behind the kitchen, to the street.

Gilberto, then, was a chubby kindergartner who slept, hugging a toy panda, in the same bed with her.

Now—next week—he would be thirteen; half boy and half band-aids over football wounds.

And how many years was it since she had a man—either for pay or for free? If, as the legend said, it grows back after seven years—she smiled—she had one more year to go.

Leaning against the cold juke box in the Orizaba Cafe, she hefted the coins in her apron pocket; tips. Four dollars, plus; and people still at three of her tables.

She couldn't complain. Up to two years ago, during the war, times had been better. But she didn't wish them back. Then, they used to practically drag people in to work at Douglas, Lockheed, and other places all over the city.

At Consolidated, they put her down for $1.02 an hour, wheeling a cart of iced aluminum rivets up the line in Wing Assembly. She had been working two weeks there, made over $112 when this chest X-ray business happened. They took people out, a hundred at a time, and one by one had them stand up against this machine. The next day, she got her severance slip and was advised by Personnel to go to the Community Chest for information about where she could get treatment.

In those days, waitress jobs went begging. The Union gave temporary work permits to anybody who asked. She worked at a couple of large hotels and for one of the restaurant chains. But the bigger the outfit, the harder they drove you. When she got home, she used to fall asleep while Gilberto was doing his homework.

It was better here, at the Orizaba. The hours were from six in the evening to closing, around two a.m. She could walk to work. It was a small place; eleven tables between herself and another girl, with Verónica La Negra helping out. Twelve steps only, from her furthest table to the kitchen service counter. The patrons were almost 100 percent Spanish-speaking, and now, after two years, Elvira had her personal clientele. The menu was simple: a thick soup, garbanzo or a caldo of meat and vegetables, a choice of two main dishes, Mexican, naturally, and either custard or ice-cream for dessert.

Efrén Samaniego, who took the cash, was the owner. Nobody called him anything but Yerno, which means son-in-law. It was Verónica La Negra, his wife's mother, who really ran the business. She came from Michoacán, in Mexico, and after 20 years she could speak about a dozen words of English. One of them was Michigan, which she answered, laughing, when somebody asked her where she came from.

Yerno was itching for a liquor license—they had one for beer—but Verónica said no, and her word was law in the Café Orizaba.

By around one o'clock in the morning Elvira had served the last order of pozole—scraped from the bottom of the pot. Her feet hurt and her wrists were so weak, she could hardly mark the checks. The place was noisy; everybody seemed to be yelling. It would have been worse if the juke box was not out of order.

Right next to where she stood, there were these two men who had been coming in regularly for some weeks. They were foreigners, Argentines, and they had with them a guitar and an accordion. "Why don't you play?" she asked them.

"Is it all right?"

"Why not? Anything is better than this." And, tired as she was, she gave the juke box a good kick.

They played a tango, and a few customers turned to look to be sure it was live musicians they were hearing. They weren't Vicente Gómez, but they were good.

Then they asked her if there wasn't anything she would like to hear, and on the chance she asked them, "You know anything by Agustín Lara?"

Yes, they knew "Granada." They played that.

"'Noche de ronda?'"

"That, no," the guitar player said. "But do *you* know it?"

"Sure."

"Then go ahead, sing. We'll follow you."

She began low—just for the musicians and herself. Anyway, it has to be low—a girl talking to the moon that is making sad shadows on her balcony, begging it to find her man and send him back.

The noise in the restaurant stopped. In the haze of cigarette smoke, everybody had turned and was looking at her. She put the pad of checks behind her and kept on singing.

Nobody moved, not even to lift a fork. Yerno sat listening on his stool at the cash register, his hand motionless in the open drawer. Verónica La Negra stood in a halo of steam in the open kitchen door, beckoning the cook and dish washer to come and listen.

Like in a theater—not a sound till her last note. Then—Yerno was the first to shout, "¡Olé!"

Verónica La Negra stamped her feet and yelled, "¡Olé con olé!"

People were applauding, banging their fists and bottles on the tables and calling, "¡Otra!" and "¡Más! ¡Más!"

Verónica rushed up to her, gave her a big hug and took the checks out of her hand. "You go sing. I'll serve your people."

"'Te quiero morena,'" a girl in the back called. A morena herself, a brunette, she held her escort's hand as Elvira sang it.

Somebody pushed a five-dollar bill in her pocket and wanted "Borrachita." Then, the two Argentines asked her to sing the tango "Celosa."

One of a party of four shouted, "¡Somos de Tehuantepec—somos istmeños!" They were from the Isthmus of Tehuantepec. They wanted the "Sandunga."

"Ay, Sandunga, Sandunga, mamá por Dios . . ."

That night she had $25, including her regular tips. The musicians had $15 each. Not bad; not bad at all. But she couldn't do that every night, nor did she want to.

Between Verónica La Negra, Yerno, and herself, they settled that she would sing on Sunday nights, Family Night, at the Orizaba. They would get a substitute waitress. Elvira could come in at ten and sing whenever she wanted to.

So, Sundays turned out to be very pleasant days—and nights. She and Gilberto would get out of the movies at nine and have their supper with Verónica and Yerno.

Señor Pérez, who owned the Teatro Luna, out on Avalon Boulevard, joined them on one of these nights. "Without presumption," he said, "and, as between artist and manager, I should like to engage your talent for an evening."

Next week, he explained, the Luna would show a new Mexican film, starring María Félix. If Elvira would sing three songs—the theme song of the film and two others of her own choice—he was prepared to pay "an honorarium such as his advertising budget would encompass—forty dollars; fifteen dollars each, extra, for the musicians; and, of course, their fares in a taxicab to and from his theatre."

"But for such a gala," Elvira said, "I could not appear in anything but an evening gown."

"To be sure."

"And I don't have one."

Señor Pérez struck his brow. "Do not preoccupy yourself. The señora-my-wife will lend you one."

The señora-his-wife sat, beaming, with the five little Pérezes at a nearby table. She was as tall as Elvira, and a good thirty pounds heavier.

"She is an excellent seamstress, my wife, and she can reconfect her handsomest gown. May I take your hand in agreement, then, señorita?"

"It will be announced, though," Verónica insisted, "that she may be heard, whenever one chooses, at the Café Orizaba, at this address?"

"With pride," Señor Pérez said, bowing.

Gilberto beamed. "Gee, Mom, forty bucks for one night! That puts you right up there with Betty Hutton and them. You going to quit here, now, huh, Mom?"

Not yet. Not even for the Club Tapatía, which offered her a two weeks' guarantee at $75 a week. That amount wouldn't pay for the clothes and shoes she would need. In addition, she would need a complete set of arrangements for a 20-piece band. Not yet, son.

If it weren't for those Sundays, she didn't know how long she could have kept going. Waiting tables, you had to expect your back, arms, and legs to hurt. But now, every time she carried back a stack of dishes, she was afraid she wouldn't be able to put them down in time. If a coughing spell got her when she had a full tray in her hands, it was just too bad.

Some Sundays she sent Gilberto to the movies alone and didn't get out of bed at all, except to pack the boy's lunch, until Monday's time to go to work.

She was ready to drop the night Verónica and Yerno made her stay after the place closed.

Yerno began by saying, "The extra girl—she's been working enough Sunday nights so we could put her on steady."

"Shut up," Verónica said to him. "You sound like you want to fire her."

That's just the way he did sound. "Then you tell her," Yerno consented.

"Then, listen," Verónica continued. "We're taking over another place.

The Maya, it's called; on Melrose Avenue. Today we signed the lease. It's small, only eight tables, and straight lunches and dinners. But Efrén and I, we'll have to be over there all the time till it gets running good; six or seven weeks, maybe longer."

"Tell her what we want to do with her," Yerno urged.

"You're going to get off your feet, that's what," Verónica said. "Take the cash here. Sing if you want to. And if you don't, don't. Just take charge. I'll be popping in and out from the other store, so if there's any trouble."

"I appreciate what you're trying to do," Elvira said. "But can I afford it? Gilberto's in junior high now and I want to keep him in school."

"And I don't? What have you been averaging here?"

"Thirty, thirty-two, thereabouts."

"We'll make it thirty-five straight. Forty in two weeks if the receipts stay up. Efrén, take her home!"

The receipts stayed up, and even got higher. With the extra money, she moved into the two-bedroom dinette apartment on the floor below the old place. Gilberto needed more space, much of it for his books. He would take as many as six at one time out of the Main Library.

The arrangement at the Orizaba stayed. Verónica La Negra popped in less and less, after a while only at closing time to pick up the cash. Then she handed the job of banking the receipts over to Elvira altogether. "En un ratito," Verónica assured her, in a little while, she would come back; the new place still needed building-up.

Elvira enjoyed the sense of managership. She felt like singing oftener than Sunday nights, but her arrangement with the two musicians was for only once a week. The man who serviced the juke box said, "It's a good thing, or you'd put us out of business."

That was nice to hear. Then, there was this fellow who sat by himself, and there was something professional in the way he listened: with one hand cupped over his ear, nodding and sometimes frowning.

But there was cash to be taken, and she forgot him, until, when he paid his own check, he dropped a card beside the register and said, "Look me up one of these days, like soon. I may have some news for you."

The card read: "J.M. 'Chuy' Heredia—Leader & Manager—Chuy Heredia & His Rhumbaleers."

It gave a Hill Street address, but no telephone number. She neither rubbed her fingers across the print, nor noticed that it was grimy and furred on the edges from long storage in his pocket.

Two weeks later, he was back. "Why didn't you drop around?"

Actually, she had forgotten. However, she said, "I couldn't just take off the time. I only work here, you know."

"I work, too," he said. "We all work. If I should take it into my head to quit, half the name bands around here wouldn't let me."

When she didn't ask why, he hastened to explain: "I do most of their novelty orchestrations. They call me in for ideas. Like you, I work. But that doesn't mean I don't want to better myself. Why should the other guys get fat off me? So I got together my own band, and *I'm* the one to say how the music has got to be played."

His talk, more than the legend on his card, showed that he was a professional. And more, he was talking to her on that level.

"But bands don't grow on trees," he went on. "You build them. Takes a while."

Oh, yes, Elvira knew about the time it takes to build something, even something like a restaurant, where talent is no factor.

"Glad to hear you say that. Not only it takes time, but *timing*. Take building your crew, alone. You can go down to Local 802 and there's always enough guys willing to stop playing pinochle long enough to try out for a combo. No! You got to pick and choose, pick and choose, till you get the best instrumentalists."

Instrumentalists. She liked that word. There was a craft feeling about it that neither combo nor crew contained.

"Then you start building again. A reputation this time. Build wrong, and you fall on your face. Like for example: I send out a wax to all the networks. A medley like. Standard numbers to give them a comparison. And right away the Metropolitan Chain sends for me. I swear to you, the manager didn't have time for more than one spin, but he could *feel* the quality. Do I want to go on a sustainer, regular union scale? Time and stations, I want to know. So, what does it turn out to be—a foreign-language quarter-hour. Spanish! 'What do you think I got here,' I ask him, 'a mariachi? Excuse me,' I say, 'while I go play for a Polish wedding.'"

Elvira didn't understand most of it. But it sounded like something you read in Downbeat and Billboard.

"Would *you* go for that kind of an offer?" he asked her solemnly. "Considering it's not like from hunger."

She wanted to say something safe and not patently amateur. "I guess you knew what you were doing, all right," she ventured.

Heredia nodded. "I see you got a good head on you," and paused to light a cigarette. "I'm cutting another disk next week. This time with a vocalist."

Vocalist. If he were speaking to anybody else, Elvira was sure he would have said singer.

"A good band needs a good vocalist," he continued. "Cries out for it. I've been checking around. Been in most of the downtown spots, and I don't mind telling you, they all could use something you got. A quality like."

"You're not offering me a job, by any chance, Mister?" Elvira said, with the tentative aloofness of a waitress, or a salesgirl, who thinks she is being jollied.

"I wouldn't insult you," Heredia said, gravely. "People with me make their own jobs. I don't want anybody just rides with the tide like."

He would pick her up next Tuesday afternoon. Take her over to the rehearsal hall; meet the boys and listen for an hour or so. Maybe even favor them with a number?

"That is, if you're in the mood like."

The rehearsal hall was in an office building on Fifth, near Western Avenue. When she and Heredia arrived sharp at two o'clock, they were the first. The room, with fourteen chairs and music stands set up, was still smoky from an earlier group.

When the first two of his men entered, Heredia glared at them. "This is costing me," he muttered.

These two had news that three other men weren't coming at all. They had been called that morning for work in a musical at Paramount studio. Within the next few minutes, five more men came in a bunch, and later, another group of three. Every one of them gave Elvira his own particular kind of glance before sitting down. Heredia made no effort to introduce her or account for her presence there in any way. He kept puttering with a heap of music on top of the upright piano. She continued to sit on a folding chair, ill-poised and uncomfortable.

As he handed each musician a folder of lead sheets, he kept glancing over his shoulder at the door. The men took final drags at their cigarettes and ground them out on the floor.

In the cricket hum of tuning fiddles and the gurgling of clarinet and sax, Elvira forgot her own discomfiture. She was going to watch hand-picked instrumentalists at work.

Heredia came back and glared at the piano stool, demanding, "Now where the hell is Paredes?" A few of the musicians shrugged, others smiled.

"All right!" Heredia warned, his face black and angry. "This is the last time! I had it up to here—" He slashed his throat with a finger. "Up to here from that cathouse piano player. Today, his name goes to the union. I'll put him up on discipline."

Stalking to the door, he flung it open for a look down the hall, then slammed it shut. He charged at the piano and began shuffling music about on the rack. Spinning around, he snapped, "And that goes for anybody in this band who don't come out of a grifa-jag by the time I call a rehearsal. Now let's get some benefit out of the time we got left. Number Fourteen—'Amor perdido.'"

He smoothed a piece of music flat. "Here's the new intro." His stubby fingers clawed at the keyboard, and the music began.

They played an entire dance set: "Suavecito" and "King Kong" for the fast ones. The rhumba-lento was a number called "Nostalgia," and they finished with a samba.

"Take five," Heredia announced, remaining at the piano, pencilling over some music, while the musicians lit fresh cigarettes. Elvira waited for Heredia to turn around so that she could smile or say something approving. But he kept busy.

Finally, he rapped with his pencil and beckoned to her with a jerk of his head. "Come up here, kid." As she rose he told the musicians, "I'd like you to hear how she delivers a number. Diction is good, and maybe she's got the beat. I say maybe. I don't know. Not much professional experience, so don't go too critical on her. Save the comments till later."

He hadn't even mentioned her name. Perhaps, Elvira thought, this was the easy, off-hand way professionals were made known to each other.

"What do you want to sing first, sister?"

"'Noche de ronda'—?"

"A little on the slow side," Heredia said, sourly. "But if that's what you want to do—"

"'Mujer sin corazón?'" she suggested timidly.

"Okay. She's going to sing 'Woman Without a Heart.'"

In the middle of the second chorus, Heredia increased the tempo. "Come on, bounce it," he said.

It was the first time she had sung that number in the swingy way called for by his accompaniment. She knew that she was slurring, and biting off all but the last words of some phrases. But Heredia grinned and nodded as if he liked it.

"You caught on," he said when she finished. "Now let's try 'Farolito' with the same beat."

She knew she was doing it well when Heredia toned down on the piano and waved the strings and brass in.

"Hey, Chuy," one musician called, "how about that 'Noche de ronda?'" She nodded to Heredia—yes, she would like to sing it.

"Go ahead," he said, indifferently. "Maybe you want to prove something."

She sang it her own way. The musicians applauded.

"Good here, too," Heredia admitted. "In a musical way, I mean. But it's still a torch song. And by me, torch songs are cold as Kelsey's. The public's tired hearing about My Man—in any language. It's only words. Right now, what counts is the bounce."

He started pawing through a heap of music. "I laid aside a number here, someplace. A real oldie, but I worked it over. It happens to have—ah, here it is!"

He brought out a lead sheet all pasted over with manuscript, spread it on the piano and beckoned Elvira to come closer. "Here's one you'll really be able to tear into—'El Caimán'!"

Number 4 lit up and continued flashing on the annunciator board.

"That's Sophie," said Miss Horowitz, touching the switch that extinguished the number and darkened the panel again.

"I'll go," said Miss Gerson, dusting the powdered sugar off her fingers. "You've got that paperwork."

"Okay, thanks. She gets ascorbic acid, five grains."

As Miss Gerson left, Number 7 flashed on, then 4 again . . . 8, 5, and 10—all of them in the ward—except 6.

Trembling, Miss Horowitz spattered ink all over the chart she was working on. Miss Gerson, back, picked up the interphone. "Dr. Bergman, please—*please!* Women's Ward B, Nurse Gerson. Yes . . ."

Still holding it, she pushed Miss Horowitz, "Where's your telephone list?"

The interphone clicked. "Dr. Bergman . . . yes, Doctor. . . . Definitely cyanosis."

The younger nurse put the pen holder in her mouth, like a bit, to keep from crying. It snapped between her teeth. Anybody else, she'd be running—

"Stop this!" Miss Gerson snapped. "What's the matter with you! Get on that telephone and call Dr. Eisen."

4

It was the same desk that Gilberto had sat beside in the Social Service bureau many visiting days. Miss Meyers, the worker to whom he reported, never kept him more than a few minutes. Was he working? Yes. At the same place? Yes. Living at the same address? Yes, c/o Romero. Still paying ten dollars a week, including breakfast and supper? Correct, Miss Meyers.

She had always called him Mr. Reyes. But this new worker, Mrs. Schwartz, began right by calling him Gilberto.

"I'm Florence Schwartz," she said. "I'm taking over some of the cases from Miss Meyers's file. Your mother's is one of them. In fact, I've just been going through it; that's why I asked you to drop in. But if you have a heavy date—"

Immediately, he felt more at ease with this woman than with Miss Meyers. He smiled. "I got all the time in the world."

This one seemed to have a lot less facts, but she sounded genuinely interested in his mother when she asked him things. She said she meant to have a long talk with her, one of these days.

"She'll sure appreciate it," Gilberto said.

Without being brusque about it, she got around to the subject of the interview. "I hope you have been thinking of the fact that your mother won't be here forever. She'll want a home of her own again some day."

Gilberto smiled. He was glad she brought that up. "I think I'll be able to arrange that."

"I'm certainly glad to hear that, Gilberto. Things getting better?"

"It depends on how you look at it. Fact is, I'm going in the army. I just got my induction notice."

You could see how she looked at it: none too cheerfully. She wrote something down on her pad and said, "Did you tell the draft board about your mother?"

"Yes, ma'am; they've got my whole history. In a file, like yours."

"That she was sick? That you were her sole support?"

"That's the point, Mrs. Schwartz. They know I'm not really supporting her. How could I? They told me about the allotment she'd get once I was in uniform. In dollars and cents, it comes to more than if I stayed working, gave her my whole salary and tried to keep two people alive on that."

"I see," Mrs. Schwartz said. "When do you go?"

"Right away. Friday. I report in the lobby of the Federal Building, Friday seven a.m."

"Then this was your last visit. Does she know?"

"Well—no," he dawdled. "I was going to write her from camp." He added, more thoughtfully, "Maybe I should have. But I don't think she was feeling too good. So why give her that worry on top of everything?"

"Perhaps you're right." She glanced at the folder on top of which she had clipped a memorandum to herself. "It may be that Miss Meyers left some data out, but I notice there was a period of about three months when you didn't visit your mother at all."

"That was when I was away," he said sharply.

"Away? Out of town?"

"Work camp," he said in the same challenging tone. "Miss Meyers knew about that."

"I'm sorry."

"Nothing to be sorry about." His voice softened. "The only thing is that my mother thought I was really going to forestry school, like I wrote her."

"Then, as far as this bureau goes, she still thinks so," Mrs. Schwartz assured him. "Did you learn anything in that time?"

"A lot," he said, enthusiastically. "All that the experts could teach us about tree diseases, scale, blight, fungus, and how to fight them, both by surgery and chemicals."

"That's wonderful."

"I was put in charge of a squad of twelve fellows. I figure we saved about eighty acres of jack pine."

"You liked it?"

"I'll say. Why, even today, if they'd give me the cement and stuff I need, I could bring back a dozen sick trees, right here in Pershing Square Park."

"So you're a trained tree surgeon," Mrs. Schwartz said admiringly.

"Well," he laughed, "I haven't got a degree. Incidentally, Miss Schwartz, whoever did the cavity work on that big cypress on the Sixth Street side, left out the most important part of the job—bracing the crotch. First real cold day and it'll split right in half."

The woman laughed. "He should have his license yanked. Anyway, the trade you're learning now is just as important."

Gilberto looked puzzled. "Me? What trade?"

Mrs. Schwartz glanced hastily at her notes. "Aren't you working with a mechanical dentist—let's see—M. L. Richardson, Wilshire Boulevard?"

"I did—until yesterday."

"And you were getting twenty dollars a week? Is that right?"

"Yes, ma'am. I'll explain it: I couldn't pick my own job after I finished work camp. This is the one they sent me on, and you have to take it. What I do—did, that is—is deliver dentures, bridgework, partial dental plates to dentists all over town. On a bicycle. That was the work."

"Was it a part-time job?" Mrs. Schwartz asked. "What I mean is, it included training in mechanical dentistry?"

"No," Gilberto said. "Three Japanese people do all the actual work. Mr.

Richardson checks it over, and I deliver the impressions and the finished pieces."

"What were your hours?"

"Regular. Nine to six. But many times I didn't get through till about eight."

The woman slammed the folder shut and, slapping her hands flat on her desk, she stared at him. "Did you know you were being cheated?"

"You mean the overtime?"

"That's the least of it. By the way, Gilberto, do you have a Social Security card?"

"Yes, ma'am. The number is 563-05-7786."

She wrote it down. "Do you know what the minimum hourly rate of pay is in this country?" she asked.

"No. I should have mentioned, when I told him I had my induction notice, he gave me an extra week's pay."

"That's very big of your Mr. Richardson. But he still cheated you. The least an employer must pay anybody working for him is seventy-five cents an hour. That's the law. And—" She stopped abruptly, then resumed quietly, "Wait a minute. I just remembered something—that dental business, it's purely local; he does work only for dentists in the city."

"No," said Gilberto. "He's got customers in Tucson, Arizona; Carson City, Nevada; lots of places. The stuff goes airmail."

"Wonderful! Does he keep time cards?"

"No. Mr. Richardson is always in before eight o'clock, and he knows when people come in," Gilberto explained.

"I'll bet he does. Look, Gilberto, even if we can't prove you worked more than forty hours a week, he still owes you two dollars for every day. You say you've been there less than a year?"

"Ten months exactly. I started on the ninth of January. It's now October the tenth."

"Any vacations—time off?"

"Only when everything was closed."

Mrs. Schwartz's pencil was busy for a minute. "You've got four hundred dollars—at least that—coming to you. And we're going to collect it. You're going to get your mother the prettiest bed-jacket in the ward, you hear. What's that address on Wilshire?"

"It's right on Normandie," he said. Timidly, he asked, "What are you going to do? Put in a claim?"

"First I want to see what kind of a louse this is—"

"Excuse me. Maybe I better talk to him, Miss Schwartz."

But that's what we're here for, to look into things like this."

"I'll see him myself," Gilberto promised. "First thing in the morning. It's no use—"

"All right. But if he doesn't come across immediately, you let me know."

"Yes, ma'am."

Gilberto got off the high-stooped trolley car at Ninth and Hill. During the entire ride, covering two fare zones, he had been thinking gloomily about his promise to go to Richardson in the morning.

He stood now under a hissing green and orange neon sign reading: Daffy Jaffe—Nearly New Cars.

Seeing Richardson was one thing. But going there to demand $400 was something else again. He should have let Miss Schwartz, who was so eager to tangle with him, handle the whole thing. You can't just walk up to a guy whom you were supposed to have seen for the last time yesterday and say to him, "You owe me four hundred bucks, so hand it over now, in large bills."

It's true that Richardson was the type who had that sort of thing coming to him. From the first day, when Gilberto walked into that place with the letter from the juvenile people, he was so confident that Gilberto would go right to work that he had twelve packages, in strong manila envelopes all tagged, ready for him to deliver.

"Those are worth from seventy to two hundred dollars each, for the metal alone, gold and palladium, not counting the work," Richardson said.

"But I figured the job would pay more than twenty a week, Mr. Richardson."

"Look, my boy, I didn't send for you. But I'm willing to take a chance on you even though I can't get you bonded on account of your record."

The thing to do when dismal thoughts like this started getting you down was take in a movie. Nor was that easy, for somebody who sees as many films, sometimes three a week. Unless you take careful note, you might find yourself seeing the same ones over again.

He walked over to the Million Dollar, checked the lobby display and the stills from the picture, and entered, in the middle of the feature. There was a wedding. The man was in regimental full dress, and he led his bride out of the chapel under an arch of swords. This was England somewhere.

The reception was in the garden of a castle; the guests all generals, admirals and diplomats. The bride's father was an earl, as well as "the outstanding nuclear physicist of our time, who holds locked in that colossal brain, the secret of our survival—the salvation of Christian Civilization from the teeming hordes of the East."

It turned out as he knew it would, as in most of the radio serials and films he had seen: The handsome officer was a foreign agent working for Russia. He is finally killed by his own bride, after he injects the old earl with a truth serum and is sitting by his bed, ready to take down the formula.

Most of the newsreel was about the Korean war. "American B-29s Clobber Red Supply Depots Fifth Straight Day." The screen showed a tilted landscape, almost obliterated by smoke.

"Hostile North Korean Town Burned Off Map in Rain of Napalm." This showed only a few walls and some dogs tearing at a bundle on the ground.

"Telenews Interviews Battle-Hardened GIs." A platoon of soldiers trudging toward the camera. Gilberto fingered the wallet into which he had tucked his induction notice. It meant that in a few months he would be carrying one of those slim carbines by the shoulder strap and slogging through mud in a pair of parachutist's boots. Ah, but it couldn't last much longer. How could it, Chinese-type people against Americans? He had seen pictures of them, prisoners, holding up their fists to the camera. They actually had tennis sneakers on their feet. It looked to Gilberto about as uneven as matching the Southern California varsity against eleven Chinese laundrymen.

There were no bayonets on the guns of the veterans in the picture. That meant to Gilberto that this business you read about hand-to-hand fighting was merely a colorful newspaper phrase. In all his life—even as a kid, in so-called tough East Los Angeles—he had never had a fist fight. And in his year on the McVeigh High basketball team, he had only one personal foul called against him.

A soldier stepped out of line. "What's your name and home town, soldier?"

"Private First Class Stan Wisoczki, Hamtramck, Michigan. H'ya, Mom—and Jeanie—and Teddy—"

"When do you expect to be rotated home, Stan?"

"Not till we kill every ——— Gook and Chink between here and Manchuria."

The missing word had been rubbed off the sound track, but from the movement of the soldier's lips, there was no doubt what he said.

"Generalissimo Chiang Kai-Shek Pleads for Green Light from Allied High Command to Launch Invasion from Formosa." The thin, bald man, with a face like a badly-fleshed skull and loose-fitting dentures, read something from a paper. The teeth reminded him uncomfortably of Mr. Richardson.

It was nine o'clock when he left the theatre, without waiting to see the beginning of the feature. He was hungry, and there was a cafeteria on Olive where the prices weren't all in multiples of five cents. He had a Salisbury steak with spaghetti, 32; a side-order of cottage fried potatoes, 13; a piece of boysenberry pie, 17, and two glasses of milk, 14.

Walking down Main, toward the Plaza, he stopped at the edge of the curb in front of the burlesque theatre. Last week, the strip teaser was called Atomic Anne. This time, the flapping oilcloth banner read: "She'll Send You—From Out of This World! SUPERSONIC SUE!!"

The barker, made up like W. C. Fields, walked up and down in front of the box office, making his spiel in short yelps at whomever passed, or even slowed up. "Plenty of choice seats right on the runway, gents. It's got pepper and spice, boys."

Gilberto had no intention of going in. He couldn't if he wanted to. That was one of the conditions before they discharged him from work camp.

A car, heading uptown, slowed and the barker called, "Stage full of girls, but it's a man's show, men." The women in the car giggled, and it moved on.

The barker spat behind his hand and pointed his cane at Gilberto, calling to him in the Pachuco jargon, "¡Orale, chicano! No bofa tonight?"

Bofa meant a dirty, diseased woman. Gilberto wanted to ignore him and go away, but not without a look at the clown, who had an ugly, moist-lipped mouth. If anything, this was a bofo. Even if the word didn't exist in Pachuco, it was a good name for him.

As the man came closer, Gilberto pretended he was looking at one of the lithographs. But the voice was right at his ear. "What do you say, carnal? This ain't no shooting gallery, but you can get your gun off."

Feeling hot and ashamed, Gilberto started away.

"Leaving?" the man said. "Well—ay te huacho."

The dirty, gabacho bastard, Gilberto thought. He had a right to call him that—a name more contemptible than gringo. The louse had called him a Chicano, which one Mexican American could call another in a friendly way, but not the way that bum said it.

El me huacha, huh! He'd be seeing him, all right. In uniform, the next time, when he would proceed to beat the crap out of that jerk. And he'd get his gun off, too. Plenty. The works. Till they hollered for help. He'd waited long enough to pay them back.

Not *them*—you can't take them *all* on to collect on what only one of them owed him. Carolyn . . .

That last game against Fairfax, with the score 26-26 in the last half and only seconds left. Everybody said Reyes' field goal was a luck-shot. It wasn't. He could have done it blindfolded because her promise had made him infalli-ble—like Ivanhoe. And she kept making it; but that's all.

Lying with her, side by side, in their bathing suits at Hermosa Beach, it was always either "too many people around," or, it was "too cold," or she had the moon-sickness.

All those nights at the drive-in theatres, with the whole rear seat of the Plymouth to themselves, dizzied with kissing, both groaning with the hunger.

"Carolyn—honey—"

"No, Gil, no. I don't want you to."

"But you said—"

"It's too—too noisy."

"Then when?"

"Now don't be like that!"

"Then I guess you don't care much about me."

"Oh, pooh! You know I like you. It isn't as if—well—you know—you're a *white* Mexican."

It was no use telling her over again that he wasn't a Mexican, any more than she was a German, because her name was Muller.

And always the bus ride home, his lips bitten through by her sharp, adolescently gapped teeth, shamed by the cold burden of his passion.

The last time he saw her was—yes—in the Art class. Mr. Jolliffe, the instructor, had the group drawing a vase of yellow chrysanthemums and talked to them about Van Gogh. "You've all seen that self-portrait; the one in which he is wearing a bandage."

Gilberto had read the book. So had Carolyn. He saw her looking at him, past her drawing board. He held up a finger and nodded yes, touched his ear and shook his head no.

That afternoon, when Dickie Collins stopped him in the hall between classes and said, "Gil, I got to see you. Meet me outside right away," he thought it would be a message from Carolyn. She and Dickie lived on the same block in Hancock Park.

"Wait by my car," Dickie urged. "It's mighty important."

He spotted Dickie in a huddle with four other students, two of them seniors, and they broke up as he approached. Collins took him aside. "It's about Carolyn," he said.

"*What's* about Carolyn?"

"I just got a message from her."

"For me?"

"It *ought* to interest you, Reyes. Anyway, here's what happened: This morning her mother looks in her purse—Carolyn's I mean—for some change and she finds three rubbers, Rameses. She gets in touch with Mr. Muller at his office and Carolyn is yanked home right after the Art class. Her old man's been in to see The Dutchman."

The Dutchman was Dr. Van Kliek, principal of McVeigh High.

"Where'd you get all this?"

"From her, Carolyn, at lunch time," Dickie Collins explained. "Lucky I called. Her folks just finished giving her the third degree, but she swears she didn't mention any names. Just the same, I'm tipping you off."

"Me—?

"You were banging her, too, so don't act innocent till the time comes you have to."

"That's not true, Dick. I never did."

Collins shrugged. "Have it your way. But that don't get you off the hook. You're in it with the rest."

"The rest—who?"

"If you don't know, it's just as well. You won't be able to spill anything."

"You know me better than that, Dickie."

Collins put his arm around Gilberto's shoulder. "I shouldn't have made that crack, I know. You know what I said to the fellows? Don't any of you worry. Gil Reyes is a *white* Mexican."

That was when he should have gone right to his locker, got his things, and never come back. Instead, he went to the Science class after the lunch period.

It was Morrissey, the physical ed. instructor who also coached the basketball team, whom The Dutchman sent to bring Gilberto down.

"And don't try anything," Morrissey warned, as they walked down the stairs, "or I'll break your arm like a twig." He could have done it, too, being a judo specialist.

The first thing The Dutchman said was, "There's no sense in your denying anything, Reyes. I have the girl's statement in writing. She says you
forced her into this relationship."

Gilberto was standing. If The Dutchman expected him to go weak in the
knees, he fooled him. He also surprised himself at the calm way he received
the news that he was the patsy.

Morrissey leaned over and whispered something to Dr. Van Kliek who
nodded and asked slyly, "Did you induce her to smoke marihuana?"

Give them straight answers . . . "No, sir."

"But you know what it is."

"Yes, sir."

Van Kliek said, "Of course you do. It's in common use among you
Mexicans."

Gilberto was about to say, "I'm not a Mexican." But not to have said it
just then made him feel better.

"It's a good thing for you that the girl's father didn't go straight to the
police," Van Kliek said. "They would have handled this matter differently.
Nonetheless, I'm going to clean house here at McVeigh. Root out every single
one of you."

"If we'd just let out a hint about this, "Morrissey said, "the white student
body will do the purging."

"I don't agree," Van Kliek said. "We don't want any race riot on campus,
or anywhere about. That would be playing right into their hands." He looked
up through the upper half of his bifocals at Gilberto. "That's what you'd like,
isn't it, Reyes? To parade at the head of a picket line around the school. Well,
I'm going to cheat you out of that pleasure. Mr. Morrissey—"

"Yes, Dr. Van Kliek."

"March him to his locker, observe that he takes nothing off the school
property that doesn't belong to him, and see that he keeps marching. And,
Reyes—if you're thinking of transferring to any other high school in this
county, you'll find that your record has gotten there ahead of you."

In the space of five minutes, Gilberto had been called a rapist, a weed
smoker, a crook, and a Mexican. And the way The Dutchman said it, a
Mexican meant all of these.

That happened before Dr. Eisen got his mother moved to the sanitarium.
She was still at County Hospital. He said nothing about being canned from
school until he began to earn some money. He brought some presents: a box
of See's chocolates for each of the three nurses and a pair of satin mules for
his mother. And, into each of the slippers, he tucked a five-dollar bill.

She wasn't happy when he told her that he quit. He was making $30—as
high as $45 a week—in his job. He told her what it was: selling car radios,
used ones, for $25 apiece. His commission was five dollars on each one.

She felt a little better about it when he told her, "It's only until you're
better, Mom. Right now we can use the money. Save it up so you could have

private treatment. Then I can make up the credits in night high school and get my diploma."

"I think about you all the time," she said. "I want you to be somebody."

A couple of days after that, when he went to the radio shop on Hoover to turn in the money for two sales, Probert, the owner, acted very peculiarly. "What is it you want, young fellow?" he started, as if he had never seen Gilberto before.

"I got rid of that Majestic and the Motorola," Gilberto said.

Trying to wave him out, Probert said, "I'm sorry I don't have a one in stock."

Gilberto didn't get it. "Well, here's forty dollars for the last two," he said, putting the money on the counter. A man who seemed to be reading the price tags on the shelves quickly slapped his hand on the money, and a second man came through from the repair shop holding a gun.

Gilberto put up his hands. "Put 'em behind your back and lace your fingers. We're police officers."

They searched him and took all the money he had, including the small change. "Who'd you sell those two sets to?" one of the detectives asked. "Happen to remember?"

"The first one, the Motorola, to a fellow in a 1946 Buick, and the other one to an old La Salle," Gilberto answered.

"How about yesterday?"

"You don't have to say a thing," Probert warned him.

"The man is right," the second cop agreed. "But I think you will, kid. Take him in the back, George."

Gilberto thought he was in for a shellacking. But all that happened was an occasional question from George.

When Gilberto told him his age, the detective seemed surprised. "Still, you may need a lawyer," he said. "Do you know one? You'll be able to call him as soon as you're booked."

"No, I don't."

"You know *anybody* might be able to help you?"

"Does he *have* to be a lawyer?" Gilberto asked, seriously.

The detective shrugged.

The judge himself said that no amount of lawyers could have done for him what Dr. Eisen did.

First, Dr. Eisen was in with the judge for almost an hour, while Gilberto sat on a blue leather chair in the ante room. Then a buzzer sounded and the secretary said, "You may go in now, Mr. Reyes."

He walked in on both Dr. Eisen and the judge laughing about something. "This is my friend, Gilberto Reyes, Your Honor," the doctor said. "Judge Bryant."

Gilberto stepped up to shake hands. "There's more of you than I thought, Gil," the judge said. "Do any athletics while you were at McVeigh?"

He became frightened at the mention of school, and prayed they wouldn't bring that up. "Basketball," he said.

"How many games did you throw last season, and for how much?"

Both men laughed. Gilberto grinned. This was going to be easy.

"You smoke, Gil?"

"Yes, sir, sometimes, not much."

"Have a cigarette then," the judge said, snapping open a box on his desk. "It may be your last for some time."

He wondered what the judge meant by that remark. Leaning over to take the cigarette he saw a big, white card with fingerprints on it and the picture, front and profile, of a young girl. The judge quickly turned it face down.

"You know what's going to happen to—what's the fellow's name—"

"Mr. Probert?"

"Yes. *Mister* Probert will very likely get three years in San Quentin before Judge Normand, in the Criminal Part." There, he seemed to forget about Gilberto, turning to Dr. Eisen. "Personally, I think it's too harsh. But it's the statute and the auto insurance companies have been moving in on those theft cases as amicus curiae."

"They want 'examples' I suppose," the doctor said.

"Off the record, Sam," the judge went on, "fellows like this Probert are public benefactors. I think a radio in any but a police car is a menace."

"Depends on what you listen to," Dr. Eisen answered. "If it's Fulton Lewis, I agree with you. Let's get back to this public benefactor." He pointed to Gilberto.

"Very well," said the judge, much more serious this time. "Reyes, I'm still doubtful about your story that you didn't know you were peddling stolen goods. Your common sense, if you have any, ought to tell you that hundred dollar sets, a lot of them brand new, don't go for twenty-five, unless they're hot."

"I wouldn't have touched them—"

"Let me finish. You're over sixteen, and if it hadn't been for the doctor here, you might have gone on trial for a felony. But being a dope doesn't carry a penal sentence in my book."

He finally came out with it. Work camp. The people there would learn more about him in a month than Gilberto could tell about himself in a year. They would find out if he was a subject for reform or correction. If reform, he would be transferred to another type of institution.

Dr. Eisen, at that point, made one more try. "Excuse me. I don't know of any character defect in this boy that needs correction; institutionally, I mean. I'm asking, respectfully, that you think it over."

The judge did silently, for quite a few minutes. Finally, he said, "No, Sam. He's going to benefit by this place."

"Would you send your son up there?"

"If he peddled stolen radios I would. Then I'd resign and go up there with him. Look, Sam, if Reyes here is the essentially decent character you say he is, then *he* can do some good up there. There are younger boys up there to whom he might be—you see what I'm getting at?"

"From 'example' into exemplar," Dr. Eisen said. "I see I didn't move you."

"You did. More than you suspect." Then the judge turned to Gilberto. He explained everything. "Consider this place a camp, a school, a job—anything but a place where the idea is punishment. You'll live in dormitories. There'll be no guards, no locked gates. After the first month your parents will be allowed to visit you. After the third month, if you have no demerits, you can visit them, at home, every other weekend. Six months is the initial term, and few boys stay longer than that.

"I'm going to send you up there alone, Gil," the judge said. "I mean you'll travel up there by yourself. You'll pay your own railroad fare. Wednesday all right for you?"

"Whenever you say, Your Honor." His tears were beginning. "How—how is my mother going to get along?"

"I'm having her moved to another place," Dr. Eisen said. "Much nicer, and the best treatment there is."

"But how am I going to be able to pay?"

"We'll take that up later," the doctor said. "Let's go."

The judge go up and shook hands with him. "Good bye, Gil, and good luck. And drop me a line. Which reminds me, Sam—I got a postal card the other day, anonymous of course; a picture of Alcatraz. It said, 'Wish you were here, you dirty bastard.'"

Gilberto heard it. It was funny, all right, if you had nothing else on your mind.

He sat down on one of the stone benches in the Plaza. The tree directly above him, he noticed, was a honey locust. There were traces of blister rust on its lower branches.

A minty smell from trodden eucalyptus buds evoked the odor of the dental laboratory and Richardson, and having to go back there in the morning. Four hundred dollars. Certainly worth taking the elevator up to the fourth floor for that kind of money. A hundred dollars a floor.

His watch said ten after ten. On ordinary Sunday nights, he would be in his room at the Romeros' yawning over the Los Angeles Sunday Times. That's where everybody must be at this hour: in bed, or getting ready for it, except, naturally, huddles of little kids, playing in the dirt around the benches.

As he got up and started diagonally across the Plaza, he decided to drop in at the Orizaba, only a couple of blocks away. He hadn't been there in a long time.

Verónica La Negra jumped down from the cash desk and gave him a big hug, Mexican style. "Sit down, you big ox," she shouted, pushing him over to the table where she ate her own meals. "Sopa de albóndigas tonight. Good. Take a plate."

"No soup, thanks. I just ate. Been to see Mamá."

"How is she? Have something."

"A bottle of beer, if you have one with me. She wasn't feeling too good."

"Ay, pobrecita," Verónica sighed. "Rosa—the kindness of two bottles of beer. . . . Listen, Gilberto—just between the two of us, tell me—they treat her all right in that Jew sanitarium?"

"The best."

"¿De cincho?"

"Certainly. Why?"

"Because maybe she would get better sooner in a private place. I've got a little extra money and there's no better thing I could do with it. I say this from my heart."

"And from there I thank you," Gilberto said. It was the way you put it, in Spanish. "And I'm sure she does, too. But it's better that she stays there."

He decided not to tell her why—that he was going in the army in a few days. It would bring on either a celebration or a gush of tears, and he was afraid of both.

Sundays were still Family Nights, and the Orizaba was crowded. Verónica didn't want him to leave. "Don't fly off like a tzin-tzan-tzun," she begged, as she sprinted from the register to the kitchen and back again. "I want a word from your mouth."

At around midnight, the last party of diners was paying its check. Gilberto strolled over to the juke box, put a quarter in the slot for five plays, and pushed four buttons at random.

"Number Twenty-four," Verónica called, as she was locking the door.

The first four records spun away by the time Verónica came back to the table, carrying her cup of special, extra-strong Mexican coffee.

Number 24 started up. It was "Noche de ronda"; the only song recorded by Elvira Reyes. "With," the label read, "Chuy Heredia & Rhumbaleers." The only time Verónica La Negra let the collector for the box touch that record was to exchange it for a fresh one.

"How smooth—How beautiful," Verónica sighed as she listened. She put her big hand on his arm. "How good that you came, hijo." Tears began rolling down her brown cheeks. "You are the dearest to her, boy, and I am the next. But we love her equally. Not true?"

"Sure, sure," he said, hoarsely. "What are you crying about?"

"I don't know. . . . I have the sadness."

With all but visible tears, he was crying, too. For what, he didn't know, either. The Mexican explanation: la tristeza, the sadness, covered it. It took in his mother, Verónica La Negra, the blonde woman in the steamer chair on the hospital lawn, the little Chicano kids playing with bottle caps in the dusty Plaza, the sick trees in Pershing Square Park.

When he got home to Boyle Heights, the Romeros were all asleep. There was a pile of tortillas, a plate of chiles rellenos, and a square of orange Jello covered with a napkin on the kitchen table. He smiled; everybody was always trying to stuff food down him. He didn't take any of it, but it wouldn't be wasted. The Romero kids, Paco, who was seven, and Luz, four, would have it for breakfast.

This was the only real Mexican family he knew; all, even the kids, born there. Serafina—Señora Romero, who was born in the State of Jalisco, had reddish-brown hair, a rubia. She and Tomás, the husband, spoke only Spanish to the kids. "They must not lose domination of Castellano," Tomás said. "You, as well, Señor Reyes. There are other Américas besides this one."

Gilberto wrote on the slate nailed up over the sink: Just coffee—. Quickly he rubbed it out and began: Solamente café—

5

The elevator starter, Jeff, rattled his castanets, sending Gilberto up alone in the first car. It was only a few minutes after eight. The door of Richardson Dental Lab was locked, but he could hear one of the buffers going inside. He knocked, and Richardson came to the door.

"Well if it ain't Pancho! What happened? The war over, or something?"

The entire routine Gilberto had been rehearsing on the bus coming here fell apart. "I'm sorry to have to bother you," he began. "I dropped up about—"

"I'm busy this morning, you can see," Richardson said impatiently. "What's on your mind?"

"Well, I've been talking—they told me that there's supposed to be some money coming to me. I mean besides—" He stopped, as Richardson turned to shut off the buffer.

"What is this?" Richardson said slowly. "What are you giving me?" He put on such a scowl that Gilberto was convinced he was acting.

"According to the law I should have been getting thirty dollars a week," Gilberto said, feeling surer.

"They've been ribbing you, Pancho."

"The minimum is seventy-five cents an hour."

"Who told you that? A lawyer? That applies only to firms in interstate commerce."

"Arizona is interstate commerce, Nevada is interstate commerce—"

"You've been to see a lawyer!" Richardson shouted. "Going behind my back!"

"No. But somebody who happens to know. Miss Schwartz, the lady in social service over at the Beth Zion sanitarium," Gilberto said.

"So that's it! Some goddam Jew communist—"

"Now, wait a minute, Mr. Richardson—"

"What the hell are we fighting this war for if not to wipe out that scum? Instead of that you let them turn you into one of their dupes. I'll find out who put you up to this. I know ways to—"

The telephone began ringing. "I didn't come here to make any trouble for anybody," Gilberto said, walking after Richardson. "That lady says it's the law. And either it is, or it isn't."

"Dental Laboratory, Richardson speaking. . . ."

Gilberto was close enough to hear most of what was said on the other end. He heard: "Florence Schwartz . . . service . . . Beth Zion . . . speak to . . ."

"This is a business phone," Richardson snapped. "No personal calls. No! . . . And no messages, either. He's here, but I'm not his secretary."

Then Richardson listened while Mrs. Schwartz said something about her trying to get in touch with him. He made out the phrase, "an hour ago."

"Then you better tell him yourself," Richardson said. "Oh, you want to talk to me first? Well, I got nothing to say to you." But he didn't hang up. He listened, and Gilberto, having moved up, could hear Mrs. Schwartz's loud voice.

"Have you settled that matter the boy came to see you about?"

"It's between him and me," Richardson answered. "We'll come to an agreement."

"He's to get four hundred dollars—*even*."

"What *is* this, a holdup?"

"Would you like to go to court about it? We're ready to take the boy's case."

"Four hundred dollars," Richardson said slowly. "I don't have that much on me."

This elated Gilberto, not because Richardson was giving in on the money, but on account of the way Mrs. Schwartz was letting him have it. No nonsense.

"Then have it here, the Beth Zion Sanitarium, on Mission Road, just before you get to Alhambra. In cash, preferably, by twelve o'clock."

Richardson got a little angry. "Or what?"

"Or have your books ready for a government inspector by one. Now put the boy on."

"Hello, Mis' Schwartz. Did you want to tell me anything?"

"Yes, Gilberto. It's bad news . . ."

Funny, he could hear her so well before, when she was talking to Richardson; and now—"What did you say, Mis' Schwartz—huh—"

"Quietly, in her sleep. I'll wait here for you."

No matter what, unless they were there to see, she always said that it came quietly, in their sleep.

Gilberto sat up angularly, to make it appear that he had not been dozing, when he heard Dr. Eisen enter. He was carrying, in addition to his own, a plastic zipper bag. Gilberto recognized it as the one in which his mother used to pack their bathing things. He started to get up.

"Sit," said Dr. Eisen. "We're going to have a drink. You like cognac?"

"I never got used to anything besides beer."

"Then don't get used to this stuff, it'll keep you broke." He took a bottle, Courvoisier, and two small glasses from a cabinet behind his desk and poured. He drank his right down; Gilberto took a moderate sip.

Touching the zipper bag, Gilberto said. "That's what they wanted me to come back and sign for."

"I had to stop by, so I thought I'd save you the trip."

"Thanks a lot. Is it all right to open it?"

"From the weight, there can't be very much in it. The nurses told me she gave most of her things away. A suit, nightgowns, underwear—finish your drink."

"I'd like to ask you something, Doctor. Do you think she knew; ahead of time, I mean?"

The doctor tilted the dregs of brandy into his mouth. The answer was still in his pocket. It had come in the mail, to his office, the previous Monday.

Dear Dr., When I am gone you will be stuck with a very large bill. On account of Religion and family, bodys are hard to get for Drs. to experament. Having no money or jewelery but only Myself, I wish to hand over my Body offical to Dr. Samuel Eisen M.D.

Yours truly, Mrs. Elvira Reyes

"Yes," said the doctor. "She knew better than we did."

Gilberto opened the bag. On top were the satin bedroom slippers with pom-poms of blue feathers that he had got for her; still brand new. He would give them to Mrs. Romero. There was an old chenille bathrobe. Under that, a small wicker basket with Chinese labels that once contained tea. He lifted the lid and took out an envelope. "It's a letter from Mexico," he said, and put it aside.

Dr. Eisen picked up the envelope as Gilberto looked at the rest of the things: a tiny carving of an elephant, less than two dollars in coins, and a faded, tin-backed photograph of a fat baby.

"Postmarked ninth February, nineteen forty-nine; three years ago," Dr. Eisen said.

"From Mexico."

"Zaragoza, S.L.P. That's San Luis Potosí, the State," the doctor said, handing the envelope to Gilberto. "Know anybody there?"

The address was typewritten. "It says Doña Elvira M. de Reyes—to our old apartment—Cuidad de los Angeles, Estados Unidos. Skipped the state," Gilberto commented, "but it got there."

He drew the letter out of the envelope. Unfolding it, a small silver medal strung on a slender blackened chain slipped out, tinkling on the desk. The letter itself, typed in the same chemical purple as the envelope, was a single sheet of tissue-thin paper.

"On the top it says Tres Cenotes. That means three water holes; something like that."

"That's probably the name of the house, or farm," Dr. Eisen said. "Zaragoza is the city; has the post office."

"Must be a relative I didn't know we had. The name is Esperanza S. Viuda de Reyes."

The doctor glanced at the paper. "That thumb print; that's her signature.

She must have had the letter typed by one of those escribientes públicos."

"Here, you want to read it?"

"No, you go ahead, Gil. I learned my Spanish off phonograph records, not like you."

"Okay. It starts, Dear and Esteemed Cousin. She received the giro— that's a postal money order—for fifty pesos for her daughter Inés's confirmation dress and veil, and thanks us both in her name. After paying for the Mass, there was enough left over for a first class lunch—una comida primorosa—for many friends and neighbors, which she is sorry we could not partake." He looked up from the letter. "How much is fifty pesos?"

"About six dollars U.S. Read some more."

"She suffers from deep shame that she has nothing to send back except this little medal of Our Lady, the Highly-Sainted Virgin of Guadalupe, whom she begs, all the time, to intervene—"

"Intercede, I guess she means," the doctor said.

"Yeah, intercede with her Precious Son, the Señor Jesucristo for all that we desire. My house is yours and everything that is in it. Your most obedient servant and affectionate Esperanza S. Widow of Reyes; then the fingerprint."

He put the letter, the medal and the rest of the objects back into the bag. "The name Reyes makes her an aunt, or something. I'll drop her a line telling her."

Eisen nodded. "Do that."

Gilberto studied the brandy in his glass, picked it up and gulped. Rising to put the glass back on the desk, he tugged the wallet out of his pocket. "Look, Dr. Eisen—I know we owe you plenty, and I'd like to clean it up. If it comes to more than four hundred dollars, I'll send you the rest, as much as I can, every month."

"Sit down, Gil. The bill is paid. Your mother settled it."

"You're not kidding *me*. She couldn't have saved up that much out of what I gave her," Gilberto protested.

"She had it all the time," Eisen said. "I'm the only one she told."

Gilberto shook his head, puzzled. "Then there's the bill for the funeral. I don't want that hanging over me."

The doctor said airily, "That's taken care of, too. By the sanitarium, out of a special fund."

Gilberto put his wallet back slowly. "Well, then—"

Eisen felt his hands getting moist, as if he had them in rubber gloves. The boy was going to leave. He was getting ready to babble out how thankful he was again—and goodbye. He wanted to keep him there, five minutes—ten, or only a minute, if he could find the courage. Now!—or let him go. "So, Gil—"

"What'd you say, Doctor?"

This was good. He had said nothing. The boy knew it and this showed that he was keeping himself within range.

"I said, so you're going Friday?"

"There's nothing to keep me now."

"Four hundred dollars—"

"Four thirty-two, to be exact; less what I'll owe Mrs. Romero on Friday."

"That money will go a long way," Eisen said.

"In the army? What for?"

Eisen had begun wrong, too slyly. There has to be a crack in the mass before you could drive in a wedge. Maybe it was there, in the shadow of his grief. "I'm trying to think of what she would say if she knew."

Gilberto spread his hands. "What *could* she say? She'd have cried, that's all."

"Why? What difference would it have made? She knew *she* was going, and she didn't cry then."

Gilberto looked down. "I caught myself a couple of times last Sunday trying to tell her, in a roundabout way, sort of. About the allotments that would come to her every month. Then I said, no, it's no use."

"She couldn't have stopped you from going; that's what you mean."

"Well, how could she?" Gilberto's voice rose. "I've been through the whole routine, from the registration on up. Now I'm inducted. Friday I'm sworn in."

The fissure was there. Eisen saw it in the boy's vehemence. "If you made it sound as reasonable as all that, there is only one way she could have taken it: Goodbye, son, take good care of yourself, write often, and God bless you."

"Aw, I wouldn't expect that. Not from her."

"Then, excuse me, Gil, I think I know what you did expect; that she would say, 'Don't go!' "

"Well, naturally," Gilberto said, twisting a bit, "no mother, deep down, *wants* a son of hers in a war."

"You don't get me, Gil. I don't mean she would have stopped at 'I don't want you to go, son.' "

"You think she'd actually try to stop me; like telling me to desert?"

"It isn't desertion until you're actually in the service," Eisen said casually, "and you're missing for fifteen or thirty days. I forget which. However—"

"She'd never suggest a thing like that, no sir." Gilberto wagged his head.

"Then why didn't you tell her?" Eisen demanded.

"Because—," the boy faltered. "Well—her having gone has got me all mixed up. But you know as well as I; she read the papers, she listened to the radio, she knew what was going on: the Korean War; people were being drafted." He paused and felt himself on a maturer level. "The world would be in one hell of a shape if every fellow's mother said, 'Don't go. Run away.' "

"Would it? I wonder," Eisen spoke quietly. "I wonder what would happen if every mother said 'no.' "

"I guess, in a way, they all do," Gilberto acknowledged. "At least they don't go chasing them down to the recruiting station."

"Here's one whose mother did," the doctor said, taking out of his desk an unframed color snapshot. "My wife's brother."

"Looks about my age," Gilberto commented.

"He was when this picture was taken. Cadet-Major Charles L. Devlin, of the R.O.T.C. The L stands for Lindbergh."

"Say, wasn't he a crack middle-distance runner at Westwood?"

"Tennis," Eisen corrected. "Here's the next picture of him two years later."

It was an official War Department photograph of a new grave. The cross was stencilled: 1st Lieut. C. L. Davlin—a Corpsman's error.

"Korea?"

"That's right. Charley, however, didn't die in vain."

"I should say not," Gilberto agreed, with sympathetic conviction.

"He died to show us what the next war will be like."

"How do you mean, Dr. Eisen?"

"Well, here's what happened: Charley was leading a night reconnaissance patrol and, coming back with prisoners, they were jumped."

"By the Chinese reds?"

"Chinese, North Koreans, or guerrillas, we don't know. The official account said, 'a superior enemy detachment.' In the fight, three of his men were killed—knifed. But Charley and the others got away. First he made his report and then had some tooth marks on his arm dusted with sulfa. In a few hours, they couldn't bandage the arm fast enough to keep up with the swelling. The following night he was dead."

He stopped to watch the effect of his narrative on Gilberto, whose expression showed nothing besides grave interest.

Eisen was almost angry—at himself. His minor reputation as a raconteur at the golf club, in medical meetings had trapped him into dramatizing something that should be told straight out. "You don't get it," he said, with the awkward feeling of having to repeat the punch line of a badly told joke. "In the Atomic Age, a soldier is killed by a human bite."

He braced himself for that short, scornful phrase that he had been hearing all too often: the cynical, pigheaded, "So what!"

But Gilberto didn't say it. He was silent for some seconds, then, "I'm only one out of 350,000 men drafted this year."

"Men? That's not enough. Ten times 350,000 wouldn't be enough." Eisen wanted the boy to ask him enough for what, because from there, he could take him slowly.

"We're not in this alone, exactly," Gilberto said. "Greece is in with us, and the Turks."

This was good, Eisen thought. The kid had some facts, out of those grew truths. "England, too. And Canada," he suggested.

"Canada, naturally. She *has* to be in with us."

"Why?" Eisen asked simply.

"Look at your map. Neighbors; common border, three thousand miles long."

"What about Mexico? Neighbors; common border, three thousand miles long."

"The same thing goes."

In a tone of casual inquiry, Eisen asked, "About how many men would you say Mexico has over there?"

Gilberto tried to remember what he had read recently about Mexico. Or had he? "Mexico belong to the United Nations?"

"Very much so. In fact a Mexican is chairman of the Assembly this year," Eisen informed him.

"Then they send men according to their population," Gilberto said, guessing.

"India has twice the population of the U.S., more, in fact. How many do you suppose they've got?"

"I'm not up on that," Gilberto admitted.

"None," said Eisen.

"Oh, well," Gilberto brightened, "they're colored people."

"So are the Abyssinians, and they've got, oh, a battalion, I guess. But we were talking about our neighbor to the south, Mexico. How many men?"

"What do I win, a refrigerator?"

Eisen laughed. He was glad the boy's spirits were lightening, while at the same time fearful of his own tone, which was veering on the superior. He corrected it. "I don't blame you for not knowing, Gil. That figure is a sort of a military secret. None of the newspapers we read will give it away. The answer is, one." He held up a finger. "One! ¡Un solo mexicano! An observer."

"That's one for Ripley!" And with mock sincerity, he added, "It's too bad I'm not a Mexican."

The doctor widened his eyes theatrically, "You're not? Since when?"

"Since the day I was born, right here in L.A. Doesn't that make me an American?" He sounded too serious; this might be one of Eisen's jokes. "Or did they change the law? Okay, Doc, I'll play straight for you. What's the gag?"

"No gag, Gil. The law is the same. And under it you and I are equal, and both of us are equal with the rest. Fact is, you're more American than I. Your people were in America long before Columbus. The first of mine didn't get here until the year 1768. Isaac Eisen landed at Newport, Rhode Island with nothing but a tailor's shears and a package of needles."

"The time of the Revolution!" Gilberto was impressed.

"A brother of mine in New York has a funny collection of letters, written on the back of his own, to old Ike Eisen from some noted Revolutionary characters. He made their uniforms."

"George Washington?"

"No, I don't know who made his; maybe Martha. But I'll tell you the ones who paid him. General Israel Putnam, Commodore John Paul Jones, and Colonel Alexander Hamilton."

"Actually? The first Secretary of the Treasury; the man who wrote The Federalist papers?" Gilberto marveled.

"I see you didn't forget your American history."

"I only wish I'd learned more." Gilberto smiled. "Anyway, I did, just now. Nobody is going to stick me with the question: Who was Alexander Hamilton's tailor?"

Getting late—the phrase alone leapt to the doctor's mind and nudged him. It was the imp of his professional, middle class existence. Getting late. It had to do only with time, not with material existence. Late for what? Rarely did anybody, even himself, expect an answer. Getting late; that was enough; it stood by itself.

Tonight, perhaps it meant that his desk lamp, which was good enough twenty minutes ago, no longer gave enough light. He walked to the door and switched on the ceiling light. Maybe the boy was thinking it's getting late.

"You know, Gil, between sewing uniforms, he had to fight. He was in the Battle of Brandywine and in what they called the Paoli Massacre that wiped out half of General Charles Lee's army. The general himself was found lying drunk as a goat in a farmhouse. By the way, have another drop of that and I'll put it away."

"No thanks, Doc. But this is marvelous: hearing about history from somebody whose ancestor was in it."

"Somebody said we're all our own ancestors." Eisen took another drink and put the bottle away.

"This original Eisen, was he killed?"

"Hell, no. According to his headstone in the Jewish cemetery in Newport, he lived to be eighty-three." This was careless, this talk about a cemetery, with the dust of one still on the kid's pants' cuffs. "He had eight children: five girls and three boys. Which makes me suspect; for a Continental militiaman to take that much time out of fighting, he must have been one of those 'summer soldiers' Tom Paine talked about."

"We had something about Tom Paine in history," Gilberto remarked. "Just a paragraph, about how he kept up the spirits of the soldiers in the time of Valley Forge, with his pamphlets."

"What else?"

"But it turned out that was wrong. This particular textbook was biased. They said it should never have gotten into a decent American high school. Also, on account of some of the language in it."

This was interesting. Here, Eisen recognized, was a point where some honesty could be adduced. A septic area of pernicious, laboratory-grown ignorance. He could disinfect it if he could check himself in the habit of dialectical levity with a dash of Talmudism. Not long ago, he overheard a conversation, about himself, between two other doctors: "Don't tangle with Eisen. If you quote him something, he's read the book and he can quote it right back at you; kill you with it—I heard him last week at the County

Medical meeting cut down that A.M.A. stooge, a fellow *paid* to have all the arguments against compulsory medical insurance. Eisen made him look like a cretin."

He wanted to know a little more about this history textbook. "Who said it was biased, the teacher?"

"No. This booklet. She passed out the whole batch of them. We had to read them and then devote the rest of the history period to a discussion. She just asked the questions that were on the last two pages."

"What kind of questions; do you remember?"

"The usual kind. You know: 'What stands as the biggest menace to the American way of life? Answer: Communism.'"

"Godless Communism," Eisen suggested smiling, and Gilberto nodded. "Say anything about Fascism?"

"Red Fascism," Gilberto said offhand.

"Who put out this booklet?"

"The Legion; Americanization Department. It was called a supplement; supposed to be read along with the book."

"I'm interested," Eisen said. "Did it mention Tom Paine?"

"Oh, yeah. It straightened us out on him. He was a dangerous radical, and an atheist on top of that."

"'Dirty, little atheist?'"

"Aw, you must have read the book," Gilberto complained.

"No, really; I'm just quoting an old Legionnaire, Teddy Roosevelt. What else do you remember about Paine?"

"Well—let's see—he wrote these subversive pamphlets to weaken the fighting forces. That if Washington hadn't prayed to God, the Revolution would have been lost; that being Paine's idea all the time."

"What about this indecent language they complained about?"

"Oh, I guess they meant the part, just before the Battle of Trenton, when Washington crossed the Delaware—you know the picture. Well, according to the textbook, he, Washington, called out to one of the officers, 'Move your rump, sir, you're rocking the boat.'"

"No wonder," Eisen grinned. "You know what Washington actually said: 'General Knox, be so kind as to shift your fat ass and trim the boat.'"

The boy had a full, thoracic laugh. Like Charley's, the doctor thought. A doctor ought to include that as well as auscultation. "Say ah. Now laugh for me."

Charley Devlin would have laughed longer. There were very few things he did in his life that weren't "for laughs." Now, the last laugh, the risus sardonicus, was frozen on his face. It will be there forever. There is no skull that doesn't grin.

But between laughs, he had been able to teach Charley some things. Living in the same house, the opportunity was there. At mealtimes . . . "Hey, Sam, what's Lancashire Legs?"

"Where do you see that?"

"In this short story by an Englishman . . . 'straggling into the pub on their Lancashire Legs.' " The story was about millhands, in the cotton factories of Manchester.

"Rickets. Lack of Vitamin D. Makes children grow up bowlegged. The time you're reading about, Charley, people thought it was due to living in Lancashire."

"Wasn't it?"

"No. It was due to *working* in Lancashire; beginning as children, from the age of seven, or eight. They used to breathe in all the lint. I'm surprised they didn't call consumption Lancashire Lung. The factory owners had their own infirmities."

"Nothing like Lancashire Leg, though."

"No. Foxhunter's Foot, gout, Madeira Liver—"

So when the show-down came, Charley was beginning to get a vague idea of the score. But this brown Charley—he doesn't even know there's a game on. How do you go about telling him the ground rules when he's already half in uniform?

Put your hand on his shoulder in a fatherly way? Tell him, "Look son, I was very close to your mother. If she wasn't a sick woman, I'd have fixed up a nice apartment for her; somewhere I could drop in a couple of afternoons a week; saw to it that she got enough every month so that you could keep on with your education—."

It was too late for that; too late all around.

There was irony: This Mexican American boy was more of a patrioteer than the fair Celto American Charley Devlin. Charley would go to the American Legion's sponsored prize fights every Friday night, often "for laughs." That's all they were good for; that and to show up in parades. Gilberto Reyes bought his American history from them.

Eisen walked to the window and pulled up the blinds. Traffic was light on Wilshire Boulevard. Big street. It ran all the way from the heart of downtown Los Angeles to the ocean. Keep going and you'll wind up on the coast of Asia; Korea, if the winds are fair. The splotch of dark on the other side of the boulevard was the park surrounding the La Brea Tar Pits. Out of those jet, bubbling pools, they dredged the bones of animals that stood 18 feet high when man was still a blob of his own sperm.

Getting late—the imp elbowed him again. Yes, Eisen thought, it's getting on to Friday.

Gilberto was still smiling. "A thought just came to me: Thinking of the names, maybe Ike Eisenhower is related."

The doctor shook his head. "No. The old boy's name was Isaac, not Dwight."

"You think he'll get in?"

"I certainly hope so," Eisen answered.

"Yeah," Gilberto agreed. "Stevenson sounds a little more like he's for having the government pay for everything. Eisenhower is against that."

"He shouldn't be," the doctor said. "From the time he was seventeen, the government paid for his education; for every stitch of clothes he's worn; every house he's lived in. It paid for every aspirin he ever took and for every Eisenhower baby that was born." He smiled. "It would be almost a shame now to tear him away from the public titty."

"Why doesn't Stevenson bring that out?"

"Stevenson is a gentleman." Seeing Gilberto's puzzled expression, he went on. "Such a gentleman, in fact, that it never occurred to him what the rest of the country—which is composed mainly of non-gentlemen—wanted most. That's what's going to lose him the election."

In complete, childish bafflement, Gilberto asked, "And what's that?"

"A quick end to the Korean slaughter!"

"That's okay with me," Gilberto said. "Too bad I can't vote for him, too." He pointed to Eisen's commission, framed on the wall. "You fought with him and you're going to vote for him."

"Yes. And I hope I'm not making the same mistake as my grandfather when he voted for General Grant."

"Gee, you people must have been in every war."

The doctor nodded. "All of them—good and bad—that this country ever had. Yet—" He felt something touch his brain, in the pre-frontal area, that was like an electric charge. As the sting subsided he knew why Sam Eisen, if he were 19 today, would not have gone. Gilberto Reyes had the same reasons. He must show them to him. It was getting on to Friday; getting late. "—do you think that serving the United States from Monmouth to Remagen Bridge makes me an American as good as—let's say—Gabriel Heatter? No sir! Not to us. They go by our noses, by our names, and, if we have any, by our ideas. Those make me a Jew, and that's all! Just as your dark skin, the bones of your face, and your hair, make you—"

"A Mexican, I guess—"

"You *guess*? You don't *know*?"

"I mean," Gilberto stumbled, "I don't take it as an insult. Depends on how they mean it, when they call you one. I figure it this way: I never was in Mexico, unless you want to call Tijuana Mexico. Sure, I speak Spanish almost as good as English, but they teach that here in the schools. But if I was to take being called a Mexican as an insult, it would be *me* insulting all the real Mexicans. Isn't it the same with a Jew?"

"It's a good question, Gil; and I'm going to try to answer it. I may have to bring in my own experience. But the chief point is, when a man who has never seen you before, who doesn't know what your religion is, or if you have any at all; when he calls you a Jew, he *means* to insult you. Maybe that's too strong. But the least it means is that you're not an American; and if you are, by nationality, you're an inferior one. 'What the hell do you mean by being born here!'"

"That," Gilberto said, pointing to Eisen's army commission, "'The President and the Congress of the United States—'"

"That has its little story. When I was sworn in, they wanted to know what letter to put on my dog tag: H for Hebrew, P for Protestant, or C for Catholic. I said I didn't want any. I had no religion. They insisted 'everybody has to be something.' What if I was killed; what kind of service would they say over me? Give me all three, I said. If I'm killed, let the chaplains fight over me. But never mind that. See the paper next to it?"

"Diploma," said Gilberto. "It's all in Latin."

"Tufts. But that wasn't the medical school I wanted to go to. It was the only one that would take me in—that year. The others, they had enough students named Eisen, or who looked as if that ought to be their name, or Shapiro."

The Dutchman's threat: "I'm going to root out every single one of you," came back to Gilberto. "Or Reyes," he said. "Some places wouldn't let in a Mexican—I mean somebody who looks like one."

"Not many," said Eisen, with a half smile, "that wouldn't take you on as a bus boy, where I'd be turned down. For example, the Lakeside Country Club out in the Valley."

"That's where Bob Hope and Bing Crosby play. You belong there?"

"Belong—hardly," Eisen began wrily. "I had lunch there once; part of a lunch, anyhow. Even that, I had to throw up."

"That awful?"

"It was poisoned, *after* I swallowed it. A waiter brought over a note intended for the man who invited me, a patient of mine. But it was handed to me by mistake. It said: 'If you must eat with kikes, get in the trough with them. Don't bring them here.'"

"Son of a bitch!" Gilberto swore. "Did you find out who it was?"

"Right away," the doctor answered. "All about him. And why he hated Jews."

"Did they do something to him?"

"Plenty. First of all, the producer he works for—getting two thousand dollars a week as a film writer—is a Jew. His psychoanalyst is a Jew. His secretary, whom he's been trying to lay for a year, and who wants no part of him, is Jewish. And his wife, who had been posing as a refugee German baroness, brings her family over from Europe—a troupe of orthodox Polish Jews. Now he runs the only kosher house in Bel Air."

Gilberto began to laugh again, until Eisen said, abruptly, "Wait. The main reason is that two thousand a week salary. He thinks it's Jew-money because he has to kiss a Jew's ass for it. He forgets that his producer has to do the same thing to six Episcopalian bankers to keep his job."

"What gets me sore," Gilberto said, "is they have to use those disgusting names, like—"

Eisen said them for him, "Kike—sheeny. Uh-huh. But they must have some pretty fancy names for you, too."

Gilberto remembered the slack-mouthed clown in front of the burlesque house. "Chicano is what they use mostly, around L.A."

"Yet there's something worse than those labels," the doctor said thoughtfully. "It's when they want to be nice, or praise you, and, at the same time, don't want you to forget that they're bending over to pat you on the head. 'Nice boy, good Jew.' And there was one expression I haven't heard since I was in high school, in Providence—white Jew."

Barely aloud, Gilberto said, "You, too?"

"What?"

"Nothing—I just—"

"That was the worst," Eisen continued. "I wanted to act like a black Jew, a red Jew, or a Jew Jew. But I didn't know how. All I knew about Jews was what I learned in a Quaker Sunday school."

Gilberto sat silently. He wanted to, but couldn't, bring himself to say, "I know how you felt, Doc. I was in the same boat." Then, he would have to tell him about Carolyn Muller, and Dickie Collins and that essentially, there was no difference between their calling him a white Mexican and the kind of Mexican The Dutchman and Morrissey called him. Yes, there was a difference now: he preferred the way The Dutchman and Morrissey put it.

Eisen pressed his hands on the desk top. This was the point at which he should rise, say something about their both having had a tough day, and write the whole attempt off. He had failed; passed him in the dark, an obscurity of his own making, to cover his own fear that he might succeed.

He had conjured with love: Elvira's love for the boy; the profound, though unvoiced devotion of Gilberto for his mother. Those were constants. The boy loved as he breathed. In telling him about Charley, he had invoked fear. He possessed that, too, but not abnormally. If he had added that what happened to Charley happened also to 25,000 other American soldiers, Eisen doubted if that would have made any difference.

It was clearer now. The boy had love; he understood and respected fear. What he didn't know was hate.

Was it possible that he was pretending not to see, or to be inured to the most nauseating fact of his existence? Where he "belonged." In the steerage of the Ship of State, was the phrase that occurred to Eisen. With a kick in the face for his trouble if he as much as stuck his head up onto B Deck.

"Well, Gil," Eisen began, rising, "it looks like we both put in a pretty tough day."

The boy stood up. "I'd like to ask you, you ought to be the one to know, how is it in the service?"

"How do you mean?" Eisen asked, riffling through his appointment book.

"You know—what we were talking about—is there much of that in the Army?"

"You'll meet it to about the extent that it exists in civilian life, but not as much as in the Navy. There's a peculiar reason for that."

Gilberto had more questions. He tried not to appear impatient with this latest of Eisen's anecdotes. It was getting him off the track.

"Shortly after the Revolution," the doctor continued, "no, it was after the War of 1812, an officer named Commodore Uriah Levy won his fight to abolish corporal punishment of enlisted men. Annapolis never forgave him."

"Yeah, yeah," Gilberto said, hurriedly. "But once you're in uniform, you're entitled to certain rights. Let's say, you can sit down in a restaurant, walk along a street, stop to look in a window without a guy flashing some kind of a badge or a card and saying, 'Okay, buddy, let's see your Selective Service registration.'"

Eisen shut the book. "And when you show it to him, he looks as if he hoped you didn't have one. But does that happen to everybody?"

"No, goddam it; only to us—" He couldn't find a substitute for "—Mexicans!"

Eisen said nothing. It was evident from his expression that Gilberto had more to say. When he said it: "Pardon me for getting heated up like this," Eisen was disappointed.

"It doesn't have to, Gil." That was weak, catfooted, even cowardly, he admitted to himself. Let the kid go a little further, and he would, too.

Gilberto took two steps to the desk and put his hands on the zipper bag. He took deep breaths, and his face was taut.

"Am I going to see you before you leave?"

Gilberto didn't seem to hear him. His face, gray, became flushed as he spoke, not directly to Eisen, but at the wall behind his chair. "I've been thinking this over in my mind. My mother is dead now, and I don't belong to anybody. There's nobody I have to answer to for what I do. I mean, *she* can't be hurt any more where she is."

"What do you plan to do, Gil?"

In that curt tone, which implied that he preferred not to discuss it further, he said, "I didn't make up my mind yet."

"Before you do," the doctor said, rising, "make sure it's something that wouldn't have hurt her while she was alive. Okay?"

"Okay."

He seemed eager to go. There was no use holding him.

6

There was work he could do. Miss Carpenter, his nurse-secretary, had arranged, roughly in the order of their urgency, a heap of memoranda. There was a fresh disk in the dictating machine. The first memorandum informed him that Mrs. Garber called. Little Gregory's temperature was down to 100 at six p.m. The spots she was told to look for had started to come out. What should she do about Ellen, the older child?

It was chicken pox, all right. This was the least urgent of his cases. But Miss Carpenter was following orders: Anything pertaining to children comes first; with a sick child, we've got a whole family on our hands. He spoke into the machine: "Call Mrs. Garber. Calamine lotion; she'll need a pint. Dab lightly. It's okay to expose Ellen. Two for the price of one."

Next: Consultation with Dr. Browne, 9 a.m., Cedars. This was grave. Dr. Pincus's X-ray plates showed a considerable intestinal area affected: polyposis. Tough surgical job ahead, but George Browne was the man for it. Must explain to the patient how lucky he is.

Dr. Benjamin called. Gastro-intestinal series completed on Mrs. Kingsley—

The telephone rang. "Hello." It was his wife. "Yes, Margaret. . . . I'm sorry; I should have called, but I got tied up here. . . . No. I'll have something in the drugstore downstairs, so you and Gertrude go ahead and have your dinner. . . . Then you're going to the movies. Take the De Soto. . . . No, I couldn't. Too much to do here. . . . I don't know when I'll be home. Goodbye."

What if he had said, "And I don't give a damn if I never see what you two harpies call home again. Good-*bye*! And to hell with you and that old bitch, for good and all!"

Eisen's was a solitary rage; real enough when he was alone. But, when he came face to face with the two women, it flattened out. Meaning to sting, at the last moment, he would take the iron out of his protest and make a flabby joke out of it, one ponderous and soggy with words: "Since you have the curiosity to ask, my dear Margaret, why I flee straight to the study and play my phonograph records, I'll tell you: I have been in places where they refrigerate cadavers that were warmer than the atmosphere around this house."

More often, though, he thought his home was a steaming forge where his wife was the anvil and her mother, the hammer. "And I," he thought, "I'm something malleable that they want to pound out of shape. Why? They hate me! And why shouldn't they; they're not idiots. They know how I feel about them."

He groaned. "Oh, balls!" Here he was, dramatizing himself as a character from Dostoevski. "Stoning myself with confetti. Am I no bigger than what I'm contending with?" Margaret was once so agreeable, natural, and perfect. And how inexorably the freshness and tone of the woman deteriorated—even before the Fallopian pregnancy and the surgery that had to follow.

"Peg, you're only twenty-six. Do something with your life that I can't do for you. Would you like to own a dress shop? I've got a patient who wants to sell out—good will and all, for—"

"I want to forget," she said.

"What do you want to forget? *Tell* me!"

"Doreen—my baby."

"Margaret, dear, listen. I told you over and over that it was too early. We don't even know the sex of the embryo."

"Then maybe Dr. Nowak can convince me that I never had a daughter."

"Psychoanalysis is no solution, I told you."

"That's because you're afraid of what I might tell Dr. Nowak. If he was a greasy old Freudian—"

"Are you implying that I'm jealous of that charlatan! Listen, sweetheart, if you wind up, as you're well on your way, to becoming a broad-bottomed canasta machine, he's more than welcome."

And he could have her mother, too, in the bargain. Gertrude Devlin and her three dream-lovers! She had betrayed them to Eisen, in a series of wanton, venereal gasps, under the effects of sodium pentothal, during a minor operation. Three reverend gentlemen. Gerald L.K. Smith, Charles Coughlin, and Gerald Winrod. It's a pity, he mused, that they would never know with what virility she had endowed their shades.

He smiled at the familiar sight of her after dinner, nose deep in her copy of *Science and Health With a Key to the Scriptures,* and munching a slab of Ex-Lax to grease her leathery colon.

Which reminded him—he could use a soda mint tablet. Next to the bottle was his passbook, where Miss Carpenter always put it, after depositing the day's checks. "Security First National Bank, In Account With Samuel Eisen, M.D."

With this day's deposits, the last figure was $26,212. Another account— "With Samuel Eisen, M.D. or Margaret D. Eisen"—was always kept at a level of $5,000.

Whenever, as now, he thought about his finances, he always struck a lesser balance than the actual amount he was worth. He calculated that his endowment policies, worth $50,000 at maturity, had, today, a cash value of $30,000—make it 25. The house on Queens Road, which he bought for $30,000, was worth 40 on today's market. He owned no stocks, but he had a certificate for 20 shares, each worth $1,000, in the doctors' cooperative that owned this building. Two cars, furniture both home and office—nothing that would have to go at distress prices.

He never considered his medical practice as a capital asset; something you could fold up and tuck in a vault. Once a month, Miss Carpenter gave him a slip with the total amount in bills outstanding. The last figure was something less than four thousand dollars.

That's about where it stood last February, on the first, when she handed him the slip. The bills were already made out. She had only to type the envelopes. "Do that," he said, "but first mark all of them 'Paid in Full' and I'll initial them."

"All of them! Are *you* crazy! I could understand a few—Mr. Greenberg, the Cooper family."

"All—every single one of them."

She came back a few minutes later, with a card: L. T. Nielsen, Special Agent, U.S. Department of State. "He wants a few minutes. Official business, he says." Eisen guessed that he would be blond, humorless, and polite. He was right.

"Just a few questions, if you don't mind, Doctor, in connection with your application for a passport."

"I applied for a renewal of a passport that expired," Eisen corrected him.

The man glanced at the top one of a deck of three-by-five-inch cards. "I beg your pardon, that is correct. Technically. But an application for renewal is subject to the same regulations as a new one."

Eisen noticed that the cards had been arranged, one to follow the other, without backtracking. He saw Nielsen make a small check mark on the first card and put it behind the others. When he came to that one again, his business would be concluded.

"These are simply routine questions, Doctor, but please answer them fully." They seemed to be: pertaining to his medical degree, when and where obtained; when licensed, in what state, and, if elsewhere, where. Eisen gave the answers without hesitation.

Nielsen read from the next card: "Do you hold any degrees from Europe?"

"No."

"Have you practiced anywhere outside the United States?"

Eisen wasn't going to be trapped. "All my *civil* practice has been in this country."

"I see," Nielsen said. "And your training?"

"Tufts, P. and S., Massachusetts General—that about covers it."

"That is your answer?" Nielsen said, a little too smugly.

"Just a second, Mr. Nielsen, before you ask me any more. I want to know if I'm expected to sign any statement under oath."

"Oh no, Doctor, this is an administrative investigation."

"Then I'm entitled to know what you're investigating—the purpose," Eisen demanded.

"It's clear enough: your passport application. The questions are pertinent."

"Go ahead, then. What's the next question?"

"When was the last time, and for how long did you reside outside of the United States?"

Impatiently Dr. Eisen said, "Look here, Mr. Nielsen, are you seriously asking me that? Don't you people have any liason with the War Department? I *resided* outside of the United States from March 2, 1942, until some time in February, 1946. During that time I resided in England, France, Belgium, and Germany under the name of Major Samuel Eisen, U.S. Army Medical Corps." He added sarcastically, "Would you like to see my honorable discharge and my Good Conduct Medal?"

Nielsen didn't even look up from his cards. He read: "You stated in your application now pending, that you had a passport previously issued to you. That was in—?"

"Come now—you've got it down there. November, 1936."

"November fifth," Nielsen agreed. "You stated, under oath, at that time, that your passport was for travel in Switzerland for the purpose of study."

The doctor flushed. "Okay. You caught me. Just a minute ago I said I never studied anywhere but in the United States. Put it down, quick."

"As a matter of fact, Doctor, you weren't in Switzerland at all. You went first to France, and you were there only long enough to cross the border into Spain."

"At Port Bou," Eisen said, with clarity and anger. "At night! Through twelve feet of snow. Didn't you read all that in my file at the Franco embassy?"

Ignoring him, Nielsen glanced at a fresh card. "You volunteered your services on the Loyalist side."

"You're being polite, Mr. Nielsen," Eisen mocked. "Your friends never used the word Loyalist. Just exactly what does it say there?"

"Isn't it a fact, Doctor, that you served with the Communist elements?"

"Yes, there were Communists on my side." Eisen's voice mounted. "Also anarchists, Catholics, and Jews—lots of Jews. On the other side there were Nazis, Fascists, Moorish sodomites, and shits like you! Now what else do you want to know!"

Nielsen didn't appear in the least disturbed. "In your present application, the statement that you wish to go to the State of Israel for the purpose of study—is that correct?"

"I'll stand by what I put down. . . . And it's not *Iz*reel; it's Is-*ra*-el. Don't they teach you better than that in the State Department?" That aspersion on his bureaucratic alma mater, Eisen knew, would touch him.

"It won't help you to be abusive, Doctor."

"Go ahead with your questions."

Nielsen fed a new tip to his mechanical pencil and began on the next card. "Race?"

"Caucasian. Next—"

"What I mean is—" Nielsen hesitated.

"I know exactly what you mean. Put down non-Aryan."

In a precise, official tone, Nielsen demanded, "You are required to state your national origin."

Elaborately the doctor said, "Oh, well! Why didn't you *say* so in the first place? Let's see now—we weren't really the United States until after we overthrew the then existing government by force and violence, so I'll have to say British."

"Hebrew, I take it."

"Oh, my aching crotch!" Eisen chuckled. "You say Hebrew in the same dirty way that Senator Bilbo used to say Nigra."

"Your faith, I mean. That's obvious," Nielsen said, tautly.

"Why? My name? I wouldn't think of changing it. What would our next president say?"

"You're very funny, Doctor."

"I could be a lot funnier. My appearance? My big nose? I could take you down to a row of rug cleaning plants on Sunset Boulevard where the people look more Hebrew than a Stuermer cartoon, but happen to be more Christian than the Archbishop of Los Angeles."

"I should like a direct answer, Dr. Eisen."

"State the question, Mr. Nielsen."

"Are you Jewish?"

Eisen spoke slowly and distinctly. "I challenge the right of anybody to ask me that question."

"You may find that you're mistaken, Doctor." He skipped several cards, saying meanwhile, "I'm sorry I won't be able to report that you've been entirely cooperative."

"That's too bad. Now, if you don't mind, I have patients to see."

"Just one more question, Dr. Eisen, and I advise you to listen very closely." As Nielsen read, the doctor tasted fear, like dry cotton in his mouth. "Have you, during various dates in June 1951, conspired to violate the National Selective Service Act by means of suborning, bribing, or offering a bribe to secure evasion of military service by a person subject to same?" Then, tauntingly, he said, "Let's see how funny you can be now, Doctor."

He tried, even if it had to be gallows humor. "I see you know my mother-in-law."

"That information comes from another bureau, if you're interested. State has nothing to do with criminal complaints," Nielsen said. "Of course, it's a factor in your passport application."

"Which bureau has that?"

"Oh, Attorney General's office, or Justice. One or the other. You'll probably hear from them. Well, Doctor, I don't want to take up any more of your time—"

Good old Gertrude! Nobody else. Charley wouldn't have done that under torture, Eisen was sure. There was that note from him, the morning he left; that was a Friday, too:

> "Sam—I'm sorry but the whole deal is off. I know why you did it, not having anything to gain. Don't think I don't. The only reason I have to back out is Mom. It would kill her. She found out what we were cooking up and swore she saved up 40 seconals. That's the part I couldn't face. I put the book of Am. Ex. traveler's checks in your top dresser drawer. I'm also leaving the car in the showroom. Someday I hope to rate a Buick convertible for something better than making my Mother commit suicide. I know you wouldn't want that. So thanks for everything, and take good care of her and Marg."

Charley could have been in Guatemala now, playing tennis all day and screwing all night, if that's what he liked; instead he was nuzzling the dirt of a Korean hill named in honor of an actress's tits. But this is a break for him. Orders were probably being cut in the Pentagon, bringing him home to testify. Or, Eisen thought, he may be on his way already.

So, they were reaching back to a 1917 law to nail him; the same one, Eisen remembered, on which they sent Eugene Debs away for ten years. They had to go back that far to convict the Rosenbergs. Debs got out in four years. Those were merciful times, merciful judges. The electric chair for the Rosenbegs today. Incredible and impossible!

Eisen wondered what kind of a judge would sit on his case. A synagogue Jew, howling, "An eye for a hair and a life for a tooth!" or a weary peacock, like that Medina who had himself photogarphed going in and out of church lest he'd be mistaken for a Jew?

And what a magnificent Cornelia, with her jewel of a son Gertrude will make on the witness stand; bucking with all her might for the title of 100% American Mother-of-the-Year.

Hold it, Eisen, he commanded himself. You've been funny enough for one day. It won't be to laugh when they take you, M.D. and all, and put you to swabbing out crappers in some federal penitentiary. Nice job you did, Gertrude. I'll do as much for you, someday. The next time you go into insulin shock, I hope it happens when I'm around—to see that it's one coma you'll never come out of.

For three days after that visit from Nielsen he put himself on phenobarbital to settle down, to keep from walking into walls. The first night, he didn't go home at all. Instead, he went to the Finnish baths on Santa Monica Boulevard.

Naked, seeking a place to sit down, a voice called to him out of the hot fog. "Hey, Doc." It was Jerry Hayman, a lawyer, once his patient. "Why are you walking around with the family jewels hanging out, Doc? Sit down, have a cold lemonade."

"Watching your weight, Jerry?" he asked, patting the man's belly.

"Like a hawk. Do you think it's all right for me to eat watermelon? Wait a minute, before you answer—how much you going to charge me?"

"This one is on the house. All the watermelon you want. It's ninety-three percent water. Only don't eat it late at night."

"Hard to digest?"

"No. You'll wet the bed."

Jerry was somebody you could joke with, and Eisen wished he was more in the mood, and feeling less drugged.

"I didn't know you came to this mikvah, Doc."

"Mikvah?" Eisen assumed it was a Yiddish word. Lately, he had been hearing a great deal of Yiddish spoken: among doctors in the hospitals, among businessmen and movie people at his golf club. Not brashly, but like a secret language, in huddles, among themselves. Interrupted at it, they looked frightened.

"I *beg* your pardon, Doctor," Hayman said, bowing elaborately. "I forget you're one of those Reformed. Did you lose it in an accident, or, like that fellow, did you wear it off? Doesn't know what a mikvah is!"

"My dues are paid up in the B'nai Brith."

"But I never see you at a meeting. Anyway, I'll enlighten you," Jerry said. "A mikvah is a ritual kind of a bath that husbands are supposed to take before they give their wives a schtoop."

"In that case," Eisen said, nodding, "my compliments to Mrs. Hayman."

"Thanks. And speaking of the B'nai Brith, Doc, you didn't go to the special meeting last week when they showed 'Gentlemen's Agreement.' The President made a little talk about how, due to conditions in the world, it was time to take courage."

"Courage!" Eisen was amazed. "From that?"

"Why—what's wrong with it?"

"All the courage you can get from that picture, you can put in your eye. Don't tell me you missed the whole point, Jerry. What that picture says is, 'Don't be nasty to a Jew, he may turn out not to be one, after all.'"

Hayman pondered for a moment, finally nodding. "Oh, brother! What schmucks all of us are!"

It was time, Eisen decided, to broach his own problem. "Do you ever handle any civil rights cases, Jerry?"

"Well, it's not exactly my specialty. The last one of that kind I handled was a picketing injunction. What's on your mind?"

"A friend of mine," the doctor began, "in pretty serious trouble. He tried to bribe somebody to evade military service. Giving him money and promising to support him if he skipped. What's the penalty for that?"

"Hell, you've got him convicted already. Give me his side," the lawyer snorted.

"Well—the boy didn't take him up. He went into the Army and he's still in it. Does that make any difference?" Eisen asked hopefully.

"Witnesses?"

"The boy." He stopped there.

"Who else?" the lawyer probed.

"The boy's mother."

"Both willing to testify against him?"

"The kid will have to; the old lady is more than willing. She's eager."

Hayman sucked noisily at his drink, his brows knitted. Suddenly, he snapped his fingers. "This may work! Is this chump a Conscientious Objector, official, I mean; a Jehovah's Witness, or does he belong to any religious sect that's against war?"

"Nope. None of them."

The lawyer shook his head gloomily. "Then he's sunk. What I mentioned was his only out."

"That's what I thought," Eisen said. "But what I asked you first was what kind of a sentence would he get?"

"I should hate to guess, Doc. In these days—well, look at the Rosenbergs." Hayman put his finger on Eisen's chest. "Legally, the case against them stinks. Christ, they smell it in Pakistan, or wherever. So all right, but where's the morality! I ask you."

"I think the Supreme Court will see that," Eisen said. "That's, after all, their function—to see that the law squares with morality."

"If they don't," Hayman argued, "they might as well sit me in the electric chair. After all, during the war I gave the Russians an old wrist watch I'm sure did them more good than what they got from the Rosenbergs. So, you see, Doc, I'm not too high on your friend's chances. Explain it to him."

"I think he knows that."

"The best thing he can do, Doc, on the basis of what you tell me, is plead guilty. He recognizes his error, his nerves played him false—something like that. And, another thing—character witnesses, clean ones. You know the kind I mean: solid citizens. I'm trying to think—yourself, for instance, Doc."

The travel agency was sorry that Dr. Eisen had to cancel. "Too bad," Robbins, the manager, said. "March was such a lovely time of the year for travel in the Near East." He had even made reservations for the symphony concerts in Tel Aviv.

"I'll send you a check for your deposit, Doctor. Rather have the good will of you professional people. Just had the pleasure of serving a friend of yours, Dr. Emmerson and family. Arranged a beautiful tour: Mediterranean, fifty-nine days and deluxe all the way. Yes, and the two little girls will stay in a school, in Switzerland, meanwhile."

In not many years, Eisen reflected, those two little girls will be old enough to read their father's testimony before the Un-American Activities Committee, and spit in his eye. *He* had no trouble getting his passport! Neither did Ben Jackman, Norman Schultz, and a half dozen others. His colleagues, he thought bitterly. He had seen them, scuttling out of the Arts, Sciences, and Professions Council, like scared midwives; keeping themselves sedated out of their physicians' samples of barbiturates, paying up their assessments to the American Medical Association like good boys. And when it came to brown-nosing a hospital board, how they went at it with a zest. Physician, purge thyself!

He recalled how much better the lawyers conducted themselves during that Congressional auto da fé. Margolis, Katz, Steinmetz—he'd feel better if any of them could take his case. But he could see from the newspapers that they had more than they could manage.

He thought of calling Moe Feibush, who had been mentioned as being in line for a federal judgeship, and having a frank interview with him. Not at his office, though; a private corner of the card room at the golf club would be better. But, suddenly, he recalled that Feibush turned down a civil liberties case only a few days before. He did it publicly, ostentatiously, in a star-spangled letter to the Hearst paper. It was featured in a box on the editorial page. It ended: "And no soapbox traducer of our Christian Civilization shall find balm in Gilead, or an ally in me—Loyally yours, J. Morton Feibush."

Then came the day when Miss Carpenter entered from the waiting room with the mailman behind her. "A registered letter," she explained. "Joe wants your own signature on the receipt."

As he scrawled his name, he saw in the corner of the envelope: "For Official Use Only. Penalty for Private Use $300." He fumbled it open:

Application No. 314244.

Upon the authority of the undersigned, a passport to the applicant here named, is denied upon the grounds that it will not serve the best interests of the United States.

His hand steadied, finally. At least it wasn't the indictment. The reason they notified him at all, Eisen decided, was to get it on the record. They want to show that after committing black treason, he planned to report back to his masters, the Elders of Zion!

Shallow, twitching sleep, which did not come to him until dawn, was the best he got during the latter part of February.

On Washington's Birthday, Miss Carpenter caught him, drowsing at his desk. "I thought you weren't coming in today, Doctor."

"I forgot," he said. "Habit. Appointments?"

"None." And she urged, "Why don't you go home? Better still, you ought to go away for a while."

"Okay, Bobbie, okay. Run down the hall and borrow me a cup of benzedrine."

"Stop being funny," she warned. "One of these days you'll crack up."

She brought him a physician's sample packet of five-grain tablets, and he took one with a shot of brandy. "Amphetamine sulphate," the label read. "Stimulates the central nervous system and increases mental activity. Useful in cases of post-encephalitic parkinsonism. To be taken only on the advice of a physician."

He caught himself humming a snatch of the violin obligato from *Swan Lake* and stopped abruptly, imagining what a picnic they would have with his record collection. He would be questioned about them. Good. He wasn't a total stranger to the legal process. He'd have the answers. ("Stimulates the central nervous system; increases mental activity.") Shoot!

Q. Tchaikowsky, Iron Curtain?

A. Born 1840, died 1893, forty-two years before Josef Goebbels invented the term, Iron Curtain; not Churchill, as is popularly supposed.

Q. Stick to the facts.

A. Peter Ilyich Tchaikowsky visited the United States in 1891 and was given the honor of dedicating Carnegie Hall.

Q. There's one here—Rimsky-Korsakov. I suppose he visited the United States, too?

A. During the Civil War, as an officer in the Russian Navy; here to offer its help to President Lincoln against the South.

Q. You seem to know a lot about these Russian songwriters.

A. Yes, sir.

Q. Here's another one—Abraham Katchaturian—

A. It's Aram. He's an Armenian.

Q. It says here on the album "Young Soviet composer."

A. From Soviet Armenia.

Q. Oh, that one.

A. That's the only one there is.

Q. Was this one ever in the U.S.?

A. No, but he led the Hit Parade here for some weeks. The Sabre Dance. No royalties, though.

Less funny than what actually happened some years ago, he recalled: the L.A. police Red Squad solemnly listing S. J. Perelman's *Strictly From Hunger* among the "Marxist and subversive literature" they had seized.

Oh well, he thought nonchalantly, while he was at it, he might as well clean up the entire case.

My next witness, in rebuttal, Your Honor.

THE COURT. Proceed, Mr. U.S. Attorney.

Q. State your name, please.

A. I. Wendell Ha-Lévy. (The Witness is duly sworn.)

Q. Now, Mr. Ha-Lévy, you have heard the defendant, Eisen, act-ing as his own counsel here, questioning himself on direct ex-amination.

A. I did.

Q. You have heard him deny, categorically, any ulterior, subver-sive, un-American motive in desiring to go to the State of Israel.

A. I did.

Q. Then state the conversation you had with the defendant, per-taining to that matter, in the presence of two other witnesses, giving the date and place.

A. December of last year; during the holiday season—

DR. EISEN. If Your Honor please, it was the First Night of Chanukah. The witness should remember.

THE COURT. The witness will proceed without interruption from the defendant.

Q. And the place—

A. In the card room of the Hilldale Country Club. Dr. Eisen announced to the group of us that he was planning a trip to Israel this spring, and, knowing that I had traveled in the Near East, he asked my opinion of the country.

Q. And you gave it? Tell the court exactly what you said.

A. I said: "Sam, you're making a big mistake. I used to dish out that crapademus about the shining tents of Kedar, the Rose of Sharon, and the milk-and-honey myself, once. But what you're more likely to find is pastrami and gefilte-fish. Smell for smell, it's worse than Boyle Heights. (Laughter)

THE COURT. I must insist on decorum. The witness will proceed.

A. And politically, I said, it's as red as borscht. (Laughter)

Q. What was Dr. Eisen's response to that?

A. He said that his main reason for going there was professional. He said that it was a sick country. My suggestion then was that he picked the right place to stick the enema. (Laughter)

U.S. ATT'Y. Your witness, Dr. Eisen.

Q. (by Dr. Eisen) You gave your name as I. Wendell Ha-Lévy, with a hyphen and accent.

A. That is correct.

Q. What does the I. stand for?

A. It's merely an initial.

Q. I know. But the initial of what name?

A. Isidore.

Q. And the Ha-Lévy—that stands for Levy, doesn't it?

A. I have been known professionally—

Q. Did you obtain a court order legalizing your change of name from Isidore Levy to I. Wendell Ha-Lévy, with hyphen and accent?

A. Well—no; I didn't consider it essential.

Q. You are sometimes referred to as Doctor.

A. I hold the degree of Ph.D.

Q. What is your profession?

A. I am a motion picture producer.

Q. What are your qualifications for that work?

(Objection by U.S. Att'y.)

THE COURT. Objection sustained. This is not an inquiry into the witness's profession.

DR. EISEN. If Your Honor please, what I want to bring out is that his studio job is a false front; that he is actually employed as a provocateur, a professional stool pigeon by an organization calling itself the Film Legion for Rededication to American Principles, a completely—

THE COURT. That's enough! The jury is to disregard those remarks. Strike them from the record. And let me warn you, Dr. Eisen, you are skirting dangerously close to contempt.

DR. EISEN. I ask Your Honor's indulgence, but does the law require me to spare his reputation at the expense of my life? May I ask the witness what he did before he became a film producer?

A. (by witness) I lectured.

Q. Before that?

A. I was a member of the clergy.

Q. Isn't it a fact that in 1948 you served as rabbi of the Briscoe Avenue Temple in Brooklyn?

A. For a time, yes.

Q. And that you were unfrocked for being unpantsed with too many of the sisterhood? (Objection by U.S. Att'y.)

Great, if it could happen that way. But they would see that it didn't. Maybe Hayman had the right idea: don't shave for two days, wear a shabby suit, and "Look, Judge—I got post-encephalitic parkinsonism. God save you, Judge, from ever knowin' what that is. For months I been livin' on amphetamine sulphate. I don't know what got into me, Judge. Psychological tension—that's what it was—complicated with battle fatigue. I'm a veteran myself, Judge. Gimme this one chance, willya, Judge. . . ?"

Cringe, you bastards! That's what they wanted you to do. Assume the angle, in the army-medical phrase, so that they could plant the Cross and the Flag.

The Baltic Knights were coming . . . *"Peregrinus—expectamis—"*

That was the moment when Miss Carpenter burst into his office. "You're to go straight home, Doctor. There's a telegram. That was Mrs. Eisen called just now—"

"Get her back!"

"I think she passed out on the phone. Go on—take a cab, I'll drive your car home—"

Here then, was death and *nolle prosse*. Transfiguration into a dog-tag, impervious to acid, rough handling, and the gases of decomposition. A ritual apotheosis of formal paper: the War Department telegram first. "Of wounds . . . in action . . ."

His company commander, "Friend and companion in arms." The brigadier-commanding, "Splendid officer." The chaplain, "Eternal Glory of Christ's presence." The White House, "Profound regret." Later, a letter from a manufacturer of bronze memorial tablets, "Our representative will be pleased to show you these plaques in suitable sizes and dignified designs."

Batches of letters, but nothing from Standard Oil, Dr. Frank Buchman, Monsanto Chemical, or General Motors.

Here was victory and defeat, to each what's coming to him. Some defeat for mine, thanks, Eisen admitted. Margaret, you lost only a kid-brother; here's something to mourn on for a time. I'll have some shame with mine, thanks.

But you, Charles Lindbergh Devlin, your defeat is the greatest, because you could have been around to see the world flooded in the greatest light since Creation.

Ah, but Gertrude, you lucky bitch, yours is the victory. You weren't kidding about those forty capsules of seconal; you would have taken them if Charley lived. You can flush them down the toilet now, now that you're a Gold Star Mother. That's what you wanted to be, from the minute they brought a male out of your loins. But there is only one thing wrong with your victory, Gertrude—you'll never recover from it.

She took to having her mail laid beside her at the breakfast table, like Mrs. Miniver. Eisen would listen to her repertoire of little snorts, sniffs, and murmurs, which infuriated him. Then, when the $10,000 government insurance check arrived, she made no sound. Instead, she struck what Eisen called the Pioneer Woman pose, and let it flutter on the table. He would have said nothing if she had not batted her eyes to start a rill of silent tears.

"Don't cry; it's tax-exempt. You can declare it as earned income."

The look she gave him reminded Eisen of something by Ehrenbourg: "Persecute us and we shall go into the catacombs; there, suffering in the darkness, we shall live on the whisper of numbers, the rustle of debentures."

When Margaret came down, Gertrude had folded the voucher back in the envelope and did not mention it to her. Instead, she talked about how much she would have to do that day: the American Legion had called early. Yes, they knew that the "shipment" would arrive at San Pedro on Thursday. The "remains" would go, by army truck, directly to the military cemetery at Sawtelle. "I had to remind them that Charles was an officer before the adjutant finally promised *two* ranks of riflemen, one on each side of the grave, to fire the salute. And a bugler, for Taps, of course. I've got to bring them a list of the organizations I want invited. It'll be the Women of the Pacific, and the Pro-America girls, naturally."

Oh, she had so-o-o much to do! Would Doctor drop her at the Legion headquarters on his way downtown? Does Doctor know where it is?

"Me? A Daughter of the American Revolution shouldn't know where the American Legion is! Why, Gertrude—!" he mocked.

It all went off slick and smooth: Guard of honor, two ranks of riflemen, bugler. And the government picked up the check.

He sat up alertly. What time was it, anyhow? Twenty after eight, the hour that's shown on all dummy watches. Supposed to be the exact time that Lincoln died. Bobbie Carpenter had been gone since six-thirty. The Reyes boy had left an hour later. It seemed longer than an hour that Eisen had been lost in the thicket of the past. He had intended to do something immediately after the boy left, but he couldn't remember what it was. Oh, yes—

He clicked the switch on the dictating machine, waited for the disk to revolve, and spoke into it. "A letter, Bobbie, to Palmer Brothers, Funeral Directors—something Washington Boulevard, City.—Look it up—'Gentlemen: At the request of the family of the late Mrs. Elvira Reyes, I am sending you the enclosed check—call them up and find out the exact amount—for your esteemed services and appreciation for the manner in which you conducted her funeral. Yours, et cetera,' and I'll sign the check in the morning."

It was 8:25. No hurry. He would give the women time to leave the house. Tuesday—chicken pot pie special, if they had any left in the drug store downstairs. And then, the luxury of being alone in his study, with a new recording of Mahler's Fourth. He rose to leave and the telephone rang.

"Sam?"

"I was just on my way out—on a call. Aren't you going to the movies?"

"We decided not to. Mother's foot bothers her."

"What seems to be wrong with it?"

"Well, it's pretty badly swollen, around the large toe. It's where she cut it with the nail clippers."

"After what I told her!" he raged. "Oh, that stupid woman! The one thing a diabetic must guard—"

"Stop yelling at me, Sam. What shall I do, soak it until you come home?"

"No. Plug in the small sterilizer—you know where it is? See that there's a five c.c. syringe and needles in it. Scissors, too. There's sterile bandage in the bathroom cabinet, alcohol, and iodine. Put her to bed—no, I don't want her to walk. Make up the couch downstairs in my study. Keep her calm. I'll be right there."

Most of what he might need was in his bag: quarter-grain morphia stock tablets, novocain, carbolic lotion, bistoury, needles, needle holder, ligature. In the scramble of physicians' samples, he found two phials of terramycin. Sterile dextrose—he would pick that up in the drugstore below. As he shut the bag, the telephone rang again.

"Hello, Dr. Eisen; this is Gil Reyes."

He was about to tell him that he was in a hurry, and ask what he wanted. But, unaccountably, he spoke in a quiet, unhurried way. "Well, Gil, what's on your mind?"

"If you got a minute, Doc—"

"Just about."

"I'm down here at the Main Library on Grand, and they're getting ready to close the reference room."

"Yes?"

"Which book can I find that in; you know, the law on whether it's desertion only after—"

Eisen interrupted him; caution laid a finger across his lips. "I didn't hear you." And in the best Spanish he knew, he added, "Who told you that?"

"Huh? Oh—" and he continued in Spanish. "Some fellow I ran into on Fifth Street. Somebody I never saw before."

"How would he know? Had he ever been in the army himself?" Eisen had to hesitate until he remembered that the word for army was ejército.

"He makes the pretensions that he had served," said Gilberto.

"In that case, I'd have to take his word for it."

Gilberto spoke English again. "Didn't mean to bother you."

"Perfectly okay. Will I be seeing you?"

He may not have heard clearly. All he said was, "Goodbye."

At one a.m. he gave Gertrude the second dose of terramycin. Another one at five, and one more at nine, before going to the office. That ought to do it, he decided. Yawning, he set the alarm, tightened the belt of his bathrobe, and lay back in the armchair.

"Sam—"

It was the first time that she called him anything but Doctor. He glanced at the clock. It was 3:40. "What is it?"

"I have to get up."

"Oh, no, you don't, Molly Pitcher. Stay where you are. I'll bring you the pan."

7

The big coach hammered along the straightaway from Niland into Yuma.

Up to San Bernardino, Gilberto barely glanced out of the window. He had been that far before, so this was his real jumping-off place. Only this land was worth watching. The land and the driver. He was somebody; he was doing something. From where he sat, just back of the front axle, Gilberto watched him at work; an expert. He sat straight up, even on curves, he "walked" the bus, segment by segment; no tire squeal, like when you try to take it in one big swoop. Never touched his air-horn either, but talked the language of the highway with his lights, flashing them twice, to pass; dipping the beam for every approaching car.

Gilberto hungered to sit behind a smooth, slender wheel like that one, in one of those bucket seats, on top of a motor that *gave* when you asked it to give, and a set of air brakes that you only had to stroke to get a velvet stop.

The driver occasionally put his open hand up in front of him, and Gilberto knew what it was; he was being annoyed by the reflection of the passengers' reading lights on the windshield.

"Would you want that curtain down behind you?" Gilberto, moving forward, asked.

"If you don't mind."

Gilberto pulled down the green canvas screen from the ceiling behind the driver and buckled it to a cross bar.

"That's just fine, sir; I'm much obliged," the driver said, and Gilberto could see his smile in the glass.

He sat down again. Right now, he'd even settle for the three-ton Dodge stage truck they had up at work camp. The Cee-ment Mixer, they called her. "You take her up to the firebreak, Reyes," Mr. Lewis, in charge of engineering, would say. "And on the way, explain to your squad the reason behind double-clutching."

He tried to think which he liked better in work camp; the outside, or field-operations, as they called it; or the alternate week of inside work, called Camp Accounts Management. Making out requisitions for tools and materials on a typewriter; keeping the various inventories up-to-date; handling the single-entry bookkeeping of the commissary accounts; the miraculously accurate adding machines. . . . It was all good to know.

A woman in the seat behind him turned on a portable radio and began shopping around. The air was full of cowboy and hillbilly music. She finally made up her mind on one of them and turned the volume up. ". . . just sweeten your mouth with a delicious dipperful of Monongahela Snuff, while Alfie and Roy and me, on the 'lectric guitar, sweeten your ears. One—two—"

They played and sang fast, probably running out of time, pausing only to announce the numbers: "Put My Feet on the Road to Zion"; "Ding Dong Daddy From Dumas"; another hymn, "Give Jesus an Even Break"; and "Salty Dog Blues."

At Gila Bend, there was a 30-minute stop for fueling, servicing the bus, and changing drivers. Gilberto got out, carrying the canvas flight-bag which he bought at an Army-Navy Goods store in Hollywood. In a coin-operated cabinet, he washed from the waist up and changed his socks. Rinsing out the worn pair, he wrung them almost dry and wrapped them in a piece of toilet paper.

His supper was two hamburgers and a giant malt; "So Thick with Goodness," the sign in the cafe said, "You Eat it With a Spoon!"

For 25 cents, he rented a pillow—"Just leave it in the bus when you get off."—and took the same seat he had occupied before.

They took off, on the dot; the big wheels spitting gravel until they hit concrete. Next stop, Tucson. From there, he wasn't sure. Maybe Nogales, maybe El Paso.

The country was getting a lighter blue. He watched it lighten to gray. Hoping that when he opened his eyes again he would see green, he fell asleep.

A red glow forced his eyes open, and for the next hour, it was like watching one of those "A" Westerns in Technicolor. A horseman waved from an island of white-faced cattle. The shadow of each saguaro cactus traced a perfect h on the highway. Road runners sprinted cockily along the shoulder, their own dirt track, and lost themselves in the brush. The pungent aroma of sage brought back the taste of something exquisite he had once eaten, but which he couldn't name.

The Tucson terminal was just coming awake when the bus pulled in. Gilberto got off among the first three passengers, and when he turned to look back, after taking two or three steps, the rest of them seemed to have melted away. It was as if he had been riding with ghosts.

The refreshment stand was dark. There was nobody at the ticket counter, only a porter sweeping the litter from under the ruptured leather benches.

Gilberto checked the schedule on the wall. Nogales was out; no bus to there till late in the afternoon. El Paso was chalked up, but no departure time. He asked the porter, who told him, "It's making up now."

"Can I get a ticket?"

"Agent ain't here, yet. If he don't come by the time she leaves, the driver will take your fare. You got a whole hour yet."

He stowed his bag in a self-service locker, and while it was still open he glanced out in the street. Despite the morning chill, the sun already had a glare; just as well leave coat and necktie in the locker.

A little more sleep was what he wanted, but something to eat wouldn't hurt. No place where he might get some wheat cakes and coffee was open in the first two blocks of his stroll.

Then, around the next corner, he was on the threshold of the Mexican Quarter. The smells—burning charcoal, boiling vegetable oil; the sounds— the hammering on tin, a shrill radio voice; "¡Sí, señoras hogareñas, absoluta- mente gratis!"—these told him, before he could bring the street itself into focus, where he had ventured.

It was less ghetto-like than his own neighborhood in Los Angeles, which had a uniform, dun aspect; an impression of moist, vertical planes. Here the colors were sharp, crisp, like the air.

The stores had interesting Spanish names. A butcher shop called itself El Becerro de Oro, The Golden Calf. A small, cluttered novelty shop, El Rescate del Rey, The King's Ransom.

Gilberto stopped at a refreshment stand—La Línea de Fuego, The Firing Line. It was just opening; the hot-dog griddle was still cold, and there was nothing ready to eat except cellophane-wrapped packages of filled crackers and chocolate bars. But there was a battery of large, dewy jars on the counter, each filled with a different fruit drink.

"What may I have the pleasure of serving you?" the vendor said pleasant- ly in Spanish.

"I will take a glass of this, please." Gilberto tapped a jar of glowing ruby.

"Ah, jamaica! You chose well. It is what I myself prefer." As he ladled out a glass, Gilberto saw that he wore a Guadalupe medal on a string around his neck. He had one—somewhere—yes, in that envelope in his coat pocket. The drink, a cold, tart infusion of the jamaica flower, was delicious.

"You find it to your taste?"

"To be certain," Gilberto said. "I would like one more." He drank the second glass with a packet of cookies and walked back to the terminal.

The ticket agent was at the counter and the terminal looked alive and populated. Wallet in hand, Gilberto asked for one ticket to El Paso.

"Get a round trip," the clerk said. "You know, viaje redondo," and made a circle with his fingers. "Save ten percent. Ahorre dinero, huh?" His pronunci- ation was lousy.

"Just going one way," Gilberto insisted.

A few passengers were already seated—enough to have occupied all the window seats when he climbed into the bus. Standing in the aisle, he felt his arm touched hesitantly. A tall, fine looking man, around fifty, but with a ruddy, unwrinkled skin, edged away from the window. "Take that one," he said, smiling.

It was a good seat, same location, back of the front axle, on the right, that he had in the earlier bus. "You had it," he began awkwardly. "I could take one of the—"

"Now you go ahead, boy, and sit," the man said, moving his feet out into the aisle so that Gilberto had either to step over them or take the inside seat.

It was settled for him when the man took his bag and wedged it in the luggage rack. "Easier for me, too," the fellow said. "I can stretch out my legs."

"That's awfully nice of you, sir."

"Name's Buchanan, but everybody knows me calls me Buck. What's yours?"

When Gilberto gave his name, the man took his hand. It was a tiny hand for a man of his size. "A Tucson boy, are you?"

"From the Coast, Los Angeles."

"Got to go out there sometime," Buck said. He kept talking and Gilberto made polite answers. When they were well out of the city, he opened his copy of Popular Science magazine, and Buck was silent for a time. Then he began again.

Sleepily, Gilberto heard him talk about the movies and his hope, when he could take the time off from his business—cattle growing—to go to Hollywood and maybe see some of the stars he had been writing fan letters to. Gilberto was aware, in a vague way, that all this fan mail was to old-time leading men.

The fellow skipped from one subject to another; or, Gilberto thought, perhaps it only seemed that way because he heard him between momentary fits of sleep. Once, Buck took Gilberto's hand and made him feel the soft leather of his expensive boots.

Yes, Gilberto thought they were very fine. No, he'd never worn this type; heels were too high. Besides they were too expensive for him. "Maybe not as expensive as you think," Buck said, "for friends of mine."

This man seemed to have a lot of interests, it occurred to Gilberto. After talking about his ranch in Dona Ana County, New Mexico, he began to sound as if he owned a mine in Texas. "That's my home state; I'm a Texan, born and bred."

Somehow, the man's conversation got around to the subject of girls, and Gilberto didn't mind hearing about them from a fellow who obviously had been around. But he talked like some school kid on that subject, mostly against them; that they were mean and treacherous and were likely to give a young fellow disease—that's what he called it, "a disease." Then, he asked a very stupid question: Did Gilberto have a sweetheart where he was going? Didn't he miss the one he left in California?

"No," Gilberto said, grimly. "I got other things on my mind right now."

A minute afterward, Buck said, "I got a couple of nice, clean Mexican boys working for me on the ranch. Nothing heavy. Sort of assistants to me; I take one or the other along when I travel. Spend a few days in Deming every couple of weeks. I put up there at the Antlers Hotel. Nice to have you look me up, if you want to stop over. Just ask for Buck."

"Thanks; if I'm ever around there—"

Buck leaned over and said softly, "You'd look awful good in a pair of Levi's."

"I'm kind of tired now," Gilberto said, yawning. "Going to try and get a little sleep." Leaning over on the window, he shut his eyes. The pounding of the engine soon became just a pleasant hum, and the sound of traction a sustained buzz, fainter and fainter until it died.

He came slowly out of sleep, feeling the man's breath in his ear and a hand behind and under him. "Sweet boy—I'm goin' to be awful good to you—"

In the compound reflex to disgust, he shouted, whirled, and slammed his elbow into Buck's face. He was on his feet, his right fist cocked back, his face flaming, when the bus braked to a stop.

The driver was calm. "Now what's going on here?"

"This old faggot—," Gilberto began.

Buck waved his hand. "Now, now, Captain; nothing to take on about. It was accidental. We're going to Deming together, my friend and me."

"That's a lie," Gilberto said. "I'm going straight to El Paso. I'm no friend of his; never saw him before."

The driver, a husky, dark-browed man, waved Gilberto to his seat, but kept his scowling eyes on Buck. "You must be the old joker we were told to watch out for; picking up young guys."

"Don't you talk that way to me, you—you—." That's where he stopped, a strange, new pitch in his voice.

"Okay, Queenie," the driver ordered, "You're getting off."

"You don't want to be that mean to me, Sugar." This time, the coo stayed in his voice. "My little ticket reads as far as Deming."

"'Off!' I said."

"I'll sit up front where you can watch me. . . . You're so strong—"

The passengers laughed, and the driver, blushing, yanked Buck up on his feet. With one hand on his collar, and twisting his arm, the driver levered Buck to the door. "Now hoof it, mother, before I flag down the highway patrol."

The Texan jumped. "Puto!" the driver muttered, as he got behind the wheel and gunned the bus ahead.

Gilberto was glad he had the magazine so that he would not have to meet the stares of the others in the bus. He had come clean out of the incident. Still, there was that uncomfortable feeling that he couldn't shake.

If this hadn't happened, he would never believe that this typical, Stetson-wearing, tight-trousered citizen, who looked as if he had cut more than one notch in his six-gun, was queer. Nope, he thought, you can't tell these days who's fruit and who isn't. He mentally apologized to Tommy Rush, back at work camp, for disbelieving his story about—of all people—Wild Bill Hickok.

Tommy and he worked the bulldozer together, clearing for a fire break, when Gil heard it.

"You believe me," Tommy said, "that my old man writes about the Old West, don't you?"

Gilberto had to. Tommy had shown him evidence: a magazine article about Deadwood City and Boot Hill, with his father's name on them—

Payton Rush. Also a newspaper ad for a picture about the Younger Brothers, the bandits, "From an Original Story by Payton Rush."

Tommy himself, for that matter, was something of a specialist in that line. He knew all about what he called hand guns: derringers, Navy Colts, and Frontier models. It was on account of a gun that he was sent up to work camp. He admitted it: a Walther P-38. They grabbed him for popping glass insulators off telegraph poles while going 75 miles an hour in a hot rod.

"My old man went up there, for the research, where Wild Bill got killed," Tommy said. "Spent weeks hunting up guys—old settler types. He got told a lot of lies, but there was one he brought back was an affidavit; with a seal and all. That was the tip-off. The old guy who wrote it out was there in the barroom where Hickok was shot."

"Yeah," Gilberto said. "I saw the movie. They were playing poker and he held the Dead Man's Hand—aces and eights. It was doom."

"Well, this old type stuck around till they undressed him, Wild Bill, that is. And you know what he had on? A pair of long black silk stockings. And there was lace sewed onto his underdrawers."

If he ever met Tommy Rush again, he'd have something to tell *him*.

There were still several miles to go before reaching El Paso, but the passengers were already shuffling and fidgeting; edging forward to be the first ones out.

He waited until they had all left, and hoped that the driver would leave the platform, too. But he stood there, waiting for Gilberto. He would have to say something to him.

"I'm sorry there was trouble with that guy. I should have spotted him before," Gilberto said.

"That's all right. Nothing against you; but I tell you, kid, I had a tough time keeping my hands off that bastard's throat." His lip curled. "The dirty gabacho!"

"Gabacho texano."

"They're the worst," the driver said. "Anyway, the next time you hear them singing 'The Eyes of Texas Are Upon You,' tell them about this." He added, in Spanish, "Where you heading?"

Gilberto groped for the name of a place—any place. "Vera Cruz."

"You're a long ways from home. My people are originally from Durango City. Going by way of Laredo or Brownsville?"

"It all depends," Gilberto said, trying to sound casual.

"I'd take Laredo," the driver suggested. "It's only a five-minute walk from the terminal there to the border and you can take the through-coach, first class, straight to Monterrey." He glanced at his watch. "We got time for a cup of coffee, then I'll take you over to Joe Phillips, good friend of mine driving the Laredo Limited. If there's no seat, he'll make you one. Let's go."

8

He had slept and awakened and slept again; eaten and drunk and voided, during the brief stops of the massive silver Laredo Limited. He had ridden into the sun and under it; then, with it on his right hand and on his left, until it fell behind, to smother under red and gold banners.

The enameled shields marking the highway had changed their faces—US 80—US 90—US 277—whenever he thought to look. Texas was big all right; the way it used up highway numbers and a relay of three drivers on this one stretch.

They swept through the tattered gauze of dusk. And when the black wall of night went up, Gilberto imagined himself at the controls of this big beauty—Flash Reyes of the Planetoid Scouts, howling past Nova under 90,000 mega-pounds of thrust.

A fresh number popped up—US 83. How much longer to Laredo? Nothing to see outside the window except the occasional match-flare of burning gas on the horizon. He tilted his seat back for the dozenth time and, after a while, moved it forward. Behind him sat a man with a bubbling snore. In the seat ahead, a woman kept getting up and down, up and down, tortured by a sweaty girdle.

This was the price, in creeping time and somnolence, that a fellow has to pay for being ignorant and at the same time making sounds like a man who knew what he was talking about. So it's Vera Cruz you're headed for? Take him the rest of Texas, Joe, and bum voyage!

It was too late for Gilberto to change his story, even while they were having coffee. He thought of a number of other places in Mexico, but a person who was supposed to be on his way to see his folks can't suddenly decide to switch his destination.

Nor, could you meet a more well-meaning fellow. He, too, wished he could take the time off to visit relatives of his own in Durango City; and he would, some day. He conducted him right up to the steps of the Limited. "A friend of mine, Joe. Take good care of him, and pass the word along."

"You bet. Going far?"

"He's going all the way to Vera Cruz. . . . So long, feller, and have a nice trip."

"Goodbye, and thanks."

That was all. No names were given and none asked.

A double-headed marker showed up: US 81-83. He settled back; he wasn't going to be fooled any more by a cluster of lights ahead. Too often they meant some squat hamlet through which they breezed even before the bus could throttle down to the legal limit.

Now he could see the play of headlights, one after the other on the roof. He sat upright and, peering ahead, saw the kind of sky that glows at night only over a metropolis. The wheels began pounding upon pitted asphalt. Neon signs spat—Eats—Hotel—Motel—Cafe—Beer—Lone Star—Chile—Chili and Lone Star again.

Like the lowing of cows, the passengers began making the sounds of arrival: coughing, hawking, groaning, sighing. Some were on their feet, pawing like insects in the luggage racks. Others were crouched on the edges of the seats.

The bus drew up at a curb. "Park Street—San Bernardo Avenue," the driver called out, opening the doors. Four people descended.

The street names didn't mean anything to Gilberto. This wasn't going to catch him, as it did hours earlier when the driver had to tell him, "Take your time; this is only Eagle Pass."

He lit a cigarette as the machine turned off the road and stopped with a gasp of compressed air.

"All out! Watch your step getting off!"

It was cold and he felt the icy touch of the wind on his back and the crescents of sweat at his armpits. His coat lay folded in the canvas bag and Convent Avenue, Laredo, late at night, was not the place to unpack. Besides, he would be unpacking completely in a few minutes. The tall, red-lettered sign reading "Hotel—100 Rooms—100 Baths" was only two or three blocks up the next street.

A number of cars with Mexican license plates passed him going the other way; south, toward the border crossing. That five-minute walk he had been told about. He would be taking that stroll, but not yet. He felt tousled and dirty; not like the traveler who left San Bernardino, California, at his back and took full and glorious possession of the miles ahead. Being clean was the secret of that elation. He would recover it. Already, as he pushed the screen doors of the hotel apart, he could taste, with his skin, the torrent of fresh water.

Inside, he proceeded straight toward the far end of the tiled lobby. Somebody hissed, and he turned. A man, sifting the sand in an urn, called to him peremptorily, "Hey, you! ¿A dónde vas?"

Gilberto pointed to the desk in an alcove and advanced to it. The clerk did not, as they do in the movies, twist the register around and offer the pen, butt foremost. He waited, with a blank look on his face, until Gilberto was against the counter. Then he asked, "What is it you want?"

"The rooms have baths or showers?"

"Where you from?"

"California," Gilberto said. "I just got off the—"

"Well, this is Texas," the clerk snapped. "We're full up. No rooms." He turned to attend to the switchboard behind him.

"It's mainly the bath I wanted," Gilberto tried.

"We don't have separate baths."

"I don't mind paying for the room, too. I'll just use it to get cleaned up and change."

"Are you all that dumb in California? I said I don't have anything. Is that clear?"

Apparently, it wasn't. "What about the hotel on the other side of the street?" Gilberto asked simply.

"You'd be wasting your time. . . . Can you read English?" The clerk put his finger on a framed notice on the wall: *The Management Reserves the Right to Refuse Service to Any Person it Considers Undesirable.*

Gilberto had seen that notice, or a variation of it, many times before in Los Angeles, on practically all restaurant menus. He had thought of it as being in the same category as *No Smoking* or *Watch Your Hat and Overcoat.* In its more serious aspect it referred to drunks and Negroes. He was neither. He was an—

"Whyn't you try the Y," the clerk drawled, "or one of the baños on your side of town?"

"Thanks," Gilberto said, picking up his bag.

"On your way now."

On the sidewalk he scanned the rooftops, looking for the familiar red triangle of the YMCA. It wasn't there. Baños, the clerk suggested, and by "your side of town" he obviously meant the Mexican Quarter. He thought of going, but decided that a stranger in a public bath house took a big risk. A flip of an expert's finger and his wallet would be gone.

The wallet—! He slapped both hip pockets before he remembered, in foolish gratefulness, that it was in the inside pocket of his coat, folded in the flight bag. It wasn't the best idea to leave it there. If somebody snatched the bag out of his hand, he would be left with nothing but what he was standing in. Better to transfer it to its accustomed place, a region long-sensitized to alien fingers.

As he tugged the coat out of the bag, unintentionally collar down, the wallet thumped on the sidewalk. The letter from Mexico fluttered beside it. The thin chain hung out of the envelope as he picked it up, after stuffing the wallet into his pocket.

Drawing the medal out, he weighed it in his palm. It was about the size of a dime, but not as useful. A dime you could spend; all you could do with this is lose or mislay it.

Give it away? He wasn't sure that was the right thing to do; at least, not for the purpose of merely being rid of it. Religious objects, he supposed, were passed on to people who mean something to you, like—well—like a mother passing it on to her son. They were precious if you believed in them. He didn't. His mother didn't either, although he never heard her say so, right out. Maybe her mother did—or his father. The point was, she kept it stored away for three years.

Glancing around, to be sure that nobody was watching him in a gesture so purely feminine, Gilberto put the chain around his neck and hooked the clasp. Lifting his bag, he walked west, toward a more brightly lit street.

Here, at the corner of Hidalgo Street and Convent Avenue, he might find an open drug store, a telephone book, and the address of the YMCA. He waited for a dusty Ford two-door to pass before crossing the street. The car had Nuevo León license plates and was carrying an entire family. Less than a hundred feet onward, it settled noisily down on its bone-dry springs and stopped behind a line of cars.

Gilberto walked along, toward the head of the throbbing file of machines. Of the eight that he passed, six had Mexican plates; one Texas Mercury and a Florida Nash grumbled among them.

At intervals of less than a minute, the first car in the line would spurt ahead and the rest inched up and closed the gap.

He passed the Ford with the Mexican family. Now he saw lights on rippling water. This last street over which the cars jolted was a bridge. That water was the Río Grande on this side, the Río Bravo on its opposite bank. The pink and orange sky over him was Laredo. The pale, yellow one over there was Nuevo Laredo. This soft sucking of rubber on smooth pavement was the United States. That dust, rising in puffs from each turning wheel on the other side, was Mexico.

And this was the border crossing. This was the river that gave the Wet-backs their name. Gilberto had imagined that it would be wider, but it wasn't much different than the turgid wallow that ran past the Cudahy slaughtering pens back in L.A. This couldn't be the burden of all those cowboy songs; not this stretch of it, anyhow.

Again he saw the family Ford, which was being waved brusquely across the bridge by the U.S. guards in dark green uniforms. Except for the shiny buttons, they were cut much along the lines of business suits. The car that followed, a Pennsylvania Dodge, was stopped briefly and then sent on to the Mexican side. There it was halted by the Mexican officers. These looked more military. They wore tunics with Sam Browne belts, Colt .45 automatics, breeches, and shiny cavalry boots.

That car and another U.S. sedan with a roof carrier piled with luggage pulled over beside a building marked Aduana. For a time, he watched the Americans, grinning, nodding, showing papers, and directing porters who hauled luggage into the building, hauled it out again, and restowed it.

There was other traffic as well: foot passengers. Most of this was one-way—from the Mexican side; men alone and occasionally mixed groups. Some carried bundles or unwrapped purchases such as any tourist might make during a few hours across the border. Those who carried things displayed them briefly to the U.S. Customs guards and moved on toward the brighter area of Laredo.

Those walking across from Laredo into Mexico moved faster, more quietly, and if they carried anything, it was a tin lunch basket. The men were mostly in workshirts and overalls. The women and girls wore uniformly dark dresses, many wearing rebozos. These were obviously Mexicans who had jobs of one kind or another on the American side, and were taken no notice of by the American officers. The people, it appeared, did the same. They were like home-going factory hands, hastening to get the mill gates at their backs.

Gilberto had already decided that the U.S. guards let anybody and everybody out of the country, and that the Mexican officers let anybody come in. If it continued this way for—he determined—four more cars and the next ten pedestrians, in either direction, the pattern would be set. Then, his next move would be to blithely cross the bridge and see what was cooking in Old Mayhee-co.

A man on a bicycle—this wasn't in Gilberto's calculation, but he watched the cyclist approach the U.S. side, take a piece of paper out of his pocket, and flash it. Instantly, a guard stepped in front of him and gestured for a look at the paper. One glance and the guard beckoned the rider to walk ahead of him, pushing his bike.

Something was wrong, although Gilberto didn't believe that this disturbed the pattern of free passage, both ways. It might be that the pass had just expired, or something as minor as no tail light on the bicycle.

Two cars and then another crossed from the U.S. side. The first was waved on toward the lights of Nuevo Laredo. The second was signaled to pull over toward the Aduana. Routine baggage check, Gilberto thought, as the third car followed the first.

With relief, Gilberto saw that he guessed right about the man on the bike. He seemed to be pleading to be allowed to mount it, but the guard pushed him gently on, appearing to tell him that his machine would be right there when he came back.

Five of his ten pedestrians started across; two women and two older men. The fifth wasn't in that party at all; he couldn't be, although he was dark, wore a sombrero, and carried a corrugated paper box tied up with string. Less than ten feet from the U.S. gate, a guard moved swiftly behind him and took his arm. A second guard came around to the other side of him, and the three walked back across the U.S. gate together.

Gilberto thought that what happened was like one of those slow-paced, but suspenseful—as they called it—English movies. He moved closer, still in the shadow of a building, to see better. The two guards and the man between them were almost abreast of the customs building when the man jerked forward in a blind attempt to run. Gilberto heard cloth rip as the guard on his left caught the sleeve of the fugitive's denim jacket and spun him around. A long barreled gun flashed in the hand of the second guard, and he swung it, twice; once across each cheek of the man. Blood spurted. Gilberto wished he wasn't there and that this erection, a sign of his terror since childhod, would descend. He feared they were going to hit him again, and when they only shoved him into a chair inside, the relief brought a thin dribble of urine.

While one guard signaled somewhere down the street, the second one, Gilberto could see by the firm gesture, ordered the bloodied younger man to undo the package. Gilberto hoped it was only narcotics and not a severed human head, like in that oldie with Robert Montgomery and Roz Russell. The guard plunged his hand in the box and brought up one article at a time: a crumpled gray sport-jacket, a pair of brown slacks with the suspenders hanging from them, a sweater, and a leather toilet kit. He whisked around in the box, but there was nothing else.

With scarcely a sound, a car moved up to the building and a heavy man with something in his hand that clanked got out. It was no ordinary car; it had a red spotlight on the roof.

Gilberto got away from there, walking north. He kept going; past Grant, Iturbide, Hidalgo, Farragut. At Guadalupe he slowed down. There was a lunchroom a few doors from the corner, an all-night place, and he went in. Not that he was hungry, but he wanted to be able to sit down and think about what he had seen.

He mounted a stool, and the twitching under the skin of his calves stopped when he wrapped his leg around the stanchion. He asked for a glass of milk and chose a dish of bread pudding sprinkled with toasted coconut.

It was all pretty clear now as to how those border crossings operate. It was, simply, that you had to be somebody to cross that burbling ditch as nonchalantly as the 99 people out of the 100 he had watched negotiate it. And by somebody, it doesn't mean that you have to be at the wheel of a Buick Roadmaster full of premium gas and matched luggage. It means, in the language of the man on the street, that you have to be either a Mexican or an American—mexicano or norteamericano. The rest were culls, with an occasional sport like the guy who had been pistol-whipped and hauled away. Why had that been? If he had made it to the Mexican side, would he have gotten the same treatment? He doubted it. Certainly not for carrying his clothes in a paper box. Then, what—

It struck Gilberto with cold, sudden clarity that some people don't have the *right* to leave the U.S.; that the beaten man was one of them, and he, Gilberto Reyes, was another. But people do it all the time, Gilberto pondered, and get away with it. How many times had he seen the newspaper phrase: ". . . believed to have escaped into Mexico." If only the guy had not made himself conspicuous by carrying that bundle.

Tilting his head back to finish the milk, Gilberto momentarily saw his own face in the mirror, behind a shelf of single-service packages of breakfast cereal. It brought back Eisen's description: "Your dark skin, the bones of your face, your hair . . ." Doc was right. Those made him a Mexican from the stoop of the Romero house up to the last inch of Texas pavement.

He paid the check, and as he left he saw his full figure in the tilting mirror. That's how he would appear to Mexican eyes: in his $37.50 Meadowbrook Model Semi-Drape, his medium-short haircut—a hybrid who looks as much like a Mexican as a mule looks like a horse, and vice-versa; and was, in all probability, a jackass.

Color of skin—bones of face—thickness of hair; those are things you can't change. You're not even aware of them—why, even in that war picture, he saw himself as Van Johnson and not as the Mexican boy who played his buddy. You forget certain things involving the way you look—things like Carolyn and the Dutchman and people like that pasty faced hotel clerk. The object of those is to see that you don't hold your head up so high or walk so confidently.

Then, along comes a guy like Doctor Eisen and you take his word for it that you're as good as any son of a bitch, regardless of his name or tint of skin—and here you are! Was he proving this by being down here? He didn't see how. If anything, he was proving to the Richardsons and the Morrisseys how right they were. By being down here, by looking for a rat hole out of the army, even those who called him a white Mexican would say he was betraying his whiteness.

But they and Eisen couldn't both be right. There was another reason for his being down here that would hold just as good if his name was—well, let's say Charles Lindbergh Devlin, instead of Gilberto Reyes.

That motive was somewhere, but in bits and pieces. It was too bad, Gilberto regretted, that Doc Eisen had such a way of talking in circles. And when it came to the clincher, why didn't Eisen come right out with it in so many words and tell him to run away? No; he couldn't pin this on Eisen. But he wished desperately that he could collect all those bits and pieces of what Eisen said and knead them into the big reason that made him decide that when they called the roll in the Federal Building on Friday morning, Reyes would not be there.

9

Over the gas station on Salinas Avenue there was a lighted sign reading, "Tourist Information Here."

Gilberto strolled over. Instead of asking the attendant directly, he got a bottle of Dr. Pepper out of the vending machine, uncapped it, and drank. As he put the empty in the wire rack, the man noticed him and Gilberto asked, "This tourist information you give out—is it about Mexico?"

"Mexico and the States, both. It's all in one of those folders on the rack with the maps. Help yourself."

"Thanks. Does it tell about the rules?"

"You driving?" the attendant asked, "Or just on your own?"

"It makes a difference then?"

"I was going to say," the man said, "if you were driving, the Auto Club could help you out. But they're closed till morning."

"Good idea, thanks," Gilberto said, walking toward the map rack. The attendant called to him and pointed. "There's a fellow ought to be able to tell you; guy working on his jeep over there by the air hose. He's back and forth all the time."

The jeep stood a little outside of the track taken for servicing. Its hood was up and a man was bent over the engine, the play of his shoulders indicating that he was tugging to loosen some stubborn part. An arm flew up like a semaphore and the man leaped backward with a shrill cry of pain, alternately licking and blowing on his left hand. He saw Gilberto and grinned. "Damn near barbecued myself. You forget how hot these manifolds can get."

"Touch the exhaust? I can give you a Band-Aid," Gilberto offered.

"A little engine oil will do it, thanks just the same." The man looked maliciously inside the hood of his jeep and at the pliers in his hand. "I still haven't got that filter off the gas line."

"Can I give you a hand?"

"If you don't mind." He handed Gilberto the pliers and both tucked their heads under the hood. While Gilberto held a section of the copper fuel line away from the manifold, the driver twisted the glass filter cup.

Gilberto was able to see him very close. He was shorter than himself, about 28 years old, with sparse blond hair. He was big in the chest and his skin was naturally rosy, not sun-reddened.

He got the filter cup off and held it up to the light. "Look at that, will you! Bugs! Beetles! Compliments of Petróleos Mexicanos." He swished out the cup and wiped the inner surface carefully with his fingers. "I didn't mean anything personal. Only it isn't worth the saving of a few cents buying gas on your side if you don't keep your pumps clean."

"I see what you mean." Gilberto watched him replace the filter and buckle the hood down.

"That does it, and thanks a lot."

"No trouble. . . . The fellow at the pump tells me you go over the border a lot."

"Sure do. And I owe you a lift. But if you take it, you'll have an awful sore ass by morning."

"You going *that* far?" Gilberto said, smiling.

"If I went any further, I'd land in the Gulf. Matamoros is all. And I got to be there pretty early or the governor of Tamaulipas'll get eels in his beer."

Gilberto had never heard of Matamoros or Tamaulipas, only they sounded Mexican.

"So you're going right on through." That, Gilberto thought, was noncommital enough.

"Yup, right on 83. A good 200 miles, including the stretch on 77 from San Benito into Matamoros."

"I'd appreciate it a lot—" Gilberto began.

"I could run you down to the bridge," the man suggested, "and you could have some fun in Nuevo Laredo and later get a plushy ride on the through-bus to Monterrey."

That damn through-bus to Monterrey was always popping up! "That wouldn't do me any good," Gilberto said uncertainly.

"Why not? Where you going?"

"Vera Cruz." It was out before he could check himself.

"So that's where you're from. I knew you weren't a Tex Mex. Where'd you spend most of your time in the States?"

"I lived in Los Angeles."

The man's voice took on a more direct edge. "What part of town?"

"East; on Soto."

"Oh, yeah," the man said, in a tone of elaborate recognition. "That's practically around the corner from Macy Avenue."

"I think you're a little bit mixed up. Macy starts on North Spring and turns into Mission Road going east, after the second bridge."

The man smiled. "That shows you how much *I* know. I put in six weeks there when it was the Ninth Corps Area Headquarters. . . . By the way, what's your name?"

"Gil—Gilbert Reyes."

"Mine's Fred Bishop." They didn't shake hands. "You speak Spanish as good as you do English?"

"*Almost* as good. You know, when you're born into it—"

He stopped because Bishop was staring at him keenly; at the dangling Guadalupe medal, he realized, with slight embarrassment. "I guess you're a little bit leery about me."

"Well, figure it out for yourself," Bishop said. "Why do you suppose all these trucks you see have signs on them, 'No Riders'?"

"You got a right to be suspicious," Gilberto agreed, putting his flight bag on the flat hood. "You can look in there, if you want." He unbuttoned his coat. "You won't find as much as a pocket knife."

Bishop looked less stern. "Forget it. It isn't as if you were trying to flag me down on the highway. . . . Okay. But it's going to be a long ride and a cold one. And that bucket seat is just a steel frame with a thin cushion. Another thing, I'm not making any stops except once, for gas."

"That's all right with me."

Bishop took a thin fold of money out of his pocket, peeled off a dollar, hesitated, and added another dollar to it. Holding them out to Gilberto, he said, "Get yourself something to eat. Get plenty; use it all."

Gilberto shook his head and took out his own wallet. "This meal is on me, Mr. Bishop. You have to eat, too."

"I was going to." Bishop hesitated and appeared to be thinking hard. "Okay. I just remembered a place where we can eat together."

They sat across a plastic-topped table in a small restaurant. While waiting for their T-bone steaks, Bishop explained why he had to be in Matamoros early in the morning.

"I was only half kidding about the governor of Tamaulipas," he said. "The thing is, they're giving him a lunch tomorrow in a restaurant that's one of my customers, so I've got to be there in time to clean out the beer pipes."

"Oh."

"You say 'Oh' like you know all about it," Bishop smiled. "How much draft beer did you ever drink? Admit it wasn't much."

"To tell the exact truth, I don't remember that I ever drank any."

"Well, if you did, you'd know if the brew came out of clean pipes or those that they let get all slimy and gummy. Keeping them clean is my job. I got contracts with eighteen cafes between here and Southmost, Texas, on both sides of the border."

"That's pretty good," Gilberto said. He wanted Bishop to keep talking about his own affairs; to leave him no opportunity to ask questions. He was afraid that he would not be as lucky with the answers as he had been with Vera Cruz. "How does the thing work?"

"The whole rig is mounted in that semi-panel I had built in the back of the jeep," Bishop explained. "Air compressor and a fifteen-gallon boiler fired with kerosene. After I blow the pipes clean with air, I sterilize them with live steam."

"It's quite an idea," Gilberto said, trying to think of a way to keep Bishop talking about himself.

"It's a living. Keeps me on the go."

There, Gilberto decided, was his opening. "Sure. They can't bring the pipes to your shop."

"Right. . . . What about you?"

How little about himself could he tell? How dangerous would the truth be, and how safe the lie? "Just what you see, Mr. Bishop."

Bishop grinned. "You want me to say, 'Not much,' huh? But I'm going to fool you. I see a guy that got himself a good Stateside education."

"From first grade on up to McVeigh High."

Bishop nodded. "That explains the way you talk English. I'd say as good as anybody's *born* in this country. After high school where did you go?"

This had to be a lie. "Fillmore," he said, giving the name of the town nearest the work camp.

"Never heard of it," Bishop said.

"It's small; only about 175 fellows enrolled."

"Not coed then."

"All male."

Bishop chuckled. "Too bad. You missed out on the best part of college. Anyway, you probably got more out of it than I did in my year in Mexico City College. What did you take up?"

Another lie, on top of the last one; only not as fat. "Forestry."

"Good deal," Bishop said. "And now you're going back to Mexico."

As Gilberto nodded, the waiter brought their steaks with French fried potatoes and a stack of bread. "Tortillas," Bishop said, "and bring some salsa mexicana, too."

"No, thanks," Gilberto said. "I kind of got out of the habit of eating that stuff."

"That was for me," Bishop said. "I like it."

10

With no wind wings on the jeep, the cold swirled around them as they ground up Guadalupe Street.

More Texas. A fresh highway number—US 59 sprouted, and the jeep bucketed along.

For the first ten miles, neither of them said much. "Feel a little logy, with two beers on top of that steak," Bishop said. "You were smart to take milk."

"Habit," Gilberto said. "Coffee is what I should have had."

"Me, too. . . . I notice you keep looking at the speedometer. Forty-five, fifty, is the best these double-traction jobs can do, level running."

"Seems faster."

"That's because the road's so close under you."

"Yeah," Gilberto agreed. "It's an effect; when you look down—"

Bishop interrupted. "Why don't you lean back and get comfortable. It's all right with me if you don't want to make conversation, and you don't have to pay any attention to me if I keep on yapping. I got to talk so I don't go to sleep. I tried a radio, but it works on me like a sleeping pill."

"I could spell you, any time you want to rest," Gilberto suggested.

"Don't feel insulted if I say no. I know you Los Angeles drivers are up there with the best. But this isn't city driving. I know every dip and every cattle-crossing from here into Matamoros."

"I just made the suggestion."

"And another thing, I'm not squeamish about running over jack rabbits. I notice how you suck in your stomach every time we flatten one."

Even to explain it made Gilberto queasy. "The way they sit up, like they were frozen to the road, and then—crunch."

Bishop shook his head slowly. "That's one thing about Mexicans I can't figure out." He paused for an instant and then said, "You don't mind my talking about Mexicans, do you?"

"Why should I?"

"I mean, my being a Texan; knowing Mexicans all my life and knowing what their feeling is toward us. You probably got some opinions of your own."

"Mine are mostly about Californians. But only certain ones."

"That's what I call a fair-minded way of looking at it," Bishop said enthusiastically. "And I want you to give me credit for the same point of view. Whenever I say, 'Mexicans this,' or 'Mexicans that,' what I really mean is *certain* Mexicans."

"You started saying about rabbits—they reminded you something about Mexicans."

"Let's see, now—" Bishop had to think for a moment. "Oh, yeah; it was your reaction reminded me. I don't want you to get the idea that I enjoy killing them. Or even seeing animals killed, like Mexicans do—excuse me—*certain* Mexicans, I meant to say; a few million or so."

"Oh, the bullfights. Did you see any while you were down there?"

"Two," Bishop said. "And I'll take a good ball game any day in preference."

"It must be pretty rough on the bull."

"That's where you're wrong."

"How wrong could I be?" Gilberto said. "All he does is get killed."

"Every time," Bishop agreed. "But put it this way: If you were a bull, wouldn't you much rather go out fighting instead of getting nutted, worked till you dropped, and finally led up the slaughter house ramp and get your throat cut? You've been in fights yourself."

"Nothing life-and-death."

"Regardless. You know it's only the first punch that hurts. And if you're really in there swinging, it's an anesthetic for the rest of them you get. And certainly, the last one is painless."

"You don't think the bull feels it?" Gilberto's purpose in asking the question was to be companionable—to play along. Bishop, he saw, talked not only to keep alert at the wheel; he liked to talk. Gilberto was prepared to bet that he would talk about anything, providing he got the feeder-lines.

"Some bulls feel it, some don't," Bishop said carefully. "I saw a couple when the fight was out of them just stand there, waiting for the payoff. And when they get it that way, that must hurt."

"But sometimes the bullfighter gets it, like in that picture—"

"Yeah," Bishop broke in, "and sometimes a guy painting a flag pole falls into the street; sometimes a window cleaner's belt breaks, and both of them were doing something useful."

"But the way a bullfight brings out those crowds!" Gilberto marveled. "I saw a newsreel—"

"The crowds!" Bishop exclaimed. "I want you to see those for yourself." He snorted, then calmly, said, "Now I don't want you to take this as anti-Mexican talk. But you just mentioned a type of people that come all over themselves watching six bulls get killed, paying as high as seventy pesos every Sunday for the privilege, and on Monday they call themselves animal lovers! That, to me, stinks."

Although clearly the man's rage was rhetorical, Gilberto gave it silent respect. The man wasn't really angry about anything, but like many people he didn't simply discuss a subject, he assaulted it. To Gilberto, it was the difference between listening to a teacher explain something in the classroom and somebody haranguing—no matter what about; vitamins or the man-eating shark—from a street platform. Gilberto preferred the dedicated howler, the Bishop type.

The one thing Gilberto wanted to avoid was an argument on the subject of the Mexican personality. Despite the earlier exchange of mutual denials of prejudice, Bishop veered close to general contempt of Mexicans. The safest thing to do was not to get into the range of controversy.

Meaning simply to say something amusing, Gilberto remarked, "We started with rabbits and wound up with bulls. There must be some animal in between."

"Okay, let's take—well—let's take the burro," Bishop snapped. And he didn't sound amused. "Now you don't want a more ordinary type of animal then the burro. He's not given to committing suicide like the rabbit and he's not a fighter, like the bull. He works all his life, and if he's lucky, he may get to jump something in the female line."

"Yeah," Gilberto offered. "They got to come from somewhere."

Bishop continued seriously. "Now we're dealing with the burro—so get this: A friend of mine down there by the name of Ellis; not a GI like the rest of us, but been down there ten years, at least. He tells me this: One weekend he's in a little town in the State of Guerrero. He didn't know it, but at the same time there's a Hollywood picture company down there on location. Speaking perfect Spanish, he walks up to where there's a huddle of these picture people around one of the Mexicans with two burros. It seems they need a couple of burros in the picture and they're trying to buy these from the guy. First he says they're not good burros; there are better looking ones in the neighborhood. Then he gives the excuse that he's got to deliver their loads of leña—you know, firewood. They were offering him a hundred pesos for each, which, in those days, let me tell you, was one hell of a price for a burro. No, señor—the way Ellis told it to me—I cannot sell my darling little burritos. It would break his heart. The fellow acted like he was being asked to sell his children. Finally, somebody came up with the idea—you know these Hollywood geniuses, you come from there—they rent the burros, for something like ten pesos a day. Believe it or not, the guy said that was too much. He would be cheating them; five would be enough and he'd throw in his own services as the driver."

Gilberto began to laugh and Bishop said sternly, "Wait a minute. This is no gag."

"It's the funniest thing I ever heard," Gilberto insisted.

"I guarantee you'll change your mind. . . . The movie people told him they couldn't use him. It was a scene. One of the actors was supposed to drive the burros. It took them quite a time to convince this guy that the actor was a decent guy, a great animal-lover himself and he wouldn't hurt the burros. It was all right, wasn't it, if he just gave them a little tap with a switch? Well, this Mexican was horrified. That was no way to drive his little sweethearts! He'd show them how. . . . Now I'm not making this up; it's the way Ellis told it to me, who was there. . . . The driver pulled back a piece of dirty rag from both animals' flanks, uncovering sores as big as your fists, raw and creeping with maggots. And he had a sharp pointed stick—"

"I get it, I get it," Gilberto said, his teeth clenched.

Bishop sailed right in, like a boxer before his man could recover. "Take the dog! The way that poor bastard suffers from the Mexicans' love for animals! I tell you there's millions of them running around, starving. They're under your feet everywhere you go. You come out of a restaurant and they're out there looking up at you. I'd rather they were panhandlers; you could slip them a few quintos. But you can't be carrying around a pocket full of bones."

"They should get rid of them," Gilberto said innocently. "Painlessly, you know. Carbon monoxide gas is what they use in L.A., I heard."

"You're going to make yourself awfully unpopular in your own country, boy," Bishop said solemnly. "Let me tell you something. I was walking down a street called Bajío and I see a fairly sizable crowd around something in the street. A dog, hit by something that must have been a road-roller, from the shape he was in. It was giving out moans and screams every once in a while. And the people around, all they were doing was shaking their heads and saying, 'Ay pobrecito.' And there was a cop right there, too, feeling just as sorry; too sorry to put a bullet through him. Goddam it, I did as much for a Japanese corporal who blew his stomach open with a grenade."

And this, Gilberto thought, was the same guy who hung back about giving him a lift; timid about being held up.

"I tell you—the one time I was really afraid, and that includes sixteen months in the Pacific, was driving one night with a friend of mine down Tacubaya, in Mexico City. . . . We hit a dog and made the mistake of getting out of the car to see if maybe it was just clipped. But no, it was good and dead, fifty feet or so behind us. And when we looked up—boy! A mob closed in on us, women included. Maybe because the car had Arizona plates, but they smashed the windows, cut the top to pieces with their knives, and they would have done the same to us if we didn't run like hell—leaving the car there. . . . Now, as a Mexican, what would you say about that?"

"Why as a Mexican?" Gilberto asked, realizing that he sounded resentful and challenging for the first time. "Anybody would say it's a lousy shame."

Bishop laid the bait. "What's a lousy shame? What part of what happened?"

"The part about the mob; the way they acted."

"There!" Bishop exulted. "That's what I mean! Let me say, incidentally, your time in the States wasn't wasted."

"What's that got to do with it?" That note of challenge was there again.

"Don't go 'way; I'm coming to that. I told what happened, exactly, to a couple of Mexicans, one of them a lawyer. And you know what their reaction was? No comment about the mob action, only, 'Well, you see, we Mexicans love animals.' Get that, now—'We Mexicans.'"

Bishop paused. Gilberto admired the skill with which his companion put over an argument; he made his listener participate. "Yeah, I got that."

"Now get this: I was riding on a bus down Insurgentes, when we're stopped by a big crowd that's blocking the street. What happened? Well, a kid on a bicycle with a load of milk bottles across the handle bars couldn't stop in time, and ran smack into the side of a Cadillac that was pulling away from the curb. That stopped him, for good and all. The guy who owned the Cadillac jumped out, pulled a gun, and shot the kid right through the chest. He was still laying there. And what do you suppose the mob was doing? Tearing up the Cadillac? No! They were listening to the owner explain with tears in his eyes the damage to his car. . . . Now, what's the answer? Is it, 'We Mexicans love Cadillacs'? Be honest."

"The way it strikes me," Gilberto said, "is that people, Mexicans or Americans, can't claim only the good."

"You're darn tootin'. It cuts both ways. When it's a virtue, you can't say, 'That's us!' any more than when it stinks, 'That's him!'"

They were silent for a time; for the space of one cigarette. Gilberto tried to think of something else—not Mexican or Mexicans—that he could bring up. Bishop himself? No, Bishop might require a more detailed run-down of his own background. Recent movies were out; Bishop had cut him off before when he tried to mention them. The war—ixnay—but definitely. Texas? Well, being a Texan, Bishop would want some comment on that; praise, naturally, and so far Gilberto had nothing pleasant to recall, up to meeting Bishop.

He thought of trying to match one of Bishop's stories of violence; an eye-witness account of the pistol-whipping at the border crossing. Bishop might tell him why that happened. Gilberto already suspected, but he was afraid to know for certain when and in what city that fellow was due to answer to his name.

The headlights caught two iridescent green points ahead, and a low, gray shadow slunk out of the beam. "Coyote," Bishop said. "Comes from Mexico."

Here we go again, Gilberto sighed to himself; back to animals and Mexicans.

"The word, I mean, is Mexican," Bishop continued. "Not Spanish—Mexican. Coyotl. You also gave us the turkey—guajolotl; the tomato—jitomatl; chocolate, squash—"

"Marihuana," Gilberto smiled.

"Okay, put that in with the hoof-and-mouth disease and the cow pony. The good with the bad. And what you didn't give us, we took: California, Arizona, New Mexico—little things like that."

"Texas," Gilberto added.

Bishop laughed. "Now how did I come to leave that out! . . . I didn't have to be down there long to find out what we gave you people. They don't bother the tourists with it, but if an American is down there to stay for a while, they'll hash it over with him. And they're not any too friendly about it. For instance, there was an old portero in the rooming house I lived in, who wouldn't even talk to an American, student or no student. I found out why. His whole family was killed in Vera Cruz—your town—when the United States Navy shelled it."

"When was that?"

"In 1914. The excuse was something about refusing to salute our flag. But the real reason was oil. . . . Boy! If the Veterans' Bureau gets wise to some of the things we learn down there, they'll stop sending GIs down to study."

"In history," Gilberto said, "we learned about The Alamo."

"Yeah, all good Texans remember The Alamo, and all good Mexicans remember Chapultepec. When you get to Mexico City, you'll see the castle and look down from where a bunch of kids, none of them over sixteen, jumped. The last one with the Mexican flag wrapped around him, instead of surrendering."

"That's the first time—"

"Hang on!" Bishop warned, swinging the jeep in a swift arc around a colt trotting in the middle of the road. "It's okay—relax." Gilberto let go of the windshield frame he had clutched for balance. "I got too much invested in this nutcrusher to wreck it. And I still owe on it."

"Buy it from the government?" Gilberto asked.

"Are you kidding?"

"No; I heard they were all going to be sold to ex-service men."

"Yeah," Bishop began sadly. "They certainly crapped us up about how we were going to get these surplus jeeps for peanuts; fifty or a hundred bucks apiece. Big peacetime deal for the GIs. Yeah! So we could all go into business, get married, and join the Chamber-pot of Commerce. Well, the way it turned out, the only thing surplus about this rig is the surplus rooking I'm getting from the finance company."

"That because the Russians got 'em all?"

"Not the ones I saw on Okinawa, after VJ Day. They were piling them one on top of the other and setting them on fire with jellied gasoline. And they had *scows* loaded with them; towed out in the ocean and dumped like garbage. Well, I figured, there must be plenty of them to go around. And how right I was! In the dealers' showrooms, at the regular civilian prices."

He signaled for Gilberto to hold the wheel steady while he lit a cigarette. "I got this, though," he said, showing the lighter. "A Zippo. Cost me twenty-nine cents in the PX. Cost the civilians a buck and a half. This and my year in Mexico City, with the Veterans' Bureau paying me ninety-five a month. I used to chisel five or ten more on my allowance for school supplies. And, would you believe it, I didn't feel one bit like a thief."

"Why should you? Plenty of guys got theirs; making as high as three dollars an hour while you guys were doing the fighting for thirty a month."

"The figures are slightly wrong," Bishop said. "If the guys working in factories were to get the same pay as the guys fighting, it ought to be that way all the way up the line. That was what a couple of agitators in my outfit kept bringing up. But they didn't last long. But you're right just the same; plenty of guys got theirs. I was still doing occupation duty in Japan when I read about a brigadier general and a congressman going to the can for fraud."

"Must have made you pretty sore," Gilberto suggested.

"Sore?" Bishop said thoughtfully. "No. Only later, I got what we call in the army, 'disaffected.' I'd put in four years; left a fairly decent job and a girl likewise. In all that time, there wasn't a minute I could be sure I wouldn't get my guts blown out. The misery came after I got my discharge."

"Things were different," Gilberto said.

Bishop shook his head. "Things were the same. I could have had both the job and the girl back. *I* was different. I couldn't get interested in anything anybody had to offer. I wanted time to see if I could fit back some way. I took just enough, including one good look at those farts sitting around in the Legion Hall, and I grabbed this GI student deal. That was five years ago. I was twenty-three then."

"Figuring back," Gilberto said, "you must have been about nineteen when you were drafted."

"Not drafted," Bishop said casually. "But I was 1-A and due to be, so I enlisted. And there were plenty ahead of me down at the recruiting station before it opened on the morning of December eighth. Waiting there, and talking it over, I can give you my word that I wasn't thinking of any fifty-dollar jeeps or GI benefits."

"I can't believe that."

"Then, it was clean cut. We just hoped we could be ready to meet the Japs in San Diego or in San Francisco. But this time around—well, maybe I'm thick, or maybe I'm not looking close enough. But this time, I'm not buying. I read what they print and I listen to what they've got to say on the radio, but it leaves me cold."

"They want you back in the army?"

"Every which way; enlisted reserve, national guard, name my own ticket. So far, the best argument they gave me was that if I re-enlisted, I was practically guaranteed a commission. I made buck sergeant and they'd put me right in Officer's Candidate School. As if a lieutenant don't die just as dead as an NCO."

"Deader," Gilberto said. "I was told of a lieutenant who died from a Korean's bite."

"Doesn't surprise me," Bishop said. "You know what I told those army procurement people? I said, 'What do you need me for? You got Humphrey Bogart and John Wayne—the country is safe.'"

Gilberto laughed. "Them and the atom bomb, both."

Bishop winced. "Don't remind me about that. I saw the official War Department pictures: Hiroshima, people curled up—you've seen a cabrito al horno—"

"A roasted young goat? Is that what that did?"

"I could tell you, but I don't want to spoil your stomach. But I'll bet you one thing—if you were the Air Force guy who dropped that thing from five thousand feet up and you saw what it did on the ground, you wouldn't go around crowing about it. . . . What do you say we knock off this war talk?"

"Suits me."

"See those lights up ahead. . . ? Zapata. We'll check the gas there and get some coffee. You're sleepy, aren't you?" Gilberto couldn't deny it; he was yawning. "I admit," Bishop continued, "I didn't give you much of a chance to sound off."

"I'm just as satisfied to be listening," Gilberto assured him.

"That's a habit I ought to cultivate, but there's so much horseshit flying around, it's a novelty not to have to duck it all the time from nine out of ten people you meet."

"Well, you've been around and you know the difference," Gilberto said. "I haven't been anywhere much, outside of California."

Bishop gave him a quick, warm smile. "You know, kid, when you came up to me in that gas station, I almost had you pegged as one of those Los Angeles pachucos who'd take it as an insult if you called him a Mexican."

"That depends on how you meant it," Gilberto retorted.

"Or who's the one doing the calling. You're right. . . . Well, here's Zapata."

There was less of the town than the distant lights promised. At the eastern limit of it, the jeep crunched over gravel into a brightly lit service station. The attendant signaled them to wait while he fueled a diesel truck ahead of the jeep.

Bishop cut the motor. "She'll only take about six gallons. But I like to ride on the top half of the tank; a thing I learned to do in Mexico."

"I wish I knew as much about that country as you do."

"You will, I promise you," Bishop said. "And you especially, you're going to have to like what you find out."

"You think there'll be things I won't like," Gilberto asked, seriously.

"That's putting it mildly," Bishop said with assurance. "If you were, let's say a bracero going back after a spell of work in the States, you'd know what to expect. But it's different in your case. You'll see things that will get you spitting mad. But in time, the balance shifts and you begin to find out that there's something about the country—the people I mean—because, after all, a country is just plains, mountains, and rivers."

"The language and the customs is what makes the difference, isn't that it?"

"Both figure," Bishop explained, groping to make himself clear. "But there's something else. You'll know what it is because it will give you a glow. You'll feel it, like I did, with the difference that, on account of your blood, you'll see only the good side."

"Maybe I will," Gilberto said. "But it won't be on account of the blood I got. Chemically speaking, blood's blood."

"And coffee's coffee; let's go get some."

Bishop tossed the key to the tank cap to the attendant, told him to fill it up with regular, check the oil and water, and pull the jeep over to the side.

They entered a long, white-tiled diner, foggy with the steam of cooking food. Ten or twelve men, drivers of the trucks parked outside, were eating; or, having eaten, were smoking and talking loudly. Bishop ordered hamburgers-with: onions and "the works" and coffee. "On me, this time," he said. "You paid for the steaks."

"But you're paying the gas," Gilberto protested.

"I use just the same amount riding alone. Put your money away. . . . Okay, then, I'll match you; loser pays the check."

Gilberto lost and reserved a $5 bill, drawing it out of the wallet. Bishop saw the thick wad of bills and said, "You'll have to change that money into pesos. Once you get away from the border towns, you'll have trouble unless you're carrying moneda nacional."

"I forgot about that. Where do you change the money?"

"Any bank in Matamoros. Don't go to any of those tourist money exchanges. They'll gyp you. You should get about eight sixty-two for the dollar."

He would have about 3,500 pesos, Gilberto calculated mentally. "How long would I be able to get by on around three thousand pesos?" he asked.

Bishop thought a while. "I'll tell you what it cost me. I paid two hundred and twenty-five a month for my room, breakfast, and comida; both good, solid meals. I slipped the criada a few pesos now and then, and she took care of my laundry. For supper you're on your own, but all you'll want is coffee and cake. A couple of movies a week. Figure about three hundred, or a little more, a month."

"That isn't so bad."

"I'm talking about Mexico City and me a foreigner. You'll be home in Vera Cruz. Living there will be cheaper."

Gilberto mumbled, "Yeah, that's what I heard."

"Wonderful seafood, too. The place is famous for it."

"A guy can't live only on sea food," Gilberto said, without expecting such enthusiastic agreement as Bishop showed.

"Damn right, he can't. He's got to get his meat. Which brings us around to Subject A—getting laid. That's where the real economy comes in, for you."

"Why for me, especially?"

"Because you're a Mexican," Bishop said blandly. "It's that simple."

"Not to me, it isn't. In Los Angeles it was just the other way around."

"Who's talking about those pigs up there," Bishop said grimacing. "What I'm saying, and plenty of ex-GIs down there will agree with me, is: Take a Mexican dame—a real one; not one of these border town huarachas—and if it's a question of putting out for a gringo with money or a Mexican fellow for free, nine times out of ten it's the Mexican gets in. It happened to me enough times to know it isn't an accident. . . . Maybe it's patriotism or something, but that's the way a lot of Americans found out there are some things they can't even buy, much less grab."

Gilberto said nothing. He only nodded, pretending to be absorbed with the last crescent of his hamburger. Vaguely conscious of the tinge of incest in the image, he thought of his mother. . . . Would he be here now if his mother had put out for a gringo? Who gave a damn! He wanted to be nobody else but the son of Fernando and Elvira Reyes, and his heart flooded with love for both of them.

Bishop nudged him. "But pick your spots in Vera Cruz, boy. Like they told us in the army, quote: 'There's a mighty high incidence of the old claperoo in seaport towns, and don't let anybody tell you it's no worse than a bad cold.' Unquote."

Leaving the gas station, Bishop trolled his jeep past four giant diesel-powered trucks parked side by side.

"Look at this convoy, will you?" he begged. "This is what I like to see— good maintenance. What equipment! I bet if you put a pressure gauge on every one of those tires—and there's forty of them—they won't vary more than a couple of ounces."

"I know," Gilberto agreed. "We practically live with those trucks in California."

"You're going to have to live without them in Mexico," Bishop said, rather sadly. "That's one of the things used to bother me in that country." Shaking his head, he glanced backward once, ground off the driveway, and snapped the jeep into high on the asphalt.

Gilberto recognized that Bishop was off on another anti-Mexican riff; well—not exactly anti-, but certainly not pro-. Earlier, it was Mexicans and animals, nqw it was Mexicans and machinery.

"Take a good look at those," Bishop urged. "You'll see rigs just like them in Mexico, sure. They cost as much as a hundred thousand pesos each, but in six months they look like fugitives from a junk heap, and neither the drivers nor the owners seem to care a hang. You see them at night, blind in one headlight, or no headlights at all. Windshield crazed, sometimes without tail lights. But there's one thing you *will* see, and that's a pair of boxing gloves or the baby's shoes hanging right where they cut off the driver's vision. And always something cute painted over the cab. Either the guy's sweetheart's name or 'Come Close But Don't Kiss Me.' And there's also the type with religious slogans, like 'God is at the Wheel' or 'Jesus on My Trail.'"

"Honest?"

"You'll see for yourself; some times in ways that'll make you wish you hadn't looked. Or you'll read about them. ¡Espantoso choque! Horrible crash—forty killed; a second class bus slams into a stalled truck and gets sheared right through the middle."

"There's plenty of that kind of thing happens in Los Angeles, too," Gilberto said. "Accidents every day in the week and twice on Sunday. Right on Venice Boulevard, in broad daylight, I saw a school bus run smack into a string of flat cars."

Bishop appeared to take that as a defense of Mexican drivers. "Are you trying to prove that Mexicans are better?" he asked sharply.

"No. But you mentioned one accident and I brought up another."

"Then, fine. One is as good as another when it comes to driver skill. I'll grant you that if you want to match the number of people we kill in traffic, it would keep you guys busy for the next fifty years. It's the equipment that makes the difference. I'm not saying that it's any nicer to be spattered by a Chrysler Imperial in perfect mechanical condition, than by a Plymouth riding on its rims. But your chances are better with the Chrysler; it's probably got brakes. My beef is the kind of equipment they let run around all over Mexico; stuff that wouldn't get you ten bucks for scrap metal. Imagine! Passenger buses with the front wheels four inches out of line, rain pouring in through the roof; windows, if they got any at all, so filthy, you have to guess where you are. And when the driver tells you to watch your step, you'd better, or you'll fall through where the floor boards are missing. I've ridden in them, so crowded the sides bulging out. . . . What's the answer?"

"The more people, the more fares, I guess," Gilberto answered. "Reminds me of that picture, you may have seen it, where the cops lost Kirk Douglas in the crowded subway. They sure packed them—"

"The idea seems to be: if it moves, get on—or walk. What do you expect for twenty centavos, a Greyhound with reclining seats!"

"It's certainly cheap enough," Gilberto said. "Twenty centavos; what is that, three cents?"

"Cheap for you, maybe," Bishop said in a scolding tone, "with three thousand pesos in your kick. Well, it isn't cheap for the Mexican. It's twice the percentage of what they pay in New York." He gave Gilberto a sharp glance. "It seems to me you're going to have to get a lot of gringo ideas rubbed off you."

A gust of shame made Gilberto's face smart. That was the first time Bishop had shown anything like anger, and in defense of Mexicans. Gilberto was not prepared for anything as sudden and, as it appeared to him, as violent. This ambivalence confused him. Perhaps Bishop didn't intend to be so intensely personal, but that was the way he sounded. His expression would tell him, but Gilberto couldn't yet look at his face.

Bishop was working at getting the jeep up a long, ascending curve in high gear. The valve tappets rattled loudly.

11

The road was level and the strong little engine had settled down to a normal thrum.

Bishop felt sorry for having talked that way. He felt that he had made several earlier mistakes—not that he would take anything back—but in the strength and curtness of his tone. Just because he knew more, there was no call to bat this kid's ears down, even for such a thing as defending Mexicans from another Mexican who forgot, quite naturally, on which side he belonged.

He would have to smooth this over. "Did you catch that road marker back there a way—San Marcos—38 Miles?"

"Uh huh."

"Well, from a point about a quarter of a mile up ahead to the next marker we come to—San Marcos, 18 Miles—the whole stretch, on the south side of the highway, your side; thirty thousand acres. What do you think of it?"

"Can't see much," Gilberto said. "What is it, a ranch?"

"Used to be, when my grandfather owned it. The least amount of cattle he ran was eleven hundred head. But now it's cotton—cotton as far as you can see."

"Your grandfather?"

"Yup. And it was all supposed to have been left to me in his will. I first heard about it when I was about ten-years-old. He'd pick me up and point it out to me from the porch—of the county farm; in other words, the poor-house."

"That's too bad," Gilberto said. He suspected that Bishop had told this story to many people before, in just this way.

"I used to ride over on my pony and bring him some candy. . . . Funny, a ten-year-old kid bringing his grandfather candy, when it's usually the other way around. The folks used to talk about what a shrewd old guy he'd been. But not shrewd enough; he got screwed out of every foot of his land during the depression in the Twenties; some big cotton operators with bank connections. First he went broke in the courts fighting them, and then he went slightly off his rocker. Everybody around here remembers him—old Adolphus Bischoff."

"Bischoff? I thought it was Bishop."

"Bischoff was the name originally. My father changed it, so people wouldn't keep taking us for Jews."

"I knew some of them in Los Angeles," Gilberto said.

"Bischoffs?"

"No, Jews."

"I had a Jew for company-commander," Bishop recalled. "Captain Roy Harris. Never knew he was one, till on a special holiday they have, he broke out a box of matzoths."

"What's that?"

"Something they eat. Big, round crackers, the shape of a tortilla, but it lacks the flavor."

"You find them in Mexico?"

"Matzoths?"

"No, Jews."

Bishop laughed loudly. "We're beginning to sound like Abbott and Costello. . . . Yeah, you'll find Jews, but mostly in Mexico City. And where you'll find one, you'll find ten. They don't like to be apart from each other, and I don't know that I blame them, either."

"A friend of mine, a doctor," Gilberto said, "explained to me that even if a fellow doesn't happen to be one, he just has to look like one, or have a Jewish name, and he's on the spot."

"Well, then," Bishop continued, "the only one in my town had *all* the handicaps. His name, to begin with, was Abe Birnbaum, and he had a nose— well, if I had it full of nickels, I could retire. He owned the Spot Cash Market, but it was the only place that gave credit. I used to deliver groceries for him Saturdays and after school. . . . But they ran him out."

"Who did; the Klan?"

"I guess it was the Klan; anyway, my Uncle Paul had a hand in it, and he ran with the Klan bunch. One night, they lit a cross on Abe's lawn and watched from the other side of the street to see what he'd do. Well, he did it! He came out, pulled the shades so that his wife and kid shouldn't see, then unbuttoned his pants and pissed the fire out."

"Great! That's what I call showing them."

"It didn't end there. The next day, with my uncle and his bunch standing in front of Bradley's hardware store, Abe Birnbaum is in there, shopping. He comes out with a twelve-gauge Ithaca shotgun and two boxes of shells. . . . They got him in the end, though."

"Burned him out, finally?" Gilberto suggested.

"Just as thoroughly as if they had. One Saturday night, closing time, he called me and the clerk, Mac, over. He paid Mac, handed me ten bucks, and said he was closing. All the money he had in the world was in the cash register, he said, and what he could get for the stock at ten cents on the dollar. He was going back to Philadelphia. Naturally, we all knew that for the last couple of months he had just been hanging on; but we acted like it was a shock to us. Why? What's it all about? He put it to Mac, 'What are we getting for a box of corn flakes?' Mac said fourteen cents. 'And they cost us— wholesale?' Mac said eleven and a half. 'And what was it selling for today down at the chain grocery?' We all knew—eight cents."

"Yet," Gilberto said, "you'd think the Jews would know some tricks."

"He knew more than my grandfather; he knew when he was licked."

A town called Roma flicked past and they settled down for the stretch into McAllen. We're heading away from the Río Grande, and if the wind is right, you'll get a whiff of that salt, sea-weedy smell."

Gilberto sniffed the air. "I got it just now, Um . . . kind of like iodine. Reminds me of home."

"Yeah, down in Vera Cruz you'll have it as a steady diet."

He hadn't meant Vera Cruz; he had meant Los Angeles. He wondered if the name of Vera Cruz, which he had plucked out of the air, sounded as much of a lie to Bishop as it tasted in his own mouth.

"I never asked you, but is that where your folks are, Vera Cruz?"

It was time to lie again. "Some," he said.

"Some!" Bishop mimicked. "You guys feel like you're orphans unless you got about thirty or forty primos and primas and at least two sets of godfathers and godmothers. I swear, no Mexican I ever knew was alone, in Mexico, I mean. . . . You all set with a job down there?"

"No, but—"

Bishop interrupted, "I wouldn't worry too much. With relatives and enough dough to carry you for a while, you can pick your spots. In a seaport town, a young fellow with a good education who can handle two languages— can you type?"

"Sure. And I also handle a calculating machine," Gilberto added, with a trace of pride.

"Then you've got no problem getting a good office job."

"That's not exactly my line," Gilberto said.

"Oh, yeah—you told me—tree surgeon."

Gilberto corrected him. "Forestry; laying out seedlings; clearing, drainage—"

"Better still. They got a big campaign on in Mexico to save their trees; that is, they had, when I was down there. There's billboards all over put up by the government, telling people about it. A tree expert down there ought to be worth his weight in gold."

"It sounds like that's for me."

"Maybe the pay isn't what you're used to in the States; besides, you get your salary by the month. But I'll tell you one thing, it's a hell of a lot better than getting drafted and shipped to Korea. And you look just about ripe for that."

Gilberto felt as if an ice cube had been dropped down his collar and was sliding slowly down the furrow of his backbone. He wanted to say something, but fear clamped his jaws together. If only Bishop would keep talking, he might make himself clear as to why, out of the blue, he had struck so close. Was he like Superman or Mandrake the Magician, who could see through two thicknesses of leather and a thick wad of money right to the postal card that said, "Federal Bldg., Friday, 7:00 a.m. on penalty of . . ."?

Maybe he *had* been talking and Gilberto couldn't hear him above the surf of blood pounding in his ears. He could hear him now: "I don't have to tell you how lucky you are they can't grab you." He stopped suddenly and darted a look, weighted with doubt, at Gilberto. "Or maybe I'm talking out of turn. . . . What do you say, Valdez—am I?"

"Honest, I don't know what gave you that idea," Gilberto said with complete sincerity. "It's Reyes, not Valdez."

"Okay, then—it's Gil, isn't it? . . . Only you never know these days, Gil, who you're yacking to or when you're going to hear it played back to you. That happened to a friend of mine who worked in the post office. He's out."

"I'll forget anything you said to me, if that's what you want," Gilberto assured him.

"No! If that's what I wanted, I'd have kept my mouth shut," Bishop asserted. "But no son of a bitch, and I don't care who he is, is going to shut it for me. There's too much of that going around. Ask a guy what he thinks about something and he says, 'Leave me out of it.' Try to tell him what *you* think and he says, 'Excuse me, I got to hurry along.' Now, some of the ideas I got may be wrong, but I got a right to have them, even test them out."

It seemed safe for Gilberto to agree obliquely, with a reservation. "There's certain limits, though," he said.

"Naturally," Bishop agreed. "But I don't think this idea of mine about this Korea business is outside of them."

"What was that?" The terror had left Gilberto.

"Well, let me begin by asking you, did you ever read the casualty lists back in L.A.?"

"Once in a while; but they only have the local names."

"I *mean* the local names. . . . Now I haven't read one of your papers in years, but I can tell you the names on those lists. Listen—López, Jiménez, González, Rodríguez, Martínez—how am I doing—Chávez, Gómez, Henríquez—want more?"

"You sure got 'em down."

"I read the Dallas, San Antonio, and Houston papers, and the same type of names show up. Look at a Chicago paper, and what do you find—the 'Witzes and the 'Oviches. New York, the Cohens and the Kellys. Pittsburgh, Slovak names you can't even pronounce. Milwaukee, the 'Heims and the 'Orfs."

The Eisens, Gilberto thought, and the Devlins—or didn't they belong in this picture?

"You see what I'm getting at, Gil?"

He didn't quite, and the safest thing to do was say something that wouldn't rile Bishop up beyond the point where he was now. "I see you don't miss much."

"I don't want to make it look one-sided, so I'll include the Joneses, Smiths, Johnsons, Jacksons, and Lees—and who knows how many of them aren't Negro. . . . Now, I'll make you a sporting proposition—you give me a cent, one penny, for every name like the ones I mentioned and I'll give you a five-dollar bill for every name you spot like—well—like Dupont."

"Dupont. That's the name the Commies always bring up."

Bishop's foot left the gas pedal abruptly and he let the jeep decelerate as he steered it to the shoulder of the road. The lights began to dim under the idling motor. He set the hand brake, snapped up the brim of his cap, and faced Gilberto, glowering. "Look, feller, I don't like that crack you just made. I don't like it especially from a kid who must have got his ass kicked good in the States, or he wouldn't be going back to Mexico."

Gilberto felt himself pale; out of no embarrassment, but because of Bishop's unexpected show of rage. "I'm sorry; I didn't mean a thing by it. I only mentioned something I read."

"Then why did you say it to me?" Bishop's voice was cold now, and even.

"Honest, it was more of a gag, Mr. Bishop. You know yourself what they say, that the way to tell a Communist—" He stuttered; he was getting confused in his eager sincerity. "That is—when you mentioned Dupont—"

"Yeah! And the fact that I said Negro. That convinced you."

"No—"

"I don't call a black man a nigger for the same reason I don't call you a greaser." He tilted his head and continued in a flat voice. "I don't know— maybe you're not a real Mexican, but one of these wise-cracking pachucos who got the idea someplace that the way to be a real Americano is to call the next guy a Commie."

"If that's the way you feel about it, fuck you. I'll go my own way from here." It wasn't blurted out; his mind had framed the words before he spoke them. But they weren't enough, and cooly he added, "You're not funny any more. How much do I owe you for the time you were going good?"

As Bishop squirmed to get out from under the wheel, Gilberto braced himself for the first punch. Let him start it, and maybe finish it. He was leaving himself wide open, reaching behind the seat for his bag and watching Bishop's eyes at the same time. It seemed that Bishop was doing the same thing. This, Gilberto thought, could go on for a long time.

Bishop spoke and his voice sounded pained. "What are we staring at each other for, like cats under a barn?" He spread his arms. "Acting like a couple of punk kids. . . . Maybe I was wrong."

"There's got to be no maybe about it, Mr. Bishop."

"For Christ's sake, lay off that Mr. Bishop!" He snapped the car from neutral into second, letting out the clutch for a jackrabbit start off the shoulder. "It's Bish, or Fred. And leave your lousy satchel where it is."

There was a long downgrade, and the jeep hit 60—64—almost 70, and was leaping over the heat blisters in the road like a roller coaster. Gilberto started to say something about how they were sure bowling along, but the wind shredded the words.

"What'd you say?" Bishop asked carefully, letting the jeep coast.

"Nothing." There was no wind now and it was quiet enough to hear the telegraph wires humming overhead.

Bishop carefully raised one ham, groaned, and let go a loud one. "Tight shoes." It won the smile of amusement from Gilberto that he had calculated upon. "I'd like this ride to finish up the way it began; with no hard feelings on either side."

"None on mine."

"I know—just the same I want to give you a little background on why I jumped you back there."

"It's all forgotten—Bish."

"Sure, sure, and I don't want to rake up anything. But I want you to take this in the right sense, because the same kind of situation came up once before, me being called a Commie."

"I didn't—"

"I know, Gil. That's why I'm telling you this. But if you don't want to listen—all right, then. . . . Well, you know there's a big push on for enlistments. I don't mean just the draft, that's taken for granted; they just herd them in. It's the veterans they're trying to suck back in."

"You told me—"

"This is something else. . . . I get a telegram a couple of weeks ago from a Major J.B. Finney telling me to come up and see him. It sounds official and I think maybe it's about my GI insurance, or something like that. But no. The guy is an oil company official sitting in his own office, and he's got my whole service record in front of him. His pitch is why don't I sign up in the enlisted reserve, and he named a few outfits he could *help* me to get into without loss of benefits and all that. As a special treat, he said I might even get to Korea before the fighting ended. Big of him, wasn't it? . . . The thing is, Gil, he started out talking to me like I was a half wit; the village dope, or something. He offers me a cigar and says, 'Bishop, forget for the time being that I'm your superior officer.' Superior officer my hind tit, I told him, you're talking to a civilian. Well, one thing led to another, and when he saw that I had a few of the answers, he wound up calling me a Communist. How do you like that!"

"That time he got hold of the wrong guy. What arguments did he give you? Was that the best he could do?"

Bishop shrugged. "What arguments? The same ones you get on every side, wherever you go. It baffles me. Pick up a magazine—anything—the *Post, Colliers.* They advertise a four-thousand-buck television and it says, 'Don't Let Them Take This Away From You!' . . . You haven't got it yet, and already they want you to protect it."

"Who? Who's taking it away?"

"You see an ad for a washing machine. It used to be, don't let your poor old mother break her back; get her one of these. Now, it says something about how many man-hours a Commie has to put in to buy a shirt. Picture of an aeroplane and it's shooting down a Russian bomber."

"That all comes under the head of propaganda," Gilberto said, sounding sage. "The U.S. has got the highest standard of living anywhere in the world."

"Sure, we all know that, so why don't they let us enjoy it and stop talking about it so much. Highest in the world, you said; then why only higher than Russia? They can't be in second place to us. . . . No—there's something else behind it."

"You think so, Bish?"

"Yeah. And you know how it strikes me—" He fell silent. Gilberto turned to see if something had distracted him. Apparently nothing; he kept looking directly at the road ahead.

"Go ahead, Bish—"

"I know what they want to say—in those ads, and on the radio, and everyplace else. They get close to saying it, but they just haven't got their nerve up to putting it in plain language. And it's this: Hear this! Buck Sergeant Bishop and all the rest of you dogfaces. It was all a mistake. Big snafu all around. We were in the wrong war the last time—or in the right war on the wrong side. But this one is the real thing! Those dirty Commies are at our throats. Look how close they are to Alaska! All right, you say you're ready as soon as the first Russian puts his foot across the line; long before he starts raping your sister. Well, they tell you, it's not really the Russians; they're too shifty. They get their satellites to do the dirty work for them. All right, I say, let us be shiftier; let's put *our* satellites in. What! We don't have satellites? Why not? I'm a taxpayer. I got a right to know!"

"We got a few; Greece, Turkey,—" He couldn't remember the others he and Eisen talked about.

"Look, a satellite is something right next door to you—like the moon is a satellite of the earth. In other words, like Mexico is to the United States. But somehow, we can't sell you people on the idea. Remember—? Only last year we offered you a deal, something like a few hundred million dollars, for a starter. But you said no, thanks, but thanks."

He didn't remember; even if there had been something in the *Los Angeles Times* about such a deal, he would have passed it by. Very little about Mexico concerned him—up to a few days ago. "How big of an army has Mexico got, anyhow?"

"As I remember," Bishop pondered, "about eighty thousand; about the strength of five divisions. They keep it up to strength by conscription. They draft guys by the year they were born. Every able-bodied kid has to put in two years, and he gets a card. It's the first thing they ask him for when he goes looking for a job or anything. . . . You might as well stay over Sunday in Mexico City and see them."

"I don't know if I'll be able to."

"Aw, come on, you can't pass up a chance to see that town. Fellows who were in the ETO tell me it's just like Paris. . . . Anyway, every Sunday morning the police rope off certain streets and all the conscripts in that neighborhood fall in for drill. Some with uniforms, but most without, except for a cap. A sergeant puts them through mostly the manual of arms, with dummy rifles. . . . Maybe you can't make a regular First Marines-Iwo Jima type beach head with that kind of an army. But I'll tell you this much, and not just because you're a Mexican—no Greek, Turkish, Russian, *or* U.S. army can make a landing at Acapulco either, with those Sunday morning conscripts behind the rocks."

"It's their country—"

"You bet! When it's your country and you got a stake in keeping an invasion off—and that goes for my country, too—a machete is as good as an M-1. Right?"

"Right."

The moon blacked out and the night was getting colder. The salt breath of the near sea was on the wind. Bishop zipped his jacket to the chin. Gilberto folded his coat lapels over his chest and felt an icy touch on his skin—the Guadalupe medal. He waved aside the package of cigarettes and the lighter which Bishop offered him. "Not now, thanks."

"Then will you light one for me?"

There was something about handing the cigarette, lighted at his own lips, into the blind fingers of the man. Bishop had lit six or seven himself since they left Laredo. But this, the boy recognized, was an act of trust and friendship. "I think I will take one," he said; and as he smoked, he felt warmer.

He wanted to touch Bishop, smack him on the shoulder, know how his handshake felt. He remembered how the Romeros always clasped the shoulders of their friends. Other people did the same, often spontaneously, in the middle of a conversation, in a place as public as the Café Orizaba. Probably because, in a big town like L.A., they were lonely among so many Americans. Yet, they did it in Mexico as well; he had seen it in Mexican films. The explanation that made the most sense was the simplest: they were Mexicans, that's all. That was the way Mexicans acted.

"What do you say we coffee up in Harlingen, huh, Gil?" Bishop tugged the brim of his cap down against the line of pearl gray widening on the horizon.

"Whatever you say."

"It's five after five. I figure on getting into Matamoros about a quarter to seven. What do you want to do?"

It wasn't meant that way, but the question sounded imperative, unfair, Gilberto thought. He was about to ask what *does* one do in Matamoros. But he had already said that his destination was Vera Cruz; and if Bishop persisted in asking what he was going to do, it was likely that he didn't believe it. The safest thing to do was show dependence on Bishop for more information. "I was just wondering—so early in the morning, what can you do in Mata-moros?"

"Well, I could drop you off in Brownsville. You can have your breakfast there, stall around a while, and do what shopping you have to do. You'll have a good five hours before your plane leaves."

Here was a fresh complication—Brownsville instead of Matamoros—and this plane business; something new. He said suddenly, "That a through plane?"

"I don't think so. I know she makes one stop at Monterrey and gets you into Mexico City in something over four hours. You make your connection there for Vera Cruz. If you have to lay over, I'll give you the address of my old boarding house. They'll be glad to put you up."

Here was that Vera Cruz lie again, standing up like an obelisk. No use trying to push it over, now that it existed for Bishop as well as himself. Walk around it and don't let its shadow touch you. "Matamoros you said, I thought you weren't going to stop on this side."

"I didn't intend to; thought you might want to kill some time there, futzing around in Brownsville. It's only a two-minute walk across the bridge. But if you don't want to, it's better for me. I got something I want to ask you and I'll feel better about it on the Mexican side."

"Sure. What is it?"

"Something you can do for me; a little favor."

"I sure owe you one."

"You don't owe me anything. Only, I'll remind you in Matamoros. . . . Look at that sun, will you!"

Nobody could look at it. It hurt even to see directly ahead, where it had already begun to play its tricks of refraction on the road, making distant oil slicks look like sheets of water. It detonated castaway bottles and powdered the highway with diamond dust. Bishop said, "This is going to be a scorcher. By ten o'clock you'll be able to fry a hamburger on the sidewalk."

Harlingen lay ahead. Bishop tapped the dial of the gas gauge with his finger. "Got plenty. What do you say we pass up coffee this time? You can get a good breakfast in Matamoros. I'll show you where."

"What about you, Bish; don't you eat?"

"Don't know if I'll have the time. I'd like to start right in on those pipes so I can finish by eleven. But you can mooch around the town, and even grab a nap in the plaza. You'll have plenty of company."

"How big is this Matamoros? What's it like?" What Gilberto actually wanted to know was how the vigilance is kept on either side of the border. "Is it anything like Nuevo Laredo?"

"Lots smaller, and it doesn't get anywhere near the kind of tourist play of border towns like Nogales, Juárez, or Tijuana. What'd you think of that joint?"

"Lots of drunks," Gilberto said. "Cheap liquor, I guess, that's the big attraction in Tijuana."

"For my money, that's the crummiest border town of all. Try buying anything there, a drink, a postal card, a novelty with a Mexican peso, and they look at you like you're trying to hand them counterfeit money. That— and a few other things—gave me the idea that it isn't the Mexicans at all that are running that town."

"You're right. It was the Japs. They owned the big whorehouse just as you come into town. Used it for spying. It was all in the papers."

"I'm thinking of much later," Bishop said. "After the war; the last time I was there. . . . I remember one joint there; the only one of its kind I ever heard of."

Why, Gilberto wondered briefly, hadn't he gone to Tijuana, instead of two-thirds of the way across the United States? Tijuana was Mexico, too, despite what Bishop experienced there; just as Mexican geographically as Laredo or Matamoros. It might have been that he wasn't sure that Mexico was where he wanted to go. Neither was Texas. There was a bus that was going to San Francisco and another to Salt Lake City ready to leave from the same platform. What made him decide to take the one that said Phoenix-Tucson? And, since he was thinking along those lines, what made him, about a year ago, decide to cross over on the opposite side of Pico Boulevard, just ahead of an explosion in that welding shop that killed two pedestrians . . . ?

"What's this place you were talking about, Bish?"

"It's about four blocks after you make the first turn into Tijuana, on a side street; looks like a regular bookstore. You know, with piles of books, new and second hand, in the window. You go inside, and if you're alone—that is, without a girl—the clerk comes up to you, pulls aside a curtain, and says, 'Don't you want to step in here, please?'"

"Oh, I get it."

"Oh, you *think* you do! Well so did I. But it's a different gimmick. There's a room with four or five soft chairs, reading lamps, and shelves of books; just like a library. But you know the kind of books—*Art Studies* and stuff like that. But there's one special shelf. . . . Say, did you ever hear of the Kama Suder, or something like that? . . . Well, it shows the 660 ways the Hindus do it. Not 660 separate pictures, but enough to show the basic moves. Well, it cost a dollar an hour to sit down and read. There's also a table laid out with chili peppers, little dried fish, and other stuff that's supposed to act on you like hardónica. That's the buildup. When the customer has read enough and wants action, the fellow in the book store slips him a card to a cat wagon parked down the street."

"I never heard of a cat wagon," Gilberto admitted. "But I can guess what one is."

"Yeah, a house trailer; a regular hookshop on wheels. No protection to pay and no rent. The pimp drives and they can even do business while moving the location."

"Pretty smart, whoever thought that up."

"One thing I'm willing to lay my money on," Bishop said forcefully, "is that it wasn't a Mexican's idea. That's what I meant to tell you before, when I mentioned that I didn't think Tijuana was run by Mexicans at all. That bookstore idea is *imported*. I say that because—well—Mexicans are—well—*cleaner* about it. Maybe, as you say, Gil, the idea comes from the Japanese. But I've been there, and they've got their own style, but at least they show you the women first—not books. Mexicans, though—well, I don't have to tell you—Mexicans take it for granted that a guy old enough to shave has got himself a babe. Or, if he wants it a-la-carte, he knows where to go. Right?"

"Right!"

The wind still had some freshness, but the sun was boring into their backs. First, Gilberto squirmed out of his coat, folded it, and wedged it into the space behind his seat, next to the flight bag. While he held the wheel steady, Bishop unzipped and peeled out of his jacket.

In the glare, any unpainted object—roadside structures, houses, bare billboards, fenceposts—stood out bone white.

The jeep struck a stretch of asphalt paving and the tire treads geared themselves into the softening tar.

They flashed past a road marker with Brownsville on it, but Gilberto didn't catch the mileage figure. He was going to ask, but Bishop brought up the subject of beer. "Let me give you a tip; most Mexican beers are better than what they brew in the States. But Orizaba beer, that's the best there is. As for tequila, they can pour that back in the horse—" Abruptly, one hand left the wheel and he pointed ahead. "The dirty sons of bitches!" he shouted and braked the jeep to a stop, half off the road, behind two rocks, each the size of a good head of cabbage. Too angry to talk, he pointed to the stones, both well in the center of the right lane of pavement and about five feet apart. "Curse those bastards!" he finally muttered. "You can always tell where a Mexican driver has stopped to take a leak." Gilberto, somewhat puzzled, followed him out of the jeep. As he picked up the nearest of the stones and hurled it as far as he could into the scrub, Gilberto heaved the other one after it.

With grimaces of mock amazement, Bishop scratched an imaginary X with his toe. "Now I've seen everything! Right there is where I'm going to put up a bronze marker!"

"What brought this on? All I did was move a rock off the road."

"You call that *all!* I'll tell you what—when you see that happen in Mexico, let me know, and I'll come down there to live."

"You seem to be kind of hipped on the way Mexicans drive."

"Why shouldn't I be; tell me! I spend half my life on wheels, most of it on your side of the border, and I want to be around for the other half. Is that asking too much? But many a night—let's say on a run between McAllen and Cadeyreta, I'm not so sure. Camino Number 30 is typical—a car is coming toward me; if I don't see those rocks, I hit them and turn over with this thing on top of me. If I *do* see them and turn out, the approaching car clips me, if it doesn't do worse than that."

"I got to admit that's pretty dangerous; especially at night."

"You can drive a thousand miles in the States and not see a thing like this once." Bishop was assertive. "In Mexico you couldn't drive ten. The bastards stick them under the wheels while they're having their lunch or a nap and just calmly pull away. I've seen them right under signs that say, 'Don't Leave Stones on the Road.' It seems to be, with them, a case of the hell with the next guy; and the next guy is that way about the guy coming up behind him. . . . Don't get me started on Mexican drivers."

Smiling, Gilberto said, "I thought you finished."

"On that subject I could go on till the cows came home. I found out from somebody that the Aztecs didn't know the principle of the wheel. Well, I can believe it—they don't know it yet."

He talked rapidly, in pace, it seemed, with the accelerating jeep, which he drove smoothly and expertly, in a subconscious demonstration of his own familiarity with machinery. "I'd sooner run this off the end of a dock than let any of them do a major repair. Nothing bigger than changing a tire. And even then, better count the wheel lugs afterward."

"I don't have a car," Gilberto said, "so I won't have that worry."

Bishop looked at him with a brief but keen glance; the sort with which to make a quick assay of the listener's capacity to understand a philosophical concept. "It's something more than you owning a car, or the other guy owning one. What I want to get over to you is this—using cars puts everybody on a different level than when they were using horses or just their feet. I'd say, it even brings them closer."

He shook his head impatiently when Gilberto said, "In distance, sure."

"No, that's something else again. Look at it this way: With cars, people have to use the same highways, public roads. They got to follow certain rules. It's different if you're walking, regardless of whether it's Main Street or Avenida Madero. Do you worry that the man behind you or the man ahead of you, also walking, could kill you by moving his wrist two inches? No! But you're driving, and it's just the opposite. Everybody's life is in everybody else's hands. That's why I say the car brings people together. The least they have to have is respect for each other."

"In that way, you're certainly right. I'll certainly put in with you there."

"Then you've got to go all the way—I don't mean you, personally, Gil; but that's something Mexicans still have to learn. For their own good. People shouldn't have to be afraid of each other—a strange face, or a strange car, or both don't mean that it's an enemy. . . . One red-hot I knew down there, fellow named Ortiz, when I tried to tell him just what I told you, says to me, 'No Mexican is afraid of anything!' Just like that! Well, I showed him what I meant. There was a guy ahead of us, on a kind of narrow street, Tapachula, I think it was; but with enough space for a car to pass."

"You were in a car?"

"That's what I'm talking about. . . . We signaled him a couple of times that we wanted to pass, but he wouldn't give an inch. When he had to stop at the corner, he deliberately took the middle of the street and blocked us off, so that when we could go again, he'd be first. There, I told Ortiz, what's that guy afraid of. Nothing, says Ortiz, he just doesn't like anybody to get in front of him. Well, I said, that's fear enough for me. Ortiz had to admit, 'The fellow ahead knows that, if he lets you pass, you'll think you're better than him.' "

"Did he mean you were driving a better car, or were better-looking, or had more money in your pocket?" Gilberto asked.

"That's just the way I put it to Ortiz. Better in what way? 'Just better,' he says. Well, after being down there a year and getting to know a lot of Mexicans, the nearest I got to finding out what they meant by better is that it has something to do with how good a lay he is. They use the word macho."

"That means male," Gilberto offered.

"Yeah. Muy macho—*very* male," Bishop said contemptuously; then with some heat, "Now what the hell kind of a talent is that to boast about, I ask you! There's better ways to prove it than driving faster, drinking two bottles of tequila to your one, or shoving you away from a post office window when I'm in the middle of registering a letter; not just once, but a number of times. And not just because I was a gringo, either."

"What did you do?"

"What did I do? You don't think I stood there in the post office and matched balls with him, or stopped to tell him how I bayonetted a Jap major on Buna! I did exactly nothing."

"You had to take it—"

"You mean as a Mexican you won't have to? Well, don't kid yourself. You'll get shoved, too; and one reason is that you don't look like the kind of a guy that pushes people around."

"Why should I?"

"Why should anybody?"

"That goes for the States, too," Gilberto said.

The sign ahead read: BROWNSVILLE, Pop. 23,000.

12

With its familiar chain stores advertising the same "Specials" and "Introductory Offers," Brownsville could be—except for the salt smell—a Los Angeles suburb, like Watts or Canoga Park.

On the main street, whatever stirred, man or machine, gave the impression of being in fluid slow-motion.

Only the jeep seemed to have gotten up some terminal velocity. It moved at a normal traffic pace toward the border crossing.

Here, it looked as much like Laredo as one post office looks like another. Elizabeth Street, Gilberto read.

Bishop made a right turn onto a narrower street. There was no waiting line of cars and nothing was behind them. But many Mexicans were coming from across the river, the men in denims, the women in shawls; walking with a limber stride, their bodies tilted slightly forward.

The jeep shuddered as Bishop shifted down from high to second gear. The front wheels bit into another type of road surface: the bridge.

Gilberto forced his clenched hands across his stomach, inside of which he felt a roiling. This was fear, he told himself. You feel it in your guts—the way they uncoil inside of you. A bullfighter knows enough to wrap his belly up tight in yards of silk. A motorcycle racer straps himself with a wide leather belt. It's all in the guts.

"There she is," Bishop said, pointing twenty yards ahead to the flag hanging limply from its pole. "Prob'ly the last you'll see of it."

"I don't know . . . Every time I said, 'I pledge allegiance,' I meant it."

"So did I every time I stood up for the Mexican flag. I didn't feel like that made me a traitor. . . . Come on, Gil, salute her anyway."

Gilberto did, and held it until they passed. Bishop thumped him on the shoulder. "I'd like to invent a flag that will salute back to the people," he said, and pointing ahead warned, "Oh oh—"

Only a few yards ahead, a man in the faded green uniform of the U.S. Immigration Service sat on a tall stool, drinking coffee from a thermos bottle. The jeep would have to pass him by mere inches. The officer grinned and stuck his foot out in the path of the jeep.

"Wise guy," Bishop said. "Watch me knock him off that perch," and he raced the engine. But he stopped, using both the brake and clutch, holding the latter disengaged. Aside to Gilberto, he said, "This guy thinks he's funny. Get a load of him."

"Who's the gentleman with you, Bish?"

"A friend of mine. What about it?"

"I thought maybe you hired yourself an assistant."

"Come on," Bishop said impatiently. "Get started if you're going to make like Bob Hope."

"I got a little job for you when you're through down at the café," the officer said. "I got a toilet that's stuffed up."

"Yeah? How would *you* know it!" Bishop called, racing the engine and moving ahead. He laughed in loud satisfaction, nudging Gilberto. "Right between the eyes! I usually don't think of a comeback that quick, but this time I handed it right back. Right?"

A muffled yeah was all Gilberto could answer. His eyes were on another uniformed man, a Mexican, on the opposite side, who apparently was waiting for the jeep to approach.

"That's Captain Bermúdez," Bishop said. "Nice fellow. Want to meet him?"

"I don't want to hold you up, Bish."

Abreast of the Mexican officer, Bishop slowed and exchanged a military salute with him.

"Oh, Mr. Bishop," the captain called as they were passing him. Bishop stopped and the officer asked, "Are you going to the game tonight?"

"I don't know, Captain. I wish I could—" He turned to Gilberto. "Maybe you'd like to stay over, Gil. Basketball; San Benito against Matamoros. There's a dance afterward."

The captain looked at him. What would be the safest thing to say? And how should he say it? He had it! "Con todo gusto—if I stay over."

The officer smiled to him and said, "Espero que pueda usted venir."

"Gracias—adiós," he called back, as the jeep bucked over a lump in the pavement. Straight ahead were trees; big, fat billows of dark green, motionless under their cloud counterparts in a pale blue sky.

These trees, and that sky—they made it Mexico, not just the flag lolling on a pole over the Customs House.

Bishop turned left, and right again, to the central plaza of Matamoros. Here were the trees, the thick black trunks which supported the dense, cloud-shaped foliage. Some type of laurel, Gilberto judged. They must have been planted here a long time before any of these buildings had been put up. He pointed. "A fellow could hide in the tops of those trees; live there."

"Like Tarzan." He glanced at his watch. "Still pretty early; not eight yet."

"Well, you were going to get an early start," Gilberto reminded him. "Wherever you want to stop, I'll—"

Bishop shook his head and tramped on the accelerator, making a left turn to the east side of the plaza. "There's no hurry." He seemed a little embarrassed. "I wanted to say something before you took off, and I might as well—" Instead of finishing, he twisted the ignition off and let the jeep roll up to the curb.

"Something you wanted me to do for you, wasn't it? A little favor." Gilberto was glad he remembered.

"Before I ask you that, I want you to understand that anything I said to you out of turn, I didn't mean it to be personal. And if it was, I take it back."

"Is *that* what's on your mind? I wish you'd forget it."

Bishop insisted, "A couple of times there I went overboard against Mexicans, and when you tried to stop me, I talked you down."

"There were a lot of times you didn't give the U.S. the best of it either, Bish."

"There I don't take anything back. There I got a right to say what I don't like. I'll even grant *you* that right, Gil, even though a lot of people wouldn't."

"Thanks," Gilberto smiled.

"Don't thank me. It's not a personal gift I'm giving you. . . . Anyway—"

"Now what was the thing you were going to ask me to do? What about it?"

Hesitantly Bishop said, "If it's too much trouble, just say you can't."

"I don't know what it is yet."

"I'll tell you—according to your schedule, you'll be in Mexico City late this afternoon, and what I want will take only about an hour, if that much. First, I'll give you an address here in Matamoros where it'll reach me."

"A message, or you want me to buy something?"

"Something special." Bishop took some money out of his pocket. "Five bucks ought to cover it, mailing and all. Here."

Gilberto pushed the money aside. "You didn't tell me what it is yet."

"That's right, I didn't," Bishop said with a thin laugh, in pretense that it was an item of little importance. "It's a Guadalupe medal. . . . I know I could pick one up here, even anywhere in Texas, for that matter. But Dolores—that's my girl—we're engaged. The kind she wants is one right from the Guadalupe Shrine; one that's been blessed by the bishop, or whoever is in charge of the place. You know what I mean." He waited only for Gilberto's nod to add hurriedly, as if eager to end the subject, "You take a Peralvillo bus straight out to the Shrine. You can't miss it—better still—here—let me give you enough for a taxicab—"

"Now wait a minute; put that dough away," Gilberto said firmly. "I owe you a lot more than the little favor you're asking. Not only for the ride down from Laredo, but breezing into Mexico like a duke. Without even being stopped to show my baggage, or papers, or anything."

"Well, they know me pretty well," Bishop said modestly. "You won't be bothered till before you get on the plane. Better check to see you got all your papers in order."

Pale, Gilberto turned and fumbled with his coat, folded behind the seat. He was relieved when paper crackled: the old letter to his mother from San Luis Potosí. He put his hand on it and made it whisper. "It's okay." As he bent lower to reach for the handle of his bag, the thin oval of silver hung directly below and so close to his eyes that the stamped figure on it seemed elongated, as in an El Greco. He sat up, bag and coat on his lap. "I don't want any more arguments about this, Bish. I'll go out there and get that medal if you want, but I don't call that a favor on my part; not the kind you've got coming."

"It's something I wouldn't ask anybody else to do," Bishop said. "I want to show you who'll be wearing it." He opened his wallet and showed the picture of a plump, smiling girl. "This is Dolores. We're getting married right after the first of the year."

"Nice, real pretty."

"Not posed, either; that's her natural smile."

"I can see that," Gilberto agreed. "She looks Mexican."

"Why shouldn't she? She *is* Mexican." Bishop sounded boastful. "Her folks are fine people—from Sinaloa. We made up our minds we're going to have four kids and then close the books."

"Best of luck," Gilberto said, as he began unclasping the medal. Handing it to Bishop, he added, "And this goes with it."

"What do you mean, Gil!"

Smoothly and confidently he answered, "That's what she wants, isn't it, or were you just ribbing me?"

"Certainly—but it's—"

"It's the real thing. Comes right from the place up there. Belonged to my mother. She left it to me."

"Then you don't want to get rid of it."

"Not the way *you* say it; I'm not getting *rid* of it. I'm giving it to you, for your girl." He closed Bishop's hand over it.

"All right," Bishop said, putting the medal reverently into the zippered section of his wallet. "I don't have to tell you how much I appreciate this. Even more how much it's going to mean to Dolores. Anybody could buy one of these at the Shrine, but to get it this way—"

"That's what I mean, Bish."

"When I tell her, she'll say it's a miracle; the Guadalupe worked it out this way. I don't know how to thank you, Gil."

"I don't want to hear it."

Bishop put the wallet in his shirt pocket and patted it. "Come on—I'm going to buy you the best breakfast in Matamoros."

"I thought you had to go to work."

"The hell with that! This is the last meal we're going to have together. Ever eat a pink shrimp omelet—?"

Locking Gil's bag carefully in the back of the jeep, Bishop explained, "Lock up; even if you're just ducking into a store for a pack of cigarettes. And don't leave anything where it can be seen. You can't get any theft insurance in Mexico, you know. Take a look at my tires—you'll see four dust caps, and I'll bet you that when we come out of the restaurant, they'll be stolen. . . . Christ, here I go again, on the same song-and-dance. I'm sorry, Gil."

"Who's saying anything? What's right is right."

"I shouldn't be making a big stink when there's maybe a peso involved, and the guy wouldn't steal them if he wasn't hungry."

After breakfast, they walked across the plaza, back to the jeep. Gilberto felt Bishop's arm on his shoulder, and he walked slower. The freshness and luxury of the trees were good; he could have all of that he wanted, but only minutes more of companionship.

It was a struggle, during the meal, not to mention Dr. Eisen. But mentally, he equated him with Bishop. Neither man, he reflected, knew, could have known, or would ever know the other. The affinity between them existed only in his perception that they shared, between them, the contents of a secret book. He imagined them as members in different lodges of some big organization like—the Elks was the only one he could think of.

They broke out of the shade where the jeep was parked and Bishop unlocked the back of the panel. Instead of swinging it open, he said, "Say— why don't you leave your stuff in here for the time being? You got some things to do—the bank to change your money; the airplane ticket—Oh, and if you want to see that game tonight, maybe I could arrange to stay over."

"I just remembered—I won't be able to make it."

"Well, anyway, it's going to be a long morning for you. The plane doesn't leave till about half past one. So do what you have to do. Meanwhile I'll be working over at the Café Tupinamba—it's not far from here. Come over around one o'clock. We could have a sandwich and a beer, and I'll run you down to the airport. How about it?"

"I hate like hell to say no, Bish, but I held you up long enough as it is." That much was sincere. But Gilberto needed a better excuse to get out of being driven to the airport. "Besides, I need to have the bag; some things in it."

"Well, I kind of hate to see you go—"

"The same here, Bish."

"I gave you my address, on the back of the card. You'll let me know how you're making out in Vera Cruz, huh?"

"Sure will; drop you a card."

"And if I ever get down that way, I'll look you up and we'll break a crab together."

The frank pressure of Bishop's hand shamed him. He could end this mortification by saying, "Forget Vera Cruz. I got that one out of a hat; I never meant to go there. I've been lying to you all the way. And I still don't know *where* the hell I'm going!" But his throat felt as though there was a hand pressing on his windpipe.

The starter growled, gears rasped, and Bishop called, "Adiós, Gil, the best of luck."

"So long—and thanks again, for everything."

He watched Bishop turn left at the next corner and sat down on an iron bench under one of the big trees.

The mounting sun, weaving through the leaves, laid a mosaic carpet at his feet. He lit a cigarette, his second smoke from a package of Mexican cigarettes he bought in the restaurant. He had given the cashier a dollar, and received eight pesos in change. The smoke of it was purple in the sunlight. Leaning back, he felt a pleasant indolence; a delicious weariness of the bones that overtook him usually on Sunday mornings, when he knew that he didn't have to get up. No more than he had to now, he thought. Glancing at his watch, he saw that it was ten minutes before nine o'clock—and Friday, too. Clearly, slowly, and with no alarm, he calculated that he was two hours and some two thousand miles away from where he ought to have been this morning.

And why wasn't he there? He laughed to himself and thought of the way a comic Mexican—the kind they carve in pairs, seated asleep, as book-ends— would answer: Poor Pedro—might as well make it Gilberto—poor Gilberto ees not there, señor, because he ees here, I theenk.

Sometime, but not right now—he would think it out, in full seriousness, the hard way. Just what was it that brought him, this bright Friday morning, to a bench in the plaza in Mexico? Eisen tried to get it over to him that he would be carrying out the unuttered deathbed wish of his mother. The doctor had something there; you couldn't deny that. Bishop was in on the deal; how else could he have let himself be fooled into thinking that this joker beside him on the ride was anything *but* a genuine Mexican. Then, Gilberto thought, there was me! I had more to do with it than any of them—and *before* any of them got into the picture. Just how—well, that he would figure out later; some other time. You don't just plunge into such a complicated mental exercise. Tomorrow would do. He couldn't help smiling at that. One hour in Mexico and he was gone native—already saying, "Mañana."

A dog, gold in the sunshine, came pattering down the walk, his tail curled in a tight O. Gilberto called, "Here, boy," and the dog kept right on. Wrong language. "Ven acá!" Nothing doing. He knows a gringo from afar. Another thing that dog knows: he knows where he's going; certainly not anywhere he'd be asked for his papers.

His eyes half shut, he watched an old man sweeping litter in the street and working his way closer. Each time he gathered up a small mound of litter, he moved his cart a few feet toward the bench. Finally, he stopped at the fenced plot of grass opposite Gilberto, raised his hat, and wished him a good morning. It was pleasant to hear the greeting in Spanish, to answer, and to be asked, "You find a cigarette savoury; to your enjoyment in the morning?"

"Greatly so. Please take one," Gilberto invited, gapping the package.

With one hand, the old man raised his hat, and with the other, he daintily selected a cigarette. "A thousand thanks for your kindness, señor."

"You are welcome," Gilberto said, and smiled at what he saw lettered in whitewash on the dirt cart—"En Busca de Novia."

"It is a joke," the sweeper said. "Me, your servant, the father of thirteen, looking for a sweetheart."

"Yes. It amuses people."

"They can laugh all they want—" Then a bluster entered the old man's tone. "But if any cabrón thinks I can't handle one with the best of them, I'm ready to show him."

Despite the slurred and rapid Spanish, Gilberto missed nothing of the boast. This sudden, unaccountable assertion of machismo—this stallionship, was what Bishop meant; the thing you don't contest. "Absolutely no doubt," he said.

It was apparently the right thing to say, since the man repaid the compliment. "One can see that you haven't been gelded, my chief." Jaunty in his maleship, he tucked the cigarette behind his ear and studied Gilberto admiringly. "You are not of Matamoros."

"That is so."

"Nor even of the State of Tamaulipas, one can guess."

"No. I am from further away."

"Then you are going, with God, back to the capital."

"Yes."

"How fine! Thousands upon thousands of people all rushing about in and out of those monstrous buildings. It must be like a bee farm. Tell me, please, is it as miraculous as they say?"

"More so; it is magnificent. It is like Paris."

"It is good here, too," the sweeper said with quiet pride. "This also is Mexican earth. . . . You are very early, my chief."

"It is just nine hours."

"Then your bus does not leave for two hours yet. Besides, it is only a scant hundred steps to the terminal." The man pointed behind him, to a block of yellow buildings.

"Isn't there an earlier one?"

"Yes, but not for you, my boss. There are several of the second class. But you watch—you will overtake them before they have gone fifty kilometers. You will fly past them in your machine of the first class, with the numbered seats."

"I see. And do these earlier machines go to the capital also?"

The sweeper shook his head. "They have not the force to go beyond Cuidad Victoria. Some to El Mante, with the help of God."

Gilberto got up from the bench and lifted his bag. He remembered that you don't part from a Mexican with merely a curt "So long." You ask his leave. "I have some matters to attend to; so, with your permission—"

"Let me not detain you. Adiós."

13

The terminal, a jerry-built shed in a rutted vacant lot, had the unkempt look of a suburban streetcar stop.

A buff and green bus marked "Sta. Teresa—Servicio Mixto" was pulling out past a narrow arch, littered with peeling announcements. Gilberto watched it stagger past him.

Every seat was occupied, and some passengers were standing in the narrow entry beside the driver. The railed top was loaded high with bundles and willow crates. The bus itself was ancient; wooden ribs of the coachwork showing through patches of rust-eaten metal skin. Below, gray streaks of tire fabric showed under the worn rubber. Motor wise, Gilberto judged by the rattling, like marbles shaken in a jar, that the engine's main bearings were shot.

A second bus, newer—at least cleaner—sat with its motor idling, its exhaust drumming against a rotted fence. Some passengers were already inside.

"GLORIA," painted in red enamel with little blue flowers between each letter, blazed on the sloping front of the roof. Did it mean glory, or, as Bishop suggested, was it the name of the driver's girl? What interested Gilberto more was "Cd. VICTORIA" painted on the entire right half of the windshield.

Ciudad Victoria. Until the street sweeper named it, Gilberto did not know that such a place as Victoria, City of, existed. Even now, it was merely an additional place-name. But seeing it chalked on a bus as a destination made him feel again like a traveler. He experienced that same flush of poise as when California first began rolling back behind him.

He stood beside the door of the bus, waiting for the driver to finish his conference with the cobrador, his lackey, whose place was on the narrow iron ladder at the back of the machine or on top.

"Ready to take off?" he asked when the driver noticed him.

"This moment. Take a seat inside."

"What's the fare?"

"How far are you going?"

"All the way—Victoria."

"That'll be six-fifty."

As he took out his wallet, Gilberto realized that it had only U.S. dollars in it. He put it back quickly and brought out the limp Mexican currency and paid. "Do you suppose I have time to run across the street?"

The driver looked dourly inside the bus. "People are waiting, you know."

"Just over to the bank—to cash my paycheck. They don't know me in Victoria."

"Go ahead, then. You can leave your valise."

Hurrying, Gilberto realized, with no little admiration, how shrewd he had been to mention cashing a paycheck. How things clicked in his mind. And putting in that extra flourish: "They don't know me in Victoria."

It took less than five minutes to change his money at a window in the bank. The rate was 8.62 to the dollar. It was the first time he had seen a bank clerk on duty, smoking and drinking a bottle of soda. Taking most of the Mexican currency in 50- and 20-peso bills, he retained five U.S. $20 bills, tucking them away in his watch pocket, and kept twenty 5-peso bills handy in his trousers pocket.

When he returned to the bus, the driver had secured the seat directly behind his own by leaving the bag on it.

There were now—he counted them—sixteen passengers, including himself. They all sat straight, but not stiffly. None, except two women in mourning black, appeared to be travelling together. The women in black were no novelty to him. Identically dressed, even to the jet earrings, he had seen their sisters hundreds of times in Los Angeles.

The men were the curiosity. Not that there was very much difference between them—as individuals. But they were different, as a group. He suddenly understood why: every one of the men, and there were twelve, wore a hat; a sombrero of one kind or another. He recalled, wonderingly, that he never in his life owned a hat.

Even the driver wore one, a baseball cap, tugging it on as he started out of the terminal at a creep. The cobrador ran ahead of it and posted himself in the street to guide the bus forward with elaborate gestures.

The long main street sliced through the populous southern end of Matamoros, crossed an iron bridge with no warning and shot into open country, losing iself in the distant hills.

Now the land lay flat, only slightly creased, like a thrown cloth. Ahead, through the windshield, Gilberto saw buzzards convoked around a bloody patch. Like unhurried pedestrians, they broke up, some walking, as the bus rolled toward them.

He glanced at the speedometer: 40. It didn't seem that fast. Must be a good, tight motor, he thought, until he realized that the dial was calibrated in kilometers, making the true speed about 25 miles an hour.

The driver was doing a good job; didn't hesitate to shift down at the first sign of engine strain. One thing he failed to do was give hand signals when he turned out to pass anything. But it was in his favor that he gave the driver ahead plenty of warning, instead of waiting until he was on top of him. All in all, he was doing all right. Bishop might have to take back some of the things he said, if he were along on this ride. Yes . . . he might find some objection to half the windshield area smeared with white paint, but none to a 6-volt bulb burning under a picture of the Virgin of Guadalupe. That was safely above the driver's line of vision. As for a narrow vase of fresh flowers—well, that was in a bracket fixed to the center strip.

He admired the wristwatch of the driver and its heavy gold band. It was one of those chronographs with three auxiliary dials. The hands pointed to 4:10. Obviously he had forgotten to wind it.

The landscape had become, for the last couple of miles, a tremendous planting of henequin, unrelieved by fence or tree. So evenly spaced, each green plume, he mused, must have been laid out by engineers.

As he lit a cigarette, the driver called, "Got an extra one of those?"

"Sure, plenty."

"I see they didn't hold you up long at the bank in town," the driver said, handing back the package. "They must have known you there, like you said."

"They identify by the signature," Gilberto answered.

"Did you speak English to them?"

A trap, Gilberto sensed. He had put his foot in it when he used the word signatura instead of—what was it again?—firma. "No," he told the driver, "but I'm sure they can talk it better than I can."

"I wouldn't say so. You learned to speak it in the States."

It would be dangerous to deny it. "Yes. Studied it so hard, I even talk Spanish with a gringo accent."

"You're telling me! Why, man, you even dress gringo."

"Oh, this number—I got this in San Diego, California. I'm on the West Coast a lot."

"Baja California?"

"Mostly."

"Sinaloa, too, I suppose."

This was getting too much like a third degree. He had heard the name Sinaloa from Bishop, but he had no idea where it was. If you can't play it safe, play dumb. "To tell you frankly, this is my first time out of that territory." Whatever that would mean to the man, it sounded, at least, like a salesman talking.

It worked. "What line are you in?" the driver asked.

"Dental—dental supplies; dealing exclusively—"

"Excuse me," the driver interrupted, pointing ahead and braking to come even with a group of seven passengers waiting at the side of the road. There were three men and four women, and between them, a mound of bundles. The men came aboard first, looking almost military in their white shirts and trousers, identical sandals and machetes. They gave polite way to each other, and there was dignity in the way they made a greeting out of paying their fare, so that it seemed less of a cold transaction.

The women, meanwhile, handed their freight up to the cobrador to be stowed on the roof. Past Gilberto's window rose a woven crate in which two suckling pigs screeched as though they were being branded. A cluster of live chickens, their legs trussed, followed the pigs upward.

Three of the women, relieved of their burdens, took their seats quietly. The fourth tried to bring her goods—a large cluster of pottery jars, threaded on a string by the handles—into the bus. She tried to back in, lugging the stuff. All watched, but nobody tried to help her. And when she turned, panting, the driver said, "Upstairs with that junk."

This wasn't fair, Gilberto thought. The driver should have told her sooner, and he was sorry for the woman, who was probably taking those jars somewhere to sell. She glared at the driver, her bare feet planted wide apart and solidly on the floor. She was young—younger in the body than the face— perhaps in her middle twenties. She was close enough for him to see a row of pock marks, too small to be disfiguring, across the bridge of her nose.

"Be a sport," she said to the driver. "Let's not hold everybody up."

"No, doll," he answered. "Hand it back to the boy and sit down nicely."

"I'll hold these few little jars with me. That won't be any skin off your ass."

Gilberto was amused. This was telling him.

"Look, sweetheart," the driver told her, "you and your fine porcelain won't fit on one seat, and I won't let my own mother spread herself on two."

Pertly she answered, "Your own mother can go spread herself in a ditch, where you were conceived, you burro's bastard."

This, thought Gilberto, is where the driver slaps her in the face. Instead, the man said, unruffled, "Come on, come on, or I'll leave you by the road for the vultures."

She turned as the cobrador hauled the pottery out of the vestibule. "If anything breaks, I'll let your blood out, you unbaptized louse," she warned the boy. And, while unknotting a piece of cloth to get the money for her fare, she took off on the driver again.

Some of the coarse phrases Gilberto understood: about the driver's wife, who at that moment was putting the horns on him; but he needn't worry, it wasn't anything human. The rest of the passengers, more familiar with the pungent idiom of rural Mexico, smiled; the men broadly, the women with their eyes downcast.

"But what am I wasting my time for on a specimen that hasn't the virility of a yearling butterfly?"

Now she's going to get it, Gilberto thought. Even in Los Angeles, it was the supreme insult to refer to a man as a mariposa.

"And that," she finished, "goes for your catamite on the roof!"

"Olé!" called the driver, starting the bus with a jolt.

As the pottery woman stood there, surveying the seats, her sharp glance fell on Gilberto, and he dreaded that she would take the seat beside him. With relief, he saw her stride to the middle of the bus and look around again before choosing a place on the aisle, next to the best looking of the Mexicans. He had a thin, carefully tended mustache, and dimples showed as he smiled to indicate to the others that he was helpless.

The pottery woman looked around to assure herself that she still had her audience; looked frankly at the young fellow and pinched his ear. "Well, lover—what'll it be; a kiss or a cigarette?"

With cringing haste, as everybody laughed, he handed her a cigarette. "Come on," she urged, "a light, or I'll take the kiss, too."

Gilberto was sorry for the guy, but it was a diversion. You can rely on it that there will be one of these comic extroverts, usually mild drunks, in every public conveyance. And this was diverting in another sense, useful to Gilberto; he would talk about this to the driver instead of answering questions on which he may trip up, sooner or later. Forcing a chuckle, he said, "I'm lucky she didn't pick on me."

The driver heard him, but he was intent on letting the bus coast, after a burst of running in gear, along the edge of the road. Gilberto looked for his target—perhaps more passengers were waiting. There was nobody. But well ahead, and looming closer, a curving driveway led off the highway, toward a blocky, concrete building. Four sedans were lined up under a shed extending from the roof. He caught the colors of the license plate on the last car; yellow and black. California.

Now he knew where the driver was heading—a big sign reading "¡ALTO! INSPECCIÓN"—and why!

That's what the rat had done; doubled back in order to deliver him up to the authorities! At Matamoros there was only one official. Here there were four. And they were thorough, they had the passengers of the cars out and on their feet, papers in hand.

The bus swerved off the road and took the curving driveway, stopping a few feet ahead of the first car. Gilberto stared at it stupidly, as if he had never seen a green Pontiac with Michigan plates.

The driver honked twice and levered the door open. A stocky Mexican officer in light brown breeches, riding boots, and a darker brown blouse leapt up on the step.

"What do you say, cowboy?"

"The captain around?" the driver asked.

"Got something for him?"

"Yes—"

Gilberto wondered why he was fumbling; why he didn't say the rest of it: "A suspicious gringo, trying to pass himself off as a puro mexicano"?

But there was only a ruffling sound as the driver felt in the space between his seat and the bulkhead and brought up a magazine. "Newsweek," he read. The officer took it.

"Tell the captain it's two pesos-seventy."

The bus swept back on the highway. Gilberto smoked in relief, dragging deeply. Two minutes later, the Michigan Pontiac, with a man and a woman in it, snarled past.

Now it was safe to talk. "Do they stop every private car back there?"

"The checkpoint? No, strictly North Americans. Make them stop and show their tourist permits and whatever else they are supposed to have."

"But they already crossed the border."

"Sure," said the driver, "and they think they are in the clear. This makes it a double check. Anybody can cross at Matamoros, but here's where they spot anybody that's hot; crooks, deserters, anybody that's wanted."

"It seems to me, in that case, they'd be a lot smarter just to lay around in Matamoros," Gilberto contended.

"You'd think so. But they get panicky so close to the States, and want to get into the interior. Well, they get just so far." He pointed backward with his thumb.

"That's assuming they don't know about it. But if they do," Gilberto argued, "and pour it on."

The driver snorted. "I don't know how you handle it out in your part of the country, but here in Tamaulipas—did you see those motorcycles? And the kid I gave the paper to? Well, it just happens that's Sergeant Falcón, the best pistol shot in this part of the Republic. And the rest of them are right up there with him."

The driver went on enthusiastically, as if he were praising the home team. "Meantime, the telephone is busy and they put up a road block ahead. This time it's the military, with rifles." He took both hands off the wheel to aim. "Zas!"

"Pow!"

"That's nothing. Suppose by some miracle this mister gets through and almost reaches the capital. Mind you, I said *almost*—when suddenly he finds himself smack up against the Federal District Secret Service lads. . . . Hullo, Joe, whaddya know; what you doin' in Mexico! Papers, please!"

The last was in English, of a sort. Gilberto felt he should show some admiration. "Hey, that's pretty good. Where did you learn English?"

"Oh, you pick it up. I wish I'd put in a few years steady at it, like you."

"At the expense of my Spanish, though. You spotted that."

"Not much, if any," the driver assured him. "Maybe you forgot a little, or you missay a word now and then. But you didn't lose the real accent. That's in the blood."

Here was somebody else trying to account for something by blood. In this case, the durability of Gilberto's accent. Bishop, when he brought it up, meant something quite different: That on account of his blood, Gilberto would feel, judge with an inbred charity toward anything and everything Mexican. Conversely, it meant that this blood would boil up at the faintest shadow of arrogance.

Well, he thought, Bishop was all wet. His blood stayed cool under a good deal of provocation; most of it ignorant. If Mexican blood showed in the bones of the face, the color of the hair, and the skin, you couldn't go around saying you were a sunburned Anglo-Saxon. Does a dog bristle when you call him dog?

No—absolutely. Bishop couldn't be right, Gilberto decided. The worst he ever felt at any disrespect was shame, and he paid that back with con-

tempt. . . . That crud in front of the burlesque house . . . "Orale, chicano—"
The Dutchman . . . "You Mexicans—" Morrissey . . . "A hint to the white
student body—"

The best thing to do was to forget these ignorant bastards—like that mop-
jockey at the hotel in Laredo, calling to him, "Hey, you, adónde vas?" Richardson . . . "*Heel*-berto—is that the way to pronounce it? Well, this is an
American place, so suppose you answer to the name of Pancho." The chairman of the draft board, *that* horse's ass . . . "You're in, boy. You won't have to
worry now where your next plate of tortillas and beans is coming from." The
draft board doctor, with the bad case of B.O., telling him, "Pretty good
specimen—for a Mexican."

Time to forget them. Then why was he remembering the old as well as the
recent ones? The draft board was a long time ago; something that he had
forced to the outer rim of memory. But it was growing now, and flooding his
consciousness like a gas, acrid and ammonic—the smell of the specimen
bottles and sweat, the same smell that enveloped him when he lay on that
cold metal table.

The chairman of the draft board had been talking across him to the
doctor, telling him a joke. "Well, after this GI had been home for a few days,
just lazing around, his wife says to him, 'When are you going to wipe off all
those dirty things the kids chalked up on the fence?' 'Right now,' this GI
says. 'I'll wipe off all but one—Fuck MacArthur!—that stays!'"

When they both finished laughing, the doctor walked the chairman to the
door and said, "I'd be careful about telling that one around draftees."

"What do you mean?" the chairman asked. "That it might get back to
me?"

"That's right," the doctor said, pointing back to Gilberto.

"Who the hell is going to listen to him, a Mexican?"

These things he couldn't forget. No foreign sun could bleach out his
shame at remembering. If he had to drag them along with him everywhere he
went, how could he ever be his own man? Or would it be better to be free only
in the intervals between remembering? No; that way there would never be, for
him, any starting from scratch.

He would make one last mental pass at this galling problem; let's see:
Contempt—insult—reaction to—equals shame, i.e., taking it and wiping
your nose;—except once, when Bishop called you a wise-cracking pachuco
and you almost blew your top, out of a deeper sense of shame. What else
could it have been? What was a synonym for shame? What was the opposite—or to be fancy about it—the antonym—?

He was losing himself in it. Better, he thought, to take a little sleep now,
and later attack both problems—this one and the unfinished business of the
morning in the plaza; the answer to what blasted him out of L.A., himself,
Doc Eisen, his mother. He had gotten that far in the calculation when that
mañana feeling overtook him, he recalled.

The two ideas—his mother and mañana—fused. They meshed, in his drowsy mind, into a bulky, vulgarly lighted jukebox; one he had seen a hundred times, in the Café Orizaba.

"Mañana"—that was the record it was playing one Sunday night when he and his mother were there together, having supper. Quite a number, too; sung by Peggy Lee, in a drawling, lazy Mexican-American dialect. Each new chorus was a gag about how shiftless and dumb some Mexican girl was; how it was no use fixing the leaking roof because it wasn't raining, and stuff like that.

A lot of people were listening, and, suddenly, in the middle of it, a beer bottle crashed right through the front of the jukebox. Everybody saw who threw it: Baby Torres, the fullback of one of the big West Coast pro football teams. When the record still kept on playing, he pulled out all the broken glass, stopped the turntable, and, taking the record out, smashed it to the floor.

Only Verónica La Negra had the nerve to walk up to him, thinking he was drunk—and he may have been. But he just pushed her gently aside and stared at everybody in the place, from one table to another, moving his whole head, like a big bear. Yerno sidled up to him. "Now, Baby, let's sit down—"

"Callarte!" Torres yelled, and Yerno shrank back. The people watched to see what the big man would do next. He just spoke, in good, clear Spanish, and he had one of those high-pitched voices, not unusual for athletes. "What's the matter with you people, anyway? Don't you have any shame—at least before each other?" He waved his hand toward the smashed jukebox and it seemed, for a second, as if he were going to cry. "You listen to songs like that and smile as if somebody else was being made fun of, and shove in another nickel. Don't fool yourselves, my friends—you yourselves are the clowns. If the best you can be—if it doesn't disgust you, being a cheap joke to other people—I'm ashamed of you."

That was all he said, but his face was white when he finished. Anger had dried up his eyes. Nobody said anything for a long time after Torres left. A week later, "Mañana" was on the Hit Parade, but it never played in the Orizaba again. They remembered with shame.

There was Gilberto's answer: Sure, remember, don't ever forget; but with anger—not shame.

Now, he could sleep.

14

At each jarring stop, his eyes twitched open, looked nowhere, and saw nothing except the heaving floor of the bus. The last time, when he tried looking up, the sun on the driver's wristwatch drilled him through the brain.

A jolting, vertical slam that threatened the front axle brought him fully awake. The lassitude was gone, but he was alertly uncomfortable, his neck stinging with sweat. The driver grinned into the mirror. "You were really scratching the drum there for a while."

"I must have slept for—," Gilberto yawned.

"All of half an hour."

He smoked, but it did nothing for his impatience with the slowness of the machine and the sedate mobility with which old passengers left and new ones entered. What he had once admired about them, their calm and patience, he began vaguely to resent. The way they sat, perfectly still, except for their eyes, bright with secrets of things that lay beyond the monotonous kilometers of pocked highway. Perhaps they were playing some kind of game with him; for, whenever they stared greedily, as if watching a parade, it tricked him into looking. And what *he* would see—for the twentieth time—was either a herd of goats, a string of burros, or a cluster of farm buildings.

Once, the song of a bird—a riff—six liquid notes penetrated the shivering metal of the bus. Everybody smiled; at each other, and at him. Later, when a donkey brayed, Gilberto offered a grin all around. There were no takers. A bunch of deadpans, he thought; to me, that jackass was funny.

Amid ship, the pottery woman, he saw, had gotten to first base, and even beyond, with the good-looking machetero. Her head was on his shoulder, and it was plain that his left hand, which she covered with her rebozo, was inside her shirt.

He recognized the vast fields of evenly planted shrub, with its pearly blossoms, as cotton. There—again he saw a burro nursing her young. The mother stood on the bank of the ditch, while the baby reached up, from below. This he admired as exceptional intelligence and wondered if it had been observed before by naturalists.

The driver made a smooth and careful stop for an old man with a whispy beard. He was barefoot and carried a bunch of marigolds, a whole sheaf of them, the color of brass. Their gunpowdery smell excited Gilberto in an odd, sensual way.

As the old man started drawing the strings of a cotton purse with his teeth, the driver said, "In place of the fare, you may give me some of those flowers."

"Many thanks," the old man nodded, "but no need. I have the money to pay."

"Very well, then, how about selling me a tostón's worth?"

"With your permission, allow me to pay instead."

"But you're stuck with them," the driver reasoned. "You didn't sell them off."

"No, señor, I bought them, for their beauty and freshness."

"Then I ask your pardon."

"But," the old fellow said, "if you will be so good as to take some, as a gift."

"With great pleasure."

The old man separated a third of the bunch, tied the stems with a piece of twine and laid them across the steering wheel. The driver said, "A thousand thanks. And may I offer you a ride into Jiménez?"

"It chances that my way takes me to Jiménez. I am grateful."

A warmth-upon-warmth suffused Gilberto as he witnessed that. It brought back to him something that Bishop said: "There's something about the country—the people, I mean to say—that gives you kind of a glow." The Spanish word, brillar, didn't quite fit. Calor sin llama—heat-without-a-flame, was not it, either. Glow, after all, was the word.

He became drowsy again, watching the cotton bordered by the road and the pink horizon.

Later, awake, but with his eyes still shut, he heard the purr-gallop-purr of the idling motor and knew they had stopped somewhere. Maybe Victoria, he thought. No, still in the cotton country.

He was alone in the bus. The hood was up and steam rose from the open radiator cap. The bus had toiled up a long grade and, looking ahead, he saw that the road ahead ran steeply. He appoved the driver's caution in not shutting off the motor. Here was one chauffeur in ten who knew that to pour cold water into a red hot engine block without the pump circulating was begging for a cracked casting.

The driver poured two pails of water, filled from the ditch, into the radiator before the heat gauge dropped to around 180. While the cobrador buttoned down the hood, the driver called the passengers to get back in and took his seat. Glancing around, he made a quick census. Somebody was missing. Shaking his head, he sounded a long bleat on the horn and raced the engine.

There was a movement in the scrub which lined the road, between the ditch and the cotton field. The young machetero appeared first and leaped the ditch. As he got aboard, he jerked his head backward and went to his seat.

The pottery woman scraped the loam off her feet before entering upon the first step, where she stopped. Gilberto was strangely eager to see her face—a woman fresh out of the hay.

With a great show of patience, the driver put both elbows on the steering wheel, as the woman shook out her rebozo. "Take your time, princess. It's part of the service on this line."

She came right back at him. "That's what your sisters tell me."

When she wiggled past him, he called, "Don't forget to have it sprayed for the boll weevil."

Gorgoja—boll weevil. Gilberto laughed with the others, louder, and with a grace note, to show that he had a keener relish for the joke. Then, it puzzled him why the gag was on the woman, instead of the man. In the States, it was just the other way around; the fellow would have to take all the ribbing. As for the woman—why, one crack out of the way to her, and you'd have everybody down on you. Maybe it was because there, the dames, no matter what kind of tramps they were, had a way of looking as if they thought a fly had wings instead of a zipper. But this baby here—you could see immediately that she was ready to go to the mat any time with anybody.

Her boyfriend was no longer sitting with her, but had taken an aisle seat nearer the front of the bus, his sombrero tilted down over his eyes. And why shouldn't he, Gilberto thought. He owed her nothing; she was the one who went on the make.

Gilberto had not gotten a full look at her. There must be a difference as a result of what happened there in the cotton, he was sure. Anyway, he meant to let her know with one of those looks that Spencer Tracy, whenever he plays a priest, can level at a tart, just what he thinks of a hustler.

She sat three rows behind him. As he turned slowly, intending to discover her in the sweep of his view, her eyes caught him first and held him clamped in the narrow limits of her gaze. He, who meant to give her the old Spencer Tracy withering look, was being stared at in a way that made him uncomfortable. There was no scorn in the way she looked at him. If it had been that, he could snap his eyes away and pretend he wanted to look elsewhere.

When, finally, he was able to do just that, he knew that she was through with him. She saw all she wanted to see and cared no more. There was an edge of pity to her dismissal.

He felt bitter against her because she had read the secret of his oppressive celibacy—and pitied him.

What's good for pity—? Hate her because she knew, as well as if he had written out a confession, that he flogged his dummy? No—he had a good look at her, too; and that entitled him to a few conclusions of his own. If, when she first came aboard, he had just moved his knees an inch, she'd have sat down with him, and he'd have scored with her during the wait to cool the engine. So, what was the use of wasting his time being furious at her, when he could get some *benefit* out of having seen—yeah, and even smelled her.

(Men forced into continence had paid premiums, in experience, upon which they could draw for certain benefits. Signalman First Class Verne Waddell, for one, could redeem whatever sublimities or dishonors that fell to him here, alone by the yardarm blinker, and long at sea. He had mementos. The silk pants of some bigshot's private secretary he'd met at the U.S.O. A Parker "51" from the two college dames he'd had a regular circus with in La Jolla. The Armenian girl, with legs as hairy as a bear's ass, whose father cried in front of him and offered him half the raisin farm if he would marry her. Lois—he forgot her last name—who was a buyer for a department store and looked like something that stepped out of *Harper's Bazaar*. He still had the paper napkin on which she had marked with lipstick, "Rm. 614—in 10 mins." The trap-drummer in that girls' hillbilly band in San Diego. The married woman in the Lincoln custom job— So what! So every son of a bitch and his brother on this battle wagon claims he's been picked up by a married woman—and always in a custom job. So she gets around! Does that mean it couldn't have happened to him?)

Gilberto Reyes had nothing to recapitulate; no souvenirs—ni de seda, ni de papel.

(Thomas Keeting, for another. Long timer in Ossining, reading, in barred sections, the sky, black above him; tinged with red and yellow downriver. He watches for her searchlight—the dear, sweet, heavenly Albany Night Boat. The world's biggest marquise diamond! The people aboard her think the light is to show them Sing Sing and the cell blocks. Nothing like it! It's for him, Tommy, and nobody else; like it's been for eleven years, four months and twenty-six days. It talks to him. It says, "All set, Tom. Come on aboard. The stuff's here and it's mellow." He takes his time—the first cabin in which the light goes out is the one. And what'll he draw tonight? Something plump and juicy, and hot as a meatball, like Molly? Scratch that! Molly is for Saturday, which used to be their regular night for going down to the bungalow in Arverne. Then how about something lean as a snake—like Pat Braidwood's sister, who you had to beat with a hunk of clothesline to get her fired up? Maybe this time it'll be a redhead, with a skin on her like pongee silk—and a black shimmy. . . . Funny, their always asking, "Why, Tommy Boy, how'd you get into my cabin?" A nuisance—always having to explain how he slid down on the searchlight beam.)

Gilberto had no Mollies, no redheads, no smart lady buyers. And he had forgotten Carolyn. His were total fantasies, frothing up out of a single, broken look at a sturdy brown woman.

Now he'd give it to her! He'd do everything but put his lips anywhere near that wide mouth of hers, big enough to cram two pork chops into and she could still whistle "Yankee Doodle." He didn't have to guess about those hips—firm under the single ply cotton of her dress; the kind of can that didn't flatten out around her like melted tallow when she sat down on it. His fingers clawed his own knees as he saw himself, grappling for purchase on smooth, pneumatic globes. And what a pair of water wings! Like big pears, with the tips *out*—pointing away from each other. He brought a companion into his fantasy—anybody—a guy, so that he could make a little bet with him before he stripped her down. "Bet you any amount, the space between those pumps and her box is flat as an ironing board." He was helping her, with slow, salacious fingers, when the illusion ended in glaring blankness, as on a movie screen when the film breaks.

Let it go, he thought. If it was true—what Bishop said—that every guy in Mexico who could use it, was getting it regular, then there ought to be enough to go around. . . . He could sure use it.

Bishop said—well, just how much of what Bishop said was merely to hear himself sound off?

The bus strained to a jerking start and groaned uphill in compound-low. Gilberto looked out through the rear window. This time, he had to hand it to Bishop—where the bus had stood while taking water, were two stones, each as big as his head.

15

For the last hour, Gilberto had been feeling hunger sharply. The piece of chewing gum in his mouth no longer diluted the sour gases that burbled up from his stomach. Another cigarette, he was convinced, would make it worse. Cupping his hand over his mouth, he tested his breath. It was sour. A big glass of orange juice would go good right now, just to lubricate the ways for a triple-decker sandwich. A tuna salad and melted cheese, or a peanut butter and bacon, helped down with a skyscraper malt.

His stomach rumbled loudly enough for the driver to ask, "Hungry?"

"I could stand something—a hot dog."

"A taco do you?"

"Sure," said Gilberto, remembering the noontime appearance around McVeigh High of the hot tamale cart. Thick cartridges of warm, moist, cornmeal, with a stuffing of peppery beans and slivers of meat. They tasted good. But what were tacos? He had heard of them in L.A., naturally, but none had ever showed up at the Romeros' table.

"There's a stand, up where we stop to get on the ferry, that makes a good taco," the driver suggested. "Ask if they have barbacoa with drunkard sauce."

"I sure will—how about you?"

"I had breakfast. I eat again when we get into Victoria; then I stoke up and sleep till it's time for the return trip."

"Well—if you change your mind—"

"Thanks just the same."

They began the descent of a long grade. He could see the stream which they would have to cross, and the ferry; a barge, almost as long as the stream was wide. Four cars were ahead of them on this side, and three more waited to be ferried over from the other shore.

"I figure about a twenty-minute wait," the driver said, as he brought the bus to a stop behind the last car and cut the motor. "Maybe half an hour, if an Obras Públicas truck comes along; they have priority. . . . Oh, the taco stand—behind us, on the left."

"You sure you don't want anything?"

"All right—a beer, for sociability's sake."

The stand was an open-front clapboard hut with a counter open to the road. Under a cloud of flies were two deep, wooden trays, and between them a stone basin of pungent, olive-green sauce. A fat woman smiled to Gilberto and prodded something in one of the trays with a carving knife. A little girl, perhaps nine years old, with a clogged nose, was bent over a brazier, puttering with a stack of tortillas; sousing them in smoking fat and laying them aside, to be filled with meat.

The woman tilted the filled tray toward him; something covered with large banana leaves. "A taquito, little chief?"

"If you please, señora."

"Of barbacoa, fresh and tasty—" She lifted some banana leaves with the tip of the knife, unveiling a bisected sheep. It looked and smelled as if it had been steamed, rather than barbecued. Its poached eyes looked at him. The lips had shrunk back over the teeth. "Or," she invited, pointing to the second tray, "of young pork, very rich and fine." She offered him a dice of meat from the heap.

"The pork. And a beer—two beers; one for the chauffeur."

The child probed in a wooden chest, and sluggishly opened two bottles. She set one down on the counter and carried the other to the bus, handing it up through the window. "Salud," the driver called and drank. Gilberto sipped his. It was warm.

The woman troweled a handful of the minced pork across a tortilla and invited Gilberto to spoon up some of the green sauce from the basin. He slopped on a good amount.

"Have a care, hero," she said. "I make my salsa borracha with the chiles of Jalapa."

He bit into the taco and knew why she called him a hero. A gulp of beer spread the burning area from his mouth, deep down into his throat. He chewed rapidly, and the rich juices of the meat helped. He called for another taco, and this time declined the sauce. Hungrily, he crunched upon delicate cartilaginous lumps. Some morsels had the flavor of the tiny, gristly bones on spareribs. The best, though, were thick, striated wedges, like chicken gizzard.

"It pleases your taste?"

"It's a real treat."

"A young boar, that was," the woman boasted. "And only the most delicate parts—ears, snouts, palate and quartered stones. One more?"

"No." He dropped the last bite on the ground. "How much do I owe?"

"Two pesitos."

"And the chauffeur's beer."

"Included. Thank you, little boss, and return soon."

Leaning against the bus, on the driver's side, he lit a cigarette and probed with his tongue between his teeth. "Finished already?" the driver asked. "It'll be another ten minutes or so before we can cross."

Gilberto shook his head and came around the front to enter.

The seat next to his, on the aisle, was occupied by the first fat man he had seen since leaving Matamoros. His face was round, with a deep cleft in the chin. The skin was of a peculiar color, like manila paper. He had a small, black satchel on his lap, with his jacket folded under it. Over a soft shirt, he wore a light blue pullover with Donald Duck stencilled on it. Smiling, he angled his legs so that Gilberto could get into his own seat by the window.

The driver pulled the beer bottle away from his mouth and pointed with it. He spoke in English. "That feller is priest. All right with you?"

"It's all the same to me. How's about another beer?"

"I don't think so, thanks. Don't wanna go to sleep."

The priest smiled, amused by the brief exchange in English. "My companion, I see, is a norteamericano."

Gilberto let the driver answer. "No, a national; only the doctor has spent some years in the United States of the North."

"In California, mostly," Gilberto added. "And may I offer you a beer, señor priest?"

"I would take it with pleasure."

"Meanwhile, a cigarette?"

"Many thanks, señor doctor."

Gilberto passed a peso out through the window to the child and ordered another bottle of beer. When it came, the priest wiped first his mouth, then the bottle with his palm. He nodded, "Salud," and took a long pull. Spitting tiny flecks of beer, he said, "In a sense, young man, we are colleagues. You heal the body, which was blessed unto us as a vessel for the eternal soul, and I—"

"Bullshit!" said the driver.

The priest shook his head, "Some day, Anselmo mine, your throat will burst open like a rotten gourd for blaspheming against the Most Holy Mother of God."

"*There's* the Holy Mother of God, you gachupín faker," the driver snorted, pointing to the Guadalupe image and rapidly crossing himself. "And damn well he knows it, too! Why, any schoolboy will tell you that when it comes to a showdown between Our Lady of Guadalupe and his Virgin of Los Remedios, She—" he jerked his thumb upward and crossed himself again— "She always came out on top. And don't let His Eminence there, Padre Don Iñigo Rubirosa, tell you different."

The priest clasped his hands over the beer bottle and mumbled something.

"There he goes," the driver explained. "Excommunicating me again. That's the third time this week." He glanced ahead. "Come on, Don Iñigo, drink up your beer. We're moving."

The bus slid, with a thump, into the ferry. Shaking his head, the priest turned to Gilberto, "A Saracen, that fellow. You hear how he talks, a Moor, eh, señor doctor?"

"Thanks," Gilberto said. "But I don't have a title."

"He's in the dental profession," the driver affirmed.

"Ah, so—maybe you will be good enough to sound this tooth for me." The priest pulled down his lip. "This one. It torments me when I take something hot."

"Probably needs to be filled. A dentist could tell you. I only sell them supplies." He hoped he would not have to do any more talking until the gripping pain he felt, let up.

"You know, His Reverence here, is a Porfirista," the driver said, grinning and pointing backward. "Because I belong to a sindicato, the Alliance of Chauffeurs and Omnibus Pilots, he claims that makes me an atheist."

Gilberto didn't know what a Porfirista was, and didn't care. The greasy pork giblets were rolling in his stomach like pieces of broken crockery.

"Anselmo," the priest protested, "you are stuffing words in my mouth." He nudged Gilberto. "What I said was that when the servant rises up against his master, it shakes the throne of God."

"And I say, if it's that weak, it's going to go over one of these days."

Gilberto smiled wanly. The surge of water under him and the sight of it lapping against the opposite bank brought on another vehement urge. He pressed his tight groin and tried to get his mind off the pay booth in the Los Angeles Union Station—the apparatus for serving sanitary paper collars to lay over the cool ebonite seat. A guy could read a paper— The pain began letting up; backing off like a receding wave.

"The padre's got some funny stories about those Porfirista days." Anselmo began chuckling. "I wouldn't mind hearing the one about the Mother Superior and the pig, again. Go on, Don Iñigo."

The pain came flooding back again. Did it *have* to be about a pig! He eased his belt. The priest cleared his throat as the bus started rocking up the incline from the ferry.

"Listen, then," the priest began. "It was in the golden days of that noble chief of state, Don Porfirio, that there flourished, in Puebla, an edifice peopled by saintly women, dedicated to chastity—"

"Naturally," the driver sneered.

"Poverty, and good works."

"He means a nunnery. . . . Don't mind the way he talks," the driver said, "like reading from a book."

"This convent, then," Don Iñigo resumed, "was under the guidance of the Most Reverend Mother Inocencia de la Cruz; and very aptly was she named, as you will see. It passed that there was given to the nuns a suckling pig. It was of an age, and a succulence when it should have been eaten. Stuffed with a forcemeat of its own tripes, green plums, pounded brains, and pine nuts, it would have been fit for the table of an archbishop." He smacked his lips.

"Oh, Christ!" Gilberto groaned, in English.

"See what I mean," Anselmo said. "The way he tells it, you can practically taste it. Go ahead, padre."

"However, none of the good sisters could bring themselves to take this tiny animal, the color of a rose petal, and cut its dainty throat. So, it became a pet. They built for it a little sty and fed it, literally with their saintly hands."

"Okay, cut out the trimmings. It turned out to be a big, fat, roaring sow."

"As Anselmo says. And Mother Inocencia knew from the twelve dugs upon the sow's belly that the Order would have, in God's good time, a litter of little pigs. They waited, and the convent sow grew leaner and uglier in disposition, and often she complained in the night. But no tiny pigs did she yield up.

"In remarking about this to His Eminence, the Bishop of Cholula, who came to confess them, he pitied the unworldliness of the nuns. He told them that their sow must be coupled with a boar for the increment that they wished, and rode off on his fine mule.

"Mother Inocencia learned that there was a boar in the herd of a campesino, some two kilometers distant, and resolved that, since that was the custom, to bring her sow there.

"Now—and needless to say—it was not seemly for a godly woman to drag a leashed pig two kilometers along a highway. So, with the help of Sor Prudencia, a robust novice, the good Mother Superior lifted the animal into a handbarrow and brought her, in state, so to speak, to the headquarters of the boar. And the two beasts, after a manner of speaking, rushed into each other's arms. You may be assured that the Reverend Mother and her novice averted their faces while the boar conducted himself with the convent sow as nature ordained."

"In plain language," Anselmo elucidated, "he put the blocks to her."

"In the morning," Don Iñigo continued, "they looked in the sty. The sow was at peace; luxuriating in her wallow. But there were no sucklings. So, after Vespers, the pig was again put into the barrow and delivered to the boar, who, though he had ministered earlier to his own household, acquitted himself as commendably as on the previous day."

"Better, as a rule," the driver commented.

"At any rate, Mother Inocencia's disappointment was profound when she saw no young at the sow's teats the following day. But, dauntless, she and Sor Prudencia conveyed the stubborn sow once more to her cavalier and home again to the convent.

"On the fourth day, neither were there any little pigs, nor—to the horror of all—was the sow anywhere to be found. They looked among the stalks of maize and in the bean patch. They searched the barranca, where wild berries grew. Again in the maize and among the melons. And just when they had despaired, Sor Prudencia herself found the sow and called the others to see where: There! Perched comfortably in the hand cart—and waiting."

Gilberto owed them both a show of appreciation; the priest for the entertainment, and Anselmo for having stage-managed it. He tried to laugh heartily, and the stomach muscles brought into play, forced a risky spasm of his bowel. Even smiling was risky, but he wanted very much for them to see that he was companionable. The best he could manage was a slack-jawed grin.

Anselmo glanced around at him. "Don't you feel good?"

He tried to answer, moving his lips as little as possible. "Kind of dizzy. Must have eaten too fast. I'll be all right."

"Doesn't he look kind of gray to you, padre?"

The priest brought his face squarely in front of him. "Pallid, I should say, and no wonder; it is Satan's own stench up here by the machinery." He tugged at him. "Back further in the coach, there is a current of cool air."

He couldn't speak; his lips felt frozen. He had an impression that the wheels had left the road, but he was still in motion, sidewise, in an orange-colored fog. All sounds were muffled; the engine was no louder than the one-fifth horsepower buffer in Richardson's laboratory, which had a high-pitched sound, barely within the threshold of hearing.

He reached forward to turn it off.

There was a breeze on his face when he opened his eyes; Anselmo was fanning him with his cap. The bus was stationary, in the shade, and there was no sound.

"Feel better?"

"Yes, thanks. Are we here?"

"Yep, Ciudad Victoria. You'd better wipe your face."

He put up his hand. His neck and chin were clammy with drool. Mopping it off with his handkerchief, he tried to get up. "Take it easy," Anselmo urged. "Sit there as long as you like; you must feel rocky."

"Thanks, but I'm fine now." It was the truth; as if he had a refreshing sleep. "How long—"

"You were under for a good thirty minutes. At first I thought you were corking off for a nap. Then, Don Iñigo said you were twitching. He claimed you had the epilepsy and thought maybe he'd better give you Extreme Unction, in case you didn't come out of it. So I stopped for a minute back there and had a good look at you. . . . You want a piece of advice—get yourself a hat."

"Yeah, the first thing."

"Don't be a wise guy. The sun in this part of the country is liable to bake out your brains. Get one with a good, wide brim."

Anselmo handed the bag down and watched him get off the bus. The parking area behind a row of buildings was spacious and the surface was smooth cement. Dishes clattered somewhere near and he smelled coffee. At first he enjoyed the fragrance, but after a few sniffs, a faint nausea returned. "I guess I'll get to a hotel."

"There's the Palacio about three blocks over. But if you want a cheaper place—"

"The Palacio'll be okay. And thanks for taking all that trouble with me. It was the first time a thing like that ever got me."

"No trouble at all."

They shook hands and he walked. For three blocks, he was able to keep in the shade of the buildings. As far as the main plaza, larger than the one in Matamoros, but with fewer trees. With less shade, the sun angled off the smooth tile walks. His head began throbbing again. But that was bearable; nothing like that ghastly churning from which he suffered on the bus. What happened there? Better not think about it now, or it might overtake him suddenly. Anyhow, it would have to be attended to, the sooner the better, or it would poison him. As Miss Gormley once told the biology class, that was why the bite of the gila monster was poisonous, even its breath sickening; because it had no hole—excretory orifice, she called it. Everything it eats stays with it, and the entire animal becomes a sponge of corruption. Later, he decided, he would stop at a drug store and take a good dose of something.

Across the street from the plaza was the hotel. El Palacio—Filtered Water—Air Conditioned. Four of the six cars parked nose-to-curb in front of it had U.S. plates. One Texas Ford, one Utah station wagon, an "America's Dairyland," a Michigan Pontiac, the same one he had seen at the Inspection Station that morning.

There were a dozen reasons, he said to himself, for staying away from that hotel. For one, the act of registering itself; walking into a lobby full of U.S. tourists and being pinned down, asked a lot of questions, either beginning or winding up with where was he going. And how could he be sure they were merely tourists, or just using that as a front? That Michigan Pontiac didn't look kosher to him—it had gotten away from the Inspection Station much too soon.

For two—not so easy. He started out with a dozen reasons for not crossing the street, and even the first was more or less imagination. Suspicion began to dislodge fact in his mind. Take this bus driver—Anselmo, he called himself—a nice enough guy, as they come. But why did he recommend the Palacio? Suppose after a little while, Anselmo came up to see him and started out, "Okay, feller, what's the pitch? I looked in your grip while you were out cold, and the only thing in it resembling a dental supply is a toothbrush. But I took a quick hinge in your pockets, and you're kind of slightly loaded. . . . Let's face it—you're no more a mexicano than I am a Swede. You're a pachuco, trying to pass yourself off as a man, and if you want it to stay that way, just count out a thousand pesos. On second thought, better make it two."

The other ten reasons could wait. There must be another hotel where he could hole up for a while. For how long didn't bother him, as he walked down to the end of the plaza and entered a narrow street. He continued on that to where it ended, in a right-angled wall. Turning left, an alley led him to a wider street, two blocks from the one which he entered off the plaza. Over a narrow gateway cut into a long, one-story stucco building was a sign: Hotel—LA RECIA—Plano E. o A.

Within was a flagstoned patio, a simple quadrangle with doors numbered from 1 to 14 on three sides of it. A boy, who seemed not older than twelve, watering plants in red painted nail kegs all around, looked up, but didn't stop his work when Gilberto entered. He answered, "Sí, señor" when he was asked if there were any rooms.

"With bath?"

"Shower only, señor."

"Good enough. Which room?"

"Whichever you like—four, five, seven, eight, ten, or twelve."

There were keys in all the doors enumerated by the boy. Gilberto pointed to 5, the nearest. "That one all right?"

"Why not?"

"Is there hot water?"

The boy touched the stream from the hose. "Not hot, not cold."

The room was clean. The window, opposite the one facing the patio, looked out on the street. Sunlight came in, lemon-yellow, through the half-closed slats of the venetian blind. The bathroom was a doorless alcove.

When Gilberto saw the toilet bowl, with its overhead flush tank, his stomach began to seethe again. He prepared slowly. As he locked the door, the boy knocked, bringing with him a printed card and the stub of a pencil.

There were spaces on the card for his name, place of residence, and occupation. "How much is the room?"

"Twelve pesos."

He gave the boy a five- and a ten-peso note. "I have no change. The boss is lying down," the boy shrugged.

Gilberto thought a moment. He had cigarettes, matches; he would want something to read. "Can you get me a newspaper?"

"Of the capital?

"It doesn't matter, but bring it right away. Meanwhile, I will fill out the card."

Name. . . .? Leaning on the dresser, he fished for a name with the initials G. R. George—no; that would be Jorge. He wrote: Gustavo. Romero—no; that could possibly involve them. Ruiz was good. For Place of Residence, he wrote Monterrey and put a dash next to Estado; he didn't know what state Monterrey was in. But he was confident that this was as ordinary as a traveler in the States writing simply Chicago or San Francisco.

He puzzled for a time over Occupation. Viajero—viajador—those meant simply traveler, not traveling salesman. Vendador—seller. Comerciante—businessman; that would do. Date—he wasn't sure whether he left on the 12th or the 13th. The newspaper would tell him.

Stripping off his sweaty shirt, he proceeded to lay out his shaving things, toothbrush and paste. When he checked that there were towels and soap in the bathroom, the boy returned with the newspaper and the change: fourteen pesos and sixty centavos. "There's the twelve for the room, and one for you."

"You are giving me more than the newspaper cost."

"That's all right; put it in your pocket."

"Many thanks, my boss. If you wish anything, cry out for me, Mauricio-at-your-service."

Mauricio-a-sus-órdenes—it sounds as if the whole thing was his name.

16

It was already twilight. The shower had been refreshing and he had given himself the Sunday-shave—once down and once against the grain.

He lay on the bed in his shorts, the newspaper on the floor, where he had let it slip after barely glancing at the front page. Except for the language, it had pretty much the same kind of stuff as the Los Angeles papers—"Moscú," "Kremlin," "Comunistas," "José Stalin" sprinkled all over.

He would like to have gotten hold of a *Los Angeles Examiner*, for a look at the School Page. There was always something on it about McVeigh High. They must have a pretty strong basketball team this year—the kid, Chambers, who was a freshman, should have developed into a crack center by this time.

Lying here, comfortably like this, a man could think things out; not his whole life plan, that is to say, but the next stage, anyhow. He knew where he was now, but tomorrow—where would he be? Yes, sir—time for a man to think of where he was heading. Got to close that gap between getting *away* and getting *to*. Not that a little clarification on what he got away *from* would hurt; but he blew that bridge, so *that* story could wait. Later on, when he got to writing his memoirs, was the time to think of that. Right now, the main thing was to get one day ahead of mañana, instead of staying behind it. The trouble with Mexicans—he lit a cigarette and blew a puff of smoke up into the ceiling fan—yeah, the trouble with Mexicans—what kind of an electric fan is this, anyhow? It sucked up the smoke—ah—the blades were pitched the wrong way, that was it. The same with the light switch; the indicator said ON when the light was off. Then, too, he had bruised his knuckles opening the door because of the way the knob was put on, half an inch from the frame. Pretty sloppy work all around. But the bed was good; a big matrimonio. Lying in the middle, he could barely touch the sides.

Of course there was nothing like the first hotel he'd been to as a kid; that one in Los Angeles. What a layout that was! He and his mother drove to it in a taxicab. She let him hold her make-up case and she held her evening gown on a coat hanger so that it wouldn't get wrinkled.

They turned off Wilshire Boulevard onto a curving driveway lined with palm trees up to the entrance. When they got out, a man was waiting there. "Miss Reyes? . . . Don't bother about the meter. And who's the young man?"

"Gilberto, my son. He's almost twelve. I thought I'd send him to the movie downstairs while—"

"That's all right, unless he wants to go. He won't be in the way," the man said, leading them into the beautiful crystal and emerald lobby. He gave her a room key and asked her if she would like to rest before rehearsal, and had she eaten? "Anyway, you should have something. Go right into the dining room, order anything you like and put down the room number when you sign the check, or just say, 'Sheriff's party.'"

He had a waffle with pecans baked in it and strawberry jam spread on top. His mother had a club sandwich—beautiful—without crust on the toast and coffee out of a silver pot. She signed the check and left the waiter a dollar. Then they went into the big ballroom where she was going to sing later at this Sheriff's Benefit. There was a dance-team already rehearsing with the orchestra, and she was down for an hour later, to go over her music.

They walked around the hotel grounds for a while and sat down under a big umbrella, by the swimming pool. There were only a few people in the water, which was blue and splashed up silver when anybody jumped into it. A waiter came up and kind of fidgeted with a sign on the table. "Reserved for Guests of This Hotel." "Wish anything?"

"Not now, thank you," his mother said, letting the waiter see the big, bronze room key, and he backed off, saying, "I beg your pardon."

A kid about his own age in purple knitted trunks, no shirt, and a white bathing cap climbed to the high diving board and did a neat one-and-a-half gainer. He saw it was a girl when she came out of the water, peeled off the cap, and shook out a cluster of brown curls.

Love for her overcame him and he wanted to get away from there, quickly, before she could look at him. He wasn't ready for that. She could see him, all right, later on, after he had brought the big transport down, two of its motors dead, in a cross-wind belly landing, without a single passenger hurt. And he, staggering out of the shattered cockpit, blood streaming from a cut on his cheek, and the crowd saying, "Nobody but Hot Rock Reyes could have set that ship down in one piece."

The room looked out over the pool, but the goddess had gone when they got upstairs. A good thing, too, because it was getting chilly and he didn't want her to get pneumonia. But maybe—

"Are you sure, hijo, you don't want to see the movies?"

"No, Ma, I'd like to stay up here and look out."

When it got really dark, he explored the room; a treasure house, with everything in it monogrammed A—on the covers of the twin couch-beds, on the glasses that stood in holders in the bathroom. There were three faucets over the sink. Hot, Cold, and Filtered-Ice. He tried them all. A pile of thick towels. He unwrapped a piece of soap, inhaled its perfume deeply, rewrapped it, and slipped it in his pocket. He felt the toilet paper—so thin and yet strong, that he folded a piece of it over his pocket comb and played "Praise the Lord and Pass the Ammunition."

Oh, there were more wonderful things! On top of the writing table was a leather portfolio containing a magazine—all about the hotel. In the drawer there were two pens, one stub and one with a fine point; an inkwell that didn't spill when you tipped it over. There was writing paper of three sizes and Airmail, with envelopes to match; a pad of laundry lists; a few trunk tags; paper clips. What a hoard!

But of all those things, he appropriated only a blotter (and, of course the piece of soap) to show the kids in school, in case they doubted that he had stopped here.

His mother came back and said the rehearsal had gone fine. She would be appearing second on the program and would be through by ten o'clock. No, she wasn't being paid for singing tonight, but, she explained to him, it was an honor. This was a dinner to raise money for some charity that the Sheriffs were behind. For her, it was a chance to sing before some very high-class people.

After she came out of the bath, she put on her evening gown. He helped her with the shoes and looked to see if the seams of her stockings were straight up and down. And, while she fixed herself up at the mirror, with all the lights on, he glanced through the magazine about the hotel once more.

It hit him like a punch in the ribs when he saw *her* picture on a page that said: "WE HAVE WITH US—" It showed her, her legs dangling over the edge of the pool. Under it, he read:

MISS JENNIFER BAXTER, a lovable little mermaid from the Canal Zone, makes her beach-head at this hotel, while her daddy, Col. Norman L. Baxter, of the U.S. Air Force, sweeps Hirohito's monkey-men from the skies.

He held his finger on the page until his mother left. "You'll be all right, now, won't you, hijito? You won't be frightened till I come back?"

Frightened! "Me? What are you talking about, Ma?" She threw him a kiss and left. And he didn't like her to call him hijito, either. Frightened! Hot Rock Reyes frightened; that was a laugh. He opened the book.

"Jennifer—Jennifer, I love you."

"I love you, too, Hot Rock. You are my shining knight of the stratosphere."

"Colonel Baxter, sir, I want to ask the hand of your daughter, Miss Jennifer Baxter, in marriage."

"We're in a war, Lieutenant."

"Yes, Colonel."

"Bloody war!"

"Yes, sir."

"And no daughter of mine marries anybody but a full ace. How many Nips you got so far, Lieutenant?"

"Two, sir; a Zero and a medium light bomber. But I only just started this morning. It was my first mission."

"Well, then, don't stand there! Get into that P-51 Mustang and don't come back here till you nail three more of the yellow bellies. Now, scramble!"

Boy, was this a cinch! He swept right in among them, gutting everything with a meatball on its wings that got in front of his guns. The last one was a black Nakajima troop carrier. Well, you might call it a little grandstand play—this coming around it in a screaming power dive and gutting it from below. But there it was, going down, flaming, in a flat spin. It seemed to take hours—

He listened to loud whispering outside in the corridor. "I hope you didn't lose the key. Give it to me, I'll open it for you."

It was right outside this door, because he heard his mother say, "No, please, Mr. Andrews. Thank you, but you don't want to keep your friends waiting—and Mrs. Andrews."

"Shhh! She thinks I'm in the Committee Room stagging it. Here, gimme the key."

"Besides, I don't have anything in the room."

"I'll run down and get a bottle—"

"Yes, do that."

"Later on," the man said. "Right now—"

Gilberto got up from the couch and walked closer to the door. His mother laughed lightly. "No, I'll tell you why you can't come in. There's somebody asleep inside—my son."

The man laughed. "Come on, sister, I heard that one before."

"It's true, Mr. Andrews. He's just a little fellow."

The man's voice got hoarse. "I don't know what your game is, but I'm going in there with you, see!" The knob shook. Gilberto wanted to shout that his mother was right, he was in here, but he was afraid to, in a high-class place like this.

"Please, Mr. Andrews . . . I had a nice time—"

"Well, I want to be able to say the same."

"So, please don't spoil it."

"*You're* spoiling it! It was me that fought to get you in on this program. You know what that could mean to you."

"I appreciate it, Mr. Andrews—"

"Well, you're not showing it."

There was a bump against the door. Gilberto put his hand on the knob.

"No, hijo, don't open it!"

He stood there, frightened, and heard the man start in again. "Maybe you take me for one of your zoot-suit congaline boys, huh! Well, I'm a business-man—Hon'rary Sheriff's Deputy, see. I own Andrews Motors, in Glendale." He began to plead. "Let's go in, huh; and tomorrow, whenever you want, come around, here's my card—take anything you want off the used car lot. How's that?"

"I couldn't, no. I can't afford a car."

"I'll make it up—in cash."

"You'd better go, Mr. Andrews, good night."

"Look, baby—the hall is empty. . . . The least you could do—"

They slammed heavily against the door and his mother yelled, "Let me go! Gilberto—sonny—call somebody—the manager—on the phone."

Sobbing, he started to struggle with the door latch and heard the man, "No goddam greaser bitch is gonna give me the runaround!" A hard bang against the door followed that, just before he got it open.

His mother stood there, trembling. The man had run away, leaving a stale whiskey smell near the door.

The front of her dress was torn open and there was blood on her lips. She took him up in her arms, but he struggled. "Lemme go, Ma—lemme catch him! He hit you! I'll catch him and kill him!"

"Let's get the hell out of here!"

Never letting his hand go, she grabbed her things, makeup case and all, and pushed him out first. He forgot the blotter and something else he wanted very much as a souvenir—a pincushion stuck with threaded needles.

At the door, she stopped for a second, turned back, and spat on the light green carpet.

He dropped his cigarette butt into the ashtray on the chair beside the bed and wished he had that pincushion here, now, with its threaded needles. He had use for it, here in Mexico especially. Anyway, as soon as Mauricio-at-your-service came back with his pants from the cleaners, he would send him out for it. Borrow it, most likely. He reflected on the utter cheapness of such useful articles as needles. Once, in the Subway Terminal Arcade on Hill Street, he bought a package of them. Not that he had any special need for them, but because they were four dozen for five cents; all assorted sizes. Some were extremely fine, with gold eyes; and there were several thick enough to sew up the torn seam of a practice basketball.

A basketball—the thought of it was a hinge on which another door in his memory swung. This had to do with a hotel, too—the only time he'd stayed overnight in one. That was in Ventura, when McVeigh played Ventura Central, and there was too much fog on the Coast Highway to go back the same night.

After the game, there was the usual dance in the gymnasium. But Morrissey warned the squad that they were still in training, and everybody had to report back to him in the lobby by twelve midnight, sharp.

All the squad made it, except Nick Keaney, who blew in twenty minutes late, and anybody could tell he'd had a good shot of something with his Cokes.

It was plain that Morrissey was stalling to give Keaney time to show up. Ordinarily, Morrissey would give one or the other of his two standing lectures. But this night, he worked both the "Your God" routine and the "Self-Abuse" spiel into one. When Keaney finally showed, Morrissey raced to the finish; something like: "The Great Power outside yourselves, which gave you this victory of 48 to 26 tonight, and another leg on the Southern District Inter-High Scholastic Trophy. . . . So, no matter what faith or religion you belong to, before you and your teammate turn in, each, after your own fashion, give humble thanks to Him, Your God, Amen."

A couple of the fellows said, "Amen," after him. But Keaney, standing right next to Gilberto, said, "Oh, the mealy-mouthed bastard."

"And now, men," Morrissey finished, "don't forget—hands on top of the covers."

Keaney let go with a loud razzberry, and everybody waited to see what Morrissey would do about it. Not a thing! All he said was, "You all have your room assignments—hike!"

In the morning, at the so-called training table, Keaney pulled another one on Morrissey, even rawer than the night before. When the juice was all served, Morrissey rapped on the table, bent his head, and said, "Dear Lord, our Father, bless this food to our use and us to Thy service, for Jesus' sake. Amen."

When he looked up, Keaney had finished his juice and was wiping his mouth. Morrissey looked over to him and said, "I gather you didn't like my offering of thanks, Keaney."

"Thanks for what?"

"Well, isn't there anything said at your house before meals?"

"All the time," said Keaney. "Every meal."

"Would you mind repeating it for us, here. Perhaps we could benefit."

Without being snotty, or anything like that, Keaney said, "Would you really like to know, Mr. Morrissey?" Just suckering him into playing straight. "My dad always says, 'Butter's up to ninety-two cents a pound, so go easy with it, for Christ's sake.' " The howl that went up . . .

On the way back to L.A., Gilberto, sitting in the back of the bus with Keaney, brought the subject around to how he was able to get away with riding Morrissey like that.

Now, Keaney was really eager to let somebody in on it, but he prefaced it by saying, "I don't mind telling you, Reyes, but it's got to be strictly masonic, and I know you're not a blabbermouth. I may have to use it against him some day—on something big—and I don't want it to piddle out. He suspects I got something on him, and I want him that way—just simmering—till I'm ready to take the lid off, and then—Whoosh!"

"Sounds atomic," Gilberto said. "Don't keep me in suspenders."

"Well, it goes back to a sloppy Saturday—come to think of it, it was just three weeks ago, today," Keaney began. "And I had a thing on with—never mind who. A matinee. So we haul over to the Gray Bonnett Motel—you know the place—out on Sepulveda."

Gilberto knew *about* it. They called it the Quickie-Biltmore and all the bigshots in the senior class took their girls there. "Oh, sure," he said.

"I put Toots in Cabin Number Three, and I'm coming back from signing in as Mr. and Mrs. Bullock Wilshire, when I spot this dark blue Chevy coup parked by Number Eight, just across the strip from us. And it looks migh-ty familiar. So, I ramble over for a look at the certificate around the steering post. Sure enough, it's Myles J. Morrissey, something-something Gardiner Avenue—inside, blasting away at something."

"Terrific!"

"Hold your water—let me get to the punch line before you start cheering. . . . I try to keep an eye on his car from my bungalow, so's to spot who he's got in there with him in Number Eight. But, the babe I'm with is hot as a pan of biscuits and she wants action. I could use a little myself, but I'm afraid to take my eyes away from those window slats. Well, the chick starts razzing me—Who did she come here with, A Peeping Tom or some kind of degenerate?—so I have to deliver. But I'm telling you, Gil-boy, all the time I'm giving her the treatment, I'm worried that I'll lose my man."

"What a spot to be in," Gilberto said sympathetically.

"By sheer luck, the operation is timed to a hair. I hop back to the window, just in time to see Morrissey unlocking the right-hand door for this buffalo he's got with him. But her back is to me, and it looks for a time like they'll get away without me seeing her pan. So what do I do but rap on the window, and she whips around like she'd been goosed with a soldering iron."

"Somebody you knew?"

Keaney answered in a pretty good imitation of Ronald Colman. "Slight-leh—only slight-leh, dear boy. We all know her slight-leh. But, of course, Mr. Morriss-eh and Dr. Van Kliek know her more intimate-leh."

"I got it! Miss Nixon, The Dutchman's secretary."

"Close," Keaney said. "Close, but no cigar. . . . The Dutchman's wife."

Lying here in the high, wide bed, he regretted not dropping that surprise package between Morrissey and The Dutchman when they had him in there. The fact that he didn't, gave him a fleeting sense of nobility, which, he promptly admitted to himself, was false. The truth is, that he had forgotten, even while they were raking him over the coals. Yet, he could have remembered if he had not been so coldly, bitterly angry, or had paused to pity himself.

Still, he meant to get some benefit out of Keaney's story. Someday, if the time came, and he was in goodly company, he would change roles with Keaney. He would make his awed listeners marvel at the kind of life he led in the States, the quality of the sport he had pursued as a crack athlete, the forms of recreation that came with the laurels. The hot-rods, the Cuba libres—and the dames to share them with. The signings-in at motels as "Eric Shawn & Wife." Sports jackets from Pesterre's in Beverly Hills, with matching slacks. . . . They'd want to hear more about those chicks and their wonderful, cup-like handfuls with strawberry tips; their smooth, white throats—one whiter than the rest. He kissed it to cool his lips. "Oh—Miss Jennifer Baxter—my lovable little mermaid . . ."

"Gilberto—my darling lover, you know you are the first and only. Can't you see—there, on the carpet—the blood?"

"Lieutenant Reyes! What is the meaning of this?"

The slender arms and the crisp brown curls vanished. He wasn't the first and only—not by a long shot—here, now, amid the mingled fumes of gasoline, dusty upholstery, and hot metal. He tasted the familiar, acetonic moistness of the darting tongue; the scent of Shalimar warmed by grinding thighs. . . . "Don't tease me now, Gil—please. Haven't you punished me enough? Didn't I always say you were a white Mexican? . . . I want you—"

"Órale, chicano—"

17

After a single, sharp rap on the door, Mauricio pushed it open. It had been unlocked.

"Pardon, señor, you were asleep."

"Just resting. Let's see the pants. They look all right. Just drape them over the end of the bed."

"Is there anything else you wish me to do, señor?"

"Yes—can you get me a needle and thread, it doesn't matter what color, and I'll pay you all together."

"If there is something to sew, señor, the galopina will do it for you," the boy suggested.

Galopina—it was the first time Gilberto heard that word. From the sound of it, he judged, it must mean something less than a recamarera—a chambermaid. "I'll take care of the sewing myself. Just ask her to lend me the needle and thread, huh."

Certainly a secret pocket was no secret if somebody had to make it for him. Like in that picture—where the scarred-face pirate had his men bury the treasure; deeper, deeper, they were getting more and more afraid that he'd bury them with it—which he did.

Perhaps, he thought, he was still acting with an excess of caution. Had he been tipping the boy too liberally? Wouldn't that kind of fix him in the kid's mind later, if questions came to be asked?

He would have to start acting more—well—Mexican toward those people. Well, maybe he didn't mean it that way. It was simply that he had seen, even at the Café Orizaba, how the customers behaved to the help. Verónica La Negra, too, for that matter, big-hearted as she was. Things like, "Hey, you—girl!" barked at them, or that hissing business, "Pssst!" to get their attention. Very rarely did anybody say, "Please," to a waitress. Not like in the Americano places. There, they put the menu down in front of you and stood by with a pencil. And if you didn't make up your mind right away, they'd go off, and you could hiss at them till you got blue in the face.

In a way, he felt, it's partly the fault of these people. There's a point at which service ends and flunkyism begins. Take this boy, Mauricio, for instance. Every time he opens his mouth, it's not without, "Para servirle, patrón."

There—that knock; that's what he meant. It had a servile *sound*. He opened the door. A woman stood there who was about the age of the one he had seen on the bus. She was almost as tall as himself and wore something resembling a pinafore. Her thick black hair was combed smoothly and tied up with colored yarn, and she was barefoot. The first thing she said was, "Your servant, señor." Su servidora—holding up the threaded needle. "You wished me to mend something—"

"No, but if I can borrow this for a while—" He took the needle from her fingers.

"If it is a fallen button or a—"

"Nothing like that, thank you."

The woman looked almost frightened as she backed away, saying, "Pardon—your permission—"

"That's all right."

Uncomfortably he realized that he had spoken curtly, perhaps harshly, and that he had given her no tip. Well, he'd square it with her; when she comes back for the needle she'll find it pinned on a one-peso bill. She'd get a bang out of that—a glow, that is.

Locking the door, he got his razor and removed the used blade. Then, seated on the bed, he carefully slit open the seam of the striped lining on the inner waistband of his pants, making a four-inch gap.

The money made a fat pile. There were 1,000 pesos in fifties; 1,500 in twenties; and 100 in five-peso bills. The five U.S. $20 bills were in a separate wad. Putting aside 500 pesos in twenties and fives, he carefully folded the rest of the Mexican currency around the U.S. bills and wadded them into the slit waistband.

Sewing with small stitches, it became dark before he was half finished. Grinning, he snapped the light switch to OFF. The single, unshaded bulb in the ceiling was a 60-watter, but it gave sufficient light.

Finished, it seemed to him that the money made a quite noticeable bulge, but he could judge better if he slipped the pants on. The bump was prominent, all right, but it didn't matter, because the coat would hang below the waistband.

Now what—with the whole night ahead of him? A little bookkeeping right at this time wouldn't hurt. Adjusting the pillow against his back, he calculated: Since he crossed the border, he had spent roughly 20 pesos. That was twice as much, according to Bishop, as living here would cost him. Still, it was less than $2.50 U.S. But wait—those 20 pesos included transportation, getting 140 miles or so into the country. And what's more, this hotel room, that would have stood him at least three bucks in the States, was already paid for. Supper, later, might cost another couple of pesos. Not so bad, for around three dollars to be living, as Keaney used to put it, like a belted earl; handing out lavish tips, buying beers for bus drivers and priests, smokes—lunch—

At the thought of that lunch, his stomach shuddered with revulsion. He would have to force himself to eat another speck of food tonight. Anyway, he'd go out and see what Ciudad Victoria looked like after dark; maybe take in a movie.

Half-risen, he slumped back on the bed again. No, a man doesn't take chances in a strange city, carrying around a bundle of 2,600 pesos, plus; plus the equivalent of 860 pesos more in U.S. money. Even if there was a safe here in the hotel, he'd either have to rip the seam again, or deposit the whole pair of pants. For that matter, just having all this plunder on him was taking chances.

Who knows what could happen? After all, the situation was something like the one he'd listened to on the radio once: A young fellow, who'd been away in the States for a long time, returns to his home town, somewhere in Europe. He'd made his pile and he wanted to surprise his mother and father, who didn't recognize him when he asked for a place to stay overnight. He was going to tell them who he was in the morning and they'd have a big family reunion. The old folks were poor and they happened to catch sight of his bankroll. So, during the night, they cut his throat—aaargh! And when they started to get rid of the body, they find out from his papers that they killed their own flesh and blood. Blackout.

The listeners were asked to send in letters, along with a box top from soap powder, and say, in not more than 250 words, what they would do if they were the parents. The first three prizes were $50, $25, and $10, and the next hundred best letters would get a pair of scald-proof tongs for lifting spaghetti out of boiling water.

He worked a long time over his letter, writing in ink, on only one side of the paper:

> My entry is as follows. That they shouldn't do anything. Even if the
> Law fines them guilty of first Degree. As they are old anyway they
> should be put in solotery with a picture of their son in there cell with
> them as a reminder. Let them live and sufer!!! Respectfully yours,
> G. Reyes, Age 13.

He waited and waited, and when they didn't send him even the spaghetti tongs, he decided it was a fake.

A deep yawn let him down into a balmy swoon that lasted several seconds.

A deep-toned bell somewhere in the city rumbled nine times. His own watch said five minutes after nine. The clean shirt and socks he was going to put on were in the bag, on the opposite side of the bed, and as he started to lever himself to a sitting position, he heard the rain. It may have been raining for some minutes, for that matter, before the soft, scratching sound of it on the window screen reached him.

That meant he would have to stay in, at least until it let up. And if it didn't—incidentally, what was wrong with getting a good night's sleep? He'd need all he could get if he was going to make a start in the morning.

From now on, it was going to be no more panic, no forced marches. He could think better if he hoisted his legs up on the bed.

Now he pondered Ciudad Victoria itself. It lay a good distance *within*

Mexico and was, when you come to look at it from the standpoint of wear and tear on the nerves, the toughest stretch. Having made it, didn't he owe himself a few days of leisurely exploration? He decided, no. Victoria was still on the tourist track; merely a prolongation of U.S. 83, only at right angles to it. Yep, tomorrow was the date, but Victoria was decidedly not the place.

This was good, he congratulated himself. This was thinking along the constructive line.

What about Vera Cruz, now? That being the first place he named. It just popped out of him; a pure hunch. Yet, it came from somewhere—like a signal beamed at an extra-sensory coil in his brain. No, this line of thinking wouldn't do; it's something right out of a *Space Cadets* comic book. . . . This was a hell of a fine time to start figuring out an itinerary! It's what he should have been doing months ago—

A sound distracted him—not the rain; a snarling flourish of drums that broke off, without an echo. Then music somewhere near; at the plaza, three blocks back. A band concert was beginning. He recognized the Mexican National Hymn: "Me-xi-ca-nos al gri-to de gue-rra"—

If he were outside now, he'd be standing, with his right hand on his heart, the way he had seen them do in Los Angeles on Mexican holidays. But, since he was here, lying on his back, he could at least think respectfully of the country. He recited to himself, almost by rote: Mexico is a Latin-American republic, bounded on the north by the Río Grande River; on the east by the Gulf of Mexico; on the west by the Pacific Ocean; on the south by—He couldn't remember. He knew that it comprised 28 states, but he could name only two. Tamaulipas, because he was in it, and Durango, from listening to *The Durango Kid* program on the radio.

Topographically, he pictured the country as having the shape of a pork chop. Mexico City, being the capital, he felt certain should be smack in the middle. Three million population, and, according to Bishop's informants, it was supposed to be on the order of Paris. Well, they ought to know. But outside of its being big and like Paris, what quality of its own did it have? Well, here was a Mexico City paper that he had barely glanced at; see what it could give him of the feel of the city. And who can tell—there was always the off-chance that there would be something in the paper just for him. Like, say: "YOUNG MAN, strong, athletically inclined. Must know perfect English. Excellent salary and advancement to right person."

Who else could they mean?

There was no classified ad section. The paper was an edition of 16 pages for circulation in the provinces. He turned the paper to the last page. There, like a good omen, was a large map of Mexico. It illustrated an advertisement for a soft drink. This showed him that he had been mistaken about the country's resemblance to a pork chop. It was almost a perfect cornucopia, with the mouth open at the U.S. border. And Mexico City was not in the middle, but about three-fourths of the way down.

He skimmed past the amusement pages, the sports section, two pages of society news and pictures, the financial page, and fetched up on page 8.

Gilberto had an experienced newspaper-reader's eye. Nurtured on the morning and evening and Sunday Los Angeles papers, he had developed a capacity for scanning a page of type and rapidly picking out his specialties. In headlines, he ignored proper names, even those of film and radio stars, unless they were joined to verbs like "Slain . . . ," "Held . . . ," "Named . . ." He would read well into the account if it was garnished by ". . . in Girl's Ap't," ". . . by Vice Probers," or ". . . After Yacht Orgy."

He knew from long readership that almost every story was heavy with those murky phrases like, "suspected of," "believed to be," "alleged to have." And whenever they used the word "assault," it might mean a rape or a mere slapping around. In rare instances, they went as far as saying, "statutory assault."

But this Mexico City newspaper was amazingly different. They came right out with it. "Capture of an Ugly Delinquent." Nothing "alleged to be" or "suspected of" about this one: ". . . a hardened scoundrel, whose offenses number murder, robbery, and peddling enervating drugs. . . . This monster answers to the name of Heriberto Guzmán G.

"Infanticide in Tepatitlán.—Savage dogs, fighting over the bloody contents of a paper bag, attracted—" Enough of that one.

Here was a boxed story, datelined México, D.F. These usually are funny. But this was written with a straight face; about a city ambulance which they couldn't locate to answer calls for an entire day. When finally caught up with, the driver admitted he had been cruising up and down, taking passengers at a peso per head. His story was, he needed 100 pesos "to repair an indiscretion. This shameless abuser of confidence will be put under discipline of the sternest."

Gilberto began to enjoy reading Spanish. It practically translated itself and reminded him, in certain rounded phrases, of the way the priest, Don Iñigo, spoke. He turned the page.

The rain had stopped and the music from the plaza bandstand sounded clearer. The piece they were playing now was the "Rakoczy March," an old standby of the McVeigh High School orchestra. He shouldn't laugh—they weren't that bad—but because the faculty conductor was Prof. Maurice Whyte, they called it "Maurice Whyte and His Musical Shites."

Page 4. Right at his thumb was something he couldn't pass up; an ad:

THE URINARY TRACT—Once that is gone, ALL is gone! Treatment, modern and efficient, of Chronic Genito-Urinary Disorders which have resisted recovery by Penicillin. ACUTE GONORRHEA cured— with microscopic examination before and after, 15 pesos. Consultation alone, 5 pesos.

This ought to support the minority claim, during all those locker room arguments back at McVeigh, that there was a type of dose that penicillin didn't cure. He could send it back there in a plain envelope—to Morrissey.

Page 3 was solid with type. "Comunismo Mundial Peor Que Nazismo." . . . Well, maybe it was. Who knows? . . . "Yo Fui un Prisionero de José Stalin." . . . . "Truman Atacó el Plano de Rusos."

There was one headline he translated carefully: "Either Universal Military Conscription or Three-Year Draft in Prospect for EE UU." EE UU— Estados Unidos—the good old U.S.A.

This ought to be good: "Jealous 70-year Old Lover Attacks Sweetheart With Dagger." This Lotario anciano, as the paper described him, had been "housed" with his victim in perfecta harmonía for four years, until recently, when she had taken to leaving the house of the old boy, Neftalí Cerdan. Her last promenade, the neighbors observed, was "upon the arm of an individual, short of stature and complexión robusta." Having reached home before her return, "Neftalí disbelieved the explanation of his 54-year old Dulcinea,that she had been to visit her godmother. As he secured a knife from the cupboard, the woman attempted to flee. But, with an agility uncommon for a man of his age, Neftalí overtook her in the patio, dealing her two stabs in the flesh of the posteriors."

The magnetic combination, "Homicidio y Suicidio," tugged Gilberto's eyes toward the opposite page. The account was almost a column long, and the first few lines were in the style of an American lead paragraph: "Tormented by poverty and brutalized by alcohol, Adalberto Ruiz Patlán fatally wounded his wife, Carmela, with one blow of his machete, and ended his own life by swallowing a large quantity of insecticide."

As he read further of the tragedy of Patlán, narrated in solemn Castillian, Gilberto became aware that it was not only the language that made the difference between this account and the many, many reports of similar, even identical calamities he had read over the years. He had been accustomed, in the Los Angeles papers, to see, played-up, the savage nature of the atrocity and all the specifications of the outrage. But when he read those things, they were never about Patláns! In his experience, the principals in a crime, whether they were the murderers or the murdered, had to be either "prominent," "wealthy," or "famed."

Here, the newspaper was calling Patlán "un hombre infeliz"—an unfortunate, a poor devil. The more he read, the more Patlán appeared to have been the victim, along with his wife, of some vicious force they could not escape. It made it look somehow that the machete and the poison had less to do with the deaths than what it said here—"hopelessness," "hunger," "unbearable misery."

Los Angeles had its Patláns, too. There was that whole family—mother, father, and three little kids wiped out last year when that condemned building on Temple Street fell in on them. They had sneaked in there to live after being put out of their cellar apartment. The father tapped the gas line from the adjoining building so they could cook something, and there was an explosion. Gilberto was there when they dug them out. Their name was Peralta. It never got in the papers.

The band cut loose with a paso doble, underlaid with a gritty, scraping sound by which Gilberto knew that people were dancing on the tiles of the plaza. Had he known that there would be dancing, he might have gone out; maybe done himself some good. Ah, but that would mean getting dressed— he would just glance over the front page and turn in.

Hell, he thought, as he saw the first two items, Bishop must be the editor of this newspaper. The first said, "BLOOD RUNS ON THE ROAD TO PACHUCA; Six Dead and 24 Injured in Violent Collision Between Truck and Bus Laden with Passengers."

The second story was a straightaway, eyewitness account of the sudden death "by two bullets, of a braggart, who, in life, called himself Juan Mondragón Vega." The shooting took place in a grocery store, known as "La Guadalupana, where intoxicants were surreptitiously dispensed."

"At 22:30 hours, approximately," the story ran, "Guillermo Hernández H., another patron, entered the place to obtain a stimulant. Very soon, the now extinct Juan Mondragón Vega commenced to shout, 'I am muy macho!' Not content with this assertion, he drew a pistol, flourishing it threateningly. At this, his fellow client of La Guadalupana freed his own weapon, discharged the two bullets which gave Mondragón his death, and walked to the street en forma casual." Thirty!

Bishop wasn't fooling. This machismo was a serious business.

The paso doble ended; applause won the dancers a waltz. Played too fast, Gilberto thought. Ten minutes to eleven—maybe the band was anxious to knock off. Anyway, the music was soothing; distant enough to be filtered by the soft night, which sweetened the brasses and took the rasp out of the cymbals—making them sound like cut-glass snapped with the finger. . . . Nothing finer than live music—better than listening to a bedside radio. How could anything leaking out of a five-inch paper cone be called music? Besides, music wasn't supposed to be a soporific; not for him, anyhow. Kids, maybe; but being made to listen to those droopy lullabies makes them go to sleep out of sheer boredom. Didn't his mother tell him they had music going all day in that war factory where she once worked? There was proof. Personally—well, take Stan Kenton's orchestra. Every time he heard it, the music went to his head instead of his feet; made it clear as a bell.

That managerie out there in the plaza wasn't Stan Kenton. They didn't have to be. The old head was as clear as it ever was; clearer, in fact. He was a sucker to doubt that he wasn't on the ball, every inch of the way.

What led him here, to this hotel, where a chump would have gone straight to one of those tourist joints with air conditioning? Fate? Fate, my ass! It was the old skull working; with built-in air conditioning of its own to keep it clear. Anything wrong with the way he handled that bus driver, Anselmo? Like a toy! Had him so convinced he was a dental-supply salesman that the fellow called him Doctor, out of respect. So—! Don't let them kid you that Old Gil Reyes didn't have a grip on things from the start.

The waves of confidence rolled over him, and through him, in cadence with the music outside. The beat was right; not too fast, as he thought at first. His thoughts began racing faster than the music when his hand fell on the money in his belt. There was power there—his own, personal atomic pile. A much more convenient article to have in your pants than what those machos are always boasting about. Gets you a lot further, too. And if you don't believe that it makes a better showing than a gun, ask Juan Mondragón Vega, who pulled his out like it was a prolongation of his jock. A roll of currency would have looked much more like one, and would have saved his life.

Smiling, he hummed, Juan Mon-dra-gón *Ve*-ga-*ta-ra*, Juan Mon-dra-gón *Ve*—there the music ended with a ragged crash. Too sudden—he had outrun it.

The silence made the room seem chill. The exuberance was draining out of him. The wad of money—the atomic pile—felt like nothing more than a brick of lead under his hand.

Alone—twice-alone—in the silence, a great weight of shame pressed down on him. He had his moment of invincibility—then the plug was pulled. At the peak he had been humming a dirge for Juan Mondragón Vega in three-quarter time—

This is crazy, he thought, but *I'm* Juan Mondragón Vega—*me!* Why couldn't he—I—we—climb down off our own erections, admit we're just a couple of guys named Pinky, and buy a drink all around!

Maybe Mondragón had had a few drags on a reefer or a crock of mescal that made him so macho. Me—nothing.

That's what he thought. He couldn't know that what set him up was that extra lungful of copper-tasting, ozone-impregnated air bearing that special molecule, which—only in Mexico—bursts in euphoria. Why only in Mexico? Ask the eagle in his lonely sweep high above shrouded Ixtacihuatl.

Gilberto wondered what's with the music. There—no, that was thunder, far away. The light bulb flickered, paled, and went out.

Now—a slow unwinding of cornets. "La Paloma," of all things, he groaned. Dreary . . . dreary; as if a band in the States should choose to play "My Old Kentucky Home." He'd just as soon sit this one out, he mused, covering his eyes with his bent arm.

Anselmo, in a leather flying jacket and wearing a baseball cap with "Gloria" embroidered on it, was making a speech from the bandleader's platform in the plaza. All the chairs behind him were occupied by people Gilberto knew—men and women—but he was straining too hard to listen, to be able to identify them individually.

Anselmo's mouth was working, but there was something wrong with the sound track. It came back on again and he heard, "Yes, fellow Mexicans, I'd have him up here, but he's the shy, retiring type, as all of you folks know. Looking at him, could you tell that only up to a short time ago he used to hold still for every swift kick-in-the-behind that came along? . . . Turn around, Gil, and show the folks the bruises. . . . But no more! I state, without fear of successful contradiction, that it's over and done with. For days now, he's been led by the little hand. Born at an early age, poor but honest, he became a rich orphan practically overnight. And today, he's well on his way to becoming a perfect horse's rosette. You wouldn't believe me if I tell you, that after the rough day he had today, he not only went to the toidy-seat himself, but sewed up his own pants. That takes clearheadedness. ¿No es verdad? In conclusion, I want to say, my friends, that he was more of a man when he was ten years old than he is today. I thank you for your kind attention."

Straightening up to take a bow, his eyes opened to the full glare of the ceiling light, which had gone on again, brighter than before. Sitting straight up, in the nest of scattered paper, he saw his face in the mirror on the wall. It was gray; pools of viscous matter had formed in the hollows under his eyes.

Thunder snarled, now much nearer. The light flickered, faded, but stayed on with a faint, reddish glow.

There was a silence within a silence, then the inner globe broke as a reed vibrated and the music walked toward him on slow feet. They were playing "La Sandunga."

He turned over, with his face in the pillow. . . . That, which he had just got through dreaming, must surely have happened. Otherwise, how would the bandleader know that was the cue for the "Sandunga"?

He let himself go, and the music settled over and around him, as if it had weight and warmth.

Like that gray-and-green serape, she drew over him, singing, "Ay, Sandunga, Sandunga mamá por Dios . . ."

"It's short, Ma, it shrunk."

"No, it's you getting bigger, hijo—ten years old."

"Goin' on eleven."

"Uhmm-huh. . . ."

> Sandunga no seas ingrata,
> Mamá de mi corazón.
>
> Perdóname, mamacita—

Please, Mamá—please excuse me. Don't hold it against me for not asking you before you went away. Even if this was what you wanted, I'd never have left you—I swear—listen—

> Por vida de ese lunar
> Que tienes en tu pechito,
> Mira, no le pagues mal
> Al pobre de tu negrito.

18

His face lay in a damp oval on the pillow. The sun was battering at the window blinds. It was 5:05 by his watch, which had stopped.

He stripped off his badly wrinkled pants. They would have to stay that way. Walking across the warm tiles, he parted the slats. The sunlight was glaring as it might be between seven o'clock in the morning and noon. His guess, based on how he felt—refreshed, slept-out—was ten o'clock.

After brushing his teeth and taking a shower, he rubbed a palmful of unscented Vaseline hair tonic in his hair and combed it carefully. He had an expensive ten-inch comb, the type used in beauty parlors. His thick hair was parted 70/30 and smoothed back over each ear in a modified duck wing lie; nothing extreme like the pachucos, who wore the wing tips overlapping at the back of the head.

There were three clean shirts still in the bag. The two he had worn, a pair of shorts, his handkerchief, and a pair of socks were wadded in a slightly sour bundle. Mauricio was the man to consult about this. He was sweeping in the patio.

"What time is it, Mauricio?"

"I am unable to tell you, señor."

"Will you find out for me, please."

"The galopina has an awakener. I will ask her."

"What is she called?"

"Rafaela, señor."

"I would like to see her." Mauricio nodded, but went on with his sweeping. "Right now, I mean."

Gilberto had pushed the borrowed needle through a folded peso when she called from the door, "Good morning, señor."

"Ah, Rafaela—"

"Yes, señor, at your service."

He handed her the peso. "And many thanks for your kindness. And Rafaela—I have some clothes here. Can I have them washed?"

"And ironed," she suggested.

"Only the shirts to be ironed."

"Yes, señor; with pleasure." She took the bundle.

"How soon can I have them back?" Gilberto asked.

"Before noon; the sun is strong."

"Not sooner—?" Why was he rushing? No more need for that. He could do things normally now—

"If you wish, señor."

"No—noon will do."

No more of this idiotic haste. He could take it easy from now on. He knew where he was going.

In the plaza, he stood for a moment gazing at the place where Anselmo stood, behind the iron railing, to make his speech. Of course, you don't have to be an expert to interpret that dream, he thought. That was himself making the speech; Anselmo was just there as his mouthpiece, his medium. Doing him a favor, when you come right down to it.

Chimes sounded diagonally across the plaza, from a clock tower that looked strangely solid among the one-ply stucco buildings surrounding it. The bells were unintelligible to him, but the clock said 8:15.

He wound and set his watch. The hotel room was his until six o'clock in the evening, ten hours. How much of that he would use up depended on what he could find out about transportation. This wasn't as simple as just inquiring from the first person likely to know. First of all, he had to position himself in relation to where he was going, then find out the means to get there. Was there a plane, a train, or would he have to go for another one of those bone-crushing rides in a camión?

The plaza was empty, littered with lollipop sticks, candy wrappers, and bottle caps. The iron benches were moist; the grass and the trees still smelling of rain. The air was brilliantly clear and distant objects showed up as sharply as through a pair of 8-power binoculars. The clock tower, the big stone blocks of which it was constructed, was seamed, like fine hemstitching with smaller stones set in the mortar. A shadow which flashed on the walk was that of a blackbird. He could see its yellow beak and clearly hear the mewing sound it made.

Not that it was a matter of elevation or rarity of the atmosphere, but he was conscious that he was breathing far more deeply. Catching an exquisite scent, he identified it immediately: frying doughnuts. The only likely source was the kitchen of the Palacio hotel. He looked, but there was no vat of boiling grease in the window of the restaurant there. He walked to the corner and proceeded up the street, and from there he could follow the aroma with his eyes shut.

It came from the opposite side of the street, near the corner. Posada La Linterna—Lantern Inn. Donas—Milcheques. Donas was easy to figure out—doughnuts, they were being fished out of a bubbling tub.

The interior was narrow, with four stools at a counter and two oilcloth-covered tables. A battery of nickeled mixers on the back counter explained what milcheques were.

Gilberto entered, passed the girl tending the doughnut vat, and took the stool farthest from the door. The girl signaled, by holding two fingers up as though holding a cube, that she would attend to him in a moment.

The menu was written on a large mirror, so that every item on it appeared twice. Donas (3) con milchec 80; con leche malteado 90. Bolas extras of ice cream in either were 30. Eggs (2) with sausage or bacon, 140; with ham, 160. There was a basket with four pan dulces, rolls of slightly sweetened dough, in front of him. The girl approached and added two more.

When he ordered two fried eggs, with ham and toast, the girl mumbled it after him. "And while I'm waiting," he added, "I'll take a glass of orange juice. And coffee—when you bring the eggs, please."

When the eggs came, an older woman brought them out. The girl had gone back to her vat of doughnuts, forgetting his coffee, and he had to call her.

The ham was thin and had cooked up into crisp curls, but it tasted fine, blended with the warm yolks. The coffee was half hot milk. When he had almost finished, he called the girl again. She might know something about transportation out of town. But he meant not to ask her bluntly; merely to let the subject emerge so that it wouldn't appear to her that getting away was an emergency.

He finished the coffee and smiled. "It's good. I think I'll have another cup and some doughnuts. Or, wait—" He looked gloweringly at his watch. "Maybe I won't have the time."

"As you choose, señor."

"Transporation being what it is—"

There, she was supposed to ask him, "Transportation to where?" Instead, she asked dully, "Coffee and what else?"

He understood the type—strictly business, career girl. Nothing to be got out of her. "Never mind. What's my bill?"

She began a confused struggle with numbers. Her eyes rolled to the ceiling and her fingers twitched as if on the key board of a comptometer. Now he understood—she wasn't unfriendly, just dumb; afraid somebody would ask her how much is two times two. His getting up made her confusion even greater. "Two pesos," she blurted, "no—two-twenty."

"Orange juice, ham and eggs, toast, coffee; I make it two-fifty." He was sorry for her. "And how much extra for the sweet rolls?"

"That's with the coffee." She gave him the change, out of a shoe box, from three pesos.

He left the fifty centavos on the counter and walked out, taking no notice that the girl did not thank him. He estimated what a breakfast like this would cost him at the Owl Drug in L.A.—two plain fried or scrambled eggs were 49 cents, 65 with two snips of bacon. Orange juice—you'd think that it would be cheap in California, but they charged for it like it was their life's blood. Coffee was a dime; and catch *them* giving away coffee cake on the house.

On the side street, out of sight of the plaza, he felt conspicuous. Three out of the four people he passed since he left the restaurant nodded to him and said, "Buenos días," as to a neighbor.

Again in the plaza, he trod on the long shadows of people who were hurrying on the transverse paths. Victoria was a late-rising town, but it was coming alive. Up ahead, near the end of the walk, was somebody who certainly ought to know; a railroad man, if ever he saw one. He was having his shoes shined, looking ready for work in his gray-striped overalls, bandanna, and peaked cap. Almost abreast of him, Gilberto slowed and frowned at his feet.

"You're next, señor," the shine boy called.

"Very well." He sat down, first asking the railroad man's permission.

"With great pleasure . . . And did you have a good meal at the Linterna— I saw you leaving."

"Yes, very good, thank you. . . . May I offer you a cigarette?"

"It is kind of you, but I do not use tobacco."

"Then, may I have your permission—?"

"To your taste. . . . And are you staying long in Victoria?"

Gilberto felt it was natural for a citizen to spot him as a transient. "No," he said, "as a matter of fact, I am obliged to leave this very day."

He deliberately, though casually, left it wide open for being questioned as to where he was going. But, like the waitress, the man showed no curiosity. The notion that this was simply politeness did not occur to Gilberto.

"I have to leave for Zaragoza." The boy was working on the second shoe; there was not much time left. "I wonder if you could tell me the quickest way to get there."

"To Zaragoza?" The man smiled. "There are Zaragozas and Zaragozas; six, I think, in the Republic. One in Nayarit; two, I think, in Jalisco; one in San Luis Potosí; and—let me think—"

"I mean the one in San Luis Potosí."

"Ah, yes, that one. . . ." He looked down at the shoes and nodded to the shine boy. "A touch more with the cloth, Benito. . . . Zaragoza, S.L.P. . . . Now, the train which is in my charge and leaves at eleven hours can take you to Calles, where you will be required to change to the narrow rail to Zicoten-catl, and thence to—but perhaps your trip is urgent."

"Well," Gilberto said, "I have a client—"

"A commercial matter, I see," the engineer said. "You will, I think, be better served by going over the highway. In your own machine?"

"No—you see—"

"In any case, I can mark your route on a map."

"I'm sorry, I don't carry one."

The railroad man tapped the bootblack on the head. "Hop across the street to the gasolinera, Benito, and bring me back a map. You may say it's for me."

"Yes, Don Aníbal."

The boy started across the street to the cream-and-red Pemex service station. "This is very kind of you, señor," Gilberto said. "But I don't wish to delay you."

"It is nothing—" He reached for the map which the boy brought back and unfolded it. With his pencil, he pointed. "Observe. Here is where we are,

Cuidad Victoria. Your way lies south, as far as Ciudad Mante, then west, to Ciudad de Maíz."

It looked clear enough on the oil company map. "And Zaragoza?" Gilberto puzzled aloud.

The man's pencil marked a dot in a blank area bounded on the east and south by clear red lines. "I would locate it about here. And if the road from Ciudad del Maíz is not washed out, nor the bridge down, you will reach Zaragoza."

"I am very thankful to you for showing me."

"However, young man, if the road *is* impassable, descend at Antiguo Morelos, ignore Ciudad del Maíz as if it were not there, and continue on the highway to San Luis Potosí, disembarking at Presa. There, you may hire a mule."

"Your advice is very helpful, señor," Gilberto said as the bootblack moved his box toward him. "If you will allow me to pay for both our shines—"

"Not at all."

"But you have helped me."

"My privilege." He paid the boy, shook Gilberto's hand, and parted with, "I wish you a happy trip."

"That's a fine man," Gilberto said to the bootblack.

"Don Aníbal, to be sure."

Instead of kneeling, like the shine boys in Pershing Square Park, this one did his work seated on a tiny stool. His equipment was complete; each polishing cloth rolled up in a tiny cylinder. Everything fitted neatly in a box decorated with chips of mirror and upholstery nails. Lettered on the side of the box was the information that he was Member No. 9 of the Syndicate of Polishers of Cd. Victoria, Tamps.

At a light tug on his cuffs, Gilberto looked down and saw that it was the most brilliant shine he ever had applied to these or any shoes. In L.A., an ordinary shine was 25 cents; a "special" like this one would be higher. The official price here was 40 centavos—six cents. "A very neat job, Benito," he said, giving the boy a 20-centavo tip.

"I am glad you are pleased, my boss. . . . I see another client; so with your permission—"

The sensation of nervous alarm with which he entered the city had left him. There still remained, however, a sense, on the lower scale of recognition, of being misplaced.

But that, too, passed, as he watched three—four men of his own age, who looked, singularly, like him. They wore dark suits like his. Their coats may have been an inch or two longer, the cuffs narrower than his own 16-inchers, and their lapels had a more pronounced roll down to the bottom button. A boy rode past on a bicycle, carrying a package on the handlebars, who could have been Gilberto Reyes leaving Richardson's laboratory on his first delivery of the morning.

Although this feeling of integral anonymity was one he sought and which, to a degree, was self-induced, the tendency to suspicion persisted. This was a habit; a channel of thought into which he maneuvered easily. In his experience—almost totally a vicarious participation in all lives but his own—he sought a villain. It did not have to be the principal "heavy." A minor plotter would do in the role of "rat."

Who in this case? The bootblack, naturally. Wasn't it always a charwoman, window cleaner, or—well, let's face it, a bootblack. Take this Benito; delivers a neat shine, which doesn't mean that he couldn't also be one of those smart cookies. By Jesus! It *was* a bootblack in that terrific movie where the formula was stolen out of the safe by old Tony who used to come into the executive offices to shine the staff's shoes, and nobody paid any more attention to him, kneeling there, than if he had been a wastebasket. It was on its way already to the Marx-Lenin Institute, when the Special Section took over—the two Bobs, Montgomery and Taylor. . . . Finally the word came: "Polo Fox to Union Dave—bandit courier plane—modified TU-27, Red markings—now taking off, Templehoff. Over and out!"

Then The Chief: "You don't know what's in that Russky plane and *I* don't know. We're not supposed to know! Only that it's got to come down blazing."

"But, Chief—they'll take good care to fly the corridor; they'll stick to it as if pinned there till they meet their MIG escort."

"I said in flames. Those are your orders!"

"Son—there's things worse than war," where the Chief's voice broke and he finished, "I've got the letter you wrote to Millicent—in case anything happens. Pray God I won't have to send it!"

He didn't, either. And what happened to that Red courier plane shouldn't happen to a dog.

A few benches down, Benito slapped his cloth bravely on his new customer's shoes. He smiled brightly, nodding to Gilberto, as though seeing him for the first time that day. He must be okay, Gilberto thought. A secret agent would now be transmitting the information that the subject was heading for Zaragoza.

He unfolded the map. It looked simple, almost hand-drawn. From Victoria, the road going due south divided at Ciudad Mante. The easterly fork went to Tampico; the one to the right, to the city of San Luis Potosí, via Ciudad del Maíz. In the center of a liver-shaped, apparently roadless area, Don Aníbal had pencilled the mark signifying Zaragoza. A dotted double line ran from C. del Maíz upward. That kind of road meant it was only good in dry weather—transitable en tiempo de secos.

The arching sun blasting through the thick branches became so warm that his scalp began to itch. He would have to get that hat, but not one of those ridiculous sombreros. He would look for a light felt, perhaps a straw, in the shape of a panama.

A moist, dirty-yellow gob hit his shoulder. Cursing, he wiped if off with his handkerchief. After hating birds for a livid instant, he relented. As a tree expert, he knew their uses. Put enough of them in a tree, and they'll eat more insects than a man could destroy with a power spray. And, he mused, they shat as fast as they ate. Anyway, if he was going to do much sitting around under trees, or, for that matter, walking under them, that hat would have to be one with a good, wide brim.

He looked up slowly on hearing a metallic scuffle across the street. It was the people with the green Michigan Pontiac, loading their luggage in the trunk compartment.

The man was fat and wore both suspenders and a belt. But he moved spryly. The wife wore a coolie hat, orange-colored slacks and spike-heeled shoes. She did little to help the man, handing him things to put away in a dawdling, listless manner. Before getting behind the wheel, the man clipped a pair of tinted lenses over his glasses and adjusted an air cushion on the driver's seat.

As the Pontiac backed out, Gilberto saw that the right rear tire was flat. When it came abreast of him, still backing, he called, "Hey!" and pointed. The man glared at him, and Gilberto pointed again to the rear of the car and down.

The man stopped parallel to the curb, and his wife came around from the other side.

"A flat," she said. "That's what I was afraid of."

"A slow leak."

"It's flat, just the same. I told you yesterday she was steering kinda heavy."

"It's the back wheel," the husband said. "It don't affect the steering."

"Still and all, Alvin, if you'd only listen to me once in a while—"

"All right, all right. Get me the keys."

When she plucked them out of the ignition lock and handed them to her husband, he said, "And pray the spare ain't down, too."

"For a man who's supposed to know all about cars—"

"You starting off again!" he growled.

"Just remember," she whined, "it wasn't me who racked up four traffic fines so far this year."

Michigan said nothing, but started hauling the jack out of the trunk. Gilberto wanted to tell him that there was a service station, the Pemex, just a few feet around the corner. But it rankled him, in a nebulous way, that neither of them offered the slightest recognition of the fact that it was he who called their attention to the flat tire. Then, too, it amused him to listen to them—like a *Ma and Pa Kettle* movie.

"It's a good thing," she started again, "we didn't bring Alvie on this trip. He's better off in camp."

"I'll say he is!" He gave the jack such a yank that one of the straw baskets fell out.

"You don't have to throw my things around just because you're mad at your own stupidity, Alvin, must you now?"

"For two lousy cents, I'd put you on board the next plane for Flint."

"And don't think I wouldn't go," she said evenly. "Gimme a Lucky."

"The pack's sitting up on the dash. Light me one, too."

When she came back with the two lighted cigarettes, Alvin had the jack erected under the bumper and was unbolting the spare tire. He pounded it and grinned. "It's inflated, all right."

The woman glanced at Gilberto and called, "Alvin—"

"What do you want?"

"Why don't we get one of these natives to do the hard part? Offer him a *pay*-so."

"Those lazy bastards! You couldn't get them off their ass for the U.S. Mint. Didn't you read that piece in *The Defender?* The one that was called 'One Faith—One America.'"

To Gilberto, the man took on a sudden repulsiveness. If he sat there any longer, he would be tempted to say something right back at him, in good, clear English. He had it coming, too, on several accounts. One, for taking him to be a Mexican; two, for talking about Mexicans the way he did. Okay, then, either spit in his eye or walk away.

He got up from the bench. The woman kept looking at him and fumbling in her purse. She unfolded a peso to its full, pink length and dangled it toward him; waving it like a fish lure, toward the rear fender. "Hey, *seen*-yor!"

He looked at her so keenly that he could see the oozing pores in the wings of her sharp nose. Then he turned away and spat.

Behind him, he heard Michigan say, "What did I tell you!"

(Alvin M. Nichols, 47, of Flint, Michigan; married; father of one son, Alvin, Jr., 13, and a daughter, Alvene, 11; inspector of hydraulic valve lifts by occupation, tossed down a lug wrench and hated Mexico. He cursed its sun, which was making the sweat pour down his back and into his bung, at which he clawed luxuriously, with all five fingers, ignoring his wife's shocked "Al-vin!" He resented a small audience his labors had attracted. He screamed, "Hey! Watch where you're going!" at a tremendous wardrobe with two mirrored doors, which bore down on the right front fender and barely missed scratching the paint. It veered off, just in time—on a pair of human legs.)

(Pedro Urzúa, cargador—burden-carrier-at-your-service, could see only the ground when he had something as big as this wardrobe to haul. He had only eleven more squares and a flight of stairs to go before he could put it down. He was 61 years old and owned nothing in the world but a serape, pants, shirt, and huaraches; the rope and headstrap which he had woven himself; a half-dozen cigarette butts

and an entire lemon which he had picked up in the street. After
finishing this job, he would have one peso and fifty centavos in
effectivo—ready cash. He weighed 117 pounds; the wardrobe, 124.
He was 5'3" in height, but he once stood 5'10". He would die eleven
years later, at the age of 72, from the thrust of an icepick under the
ear, inflicted by the husband of his mistress. It would have made
Pedro Urzúa very sad to know that the man whose car he almost
scratched would be dead in three weeks. Dead of fright, while being
administered an enema in preparation for surgery to correct a slight
hernia. In the hospital, he said the heaviest work he had done in
years was changing a tire—in Mexico. When asked casually how he
liked Mexico, Alvin M. Nichols replied, "Great country. Just
great—all except for the natives.")

At eleven o'clock on the morning of the same day, Señora Lucía Mora de
Durán, in Sanborn's, the House of Tiles, on Avenida Francisco I. Madero in
Mexico City, was eating a second breakfast and reading a copy of *El Universal*.
She had driven down from the Colonia Condesa, attended Mass in the
Church of San Felipe de Jesús, and bought a fresh vaginal diaphragm.

She read only the Society Section as a rule, and often saw her picture in it.
Today, somehow, an unpleasant story had leaked over to stain the happy
pages. It was about a 14-year old Otomi Indian girl, from somewhere in the
State of Hidalgo, who had come all the way to the capital to look for work as a
domestic. Frightened, even before she entered the city-proper, and caught in
the heavy traffic on the Boulevard Ramón Guzmán, she was crushed to death
under the wheels of a streetcar.

Doña Lucía read further:

The parents of the unhappy child are poor people. They live miserably, like thousands of natives in that district. They do not own
land. The father works as a peón in the field for two pesos a day. To
earn this ridiculous amount, he is obliged to work from sun to sun.
The dead girl was the eldest of seven children.

"Eh!" Doña Lucía said, quite aloud. "¡Qué barbaridad!" She meant it as,
"What rashness!"

19

Gilberto studied the contents of the show window. The display was neither artistic nor a jumble. Things were simply laid one next to the other on the floor of the embrasure; shirts, ties, handkerchiefs, underclothing, some cheap masculine jewelry, and hats.

He looked forward to entering for an experience above that of simply making a purchase. It would be his first contact with a businessman, a retail merchant, in Mexico, and he would see how it was done here.

Here was an establishment, the whole of which could fit in one corner of Silverwood's, in L.A. He'd been in that shop once, for a pair of swim trunks. They were $3.75 there, same as anywhere in the city. He was waited on by a polite, middle-aged man, who took pains to see that he had the right size and just the color he wanted. "And if a seam rips, or the colors run, you bring them right back, sir, and we'll be glad to exchange them, or refund your purchase price." And while he was making out the sales slip, thanking Gilberto and asking him if he could serve him in any other way, a young clerk came up and said, "Excuse me, Mr. Silverwood, but could you—"

No fancy goods, this time; just a hat. As he entered the narrow, gloomy place, the owner glanced at him over his shoulder and continued arranging some boxes on the shelf. Gilberto waited a while before the man asked him, "Do you wish anything?"

"A hat of some kind."

"There," the man said, pointing to a narrow, vertical case with ten or twelve wide-brimmed felt hats in it. Gilberto took one out and glanced at the label—Stetson. The price tag was marked $125.00. That was a lot—fifteen dollars, U.S. Just to be sure, he asked, "How much is this type?"

"A hundred and forty pesos. They're all the same."

"But it is marked a hundred and twenty-five."

"Then that is the price."

"Do you have any other kind?"

"That's all," the owner said and turned back to his shirt boxes.

Gilberto muttered, "Thanks," and left. Perhaps, he thought, the man had been seriously preoccupied—business worries. Or he may have taken Gilberto for one of those people who love to go into stores, just to handle and price things. Still, he knew from many Saturday-morning shopping trips with his mother that business people made an effort. They'd say, "I'm sorry we haven't got it in stock," or, "Can I show you—"

He walked another block aimlessly, but keeping to the fringe of the plaza.

There was a drugstore. Not that he needed anything, but once inside a drugstore, there's always something you see that you can use. He would go in, anyhow, if for no other reason than to get over the haberdasher's crude indifference.

A poorly dressed woman entered ahead of him, past a pulpit-like structure near the door. There was only one counter at the rear and every article in the place was behind closed glass shelves. Two very young girls in white jackets waited for him to approach, appearing to ignore the woman who was ahead of him. At the counter, she held up an empty medicine bottle and prescription. Neither of the two girls paid any attention to her, but one lifted her head to Gilberto. "Yours?"

"A package of Gillette blades, please. The kind that come twenty in a plastic container."

The girl went behind the case before he finished and brought back a paper-wrapped five-blade package. He repeated, "I'd like the other size."

"These are Gillette blades," she said, dropping them on the counter.

"I asked for the ones in a plastic case."

"We don't have any."

"Okay, I'll take these. How much?"

The girl didn't answer. Instead, she bent over a pad of sales slips and wrote, *Hojas 1.80*, pushed the slip toward him, and said, "La caja."

"What?"

"La caja, la caja," she repeated impatiently, nudging the slip again and pointing to the pulpit behind him, at which a man was now seated.

Taking the slip, he walked back, the entire length of the store. The cashier-proprietor took his two pesos, slowly and carefully entered the sales amount on a sheet of ruled paper, stamped the slip PAGADO, and gave it back to him with his change. He uttered no thanks.

When he returned to the counter, the woman was still waiting with her medicine bottle, but both girls were behind the prescription cabinet. There passed another long, humiliating minute until one of them, not the one who had waited on him, emerged. After examining his receipt carefully, she handed him the blades. There was something mocking in her deliberateness. "¿Qué otra cosa más?" she asked flatly. Anything else?

"Yes," he said in English to himself, "Kiss my ass."

Walking past la caja, he heard it again: "¿Qué otra cosa más?"

"You, too!"

What a way to treat a customer! With their backs up, as if he had come in to sell pencils. And he didn't even need the blades. He had gone in, rather, to trade for a warm word. Do they make everybody—even the purchaser of a single, five-centavo aspirin tablet—run back and forth to la caja? In the great capital, Mexico City, too?

Yes.

Bishop could have told him, had they gotten around to the subject. He could have told him about his tennis shoes. About sitting in the shoe department of Sears on Insurgentes for half an hour, with his shoes off, before a clerk came over to him. Then, being told he would have to go upstairs to the sporting goods department for tennis shoes. On with the shoes and upstairs. Another twenty minutes in his socks. "Tennis shoes? Not up here. Downstairs, in the shoe department."

But that was nothing compared to the deal with the gabardine slacks in that shop on Calle Gante. He tried them on, the way they came off the rack, with the raw, unfinished cuffs. The tailor marked off the proper length.

"When can I have them?"

"This time, on Friday."

"No good. If I can't wear them Thursday to a dance—"

The salesman took it up with the manager. Thursday would be all right. About 4:00 p.m. The clerk made out a slip. "La caja—"

"Seventy-five pesos," the cashier said.

"Why, that's the full price of the slacks," Bishop pointed out. "I haven't got them yet; not till Thursday. I'll give you a deposit on them. How much?"

The cashier pointed to the amount on the slip. He still wanted 75 pesos; that's what was written there.

"Sure, sure," Bishop insisted. "Twenty now, the balance when I pick up the slacks."

The cashier called the manager, who spoke very good English. He explained to Bishop that this was the way they did things—never mind the United States—in this store. The customer ordered the alterations, therefore, he must pay the full amount to insure the store that he will accept delivery. Otherwise—sorry, but it cannot be considered a transaction. Okay. Bishop put down the 75, got his slip marked PAGADO, and said, "Thursday for sure, now."

Thursday at 4:00, they told him the slacks were at the presser's, just a short distance away. Would they mind telephoning to say that the customer was waiting? Finally, at half past five they took his address and told him not to worry; they would rush them over, special delivery, by motorcycle.

At a quarter of eight, all duded up, except for the slacks, he called the store. A porter answered and said they had been closed, as usual since seven. At half past nine, he went to the dance in a pair of old moleskins.

That wasn't the end of it. He called the place the next day and held the wire twenty minutes till the manager got on. "What! You didn't get your slacks? Are you sure, señor?" The explanation now was that the steam had failed on the pressing iron, but he certainly would have the slacks Saturday; yes, before noon.

Monday—no slacks. After classes he went down to the store. Now they had a brand new alibi—that when the tailor began altering the cuffs, he found another set of measurements for that very pair of slacks. They had been marked for an earlier customer. Could they show him another pair?

The hell they could! They could show him the color of his money. Here was his receipt for 75 pesos. That, they were again sorry, they couldn't do.

The money was already entered on the books as a sale. He could look around and select any other merchandise to the value of 75 pesos. The hell he would! Not so much as a pair of shoelaces in this goddam den of bandits. "Gimme my dough!"

The manager had somebody bring a cop in from the street and pointed Bishop out as the fellow he wanted ejected. The cop made no bones about it. He told Bishop he'd better go, or he would beat him to a bloody gringo jelly.

A few days later, he gave the sales slip to one of the fellows in the boarding house and told him to get the two 30-peso shirts and something for himself with the balance. The kid came back with three horrible hand-painted neck-ties and a jock-strap that wouldn't fit a twelve-year old boy.

"Shirts, socks, and stuff like that, sure they had 'em," the fellow explained. "On sale, for cash. What you sent me in there with was an exchange slip. For that, they had these things on a special counter."

Bishop, at that time, was still new to the student group in the boarding house. And because he was the only Texan among men from New England, New York, the Midwest, and several Mexicans who were taking English courses, he kept pretty much quiet about his own beefs. He had a word— mexicanismo, for everything that offended him. Mexicanismo was the failure to signal a turn or an intended stop. It was the habit of promiscuous spitting on the street which prevailed, even among an amazingly large number of women. The airy way so many Mexicans had of being late for appointments—or not keeping them at all. Informalidad, they called it. Mexicanismo was the label he put on it.

But he had to tell the gang around the table in the boarding house after supper about the royal screwing he'd gotten. These were pretty well educated fellows and they'd know how to cope with this mingled contempt for the customer and greed for his money at the same time. "How do they get that way?" was the key question here.

"It exists; that we know," said Howard Ellis, the oldest of the student-veteran group. He was working for his Ph.D. "But it's an inherited, rather than an inherent, disposition. You'll see that if you understand something of Mexico's colonial history."

A fellow they called Ranger, who was in the first wave on D Day, said, "There's sure a difference between here and, let's say, England. Ever try browsing in one of those bookstores on the Avenida Juárez, like they ask you to do in London? Start reading a few titles, or open the cover of a book here; they don't exactly throw you out, but they don't make you comfortable. You're supposed to know what you want, pay the cashier, and blow."

"In Italy, too, they treat you nice." That was a kid everybody knew as Geronimo. He had been in the paratroops. Married, and had brought his wife down from the States; but he still liked dropping in at the boarding house several nights a week. "But not in North Africa, where most of the stores belong to the French people."

"There," said Ellis, "Geronimo has made my point. What we see here is the French influence. For a long time, even before Maximilian came here as a stooge for Napoleon the Third, the French controlled the retail business of Mexico. There was gold here, and they gave away as little and as ungraciously as they could, for as much of that gold as they could get. The Mexicans, malleable and, like the rest of us, quicker to learn bad habits than good, adopted the petit-bourgeois practices they saw. Look at the whole chintzy idea of the cashier's desk, a combination shrine and observation post; strictly French."

"And they make the customer work for *their* money," Geronimo said. "What I mean is, last week I had to get a paper photostatted, so I go to this place on Dolores Street. One girl takes my order and I ask her, 'How much is it going to cost?' She doesn't even tell me. Instead of that, she writes in a sales book, hands it to me, and waves me over with it to the cashier. The whole book! There, I have to hand it in, pay my twelve pesos, and bring the book back to the girl before I get my receipt."

"Small business in the States is different," Ranger commented.

Ellis stopped him there. "You'll forgive me, if I submit that you're merely using a phrase you've read somewhere. I doubt if you're old enough to have had anything much to do with the vanishing corner drugstore or little grocery. Either the chains have bought him out, or—"

"Ellis is right," Bishop remarked. "I saw it happen, right in my home town."

"But chains make for efficiency," Ranger said. "That's one thing."

"I can give you proof that they do," Ellis smiled. "They began getting efficient long before any of you were born. My father was a clerk in one of those chain groceries in Boston; the Mohican Stores. Every store in the system had a quota of cash sales for the week. If it didn't meet that quota by Saturday night, the store would be closed on Monday and the manager and staff automatically fired. Many a Saturday night, half my father's pay went to buy groceries we couldn't afford to eat so that he could keep a job he couldn't afford to lose."

"That must have been pretty rugged," Ranger said. "So what's happened to the small businessman? Ain't he one of the things we fought for?"

"Him and Mother's delicious blueberry pie," Bishop said.

"And Nash-Kelvinator," added Geronimo. "You mean the little guy is washed up. Still, there must be some types that are so small, it wouldn't pay the chains to take him over."

"Perhaps you're thinking of the little shoemaker; the harmless cobbler at his last—" Ellis began.

"Something like that."

"I was thinking of him, too. Always pictured as a philosopher. Sort of a poor man's Socrates, Kant, Schoepenhauer, Spinoza, or what-have-you. All day at his bench, with a mouthful of little nails and wisdom."

"Don't tell me he's a chain store now!" said Ranger.

"Believe it or not, he is, in Los Angeles, anyway."

"Ellis is right," Bishop said. "I've been in them. You sit in a booth and they hand you a pair of bedroom slippers and a magazine to read while they're fixing your shoes."

"Yes, our cobbler now wears a surgeon's gown," Ellis added, "he's eighteen to thirty-five, and a white Christian American." He pointed to Manuel Fuentes, across the table. "No others need apply."

"Let's stick to Mexico," Bishop said, whose complaint about the slacks started the whole discussion. "Whipping the stores here into a chain might be an improvement, to my way of thinking."

"That is bound to happen," Ellis said. "Perhaps, after they've weeded themselves out. What I mean is, you'll find four grocery stores on a block that can only support one. This leads not only to rivalry, but to recklessness and fraud. . . . Look at today's paper—thirty bakeshops padlocked for short-weighting the rolls; a dozen places fined a thousand pesos each for making six liters of milk out of five."

"My gums bleed for them," said Geronimo bitterly. "Let me tell you what happened to my wife in one of them abarrotes the other day. . . . I come home and she's crying—really. As a rule, she takes the car down to the Supermercado to do the main shopping. But this time, she went to the tienda on the corner to get a can of tuna fish. Of course, you know, nobody ever waits their turn, so every now and then she calls out, 'Una lata de tuna, por favor.' And the way she told it, everybody in the place starts laughing. Then, when the store is finally empty, she asks him again. This time, the storekeeper is the one who laughs right in her face. He tells her that tuna is what they call cactus pear; the fish is atún. So she learned her lesson. All right, she'll take a can of atún. 'No hay,' he says. There wasn't any. He just kept her there for laughs."

Ellis and the others couldn't help smiling. "It's not funny by me," Geronimo protested. "I want to get something out of my time down here, and it don't include having my wife clowning for these people."

"I wasn't amused," Ellis explained. "I met with a similar experience yesterday. Went to eight places on the Avenida 16th of September, around the corner to Bolívar, before somebody would sell me a typewriter ribbon. Nothing special; an ordinary black ribbon for my portable."

"All-black, huh," Ranger said. "That's what threw them. Everything they write here is two colors."

"You got the 'no hay' business, too?"

"Yes; several times before I finished saying what I wanted."

"I figured out," Bishop commented, "that a store in Mexico is like an Indian trading post. If you don't see what you want and point it out, don't even bother asking for it."

Manuel Fuentes, who nodded through most of the conversation, cited an experience of his own, finally. "I went in a place—a papelería, on Cinco de Mayo this was, for one of them hole-punchers for a loose-leaf notebook. This one does not even say to me 'No hay.' He shakes his finger in front of my face only, which you do when somebody asks a foolish thing. So, when I am walking out, I see a whole box full of those punchers."

"What did you do?" Bishop asked.

"I take this bastard by the arm and show him. 'You sinvergüenza son of a bitch; maybe you want I should rub your nose in it!'"

"You're the guy I want to go shopping with," Geronimo said.

The Mexican smiled and said, "You stay home, I'll go with your wife."

"Why, you dog, I wouldn't trust you out with my grandmother."

"What's the matter with her?" Manuel asked blandly.

Ellis wound it up. "You men know how long I've been in this country. . . . I read two Mexico City papers—everything in them—every day. And so far, I have yet to see the word courtesy in a store advertisement."

20

At an outdoor stand piled with towers of sombreros, Gilberto bought himself a hat. It was a palm straw job, medium wide in the brim, and stained gray with deck paint. The vendor made him try on five or six, and kept urging him to take one with a wide, curled-up brim, decorated with a row of tiny plastic guns.

"Orgulloso," he pronounced it; a proud hat. To go well with the young caballero's distinguished clothes. The more modest gray one, Gilberto insisted, was distinguished enough.

"Six pesos, then."

When he frowned, quite accidentally, the price fell to five. If he had offered three, he could have gotten it for four.

"How will it stand up in the rain?"

"Like a fort," the man said. But to make sure, he produced a plastic tent that would fit over the entire hat and which in fine weather could be folded up like a pocket handkerchief. "A single pesito. But since you are the owner of one of my hats, take it as a gift—fifty centavitos."

A regular Mr. Silverwood, Gilberto thought.

His first hat. Perhaps he never really needed one in California, but down here it was a useful item. It weighed hardly anything and kept his brow and the back of his neck cool.

It was eleven o'clock, and as he craned for another glance at himself in the hatter's chipped glass, a beggar stepped forward; a man, holding a wooden box painted green and gilt. It was constructed to resemble an altar, with a religious picture and a printed prayer. After Gilberto dropped two coins into it, the beggar mumbled something and presented himself to the hat merchant.

"For what this time?" he asked.

"As before, señor," the beggar said, "For a chapel of the holy San Jerónimo."

"And not to stuff your own belly?"

"For the love of God, señor."

He waved the beggar away and turned abruptly from him. The manner reminded Gilberto very much of Richardson and the way he baited people; canvassers, and some no better than panhandlers. He would let them start: "Beg your pardon, sir, but we're trying to help out the veterans by distributing these official pictures of Old Glory in natural colors, with the Pledge of Allegiance." Sometimes it was a poem entitled "My Buddy," and there was one with the slogan, "My Country; May She Always be Right—But Right or Wrong, My Country!!!!"

If these peddlers seemed to slow up with their spiel, Richardson would encourage them with, "Come on, what's the rest of it?"

"Something every loyal American should be proud to display in his home, shop, or office. There's not any set price on these, sir; just what you want to give."

Then Richardson would say, "Did you see the sign downstairs in the building, 'No panhandlers allowed'?"

They would answer something to the effect, "You got me wrong, mister. We're not asking for anything for nothing. We're selling these patriotic pictures."

"Okay, then," Richardson used to say, "let's see your peddler's license."

That would usually get them out of there in a hurry, and Richardson would laugh. "That's showing 'em they can't pull any fast ones on me, eh, Pancho?"

Gilberto never could get up the nerve to tell him what a cheap way this was to browbeat people, even if they were panhandlers. Either hand them a quarter or say he doesn't want any, or he's too busy, or something. Not send the guy out feeling lower than he came in.

So, when this man came up with the religious almsbox, Gilberto felt snared. When it comes to country or religion, there's no easy way out of it. Like that time in front of Grauman's Chinese, when he was looking at the footprints in the lobby and somebody tapped him on the shoulder. "Hey, buddy—"

When he turned around, a fat, red-faced fellow in one of those little First World War overseas caps, stuck a red paper flower on his jacket. His partner, in a khaki blouse and pants, shoved a coin box in his face and Gilberto put a dime in it.

"Is that the best you can do, feller?"

"It's all I got, outside of my fare downtown."

They left him then and turned to a woman, who was apparently waiting for somebody. With her, they didn't do even that well. When the fat guy tried to pin one of those flowers on her, she slapped his hand away.

"It's a Buddy Poppy, lady."

"I know what it is," she answered.

"Well—?"

"And I don't want it!"

"You mean," the man with the coin box said, "you don't want to give anything for the Wounded Veteran?"

"No!"

"Not even a dime?"

"Not one cent," the woman said.

"Congress passed the law, lady. It's Buddy Poppy Day, for the rehabilitation of the Wounded Veteran."

"Congress also passed a law giving eight hundred million dollars to buy cannons for the Turkish army," she said. "Take my dime out of that."

"Aw, come on, lady, you don't want to sound like one of these Commies Hollywood is full of," and again the first fellow tried to stick her with the flower. She hauled off and gave him one across the fat face with her handbag and said that if they didn't stop bothering her, she'd call a cop and accuse them of trying to slip her a free feel.

No doubt, they were right about her being a Commie. But, as he thought of the way those two patriots took off from there, like they were jet-propelled, he couldn't help smiling.

He touched his new hat from time to time as he strolled. People kept smiling at him and nodding. The pulse of congeniality was something new to him, and he felt easier and more composed.

He stopped to light a cigarette. The smoke from it hung in the still air, a faint, violet cloud. The tops of the tallest trees were as fixed and frozen as the deepest of their roots. A feather fallen from the highest nest would have dropped straight down.

The birds felt it first and broke from the trees in twittering packs, an instant before the air trembled. With palpable sound waves, the bells in the tower struck the quarter hour. The last and deepest bong sucked all the vibrations back and serenity returned.

A man stopped in front of him and requested a light. He watched the man light a match and dab some of the melting wax on the mouthpiece of the cigarette before lighting it.

"Pardon me," Gilberto said. "I have noticed other gentlemen doing that. Is it for any special reason?"

The man glanced at Gilberto's cigarette and said, "You smoke a superior brand that does not stick to the lips; it is already waxed at the factory." Handing back the matches, he remarked, pointing beyond the trees, "What do you think of this sky?"

He shrugged one shoulder. "Who knows what to think."

"I don't like it; not one bit," the man asserted. "If we are not afflicted with a norteño by fourteen hours this afternoon, I will submit to having my tongue cut out. Adiós, señor."

"God forbid it. Adiós," Gilberto called. A norteño, a northern, that would mean rain—lots of it; roads washed out, bridges down. It would be a good idea to check at the bus terminal. If Anselmo of the Gloria was still there— well, he meant to tell him that he decided to stick around Victoria for a while and make some contacts with dentists. That was easy.

Walking, he heard a pattering beside him; not like a dog's, but a heavier slap-slap. A deep, gravelly voice called, "Socorro, señor—por Jesucristo—" but from well below, near the ground.

Pity won over the first pang of revulsion and he glanced down, at his side. It was a man, moving on all fours. Pads of rubber were laced to his elbows and knees. The hands and wrists were shriveled; the finger, clenched, looked no bigger than a baby's fists. The naked feet were toeless and calcified into a pair of useless hoofs.

"En nombre de Dios, patroncito, una limosna—"

Gilberto dragged coins out of his pocket, heard them fall to the sidewalk, and moved rapidly on, out of the hearing of the cripple's blessing, before looking back.

The man was rooting the money out of the dust with his mouth.

The bus terminal was crowded with coaches—to everywhere. The drivers, cobradores and porters were calling out destinations. "¡Valles! ¡Vámonos por Valles!" . . . "¡Hay asientos! ¡Hay lugar en El Costeño!" . . . "¡Aquí, damas y caballeros! ¡Tampico y puntos conectados!"

One machine, full to the doors, roared out, and Gilberto asked the nearest man, "I didn't miss the camión to El Mante—?"

"I believe not. There's the ticket window."

Learning that there would be no departures for Mante before 14 hours— two o'clock—he bought a ticket; Seat No. 12. A Greyhound-type, blue and white coach, but smaller, backed against a low wall was marked: *Tampico vía Cd. Mante.* The driver sat on the step, weaving a hatband out of strips of colored plastic tape.

"When are you leaving, chief?" Gilberto inquired.

"At fourteen hours, on the dot."

"That gives me enough time . . . Have a smoke." They lit up and Gilberto put his foot on the step. "Norteño or no norteño, you leave at fourteen hours?"

"What's this talk about a norteño," the busman mocked. "Just look at that sky—as peaceful as the Mother of God's smile."

"Maybe." Gilberto looked up. A rag of sooty gray cloud was going somewhere at a hell of a clip. "I'm only making the run to Ciudad Mante. How long do you figure for that?"

"We pull in at Mante at seventeen hours, on the dot. . . . You in the transportation line yourself?"

It was time to give up the dental-supply front. "No, radio."

"Hey, maybe we could listen in on the Mante-León fútbol game," the driver suggested.

"Too bad we can't; I only carry parts. Next time, though."

"That's all right. Going all the way to Tampico?"

"Just Mante." This was the time to get a little more data on Zaragoza. "I hope to make a town called Zaragoza some time today."

"Then you're smart going with me to Mante," the man said. "Somebody who doesn't know the ropes would go there by way of Jumave or Palmillas. But you're making the jump—"

"To Ciudad del Maíz," Gilberto cut in.

"Right. . . . Got your ticket? There may be a rush the last half hour. You know how it is on weekends."

He showed it, with the air of a veteran traveler. "Well—time to get back to my hotel, pack, and still have ample for a light lunch."

"So early? We stop fifteen minutes at Limón; wonderful tacos there."

"I know those roadside tacos," Gilberto said. "Strictly hit and run. They hit and you run."

The driver grinned and waved. "See you later."

He strode fast and confidently, elated at the way he was able to make easy talk with people to whom you *had* to talk; bus drivers, especially when they had time and curiosity, being in that group.

When he reached the hotel, it was still only 11:30. The bare patio looked white hot. Unlocking his own room, the clinking of the metal window slats suggested that a breeze was coming up.

The room had been cleaned; the bed was made and the newspaper lay folded across the foot of it. He put the bus ticket on the dresser and weighted it with the key. Beside it, he put his money; the ready-pesos, which still made a substantial wad.

The open canvas bag reminded him of his laundry. Better start hollering for it or at least let the galopina—Rafaela, that was her name—know he was back.

As he hung his coat on the horns of the chair, the wallet in the inside pocket drew it down on that side. He lifted it out, with the idea of going through it, and that way kill some time. Unbuttoning his shirt, he sat on the edge of the bed, facing the outside window. A faint current of air touched his hairless chest.

What made the wallet so thick were the five cellophane frames built into it. In the first was a picture of his mother, reduced from the 8 × 10 "professionals" made when she was with Chuy Heredia and His Rhumbaleers.

The second frame was empty. It once had a snap of Carolyn Muller and himself in bathing suits. *That* little bitch! If only he had her down here—he'd fix her dirty little wagon. . . . In the picture, she was sitting across his legs; the satin of her thighs. . . . He snapped the wallet shut—veering, a frightened swimmer, out of the swift current of thoughts about Carolyn. Now he was free, but still floating in a turgid stream of longing. He caught at effigies and patterns. Random forms fitted themselves together into a phantasmagoric sexpot. The cropped, blonde hair of a girl at the La Cienega tennis courts and the arched black eyebrows of Mrs. Sophie Neff. A sharply pointed chin, peppered with Miss Jennifer Baxter's freckles. One leg, that of the girl climbing over the fence on the Canada Dry billboards; the other leg, in fishnet, belonging to a tap dancer in a film musical; but both dangling from the immense pubic bush of a stout woman whose skirts were blown up by a concealed jet of air in the Ocean Park Fun House.

Himself—in a pair of Jantzen swimming trunks, white; a wonderful bathrobe of toweling, also white, with the intials G. R. on the pocket. He was standing against a tall urn, overflowing with flowers, in a romantic Pond's Cold Cream moonlit garden. Two violinists—Guy Lombardo, "The Sweetest

Music This Side of Heaven," and Jan Garber, "The Idol of the Air Waves,"—both masked, were playing Dvorak's *Souvenir.*

"How brown you are, Gil—how strong—and yet, so gentle when you take me in your arms." The voice was low and husky with cigarettes and desire. Now that speech he remembered from a Hedy LaMarr movie— "And you are like a pale, waxen taper that my kisses will set to quivering flame." Advancing, shrugging the robe off his shoulders—

The door hinge squealed, a draft swept in, and the chimera fell apart like charred paper. Pretending to fumble with his shoelaces, he looked behind him. "I was just going to call you about those shirts. One second—"

For the gymnastic concealment of his state, he put his hand into his pocket, bending forward, pretending to grope for money—on the dresser, in plain sight.

Rafaela, her arms extended as if bearing a tray, held a thin, paper-covered package; simply held, not offered it. It was his, but he could not make the first move toward taking it; concluding a homely and essential transaction over some washed linen. But her long eyes were on him; when he moved to the dresser, at the foot of the bed, they followed him levelly.

The light, coming from the window behind him, allowed him to see her better, and with less frankness in his stare. She looked taller, with her hair up; straighter, from the belt of her narrow skirt to the thongs of a pair of green slippers. Above the skirt, she wore a blouse of white cotton with a narrow embroidered band around the top.

"Thanks for bringing it—Rafaela. How much do I owe you?"

He reached for the pile of pesos, but she covered it first with the package. He lifted the paper and saw the shorts, the socks, handkerchief, and only one shirt—there had been two. Her eyes were directly on him. He couldn't say anything because he saw her lips apart. There were tiny globules of moisture on the soft, dark fuzz at the corners of her mouth.

"Wasn't there another shirt, Rafaela?"

"Yes, there were two," she answered softly. She left out the "su servidora" humility, and she didn't say "señor."

"Then—" Oh, you chump! he screamed at himself. Can't you see what the dame is out for? Wave a bill at her and start going to town! He could only gasp. "Well, then—I think, maybe—"

At last, she was going to speak, he thought thankfully. She was going to save him from foundering; perhaps, even from putting his foot in it; misjudging her.

Her voice was a little above a whisper. "You are in need of a woman."

"Huh?" He had heard well enough, but there was a typhoon in his blood.

Together, they moved one step—mere inches, toward each other. The thin ribbon at the front of her blouse moved with her breath. "If I can please you, it will make me also very—"

He could make only a low, sad cry as he put his arms around her, and his mouth found the cords in the side of her neck. Her palms pressed and stroked his naked ribs under the shirt. As he pressed her, one arm across her back and with the other drawing her with eager firmness against him, she begged, "Wait—"

He couldn't; intent in a blind duel to get her softest flesh against his own, drawing up the loose blouse. As he felt the granular tips of her breasts flex of their own hungry volition, he wanted his first intelligible words to be in Spanish, her language; but he could think of them only in his. "Baby— honey—sweetheart—"

Trembling, as he repeated these strange, neighing words, she tried to help him; to lead him when he pressed her down, across the bed. Only to detain him, she took his hand. But his fingers were hot tongs, too crude to find a tiny clasp here, two little hooks there. With his weight upon her and his mouth sealing hers, he tugged awkwardly at her clothes and his own. How to tell him, past those hot, hungry eyes, that his frenzy was hampering her as well as himself?

His lurches ended with a hoarse sigh. His mouth touched her cheek on its way to her shoulder, and there it remained when he moved to be at her side.

She paced off his sweaty face, by fractions of a millimeter, until it was cool again under the touch of her fingers. When she moved away, gently, he slowly closed his eyes and said, "Rafaela . . . honey."

When her hand was on the knob, he called again, "Rafaela—" and heard only the covert sound of her leaving.

21

So, Pinky—excuse me—pinky; so you made it, at last. After nineteen years—two years behind Bishop's schedule, at that.

So, this was the slashing, tearing revenge he was going to take on all of Carolyn's surrogates; wallop away at them until they screamed for help. Yeah! The way this one must be screaming outside now—with laughter.

> Teacher: What did the gentleman-rabbit say to the lady-rabbit?
> Johnny: Bam! Bam! Thank you, ma'am.

Yup, Bishop had it right—down here you better not play macho unless you can show your medals. Even that old street sweeper in Matamoros belted out—how many?—eleven, thirteen kids. And that must have taken some homework, because you don't ring the bell every time.

As he lay face down on his arm, the room became darker. The metal blinds were clanking against the window frame. Strong gusts of wind vibrated the panes and whistled in the patio. He got up to shut the window. Rain; great big bullets of it slammed suddenly down on the street and lay there. It had turned to hail.

This must be the norteño the man had predicted. The bus—! He looked at this watch—five minutes to twelve. He couldn't believe it; how could this interminable wretchedness have borne down on him in such a short time? Would the next hour seem again as long? The next month—would that be a year?

Standing there by the quivering window, engrossed by the size of the hailstones, he heard behind him the soft closing of the door. Rafaela had come back. She had the other shirt in the crook of her arm and held an orange. She pouted at him, but her eyes smiled. That made him forget his shame and he said, "Hello, Rafaela."

"Baby—?"

"Yes—and honey."

"I know baby," she said, coming to the window. "But tell me what is honey."

"Miel," he said. "The sweetest thing there is."

She gave him the orange and put her hands on his face. So simple a thing in itself, but the way she looked at him at the same time, so slowly and with so much meaning, the natural thing to do was to put his arms around her. He did it so softly, she couldn't draw away.

"Go wash," she said, and took the orange. "I'll peel it for you."

His laundered shorts were on the dresser, and she saw him reach for them and got in his way. "Go wash," she said again.

The first time she said that, it was an echo of the many little sounds that used to beat about his ears, long ago. "Brush your hair . . . Put on your sweater . . . Wipe your feet." Sounds he would hear, but scarcely mind. The second time she said it, it was different; it reached deep. It had that tone of gentle command which he always obeyed.

Dropping his clothes in a heap on the bathroom floor and about to turn on the water, he heard the rasp of a key in the door. His money! Something like 450 pesos, laying there in plain sight on the dresser. If she lifted it and was gone, he was good and stuck. He couldn't go to the police, who would naturally want to know all about him first; maybe search him and appropriate the rest of what he had. Meanwhile, the woman held all the aces. She could accuse him of raping her—

As he stood there in the shower stall, which was no bigger than an upended coffin, he heard a soft thump, then another; pieces of orange peel dropping into the tin wastebasket by the bed.

The water was cold from both taps. Snorting and slapping his chest made too much of a din; giving the Tarzan yell on top of that would have brought the booth crashing down. Then, standing quietly, he let the water slide over him. If it were any warmer, he thought, he could go to sleep standing up.

Rafaela—she was back. Her body was still unknown to him; land over which he had run in the dark. She didn't tell him she was coming back, but *she* knew it—and he should have known it. Bringing back one shirt and leaving the other to go back for later. Christ, dames are cute. The way they plan things out, like an engineer.

While drying himself, he heard other quiet and electric sounds. A hiss of air, displaced by the bed covers being flung back. The rustling—the crackling of nylon drawn over skin and hair.

He wound the moist towel around himself and snapped off the light in the bathroom.

The bedroom was a leaden, twilight grayness, and chilly from the rainy gusts which broke against the window. Rafaela's face was a burnt gold oval, framed between her black hair and the arc of her shoulders. Covered only with the sheet, she looked thin and long.

As he moved over the tiles, her eyes were shut, but she was smiling. His own lips were parted, but only to take in air and relieve the gasping labor of his chest. Kneeling with one leg on the rail of the bed, he ran his hand along her side. She opened her eyes, and with her look, guided his own to the chair beside the bed. There was the peeled orange—and beside it, the door key.

Then she touched him. The lightly knotted towel dropped to the floor. Her thin, strong arm drew him beside her; it had the strength of strap steel, but suddenly it became silk.

Their hands tangled, like ravenous snakes in a cave. His mouth battered her lips, but in the siege his tongue came against clenched teeth. Her body arched away from him and she tugged at his hair with both hands. What did she want—? This—his mouth at the root of her breast, captive in the faint musk of her armpit. He bit suddenly and sharply, and she cried out, but did not shrink.

"I didn't mean to, honey—"

She shivered and her fingers kneaded his back. "Querido—baby—"

"Call me by my name," he whispered.

"Gustavo—mío."

"No—Gilberto."

"Gilberto—honey—" Her teeth clamped onto his shoulder, and her body became a cradle to contain him.

Far, far out, from where the spires of Venice Beach were only distant spear tips, a wave, darker and greener than the others of the cavalry that flanked it, was bringing him in. . . . It left him, feeble in the oozing silver of the beach.

He couldn't believe, until he saw her tears and wiped them away with the heel of his hand, that she had wept for a time afterward. If it was he who hurt her, as he feared, she forgave him—she kissed his palm.

He felt like having a cigarette, but he would have to look for the package. He took the orange instead. Parting it, he offered her the first wedge. "It's for you," she said.

"Can I get you something? A glass of water?"

Nothing. She wanted only to lean on her elbow and watch him.

It was getting lighter in the room. The sound of rain had stopped. A wedge of sunlight knifed in through the top slat of the blind, stayed for a second, and vanished.

"Rafaela—"

"Cariño—"

"It's wonderful to be with you." He put the orange back on the chair and lay close beside her. "Did you hear what I said?" Again, brushing the hair away from her ear, "Did you?"

"I heard," she answered. "I also want to say things that will sound wonderful to you, but I have not learned them."

"You don't have to say anything, Rafaela—you showed me. You made it so that I don't want to leave here—leave you."

"But you are going; you already have a ticket for the voyage."

"I'll tear it up—I'll show you . . ." He moved, but she held him there.

"I am going, too," she said. "Back to the land. It is very far—Campeche; and already a day is lost."

"You mean, you *meant* to go?"

"Yes, this day; early this morning I would have been gone. But last night—"

"Tell me," he said, "what about last night?"

"I came to your door. In the dark, I stood by your window and I heard . . . you were weeping. I saw you; you were asleep—but you were weeping."

He thought hotly, perhaps he was. "Why should I be crying? I'm no kid."

"Each has his own reasons."

"That's funny . . . So, I was snivelling in my sleep. And you went away because of that?"

"No," she said. "Because of that, I came back."

She drew him deeper into her arms and smoothed his hair with slow, lengthening strokes.

"Maybe I was having a dream—" Maybe! He knew damn well that he was, and all about it. "—a nightmare like, where you're tortured—"

She put her fingers across his lips. "Now you have one reason not to be anguished. You will not need any more to be frightened, or ashamed with a woman."

"There won't be another one like you, Rafaela." He meant that and he wanted to show her that he did; not by saying it again differently, but as a lover. His hand, upon the skin of which he concentrated all the hunger of his nerves, moved—loitering, barely touching—across the tip of her breast, descending toward the curve of her hip. She trembled, bowed strongly against him, and her throat swelled with a captive moan.

"Tu boca—Darme tu boca!" She sobbed, twisting to find his mouth; her own hungrily open. It tasted freshly of the milk of young corn.

A gong throbbed, bronze in his chest. Silver geysers of sound rose out of blue water, a mile into the air. They burst into stars, whirled and formed themselves into ropes of gold and descended slowly, all around him and upon him, weightlessly.

When she took his arm, to raise it from his eyes and to kiss him gently, he felt also the cotton of her blouse brushing his chin. She was dressed and she whispered, "Sleep a little more."

"Rafaela—over there—on the dresser," he pointed. "Take what you want."

She nodded. Some paper rustled, and she turned to show him what she took: the handkerchief, his best one, with the rolled hem and embroidered initial. "This I will take."

"There's money—"

Again with his eyes heavy, he watched the motes swim in a beam of sun and heard small sounds—the scrape of a fingernail, the hiss and crackle of a comb, and a sandal on the tiles. But the rattle of the door closing did not reach him.

22

The cordiality he expected on his return to the terminal, as a somewhat privileged passenger, was lacking. The driver insisted, even, on seeing his ticket, before waving him aboard. His own seat, No. 12, a good one by the window, was already occupied by a man in a white linen suit, who was reading a newspaper. The cobrador, to whom Gilberto made his complaint, told him impatiently to sit down anywhere, and please not block the aisle.

He picked a seat near the rear, put his bag up on the rack, and settled down.

It was fifteen minutes after "fourteen hours on the dot" before the driver and three passengers with whom he had been chatting on the platform took their seats. With the help of the cobrador, the coach was warped out of the station and into the channel of street traffic.

From the racking thumps, as the wheels pounded the uneven pavement, he realized that his seat was the worst he could have picked—directly over the rear axle.

The old woman who sat by the window next to him must be feeling it more, with not an ounce of meat on her to take up the shock. He guessed sympathetically that she must be well in her seventies, although you can't tell about Mexican women—they could be either forty or ninety. That's what he'd heard.

There was a burst of ragged laughter, some of it forced, up front, among the driver's friends, and he heard the word "norteño." They had turned and were looking at him, but he wouldn't give them the satisfaction of recognizing that he was the subject of their joke. He pretended to be looking out over the sloping land, bright with sun, and was glad that he didn't get the nearer seat; also, that his companion, this vieja, would not tempt them to make any more jokes.

He looked at her more closely. She did not appear to be a woman of the peón class. Her fingers were thin and brown as fallen twigs, but the nails were clean and trimmed short. Her black rebozo was of soft, knitted wool, and had a lengthwise crease which showed that it was not used for lugging stuff in. He wondered if she had any children, and how many. But he couldn't, he realized, concern himself exclusively with this problem for the next three hours or so. Better to think of his next jump. Would he have to hire a mule to get him to Zaragoza? Even then, Zaragoza wasn't his final destination; that was Tres Cenotes. He would have to look at that letter again to get the name of his mother's relative straight. He felt for it; it was there. However, there was no hurry.

He lit a cigarette, intending to ask the old lady's permission, but she turned her face to him before he could speak. Thinking he saw her frown, he said, "If the smoke torments you, señora—"

"Not at all," she said. "I would enjoy one with you, but I had no time to buy any."

"Then, please accept one of mine, if they are to your taste, señora." He was amazed at how natural that had sounded—to himself.

The old woman took a deep pull, holding the smoke in for an astonishingly long time. Exhaling, she nodded and said, "I have the honor to be, your servant, Regina Castillejo, viuda de Campos," and gave him her hand. Smoke was still coming from her nostrils.

"And I am Gilberto Reyes, at your service." He would have given her the name he signed at the hotel, but he had forgotten it.

"You are going to Tampico to fish in the sea, like the other young men?" she asked, pointing to the passengers down front.

"I would be happy if I could. But I am going to Zaragoza." As an afterthought, and deliberately in the hope of possible comment on the place, he added, "The Zaragoza which is in San Luis Potosí."

"That one, naturally. Then you will alight at Ciudad del Maíz."

"That is my plan."

"You are not from there, one can see, but you have relatives in Zaragoza?" The word for relatives was parientes; another tricky one, like firma, that almost caught him earlier.

"Unfortunately no; not relatives. I go on business," he said.

"With Don Solomón?"

She knew Zaragoza all right; she knew it too well. "I suppose so," he said.

"Everybody in that region speaks well of Don Solomón."

"I imagine they would." Better not get too deep in this admiration of Don Solomón, whoever he was. "And you, señora, you are going far?"

"I alight at El Limón, with your permission. Five of my children live there. . . . You, señorito, are from these parts?"

"No, señora; from the Northwest." He waved, vaguely behind him.

"Good. That also is Mexican earth."

Exactly what the old man in Matamoros said, he remembered.

In the time that it took him to look down at the floor of the bus to locate the cigarette butt he dropped, so that he could grind it out with his heel, it had become dark. The people twisting in their seats looked agitated and talked to each other excitedly, pointing to the horizon. It was the one line of light, jagged with scudding clouds.

There was a roaring, louder than the sound of the engine, and wind struck the side of the bus with the force of a giant fist in a boxing glove.

The first rain splashed against the windows, coming horizontally with the force of a riveting gun, driving it through the narrowest fissures. Gilberto felt it on his face.

The old lady crossed herself and said, "The norteño." The ceiling lights went on and he saw the driver's friends glaring at him—as though he had brought it on. He hoped he did. Now let them laugh.

In gusts, the wind pummelled the bus and was threatening to break the backs of the trees. When the machine hit the low spots in the road, water splashed higher than the windows. The lightning didn't merely flick by; it hovered like a flare, revealing the ditches coursing with water that looked as if it were boiling.

A spray caught the old woman in the face and she looked frightened, wrapping the rebozo around her head.

"Let me change seats with you," Gilberto suggested, rising to let her move into the aisle seat.

She smiled thankfully and said, "God bless you, my son."

He didn't mind the occasional jet of rain. Only when the lightning flashed could he see *out* of the window. But looking *at* it was almost as interesting. Leaves slapped against the glass and remained pasted there, like specimens for study. Then, the rain would wipe them off, and the wind replaced them with another kind. Once, something heavy hit the glass and he flinched, but not before he had seen what it was—a bird, a big one, with topaz eyes and a hooked beak; maybe an eagle.

Then it became lighter, and he saw strange and wonderful things—clouds unrolling like tremendous scrolls and the voice of thunder reading the proclamation off them. A knobby, brown and white calf looking brightly around the corner of its mother's broad flank. A flock of tall white birds standing with their thin legs as if glued in a lake of mud. And again rain, coming on broadside, colored like tracer bullets by the lightning.

An hour and twenty minutes had passed since they left Victoria. It was raining less, but the wind was still strong—and getting stronger. It would hit suddenly, like a battering ram, take a breather, and start pushing like a freight locomotive. The driver had his work cut out for him to keep the car from weaving. And just as important, to keep alert for washouts across the road. Every time the transmission growled and slapped into second gear, the passengers braced themselves for a bucking plunge in and out of a deep wash. Grrr-——umph!

As the coach listed, taking a wide curve, Gilberto saw a road marker with TROPICO DE CANCER painted on it, clear and sharp. It struck him with wonder—an early fable of geography come true. Sure, and this was a tropical storm; the kind they have in miniature in those classy bars in Beverly Hills, where they serve those fancy, tall rum drinks, with names like Missionary's Downfall and Serpent's Tooth. Not that he'd been in any of them, but there had been a run of movies which had that kind of background.

Nobody else in the bus appeared to be aware of this remarkable trespass.

Maybe they missed seeing the marker. Anyway, he owed it to the old lady to inform her. "We just crossed over. We're now in the Tropic of Cancer. Did you know that, señora?"

"Yes, the Tropic," she said flatly. Her reaction might just as well have been, "So what?"

So nothing. . . . Sorry he brought it up; just forget it, lady. He was piqued at the offhand way she took the news of their leap into another zone; acting as if straddling the latitudes was nothing more than skipping the gutter. . . . So she was old—so what! So let her sit there and suck her gums.

Bustling, he whipped the Pemex map out of his pocket and unfolded it. Ciudad Mante was still a considerable distance down the red line. The tiny numbers between towns—22, 15, 7—were kilometers, not miles, thank Christ. After Mante, they totalled, to Ciudad del Maíz, 115. A tiny green G meant there was a gasoline station there; a hotel, too, he hoped, in case he should be stuck there overnight.

Up ahead, the windshield wipers had begun to squeak on dry glass. The rain had stopped altogether and the sun was beginning to suck everything dry. Somebody raised a window and air fresh as peppermint flowed in.

For some reason, it made him want to think of Rafaela. Half shutting his eyes, he had begun to, but stopped when he realized the old lady was still beside him. To relive his hour with a woman now would be more than disrespect to the vieja; it would be an irreverence. There persisted in him a vague moral notion that children and old people must be kept insulated from the coarser facts of love.

Now, however, if he could think of Rafaela as a person—a woman—apart from the sex thing, he didn't think he would be doing any violence to that code.

She—Rafaela—she had character. Anybody could tell that she wouldn't walk into just anybody's room, unless the guy had a special appeal . . .

Useless, he decided, to try to hold his thoughts about her in these limits.

They ought to be getting to El Limón—not that the old lady was a mind reader, but he would rather wait until she was gone.

23

Rafaela—suppose this thing with Rafaela had developed in Los Angeles. It would make it a little awkward. Unless, of course, he wanted to keep her under wraps. But she was entitled to more than that. Where would he take her, say on a Sunday afternoon? Down to the Venice Pier, Ocean Park, Santa Monica Beach, or would it have to be Cabrillo Beach, where mostly Negroes and the poor class of Mexican-Americans went? And if he met anybody he knew, people seeing him with Rafaela would know just what was going on. It would make it very embarrassing. Not because she was an ex-galopina from way down in Mexico—that wasn't the reason. He'd feel the same way if the woman was a blonde West Adams divorcée.

And if he took her to the Café Orizaba, which was the natural place, he knew just what would happen. Verónica La Negra would be very polite and all that, but when she got him aside, he could just hear her. "I know, chulo, she is a fine *woman*—muy simpática. But *joven*—" Yes, the stress would be on her as a woman, and him as a boy.

In that respect, Verónica was like his mother. Neither of them had ever talked to him about girls. Knowing a lot of people, did Verónica ever come up with a jovencita to match his juventud? In a pig's— Well, maybe she would have, if he had shown any interest himself. She might have introduced him to some parents among her customers who had young daughters. Solid people; businessmen, manufacturers, a couple of professional people.

He had met several of that type—one, anyway—but not through Verónica's connections. There was Chiqui Menéndez, a year younger than himself, but already a junior at McVeigh.

They would always find themselves at the same table in the school cafeteria. Then, it got to be the natural thing to sit outside with her on one of the campus benches until the bell rang. She was a neat dresser, talked intelligently, and said herself that she couldn't see anything in a fellow who was an athlete pure and simple. "More simple than pure," she used to say, which was more truth than poetry.

Gilberto wasn't in love with her, but he felt flattered when people used to say they made a nice couple; looked like some high-class dance team that they'd be paying a hefty cover charge to see perform some day at the Coconut Grove.

That was before Carolyn.

Chiqui would come to all the Friday night basketball games and dances that followed. The first time he asked if he could take her home, he found out she always came with her brother, Paul. This Paul was always rooting for the other team, no matter which it was, and Gilberto found out he had flunked out of McVeigh and gone into business with his father. Paul had a car, and Gilberto would take a lift as far as Seventh and Alvarado, which was taking them out of their way some. Every time they had malts and cheeseburgers at the drive-in, Paul would always pick up the tab and wanted no arguments about it. Finally, Gilberto felt he ought to do something and asked Chiqui if she'd care to see the new Fred Astaire picture at the Egyptian.

"I've been wanting to see that one," Paul put in first. So, naturally, he had to be included; and Chiqui seemed to take it as a matter of course that Paul went everywhere with her.

"Pick me up early," she said. "About half past six. Want you to meet the folks; have a snack before we go."

He had an idea that her folks were pretty well-off, and there was no doubt about it when he saw their house. A ranch-type layout, in the Silver Lake district. When he touched the doorbell, the chimes played almost the whole of "Home, Sweet Home." A colored girl opened the door.

"Good evening, Miss Menéndez in?"

"You the gentleman?" she asked pleasantly.

The place had real class. Wall-to-wall carpets and a huge black and red Stromberg Carlson television, with radio and record player in the same cabinet. There was a bridge table all set up for canasta. Pictures, but nothing religious; no Bleeding Hearts and no Descents from the Cross, as in most poor Mexican homes he had seen.

Chiqui came in first. "Greetings and salutations. Glad you came on time. Come out on the terrace." They walked through a pair of French doors.

Mr. and Mrs. Menéndez sat in big, fan-backed wicker chairs, facing a large, sloping lawn. There was a birdbath carved in the shape of a kneeling figure holding a basin.

"Reyes?" Mr. Menéndez said. "Any relation to Mike Reyes, the insurance man in the Taft Building?"

"No, I don't think so, sir."

Although he didn't get up, you could see that Chiqui's father was tall, over six feet. He was wearing slacks and one of those rogue-shirts, like President Truman. He had thick ankles; the kind you see on a man who suffers with his feet all his life.

Mrs. Menéndez was darker-skinned than her husband, which you could see, even under the heavy patina of sunburn. She wore dark glasses; thick prescription lenses in harlequin frames. Her hair was tawny blonde to about an inch from the scalp, where it was good and black. The coolie coat she had on over a sun suit reached to just about the knees, the backs of which were discolored like a bruised eye. Her name was Rita. She called her husband Frank, and several times, Paco.

"What line are your people in?" Mr. Menéndez asked.

Before Gilberto could say anything, Mrs. Menéndez said, "There's Cokes, or anything else you wish."

"Please don't bother; I'll pour one out for myself." He was pouring the drink when Paul came in and immediately began talking about last night's game with Glendale. His theme was that, although McVeigh won, Glendale showed better team play.

"Maybe so," Gilberto said, "but the score tells the story." He glanced at Mr. Menéndez for agreement, but there was no expression of any kind. "When Graves passed to me—you remember, when it was tied up at four-teen-fourteen—how he flipped the ball backward, over his head. He didn't have to see me there; he knew I'd be there to take it. Now, if you don't call that team play—" By this time, he hoped, Mr. Menéndez would have forgotten the question, because Gilberto had no answer.

"I'm starved; let's eat," Paul said. "It's probably going to be a long show."

"You could always eat popcorn in the theatre," Chiqui said, as a joke. But Gilberto was glad she mentioned popcorn; he could tell the Menéndezes an amusing thing about that.

"Yes," he began, "they even put a popcorn machine in the lobby in that theatre on Main Street; the one that shows only Mexican pictures."

Since they were all listening now, he waited for them to acknowledge that they knew the place he was talking about. But they said nothing. "Well," he continued, "you know what they advertise the popcorn as?" Mr. Menéndez had that get-to-the-point expression. Gilberto finished, "They call popcorn palomitas de maíz—little doves of corn."

Chiqui said, "Cute." The rest of them—nothing. Especially Paul and his father. They looked at him as if he had been careless enough to let one go, noiselessly, but with a brutal stink.

He had done worse than that; worse than twirling a rope in the home of a hanged man. He had spoken Yiddish in the House of Rothschild!

"You go there much—the Main Street joint?" Mr. Menéndez asked.

"Every time they change the bill; about once a week."

"What for?"

"The popcorn, maybe," Paul snickered.

"I started going there with my mother when I was just a kid. I got into the habit, sort of."

"I mean, what's the *idea*?" Menéndez insisted.

"Well, mainly, it keeps up my Spanish. I don't see many people who speak it, outside of the family I room with." He smiled around at his hosts, "And you folks."

"We talk English here," Menéndez said. "I made Chiqui take French in school."

"I took German," Paul elaborated.

"Oh, let's listen to some music," Chiqui said.

"Yeah," her mother agreed. "Put the Swing-and-Sway With Sammy Kaye album on."

Paul went inside to the living room and put on some piano music by Carmen Cavallero, and stayed there until the maid brought in the food, buffet-style, laid out on the Ping-Pong table.

There was nothing Mexican about the way the food smelled or tasted. Fried chicken in a big casserole, whipped potatoes, peas. Gilberto took a wing and a leg, a spoonful of potatoes, and a hot corn muffin, already split and buttered. He passed up the salad, which was a ring of tomato aspic around a mixture of ground up raisins and carrots.

Chiqui had barely a mouthful and said she was going to get cleaned up and change out of her sweater and skirt.

"Pull up a little closer here," her father beckoned. "And Paul, turn on some lights. More chicken, Reyes?"

"No, thank you. It was very delicious."

The maid brought out a lemon-coconut pie and coffee. He noticed that whenever she was in the room, the family clammed up until they could hear that she was back in the kitchen.

"I heard you mention," Mr. Menéndez said, "you lived with a family—"

"Yes, sir; people named Romero. He's a foreman in the Southern Pacific shops. Raised himself up from a section hand."

"You mean, you're a boarder—you pay them rent."

"Eight and a half a week. It doesn't seem much, but it pays their rent for the flat."

"Whereabouts?"

"Over on the East Side, near Michigan Avenue." He wished the man wouldn't keep asking him about things in the present. He was going to school—that was plain enough. The years ahead, what was coming up, that's what he would prefer to talk about. About how he was planning the pre-engineering course at L.A. City College; his eye on the great big field of industrial engineering—

"That's over in Boyle Heights," he heard Mr. Menéndez say, and he nodded.

Paul and his mother skidded their chairs closer and sat like spectators at a tennis game. Every time Mr. Menéndez said something, they swung their heads toward him, and back again to Gilberto when he answered.

"Your own people; aren't they living together—separated or something?"

"No, you see, my father died right after I was born."

"Where?"

"Me? Right here in L.A."

"Your father, I mean," Menéndez said rather sharply, like an employer who expects his people to give clear replies, even to somewhat unclear questions. "What business was he in?"

"I couldn't tell you exactly, Mr. Menéndez. He was on a trip; traveling somewhere, when he passed away suddenly. My mother—"

"She got married again?" Mrs. Menéndez asked. Her husband scowled at her; he was conducting this interview.

Personal, even intimate as these questions were, Gilberto assumed they were asked out of genuine interest in him—one of their people, a Mexican-American like themselves; a double compatriot. Maybe they weren't as simpático as the Romeros, but he was their guest; he had to be polite.

"He must have left you enough to get by, huh. Insurance—something you could draw on?"

The right answer was, not a cent. But he said, instead, "I really don't know. Anyhow, we made out. My mother worked."

"Worked?" Mrs. Menéndez said in such a tone that it kept him from explaining that she had been a waitress in a Chinese restaurant once. Anyway, he had something more interesting to tell them.

"Yes, ma'am; she's a singer."

"Yeah, what kind?" the woman asked eagerly. "Where'd she sing?"

"The last time was at the Troc." You didn't have to say the full name, Trocadero, to these people; they knew what you were talking about. "But she had to lay off for a while."

"What name did she sing under?"

"Her own name, naturally—Elvira Reyes; featured with Chuy Heredia and His Rhumbaleers." This, about his mother, was really holding them. "Maybe you might have the record she made. They say it's the best rendition of that particular number."

"Which number is that?" Paul asked.

"'Noche de Ronda.' If you'd like to hear it, I could give it to Chiqui Monday."

"So she's not singing now?"

"On account of sickness," Gilberto said.

"What's she sick of?"

He recognized that she used the Spanish form, in which you say a person is *sick of* his stomach, *sick of* his throat.

"It's something with her lungs," he explained. "The doctor says she'll get along fine after the spring, when he can get her into a new place."

"Where is she now; in the hospital?"

"Yes, ma'am. In the Doheny Pavillion."

Paul piped up, "Ain't that the County Hospital, where we had to send Joe, the gardener?" Nobody answered him, but Mrs. Menéndez got up and said she had better go and see what was keeping Chiqui.

"I'll go," Mr. Menéndez said. "You stay here, Rita. Paul, I want to see you."

Left alone with Mrs. Menéndez, he started to tell her how much he enjoyed the dinner. A mistake—you don't praise the cook to her mistress's face. You compliment the lady on her "planning of the dinner," on her taste in porcelain, and on the weight and quality of her silver.

"We like cold fried chicken after Mass," Mrs. Menéndez said listlessly. "Where do you go?"

"I beg your pardon."

"What church? Near where you room? We used to go to St. Ciprian's on South Figueroa, but we go to St. Vibiana's now, in Beverly Hills. Monsignor Phelan happens to be a friend of Paco's—Mr. Menéndez's."

He'd better be careful here. "I wouldn't know what to tell you about going to church, Mrs. Menéndez. The Romeros go; three times a week, at least. I went with them once, to a raffle. They had bingo games and bridge going in the cellar."

"We were talking about church," she explained to Paul as he came in.

"Go inside, he wants to see you," he said to his mother, and sat down when she left. "We go to St. Vibiana's in Beverly Hills," he began. "Monsignor Phelan—"

"I know; your mother just told me."

"Where do you go, Reyes?"

"Fact is, I don't." No use saying he did, when he didn't. "But that don't mean I don't *believe*. It's just that I've never been."

"But you're Cath'lic."

"Sure I am."

"And you say you never *been*?"

"Not that I can remember—outside of this one church bazaar."

"You mean, you didn't take your First Communion?"

"I wouldn't know how to go about it."

Paul hesitated a second and then got up and went inside, like a man with important news; without saying excuse me, or that he would be right back. Gilberto sat there, listening to the piano music on the record player. A door further back inside the house opened and shut, and he hoped it might be Chiqui, ready at last. It was her mother again.

He smiled and said, "I hope the princess is out of her bath," expecting at least a matronly smile, and an opening to talk about Chiqui. He wanted Mrs. Menéndez to know, and through her, the rest of the family, what a swell girl Chiqui was. They had a right to be proud of her. Not that they seemed to need the assurance. But they ought to know that, in Chiqui's case, her Mexican background didn't hold her back one inch, scholastically or any other way. There wasn't another girl in the junior class who could—

But the woman didn't look as if she were prepared to listen; her mind was somewhere else, hearing things in the other parts of the house which were inaudible to him. Suddenly, out of nowhere she asked him a question: "You think Fred Astaire is as good as Leo Carrillo?"

He could have laughed right out loud. It was like asking if Bing Crosby was as good as Gene Autrey. Where has this woman *been!* Let her down easy. "As what? How can you compare them?"

"As an actor, I meant to say."

Good, then. She wanted an expert opinion, no doubt. Well, she was asking the right guy. "Personally, I don't see how you can consider Carrillo in the same class with Astaire—as an actor. You see, ma'am, Carrillo is what we call *typed*. He's a one-note character. To prove it, take the last thing he was in —"

Paul bustled in again and, standing some distance away, tried to get something over to his mother. But she was slow. She pointed to Gilberto and said, "Your friend here, he don't like Leo Carrillo."

Paul's sly smile made Gilberto think he agreed with him. As if there could be any argument between people who knew pictures, on that subject . . .

"So you don't think Leo Carrillo's a great actor?" Paul said.

"Not for my money."

"Just what don't you happen to like about him?"

This called for some genuine criticism; not prejudice, or even opinion. "Like I said to your mother, he's one-note. What's he good for, outside of taking the parts of Mexicans; singing bandits, things like that? And that phoney Mexican accent he puts on—qué chistoso!"

"It just happens that he's Spanish—not Mexican."

"Spanish, huh," Gilberto retorted. "Then what's he doing in Mexican night clubs—the Serape, and places like that—all the time? And riding a horse in every Mexican parade!"

"He goes with his friend, Sheriff Biscailuz," Paul snapped.

"Who ain't a Mexican either, if you want to know. He's a Portugee." Now he was going to dish out something you don't read in the fan magazines. "You want to know something, Paul? He'll go anyplace, a hamburger stand, even, where they'll call out his name so he can take a cheap bow."

"Hey, Rita!" Mr. Menéndez's voice was loud in command. His wife got up quickly and went inside.

Paul jerked his head forward. "Now I'll tell *you* something, feller. Leo Carrillo is one of the early California Dons—if that means anything to you. His people owned all the land around here."

He wondered what Paul was getting so sore about. He didn't want to carry this too far, but he could stand for one more dig. "Then why doesn't he retire and give an *actor* a job?"

"You think you're funny, don't you, Reyes? He got all that land in a royal grant from the King of Spain." Paul looked furious.

"Okay, okay—but don't talk about him as an actor."

That did it. Paul got red in the face and practically shouted, "Look, fella! I don't like the way you're talking about a friend of ours, see! Leo Carrillo happens to be my padrino—I mean, my godfather." With that, he turned and walked swiftly inside.

Gilberto realized that he stepped on this family's corns. Chiqui should have warned him. Anyway, it was too late now. There was no way of weaseling out of it, and what he said would have to stand. He would see how Chiqui felt about it. With all this running back and forth of the folks, that ought to be her now.

It was Paul again. "This movie deal is off. Chiqui's not going."

"What's the matter—what happened?"

"Just what I said; the date's off."

"Well—I'm sorry. How about you two taking a rain check?"

"Save it," said Paul, holding the French doors open for him to step through.

"I'd like to tell Chiqui—if I could see her for a minute."

"Get wise to yourself, Reyes. It's better if you don't see her at all—get me?"

"If that's the way she wants it—"

"Never mind how she wants it. *I'm* telling you." And there he opened the front door.

Gilberto remembered that all this happened on a lovely, cool night; hardly the kind you'd want to spend in a movie house. And that he whistled as he walked all the way down to Sunset and Echo Park, and took the streetcar to the Orizaba. Also, that the first thing Verónica La Negra said to him when he entered was, "Guess who was here tonight?"

He laughed and said, "Leo Carrillo?" And that's how he felt about the whole deal at the Menéndezes.

With Ciudad Mante coming up in a few minutes, he should still be laughing. But now, there was something bitter and definitely unfunny about what happened there and why.

It was something Dr. Eisen never brought up—he might have, if Gilberto hadn't rushed away with his mind full of pinwheels. Eisen showed him where he stood with certain types of americanos—the kind that wanted him to lie down and be a good mexicano. But he didn't know about people like the Menéndezes. And that's where he could tell Eisen something . . . "We speak English in this house. . . . St. Vibiana's—in Beverly Hills. . . . Paco—I mean, Frank—"

It wasn't his remarks about their friend Carrillo or that he didn't go to church. It was his mother, in the County Hospital, where they had to send their gardener; that she made a phonograph record in Spanish; that he was a roomer in the home of a Mexican famiy named Romero, the head of which once worked as a section hand.

Should he even be a little sorry for the Menéndezes because of the scare he gave them? What a disaster to have a Chicano—a real, dark, idioma-speaking louse—in a family that wouldn't be seen near a Mexican movie even.

Ah, but all would be forgiven—even his mother—if he knew *only* enough

Spanish to get a passing grade in school and if his name was—well—if his name was Charley Devlin.

And piss on their fried chicken! That sopa de albóndigas, which he ate later with Verónica and Yerno, had it all over that tearoom food of the Menéndezes like a tent.

And wouldn't Rafaela enjoy a plate of that with a couple of bottles of beer; and afterward, go to her place. It would have to be a hideaway somewhere in the downtown neighborhood. Just a small place that would probably have a Murphy bed. You couldn't expect a matrimonio like that one in the hotel. What a workbench that was! Yes, he'd done all right. He didn't have to take his hat off to anybody.

There was this fellow, Eddie Fowler, back at McVeigh, who knew what he was talking about. He said that coming right down to it, for *real* satisfaction, give him an older dame. "Not," he added, "that I'd turn my ass to some of the younger talent we got on the campus here."

"Dissolve . . . twenty years later! Old Ed Fowler leaving the gates of San Quentin!" somebody else in that bull-session hooted.

Another fellow urged Fowler on. "Let's have it, Ed; what's your theory?"

"All right, take your quail—she's with you tonight. But instead of having her mind on her work, she's wondering how it's going to be with the next Tom, Dick, or Harry. That's why, I figure, they have that dreamy look."

The same joker hollered, "Not with me, they don't."

"I'm serious now," Ed said. "Let's keep this discussion on a high level. . . . You take an old dame—say twenty-five and up. They figure this one might turn out to be their last, and so they make it good."

"Stands to reason," Gilberto said.

Later that afternoon, some of the football squad came in and the gang really buckled down to Subject A. The question came up as to which was the best each fellow ever had; not just good, but *the* best.

Somehow, every one of them mentioned the nationality of the babe. Pete Glennon told about the French number—*his* best—who worked in a beauty parlor. "And boy! Was she an operator!"

Lew Mitchell said the best he ever had was a Jewish broad. Another fellow, Cloyd, said, "You'd think a Norwegian would be a cold proposition. Well, I'm here to tell you different."

Gilberto was fascinated. These fellows, mostly seniors, with cars of their own, they lived it up.

Harry Earle said that if he ever got his hooks on another one like that usherette at the Pantages, he'd have it stuffed and put under glass. "Greek," he added.

Dickie Collins started, "I remember this Mexican—nothing personal, Gil—"

Gilberto came right back at him. "It wasn't me, so you don't have to apologize. And I don't have any sisters."

Mickey Rosenstock appreciated that the most, and patted his back. There was a guy, that Mickey. M. R., they called him. On top of being the best all-around athlete at McVeigh, he scored A's in all of his subjects. His folks owned a sportswear factory where 400 women worked. "About as much as I can handle in my present condition," M. R. used to say. He was the one who said the whole idea of nationality was nonsense.

Dickie, who was sore because M. R. stepped on his story of the Mexican girl, cracked, "It don't make any difference to Mickey, so long as it's got hair."

"Hair or crepe de chine, it's all good," M. R. said. "The point we're hammering out is, what's the best? I used to think the best was the one you just had. Well, I was wrong."

The wise guy, Dickie, mocked, "What is it, then; the one you haven't had yet?"

"*Give* that gentleman a giant economy size package of chocolate-covered buffalo chips," M. R. said, like Dr. I.Q. on the radio. "That's exactly the right answer." He looked at Gilberto. "No?"

"I'll say!" Gilberto agreed.

He was, then, just starting to go around with Carolyn Muller.

24

The Sheik of Araby, they told him in Mante, made the 112 kilometer run to Ciudad del Maíz.

The day was burning itself out. The sun had not time to finish wringing all the water out of the leaves and, as Gilberto crossed the rutted, diagonal path through the central square, drops rattled on his new hat.

"El Jeque de Arabia" was lettered in alternate white and yellow on the prow of the bus. The door closed, and it started as soon as he stepped aboard.

It must be the driver who rejoiced in the name of El Jeque, not the bus. He might be an Arabian or a gypsy, Gilberto thought, from the color of his skin. His hair came down to the line of his mouth, in long sideburns. His clothes were dead black, of hard finished worsted, and he wore high-heeled shoes with rubber side-gussets. When he accepted Gilberto's fare, he thanked him and gave him a thin strip of ticket. He handled the car well and without theatrics.

Gilberto had learned to look, out of simple curiosity, for the religious image at the top of the windshield. This one was new to him. It was a little doll, not more than four inches tall, with fine hair and a tiny gilt crown. It was draped in a flaring cape of the same yellow material out of which rain-slickers are made. On each side of the image, in miniature vases, were buds of jasmine, fresh and sweet-smelling. "Nuestra Señora de San Juan de los Lagos," he read.

Quite as prominently displayed next to her was a picture postcard in color, showing a bullfighter leaning over between the bull's horns and putting in the banderillas. The title under the picture was *El Par de Gaona*.

There were four other passengers in the bus; five, counting a baby, whose little paw stuck up out of its mother's rebozo.

The interior of the bus was plastered with stickers. Facing the entrance was one "supplicating" you to pay your fare in "fractional money." It was "sternly prohibited" to carry explosives or combustibles aboard. There were warnings against spitting, projecting heads or arms from the windows, and ejecting garbage. "No Distraiga al Chofer." For the departing passenger, a placard read "Dios Te Acompañe." The bottom and greater half of all the cards advertised a nasal jelly.

He watched the scenery—eroded bluffs, mouse-bitten cakes of differently colored layers. Flat patches of land had a burnt-toast appearance. A hemisphere of sun still showed over the hills ahead.

They climbed for a long time and he saw tall, thick-trunked trees, with their lowest branches higher than a man could reach. Norway pines was his first guess, but he knew that was wrong. What were trees of the fir family doing down here, in the Tropic of Cancer? Bananas belong in this country; plantain, cassava root, quebracho should be flourishing here. Outside of bananas, he had no idea what the other things were. But he had read about them and, of course, seen the movies—the ones in which the steaming jungle breaks down the moral fibre of the white man, unless he is of the stuff that—

> *"Rick Reyes, Commissioner, the young man we're sending down to the Mana-*
> *jora Station to relieve— Ah, yes—poor Davy Niven—we're taking him out—*
> *if there's enough left of that fine public school mind to bother saving. Bleeding*
> *shame a dart from a native blowgun didn't get him instead of the sweet poison*
> *of that native woman, Ngoona. Be careful of her, Rick, my boy—that's a witch*
> *incarnate. Keep yourself clean, boy—for her . . . "*

Jeez, how he missed the movies. Must be ten days now since he'd seen a good picture. And there's nothing like a good "A" production. It's not only while you're watching it; it's that it *leaves* you with something. You come out of the Four Star and the people you see around you look like the inside pages of yesterday's newspaper. And if it's a really super film, that feeling you came out with could last as much as a couple of hours.

A flock of shrieking birds hurled themselves across the road. There was enough light to see that they were big green and yellow parrots. It didn't surprise him; he felt as if he ordered them to be there.

The baby across the aisle let out a few tentative wails and thrashed its fists, as brown and about the same size as walnuts. The mother unveiled it and it stopped crying immediately. All it wanted was to have a look around; it had a right, and he was glad to see that its mother recognized that. She was aware of his glance and deliberately turned the baby around in her arms so that he could see it better. He looked at it, and it looked straight back at him; its little mouth like a third eye. The mother watched him, too; hungry for the praise, implicit in a stranger's slightest smile. Well—what would it cost him to crack a little grin? It promptly started to wail again, working its lips, fishlike.

"Ay, greedy—you little bear cub," the mother scolded. And without un-buttoning anything, with just a twitch of one shoulder, she exposed a tawny brown, globular breast.

He felt a slight revulsion at first, and gradually took a clinical interest in the apparatus. When the baby clamped onto the thick, almost black nipple, the mother's face softened. It looked to him as if she was getting as much kick out of this as the baby.

After a few minutes, he saw her wince and suck in her breath, in pain. But the smile didn't leave her face. He was aware that the baby had bitten her, but he was sure that no expression of sympathy was called for.

"Wolf!" she said to the baby. "Tiger!" and explained to him, "Teeth like needles; four of them."

"Pretty young to have that many," he said.

"Five months."

The little son of a gun—as if it knew they were talking about him, or her, took its mouth away, turned completely around, and looked Gilberto straight in the eye. It rather pleased him to get this recognition from the baby.

"Boy or girl?" he asked.

"Girl."

"And what is her name?"

"María Luz Gutiérrez, a sus órdenes."

He wanted to say something very nice about María Luz Gutiérrez, and finally settled on, "She will get a very handsome husband."

"You are very agreeable to say that, señor. . . . Do you hear, you ugly one, what this gentleman wished for you?"

The thing bored her and she went to sleep. It was night, anyhow. Green had become black. The Sheik had switched on the headlights.

Reaching into his coat pocket, Gilberto, by tactile sense, distinguished the separate textures of the contents until he felt the membrane-like air mail envelope and drew it out. Soon he would have to be inquiring about this relative, and she had a rather complicated name.

As he opened the letter, the dome lights in the bus went on. The Sheik must have seen that he was trying to read.

He glanced at the "signature" first—Esperanza Santibáñez Vda. de Reyes. Then a snatch here and there— "I have the pleasure to advise you— your gracious gift—Humble thanks in my own name and in the name of my daughter, Inés.—To you, Dear Cousin, and to your son—deep shame only this little medal to send you—"

He put the letter back in his pocket. . . . If Mrs. Esperanza Santibáñez And-so-forth could know how handy that little medal turned out to be! Without it, he bet he would still be in Laredo or somewhere, with his skull bleaching on the desert. He admitted to himself that it was a pretty cheap trick to palm it off on Bishop as something blessed by a high Church dignitary at the Guadalupe shrine. And the way he acted over being handed it— like it was the jackpot on one of those big quiz programs. Well, he wished him and his girl luck with it.

Now—what was he going to call this Mexican lady when he finally got to see her? If, as she signed herself, she was his mother's cousin, it might be the proper thing to call her Aunt—Tía. Tía what? Tía Esperanza or Tía Santi-báñez? He would see. And this kid who got the confirmation dress—she was probably entitled to be called Cousin.

Whatever it was, he assumed that he would get a friendly reception. She had written, "My house is yours and all that is in it." And right under the thumbprint, there was the typewritten phrase which served as her address: "Conocida en el Barrio Tres Cenotes." That means they knew her in Three Wells. It might also mean that she was prominent—

Maybe she had a ranch, like the Widow in the Red Ryder westerns—

> *"Listen here, all you vaqueros, want you to meet my nevview, Slim Reyes. Never laid eyes on him till now, but I can see he's a Reyes down to the heels. So let's knock off and git ready for a big barbecue in this boy's honor. Tune up your guitars, and tell all the muchachas to put on their best bib and tucker."*

How childish this was, he reflected, but it amused him, so why not play out the whole silly string? . . . In the morning, naturally, the hands would slip him a poison-mean, man-killing bronco to ride, just to see if he could gentle the cayuse. In one minute he would have it caracoling like a circus horse, and he would ask those waddies, "Where'd you get this one—off a merry-go-round?"

Better than a cattle ranch, he wished his aunt owned an orange grove; like they have between Tustin and Fullerton, back in California. Trees were better than cattle; they stay where they grow up. You take care of them, spray them, irrigate them, and they're always beautiful. When they're blossoming, the smell makes you feel as if you're walking without touching the ground. And when the fruit is ripe, there isn't a Christmas tree in any department store window that's as pretty.

And, for that matter, what was wrong with lemons? Those big, fat Ponderosas, that ate as sweet as a plum. The best he'd ever had were off that tree on the Sumimura's place out beyond Palos Verdes; from where you could see way out over the Pacific Ocean, to a big rock where the seals rested.

He couldn't have been more than seven when he met the Sumimuras; Mister and Mrs., and her brother, Frank. He and his mother had gotten off the trolley at the last stop, Palos Verdes Estates, a place with tremendous iron gates guarding the beautiful homes that stretched out in a curve beyond. They couldn't go in there, so they walked, keeping the ocean in sight, a mile or two, until they came to a place where there was no fence.

The ground was all covered with yellow poppies and they sat down to have their picnic lunch. A white horse walked up and Gilberto gave him a piece of his jelly sandwich. The horse kept hanging around and tried to get his nose into their basket. Pretty soon, a short man in khaki breeches with wraparound leggings came up. That was Mr. Sumimura.

His mother said that if this was private property, she was sorry and they would go. Mr. Sumimura said it was all right, they could stay as long as they liked. He told them the horse's name was Nikko, sat Gilberto up on him, and led him around for a while.

Later, the other one, Frank, came up to them with a little strawberry carton full of plums and said, "Please take." On his own, Gilberto insisted that the man take some cookies and eat them right there. Frank liked them, too. Then he made them come with him to the cottage for—the way he said it—remonade.

That was lemonade! Out of those big Ponderosa lemons. No sugar; just squeeze half of one into a glass of cold water, and man, you've got a drink.

They went back there—it was a tomato farm the Sumimuras leased— many Sundays after that. Sometimes Gilberto went by himself. Nikko got to know him, too. When they told him that they would have to sell Nikko as soon as the tractor they ordered came, he wanted to save his money to buy the horse.

The last time he went, the place where he and his mother used to stand and watch the seals was all torn up. Big Transit Mix trucks kept pulling up, one after the other, dumping cement. They were building anti-aircraft emplacements, and Military Police were all over the place.

At the Sumimuras' there was a new tractor, but an American fellow in overalls was driving it, tearing up the tomato plants. Inside the cottage, a radio was playing—they didn't know the Sumimuras had one. He asked about them, and the answer he got was that they were evacuated. Nikko, too—the shed in back of the cottage was empty.

The things a fellow thinks about on a long bus ride!

He still held the letter in his hand. Putting it back, he felt the wallet. The last time he had it out was back in Victoria. He had been scanning it for some reason. Flipping it open, he glanced at the first frame: his mother. Second— he'd been there before—blank. Third frame, his membership card in the McVeigh High School Athletic Association. *This is to certify that* G. REYES, *Class* SOPH., *is a Member in Good Standing*—. It had the signatures of Michael Rosenstock, Jr.—good old M. R.—and Myles J. Morrissey, Faculty Adviser. *See Other Side.* He turned it over: *Presentation of this Card Entitles Bearer to 10% Discount on Athletic Equipment (as specified) when Purchased at the Following Stores*—

That "as specified" was the joker in the deal—no discount on anything you could possibly use. But if you wanted a lacrosse bat or a three-toned referee's whistle, they'd give you the ten percent, even fifteen.

He ripped the card in half and threw it out of the window.

The fourth frame of the wallet was loaded. First, there was his original registration card. Dated more than a year back, it certified that Mr. Gilberto Reyes had complied with the Selective Service Law. It had given him great satisfaction to give the data required to the clerk and to get that card to keep. There was a feeling of belonging about that act. Several million fellows at the same time were stepping up and giving the same data, as individuals, then stepping away as members of a vast fraternity. Each one of them was no doubt told the same thing: "Carry this card with you at all times. Show it when you are called upon by the proper authorities."

He supposed those two Narcotics Squad detectives who braced him one night in a bowling alley on Santa Monica Boulevard were proper authorities.

There were maybe twenty fellows in the place, which had accommodations for spectators. There must have been twenty or more older people watching the bowling teams, when these two fellows came in and started peering into people's faces. Gilberto had a hunch that they would light on him, and they did, calling him out into the aisle between two rows of seats.

The first thing they asked for naturally was his draft card, but they weren't satisfied with that. They looked through everything in his wallet. When they were tearing the paper off some of his cigarettes to see if maybe he wasn't concealing a few sticks of tea among them, the owner of the alleys, a man named Kedzie, came over and asked them what they meant by molesting his customers.

"This punk a customer of yours?" one of the cops asked.

Kedzie, who had never seen Gilberto before, said, "He's here with my permission. This is a public amusement place, and he doesn't need it. Incidentally, let's see *your* credentials."

The cops said they already showed their shields to the boy.

"You're in my place. You show them to me," Kedzie insisted. They showed them all right. They weren't dealing with a dope.

They seemed disappointed that they didn't find a spring-knife or anything like that on Gilberto, so they went back to his draft card. "Reyes, huh? How old are you?"

"It says there."

"Mex?" They didn't even say "Mexican." And it was plainly marked on the card: *Born*: 4/12/33, Los Angeles, Calif.

"What are you doing in this part of town?"

What could he answer; that he was low on money and that it cost nothing to sit here, bothering nobody, and watching a couple of bowling teams? But before he could say anything, the owner broke in.

"If you fellows want to make a showing or something, take this fellow outside. Otherwise, if you want to bother people in here, just lemme make a note of your badge numbers."

"Wiser guys than you have been closed up," one of the detectives said.

Kedzie answered right back, "I've been in business here a long time. All my licenses—beer, City, and State—are paid up. So is my insurance against holdups—by hoodlums as well as cops—in case you're figuring on anything."

That got them out in a hurry. Kedzie asked Gilberto to show him the paper they were so interested in and nodded as he examined it. He shook his head as he gave it back and said, "Papers! I got plenty of them, too; all framed, behind the cash register. . . . I don't know what the hell is happening these days, but I remember a time when you carried your name and address in your head, and if anybody stopped you and asked you to show proof, you could spit in his eye. Papers, papers . . ."

There were two more papers in that section of his wallet—no, three, counting the letter from General Hershey.

Card number two was the same size as the first. It came a few days after his appearance before the draft board in his own district, where they gave him his first physical and took his entire pedigree. This one left out the Mr. It read simply: Gilberto Reyes, Selective Service Classification 1-A.

Then the general's letter telling him of his "selection." Finally, the ultimate postal card. He smoothed it out. The address was no longer Mr. or even Gilberto Reyes. It was Reyes, G. #23328-37, put on with an addressograph. This was the payoff—the induction notice itself; the genuine article. "Report not later than 7:00 a.m. (Fri.) 17 Oct. 1952, at Portico, US Federal Bldg., 2nd and Spring Sts."

That was supposed to be yesterday—maybe the day before. It didn't make much difference. He put the whole batch, the cards and the letter, together, and slowly began tearing them into tiny, confetti-sized pieces.

It was easy to figure what went on in the Federal Building when they called the roll and there was no Reyes, G., #23328-37. They were hunting him down, naturally; like that character carrying the plague in the picture *Panic*. Getting out the dragnet like they did for the beautiful half-Chinese dame called Sally Lung, the Leper, in another one—a re-issue; a real oldie, but good.

They were slapping it on the teletype now—*Code 44*. Tap-tap-tap-tap-tap—*Male—Age 19—White—correction Mexican—Repeat, Mexican—five foot ten—stocky build—Detain as deserter from United States Armed Forces—Visit your nearest blood bank.*

His fist was full of shredded paper. The Sheik had opened the door of the bus to let the spicy air circulate. It tasted like Juicy Fruit chewing gum.

The baby's mother sighed and fanned herself with a corner of her rebozo. "Ay, the Warm Land, at last."

She was telling *him!* Didn't he spot the sign when they entered the Tropics, before anybody?

She undraped the baby and sat it up on her lap, facing around, wearing only a little shirt that scarcely reached to its belly button.

He began whistling "Moon of Malakura"; what else would come to mind at a time like this? Talk about your theme songs; this was one for all time—once heard, never forgotten. It was like knowing one hymn and suddenly finding that the occasion calls for it.

The baby fixed its far-sighted gaze on his pursed lips, moving its own, as if trying to imitate him. Its eyes followed his hand as, pinch by pinch, he dropped the bits of paper out of the window, sowing them on the warm wind.

25

Ciudad del Maíz was entered from darkness to sudden light.

The plaza, rigidly four-square, like all of them, appeared to be hanging in space like a pavillion. What else there was of the town lay all around, in the dark blue night.

He had come through a quarter of the settlement—perhaps through all of it; he didn't know. He would find out in the morning, if he was still here; and if he never knew, that would be all right, too. He had only a shallow curiosity about the houses, the porous bulks of which he felt, rather than saw, in the quavering headlights.

These must be gloomy citizens, he surmised. Their tiny fires gave only the ruby glow of a darkroom bulb. The sounds the people made—cheerful, at first, but they fooled you. Something that started as a laugh, finished as a bubbling sob. Even the music that he caught, between the labored squeaks of the bus, was a snatch from one of the saddest songs in the language: "Borrachita, me voy; hasta la capital, para servir al patrón . . ." A guy with a hangover, telling his drunken doll that he finally has to go to work; he's two days late.

On top of that unhappy lyric, a tiny radio squawked out a commercial on the subject of dolor de cabeza latente—headache, the dull, persistent kind that will not respond to ordinary remedies.

So, here, in this plaza, must be where all the night life of the town took place. But, what he saw of it, he judged, could just as easily be conducted back there, in the shadows.

Some refreshment stands were open, and whatever it was the people bought, it was always washed down with a bottle of soda water. The light standards were too high and the bulbs too weak to give more than a pallid, amber light. Big moths pinged against them in suicide dives.

A few people—he counted four—sat, each by himself, on the benches. They seemed to sit, not for enjoyment, not to watch the strollers, or to think idly on the design of the universe; but only to relieve themselves of weariness.

He could hear music—a mambo, which ought to be played *con brío*; but it sounded like a minuet. It came from a loudspeaker wired to a stanchion supporting the bandstand. A hearty voice announced the time—twenty hours, fourteen minutes—and a couple of sopranos shrieked how they adored their slices of Bimbo Brand Bread, thickly spread with butter and mermelada.

He could go for some of that, too, right now. When was his last meal? Way back in Victoria. This was bad—this skipping meals, catching up later. First, he had a problem that was more urgent: transportation to Zaragoza. But if it had to be by horse, it would have to wait until tomorrow. Meanwhile, a hotel. Any one of those buildings on the built-up, livelier side of the plaza could be a hotel. This was rural Mexico, not even Victoria. You don't look for fancy marquees and uniformed carriage starters around here.

Whatever he encountered first—restaurant or hotel—he decided he would enter. It might be a combined establishment.

Passing them, one by one, he saw that not one of the buildings was either a hotel or a restaurant. In fact, they looked duller close up than they had from the other side of the square. One of three places that was doing business was a cantina called The Four Seasons. The second was a bonetería—a notions store, the kind of a place where you could still buy a collar button. The last establishment was a low, mud colored box, hung on the outside with strips of faded crepe paper. The place had no door, only a rough gash in the wall, out of which rolled a powerful, acidy stink. He passed it rapidly, making for the other side of the street, but still parallel to the plaza.

Here, there were no permanent buildings, only stands. These were often plain boards laid on the ground or merely a cloth. Some were slightly off the ground, elevated on bricks, tended by people seated on the dirt. Others were slightly higher, and some displayed their goods at a level that you didn't have to crane down to see.

Food—raw and cooked—was the main stock offered at all of these puestos. One had pyramids of tomatoes, each identical in height. Take your choice at twenty centavos. Dried peppers were laid out like the pelts of tiny animals. There was hard, pearly corn in measures, mounds of seeds of a kind he had never seen before, and hands of huge bananas.

Every third vendor had cooked food for sale; all kinds of stuff, ladled out on tortillas from tubs wrapped thickly in rags and newspaper. Ponds of fat bubbled in braziers and gave off the odors of charcoal and frying fish.

Somebody called to him; an old woman squatting by her fire urged him to try her tacos. "¡Son finos y gordos, y dulces como caña!" Fine and fat and sweet as sugar cane! Yes, indeed; they were all of that. So were the ones at the ferry.

At a few of the puestos, candles burned in fragile lanterns. But most of them borrowed their light from a Coleman lamp over the largest and what appeared to be the cleanest food stand. The young man tending it wore an apron and agitated some frying meat on a griddle.

The raw materials were in a row of bread tins; sliced onions, chorizo, the peppery Spanish-type sausage and the lipstick-red hot dogs of the country. And there, big as life, but many times as attractive, lay, breast upward, an entire boiled chicken. That, Gilberto decided, was for him.

"Your servant, sir—"

"If you will just lay some slices of that fowl on a tortilla, it will suit my taste perfectly."

"Breast or thigh, my boss?"

"Some of both, if you please."

Hacking thick slabs of meat off the bird, the man put them on a tortilla. "Some mole?" he asked, stirring a kettle of brown sauce invitingly.

Gilberto knew mole of old; it could be brutally hot. "If it is not too picante."

"Middling; it is of the style of Puebla."

"A dab, then."

Hey! This was good. The sauce gave the chicken meat just the personality it needed. The first time Verónica La Negra laid a plate of turkey-in-mole in front of him and said that chocolate was what gave it that color, he wouldn't touch it. "So!" she had snorted, "Christian cooking isn't good enough for you! Go! Go to the Chinese restaurant, where they cook pork and pineapple together! Ugh!"

He chewed and nodded with pleasure, motioning for one more of the same. "Got a cold drink?"

There were many varieties of bottled soda, but all of them al tiempo— lukewarm. He drank a bottle taken at random from the counter.

"Would it be worth the pain to go as far as Zaragoza yet tonight?" he asked his host as he ate.

"That is for one to choose, but the bus is still here. Who knows when it will depart?"

"Here—where?"

At the curb behind him, not more than twenty feet from the refreshment stand, was a veteran Chevrolet, school bus model; a 1936 or older. It had once been painted orange, and under that, a slate gray; but there was as much rusty body metal showing as there was paint of either color. Only two of the windows had any glass at all; the rest were boarded up, or chicken wire had been nailed over the frames. It had no door, it showed no parking lights, and, altogether, it had the appearance of being abandoned.

"That is the one, then?" Gilberto asked.

"To Zaragoza, yes. There appear to be other passengers, as well."

He counted three—a man and two women, seated on the ground, their backs against a fence.

"How long does it take for the run?"

"An hour—two; unless the machine is discomposed. But Lucas operates it skillfully, when he is himself."

"Well, thank you very much." He finished the food, ordered a package of cigarettes and one of matches; and asked how much he had to pay altogether.

The bottle of refresco was 30 centavos; the cigarettes, 45; the matches, again 30. As for the meal of chicken, the vendor couldn't say. "I leave it to you, señor, to set a fair price for that."

Gilberto declined. "Whatever you say. You know what you pay for chickens."

"I raise them. They cost little. It is hard to estimate. Please, señor—"

Too much would make him a sucker; too little, a cheapskate."Will five pesos cover everything?"

"That is too much," the man protested.

"It was worth it."

"In that case, assured of your satisfaction, I will accept it. And many thanks."

There were four people waiting for the bus, not three. The overlapping shadows cast by the fence and the bulk of the parked machine hid a child cradled in a man's lap. It was a boy about six years old, asleep in the folds of a serape. The kid slept badly, breathing heavily and grinding his teeth.

A few feet away, a thin, middle-aged woman, barefoot, sat on a sack; and beside her, a girl of about twelve. She had been watching him as he approached and, when he was near enough, gave him a long, frank look and went back to nibbling at a piece of sugar cane; stripping away the husk and tearing at it like a puppy. Her face was not clean, but she had carefully woven into her hair some lengths of colored yarn; and her earrings were ridiculously large for a kid of her size.

The two parents nodded and said good evening, and the girl piped in belatedly when her mother elbowed her.

"And a very good evening to you, damas y caballeros. You are all waiting for this camión to Zaragoza?"

The man answered in a mild, beautifully soft voice. "I go further—to the sugar works. But the ladies, I think, live in Zaragoza."

"A short way distant," the woman said. "By the Quinta Cantaranas."

"Do we start soon?"

"When there are five passengers," the man said. "Don Lucas will not carry less than five. He gains nothing, he says."

So it was Don Lucas; the man evidently had some respect for the operator of the bus. "There are five of us, now," Gilberto said.

"Four and a half," the man smiled, looking down at the sleeping boy in his lap. "He is only nine, therefore I pay for him only one-half of the two pesos, fifty centavos."

"With your permission, if that is all that is delaying us, if you will allow me—"

"No, señor; that is not just, not proper." The man looked at the woman for support of his opinion. "Have I not reason, señora?"

"Without doubt," she said. "There should be no penalty for this kind, young man." And she added shrewdly, "Unless, of course, it is a matter of great emergency for him."

"If that were the case," the man said, "one usually pays a premium for the special convenience."

Gilberto realized that his presence here served to bring people who would have remained strangers to each other, together. He had given them, also, a subject for conversation. Again, he admired the formal way in which these people discussed things. Though the man was obviously an azucarero—a sugar worker—and the woman, who knows? but certainly poor, their speech sounded educated, almost refined, to him.

"Suppose we put it this way: The señora has reason in remarking that for me, myself, to leave early is urgent. So, I will pay an additional half-fare for myself."

That wasn't the way he would have put it in speaking English, but now he found himself caught up, like the others, in the formal phrasing of the commonest remarks. He finished: "That, I think, should earn agreement."

The azucarero and the woman took a silent vote. "Agreed," she said.

"Equally," the man said. "I will go tell Don Lucas. What is the hour, please?"

"One half after twenty hours. Do you know where he is?"

"I think so." The man looked down at his sleeping son. It was a slow stare, with more than paternal devotion in it. Further, it implied that if it were not a matter of the boy's comfort, he would already be running.

Gilberto understood and offered him a cigarette. The woman declined one, saying, "But out of your kindness, señor, a match, or two."

He gave her the few that remained in his old pack of cerillos. They really were not wax, but tightly rolled paper impregnated with wax.

"I am told that this machine has no regular schedule; that one cannot rely on getting to Zaragoza within a fixed time."

This started something. "Ah, the young señor has traveled much, I see," the sugar worker began. "And he has perhaps encountered acts of God. Everyone has, who has put foot out of his house."

"That is true."

"Then Lucas Quintero, the owner of that camión, is subject to the same forces—the destruction of the bridge at Aguas Dulces, the depth of the water at the ford by Arenal, a burst tire—"

"Look—mariachis!" the girl yelled, and pointing, scrambled to her feet.

"Be quiet, slut," the mother commanded. "The gentlemen are talking. . . . Where?"

Four musicians stood across the street, by a bench beneath a tree; two guitars, a violin, and a cornet. They stood, ready to play and watching for their patrons to approach. Two women, both old, sedate, and stern-faced, with a young man walking between them, came slowly toward the musicians. The boy was twenty or thereabouts, tall, and dressed neatly in black trousers, clean white shirt, and black tie.

At the approach of the group, the musicians began "Las Mañanitas," traditionally sung at dawn to somebody having a birthday anniversary. It was the boy who was being honored. Smiling, he sat down on the bench between the two women.

Near Gilberto, and showing off a bit, the girl began singing, "Estas son las mañanitas que cantaba el Rey David—"

The mother let her sing, even nodded her head in time with the music and hummed, as the girl went on, "Y a las muchachas bonitas se las cantaban así—"

"Ay, pobrecito—to be blind at his age," the woman sighed.

"Yes, *that* is an affliction," the man said. The music woke his boy, who squirmed out of the serape and looked brightly at the mariachi quartet. "Here, son—" from under his own serape, his father handed the child a crutch; a homemade job, and it looked new. The kid tucked the crutch under his arm and stood up with his help. His right leg, from the knee, had been amputated.

Gilberto looked quickly away from the pinned-up overall leg, and to the boy's face. They smiled at each other.

The father, aside, and in a very low voice, said to Gilberto's ear, "A careless stroke with the machete in cutting the cane. . . . Perspiration gets in a man's eyes and blurs the vision."

Gilberto wanted to say, "An act of God." Instead, he asked the boy's name.

"Angel Fierro Alvarez, a sus órdenes," the father answered for him.

The boy said, "I have nine years," and offered his hand.

The girl, from beside her mother, said, "My name is Concha. I have fourteen years."

"Trollop! Nobody asked you," her mother hissed and turned to Gilberto. "And you are called, señor—"

"Gilberto—" with a nod to the others. "Gilberto Reyes." It sounded incomplete; the at-your-service was missing and his mother's family name should have been given. But he didn't think of it in time, and the attention of the others was on the music again.

The blind boy's two guardians sat stiffly, but he smiled broadly and tapped his foot. It was a new air, a paso doble.

"I can dance, if you don't believe it," Concha boasted childlishly. "Hua-pangos, jarabes, and jiterboges, too."

"That's nice," Gilberto said, and spoke louder, so that Angel could hear, too. "I'll bet Angel here dances as good as you when he gets to be fourteen."

"You joke, señor," Angel said. "With only one leg?"

"Why, I've *seen* dancers with my own eyes in theatres—people pay to see them; dancing with one leg better than most people with two." Before the boy could ask for details, Gilberto turned abruptly to the father. "What passes with the driver, señor?"

The azucarero slapped his knee, "That Lucas! I go directly."

They watched him move off to the right and enter the low, dingy building festooned with paper, which Gilberto had seen before.

The woman sighed, "Where else but in the pulquería?"

The boy, Angel, tugged at Gilberto's sleeve; something he wanted to tell him. He bent down. "It was not my father's fault. He cried more than I did."

The music finished. The trumpet stepped forward to the bench, apparently to ask what else they wished to hear. He got his reply and led the others in a fresh tune.

Concha didn't like this one; she made a face. "That old 'Tecolote'—" she sniffed. "Why don't they play something to—" Her complaint ended abruptly at the approach of a peddler selling water-ice. The vendor, bowed over by the weight of the box he carried on his back, cried, "Nieve, nieve—" and one of the two women with the blind boy beckoned him. They bought a small block of water-ice on a stick and folded the boy's hand around it.

Gilberto bought one each for Angel and Concha. Later, when the peddler was gone and he saw the hungry eyes of Concha's mother watching the girl greedily licking the ice, he regretted not having bought another.

"El Tecolote" was finished. The silence was sudden and heavy, and they could plainly hear the trumpet ask, "Now, is there something the young man would like to hear?"

The blind boy stood up to answer. "Sí, maestro; one song I like very much. It would please my taste very much." He raised his head and spoke upward, to a point over the heads of the musicians, as blind persons do. "It is called 'Baila Negra.' "

The younger of the two women firmly cancelled the boy's request by waving her finger at the musicians. They got it; at least the cornet player did and said, warning the others, "I'm sorry, we don't know that one."

The blind boy smiled unbelievingly. "It's sung much. 'Baila Negra'—" And he began, in a hoarse, cracked voice to sing, "Baila negra, ta-ta-ra-ta; baila negra, pom-pa-rom-pa—"

The woman shook her head again violently.

"Sorry señor, we can't accommodate you."

" 'La Macarena,' " the other woman called out. That is the music played at the entrance of bullfighters into the arena. It honors the Spanish Virgin of Macarena.

Concha's mother spat on the ground and cursed, "Gachupinas chingadas!"

When the last note ended, one of the boy's guardians handed the trumpeter some money. Then, both, taking his arms, faced him in the direction from which they came and walked rapidly away. The musicians stood there, staring.

"He comes," Concha's mother announced, rising and taking a few twists on the mouth of the sack on which she had been sitting.

They watched the approach of Angel's father, his arm linked with that of a squat, powerful man, whose hair was tousled as after a fight. Lucas—Don Lucas, if you please—wore patched gray trousers and a denim jacket with no shirt under it. The azucarero was carrying his hat.

Lucas didn't appear to need support. He walked straight; too straight, Gilberto thought, on second look. He had seen enough drunken men navigating a straight line on the sidewalk. And as he got closer, he caught that same nauseating smell that rolled out of the pulquería.

At the steps of the bus, Lucas shrugged the other man's arm off and sat down at the wheel. For a moment it appeared that he was "himself," until he let his arms slide off the steering wheel, to hang straight at his sides. And while he sat that way, breathing heavily through his nose, Angel's father motioned for the others to get in.

Gilberto lifted Angel into the car. Concha came up directly behind him, while he was still holding the boy. Her slender, bony little body pressed against him; her sharp, pelvic frame moulded along the curve of his hips. She squirmed, secretly hot and disturbing. What the hell is going on? he thought, and drew himself aside. As she passed him, she looked straight up into his face and said, "Hola, guapo."

"Andale," her mother urged, pushing her forward, "Stop this coquetting."

They took the two cross-seats on the right side of the bus. Angel got into the seat opposite them, behind Gilberto, who sat down on one of the two benches that faced each other lengthwise, undivided. He would have preferred to sit to the rear of Concha, but decided it would be better to stay nearer the boy.

Angel's father stood in the entrance, and touched Lucas's shoulder gently. "Let's go, Don Lucas—"

The man put his hands on the wheel again and they slipped off. His head fell forward on his chest, and he sat motionless once more.

Gilberto made a gesture of doubt and inquiry, but the azucarero answered with a calming wave of his hand and his lips formed the words, "It's all right." He shook Lucas again, and with forced heartiness sang out, "We're ready!"

"Cobrador!" Lucas shouted, standing up suddenly, swaying, and sliding back into his seat.

"Ay, the poor man," said Concha's mother. "He imagines he is still pilot of the grandiose coach of the Comet Fleet he once ran; when he had a cobrador *and* an assistant."

"The drink?" Gilberto inquired.

"The pulque. It has done worse to better men."

"Vámonos," Angel's father tried again.

"I don't move!" Lucas turned around to shout. "Not one chingada meter does this apparatus advance until every chingada soul aboard has paid his passage."

"Let's pay him," Angel's father urged, coming forward. Gilberto found three pesos and seventy-five centavos. The woman paid out of a knotted handkerchief.

Without counting the money, Lucas pushed the coins into his jacket pocket. Several coppers dribbled to the floor. Angel's father gathered them up and handed them back, remaining beside Lucas, as if for further orders.

For a minute there, Lucas acted as if he knew what he was doing. He found his keys, turned on the ignition, pulled the choke out an inch, and in general made the right moves. Then, he made one move that ruined the whole effect; he turned on the headlights before stepping on the starter.

The lights flickered and weakened almost to extinction as the starter-motor took the current. But from the sound of it, Gilberto knew there wasn't enough there to kick this motor into action. He called over, "Tell him to turn off the lights, they're draining too much juice."

The man shook his finger—you don't tell Don Lucas his business.

"Don't stand there!" Lucas growled. "Grab that chingada crank," and kicked it into view.

The man went to work with it—with the lights still on. A few turns and the engine caught, bucked, and almost stalled. And it was already rolling when Angel's father caught the handle and climbed in.

Lucas stayed in second for several hundred yards of pavement and then, slowing down, went into first just at the instant the front wheels thumped down into rutted dirt. That was okay. The man seemed to know his machine and the road, both.

This was the narrowest so far of Gilberto's entire trip; a high crowned, dusty alley between overhanging trees and out-jutting scrub. Two cars, he judged, *might* be able to pass each other—with a prayer.

Lucas settled down to his work. The sugar worker smiled pridefully from his bench opposite Gilberto; as near as he could come to his hero.

Apparently, the guy knew the road, no matter what his condition, and had lived with this heap for a long time. They were going level, the accelerator was depressed to the last notch, and still they were doing 30—around there. Unless they struck a downgrade, nothing very serious could happen, even if he left the road.

After a few kilometers, Lucas belched loudly and foully, and shouted, "Cigarro!" at the top of his lungs. While he still held the "o," the azucarero motioned to Gilberto for a cigarette, and lit one for Lucas and one for himself.

There wasn't much to see out of, except through the windshield. The window beside Gilberto was boarded up; the one facing him, caked with dirt. He just hoped for no so-called acts of God. "You said something about a bridge," he called.

"Do not pre-occupy yourself," the sugar worker said. "It is at Aguas Dulces, twenty kilometers farther on, at the head of the valley."

"How high is the Río Arenal, papá?" Angel wanted to know.

"You remember, son; or were you asleep? We crossed the dry stones."

"Has rain fallen around here since?" Gilberto asked.

"God makes it to rain somewhere—every day, señor. Is it not true?" the man asked, as if he had heard it as a rumor and wanted the facts.

"It is true—I suppose."

Concha's mother, looking as if she wanted a piece of this conversation, left her seat and came forward, first warning her daughter, "You, bitch; you stay seated." She unfolded a small piece of paper and showed it to Gilberto. "Out of your kindness, señor, would you read what it says on this little paper?"

As he took it, the woman sat down beside him. It was a leaf torn out of a notebook, and had a blurry name rubber stamped on top.

"It is a prescription. Ampules—those are little bottles of glass, señora—of Penicilina-Procaína. Four of them; each containing two hundred M—two hundred thousand units, that is to say. To be injected; one ampule every four hours."

"You have read that nobly, señor Reyes. I have the botellitas. Does it say where they are to be injected?"

"I'd say in the hip." He used the word cadera.

"Claro, in the nalgas." Her word meant buttocks. He nodded and handed the paper back. "Are you a doctor, then, that you can translate these directions so clearly?"

"No, señora."

"From your bag, I thought perhaps—"

"No; however, I have heard of this cure. It is the latest thing. You need not worry."

"It is not me you have to be sympathetic with. It is that one." She snapped her head toward her daughter, who sat behind them sulking. "It's that woman-of-the-gallant-life. That was how he translated mujer de vida galante."

"She!" the woman went on, "She's the one who has the infirmity. Possibly a bastard as well; but that we don't know for certain, yet."

Shocked, Gilberto swung his head to look at the girl again. She was waiting for this, apparently; she heard, and she knew he would look. So, she gave him something to see. She extended the red tip of her tongue provocatively between her lips, and ran it back and forth.

He blushed so that the warmth of it itched. What the hell! He was no saint—not more than a few hours ago he had been to the mat—but—well— here was a punk kid—

The woman kept on talking. "Break her shameless back, and do you think she would tell who it was who took her? And if she did, a lot of good it would do."

He wasn't listening.

26

His mind was on the frozen figures in the tableaux of that day. The paunchy man with the suspenders *and* belt sweating by his Pontiac. The Sheik of Araby. The creeping beggar. The blind fellow and his jolly birthday party. The kid, Angel, sitting behind him, missing a leg. And now this—this pissy-pants, who you'd expect to be playing with dolls, already clapped up.

And me, he thought, going along for nineteen lousy years, a shmo—Mickey Rosenstock claimed the right word was *shmuck*, which, to quote M. R., "is a Jewish term for a ball-bearing *putz*." Anyway—you go along for nineteen years in a fog and, suddenly, in one day, you know everything.

The girl's mother was still yammering beside him. "The one for injections," he heard, "is Don Solomón's Elena. A hand as light as—"

"Don Solomón?"

"You know of him?"

"No, but I had heard his name. Excuse me, señora, you were saying—"

"A hand as soft as a dove's breast. Should you require an injection, go nowhere else but to Elena."

She went back to sit with her daughter when he had thanked her for the advice. He could just see himself, baring his stern to Elena, whoever she was—

Whoa! Just a second—what about Rafaela? What if she had set him up with a dose? Son of a bitch; that made him no better and not better off than Little Miss Hotpants here.

Impossible! You could tell she was "clean." But *could* you, after all? And if she wasn't, it meant he would have to sweat it out for nine days; "reading" it every morning, "looking into its eye," as the fellows used to say.

Well, he wasn't going to convict Rafaela before the evidence was in. Funny, though, if he did catch one—stepping up to the pool table for the first time and ripping the cloth.

On this subject, although the locker-room gang back at school talked a great deal, they were still in the Boy's Department compared to Jeff Doherty. Jeff was the elevator starter who dispatched the cars by rattling a pair of castanets in the building where Richardson's laboratory was. Jeff had a better line on this field of hygiene than anybody. He had been through what he called The Mill.

"I'd just come from Alliance, Ohio, and hadn't got settled in a job here yet," he told Gilberto one lunch hour in the parking lot, in back of the building. "And you know how it is, being in a new place; Hollywood, especially. Well, a guy in a bar gives me a card to this hookshop on Franklin Avenue, near Western. A dame named Billie runs the joint. Ever been there?"

"No, not that I remember."

"Well, it's a five-buck joint, money-in-front, straight or French; and I swear to you it's the first time I ever paid for it. I could always find me a charity worker in Alliance. Nothing happened for a week, ten days, and then, one morning I wake up and I know I'd been burned."

"But you got cured up."

"Wait—like I said, I'm new in the town. Didn't know anybody but the landlady where I had my room. You couldn't go to her, asking if she knew the name of a good clap doctor. She was a Lutheran."

"And even if she wasn't," Gilberto agreed.

"Finally, I go to this guy who advertises in the men's rooms. Dr. Reardon and Staff."

"I've seen his signs," Gilberto said. "He did the job?"

"He did *a* job! But let me tell you. The first visit you make, Doc Reardon himself gives you the glad hand. A jolly old bastard. 'Well, well, young man; I see we're in trouble.' *We're* in trouble! You show him the damage, and he acts like he'd never seen one before in his life and has to call in The Staff. They each have a look and shake their heads. What they're doing is giving you the business, but you don't know it—not yet. You ask him what this is all about and he says, 'You're a *sick* boy.' You want to know is he going to cure you and he says, 'We'll *try*.' The point is to get you thinking this is a special kind of a clap that baffles science."

"Yeah," Gilberto agreed. "Like there was only one specialist—a guy with whiskers, in Vienna—could handle it."

"You get the point, kid," Jeff resumed. "And mentioning handling it—that first time they handle it like it was made out of glass, that gentle. But that's all. After that, it was like they were dealing with a piece of garden hose. You ask old Reardon how much all this is going to cost you, and he says, 'You mustn't worry about that now. The thing we got to do first is get you back in good standing. Ha, ha.' And that's the last you see of *him*. A nurse comes in and you tuck it away, quick. She starts asking questions. Where do you work? What's your salary? References? . . . Lucky, I'd been working for about a week for a tire distributing outfit. She makes me sit there while she checks on the phone to make sure I wasn't lying about this job, and she hands me a slip—appointment for Tuesday night—and wants fifty dollars down. I don't have that much on me, so she took what I had and gives me a receipt. Then, I had to sign some papers—and out."

"That wasn't the end of it?" Gilberto said.

"I wish the hell it was. I'd of saved myself a lot of misery. Anyway, Tuesday night they started me on what they called irrigations."

"That must have been before penicillin."

"Before sulfa even, I'm talking about. . . . The way they do this irrigation is, they hang up a douche bag full of purple water and you stand over a sink while they squirt this into you at high pressure. This is every other night. The fourth visit, the nurse says, 'You're in arrears, Mr. Doherty.' Huh? 'We want another payment from you before Wednesday.' . . . A couple of mornings later, I wake up and I got a swelling in the sack. I work all day, juggling a carload of truck tires. More irrigation that night. The guy handling the squirter doesn't say anything when I show him the swelling. I don't think he was even a doctor; maybe just the janitor of the building. It kept getting worse, and I knew I wouldn't be able to keep the job long. Well, I didn't. It got so I could hardly lift a bicycle tire from the pain and, on top of that, Dr. Reardon put a garnishee on my salary, which really fixed me with the boss. That was when I found out the papers I signed for Reardon was something like a Morris Plan note, to pay him five hundred bucks."

"What a gyp!" Gilberto declared. "What happened after that?"

"I got insulted, that's what happened. I went back up to Billie's joint, thinking maybe they ought to do something about it; I mean because I got sold damaged goods. There was a cop there and another feller having a sociable drink with Billie. She remembered me all right, and thought I was back for a little more of the same. But when I told her *why* I came, she sung a different tune. 'You had a good time, didn't you?' she cracked. 'Maybe,' I said, 'but not since.' The cop, who I think was the real owner, told me, 'Go back to the tall corn. We run a whorehouse here, not a clinic.' I beefed that the dame who gave it to me should have spoke up. And you know what the madam said? 'She's young; she didn't know. She thought it was a secret, because the son of a bitch who gave it to her kept it quiet.' Anything for a laugh, with those thieves."

"So there you were, Jeff, stuck—"

"Stuck for fair! No job, my dough running out fast, and sick as a dog on top of that. Then, one day I'm in Exposition Park and I'm sitting on a bench next to this citizen—an old bum, he looked like. But he wasn't, believe me. He'd been everywhere; been a merchant seaman, worked on railroads, in the oilfields, been a miner—he knew life! He saw I was walking with a cane, and he guessed what was wrong with me. I admitted it. I told him about Dr. Reardon and Staff, and that I was thinking of suing them. His advice was not to, and he said this irrigation was the worst thing they could do. That way they drove the germs *back* when they should have drove them *out*."

"That makes sense," Gilberto said.

"'Liquids,' the old guy said, 'the best being iced tea. Drink till you think you're going to founder, and then some.' That, and baking it out. He said to go down to the beach every day and sit in the sun. Well, the beach is kind of a public place, so I rigged up a screen of a couple of blankets on the roof of the boarding house and lay out there every day—drinking iced tea."

"That do it?"

"And how! I came out of it looking like a lifeguard."

"Well, it's a good thing to know. But like you said, Jeff, it's better not to get it in the first place."

"The only sure way," Jeff said, "is to keep it in your pants."

Easy advice to give, but hard to take, Gilberto was thinking, when there was a jolt, and the bus heeled far over to the left. The badly sprung body tilted so suddenly that Angel, who had been sitting with his good leg under his stump, fell forward, across Gilberto's knees. The kid said, "Pardon me," as if it were his fault.

The car straightened out normally, without Lucas having to fight the wheel. What happened, Gilberto assumed, was that it had run into a deep rut, continued the length of it, and come out, level.

He fixed Angel back in the seat and tucked the serape around his legs. Alvarez, remaining near the driver, smiled thankfully. Concha wrinkled her nose, plainly jealous. He would like to show her, too, that he didn't dislike her; that he would have done the same thing for her. Perhaps later, so that she wouldn't know about it, he would slip the mother a few pesos and tell her to get the kid something. . . . How could you hold it against anybody that young?

Suppose a thing like that happened to him when he was fourteen. It would have ruined his whole life, he was convinced. It goes on your record, the one at the draft board. The one he filled out when he took his physical had questions like: *Have you ever had (a) gonorrhea (clap); (b) syphilis (blood disease); (c) buboes (blue balls); (d) hard or soft chancre (shanker)?* And they warn you that you'd better tell the truth. It's a good thing they didn't ask, Are you still married to the Five-Fingered Widow; or, are you a member of the Knights of the Velvet Paw? There, he would be in trouble.

Morrissey had the right idea—"sublimate the instinct"—but he oversold it. Sublimate it into what? That was the point. Getting A's in all your subjects? That's past. Going out for professional athletics? You've got to have been a letter man in college. Making a lot of money, like, say, two thousand a week? The kind of money that movie actors drew down; and, oh, yes, as Dr. Eisen mentioned, screenwriters, too.

There was a thing he could have made a pass at: writing. He should have stuck to it, especially after the way Miss Andrews, his teacher in Sophomore English, praised his work. She had read his entire composition, "A Day at the Stock Car Races," to the class.

To him, personally, it was just an assignment to write 1,500 words on. His notebook read: "a public spectacle or event—examples, football games, athletic meet—but giving own personal impressions." But Miss Andrews had another slant on it. She told the class to take good notice of the original forms of expression in Reyes's composition; how much appreciation he showed for detail and how colorfully he described it. And this, she said, was a unique characteristic of many noted writers to whom English is an adopted language.

He knew of course, she was all wrong. If anything, Spanish was Gilberto's adopted language. But he was too overcome with the praise to say anything that would show her up.

Then she asked for examples of "authors of another nationality who adopted the English language."

A girl named Mignonette Forshay, who knew everything, answered first. "Joseph Conrad."

"Correct. Author of—"

"*Lord Jim, Heart of Darkness, Almayer's Folly, Typhoon,*—"

"Language of origin?"

"Polish."

Somebody else said, "Dreiser, *The American Tragedy*—"

"Language of origin?"

Mignonette butted in there and said, "If he means Theodore Dreiser, it's An *American Tragedy*, and he was born in Indiana." She even gave the date.

Another girl came up with William Saroyan, *The Dashing Young Man on the Flying Trapeze,* an Hungarian.

"Any others?"

Dickie Collins raised his hand, "Ben Hecht—?"

Miss Andrews wasn't sure about him, but Dickie said, "Well, I thought on account of a book of his my sister got out of the lending library. It was called *A Jew in Love.*"

The whole class burst out laughing, including Miss Andrews. The idea of a Jew being in love struck everybody as being funny.

Miss Andrews recommended "A Day at the Stock Car Races" to be published in the *McVeigh Vanguard*, the school quarterly. Sure enough, the Editorial Board invited him down to discuss it. It wasn't the full board, just the working committee and Dr. Throssel, the faculty adviser.

They said right out that they liked it, and the only changes they could think of were in punctuation. But it had to have a new title; the present one gave it away that it was an English class assignment. How did he like "Horsepower, Ahoy!"

He liked that fine. And if there were any changes they wanted, he said he'd be glad to do them. No changes, but Dr. Throssel brought up an interesting point, they told him. They would have to print it under a *nom de plume.*

"We'll make it by Ray Gilbert or Raymond Gilbert," the editor in chief said. "Maybe you want it Gil Raymond?"

"I don't see any of them. My name happens to be Gilberto Reyes."

"Look, it won't be any secret who wrote it to anybody in the school," they tried to explain. "It's for the benefit of the outsiders."

"I still don't get it."

"Look at it this way," the editor said. "We have to publish the term sports roundup; the scores of all our games, and so on. And that's by Ric Zamora, president of the Athletic Association. Then we're featuring three poems by

Chiqui Menéndez. We just don't want the whole issue to look like it was put out by—you get the idea, don't you, Gil?"

He got the idea, but he didn't like it. He wanted to be able to show his mother—Carolyn—his name in print. He said, "All right, give me any name you want."

It didn't matter, though, because he was out of McVeigh before the *Vanguard* went to press.

So that ended the literary career of Gilberto Reyes, and those of Gilbert Raymond and Raymond Gilbert, as well. No use grabbing at brass rings that aren't even there. Stick to something, even in pipe dreams, that's more likely to happen. Adventure—there was something!

For money, you have to scrabble. Adventure, on the other hand, is something you might meet up with around the next bend. And what was he doing now except going to meet it halfway! At Tía Santibáñez's ranch—a pushover for the kind of life in which something is happening every minute.

The name itself—Tres Cenotes—the Three Wells outfit. Already, he had a dandy idea for a brand—three interlocking circles, like the Ballantyne's Ale trademark. Gil Reyes, foreman. On second thought, Don Gilberto, administrador, sounded better here in Mexico.

> "What's that you say, Pedro? Gringo rustlers trying to make off with some head of premium stock? Well, I wouldn't disturb him now. He's up at the ranch house—hacienda, that is—with the lady-boss Doña Esperanza, makin' out the payroll. . . . W-a-all, no, she ain't learned to write her name, that's why she sent for her States-educated nevview, Don Gilberto."

The recollection of his aunt's illiteracy intruded as accidental reality into that film-born dream. She probably had a goat or two, he figured, recalling the letter, and that six dollars covered her daughter's commencement party—or whatever it was—gown and food, included. What the hell—

At the nadir of his shrug, and as he was reaching for a cigarette, the bus hit.

He threw himself forward, to keep Angel from crashing on his head in the aisle; instead, he was flung to his knees against the opposite bench. Concha screamed and clung to her mother, howling in fright. Alvarez must have hit the steel pipe that served as a handhold; he sat, dazed, his hands flat on the floor.

The sound after the impact was that of the left fender scraping and tearing, as if it were being rubbed against a stone wall and along it for some distance. This was no unavoidable rut, but a reckless veering off the road and sideswiping either a tree or an outcropping boulder. To have that happen on the right edge of the road was bad enough, but this was on the left.

Nobody seemed actually hurt, and Gilberto got up off the floor when the listing bus scraped past whatever it had hit and the wheels were again on level dirt.

From the straight position he maintained at the wheel and from the set of his shoulders, Lucas appeared to be in full control again. But to Gilberto, the fact that the man had not stopped or at least called back to find out how his passengers were, made it almost certain that Lucas had dozed off; was not fully conscious of having struck anything, but came awake at the sudden shift of balance.

"Señor Alvarez," Gilberto said sharply, as he went forward, "you had better take care of your son, while I see what's going on here." The man moved hesitantly, changing places with Gilberto.

He touched the man's shoulder. "I advise that you draw over to the side of the road and just shut your eyes until you feel more rested. We'll wait."

The driver neither felt the hand on him, nor did he act as if he heard what was said to him. But Alvarez and the woman nodded; they agreed.

"Come now, Don Lucas. There are children in this coach," Gilberto said in a louder voice, and looked at the man more closely. His hands were properly and, considering the unevenness of the road, firmly on the rim of the wheel; and they swung normally, in tiny arcs, keeping the front end in a straight line. But the eyes were wrong—too wide open and glaring.

"This man is asleep on his feet," Gilberto called back. "He's practically unconscious." With that, he leaned forward and twisted the ignition key. The bus stopped in its own length; but not for Lucas, who kept right on driving it.

"How's the traffic on this road? Would there be other vehicles passing?"

Alvarez answered, "I cannot say, señor. It is not likely, but—"

"In any case, it would be safer to pull over as far to the right as possible."

Lucas acted as if he heard and agreed. His foot pressed the starter button and the Bendix caught—but with the ignition off. Gilberto reached to turn it on. Lucas swung before he could touch the key, and the blow caught Gilberto on the temple. It wasn't a strong punch, coming from a seated man, and he was ready for Lucas when he tried it again with the other hand. Concha's mother screamed a warning, but he didn't need it. He slammed his fist straight from the shoulder into the man's open mouth, but not as hard as he could have. Lucas grabbed the arm and, hanging on to it, tried to stand up. Instead of hitting again, Gilberto twisted his hand free and slammed with his forearm. Lucas fell backward, his head against the window and legs across the pedals.

Alvarez simply stood there, like a man watching a street brawl and afraid that the combatants might hit him a chance blow. He moved alertly when Gilberto called, "Come here, you!" If the guy was going to act like a rabbit, you've got to handle him like one. "Help me pull this drunk out of here; then get down and see if there's a tail light on this bus."

Lucas was no lightweight to begin with, and tangled up as he was, with his feet caught between the gearshift lever and the hand brake, it took plenty of tugging to get him free and lay him out lengthwise on the bench.

Alvarez made a tour of the bus and came back with the report, "Both red lights behind are without glass and do not burn."

That was fine! Bishop would love this situation. There was only one thing to do: get this thing off the road. He squeezed into the battered seat, turned the key, and, after a few revolutions of the starter, she caught.

Leaning toward him, Alvarez, with a shocked expression, said, "But if you have no license to drive—"

For a second there, he felt like hitting Alvarez, too.

The pedals were smooth as glass under his leather soles. There was no floorboard between them, and he could see the clutch housing, thick with dirt and grease. Experimentally, he ran the shift lever from compound low to third and back again, through reverse, glancing meanwhile at Alvarez. Poor guy, the law must have leaned real hard on him to make him worry about a driver's license at a time like this.

Slipping into compound low, he eased the clutch and it went, although everything in the manual was wrong with it. The steering gear was loose as ashes—at least eight inches of play either way—there was blow-by from a rotten head gasket, and the timing was miles off.

Now, actually seeing the road, he didn't like it. It might look better if he wiped the windshield, and when he did, it wasn't much of an improvement. "Tell Lucas, as soon as I see a place wide enough, I'll pull over and park."

Lucas was out; he was snoring. Gilberto must have cut his lip; some blood had dried blackly.

Several hundred yards onward, the road began curving around a hill. On his left, Gilberto sensed a gloomy, cold height. On his right, an irregular planting of whitewashed rocks meant a declivity, or, for all he could see, it might be a precipice.

When possible, he coaxed it along in high gear, but it wouldn't stay there for more than a few hundred level feet without bucking. The engine acted as if the diaphragm of the gasoline pump was all flabby.

Ten, fifteen minutes, and still no place on the road was wide enough, or with even a semblance of shoulder, to pull up on.

Alvarez came forward, also to peer through the windshield and shake his head. "It is not my wish to distract you; however—"

"Then don't bother me. I'm not doing this from choice."

"Excuse me," Alvarez pleaded. "It is just to say that I am at your command."

"Then please see to it that Don Lucas doesn't jump me from behind."

Angel climbed down from the cross-seat and worked himself forward on the bench, directly behind Gilberto. Concha and her mother remained where they were.

He decided that so long as the heap was moving, he would keep going, even if he did come to a wide spot on the road. Enough gas? The needle showed a quarter full. When he tapped the dial, it jumped to full and stuck there. That couldn't be right. The speedometer didn't work and the odometer was stuck at 211,108—miles or kilometers, it didn't matter. This was certainly a museum piece.

He became more confident. This was the first lick he had at a wheel since before work camp. No resorts where liquor was sold, no burlesque shows or cabarets, and no driving were among the conditions of his release. There was another, prohibiting him from leaving the County of Los Angeles "only for the purpose of visiting relatives, but not to accept employment."

That part was funny. Wasn't he visiting a relative; his dear, old Aunt Esperanza? And, as for accepting employment—well, nobody offered him any, yet.

All very amusing, but there was serious work ahead. Rocks and ruts; a sheer drop of how many hundreds of feet on the right; and a blind curve coming up and not a stick of wood or a whitewashed rock to mark the edge. But it wasn't too bad. If the gas held out—the oil pressure hung around 30, which was fair—and if a tire didn't blow, and the road got no worse. He forgot the most important thing of all. "How much further is it to Zaragoza?"

"Not far."

"In kilometers?"

"From the bridge, you have only to ford the Río Arenal, and then it is soon to Zaragoza."

That was a big help. "Then how far is the bridge from here?"

"It is near, señor."

"*How* near would you say?" It was like pulling teeth to get information from Alvarez.

"You can hear the water."

He pushed the lever into neutral and he could hear swift water, but it was hard to tell its direction. It seemed to be roaring, now ahead, and at times on either side of the road. He strained to see through the windshield, and either his eyesight was getting weak, he thought, or the lights were dimming. Then he remembered: the sideswipe crumpled the fender and the set-in headlight, and only one was working—the right. It wasn't stupidity not to have realized this situation before; from the driver's angle, it's hard to tell when one headlight is out.

He slowed for a hairpin turn. The sound of rushing water was much louder now and unmistakably straight ahead. He felt for the switch to turn off the single bulb burning in the ceiling. That drew only a couple of milliamps, but even that little bit counts when the battery is down low. Ahead, the road looked chopped off. Slowing down, he kept the motor racing with the clutch half in, then stopped to read a battered panel: Puente Angosto, 10 k.p.h.

"The bridge," Alvarez announced.

"Thanks." Look what they called a bridge! He rolled onto it at a good deal less than 10 k.p.h.

There had been a rail on it once, but only a few snagged uprights marked its width. Made entirely of wooden planks, the weight of the front end of the bus on the first ones set all of them, the entire length, to drumming.

He rolled another ten yards at a creep, and suddenly darkness fell, utterly black and dense, as if the bus had a photographer's cloth flung over it.

He stopped, set the handbrake, and let the motor idle. The rushing water below drowned out the clacking valves and the only way you could tell the motor was turning over was by feeling the loose jointed body.

Two things more he would like to know before moving another inch: the length of the bridge and the height of the drop. He had advanced far enough on it to know that it was wide enough. There were inches of safety—in broad daylight. But no inches and no safety in this pitch blackness.

"How long is it across?"

"The Aguas Dulces is a wide stream, señor."

"That's fine! Perhaps you can tell me how much of a drop it is?"

"Fourteen meters."

The accuracy of the answer astonished him, and he became aware at the same time that the height of the bridge didn't matter. They were just as badly off at 43 feet as at 43 inches. He lit a match to see the ammeter. The needle was resting against the pin on the minus side. He tapped the glass and it remained there. When he raced the engine, it jumped; but even as he tramped down on the accelerator, it flopped over to zero again.

Concha and her mother moved up, opposite Lucas, who still lay on the bench covered with Alvarez's serape and breathing heavily.

"With your permission," Alvarez said, "I could rouse Don Lucas. He has, you must admit, driven over this bridge many times."

"Not without lights; not without being able to see what's ahead of him," Gilberto said.

Then, what is there to do?"

"This: You, the señora, Concha, and Angel, you will get out and walk across. It will be up to you—"

"Juan Alvarez, a sus órdenes—"

"You, Juan, help the others off, and see that they don't slip over the edge."

"And you, señor?" the mother asked with concern.

"And Don Lucas," Alvarez interceded.

"He stays where he is," Gilberto said. "Perhaps when you get to the other end, you can shout, and that way I will get an idea of the bridge's length."

"Or show a light," Alvarez said, "if I had a match."

A genius! The guy was a genius, Gilberto thought. He had the whole problem licked, whether he knew it or not. Probably not, Gilberto thought, quietly appropriating the idea. "Nobody leave for a minute," he announced, "until I explain. . . . The camión cannot remain here on the bridge without lights, lest something run into it behind and cause a tragedy."

"That is God's truth," the mother said.

"And I cannot risk backing up, since that is more difficult than moving ahead. Claro? . . . Therefore, please get out in this order: the señora first, then Concha, then you, Angel. And Juan, this is what you are to do: Take these matches, pour them out of the package into your hand, keeping one always lit, one from the other. Do you understand? They are wax and will not blow out."

"A flashlight would be better," Alvarez suggested.

A flashlight, sure; there must be one in the glove compartment. And there it was, in a tangle of oily scraps, next to a pair of cheap pliers. He moved the switch—nothing, not even a faint glow. Unscrewing the bottom, the two batteries dropped into his palm, corroded with fungus and useless. Angrily, he flung the flashlight out, into the water below. "Look in his pockets."

Alvarez patted Lucas's clothes and reported, "There is nothing, Don Gilberto."

So it was Don Gilberto now. He was gaining ground. It sounded all right.

"Matches will have to do then, Juan."

"Yes, Don Gilberto—"

As he reached for the matches in his pocket, he cursed Lucas. Why didn't he have something aboard that would give some kind of light; an emergency flare, something? . . . He had it! Something that would top Alvarez's idea of a match. Snatching off his hat, he handed it to him. "Here, take this. It will burn more brightly."

"Such a fine hat, Don Gilberto—"

"Never mind. Light it."

They got out carefully and lined up in front of the machine. Juan, behind, stood ready with a flaring match to touch off the hat.

"Okay, now! Walk slowly—slowly—*and stay in the middle of the bridge!* The very middle. You understand, everybody?"

Together they called back, "Sí, Don Gilberto."

"All right then—ándale!"

They shuffled, practically crept, and he was glad of it. The hat did not flare, and smoked more than it burned. Still, it gave better light than a match; enough to light up Alvarez, whose figure he kept lined up with the radiator cap. He stayed in low, slipping the clutch and working the gas pedal by slight nudges with his toe. Half the planks of the bridge flooring were loose and he could feel them sag, then spring back as the bus passed over them.

He didn't dare look anywhere but directly ahead. A glance below the left window was all he risked, and he saw a darker line not more than four inches from the line of his elbow. That much clearance and no more.

Mechanical steering was dangerous because of the play in the wheel. If anything happened—a chip of wood was enough—to cause the front wheels to veer, he'd be over the edge before he could spin the steering wheel the greater part of 360 degrees of play. The only thing to do was to hold his fingers lightly on it and let it steer itself.

He kept less than three feet behind Alvarez, who waved the hat when it started to smoulder and whipped some glow into the straw.

There was no sound above that of the water below, rocketing over stones. Then, he heard a thump behind him. It was probably Lucas's flabby bulk striking the floorboards, but he didn't want to look back to make sure. He would be on his knees now, crouching to tackle him from behind.

"Lucas—" No sound answered him. "Stay where you are. If you move, we go over the side." To signal Alvarez, he pressed the horn button. It gave no sound. Behind him, Lucas gave a deep chest groan and a sigh, which might mean that he had again lain back—maybe gathering himself for a lurch forward.

How much more of this chingada puente was there? At this pace, there was no way of estimating how far he had gone or how much further it extended. No choice but to sit tight, keep your eyes glued on that smouldering straw, and pray that nothing—a busted plank—a twig—pops up to misalign the front wheels.

Alvarez stopped and his hands danced, switching the burning straw from one to the other. The hat was almost consumed, and the last, glowing shred fell, dying on the floor of the bridge.

Waiting for him to begin lighting matches, Gilberto listened keenly now to a faint, intermittent growling of which he had been aware for the last few yards, under the hood. It wasn't an engine sound—not any that he had ever heard. It was more of a faint gargle, a low pitched vibration. . . . The horn! That was it, the horn. A short circuit in the wiring. That gargling sound was actually the horn itself, operating weakly; the same thing that happened once to the Dodge at work camp. And how fast a short like that pulls down the current!

He followed Alvarez's tiny beacon another ten, twelve, fifteen feet; then stopped when the match went out, waiting for another to be lit. When Alvarez struck it, he was no longer in line with the radiator, but off to the right—on dirt once more.

It felt wonderful to have the rubber take hold, settling into, rather than bouncing on the surface. And here was a space to the right of the bridge head, wide enough to park.

Lucas was half-lying, half-kneeling on the floor. As the others climbed aboard, he struggled to stand up, almost succeeded, but folded slowly back to his knees, remaining that way, his head on the bench.

Concha tried to snare the seat behind Gilberto, but Angel leapt into it first.

"I think I know what happened to the lights," Gilberto announced. "Don Juan,"—he felt good enough to call Alvarez, Don, too—"keep an eye on Lucas there."

He took the pliers and went to the front of the machine. Lifting the hood, and with the help of a match, he located the wires which ran to the horn from a dirty cluster, and trailed them to the terminals. The insulation was rotten and made contact along various points of channel steel. Without bothering to locate the point of short contact, he ripped them out and removed an additional eight inches from beneath their clamps. Separating them, he bent and twisted the wires away from accidental contact with each other.

Now the ammeter would tell if that was the trouble. If not, he'd be damned if he'd start all over again crawling behind a guy holding up a match at no miles per hour, for Christ knows how long. As he got back into the car, and even before looking at the ammeter dial, there was already a faint glow on the instrument panel. Success! He pressed the accelerator and the needle whipped over to the plus side, charging a full 30 amps. The single headlight strengthened, throwing a beam that was first yellow and gradually turning cream white.

Concha clapped her hands. Her mother said, "¡Qué milagro!" Angel stroked Gilberto's back in adoration as he raced the motor and watched until the needle started to drop back and remain finally a bit to the right, on the plus side. To test it, he switched the headlight off and the needle banged up to its limit of charge.

"We're off!" he called in English and swung out into the road.

Lucas, by inches, sat up. But he was not quite out of the fog; staring around him, but always coming back to Gilberto in the driver's seat. His head bobbed as he studied him, beginning to mutter, low and unintelligibly at first, then louder; cursing senselessly, with many "chingadas" and "cabrones."

"You're responsible for seeing that he doesn't act nasty," Gilberto warned Alvarez.

This was more like it. The air was just right, with just enough moisture in it to give the carburetor a mixture with more sock to it than he had felt up to now. The engine was really pulling, even in high. His pleasure in its performance was undiminished when he recognized from the angle of the light beam that they were rolling down a grade.

The time was twenty after ten; not eleven, as he had guessed. Now it was safe to throw a glance at Lucas, at intervals. Something like intelligence was coming back into the man's expression. It was almost on the verge at which you could expect the remark, "What the hell is going on here?"

The light—more accurately, the darkness beyond the light—was no longer the blackness that prevailed at the bridge, but a deep purple. This was a valley, and the stars, he believed, could shine straight down, instead of having to bounce their rays off the tops of mountains.

With the nagging roar of water past, a distant sound was as clear as one nearby. Like a pure trumpet note, the same number of vibrations per second whether you hear it right beside you or a mile away.

They were passing an occasional farm. There was a whinny and the sound of hoofs on loose rock; the bleat of a kid, like the E-flat on a tenor saxophone; a burro—to him the Satchmo of animals—sounded off.

Silence for a while, then two short yelps and a quavering howl: a coyote. Alvarez raised his head; the husbandman, alerted to his enemy. Somewhere near, a rooster on his perch caught the headlight's glowing eye or, needing only a beam, was tricked into thinking it was day, and cut loose.

"Vesuvio," Alvarez said. "Ramírez's fighting cock. Do you know, Don Gilberto, he was offered five hundred pesos for that fowl, cash on the nail, last Easter in Guerrero. Not so, Angelito?"

"Yes, papá."

"Tell Don Gilberto, then, what they say about him."

"They say Vesuvio is a pretty good fighter," the boy added obediently.

"Pretty good! You might as well say that your mother is *said* to be *pretty* virtuous! . . . I tell you, Don Gilberto, Vesuvio among birds is what Emiliano Zapata was among men. Be it an eagle or the Avenging Angel, if it has feathers, Vesuvio will fight it." He leaned across the aisle, adding in an awed whisper, "He has African blood." That secret imparted, he almost shouted, "A treasure, that fowl!"

"Must be." Cock fighting didn't mean a thing to Gilberto. The only thing Vesuvio reminded him of was that chicken and mole he had eaten back there, and he wished he had another tortilla crammed with it now.

Once more, and again deceptive as to direction, he heard the sound of running water, swift, too. "Is that the Río Arenal? It sounds like it's off to the left some distance."

"Not yet," Alvarez answered. "That is the cascade, where the Aguas Dulces takes a bend. But soon we shall be at the Arenal, and beyond it with only a slight wetting of the wheels."

With no more warning than a bird gives, Concha began to sing. "Vamos al baile, y verás qué bonito—"

"Stop this crowing," her mother called harshly. "You are molesting Don Gilberto."

"It's all right, señora; please let her sing."

"Donde se alumbran con veinte linternas—"

That was one he knew. "Let's go to the dance and see how pretty it is, lit up with twenty lanterns." The kid didn't have a bad little voice—"Where they dance the latest steps; where they dance with great—," the word there was vacilón. He made it, "where they let themselves go."

She sang like any kid, anywhere, playing a sidewalk game. "Y quiéreme, Jesusita; quiéreme por favor—" And behind him, in a quavering treble, Angel joined her, "Y mira, que soy tu amante, tu seguro servidor."

Leaning forward, Alvarez started to say, "Ahorita llegamos—," that they would soon be at the river. But Gilberto cut him off, waving to him to be quiet.

Angel and Concha were competing with each other now for loudness and speed. "Donde las niñas enseñan las piernas—"

Kids singing—that's the way it ought to be.

27

This must be the Río Arenal. He braked to a dead stop as soon as the headlight beam probed water. The sound of it was a rapid trot, compared to the plunging gallop of the Aguas Dulces beneath the bridge.

The opposite bank sloped less than the one on which he had halted. The stream did not appear to be more than twenty, at most thirty feet wide, although it was hard to judge distance in this light.

"What does it look like?"

Alvarez pointed to his ankle. But anybody could see how shallow the stream was by noticing the dry tops of even small boulders.

"What kind of a bottom—the bed; is it muddy or—"

"Stones," Alvarez said.

"Loose or—"

"What's the matter? Scared?" Lucas, coming abruptly to life, growled. "No lousy bastard that's afraid of a—" He petered out in gibberish, then slumped back, sneering.

Alvarez held his arm and said, "Take no care, Don Lucas. We are already at the ford."

"Yes, just relax, maestro," Gilberto said, somewhat cockily. "Nobody is going to run away with your limousine."

Dropping it into compound low, he let it roll down the bank. It was okay; the bottom was firm; traction was good. Moving up to first, he goosed it along until the front wheels touched the opposite slope, ready to drop back into compound low for the slight grade. The front end took it, but slid off, and he felt the rear end slew around.

As the rear wheels ground slowly, he knew that they were digging a trench for themselves, deeper with each revolution. Fighting back into reverse, he tried to rock the bus forward, but the wheels only slid in the grooves already dug.

Now was Lucas' time to really sneer. Five feet to go, and here they were, stuck. Either Lucas was having a quiet, inward laugh, or he didn't care. He simply sat, hugging Alvarez's serape around him, and glared.

Gilberto feared that they might be bogging down by the rear. To prevent this, or simply to be doing something, he called to Concha and her mother to move further forward.

"Let's have a look, Juan." They got out and surveyed the trouble by the light of matches. The rear wheels were up to the hubs in oozy black stuff, more sand than mud. "We'll have to put some of these stones under the wheels. Grab up as many as you can, middle-sized ones, and put them in front of the wheels. I'll bank them up behind."

"I will call the women to help," Alvarez suggested.

"Leave them alone; we won't need them."

Almost without wetting his shoes, Gilberto was able to pile a mound of stones behind the left rear wheel. "From here," he asked, "have you any idea how far it is to Zaragoza?"

"One may walk the distance in a few minutes; ten, let us say."

Not too bad. In a pinch, they could all walk, and Lucas can stay, if he wants to.

When there were enough stones in front of and behind each rear wheel, Gilberto said, "I'm going to try pulling out once more. Stand by here and, if the wheels start spinning, pile some more under the tires."

There may have been a gain of a foot or two on the second attempt, but that only tantalized him. The wheels bit only briefly at the stones and then pressed them into the sand.

Climbing out from behind the steering wheel, he called to Concha and her mother, "If you two wish to go, Juan says it isn't far to Zaragoza."

"No, Don Gilberto, it is quite near now."

"And if I am able to pull the machine out, it may be that I can catch up with you."

"Ojalá. . . . But if I can be of help—"

"No, thank you. Take Concha and proceed to Zaragoza."

"But this one," she pointed to Lucas, who sat now, with his arms folded across his chest, in a perverse and distant attitude, "if he should become disorderly again. . . "

"Angel can control him." He smiled at the boy and in that moment remembered that he meant to give Concha a few pesos. He waited until she got out of the bus and put his hand in his pocket, wondering what there was about the girl that impelled him to want to help her. He knew there was something more to it than making a simple present of money. Her poverty, plain as it was, was not of itself the motive.

"Here, get something for the girl," he said, extending five pesos.

"You are very kind, but I do not wish to take it," the mother said with dignity.

"It's for Concha; for a—for a hair ribbon or something she needs."

"We all need many things," she said, and turned calmly. She joined Concha, who was waiting a short distance away, and put her arm around the child's shoulder in a sudden, brief embrace. But almost immediately she pushed her forward.

He heard the woman command, "Andale, fea." Get along, ugly one. But there was no more anger in it than when his mother used to say to him, "Now stop, you little pig."

When he turned back, Juan was squatting down, chin in hand, studying the bogged wheels like an engineer on some big project. "If we had a quantity of planks now, or a few armfuls of saplings—"

"Well, we haven't. But there's something: a trick." Gilberto felt for the valve cap on the right rear wheel. "I'm going to let some air out. You go over on the other side and do the same thing, eh, Juan."

"How much air, Don Gilberto?"

"As much as you can; I'll let you know." He showed him how, by unscrewing the dust cap and pressing the pointed tip against the projecting end of the valve inside. A powerful jet of air hissed out. Regardless of the emergency, this tire, at any rate, carried too much pressure. Besides, the tread was as smooth as paper. Little wonder there was no traction.

On Alvarez's side, the air, likewise, was whistling. Sixty pounds of pressure was about normal for tires of this size, but these must have been carrying about 100. It would take a little time before they were soft enough to spread under the weight of the rear end and provide those extra inches of needed tread.

"¡Señor!" Angel's shrill cry brought Gilberto upright; whirling fast, as Lucas's arm, with the crank handle in his hand, descended in a chopping motion. It struck his shoulder so hard that he felt it down to his calves. It had been aimed for his head, and in the hands of a more sober man, the steel club would have crushed his skull.

"¡Chingado gringo! ¡Cabrón!" Lucas roared, backing off for another swing. Gilberto plunged and with his left arm deflected the blow, at the same time slamming it across Lucas's throat. Their bodies had not locked, and there was room for Gilberto's powerful stab with his right fist into Lucas's middle. The man dropped the crank handle and doubled forward, both arms across his stomach, before falling to the ground, writhing.

Gilberto stood over him, watching the agonized twitching of legs, as Juan rushed up. "He—he—might have killed me. . . . Angel cried out."

Alvarez saw the heavy crank handle on the ground and shook his head sadly. "You have hurt him badly, señor."

"Badly! I'd like to kick this bastard's face in!" It was just talk, this threat, and he knew it. He could have battered the guy before he fell or while he was hunched over, hugging his guts. He didn't do it; there was a difference between defense and punishment. The limit of defense is when you are safe; punishment is a consuming, debasing thing. "He asked for it."

Alvarez sat Lucas up, propping him between his knees. When Lucas was able to sit alone, he bathed his face and gave him a drink of river water from his cupped hands, glaring at Gilberto in a way that said, "This is more than I would do for you." And when Gilberto picked up the crank handle, Alvarez leaned over, as if to protect Lucas. "Please, no," he begged. "For the love of God."

"I wasn't going to hit him." He turned and tossed the tool into the bus. "Thanks, Angel; you're a brave fellow."

The boy, in the doorway, watching his father, looked frightened, bull-dozed, Gilberto thought; all for having interfered on behalf of a stranger, a fellow with a sack suit and a norteamericano accent—a gringo. This was the first time he had been called that—in that way—on this side of the border.

Looking at Alvarez again, he searched for something high-chinned and challenging; a trace of machismo. Blank. He could get very eloquent over the bravery of a fighting rooster, but at this moment he showed simply an abject willingness—not to fight for his friend, no indeed—but to take all the blows in his stead. A queer kind of machismo this was. He wasn't going to let this go by without some remarks.

They approached, Alvarez holding Lucas's arm. "I beg you not to attack him again, Don Gilberto!"

"I wouldn't think of it. That would be like a goddam gringo, to hit him while he was looking. I'll wait till his back is turned—the dirty son of a bitch!"

Alvarez said something to Lucas in a strange language; with many vowel sounds, it made Gilberto think it was Hawaiian. Lucas answered in the same language.

"What are you talking; what is he saying?" Gilberto demanded.

"It is Huasteca. Lucas begs you to excuse him."

"Is that his idea or yours?"

"If he were not stupified by the pulque—"

"Okay for now, but the next time he starts anything—"

Going back to finish with the tires, his first impulse was to remove the entire valve insides and let the tires go completely flat. It would pay Lucas off nicely to have the rims chop the rubber into ribbons. Better not, he decided; a thing like that might send the guy back to Ciudad del Maíz with a complaint about a strange gringo whose business down here maybe ought to be looked into. Leave well enough alone.

After operating on the tires for another ten minutes, he guessed that they were soft enough.

Just right. The bus walked out of the gummy sand like a camel. Only Angel admired his skill and patted his back. Lucas looked sour again, which was no surprise to Gilberto, who heard him complaining sulkily in the same Huasteca. Alvarez answered him, using but one phrase of Spanish—"I will mention it."

"You understand that language, Angel?"

"Yes, Don Gilberto. Lucas is very angry."

"What about?"

"The flashlight; you threw away his flashlight."

To say, "I should have thrown him after it," would get the guy sore enough to make trouble. On the other hand, to offer to pay for it was truckling; giving him a reason to boast how he forced this snotty gringo to buy him a new flashlight. Again, the best thing to do was keep quiet.

The rear end bounced a good deal on accont of the low tire pressure. But after a few miles running, it would build up.

The road was the same powdery dirt over which they had come this far. But the roadside had a different aspect; the trees which lined it appeared to be all of the same kind and planted at even distances from each other, like those which served as windbreaks in California.

The lights ahead were Zaragoza. They shed the same orangey glow that he had remarked in Victoria, in Mante, in Ciudad del Maíz. He was familiar enough with electricity to know that the current here was weaker than the 60-cycle AC.

Alvarez leaned forward, pointed ahead to the plaza and announced, "The Alameda. I will direct you to the station."

Here, it was the Alameda, not the plaza principal, the zócalo, or merely the plaza, as the central square was called in other towns. Alameda meant poplar, Gilberto remembered; and poplars grew slender and hugged their foliage to themselves. These trees had thick trunks and their branches made a solid roof.

"What trees are these?"

"Ahuehuete," Alvarez said curtly. "Turn to the right here, then to the left, and again to the left."

He looked for the bandstand in the center of the Alameda, but saw only a bare patch where one might have stood.

"There, just before you approach the corner," Alvarez directed. "Stop here—the station."

There was not even a bench where he pulled up. What apparently marked this particular handbreadth of curbing as a bus terminal was a water tap screwed to a pipe and an oil smudge on the cobbles. A simple left turn on entering the Alameda coming off the dirt road would have brought them to this point. But Alvarez, the stickler-for-the-law, had guided him clear around three sides of the square to comply with the arrows that said, "Tránsito—one-way."

Lucas turned the water tap on full force and thrust his head under it. And when he finished wiping his face with the sleeves of his jacket, he looked more pleasant.

"How do you feel?" Gilberto asked him, smiling.

Lucas ignored him and reassumed the look of a man who had been done a great injury and would remember it. Alvarez, to show where he stood, kicked the deflated tires and announced, "Don Lucas will now have to pump these up by hand."

He needed the exercise, Gilberto thought, to work up a good sweat. And Alvarez, being such a devoted friend, could help him. He looked at his watch—11:25— more than an hour had passed since they crossed the bridge. It was time to kiss these guys off, but first he asked, "Could you gentlemen tell me the best way to get to Tres Cenotes? It's supposed to be in this vicinity."

With a short laugh, Alvarez said, "It wouldn't do to walk rapidly. If you looked up at the stars you might overrun it."

"What business would anybody have in that hole?" Lucas added.

He would tell them no more than he had to. "Do you happen to know a señora Santibáñez from there?"

"Never heard of her," Lucas said.

"Nor I," added Alvarez.

He was about to give her full name, Esperanza Santibáñez, widow of Reyes, when Angel touched his arm. "I would ask of Don Solomón. His place is still open." The boy pointed with his crutch to the opposite—east—side of the Alameda.

He saw through the trees only a square patch of vibrating phosphorescent light. "Thank you again, Angel. Adiós."

"Adiós, Don Gilberto."

The two men said nothing, and he walked, as directly as the stand of the trees permitted, to the place which showed the light. It came from a tubular fixture above a wide steel curtain on which was painted EL SURTIDOR, and below it, in smaller letters, S. Gulden.

The bottom of the steel shutter was bolted to iron rings set in cement, but a smaller door was cut into it, directly under the crackling fluorescent tube. It was ajar, and beyond it, the interior of the place was lit more brightly.

Whatever kind of establishment this was, the hour was certainly too late for trade, and the fact that the smaller door was open could scarcely be regarded as an invitation to enter. It was obviously the owner's private entrance.

Knocking, then waiting to see if he would be asked in, was the reasonable thing to do. But before he could rap, a man's voice called, "Entre usted."

He stepped through as the door swung inward, and a tall man moved aside to give him room, saying, "Pase, por favor."

It closed behind Gilberto and a patent lock snapped. "You're closing up—"

"It is no matter. Come inside, please."

Gilberto remained just inside, between the shutter and the actual door of the establishment. "I have the honor to address Don Solomón?"

"I am Solomón Gulden, yes."

Gilberto saw him clearly as he reached to switch off the light outside and moved to let Gilberto pass ahead of him into the store. "I just stopped by," he began, "I was informed—"

"Permiso," Don Solomón begged, as he turned again, closed the wood-and-glass door, and twisted the knobs on two Yale locks. That made five locks, Gilberto counted; two for the steel curtain, one for the small door, and two here.

"I know how late it is—"

"It is earlier than usual that I am closing. But my clerk is away. His sister in León is to have a baby . . . mazel tov."

That last, Gilberto didn't get. But from the way the man said it, smiling and shrugging slightly it could mean, "That's *his* story." It might be Huasteca again.

He had a distinct impression that he was being regarded by Don Solomón as a salesman; dropping in, unavoidably late, on a rural customer. This was strengthened by the reference to the absent clerk—a chatty disclosure between businessmen of a minor employee problem.

"I have no doubt that he will come back," Don Solomón confided, "if not on Wednesday, as he promised, then on Thursday. But in either case, looking as if *he* had been brought to childbed. However, he is a fine boy, Felipe; and above all, honest. Be so good as to sit down." He pulled forward a stool, one of three tall ones in front of a wide counter, and by lifting a hinged section, got behind it.

For no reason, Gilberto, instead of leaving his bag on the floor, put it at his elbow, and Don Solomón kept looking at it, prepared for a display of samples.

"I'm not selling anything, señor Gulden. In fact—well—a number of people mentioned your name and advised that I see you."

"I am grateful to them. And if it is not impolite to ask, what brings you to this corner of the earth besides the camión of Lucas; or, I had better say it was you who brought the camión?"

Apparently, he knew about the trip from Concha and her mother. His smile revealed a lot of expensive gold inlay work on his teeth, the kind you don't see much of these days, Gilberto knew.

"I was in no special hurry," Gilberto said, "but I couldn't abandon the rest of the people."

"I see, then, that you are not a commercial traveler. But you are nonetheless welcome."

Don Solomón's Spanish was accentless, so far as Gilberto could judge; yet he was sure that he wasn't a Mexican. Maybe a Spaniard; many of them had red hair like his. He was between 55 and 60—to Gilberto's generation, an old man.

There was a folded newspaper on the counter, turned so that he saw its name backward and upside down: ꓕIƎHIƎꓤℲ. But the main title was printed in squat, curly-seriphed Hebrew letters. So much for his being a Spaniard. From beneath the counter he brought out a bottle and two small glasses. The label said Cognac, and he recalled the last time he drank some; wondering if Jews ever drank anything else.

"Something to clear the dust from your throat," Don Solomón said, pouring both glasses full and lifting his own. In English, half-gutteral and half-Cockney, he toasted, "Here's to your good health, sir."

"Say—!"

"Down the hatch, buddy!" He drank the brandy in one gulp, chuckling.

"Salud." The whole thing went down. It didn't bite, it warmed. "I didn't know you spoke English."

"Shipboard English. Mostly vulgarities—sonna-ma-bitch, doidy-fuckın-bestridge—"

Gilberto grinned. This old gent was easy to talk to; nothing stuffy about him. His glass was filled again. There was no "Have another?" or "How about one more?" He simply poured it out while talking. "I spoke Russian, Polish, and German from childhood on; later, French."

"Don't forget English," Gilberto said, "and Spanish, and this—" touching the newspaper. "Hebrew."

"Yiddish. That is different from Hebrew, but it is written in the Hebrew alphabet."

"I didn't know that."

"Many *goyim* make that mistake."

"That's one Yiddish word I happen to know—*goy*. I've been called that."

"It happens, however, to be a Hebrew word," Don Solomón smiled. "And I hope it doesn't offend you, because it is not a term of insult. It means, simply, a stranger."

This was all right, having a snort or two with the old fellow, but wasn't it about time to get down to cases? He was thinking that he didn't come this far just to chew the rag. Finish this second glass of cognac and make the break—

"May I ask what you are called?" he heard.

"My name is Reyes, Gilberto Reyes."

"From New York? Chicago—?"

Just a minute there, pal! No more snapping back with an answer, pulling another Vera Cruz and tripping yourself up. The first thing you know you're in the Small World Department, and if you mention a place, he'll start asking you if you know his cousin So-and-So. "Los Angeles," he said.

"That is in Upper California?"

Good! The guy didn't even know where L.A. was. "We call it Lower—that is, Southern California." He took the brandy. Mighty good stuff—smooth—and it gave you a gradual lift instead of a sock in the guts the way straight whiskey does. Cognac Remy-Martin, it said on the label. A bottle of this would sure cut deep into a five-dollar bill. "I see you know what happened on this bus ride."

"I had an account from señora Contreras, who arrived before you with her daughter."

"She was the one who mentioned you. The earlier time, it was an older lady on the bus from Victoria who said she knew you."

"Then you have come a long distance today." There was something Oriental in the way Don Solomón asked only part of that which he wanted to know. Gilberto detected that and fell into the same manner.

"And I have some distance still to go." That, he thought, ought to smoke him out. If he wanted straight answers, he would have to ask straight questions.

Don Solomón began, but went only halfway. "From here? From here you can go ahead only to Ocotal, or back only to Cuidad del Maíz. Or—"

"Tres Cenotes," Gilberto said, losing the game.

"I forgot Tres Cenotes. A person is very likely to," Don Solomón said, and poured both glasses full again, gulping his down. Gilberto took only a sip of his, being one ahead already.

"I have an aunt living there, the señora Esperanza Santibáñez, Viuda de Reyes."

Don Solomón tilted his head, puzzled, trying to recall the name. Gilberto took the letter out of his pocket, shook it open, and, glancing at it, repeated, "Esperanza Santibáñez, Viuda de Reyes. They said you might know her."

"In Tres Cenotes? . . . Ah, yes, yes—forgive me for being confused, but she has not been the Widow Reyes for some years."

"She has one daughter, Inés."

"That is the one."

"What, is she remarried?"

Slightly hesitant, Don Solomón said, "She is now called Esperanza de Vargas. Inés and Pompeyo are her children by Alvaro Reyes, who died about four years ago. José, the youngest, or Pepe, as he is called, is by Fidel Vargas."

"Inés is the only one she mentions in this letter to my mother."

"Your mother?"

"Elvira Reyes—I mean Elvira Martínez de Reyes. This is her picture." He took out his wallet and flipped it open to the first frame. While Don Solomón put on a pair of horn-rimmed glasses to look at the photograph, he swallowed the brandy in his glass. That made three, and he was feeling them.

"A very handsome lady, allow me to say."

"A singer."

"An artist, an artist—" Don Solomón mumbled and tapped his skull with a rigid finger so hard that it was audible. "Now I know! Your father was—"

"Fernando Reyes. Did you know him?"

"No, but I knew the father of your father. He and the father of Alvara Reyes, who was the husband of Pelancha—Esperanza, that is—were—"

"Brothers."

"No, they were cousins," Don Solomón said.

"That makes it pretty thin, this relationship. Just the same, since I was passing through, I thought I'd look her up personally." He paused, knowing that he sounded like a man of large affairs, with phrases like "passing through" and looking her up "personally." He continued calmly, "I know she would want to hear."

"Hear—?"

"My mother, she died about a week ago."

"I am sorry for your loss, señor Reyes." Don Solomón poured Gilberto's glass full again and handed it to him. It seemed the right thing to do—as right as shaking his hand. "She is at rest."

Gilberto nodded and solemnly swallowed the drink. "Thank you, Don Solomón, for your sympathy."

"And you came to inform Pelancha. That is remarkable."

"As distant as this woman may be," Gilberto said, "they kept in touch—by correspondence."

"She will appreciate your having come; a visitor from so far. But it will also be of benefit to you, señor Reyes. Grief is a heavy pack for one to carry alone; and if others each take a small portion—" a slight gesture of his pale hands finished it.

"I'm wondering about the relationship."

"Friendship is sometimes dearer than kinship."

Pretty corny, Gilberto thought; but a second glance, and warmed to charity by the brandy, he admitted the old fellow hit it right on the nose.

"And when you see her," Don Solomón continued, "it would be a kindness on your part to call her aunt. It will make her happy, I am sure."

"You say she has three kids—what am I supposed to call them?"

"The two eldest, Inés and Pompeyo, you may call cousins—if you choose."

The wallet still lay on the counter, with the picture face up. Gilberto's eyes became misty as he looked down at it until it seemed to move slowly around in a haze. Picking it up, he moved it slowly back and forth until he saw it clearly again. "I'll bet you, if somebody handed you this picture and didn't say who it was, you'd take it to be Dolores Del Río." Then, something thin and strong as a piece of piano wire seemed to coil around his chest and he thought, "It hurts to know I'm never going to see her again,"—not knowing that he thought it aloud.

"Sad as the passing of a mother is," Don Solomón said, "you may believe me, young man, that it is many times more tragic if she lives to survive her children."

"Huh? I didn't quite get you."

"By that I mean that my mother, as well as yours, señor Reyes, were among the fortunate ones."

"I beg your pardon, Don Solomón," Gilberto began oratorically. His mind was feeling sharp, incisive; not a sponge that soaks up any old remark at face value. "You don't mind, my friend, if I stop you right there and ask you to explain. You might be able to incline me also to the idea—" His voice trailed off, but he would have liked to repeat "incline me also." He remembered that from a debate in Civics class.

"Forgive me, then," Don Solomón resumed. "I should have remembered your recent grief and put it another way. I should have said that in the last two generations, the number of mothers who remained alive to mourn their sons was too great, too great by millions. So great that it would take a thousand years to restore the balance, the way it should be—the way life is ordained—that the children should outlive the parents."

In expansive agreement, Gilberto slapped his glass on the counter. "Don Solomón, you said something there that ought to be written down in a book. . . . With your permission—" He was aware that his voice was quite loud; can't help that, though—the man "inclined him." He slopped more cognac into his glass, spilling only a little.

"It is true, then, señor Reyes, that mothers leave us with less pain than would be their portion if we were taken from them?"

"You bet your—you're goddam right!"

"My own mother went to her rest not knowing that I had been conscripted for war."

Good thing that razor-like brain was in there slashing, or he'd let that last remark slip past him. Time to clam up—the old fox knows something; switch the subject.

Don Solomón, smiling faintly, said, "Unless the dead have ways of knowing better, I am today what she desired me to be, Reb Sholomo, Gaon of Bialystok; perhaps even Chief Rabbi of Poland, instead of Solomón Gulden, merchant of Zaragoza." As he waved to indicate his merchandise, Gilberto turned around on the stool.

"Reminds me," Gilberto said. "I want to get a few things for these people." Section by section, he took in the cluttered space around him. "Regular department store—"

More like a Main Street pawnshop expanded twenty diameters. Plows and wheelbarrows hung from the beams. Separate plowshares and smaller farm hardware, picks, shovels, hoes and machetes of many sizes and shapes hung from nails on the far wall. On a section of shelving were a number of known makes of radio receivers, spring-wound phonographs, and some cheap, factory-made guitars. The adjoining space held yard-high stacks of folded work pants. Clothing racks hung with cotton dresses and denim work jackets. Beyond that, toward the rear of the store, four folding chairs, nailed together on a plank faced stacks of shoe boxes.

A glass display case, almost the width of the store, faced the entrance, and above it hung a tray-scale with a dial and pointer, looking like a clock which had stopped at 12. Behind it were uneven ranks of canned goods, and paper sacks of rice and sugar. To the left of that, by a curtained doorway, Gilberto saw a rolltop desk, and beside it, mounted on a packing box, a small, chunky safe.

Down the center of the store, from the section of dry groceries to the door, ran a line of barrels, steel drums of kerosene, and open-mouthed sacks of beans—at least five varieties: blue, pink, egg white, dark red, and mottled brown. At the head of this battery, nearest the door, stood a crimson and white Coca-Cola freezer.

Turning again, facing Don Solomón, he felt a little dizzy. Things directly in front of him all seemed to have furry edges. Everything shiny had an aureole around it; Don Solomón's eyeglasses, a row of ball-point pens wired to a display card, and many pieces of small hardware, each fixed as a sample to a drawer.

"Yeah, don't like to go and see these people with empty hands, see. Nice rebozo or two for the aunt, stuff for the kids, you know—" Wrestling the bundle of pesos out of his pocket, he tossed it on the counter. "Whatever it costs, take it out of that, huh? If it isn't enough—there's more. Just do it up right, if you get what I mean."

Don Solomón was patting his arm and saying something, but it all sounded like a faraway drone.

"Toys," Gilberto went on. "Little trucks and wagons, huh? That's what I used to love as a kid." Swinging his arm in a circle over the counter, as if he were drawing a pull toy, he knocked over the brandy bottle. Don Solomón up-ended it quickly. "Sorry, Pop—stuff's too good to waste," Gilberto laughed and comically licked the back of his hand on which some drops had fallen.

"It has grown late, and you are perhaps very tired, señor Reyes—"

"Now just a minute, chief, I still didn't give you my order. Now get your pencil—no, never mind, forget it. Better still, you know these Widows de Reyes, so I'm going to let you pick out the stuff for them. Something for everybody, all around; and don't forget a couple of good-looking rebozos for the lady. Candy and things for the kids; and tuck in a bottle of that cognac for the old man. I'm going to leave it all to you." His voice drawled wearily. "Make up a nice package. I'll get some sleep and pick it up in the morning. . . . Right now—right now, what's the best hotel you got here in town?"

Without waiting to hear, he turned slowly around the stool and took his foot off the top rung. He would have to climb down slowly—it being such a long drop to the floor.

Don Solomón called, "Elena—"

28

He lay drunk. Awake still, but in that wretched, primary stupor, where a corrosive bile keeps the brain shrieking. He was lying on his back, undressed except for his socks and shorts, a serape over him.

The room—the area—whatever it was in which he lay, tilted as if it were being lifted by jacks; spinning, sometimes in two directions at once, until he found out he could control the gyrations. When he kept his eyes open, it was motion and confusion, and he could stop it gradually by closing them.

Then, everything steadied as he felt the grainy surface of the serape, the all-compassing armor of his childhood. The next thing, she would be singing, "Ay Sandunga, Sandunga, mamá por Dios. . . . Mamá de mi corazón—"

He dreamt. And he knew he was dreaming, because he could get outside of the shell of illusion; leave all the phantoms in it, inert as puppets, and start them going again. But what they said and did was their idea; that was beyond him.

It was the McVeigh High School Auditorium. The seats, about a third full. All Jews—with their wives and daughters. What a collection of noses! One guy with a red beard parted in the middle and wearing a long, shiny alpaca coat was walking up and down the aisles. This joker was rattling a coin box and saying, "Just come from a Jew funeral in City Terrace. Boy! You should see the way they carried on! Hey, buddy, what about a Buddy Poppy, buddy?" He called his own name, "Gilberto!" and looked all over the auditorium for himself; he knew he was there, someplace, until somebody tapped him on the shoulder and pointed to the platform. There he was, in his mother's lap, wearing only a little shirt that barely came down to his bellybutton.

The Dutchman was really in there pitching at that special assembly. Everybody had to attend, compulsory. It was about the mass meeting that was going to take place that same night, here in the McVeigh Auditorium.

"For the authorities to allow the use of a decent, Christian American public school for that element to spew their poison in, is a violation of everything we hold dear." He sort of caught himself there and said, "When I say Christian, I want to say to the many Hebrew boys and girls that I mean it in the moral sense."

Anyway, he said he had "taken steps" about the meeting tonight, and he wanted the students to show their patriotism. He called for a volunteer squad to take mops and buckets and fumigate the place with Lysol the next morning. There were plenty of volunteers, although they never swung a single mop, because the union of building maintenance employees put their foot down.

Gilberto found out what the whole thing was about when somebody asked him to sign a petition during the lunch hour. It was going to be a protest meeting called by these subversives, against a member of the L.A. School Board; a woman who slipped all the insurance on every school building in the city to her husband's firm.

When he came out of a late practice session in the gymnasium, there was a crowd already on the auditorium steps, waiting to go in. And a picket line including four women—goons, more or less—who were walking up and down, singing, "I Love America." There were some signs "Go Back to Russia!", "This is a White Man's Country," and one he hadn't seen in years, "Arms for the Arabs!"

It was only eight o'clock, and he was dateless and broke, as well. Despite the fact that it was obviously a Commie affair, it always interested him, for a time, to listen to soap boxers. So what else was there to do?

The chief speaker was good; better than the Dutchman had been that morning. He started out, "You all read on Page One of the *Examiner* this morning—before you lined your birdcage with it—"

He thought it would be all like that, full of gags, but it wasn't. He talked about a killer they executed the previous night in the gas chamber up at San Quentin. How the doctors taped a stethoscope to the man's heart and listened at the end of a long tube. And described how the witnesses watched the condemned man through a thick glass window, and the fellow was trying not to breathe when the lumps of cyanide dropped into the bucket of acid under his seat. Twenty seconds, thirty seconds, a minute, seventy-five seconds. . .

The speaker said he'd wait while the people looked at their watches and tried holding their breath for only thirty seconds. "After that, you'll want to breathe, whether it's Chanel Number Five or cyanide gas."

What all this had to do with a chiseling member of the school board, Gilberto couldn't figure. But he continued to sit there and listen. The speaker said that there would be a fellow available any day now who could do a neater job up there in San Quentin. This fellow had a lot of experience in that line, and the Occupation people in Germany had set him free. This specialist used to knock them off four hundred at a time. He used to give them shower baths, hot as they could stand. A good, hot shower not only got them clean, but it would open their pores. Then, he'd turn on a valve of special gas called Zyklon, and they'd drop like flies. Drag 'em out and bring in the next batch. "And there are people outside—you saw them as you came in—who would be willing to do the same thing to us here."

Maybe them, Gilberto thought, but not him. Anybody could see that he was different.

The Speaker came up to him, pinched his chin, nodded to his mother, and said, "Reyes, G. don't forget—Friday, seven a.m., Federal Building." Don Solomón, wearing a big sombrero, and a bald, fat little man, standing side by side and swaying rhythmically, were praying. The little man was saying, "I am the pastor of the First Christian-Jewish Church, just a stone's throw from the nearest home, where it says on the biggest neon sign in Boyle Heights, 'Jesus, King of the World' on one side and 'Yeshuah, Melach Hu-Olam' on the reverse." He was wearing an "I Like Ike" button. "It is time for the sacrament," he said to Don Solomón. The two of them came up, and Gilberto began to whimper. His mother smoothed his hair and said, "Shhh, hijito." Dr. Eisen said, "Come on fellows, I haven't got all night." There was a big sponge cake and they broke off a piece, pouring something on it from a Remy-Martin bottle. He began to suck on it. "This is my body; this is my blood." Dr. Eisen said, "Aw, knock it off," and took the wrapper off an ordinary blue razor blade. His mother hugged him. "Oh, doctor, you're going to collapse his lung for him?" He said, "Hell, no; I'm just going to cut his cock off," and she giggled. Don Solomón took the blade out of Eisen's hand. "Con su permiso, señor doctor; nuestro padre, el patriarco Abrahán—" Dr. Eisen nudged her and said, "What do you think, Elvira?" She answered "Well, Sam—if he's licensed for the work—" Eisen bowed to him, "Dispense, mi rabino." Don Solomón, the blade flashing in his fingers, leaned over him as the doors in the back of the auditorium crashed open and the Hollywood Post of the American Legion, in their blue-and-gold dress uniforms marched in, behind a high-stepping drum majorette, Miss Jennifer Baxter. . . .

He sat upright, both hands cupped over his groin. The whimpering he heard was his own.

Dazed, hollow-headed, he stared, one at a time, at the walls of the room; stained a bright blue. He counted the beams in the ceiling; eleven. The iron bars on the deep window; seven. The iron studs in the heavy wooden door; eight.

A thick shaft of sunlight from a smaller window above him made a spotlight for a spiraling insect. There was a green and yellow straw mat on the red-tiled floor and a large camel-back wooden chest, painted all over with flowers and animals. His own bag sat open on a chair.

The bed under him was a low, wooden frame with a net of rope instead of a spring, and a thin mattress. He saw his coat hanging on a hook, one of a row of five nailed to a board on the opposite wall, over a chest. Why wasn't his new hat there, he wondered. He wasn't sure now that he ever had one.

He didn't feel bad or sick or groggy; not at all like the morning he had taken two slugs of tequila on top of a couple of beers at the Romeros' once.

And this not being able to remember anything was a strange, new feeling; but nothing painful. He might have had one of those blackouts he had heard a couple of fellows discussing. They were stories about having some drinks; leaving their party for a smoke or a breath of fresh air, and waking up the next morning in their own beds, not knowing how they got there. However, as Nick Keaney related, "I not only drove myself home, but my mother thanked me for *backing* the car into the garage; and if you know our driveway, that's a stunt, even for a sober man. Yup, a complete blank is what I drew. You could come to me and say I killed a guy, and there'd be no way for me to prove I didn't."

Now, where did he draw his blank—? He went back to the missing hat and remembered about that; how he bought it in Victoria. His memory looped ahead to sweating out the crawl over the bridge, with his eye on the flaming straw and his mind on Lucas behind him.

It was later—a good deal later—that he blacked out . . . Smacking the driver—? No, later than that. Sitting at a counter—ah, it was coming! Don Solomón! It was getting clear—talking about his mother, her picture, the wallet—He jerked around suddenly, plunging both hands under the pillow. Flat! Gone; the money was gone! That's where it happened—he showed his dough, like the jerk in the radio playlet—

Snatching his pants from the chair beside the bed, he knew they were lighter by the weight of the missing pad of money. The secret pocket gaped open and empty.

Dumbly he swung his feet off the bed and, as he pulled his pants on, something fell, ringing faintly on the floor. An inch from his naked toe, he stared at it—the razor blade. Light—light from a lamp. That one, an ordinary kerosene lamp; the one on the table, right in front of him, which Don Solomón carried in. . . . "Be careful with that blade, señor Reyes. . . . Ay, hombre! You will cut yourself, slashing like that. Here, let me take it. . . . Hold still."

He put the blade down carefully on the table and remained there a moment, studying a calendar on the wall. The page was for the month of August and it advertised a coffee warehouse. The lithograph showed a dying bullfighter on a couch, gazing at a beautiful girl in a mantilla, who in turn was looking somewhere else. There was the bull that killed him; a big, black bastard, with blood on his horns and a rope of froth coming out of his mouth. There were other figures in the picture, too; but there was pressure behind his eyes, and it tired him to study it.

His shoes were by the bed, with the socks brimming out of them; his shirt, hooked over a chair by the armholes. That wasn't the way he did it; he always turned a shirt inside out if he intended to wear it the next day. And he never tucked his socks back into his shoes, either.

More and more details became clarified. Yes, it was the old man who took off his shoes for him; not just yanking them off, but holding them in his lap to untie the laces. Shameful—and that wasn't all. Another thing was his crying, and not about his mother, either; about Lucas and what a dirty, no-good heel he was to hit the poor guy.

And something happened before that—yes, stumbling on the way to this room and falling into the hammock in which Concha and her mother lay asleep. Their waking up; his making them a very sloppy lecture, half-Spanish and half-English, trying to sound like Morrissey. And the last thing—saying to Concha that he forgave her for everything and trying to kiss her . . . "Like a big brother—" Disgusting! The son of a bitch who got her in this fix must have pulled the same line. . . . Good thing this was a calendar hanging here and not a mirror.

There was also a dream, and he tried to recall what that was about and who the people were in it. But it lay in a stratum so dark and deep, that he could remember none of it except his mother's low laughter.

Sooner or later, though, he would have to look in a mirror and see what he looked like with a hangover. He had seen a lot of its victims on the screen—practically every actor. They were always yelling at their butlers for opening the blinds, clutching their heads and moaning, or gulping ice-water from pitchers.

Perhaps his head would ache, too, later on; but now it merely felt light, as after a short haircut. His mouth felt dry, but he wasn't thirsty. Churning up a froth with his toothbrush would be all he needed.

Slipping into his shirt and carrying his bag, he opened the door and stepped out on the patio. There were doors everywhere; too many. There was only one open, and he peered in, but it wasn't the bathroom. This was a bedroom, twice as large as the one he had slept in, and it had a matrimonio in it. A little woman with long, gray-streaked hair, swishing an insecticide gun around, turned and asked him, "Did you sleep well last night, señor?"

He suspected, from her wrinkled grin, that she knew all about how he slept. "Fine, thank you—"

"Margarita, at your service. I am the ama de llaves." She was the mistress of the keys, and she had a big ring of them to prove it. "I will unlock the bath for you."

It was two doors away. Now he could have a little peace. Looking at himself in the mirror, he saw nothing bestial about his appearance. Even his hair was untousled. But he could use a shave, and if that shower over the tub was warm, he would be a new man in no time.

As he peeled off his shirt, Margarita unlocked the latched door from the outside and came in with two towels.

"Thank you, but you didn't have to bother; there's a towel hanging here already."

Margarita ignored him, draped the towels over a rod, and tested the heat of a cylindrical water heater by putting her cheek against it. She didn't like the temperature, and added two sticks of kindling. She bustled about as he waited, turning the taps on and off, peering into the tub for scorpions, and

once more stirring the fire in the water heater. Finally she gave a little snort
and said, "Now, with your permission, I will go to inform the cook." And she
actually stood there, with her back to the door, waiting, until he said, "Yes, if
you please."

The water was wonderfully soft. He shampooed his hair, and in the first
rinse, plenty of dirt came out with the suds.

With everything clean on—socks, shirt, shorts—he felt one hundred percent. One thing he had forgotten: to rinse out his socks so that they would be
dry this morning. This was the first time he hadn't done that. Well, it was the
first time he had ever been drunk.

Back in the room, he locked his bag and took a minute to think things out.
What should he say to Don Solomón; be apologetic, or carry it off as if
nothing happened? If the man asked "Well, how do you feel this morning?"
just pull the pins out from under him by answering, "Fine. Why?" Then,
mention something about what a nice place he had here—you could hardly
tell from the street what was behind the walls. A little later, casually bring up
the question of the money; not bluntly, but in line with the business he came
about in the first place: the purchase of some presents for his aunt and family.
Finally, he would ask for a complete accounting, including the room and,
naturally, the drinks. After all, he had asked about a hotel, and this probably
was it.

Across the open part of the patio, opposite his room, Margarita beckoned
him toward a table. As he started toward it, she withdrew to the kitchen and
reappeared with another woman; bigger, younger, but with the same kind of a
smile. "She is the cook, señor, but she will serve you herself."

"Josefina, a sus órdenes. Is it your habit to take your coffee with cream or
scalded milk, Don Gilberto?"

"Black, please, Josefina."

She pulled a chair out for him with her bare foot. "Like Don Solomón. He
asks to wish that you will enjoy the breakfast; Doña Elena, the same. And
would you take a bottle of mineral water?"

Yes, and it turned out to be what he hoped: frosty cold, with giant bubbles
of biting gas. Nobody asked him what he wanted for breakfast, but this was
apparently one of those "family" hotels where everybody gets the same.

Josefina brought the coffee in a jar, poured it for him, then brought a stack
of four hot tortillas in a napkin. He tore a piece off one and nibbled. Delicious;
he could do away with a batch of these as fast as they could peel them off the
griddle.

Margarita scurried past, but not without stopping to say, "Buen provecho, señor Reyes."

Don Gilberto, señor Reyes—what a polite staff. He would leave them a
good tip when he settled the bill. Taking a good look around for the first time,
it reminded him of the patios in Roy Rogers westerns. Only this didn't have a
second floor, and no balcony from which Roy could leap down and land on

the heavy's neck; and no serapes draped over rails. He could see three sides from where he sat: the left, where he had slept; the passage facing him, which was the front, and through which he entered from the store; and the side with the kitchen and covered dining space. Behind him, to the rear, was a low, wide structure of hollow cement blocks, and connected with it, at an L, a two- or three-room house, with windows and a half-door. Everything was in bright, punishing sunlight. But nothing glared, unless you looked at the metal roof of the building in the rear. Whatever else there was—the grass, the moss, and the banks upon banks of bougainvillia—blotted up the sun and, it seemed, the heat.

Josefina set a large, hissing platter in front of him. Huevos rancheros, eggs fried in a piquant salsa mexicana—three of them. "Cooked in butter," Josefina said, a little sadly. "It is forbidden for Don Solomón to eat lard or the flesh of pigs. He is of another faith—here is Doña Elena."

A doña in his book—Doña Anybody—was supposed to look like a Spanish dreadnaught, looming in black lace and tall combs; not at all like the woman who came down the three brick steps from the store entrance. She came directly up to him, smiling and said, "Buen provecho." He rose and she gave him her hand—not only the fingers, but the entire hand in a firm clasp. There was an on-the-level directness, warmth without effusiveness, which made him understand, instantly, and for certain, that this was no hotel, nor a rooming house. This was a home, and she was the mistress of it.

"Did you have a good rest, Don Gilberto?"

Using the reply he had framed for Don Solomón, putting him on the spot, didn't seem the right thing to do with Doña Elena. He answered, "Perfect. And I'm having a wonderful breakfast, too."

"Está usted en su casa."

She was about the age of his mother, maybe a year or two older. Her face was oval, just a trace on the long side; but he was convinced that as a young girl, she must have been a dead ringer for Elizabeth Taylor. And he—he felt like Cornel Wilde, standing there, in a beautiful Technicolor garden. There wasn't much "Mexican" about the way she was dressed: red and black checkered skirt, a black sweater with a narrow white collar. Her hair was black and her eyes brown, and her skin, the sort of even, light brown that some women, even blondes, try to get with a tinted powder. But there was no make-up of any kind on her face. On her fingers, which curled over the back of the chair across from him, she had a gold band and two silver rings with stones.

"I'll sit down with you for a little time."

"And Don Solomón—"

"I will send him in from the store later. He talked about you last night, after you had gone to bed, and I was very eager to see you."

Then he must have told her, Gilberto feared, about how he got stinking, made a nuisance of himself, and had to be put to bed. "I'm afraid I disturbed everybody in your house, señora."

"Not in the slightest. . . . You speak very good castellano, for one who has been so long in the United States of the North."

This was strange—had he said anything that would give them the idea that he was born in Mexico? "Thank you, señora, but my accent—everybody notices that."

"Don't think about it, Don Gilberto; we all have accents, almost as many as there are states in the Republic. . . . You are eager to see your relatives, no doubt?"

He had forgotten about them. "In a way, yes. It's sort of an obligation."

"A wish of your mother. Solomón told me. I would like also to see her portrait, if you care to show it."

She looked at it for a long time, then at him, and once more at the picture. "Yes—an artist. One can tell without having known her. She has given you her eyes and mouth."

Then, as she handed the wallet back, Doña Elena did something more eloquent, more electric than her handshake: she took his wrist and turned it, so that she could see the face of his watch. "By now, they know you are here," she said. "You will receive a warm welcome. I wish I could be there, too. How proud Esperanza will be!" She got up. "With your permission—oh, let me not forget; the girl and her mother, they asked me to give you their many thanks."

"Concha—how is she?"

"She adores you—you are her hero."

That's nice! All he needed now was to have Concha on his neck. Let's see—she must have had her first injection at eleven last night; one at three, one at seven, and she was due for the last at eleven. It was a little before nine-thirty. He would be gone long before she was back.

At his side, Josefina watched Doña Elena go back in the store, and sighed deeply. "An angel! A saint on earth. . . . You do not like the eggs, señor?"

"They're wonderful. The best I ever tasted; the tortillas the same, and the coffee." As he poured more from the jar, Don Solomón appeared at the door. He blinked in the sun and appeared to be feeling for the steps as he came down to the patio level.

"Ah, *bon appétit*, monsieur," he said, sitting down. "My wife is disappointed that you didn't speak to her in English."

"I'm sorry, Don Solomón. I certainly would have; I didn't know she spoke it."

Glancing around, in mock secrecy, he bent forward and said, "Between us, señor Reyes, she doesn't, really. She studied a little in the capital, and she still has her lesson books and a dictionary." He nipped off a piece of tortilla and ate it. Gilberto saw it as a homely, easy gesture; the equivalent of Doña Elena's taking his wrist when she wanted to know the time. Those things are little acts you do at home, with people of your own circle. And he was a stranger.

"If it will make Doña Elena feel better, she knows at least three thousand English words." Don Solomón leaned back, stopped chewing, and spread his palms in elaborate disbelief. "Sure," Gilberto continued, "every Spanish word that ends in -ción means the same thing in English, only it's spelled -tion. Nación, nation; registración, registration—and so on."

"Constitución, constitution; educación, education—" Don Solomón slapped his hand on the table and rose. "Excuse me; I must tell her this!"

Josefina, grinning, watched him go. "You have given him some good news; is that it, Don Gilberto?"

"Just some information, Josefina."

He came back directly, laughing; and may have laughed too much, Gilberto thought, seeing the man's teary, red-rimmed eyes. "I told her," he chuckled. "And she called *me* a fool, but she is very pleased with you."

"I am happy to hear that. . . . She told me, Don Solomón, that the señora—I forgot her present name—"

"Do not forget, your aunt—"

"Yes, Doña Elena told me she already knows I'm here."

"Or," Don Solomón said, "she will know very soon. I sent some of the things you wanted for them with Lorenzo, the arriero, on muleback. When he comes back, we can get a fresh animal and you may go back with him. I do not urge it, but you may wish to give the children their gifts with your own hand."

This opened another area of confusion. "What was it I ordered?"

"Here is a list of them." Don Solomón took a slip of paper out of his shirt pocket. "You will see that most of the things are—"

"That's all right, Don Solomón. All I want to know is that I'm able to pay for them."

"Everybody should be able to pay as well as you, and this would be a happy land. You are, young, man, by the standards of this part of the country, a rich individual." He found a second slip of paper and brought it close to his eyes. "In my safe, you have two thousand, nine hundred and eighty-five pesos; less the ten pesos which you gave the child, Concha's mother; and one hundred United States dollars."

"And how much does all the stuff come to?"

"We will have a reckoning later; meanwhile, I will drink a coffee with you. Josefina, a cup, please."

Two things were clear now: the whereabouts of his money and why Concha's mother left her thanks. "I'm glad she finally took some money," he said.

"You started by offering her fifty pesos," Don Solomón said, smiling. "She couldn't understand why you were giving her anything."

"I suppose it's because I was sorry for them—I mean the girl. An older person could take care of himself."

"It is the girl, then, who has come for the treatment?"

"Why, I thought you knew, Don Solomón."

Looking comically betrayed, he complained, "I know nothing! I am told nothing! My wife has professional illusions with her syringes. Only when she has to inject a calf for something am I even told *whose* animal it is. . . . When you have drunk your coffee, if you will come into the store, we will—"

"I'll go now."

With the steel curtain rolled up and the doors open, the Surtidor gave directly on the street. It was bright in all the corners which, last night, looked dark and cluttered. There was more to the stock than he had observed earlier. A display of cheap men's and women's wrist watches and homelier alarm clocks; between the shoes and the hardware, a trestle was heaped with stationery; pens, ink, paper, pencils, blank notebooks; and a staggered assortment of printed material—thin books with gayly colored board covers.

The Alameda looked cool as an inland lake. A multitude of birds, but not one that showed itself, shrieked and cawed in the trees. The few scattered benches were empty. Whatever movement of people took place was on the opposite side of the Alameda, where the sun struck fiercely. The same kind of displays he had seen in Ciudad del Maíz were strung along the street.

None of the vendors called out, but sounds reached him in the doorway of the Surtidor; sounds like the conversation of many friends.

A man in frayed trousers and a washed-out denim jacket approached, crossing over from the other side of the street. A cop, Gilberto knew, more from the style of the man's ambling walk than from his equipment. This included a large revolver, a short club, and a metal insignia pinned to the front of his sombrero. As he came abreast of the store, he saluted, "Adiós, señor . . . Good morning, Doña Elena."

From behind Gilberto, she answered, "Good morning, sergeant."

"My greetings to Don Solomón, señora."

"I thank you for him." As the cop passed, she said to Gilberto. "That is Don Vicente, the chief of our two police."

"It doesn't look from here that there would be enough work for two of them," Gilberto smiled.

"On Tuesdays, yes; more than enough. That is the day of the market. You will see. In the morning both are busy settling quarrels over invasions of space. Then, at night, there is always some disorder in the Judge Not—the pulquería over there. . . You laugh at the name? There is more to it: Judge Not That You May Be Judged. Formerly it was called No Man is Wise at All Hours. But when Don Gumersindo became the new owner, he wanted a name with great morality for his place."

She had said, "Tuesday—you will see." Did she, by any chance, expect him to stick around like a tourist on the loose? He ought to give them to understand that he appreciated their hospitality and all that, but he would have to be on his merry way pretty soon. Instead, he said, "How big a place is Zaragoza?"

"I cannot say by population—perhaps six hundred. But it is on the postal route; we have the agency here in the store, and there are five telephones. . . . Perhaps you would like a small walk, with Don Vicente as your guide."

"I may do that, señora, thank you; if I have the time, later. Meanwhile, I mustn't keep Don Solomón. There's that account."

"If you are hurried," she said with a trace of a frown, and turned back to the rear of the store.

Don Solomón sat at his roll-top desk under a strong light. Pulling a board out from above the drawers, he nodded for Gilberto to take a seat. "Now, where is that list of items?" He started fumbling.

"Sol," his wife said, "if you are going to do any figuring, can it wait until after—"

"No, Elena. It is I who owes a balance to Don Gilberto. That must be settled."

As he turned to shuffle some papers, Doña Elena signaled to Gilberto, pointing to her eyes, a forefinger on each, and grimaced to show pain. Gilberto nodded—he understood; the redness, the swollen edges of the man's lids. "There is no urgency, Don Solomón. Let it go, for the time being."

"Yes," said his wife. "After Lorenzo returns."

"Very well. However, let us make a start. I will call off, since I remember, the things already sent. And if señor Reyes will be so good as to figure the amounts—give him a pencil, Elena."

Touching the rubberized cloth cover of a chunky machine on the top ledge of the desk, Gilberto said, "I may not need a pencil if that is a—" He lifted the cover; it was what he thought: an adding machine.

Both Don Solomón and his wife looked amazed. "You know how to operate that?"

"If it is in good order."

"It has scarcely been used."

Gilberto put the compact bulk on the shelf of the desk. It was a good machine; manually operated with six columns, ten keys with SUB-TOTAL, $\div$, $\times$, and CLEAR buttons. He cancelled some odd figures on the dial and said, "I'm ready."

"The first, then," Don Solomón began, "is eighteen kilos of frijol; bayo gordo, at a peso thirty-seven the kilo."

Gilberto worked the keys fast. "Twenty-four sixty-six."

"Imagine!" Doña Elena said. "Go on, Sol—"

"Cooking oil; part of a tin—make it three and a half liters—at two pesos eighty-five the liter."

There were eleven items altogether; some from his own stock, and others—like maize; a lump of lime; chile, green and dried; meat and vegetables—which he had instructed Lorenzo to buy at the stands opposite the Alameda.

"Seventy-three pesos eighty centavos," Gilberto said, tearing the slip off the roll.

"Isn't it wonderful, Elena! Look—to the last centavito. It would have taken me the better part of a half hour to work out that sum. You learned this in school?"

"Yes. There's nothing remarkable about it. I could show you or the señora how to handle it in a few hours."

"I would be willing to learn," Doña Elena said, "and then teach Felipe." She explained to Gilberto, "That is his man-of-confidence, but he is away in León for a few days."

"Don Solomón told me last night."

"He is without the alphabet," she said, "but he has numbers."

"Much too slowly," Don Solomón reminded her. "Besides, this is a machine of very delicate structure, and he is like me about machines—we are not scientists. You understand, Don Gilberto?"

"It just takes a little practice."

"Ah, to you North Americans, skills of this kind come naturally. I am prepared to say—" he turned to his wife. "Elena, show Don Gilberto the North American weighing machine from Ohio. He will know!"

"Solomón Gulden, have you no shame? Don Gilberto is a guest."

"Thank you, señora," Gilberto said. "But if it is something I could help with . . . A scales, Don Solomón?"

"A machine for weighing out things, but which at the same time gives the cost."

"A calculating scales, you mean?"

Don Solomón jutted his chin toward his wife. "What did I tell you, Elena? He knows exactly what this is! He has it in his mind's eye! All of its little wheels and levers."

"I'm not so sure. Is it a fixed scale for the price, or do you have to adjust it for each article weighed?"

Don Solomón looked trapped. "It sits on a counter. It has a fine enameled tray and shows from zero to ten kilos."

"It has been sitting in its box six years now," Doña Elena said, "and it can sit a little while longer."

"Whenever you are pleased to show it to me," Gilberto suggested. "And now this—" he glanced at the total on the dial of the adding machine. It was less than nine dollars, U.S., and all of it for food. "Shouldn't there be a separate account for those things I mentioned last night?"

"Yes—the presents you were going to bring them, in your own hands—"

"I have put aside a rebozo each for Pelancha and Inés," Doña Elena said. "Do you wish to see them?"

"Only to know which is for the mother and which is for the girl."

"The red and blue one is for Inés."

"And for the other children?" he asked.

"You would know better," Don Solomón said, rising. "I will show you what there is."

"You are going inside," his wife said. "Meanwhile, Don Gilberto may look around for himself."

They left him standing alone, in mild bewilderment as to what he would do if a customer came in. He found an assortment of toys of cheap native manufacture. Discarding the wooden objects, he selected several sets of plastic soldiers, toy guns, and imitation field glasses. Put aside, they looked puny. From jars and open boxes, he selected three of every kind of packaged candy that he could find. He went back and got plastic holsters into which the toy guns would fit.

The heap on the counter became substantial, and he wondered if these things would please two boys whose ages were—he guessed—about seven and ten. No, he decided, something was missing; perhaps only one thing that was neither something to eat nor to play with.

As his gaze roved the store, it stopped at the counter of stationery. There was what he wanted. He gathered up an armful of crayons, blank books, six pencils, several drawing blocks, and two erasers. Half-hidden among some bottles of ink, he discovered some sets in flat plastic boxes—a neatly compartmented array of pencils, pen holder and nibs, erasers, and pencil sharpener. He exchanged the loose pencils for the sets and went to the shelf of books.

Delightedly, he recognized one he had himself read when he was twelve: *20,000 Leagues Under the Sea.* He read a paragraph to see how it sounded in Spanish. The paper was gray and brittle. The price marked on the front cover was two pesos. This would do fine for the older boy. Now, which of these two—*Robinson Crusoe* and *Cielo, Tierra y Mar*—would the younger one go for? What the hell, get them both.

Doña Elena returned when he brought the things back to the counter. "Please forgive me," she said, "but his eyes were giving him much pain."

"I meant to ask you, señora—"

"After a little while in a darkened room, he will be relieved." She saw the things on the counter. "All that? You are very generous, Don Gilberto."

"I noticed Don Solomón's eyes. People with very heavy colds are so affected."

"It is more serious than that, I am afraid. For a time it was critical, and his son thought we would have to take him to a hospital in the States for an operation. But he did not wish to go."

"But if an operation would help," Gilberto said. "There's nothing more important than eyesight."

"It would not have helped, as we learned four years ago when there was a convention of specialists of the eye in Mexico. Moisés discovered a friend among them, and he sent for us. Not only this doctor, but two of his colleagues examined Solomón. One thought the infirmity of the eyes resulted from poison gas which blinded him for a time in the war. Another said it might have been from typhus from which he also suffered in those years. But all were of one mind that an operation would not help him. But two years ago, this doctor remembered his promise to Moisés, and from Switzerland he sent the drops which we have been using."

"And they help?"

"They relieve him. Twice a day. But he must lie still for at least an hour, with a dark bandage over his eyes. During that time, I read to him from the newspapers or a book. Other times, Don Perfecto, the priest, comes to visit. But they argue so violently, you could hear them in the Alameda."

"I can imagine," Gilberto smiled. "About religion."

"Naturally." She had a way of tilting her head back and wrinkling the corners of her eyes when she smiled. "The trouble is that each knows too much of his own faith and too little of the other's. To listen to them is sometimes painful and sometimes funny. Don Perfecto calls Solomón a Greek because the Jewish god requires sacrifices of animals. And because of the Sacrament, Solomón calls him 'Cannibal.'"

Gilberto was warmed by her talk; as he had been by her taking his wrist to look at his watch, by Don Solomón's absent and familiar taking a piece of tortilla from his plate—the ritual breaking of bread. What she was telling him now was not something from the secret family annals beyond which a simple gossip would not go, but particulars suggestive of her pride in the man.

Once, he, too, spoke like this, but more solemnly, about somebody—his mother. And again, about Dr. Eisen, but in that case, with a mixed motive: as a testament of his admiration for the man and, at the same time, flattering Bishop. He had given Bishop a piece of Eisen. Now, as he listened to Doña Elena, he felt she was giving him a piece of Don Solomón. She had said, "his son—Moisés," not "our son." If she had told that story to a casual listener, she need not have mentioned the son.

"This thing with Don Solomón's eyes—I thought I saw him reading, putting down figures."

"It is a show; he is sensitive and even vain," she explained. "He didn't want you to know. But he pays for it, as he did this morning." Her voice dropped. "You saw how he pretends, about the adding machine. He tried it, but the little ciphers swam away, he told me. Please, for a time don't show that you know about his difficulty."

This was the proof—not the simple imparting of a secret, shallow as it was, but being asked to keep it.

"Certainly, señora. . . ." Needless to add that he wouldn't be around here long enough even to make an accidental disclosure. "I wouldn't think of it. . . . Suppose we add up these things on the counter here, so he wouldn't have to strain."

"No—no! Let him see them and he will give you the prices, as with the other account, and you operate the machine. That gave him much pleasure."

"Sure, be glad to, señora. . . . I'd like to say something—" He heard his own voice somewhat shrilly, and in correcting it, it became hoarse. "But I don't know how to put it. . . . Not because I'm talking Spanish; it would be just as hard in English, where I have more words." She looked at him silently. That she was patient and didn't try to help him out, made it easier. "You asked me something *not* to do, which is easy, when you and Don Solomón are entitled to ask me *anything*, anything at all, that I could do. . . . You see what I mean?"

He put his hand out, supplicating her to understand. She took the hand between her cool palms, and holding it, looked at him until his struggling eyes lowered. Then her fingers touched his cheek and drew downward along his tight jaw. "I know; I know what is in your heart, Gilberto. . . . That I should be envying Pelancha of Fidel Vergas—"

"You talk about four years ago, señora, but much could have happened in that time."

She shook her head; he thought it was to deny what he said, but it wasn't that. "I had a brother; Ramón, he was called, three years older than myself. He did not go about seeking to do it, but wherever he went among people, they were sad when he left, but happier that he had been there."

He could ask about him—ask when he died and say that he was sorry, or he could thank her for what sounded agreeable. But he was impelled to tell her, "I have a very good friend in California, a doctor. He is famous, and he knows a great deal. I feel that he would know a way to help Don Solomón. I could write to him, and you could give the description of the eye trouble. He will answer you, and I know—"

"Shh, he is coming. Say nothing to him. I will speak with you later. I have already—"

From the doorway, Don Solomón said, "Lorenzo not back yet? But he will be soon. And I am very eager to hear what he says. I had to tell him to give Pelancha your greetings; to say that he was the messenger of Don Gilberto Reyes, who would come later. . . . Like an Oriental prince." He smiled. "Was that the right thing, Elena?"

"Of course, Sol. Surprises are not always pleasant. Meanwhile, look—Gilberto has been lavish."

"Ah, you say Gilberto. It does not offend?"

"I should say not. I'm not used to that Don business."

Don Solomón put his hand on Gilberto's shoulder and pressed it, once. "You have a mountain of toys there—Gilberto. They will think it is the Feast of the Three Kings."

"Los Tres Reyes," his wife said. "Gilberto is at least one of them. This is so like Ramón."

"Her brother, now dead, whom I did not know."

"The señora told me." They were trying to praise him, and it felt uncomfortable. "There is not much there, when you divide it among three children. I was wondering if there was anything else?"

"A man may bring the gift of himself."

Too quickly, before he understood fully what Don Solomón meant, Gilberto said, "I'll be taking the things up to them myself." Then, it came to him, and he added, "Oh—I hope the presents won't make them any less glad to see me. Suppose I move the adding machine up here, where it's light, and total up everything."

Doña Elena left to collect from a customer who had taken a refresco from the ice chest and was drinking rapturously. A child, who had come in to buy a bar of washing soap, stood at a timid distance, watching Don Solomón placing toy after toy in a paper sack.

When his wife returned to the counter, he bagged the last moulded plastic soldier. "One peso, twenty. . . . And now, what does your machine say?"

"Thirty-one, seventy-five."

"And seventy-three, eighty earlier, makes the sum of, let me see—"

"A hundred and four, fifty-five," Gilberto said.

"Let us call it one hundred pesos—"

"But we're not through yet," Gilberto said. "There's a few other things." He touched the place where he had put the books and the writing materials. "What happened to the pencils, and crayons, and—I put them right here."

Doña Elena, looking sharply at her husband, lifted up the outspread newspaper with which he had covered them. "You are careless, Solomón. . . . He forgets, Gilberto."

"I almost forgot them myself. I'd sooner go without the toys." He pointed to a display card—Plumas Atómicas, $3.50. "I might as well take three of those."

Don Solomón reached for the card, then turned before touching it. "Señor Reyes—Gilberto—I dislike to tell you this, but the money you are spending on these things could better go for—"

His wife intervened sharply. "Give him the pens, Solomón. . . . He means to say, Gilberto, that these people are very poor; that the food you sent them, the things to wear, they will bless you for them."

"I didn't realize that," Gilberto said. "I wish Don Solomón had said something about that before."

"They have so little—"

"That to bring them paper and pencils," Don Solomón said, "seems almost like a mockery. And books, which they—"

"Solomón!"

"Then let's figure out what they need in the line of food," Gilberto said, and realized that he was sounding like a big shot. "Or maybe we could have the aunt come in and order enough to last them for a while, like canned goods."

"There! That is sensible," Don Solomón said. "In place of these two sets of pencils, they could have a lamp for light." He moved the plastic boxes aside. "And for the price of these books, enough petroleum to last the winter."

"Fine. But I'm not cutting out the books and things. If they're going to have a lamp, they've got to have something to read by it, no?"

Doña Elena laughed lightly and patted his hand. Her husband looked serious. "I will get a lamp," he said, "and the petroleum."

Gilberto looked around. "I see you have canned milk—leche evaporada. That keeps."

"Yes," Doña Elena said, "but they are not used to it."

"I'm sure the kids will like it on their cereal, with sugar."

"A few tins?"

"A couple of dozen," he said. "And corn flakes." He pointed, "And oatmeal—and cream of wheat, that's good, too. And sugar—I don't remember if that was on the bill."

"No, but that is cheap; piloncillo, eighty centavos a kilo."

"How about flour?"

"White flour—they do not use it."

"A few boxes of cookies then. How about coffee—I see that grows around here. That ought to be cheap."

"Yes," she said, "when the people here sell it. But it is dear to buy; six pesos a kilo for the cheapest."

"We'll get ten kilos, then. How about rice; that's good and it's filling."

"And cheap; but still too dear for them, at one peso eighty the kilo."

"How much is in that sack?"

"Fifty kilos."

Don Solomón looked less stern when he returned, carrying the lamp and a five-gallon oil tin. "I found an extra chimney, an odd one, for which there will be no charge. . . . And what are you writing?"

"A list of the other things," Gilberto said, reading it off.

Don Solomón frowned, "Three hundred and fifty pesos, more or less. And so much of it things of luxury." He caught his wife's glance. "Even at the wholesale, which you will be charged. The coffee alone, at five twenty the kilo—"

"Five," his wife said.

"Five then, pardon me. But this is still more than Lorenzo can transport on one mule, since you will ride the other. And my camioneta will not run, even if Felipe were here to drive it."

"You have a truck, too, Don Solomón?"

"In the depósito, to the rear; but it is discomposed, and a mechanic has promised to come next week. . . . Ah, here is Lorenzo, at last."

"What's the matter with the car?" Gilberto asked eagerly.

"Let us hear how Lorenzo was received. . . . Come in, come in, Lorenzo—hurry, hombre."

The muleteer entered, respectfully removing his sombrero, and bowed to everybody, including Gilberto. He was a short, middle-aged man with a shock of iron gray hair; yet his big moustache was quite black.

"Now tell us, Lorenzo—"

Lorenzo nodded to Gilberto. "This, then, is the young caballero."

"Señor Gilberto Reyes," Don Solomón said.

"Lorenzo Aguilar y Esquivel, at your service, Don Gilberto," the mule driver bowed again. "With your leave—" and going to the door, he spit politely behind his hand. "Ay, it is dusty going in that canyon."

Doña Elena brought him an uncapped bottle of soda. "Your healths, all," he said, and drained it.

"And now, Lorenzo—"

"The woman of Fidel Vargas received what you sent with thanks that cannot be uttered."

"It is not we who sent it," Doña Elena said impatiently. "It was Don Gilberto. Did you tell her that?"

"Claro, Doña Elena; her foreign nephew, exactly as you told me."

Don Solomón was impatient. "There was more. How did Pelancha act? You saw!"

"As if stunned," Lorenzo said. "As I unloaded each package, it was as if she was struck a fresh blow. And then she fell to weeping."

"And when you told her that Don Gilberto was coming to visit?"

"She sent the two younger ones to bathe, and she and the girl seized brooms and commenced to sweep from the door of their jacal to the trail."

"Then—?"

"Then I left."

Gilberto was grinning and wondering why Doña Elena's eyes were bright with tears.

"Well, there is more work for you, Lorenzo," Don Solomón said. "You will need another mule."

"Filiberto Alamilla's burros are idle."

"Good; say I wish to borrow them."

"Excuse me, Don Solomón," Gilberto said. "This truck—if it is not too badly out of order, perhaps I can do something with it."

Elena! Did you hear that? He understands that as well."

"Yes—the adding machine, the scales, and now the camioneta."

"I haven't seen the scales yet, señora, but I'd like to have a look at the truck. What did your man say was wrong?"

"Nothing," Don Solomón shrugged, "except that it would not march and that it requires the services of an expert. Go, anyhow; amuse yourself with it while Lorenzo and I prepare the load. Margarita will let you in to the depósito where it sits, through the patio."

"Come, I will show you," Doña Elena beckoned.

The depósito ran the entire length of the patio and seemed to be a warehouse of the Surtidor's stock. The truck occupied the center of the space, behind locked double-doors. It was a yellow, one-and-a-half ton, stake-body Studebaker; a 1946 model, but it looked younger, due to the clean paint.

"It if lacks gasoline, I will send Lorenzo in to pump some up from that steel barrel beside the work bench, there," Doña Elena said.

"I'll open the door first, if it's all right." He unbarred the doors and swung them open to the unpaved street behind the Surtidor. The cement floor under the truck, he noticed, showed no signs of oil drip.

"If you can do this miracle—"

"It may be just a very slight thing," he said, and hoped that it was. The ignition would be the first thing he meant to check. There were some tools on the bench beside the drum of gasoline.

"I will leave you here, Gilberto. Call Margarita if there is anything you wish."

He thanked her and was glad that she would leave him. A man appreciates being alone at a time like this; having no audience for any blunders he might make.

Climbing into the cab, he turned on the ignition and checked the gas level: three-quarters full. The ammeter responded as he switched on the headlights, and again when he pressed the button with his toe for the high beam.

Next, he tried the starter and let it spin for several seconds, pulling the choke button out an inch. He could hear the carburetor sucking gas into the bowl, but the engine did not fire. Leaving the ignition on, he dismounted and raised the hood. The engine, a six, was reasonably clean for its age. The high-tension wire was well and firmly connected to the spark coil; there was a level of gasoline in the filter bowls; the plug connections were tight. There were no cracks in the porcelain of the plugs, but it was possible, he thought, that they could be badly fouled just the same. That called for a test to see if they were sparking; quite simple, by touching the shaft of a screwdriver to the plug and seeing the strength of the spark in the gap between the tip and the engine block. Pushing the starter solenoid switch under the hood with his finger, the screwdriver test showed no spark at all, or hardly any, on cylinders 1, 2, and 5. Starting from the rear of the engine, 6, 4, and 2 were weak. This meant that all of the plugs were either totally bad or that the current was not reaching them. The sensible thing to do, he decided, was examine the distributor. Unclipping the plastic dome of the distributor, he knew he had located the trouble, or part of it. The contact surfaces were badly fouled. He wiped them clean with a corner of his handkerchief dipped in gasoline, then examined the rotor and platinum points. As he feared, these were carbonized and pitted, but sometimes resurfacing them would work, but only temporarily.

He needed an extremely thin file and looked on the workbench for one. No luck. A piece of emery cloth might do, but he couldn't think of the Spanish word for it, and the idea of asking Don Solomón for it would make his triumph less, if he could get the motor started.

Then, as he thought of lighting a cigarette, a solution came to him: the striking surface of the package of matches. It wasn't emery cloth, but a fine abrasive just the same. Peeling off a thin strip, he tried it, and it worked. He blew gently, and a fine carbon dust disappeared. For good measure, he brushed the paper lightly over the contacts in the distributor head and clipped it back on.

Now for the payoff. Back in the seat, he rolled the window down. The seat was a little too far forward for him—this Felipe must be a short fellow—and he moved it back to a more comfortable position. Hand brake—on; gear lever—in neutral. Depressing the clutch—as all first class drivers do—he turned the ignition on and touched the starter for a mere fraction of a second. There was a whine and a growl, in which, it seemed to him, there was a note of impatience. He pressed the starter again, and over it went! The first explosion of the engine sounded like music. Gunning it lightly, it raced smoothly. Letting it run, he got down and tested the plugs again with the screwdriver and got a good, fat spark from each one. He raced the engine again, from the ground, using the accelerator linkage, and she snarled like a goddam tiger. One sweet bucket of bolts.

Don Solomón was standing in the patio door, open-mouthed as Gilberto lowered the hood, but raised it again, as he remembered to look at the oil level and the water in the radiator. He tried to look calm and unimpressed with his own accomplishment, while Don Solomón stared at him.

"It is going; you have made it march."

"Yes, she's running nicely. There's nothing for the mechanic to do. But I would tell him to get a new set of points."

Don Solomón nodded and alternately shook his head. There was something Semitic in the way he showed bewilderment; in the way his hands were outspread and the movement, from side to side, of his shoulders.

"I'll pull it out front," Gilberto said, climbing in. "Which way out, right or left?"

Don Solomón pointed to the left.

They were all in the doorway when he pulled up in front of the Surtidor.

"I tell you, Elena, there is nothing these young norteamericanos cannot do."

Gilberto looked nonchalantly at his grease-stained hands. "I'll just wash up a little."

"And rest for a while," Doña Elena suggested. "A cup of coffee—a refresco?"

"No, thank you." He went to the room where he slept to get his comb and a fresh handkerchief. His bag was on the chair where he left it, but the worn shirt, socks, and shorts he had put aside were missing.

Don Solomón, Elena, and Lorenzo stood silently, like a reception committee, when he came back into the store. "It doesn't look like much of a load, after all," he said, seeing the bags and boxes piled behind the cab. "Are we ready to start?"

"Lorenzo will show you the way."

"I need some cigarettes, if you have Elegantes. And what do you please to smoke?" he asked Lorenzo.

"Whatever it is your kindness to offer me, Don Gilberto."

Donã Elena brought out the two packages and matches.

"How long should this trip take?"

"It is twenty-four kilometers, there and back," Don Solomón answered. "You can be back in good time. We sit to the table at fourteen hours."

Doña Elena's "No!" was almost a shout. "He cannot leave without taking what they are preparing—in his honor. I know he won't."

"You are right, Elena. . . . Forgive me, Gilberto; it was without thought." He shook hands. "Until soon."

29

Lorenzo had raised his sombrero and nodded twice to acquaintances as he circled the Alameda. He sat proudly, as in a limousine, smoking and flicking ashes into the pullout tray.

He offered no conversation, but he answered questions; not laconically, but gravely and with all the pertinent facts.

"How much will you require for your work; the earlier trip, and this?"

"Don Solomón will tell your servant how much I have earned," Lorenzo said.

"But I wish to know."

"It will be ample. One does not regret a pact with Don Solomón. And Doña Elena, she is even more liberal."

"You have lived here long?"

"Fifty-four years, in this valley; in drought and in flood, señor."

"You must know everybody in this vicinity?"

"Yes; there are fewer to know than in former years, with so many gone to the United States of the North as braceros, to win dollars."

"They swim the River," Gilberto said. "Wetbacks—espaldas mojadas, they call them."

"The truth? I have been told that they go freely and return with golden teeth, shoes of soft leather, and much wool in their pockets." Wool, lana, was the equivalent of dough.

"Good for them."

"Yet, señor, a doubt presses upon me. I have seen them go, but none have I seen come back. Tell me, Don Gilberto, is it the women there? Does a hotter fire burn between their legs?"

Gilberto smiled; he sure asked the right guy. "Maybe they have reasons besides those of gain."

"But to live among strangers, to face away from this sun; to be forced to eat bread sealed in paper, such as I have seen. Eh—!" It was too much for the old man.

There was a lot Gilberto wanted to ask him, but he marvelled with all his senses that he was actually driving this wonderful machine. From the time they left Zaragoza, he had not needed to take it out of high gear; even when climbing, and in rough places, where he had to drop down to a crawl. It didn't take an expert to know he had a good, tight engine mounted here. And no wonder—he noticed the figures on the odometer—38,000-and-some kilometers. For a car six years old, that meant an average of less than 4,000 miles per year of use. The tires, however, were taking a beating, grinding over broken, sharp-edged slabs of concrete, half-buried under tough scrub; growths which ruined and now almost buried the road.

"This must have been a nice road once."

"Claro—like glass, and the width of eight mules; when it was built, in the days of Don Lázaro. And there was much traffic on it from the ejido, which, as you know, is again the Rancho Corona."

"Uh-huh," Gilberto mumbled, with only a vague idea of what Lorenzo meant. To stop him here and ask for clarity would mean explaining to him that he was a week, less, from California, U.S.A. "Is it?"

"Yes. Despite the Rebellion, it remains the latifundio of Coronel Carrasco, you understand."

Gilberto pretended to be busy with the ventilator handle. "I was wondering, Don Lorenzo, if you might have known my grandfather."

"Alvaro—"

"No, Gilberto; I was named for him."

"I know *of* Gilberto Reyes. I was not yet a man when he and his band attacked the Casa Municipal and shot General Zúñiga. But there is an old fellow who sells herbs in the market who rode with him against the Carranzistas, and the Huertistas, as well. Reyes and his men were, like ourselves, good Maderistas, but when Don Emiliano made his manifesto in Aguas Calientes, they became Zapatistas."

A strange kind of pride welled, only briefly. There was no hint in Lorenzo's account of whether his grandfather was some kind of Mexican hero or just a plain assassin. Anyway, he was somebody.

"You and the old fellow of the herbs will have much to talk about," Lorenzo said.

"In time," Gilberto said. "But for the present, Don Lorenzo, would you be so good as not to make any mention of this matter."

"Ah, you wish it to be a surprise! Rely on me to respect your confidence, Don Gilberto."

He asked how much further it was, and got the usual answer, "Quite near. The house of Vargas sits away from the road, a hundred meters or so. Is it your wish that I go in advance of you, with the freight?"

"No; I will go ahead, with a few of the things. . . . Tell me, did you know this son of Don Solomón?"

"Don Moisés, yes; and his sisters, the señoritas Ester and Ana."

"Younger?"

"Don Moisés is the youngest of Don Solomón and Doña Raquel."

"His first wife—"

"The European. She died of the sugar-sickness and rests in the City of Mexico, now twelve years. Don Solomón mourned long—six years—as they say is the custom among Israelites. They are something like Jews, who, according to the priest at San Pedro Mártir, are not even Christians; whereas, I thought such a thing was true only of Protestants."

"Is Doña Elena herself a widow?"

Lorenzo answered rapidly and in a sharper tone, "That, I do not know to say, señor. . . . Ahead, by those bamboos, the road goes left."

"Don Solomón isn't her first husband?"

Without looking at him, Lorenzo said, "That, you will have to ask elsewhere." And more coldly, "If it is of importance to know."

Lorenzo, the expansive, informative muleteer, bristling like his feelings had been hurt. What the hell—find out what tender spot— And before he could ask, he knew; Lorenzo's idolatry of the woman, and his own devotion, which now exalted him.

Beyond a clump of immensely tall bamboo, the shattered road ended and Gilberto followed faint wheel tracks on ridged and stony yellow earth.

"Goats."

"The herd of Narciso," Lorenzo said. "It grows. If you are not in too much haste, Don Gilberto, I wish a private word with Narciso. Or, I can overtake you."

"That's all right. I'll wait."

"It is a matter of a courtship. I am commissioned to tell Narciso that the girl will house with him when he has a roof on his jacal."

Gilberto watched the animals while Lorenzo and the goatherd, a serious young fellow with thick hair in bangs on his forehead, talked, aside. There were fourteen goats with four kids among them. The mature animals nibbled the branches of scrub laurel, standing catlike on their hind legs. The kids nuzzled at the base of rocks. One of them, the smallest, pert and a shiny copper-brown, began prancing, rattling its tiny hoofs, leaping straight up. Gilberto whistled and it cocked its head.

"Lorenzo, would you ask your friend if these are for sale?"

The answer was partly in Spanish and partly in Huastecan. "He will be taking six animals to market Tuesday, and you can offer for them."

"I'd like to get one now. That little golden one; how much will he take for that?"

"Let me treat with him, Don Gilberto. . . . The gentleman may consider buying that puny brown chiva." Lorenzo used the common term for she-goat.

"That one?" Narciso said, "That little dove—fifteen pesos."

"Hombre!" Lorenzo looked shocked.

"Does the gentleman know who her mother was? Azucena, none other!" Lorenzo whispered to Gilberto, "A famous milker."

"And this doll," Narcisco continued, "after she has been rammed—"

"The transaction is for now, Narciso."

"Fourteen pesos."

Lorenzo nodded sadly, "Narciso, my brother, don't jest about these things. What if the young señor tells them in the capital that here in the valley of Zaragoza, strangers are robbed?"

"Thirteen pesos for the chivita."

"Give him—" Gilberto began, but Lorenzo held up his hand.

"Think, Narciso, how many tiles ten pesos can buy for the roof that will shelter Faustina; but the gentleman offers eleven."

"Twelve—"

"Eleven—and fifty centavos de ñapa! Done?"

"Done!"

The delight he had taken in bargaining warmed Lorenzo again. Pinching the fire off his cigarette, he gave the butt to the kid, on the seat between them. "Here, pet; for you." It chewed daintily and thanked him with a reedy meh-heh-heh.

When it stretched and began licking the steering wheel, Gilberto scratched its hard little skull. "The Vargas kids like goat milk?"

"Who doesn't," Lorenzo answered. "The ribs and the forequarters are the best, though. . . . There, by that boulder, you may turn around and stop. Their house is on the bluff—where you see the smoke."

He saw her, standing alone, shading her eyes, until he reached the level top of the bluff. She was fifty feet distant, but she reached him before he had taken ten steps; yet she had not run. The sun was full on her dark face; so much darker than his mother's, but with the same short, narrow-winged nose, and even the spatulate teeth. Not a wrinkle anywhere on her face, yet she was old; and Elvira Reyes, who had a line, a ploughed furrow on each cheek, and whose lids were like broken leaves—she was young.

"Señora—Tía—" Her hand felt grainy, but not rough; as when you touch a birch limb.

"Gilberto—mi sobrino! Qué milagro—it is—I cannot speak—"

She put her hands on his shoulders and kissed him lightly on each cheek. Embarrassed, he smacked his lips upon air. She smelled of wood smoke and pepper.

Lorenzo passed, with the bleating kid under one arm and a bundle on his back.

"And my cousins—Pompeyo, José, Inés—"

"You know their names!"

"Inés I knew from your letter to my mother."

"Que descanse en paz." The woman dropped her head, "Don Lorenzo told me. My heart weeps. She suffered?"

"She died in her sleep. . . . Did you know you look a little like her?" He said that to make her feel good; and why not, he thought. "You could be her older sister."

"She was—" the woman began, and shook her head as though to dispel the words. "It pleases me to hear that from you . . . . I have tried to thank you for the many things, through Don Lorenzo; but now that you are here, I will express myself better—I will try."

"No hay de qué, Tía."

"I wish to have the pleasure. I know it is still too early an hour for comida, but I have prepared something for you and Don Lorenzo, to break the journey—a morsel."

She led him through a gap in a fence of nopal and pitahaya cactus. "This house is yours."

He had seen the houses of miserably poor Mexicans on the arid, crumbling fringes of metropolitan Los Angeles. And what they had in common with this jacal, this hut, was the profusion of firecracker-red flowers in rusted tins and a patch of hardpacked earth before the door—always swept, but never clean.

This had no door. It was, in reality, no house. From behind a mat nailed over a breach in the front, Gilberto heard the children's voices in admiration of the kid.

"It is beautiful!" . . . "She loves *me*." . . . "She came to *me* first!" . . . "Well, *I* am holding her now." . . . "Pompeyo! Pepe! He may hear you. How would it look—"

That was not a little girl's voice; not with that throatiness in it; as different, he thought, and arresting as a natural contralto on an amateur radio show.

A skinny rooster pecked at his shoe, raced off, and reappeared on the roof of a bamboo shed, a structure which looked more substantial than the house itself, since it was constructed entirely of one material.

The structure in which these people apparently slept and ate was put together out of everything larger than a pebble they could pick up. Around the door sill there were a few bricks set in adobe. The threshold was an unpeeled log. The lower portion of the left wall had a course of cement blocks at the base; but from there upwards, it was mostly mud with some old boards adhering to it somehow. In spots, bits of wire had been used to strengthen the crumbling mud mass, and even the bottoms of a few bottles.

An irregular hole that looked as if it had been punched out was the only window. The roof was a mattress of stalks with palmated leaves. Upon this were piled rocks, broken jars, and even some gourds that had taken root in the humus and were flowering again.

The back of the jacal was the hillside. The entire structure was smaller than a one-car garage.

Esperanza led him around a small, tin brazier with a smoky fire in it, and to a hammock slung between a tamarind and one of the posts of the shed. "Inés! Pompeyo!" she called.

The rag in the entrance lifted and two boys came out. The elder, Pompeyo, held the hand of his four-year-old half-brother and approached grimly.

"Greet Don Gilberto—your cousin."

Pompeyo dropped José's fingers, stepped forward and took Gilberto's hand, raised it to his lips, and kissed it.

"I thank you for the many fine things you sent us, Don Gilberto," the boy said solemnly and stepped away—backwards, as before royalty. The little one, laughing, charged forward and made a game of kissing Gilberto's hand, until his mother drew him away.

"Inés!" she called again.

The girl came out and stood for a second, blinking at the sun, which was now high and could not have dazzled her. She held the kid in her arms and knelt to put it on the ground.

"Enough, Inés!" Esperanza meant, stop being childish, stop pretending not to know who is here. "This is he; your cousin, Gilberto."

"I am happy to see you, señorita—prima." He did not want her to kiss his hand, but she put her lips on his knuckles. And it felt strange; as if she had not moved, but as if he had put his hand to her mouth.

"We are happy that you paid us this honor, Don Gilberto," she said slowly, her head down. "We thank you, also, for the many fine things you have sent."

It was a rehearsed speech; the same thing the boy uttered, but it was her voice that made it new. He wanted to say something that would compel her to talk again—or simply look directly at him. He was aware that Esperanza was watching him alone—not both of them—because she was no more blind than he to what the girl possessed.

The golden kid pranced up, put its feet on his knee, and tried to lick his fingers. It had tasted his sweat on the steering wheel. Esperanza was the only one who did not laugh, although she was amused. "Excuse yourself, Inés," she said and looked past her daughter, at Gilberto, in a way that meant: You have seen enough of her—for the time. "Attend to the refreshment. Pompeyo, cut some tunas."

"There is no hurry, Tía; Don Lorenzo is unloading the truck. There are some things for the children as well."

He watched Inés enter the house and imagined her dressed: white, wool tennis socks and mocassins on those narrow, brown, naked feet; a pleated skirt of blue flannel and a pullover of soft, gray wool. Then, with sudden revulsion, it came to him that this was how he remembered Carolyn Muller. When she came out of the hut with a wooden tray, he tried again: green leather sandals, a loose skirt of bright, shiny rayon, and a white cotton blouse—like Rafaela.

In the tray, which she set down on a box by the hammock, there was a pineapple, some small, fat bananas, and three spotted mangos. Pompeyo brought a handful of cactus pears and put his own knife beside them. Gilberto looked at them and asked, "How do you eat these?"

Inés showed him. She scored the skins lengthwise, and with the tip of the knife exposed half of the moist, seedy pulp. Cutting one slice, she offered it to him on the tip of the blade. When he tasted it, they all said, "Buen provecho."

Her fingers were long, and the palms of her hands were pink—the color of the inside of her mouth.

"Don Lorenzo, please sit down and refresh yourself."

"Soon," he said, "when I have finished the carting. This sack is coffee, and this box has tins."

"Milk," Gilberto said. Esperanza looked at him, bewildered. "Until the little goat grows up. . . . There are some things which I have wrapped myself, I will go back to the truck with you and get them."

"Please, Don Gilberto; this is my work. I am rested from the fine ride."

Gilberto sat on the edge of the hammock. "Some little things for the children." He looked at the two boys—no longer at Inés.

"Coffee, milk in tins, what else!" Esperanza said. "You have brought too much already. You should not have allowed Don Solomón to urge you."

"He didn't. I will have to ask the pardon of the señor, your husband, for not—"

"Fidel is at work."

"I will explain to him when he comes."

"He is working in the ixtle," the woman said hastily, pointing. "A great distance away; on the other end of La Corona. . . . He may not come."

"Then I may not get a chance to see him. I expect to be moving on. I hope he doesn't think—"

"Inés—pardon me, Gilberto—Inés, your cousin is perhaps thirsty."

The girl went back into the hut and returned with a jar and a cracked china cup. With the sun behind it, the thin dress was as transparent as glass. She had straight legs; long, narrow thighs. Esperanza smiled faintly; knowing that he had seen.

Inés poured the drink, and he took the cup from her with both hands, her fingers touching him in the exchange. They were cool and firm, like those long, Málaga grapes that come packed in cork.

The drink was jamaica. "Thank you, Inés."

Lorenzo set down more bags. "You will need a bodega for all this."

Gilberto took the paper bags and boxes he recognized. "There is something here for the boys." He beckoned to them and took out the candy. The children looked at it as if it were still behind plate glass; the little fellow's fingers trembled with eagerness to touch. "Go ahead, muchachos, help yourselves . . . . I'll leave the rest with you, Tía, to ration out. Here, Inés, try this."

She thanked him and carefully removed the tin foil for a candy bar, intact. She bit off a small piece and began rewrapping it. "For another day," she said.

He took the lid off a carton of toys, smiling at the voiceless delight of the children. "Your mother—and Inés—will have to decide who gets what."

"Can you say nothing?" Esperanza scolded.

"A thousand thanks, cousin," Pompeyo said. The little one seized his hand and kept kissing it.

He felt like an old uncle rather than a very distant cousin. As he untied the flat package containing the books and the materials for writing, he said, "But life does not all consist of playing with toys, so—"

The kids looked blankly at what was exposed. Esperanza drew them away. "What wonderful things," she said. "So beautiful to see." And folding the paper back, she wrapped the string around the package, "But we cannot—"

She turned her back to him and walked away, crying silently.

He smiled at what he thought was the profound sincerity of the woman's thanks, and, putting his hand on her arm, said, "Now, look Tía, I want them to have those things. The pleasure they'll get—"

"And Don Solomón allowed you—"

"Please," he chided, "give *me* the credit for those little things."

Both boys shouted at once, "Mira mamá!" It was Lorenzo, carrying the lamp and the tin of kerosene. Esperanza gasped; Inés stared, one hand on each of her swelling, round breasts.

"I have a nail," Lorenzo said. "You, Pompeyo, bring me a stone to hammer it in, and I hang this up, so that it will shine here like a lighthouse."

"Later—later, Don Lorenzo," Esperanza begged. "Now you must sit down and take something.

"First a draught of this regenerating jamaica." He took the jug from Inés and pinched her arm, making an ivory spot on the brown skin. "Like a mango! If I had your years, Don Gilberto, I would cut my way through a regiment of grenadiers to her petate."

She blushed the color of the jamaica in his cup, and he wanted the courage to give her his shoulder for her head, but it was nowhere in him.

If that was cowardice, it was cowardice shared. He remembered on the ride back how, after Esperanza had kissed him, she stepped aside for Inés to approach. His arms were open, and she had taken one step, two steps, toward him, but turned and ran—leaving her new rebozo on the ground.

And Esperanza said nothing; not even asking him to excuse her or go after her. She only smiled a little, as she did when she watched him looking at her body before the sun.

Lorenzo had said nothing for the first five kilometers. Unless he were spoken to, asked questions, Gilberto knew he would remain mute the rest of the way.

"I'd like to have seen Fidel Vargas. What kind of a man is he?"

"I know little of him, and most other people know less. I believe he is from Chihuahua. . . . He was gone to his work at the Rancho Corona when I came first to Pelancha's." He relit the stub of his cigarette and added, "But they could have sent for him to come."

"What does Vargas do at this Rancho Corona?"

"All who work on the land of Coronel Carrasco do as they are told." Lorenzo talked bitterly and spat.

"A tough boss, eh?"

"You ate the fruit from his trees, Don Gilberto. Was it not bitter?"

"Did they get it from there; the bananas, the sweet corn?"

"Yes—dearly. The price of those few ears was greater than all the things you brought, with all respect to you."

"I don't understand, Don Lorenzo. I saw the banana trees and the corn, just behind the wire."

"On *his* land! And sometimes hungry deer from the hills, or foxes, steal in, and Carrasco's pistoleros like so much to shoot that they do not wait to see how many feet the thief has." He spat again. "My tobacco becomes bitter in my mouth when I think about it."

Gilberto tasted a bitterness, too. "I didn't realize they were that poor."

"It is not that, señor. Poverty is our brother."

He twisted the wheel viciously. Was every son of a bitch in Mexico a philosopher? Bus drivers, mule drivers, engine drivers, storekeepers! Mention something—poverty, riches, the sky, the earth—anything, and they top you with some corny slogan. Poverty was nobody's brother; it was just one hell of a lousy spot to be in.

He cooled slowly, under the recognition that he was furious at nothing more real than his own confusion. "I'm sorry," he said, as if he had spoken aloud. "What else *is* there I can do for them?"

"Recall, señor—they have not asked for even this," Lorenzo said calmly.

It hurt. "Maybe I'll come back some day and see how they're making out."

Lorenzo turned to him. "If you do not—you will forgive me for saying this—if you do not, it would have been better that you had not come at all."

He knew that, without being told.

30

He had seen a movie once where some character from another planet put the whole town of Washington, D.C. to sleep in the middle of the day. This was like it, only in Technicolor. He did not realize how utterly quiet it was until he cut the engine. Then, near the shuttered front of the Surtidor, he could hear the secret whimper of a sleeping dog.

"At the back, Margarita or the other one will open for you," Lorenzo whispered as he crept under the truck and stretched out longitudinally on the stones.

Margarita whispered, too, when she let him in. "The señores beg you to go into the sala." She shook her keys and led him to the opposite corner of the patio, and without knocking, unlocked a heavy door.

He stopped just within a large, darkened room, and Doña Elena took both his hands. "Come in, Gilberto. I am glad that you are back."

"We heard the machine from far away," Don Solomón called from a couch in a corner. There was a tray near it with some medicine bottles. "Come sit here. . . . Elena, make a light—"

Before drawing the curtains, she laid a folded black silk cloth over her husband's eyes. "You see," he said, "this was once the sala. It is now an infirmary. Josefina will bring coffee in a moment." He chuckled, "Or do you need an injection of some sort?"

"Oh, Gilberto," Doña Elena said, "you have a present from Concha and her mother—a beautiful chicken." Josefina entered with a tray. "Show Don Gilberto his chicken, Josefina."

"It is already nude, señora, and not very young. I had meant to ask if you wished it stewed with mushrooms and little onions, enchilada de pollo, or how."

"Stewed," Don Solomón called from the couch. "With mushrooms and little onions—and dumplings."

"Sol, you are disposing of Gilberto's chicken."

"That's the best thing I'd know to do with it. I can't take it along," Gilberto said.

Doña Elena handed him a cup of coffee, and he felt enough at ease to look around the large room. It had windows both on the patio and on a street through which he could see a corner of the Alameda. The furniture was heavy and overstuffed; the kind shown in the credit furniture houses on Brooklyn Avenue. An old-fashioned radio in a tall cabinet stood between filled bookcases. He looked at a large, framed photograph on the wall: a small, pale woman dressed in what appeared to be stiff, black silk, seated, with a boy on a hassock at her feet, and two plump girls by the arms of the chair.

"Doña Raquel," said Doña Elena, "Ester, Ana, and Don Moisés."

"Lorenzo told me."

"Ana lives in the Argentine," Don Solomón said, "And Ester in France. Both are married, but they have given me no grandchildren."

Hurriedly, to carry him past despondency, his wife said, "My stepson is an engineer—for the government, in the capital."

"I heard something about my own grandfather that didn't make me too happy," Gilberto smiled. "It seems that he shot a general, way back when Lorenzo was a boy. A Huertista, or something."

"That should make him a national hero among the Zapatistas," Don Solomón said.

"Lorenzo mentioned those, and one other—"

"Carranzista? . . . That was before I came to Mexico, but I will explain."

"No politics," Doña Elena ordered. "I want to hear from Gilberto about his visit."

"Yes. How did the machine run?"

"Like a top, Don Solomón. The first thing I'd do, though, is get a spare set—"

"Was Fidel Vargas there?" Doña Elena interrupted.

"No, señora, he was working."

"Good," said Don Solomón, but Gilberto took no notice. "Pelancha—I mean, your Aunt Esperanza—they were pleased?"

To say, "Yes, sure, they seemed to be," would have served well enough as an answer. But he owed these people—and himself, in their presence—the truth, insofar as he felt it.

"I don't know—honestly, Don Solomón, señora—yesterday, at this time, I didn't mean anything to them—they didn't know I was alive. Maybe I should have left it that way."

"You mean not gone to see them?" Don Solomón said, sitting up and taking the cloth off his eyes. "That's ridiculous, my son. You have made them happy."

"That's just the point—I don't think I did."

"Come now!"

"Wait," Doña Elena said. "Perhaps I understand how you feel, Gilberto."

"I feel like I should never have gone."

"Wait, Gilberto. When you say that until today you meant nothing to them—to Pelancha, to Inés—does it not mean that now you mean too much?"

"Maybe you're right, señora—I don't want to flatter myself."

"You recognize that it wasn't the gifts you brought that made you mean so much."

"Apart from the gifts, señora."

Doña Elena smiled. "It is time to open the store. . . . You remain there, Sol. Gilberto will help me raise the cortina."

"With pleasure," Gilberto said. "I want to check on the bus back to Ciudad del Maíz, too."

"There will be no bus," Don Solomón said. "Tell him, Elena—"

In the store, she unlocked the front door and stood, holding the keys, in front of the gray blankness of the steel curtain. "Before people come in, Gilberto, tell me about Inés." She looked at him, waiting.

"Oh, yes—Inés. She's—she's—well, you know, señora, it was kind of a surprise. I had an idea of her as still being thirteen—a child—"

"And you found—?"

"A girl—and kind of pretty."

"A woman," said Doña Elena, "and quite beautiful."

Maybe it was in the idiom of Mexico to call a girl of sixteen a woman, he wanted to say. But he remembered Lorenzo's lusty compliment—he remembered Concha, and said nothing.

"Look again, tomorrow," Doña Elena said.

"Tomorrow? I didn't intend to go back there."

"Tomorrow, at the market. They come every Tuesday to sell kindling— chips of fat pine, which Pelancha cuts."

After it became dark and when there was a lull in the slowly paced but steady flow of customers, Don Solomón said eagerly, "And now, my boy, let us get at the weighing machine."

They brought it out, still in its original container, a wooden packing case, padded inside to protect the scales. The Reliance Computing Counter Scale, Model K-10BB. From the instruction folder inside, Gilberto learned that K meant it was calibrated for kilograms, 10 was its capacity, and BB was the type of finish on the metal parts—brushed brass. It fit directly beneath the old scale, between two glass display cases. It pleased rather than bothered him to have the old man hovering at his elbow.

"Will you need tools, Gilberto? Just tell me—I have everything here."

"Just a screwdriver."

The scale had two tiny spirit levels sunk in the frame and four screw legs, so that it could be adjusted just right.

"Amazing, amazing," Don Solomón clucked. "Elena, you should see what goes on here!"

"The important part of the installation is just coming up, Don Solomón: the adjustment for accurate weight. What have you got around here that weighs exactly one kilo?"

"Let me see—" He studied the shelves and took down a round paper carton of salt. "Peso neto, no menos de un kilo."

"That's not quite what we want. Something that's exactly one kilo—to a hair." Gilberto put the salt on the tray of the old scale. It weighed one kilo and eight-tenths. "At least we know you've been cheating yourself on this old scale."

"Very likely true."

"Anyway, let's try it on the new machine, just to get a rough idea," Gilberto suggested. It was way off—almost three kilos. He checked the instruction sheet and turned the adjustment screw until the dial read 1,000 grams—one kilo.

"That's not exact," Gilberto said. "How about sugar?"

"Ah! That, and rice. It comes in two-kilo sacks, packed at the mill."

Adding a paper bag of sugar brought the weight up to 2 kilos and 970 grams. "Somebody's cheating," Gilberto said. "What can we find that we know the exact weight of?"

"I have it! Aspirin tablets! I have a jar of them and we can pour out—at five grams each—two hundred of them."

"Excuse me, Don Solomón. You're thinking of grains; seven thousand grains make a pound, which is less than half a kilo—as I remember. . . . Wait a minute—" He put his hand in his pocket and took out some loose coins, among them a silver 25 centavo piece. "How much does this weigh?"

"The Hidalgo!" Don Solomón almost screamed. "The silver, five-peso Hidalgo! That has its weight stamped on it." He snatched open his cash drawer and brought one out—the size of a silver dollar. "Look at it."

"You're right, Don Solomón. Twenty-seven and seven-ninths grams. But we'll need a lot of these."

"A hundred? I have a hundred of them in the safe. I'll get them."

"First let's figure out exactly how many add up to a kilo."

"Can you do that and make it come out even? Do you require the use of the machine?"

"No, I can do this with a pencil." He began making figures. "Twenty-seven and seven-ninths is two hundred and forty-three, plus seven—two hundred and fifty ninths. That goes into one thousand—two hundred and fifty over nine—one over one thousand—cross out the two-fifty. Cross out the thousand and put down four; four times nine is thirty-six. Right?"

"Shhh," Don Solomón warned, and opening the safe, he brought out a canvas sack of Hidalgos. Counting out 36 of them, they laid them in the center of the scale and Gilberto made the final adjustment.

"Elena—" Don Solomón called, winking broadly at Gilberto. "Can you help us out here with our calculations?"

"You mean there is something Gilberto cannot do on the machine?"

"This is rather too complicated. We wish to know how many silver Hidalgos make one kilo. Here is one for you to look at. You will note that it weighs twenty-seven and seven-ninths grams."

"And a kilo is one thousand. Hmm—" She thought gravely and said, "It cannot come out even. It is a certain number of Hidalgos and a part of one."

Don Solomón looked stern, but Gilberto couldn't help smiling. She looked at him and laughed. "Is this another one of your 'three thousand words in English' jokes, señor Reyes?"

"We scientists do not make jokes, Madame Curie," her husband scolded. "The answer is right there, on the scales: thirty-six."

She glanced at Gilberto, and he nodded. Turning to Don Solomón, she mocked, "And I suppose you worked that out by yourself, Professor Einstein?"

"With a little help from Doctor Reyes here, who held the pencil."

"I'd better give you a demonstration of how the calculating part works," Gilberto suggested. "You turn this little knob on the right to the price of what you're weighing out. Let's say for example it's an odd figure, like eighty-seven. Turn it to eighty-seven, and the window right next to the one that shows the weight, shows the price. Put some more on—it reads one twelve. Take some off—sixty-five. If a customer wants, let us say, five and a half pesos worth of butter, just set the knob here to the price of butter, and when the window shows five-fifty, the person has the right amount."

"Do you think you can teach that to Felipe, Sol?"

"You will have to, Elena, I'm afraid. . . . After twenty-five years with the old devices, it is hard to adopt new practices." He spoke rather sadly, Gilberto thought. "Things, such as this, which fly under younger fingers—and that adding machine—the machines themselves seem to know when they are fumbled with by the ancient and uncertain."

"I wouldn't go so far as to say that," was the only comforting remark Gilberto could think of.

He didn't regret saying it, although he realized that its flatness made it sound insincere. It was Doña Elena who said it better: "Don't be a big baby. Go practice with the new machine." But she had the right to put it that way.

He suggested putting the truck inside and walked out to it.

They were both in the doorway, watching, as he got in and started the engine. They were standing close together; his arm around her and her hand on his shoulder. Switching on the lights, he looked at them instead of at the oil pressure gauge.

As he backed slowly to the end of the street, he was thinking about what kind of a fellow this Moisés could be.

Margarita opened the door from the storehouse into the patio. "The señores beg you to rest, to lie down. You have been since early without a siesta."

After washing up, he found the room he had slept in changed somewhat. There was a small table at the head of the bed, with the kerosene lamp on it, some matches, an ashtray, and two books. His shirt and the other things had been washed and ironed.

It was quiet and restful. Lighting a cigarette, he sat on the edge of the bed and looked at the books. *The Complete Novels of Sir Walter Scott—Vol. V—*

Kenilworth. The other was a paperback Spanish book; *Poemas líricos de Luis de Góngora y Argote.* He turned to a long poem with the title *Soledades,* and it was pretty heavy going. It was castellano all right, he agreed; but *what* Castilian! It made the priest, Don Iñigo, sound like a bum.

There was a knock. He called, "Entre," and Josefina came in smiling, knowing that she looked neat in a clean white apron. Holding out a platter, she said, "With the compliments of Margarita and your servant, Don Gilberto."

There were four round crackers, each spread with a brown paste and sprinkled with egg yolk; a small dish with cubes of melon and papaya, with a toothpick stuck in each; and a wedge of lime. "How nice; North-American style."

Josefina blushed with pleasure and put the tray on the table. "Buen provecho."

"One minute, Josefina—what is it?"

"It is the liver of the fowl, señor." She used the diminutive, la higadillita—the tiny little liver.

"How does Margarita—and you—know that I love chopped chicken liver the best?"

"Oh, señor, she will be so happy when I tell her! It is as she made it for Don Moisés—always when there was a fowl to be cooked."

He chewed one canapé quickly. "Primoroso!" he exclaimed and rolled his eyes, in the same way he used to do when he liked something Mrs. Romero offered him. "Riquísimo! What can Don Moisés get in the capital that's as good as this?"

"Oh, Don Gilberto—" The woman trembled. "Are you—is it true then, that—" Suddenly flustered, she gasped, "Permiso—," and ran out.

He finished the canapés with the melon, feeling a little guilty for having put on that act—putting the poor dame in a tailspin like that. Taking off his shoes, he stretched out on the bed. He opened the book of Góngora's poems—Déjame llorar orillas del mar . . .

The cook had been trying to ask him something, but she got panicked. It couldn't have been anything important. . . . Maybe it was *very* important. No, in that case she'd have been ordered to ask him, and she'd have out with it. "Are you, Don Gilberto—is it true that—?"

It could have been about Inés. He wished it were. Why had Doña Elena said only so much about her—and no more? Inés—she was coming tomorrow, and he would see her. Jesus! what a dish!

He knew Don Solomón was in the room, but kept his eyes shut, not to cheat the old boy out of the pleasure of waking him up. Then he heard light steps and he knew it was Doña Elena. They whispered lightly for a moment until Don Solomón called, "Gilberto—"

As he sat up, Góngora slipped off his chest and fell on the floor. It was dark, but the door was open, illuminating a patch just inside the door, where Doña Elena stood.

"I came in simply to blow out the lamp, but my wife follows to say that the supper is ready."

Gilberto grinned. "Sleep, eat—that's all I seem to be doing."

"We know how much you slept, and Lorenzo told us how little you ate."

Gilberto pointed to the empty platter. "But this chicken liver was *something*! Tasted like on Fairfax Avenue; real kosher."

"It is the recipe of Doña Raquel—"

"But *I* never got any," Don Solomón protested. "It was always for Moisés. It was too *good* for me! Ah, Gilberto, you have been making love to those women!"

"Honestly—"

"Josefina, I do not mind," the old man chided. "We can replace her. *But*, if you elope with Margarita—I warn you, joven, I will follow you to the limits of the Republic."

There was no mistaking the sentiment, the affection, in this kind of kidding. Don Solomón did something that Gilberto thought only Mexicans did: he drew his arm around him in an abrazo—a sudden, warm clasp. Strangely, to Gilberto, it was not embarrassing.

Doña Elena took his hand and guided him to the dining room, between the kitchen and the entrance to the store. An elaborate chandelier gleamed over a round table, set with a cloth. The dishes at the three places were china; the silver was heavy, European.

Gilberto drew Doña Elena's chair out—the way he'd seen Walter Pidgeon do it for Deborah Kerr—as if he had been doing it all his life.

"This is like being in Ciudad México again," she said. "We should always have late cena. You, Sol, as a merchant, should take your lunch in a restaurant—"

"Yes, an elegant one, such as Genoveva's—" He explained to Gilberto. "Opposite the Alameda, alfresco—on the curb. . . . Go on, madam."

Gilberto enjoyed this banter, nibbling a radish, he felt *almost* like—well—Kirk Douglas.

"I would be tired from bridge and cocktails," Doña Elena said, "and from dressing. But I would have an efficient household staff."

"Listen to her, Gilberto."

What would Watler Pidgeon put in here? He tried, "There's nothing the matter with your help here, señora." Lousy—even though she smiled.

"Of course a valet will lay out my esmoquin," Don Solomón said.

Gilberto laughed—too loudly, he was afraid. But that word esmoquin, for smoking—tuxedo—always amused him when he read it. And now, to hear it said, fractured him. Don Solomón took it as a compliment to his own wit and tossed his head.

Josefina brought in the first course—bite-size pieces of pickled fish in sherbet glasses—and moved slowly, with her eyes covertly on Gilberto. "Escabeche, that is called," Doña Elena said. "Have you ever eaten it in the States?"

"Never. It's marvelous."

Josefina flew out. "You see that!" Don Solomón said. "Rushing out to tell Margarita that it pleased you. What *I* think about it is immaterial. . . . Will you drink something, Gilberto; wine, beer, a refresco?"

"Beer, preferably—"

"There is something which that brings to mind," Don Solomón said pensively. "Ah, yes; could you, Gilberto, at your leisure tomorrow, do me the goodness of writing a letter in English?"

"Why do you persist in exploiting this boy?"

"It will be a pleasure to be of service, señora. . . . By hand, Don Solomón?"

"No—there is a writing machine in the sala. I assume you can perform on it."

"Reasonably well."

"There! You see, Elena!"

"You've got everything here," Gilberto marvelled.

"Whatever the ejido had for sale, including the camión, when it fell broken—in English, bankrupt, I think they say it."

"That's correct," Gilberto said. "What was this ejido; a company, a firm?"

"In a way, yes. But owned by the peasants and helped by the government through ejidal banks. It was long talked of; for far longer than the system lasted. I have a book, if you wish to read about it."

The soup came in a tureen, a sopa de lentejas, and Gilberto was served first. The tortillas for this occasion were de harina, of white flour, instead of the common ground corn softened in water and lime.

"This letter," Gilberto asked, "is it to the United States?"

"To New York, to a house which imports a certain brand of wine—Bollinger, a champagne. They have no agency in the Republic and I wish them to ship me, by rail to Cuidad Valles, or by water to Tampico, five cases. You will say it must arrive before the first of the year."

"Big New Year's celebration in town?"

"At La Corona, the ranch of Coronel Carrasco."

"Lorenzo told me something about him, too."

"I can tell you more," Don Solomón said, his eyes angry.

"Please, Solomón, another time," his wife warned, and he remained coldly silent until Gilberto raised his glass of beer. Don Solomón raised his own. "L'jaim—health to you, Gilberto. Confusion to Carrasco."

Margarita followed as Josefina, beaming, brought in the casserole. When she took the lid off, it was still hissing. Gilberto sniffed like a beagle at the perfumed steam.

"The hen!" Don Solomón gloated. "Thank God I curbed my appetite earlier."

"That is Gilberto's chicken."

"True, Elena; we are receiving his bounty. I was just going to divide the dumpling."

Margarita's eyes were fastened on Gilberto as he took his first forkful and savored the meat, reinfused with its own juices and garnished with the caps of whole mushrooms and tiny, melting onions.

"Oh boy!" he gasped. It was in English, but enough for Margarita to know. She nodded curtly and left, smiling.

"The dumpling, hombre! What is your judgment of that?"

Gilberto picked up a wedge of it, light as froth and peppered with emerald bits of parsley. "The most delicious thing I ever ate."

"Also originated in this house by Doña Raquel," explained Doña Elena, with pride.

Brother! To eat like this every day! He looked at the label on the beer bottle—Orizaba, Ver. . . . Bishop had been right again.

Almost weeping, Josefina brought the news quietly to Doña Elena: there was nothing left for dessert—"No hay postre, señora!"—nothing but a simple tray of flan and some odds and ends of small cakes, too common to be served. What a crisis!

Very calmly, Doña Elena instructed, "Find a ripe pineapple. Core it well; quarter it, but not entirely to the bottom."

"Sí, señora."

"In the ice chest, you will find a dish of sugared mulberries. Fill the piña with them."

What a way to run a house, Gilberto thought, and said, "It must be a pleasure working here. Do your help eat like this?"

"It is written," Don Solomón said, "'Thou shalt not muzzle the ox when he treadeth out the corn.'"

"That may be in your Bible, Solomón; but it is still a grossness to refer to—"

"You are right, Elena. It is also written, and I should have said, 'That thy manservant and thy maidservant may rest as well as thou . . . for, remember that *thou* wast a servant in the land of Egypt.'"

Margarita appeared at the door. "Don Perfecto begs to be announced."

"Miraculous! Cabalistic!" Don Solomón gasped. "I utter a verse from Deuteronomy and it invokes . . . a Jesuit!"

Gilberto saw Doña Elena frown slightly as she asked, "Is he in the sala?"

"He waits in the patio to finish his cigarette," Margarita answered.

"Let him come in here. Leave the chicken and send Josefina in with another plate," Don Solomón directed and turned to Gilberto. "He is a learned man, this priest. He has been to the North, to Canada, and speaks considerable English, you will find."

The priest wore a gray double-breasted suit, a soft shirt, and a ready-tied black satin necktie. He was short, about the same height as Don Iñigo, but much thinner, and younger. His hair was black, unparted, and he had a lot of it—everywhere; on his eyebrows and his pale hands were matted with it. Whatever his age, he did not look more than 35. When he smiled, it was only with his mouth. "There was an aroma flooding the callejón from your kitchen," he said, "like the kahanim would send up to Jehovah."

"Yes," Don Solomón answered. "And like the priests of my temple, we eat the sacrificial animal—in this case, a fowl. Please join us. But first, I make you known to señor Gilberto Reyes."

The priest put his hand out limply, palm down. He showed no surprise when Gilberto shook it. Josefina, who came in to set a place, kissed the priest's hand.

"I will be happy to sit, but I can take nothing," Don Perfecto said, bowing to Doña Elena. "I am back from La Corona just now."

"Ah, you supped with the Coronel—?"

"With Doña Julia. . . . But how festive!" He smiled again. "I am not participating in Simchas Torah?"

Don Solomón explained for Gilberto's benefit. "Don Perfecto has Hebrew, as well as English. . . . No, Reverend Don, the Day of Rejoicing in the Law was on the twelfth of October, by coincidence your Día de la Raza."

"Columbus Day," Gilberto suggested.

The priest nodded to him. "Here it is celebrated as the Day of our Race."

"And you are bidden, as usual, to our next Holy Day of note, Don Perfecto."

"Chanukah?"

"Yes, the Feast of Lights, to celebrate the victory of Judas Maccabaeus over the Syrians and the Greeks."

"In the histories of the time," the priest said, "that was a defeat."

"Only militarily, my good priest."

Doña Elena looked helplessly at Gilberto. "You see, this is the way it begins. . . . Margarita, a mescalito for Don Perfecto."

"Yes, yes," Don Solomón agreed, "and a rich cigar from the cabinet with it, Margarita."

"But your eyes, Don Solomón; the fumes of a puro will torment you."

"Not in the least," Don Solomón insisted. "I have rushed back and forth to the mirror today, just to be sure. I have felt *that* well in the eyes. Elena?"

She nodded. Margarita put a black, spherical jug in front of the priest. He poured a pale, sweet smelling liquor out of it, raised his glass, and when he said, "Salud," Gilberto noticed that Doña Elena was not included in the greeting. Maybe this was the way priests behaved ordinarily; he had talked to only two of them in his life.

"Then you are the young gentleman on whose account Lucas is punishing all of Zaragoza," the priest said, as Gilberto extended a match for his cigar.

"Me—?"

"What is this!" Doña Elena said sharply.

"Punishment!" Don Solomón was amazed.

"Sanctions," said the priest. "It will be a small market tomorrow. Lucas is determined to carry no one in his machine until he obtains satisfaction from the North American señor. That is what he has reported."

"I'm sorry I mixed in," Gilberto said. "What does he want? Does he claim any damage? If so, I'll certainly settle with him." Doña Elena looked at him, and he remembered that he could have found out about this earlier, when she told him that the bus would not run that day.

"You will let me attend to this, Gilberto," Don Solomón said.

"Any real damage," Gilberto said, "he caused himself, by running off the road. All I did was let the air out of the tires."

"He says you attacked him."

"But it was just the other way around. This man, Alvarez—the one with the lame boy; they saw what happened."

"Alvarez supports Lucas's story," the priest said.

"Why do you smile, Don Perfecto?" Doña Elena asked directly. "Naturally, you cannot believe Lucas."

"And Alvarez," the priest said. "Many workers at La Corona do, señora. It would be best to—"

"It would be best to put an end to this nonsense at once, Don Perfecto," she said.

"Their cura párroco is Don Cosme of San Pedro Mártir. They do not listen to me."

"They will listen to me, then," Don Solomón said.

"Look, if it's a matter of money," Gilberto pleaded, "I don't want to make a thing out of this."

"It is decidedly not a matter in which satisfaction could be obtained for money," the priest said smoothly. "There is talk of fists being used."

"I admit I hit him," Gilberto said. "But that was only after he attacked me with a bar of metal."

Don Solomón laughed. "I see it now! A matter of pride. To strike a Mexican with your naked fist—"

"Good! I'm glad you did that, Gilberto!" Doña Elena stood up, her eyes flashing. "Maybe that will teach them to strike back!"

"The señora agitates herself about something?" the priest said, with his thin smile.

"Yes, señor priest. About the sacred cudgel! That our people here will take lashes from Carrasco's whip for which they ask no satisfaction—only that they be allowed to kiss his hand." Blood was in her face as she turned and walked out.

Don Solomón followed her out immediately. Gilberto sat embarrassed. The priest calmly poured himself another mescal. "You here long, in this country, from California?" he asked in accented but clear English.

Gilberto answered in Spanish. "A week, more or less."

"You could answer me in English, please."

"Sure, why not?"

"I hear you bring many nice presents to Vargas's woman."

"My aunt—"

"How your aunt?"

"Well, she's a cousin of my mother's."

"Cousin?"

"Well, her first husband and my father were kind of related—primos or something."

"Pelancha had only one husband."

"I mean the one before she married Vargas."

"Vargas is not her husband," the priest said calmly.

"No?" Gilberto said indifferently.

"She took him in her house to live with her."

Gilberto felt uncomfortable, and even with his superior English, at a disadvantage. This guy, he felt, had an angle. "It's none of my business; she's over twelve." This ought to show him where he stood in *that* department.

Don Perfecto had a way of dropping his eyes that gave the impression that he was merely contemplating something. But you heard him. "Then is also not your business that the girl, Inés, is plenty more than twelve?"

He felt as if he had been slapped across the face with a hot, wet hand. "What do you mean by that, mister—Father?" His lips felt swollen.

"Mister is okay. You wish to know what I mean?"

He nodded, but he was afraid of the answer.

"Only, you are giving me to know," the priest said, again dropping his eyes, "that she can take a man—or a man take her—"

He didn't finish. Don Solomón entered, calling "Señores, with your permission, let us move into the sala." He took both their arms and raised them. "The girls will clear. Come; I will join you there presently. My wife begs to be excused."

If he were not sleeping there, Gilberto at this stage would have said that it was late and he had better go. He expected Don Perfecto to say it, but the priest apparently meant to stay.

In the sala, Don Perfecto again spoke in Spanish to Gilberto. "It is on my account, rather my presence, my office, that disturbs the señora. I regret it, but you understand why."

"No, I don't."

"The Church regards her as an adulteress; her husband is living."

"You mean she's divorced?"

"Such a thing does not exist."

Okay, let the smug bastard have it his way. But what was he after? What was his angle in bringing up first Inés and now Doña Elena? He was wound up to ask a lot of questions, all on the surface, polite, and that's the kind of answers he would get, Gilberto decided. He wasn't going to find a stooge.

"You find Zaragoza to your taste, señor Reyes?"

"What I've seen of it."

"This is a rich valley."

This was no question, but Gilberto decided it needed a comeback. "Rich, how?" Not too snappy, but it would do to put him on the spot.

"The soil; it yields everything that man needs to feed and clothe himself."

"The people don't look it." This was the way to handle this guy; don't just "yes" him—give him arguments.

"You observed that yourself, señor Reyes, or was that something you were told?"

Gilberto thought rapidly and was pleased with what he came up with: "Observation! I ate a banana today that was stolen!"

"True. Vargas's Pelancha is not a thief. . . . For how long will you be pleased to stay?"

"Well, I—"

Don Solomón broke in. "Drink up, gentlemen. Be more comfortable. Gilberto, join the good priest and myself in a drop of that mescal from Oaxaca. Your cigar, Don Perfecto, it draws well?" Sitting down, he still seemed to bustle.

"I don't think I'll take anything, Don Solomón," Gilberto said. "Maybe I ought to write that letter—"

"There is no haste. Commerce is suspended for the night." He turned to the priest. "It is an order for champagne, for Coronel Carrasco. A noble, Catholic drink, Don Perfecto; invented by priests."

This was the kind of patter Gilberto liked better than having the priest pitch those curves.

"It was the fashion among some orders to dabble in the chemistry of wine," Don Perfecto said, "but never of mine, the Society of Jesus." He addressed Gilberto. "Unless Don Solomón, out of his vast knowledge, can assure me otherwise."

This was good, Gilberto thought. They were baiting each other, as Doña Elena told him, and now they had an audience.

"In Europe," Don Solomón said thoughtfully, "I have encountered a wine—not to drink, mind you, out of reverence—which was called Tears of Christ, the bottling of which I hesitate to impute to anybody."

"Your respect for my faith is almost devotional," the priest said, and with hardly a pause turned to Gilberto. "And how is it, señor Reyes—and I am speaking as a priest—that you are not wearing an emblem of our belief?"

"Oh, the medal, you mean." Gilberto touched his shirt. Before he could explain that he had given it away, Don Solomón intervened. "Just because it is hidden under his clothes—"

"Like your sign, Don Solomón?" the priest smiled. "We wear ours openly."

"We, on the other hand, cannot be so frank about the Wound of the Covenant, Don Priest."

"The wound from which none have died."

"Recollect, Don Perfecto—" Don Solomón said.

"Again Torquemada, Don Solomón. . . ? This talk is for our private discussions; too solemn for our young friend here."

"No, no—" Gilberto said.

"Just let me recount this," Don Solomón resumed, with a nod to Gilberto. "I was in flight through Hungary, hiding in the city of Budapest; before your time, Gilberto, but within the memory of yours, Don Perfecto. The year of the White Terror—"

"Following the Red."

"As you say, señor Priest. . . . It was a terribly cold day; mercifully cold, because it froze the blood. The White Guards of Horthy seized every man then crossing the iron bridge which divides the city and lined them up. They were ordered to expose themselves. Those without the Sign—"

"Entire—as God made them."

"Those were allowed to go on their way. Those with the Badge—one soldier held a large, two-handed pliers, the sort used to cut barbed wire—and while four others held him fast—"

"Whew!" Gilberto said. "That's awful."

"Bolsheviks," said the priest.

"Perhaps; they didn't examine documents."

"Béla Kun could have been one of them, eh, Don Solomón?"

"They asked no names. They looked only where I told you, not on the hands for stigmata; so, it could have been Another, eh, Don Priest—"

The priest pointed to Don Solomón and spoke to Gilberto. "He smiles, our host; but inside he seethes with the wrath of Jehovah."

"I don't think so," Gilberto said cooly. Perversely, he didn't want to be on the side of Don Perfecto in anything. Dislike had something to do with this attitude; and of that animus, he was certain. And, in his mind, the way to implement it was to say no when the priest said yes.

"The mescal is good, the company is agreeable, but it is already twenty-two hours," the priest said. "I will finish this cigar—"

"This is your house, Don Perfecto. You know I retire late."

"But your guest—he has come a long way."

"Don't worry about me," Gilberto said.

"From California, I think you said, señor Reyes."

Gilberto hadn't told him; somebody else had. Give him the rest of it. "Yes, California; Los Angeles."

"A place I have long wanted to see. It has upwards of two hundred thousand people of Mexican descent."

"That's what they tell me." Gilberto was curt.

"Did you enter by El Paso or the port of Nuevo Laredo?"

He felt it in the guts again, that fear, but not as acutely as when he was in Bishop's jeep above the Río Bravo. Now he could do more than be afraid; he could be wary. This guy was no Anselmo, the bus-jockey; much less a Benito, the shine boy. This guy was asking for a purpose—calling a border town a port, and probably knowing that he didn't come in by either of them that he mentioned.

"I came in by Matamoros."

"Clear to the end of Texas! Too far by a thousand miles, at least," the priest said.

It seemed that Don Solomón was trying to help him out, seeing his hesitation. "That is nothing unusual," he began.

"Do you wish to remind me, Don Solomón," the priest interrupted, "that your people blundered forty years in the wilderness? They could have made the journey by way of Joppa and Hebron in that many days."

"No; I wish to remind you that, though God, who led them, made the Earth, He was quite ignorant of its geography."

Gilberto thought he would be laughing alone, but Don Perfecto laughed as long and as loudly. "So you cannot blame señor Reyes for going all that distance. I see."

"I was going to take the through bus from Laredo to Monterrey," Gilberto said, "but a friend of mine wanted company as far as Brownsville."

That seemed to be all on that subject, Gilberto hoped. The priest made some intelligent remarks about the elections in the States. At any rate, they showed that he knew who the candidates were, the names of the two political parties, and something about the principal issues; something more than Gilberto knew.

"I listen on the radio—mostly for the practice in English. But you, Don Gilberto—" That was the first time he had called him anything but señor Reyes, "You can tell us at first hand, whom the country will select."

"It looks like Eisenhower."

"Are you a partisan of his?"

"I don't vote for two years yet."

The priest nodded; it seemed as if he paused to make a mental note. "Though a general," he resumed, "to put him at the head would, I feel, be a mistake."

"The United States of the North," Don Solomón said, "makes no mistakes from which it cannot survive. But tell me why you regard this as one."

"Simply, my friends—by promising that he will end the war in Korea by any means, he has given the Communists a greater victory than they could gain by arms."

This isn't what Dr. Eisen told him; but this priest seemed to know, Gilberto felt.

"But Don Perfecto," Don Solomón leaned forward, "if the majority of the people make him the president, doesn't that show it is what they want as well?"

"To their regret."

"I think you're mistaken," Gilberto blurted and stopped. His dislike of the priest led him too far. Both men turned to him deferentially, waiting for him to continue.

"Please say what your opinion is, Gilberto," Don Solomón urged. "This is not Church doctrine, but a matter of North American politics; a subject on which you are better qualified than either the good priest or myself."

Gilberto fumbled; Eisen had given him nothing. Bishop had it—too much of it. He would have to bring something up out of the grab bag. "It isn't the same as after Pearl Harbor. Nobody rushes to enlist. They can't even sell the idea. They have to depend on the draft—about thirty thousand fellows every month." He stumbled. Maybe he could stop here. But they were listening eagerly. "It doesn't mean anything—except to the ones that get killed, and their mothers. And who are they, if you look at the casualty lists in the papers? López, Gómez, Chávez, Cohen, Rodríguez, Kelly—" He looked at Don Perfecto, and it was the way the priest dropped his lids, after a quick, pitying look, that made him want to go on. "Sitting on the sidelines here, you don't have any idea of what's going on."

"Naturally," Don Perfecto said politely, "we are not informed as well as you."

Bishop should be here, making with the arguments. "The propaganda that's going on—I got friends, veterans; they tell me—" He stopped to frame just one clear statement to attribute to either Eisen or Bishop.

"The other man, who opposes Eisenhower—" Don Solomón began.

"Estevenson," the priest helped him out.

"Doesn't he wish an end to the war?"

"He does. I have heard him say it, but by a total victory. Destroy the Antichrist forever."

"Rabonai Sh'lolam!" Don Solomón groaned, raising his arms in dramatic appeal to the Master of the Universe. "Again! The time to have done that was in the year 'Nineteen—thirty-three years ago, when the Antichrist had just been spawned. And they tried, hombre! We had disembarked from the train on a great open field near Chernigov in the Ukraine, to be reformed into batallions according to our nationality and re-equipped in *that* holy war against the Antichrist. We were exhorted, alternately by generals and priests; one from each dedicated nation, and one from each faith: Anglican, Lutheran, Roman, Orthodox—"

"No rabbi?"

"Indeed a rabbi! A *rav*—in full Chassidic canonicals; kidskin slippers and stockings, white as milk; black satin trousers to the knee. I tell you, gentlemen, the Archimandrite of Kiev, who was also there, looked shabby beside my rabino. And his mouth dripped honey."

"He moved you," said Don Perfecto.

"The Antichrist moved me further."

Gilberto howled, even louder when he saw the priest tighten his lips. The old boy was making a chump out of him.

"And faster," Don Solomón continued. "Budenny's cavalry had outflanked us at a place called Sumy." He continued, more seriously, while Gilberto was still laughing. "No, Don Priest—he is thirty-five years old now, this Antichrist of yours; old enough to reason with. Convert him. . . . Or is it that *you* are too old, too impatient, for that?"

Gilberto grinned and nodded to him. He felt like shaking his hand, patting him on the back. Whatever it meant, it sounded like good, strong, confident talk. A feller could learn something listening to him.

The priest rose from his chair. "I shall be going. Some time, when we have no tribune but our own conscience, we will talk about this again."

Gilberto got this: a clear slap at Don Solomón, and at him, for being a sympathetic listener.

"Come often, Don Perfecto," Don Solomón said.

"As my office permits." The priest turned to Gilberto. "And will you be seeing much of Mexico—on this visit, señor Reyes?"

The phrase "this visit" startled him. Confusedly, he answered, repeating, "This visit—? Well, as much as I can."

"There is much, or little, to see in a single month. It depends on who looks."

"I figured on more than a month."

"Then you have the immigration document that permits you to remain longer, without molestation."

"Well, no. You see—"

"¡Qué lastima! To have to return to Brownsville, to beg one of the Mexican consuls there. . . . Good night, gentlemen—hasta pronto."

31

For a time they had both remained seated, at Don Solomón's urging that this must be discussed and considered calmly. But one or the other was always out of his chair, with no order or regularity; sometimes to talk and sometimes to listen.

"I will go with you to Matamoros—"

"Matamoros is Mexico," Gilberto said. "Brownsville—it makes a big difference."

"As a citizen of Mexico of more than twenty-five years standing—as a businessman of reputation—I will bring letters of attest."

"Thanks—but don't you see, this wasn't a *suggestion* of the priest that I get tourist papers; it was a warning that I better get the hell out of Mexico—and quick."

Don Solomón saw that, and thought for a moment. "I have a plan—it just came to me. Listen, I will tell the Mexican consul at Brownsville that I am taking you back here with me to enter business. If a bond is required, I will post it. They cannot object."

"No, Don Solomón—"

"If you do not like this plan, we can devise a better one during the trip."

"It's past the time to think of ways of staying down here. The whole thing was a mistake. I didn't think it out clearly enough; I just ran. I don't know why."

"You do!"

"A couple of times on the way down, I thought I did. That I had a right to!"

"If that is—"

"Excuse me, Don Solomón—let me say the rest of it. . . . And up to tonight, there was no question about it. All I had on my mind was how good it felt to belong here."

Eagerly, Don Solomón said, "And this valley is only one fragment of the country!"

"I'm not talking about land and trees and rocks." Don Solomón looked hurt. "Or even about birds, or animals. I'm talking about people." Don Solomón smiled again. "People are what give you that—I only know the English word for it—*glow*—" He put his hands up, warming them at his own heart.

"Glow," the old man said. "The warmth of people. . . . Pelancha, Inés—"

Yes, yes, Inés; the round, bronze arms he never touched, but which warmed his fingertips—the golden crescent from her ear to her shoulder, for his cheek; the old man whose way took him to Jiménez with marigolds—Pompeyo; Rafaela; Margarita and Josefina and Lorenzo; and—Inés.

"And you," Gilberto blurted, "you and Doña Elena."

He went up to Don Solomón and gave him his hand. The man did not take it, but put both his hands on the boy's arms, looked into his face, and embraced him. "I had begun to hope—"

"I wanted you to know before I left," Gilberto said.

". . . to hope that you would stay here for a time." Gilberto shook his head to get the haziness out of his eyes. "My wife, she sees in you a younger brother—the youngest—he was as Benjamin to Reuben—"

"Yes—Ramón, I know—"

"But it is not on her behalf alone; I ask for myself. Since you have been here, the house was bright again. Elena felt it before you woke up this morning—before she knew you were here. . . . I do not know how to tell her—"

"I'll leave now, while she's asleep, if that's better."

Don Solomón shook his head. "Not in the dark."

"Then tomorrow, in the morning."

Brightly, Don Solomón said, "Wait! If the priest says nothing—if I can induce him—"

"It isn't that, Don Solomón. He didn't scare me; he just reminded me. I got to go back. He was the first one to say it; 'You're a traitor to your country!' . . . I don't want to hear it again—I don't want to hear myself say it."

"Your *country*, my son? You yourself, didn't you say a country—yours, mine—was not earth or trees; neither mountains nor valleys."

"My people then."

"Who are they, my son? They are mine, too; and mine are yours. The people of China and of Brazil are each others'; the countries of the North are of ice, those of Africa, of fire. But the *people*—the Eskimo and the Igorrote—are all of flesh and blood."

"I can't tell the government that."

"Not the government—not Pilsudski!" Don Solomón mumbled. It sounded like a curse.

"I didn't hear you," Gilberto said.

"It was nothing." He went to the door as if he meant to bolt it, but, without touching it, he turned and stood in front of Gilberto. "Look at me. . . . I will not ask you to do what you cannot and *should* not do at your age; that is, to imagine yourself as being *my* age. It is easier for you to think of *me*—Solomón Gulden—as a man of twenty-four. . . . Try not to paint too handsome a picture—" Both smiled. "Entirely different from you, son. I was sick of my lungs. I was penniless and I had no skill at anything by which a man could earn a piece of bread nor the salt with which to eat it. . . . I stood on the corner of a street in Tampico and wept tears."

"Jesus!"

Don Solomón, with a gesture, rejected the groan of sympathy. "Put pity aside, Gilberto. A Jew weeping is not uncommon. He weeps for Jerusalem destroyed and for Jerusalem restored. Pay him no mind. I turned my back upon a country and still my eyes swarmed with people. Who wishes to call me a traitor may do so."

"Europe, wasn't it?"

"A land called Poland. When I was born, and for a hundred years before, it belonged to Russia of the Czars. In the year 'fifteen, when I was conscripted, one could be flogged for calling himself a Pole. In the year 'twenty, the same man was shot for calling himself a Russian. Marshal Pilsudski changed my nationality as it suited him. I changed it to suit myself."

"I understand you fought in that war," Gilberto said. "In the uniform of some country, *as* something."

"In the year 'fifteen, in the Second Battle of Lemberg, under the Czar's uncle—*as* a Russian. Those of us who survived were sent to the Western Front, to fight beside the French as Russian-Poles. From Verdun to Valenciennes in August of the year 'eighteen, then, when the war ended, I was again pronounced a Pole, with no longer any allegiance to Russia, because of her defection in the war against the Germans, you understand."

He's just talking to get me interested in what happened to him, Gilberto told himself; to get me to forget what I made up my mind to do. Certainly, he must have had a pretty rough time of it. Bishop said he had fifteen months in the Pacific theatre; the old man had already covered three years. Wonder if he had to kill anybody, and if he did, did he have to make a prayer like Jews do over a chicken when they cut its throat. Aloud, he said, "They really mixed you up, didn't they, Don Solomón?"

"You can judge. . . . As a heroic Pole of the purest blood, I discovered myself, after the Armistice, as a legionnaire, a Falcon, under French and British command, on my way to fight the Bolsheviki."

"You signed up again?"

"How could I? I was never discharged. . . . The Bolsheviki—they were Russians, my former countrymen. There were Germans in this corps as well—my enemies of yesterday. As I told you, we were lectured by generals and holy men. The Bolshevik was the Antichrist. They had made a revolution and murdered the Second Nicholas, one of Christ's own vicars." He began to sound bitter. "They were going to distribute the land to the peasants. Their hammer and sickle was the hoofprint of Satan; Lenin was his deacon. We were the Elect of God. We were to take no prisoners. We here, and with the Americans, the Japanese, and the armies of Kolchak driving from Siberia, we were going to manure the earth of Holy Russia with their blood."

It was hard to imagine this old man with the weak, red eyes, thirty or so years back, in a uniform, with a gun in his hand, facing an enemy like that. Worse than the Japs or the Nazis, certainly tougher than those North Koreans and Chinese with their ridiculous tennis sneakers; some of them women,

Gilberto remembered from the newsreels. "They must have had the same rule about killing prisoners."

Don Solomón shrugged. He seemed to be getting tired. Gilberto waited for him to say something about this business of killing prisoners, but he acted as if he didn't think it was important enough to discuss; anyway, not until he had his fill of looking at Gilberto. When he turned his eyes to the door, to the window, the man's gaze persisted, tender, unbroken.

Gilberto experienced a sudden, derisive image of himself: an 18-karat jerk, sitting here with his shirt open, like Nathan Hale. Like *you're* the hero, and what this old fellow had been through was nothing. And if it *was* something, he's here to tell about it; and you, you're on your way to make the Big Sacrifice. . . . Jeez, Gil, if you're not the most loathesome bastard you ever ran into! Boy, when it comes to jollying the señoras, giving them the old schmalzeroo, you're all there. But now, you son of a bitch, when you want to tell this old gentlemen that his regret about your going back is nothing to what you're going to feel for the rest of your life—you can't get the word out.

He tried. "I want to say something, Don Solomón. . . . I'll never be able to forget you and Doña Elena. . . . Nothing this good ever happened to me. If I could only—"

"Stop!" The old man frowned him down. "Let us have one glass together—our last." He brought two brandy ponies from a tray on the bookshelf and poured mescal into them from the Oaxaca jug. "You don't mind drinking with an old traitor?"

"Nobody has any right to call you that."

Don Solomón smiled. "Not now. But a generation ago, when I fled—deserted—I wondered and doubted and feared. . . . across all of Europe and the Ocean, until I stood where you stand—*as* you stand, Gilberto—"

He stopped and picked his glass up by the rim, only to move it, like a chessman. He's still trying to unsell me, Gilberto thought. Should he stop him here, or let him go on? Let him. There was nothing he could say—

"No documents, either, Gilberto, and not a word of the language. I set out from Tampico as a peddler, with a tray slung from my neck. I had needles and thread and thimbles where the people had no cloth to sew; collar buttons among the shirtless; bootlaces for the shoeless. There was nowhere on my path, a soul whose name I knew, to whom I could do a kindness or bring a greeting, yet—" He suddenly raised his glass. "To you, my son; to speed you there, so that you may sooner come back."

32

He would not have to tell Doña Elena in the morning; Don Solomón would be telling her now in their room. On account of her attitude to the priest—her husband was much too charitable—she would understand that this had to happen. It was bound to, and easier all around, now that Perfecto laid his cards on the table. If he had said nothing, he was the kind who would send a letter or something to the right people, telling them where a gringo deserter was hiding out.

Before blowing out the lamp, he looked at his watch; a little after 11:30. Not as late as he thought. He was only tired, not sleepy; but the bed looked more sleepable tonight, with sheets and a real blanket. As soon as he finished this cigarette, he would ease himself into it.

Don Solomón said he would not call him "too early." Probably not until after their own breakfast, he hoped. The balance of his money would be ready, and since it was the market day, he said there would be plenty of transportation back to Ciudad del Maíz. If he didn't give him the money right away, he'd remind him, so he could slip a few pesos—ten, at least—to Margarita and Josefina. He had it all now—what the girl had meant to say when she started, "Is it true that—" She must have heard them talking about wanting him to stay.

It was going to be tough all around, that last hour or so, if it had to be that long. Some of the time could be killed talking about coming back some day. He had it! The letter Don Solomón wanted him to type out in English. That was it! He would make one draft and stall over the final one until the last minute.

It was only 158 kilometers from Maíz to Valles—less than a hundred miles—and there was a plane from there direct to Matamoros at five p.m. The flight would take an hour and forty minutes.

He lay down, smiling at the idea of walking through the plaza there. Maybe saying hello to the old macho again and asking him, "What, hombre! Still looking for a sweetheart?" Then it would be time for dinner. He'd go into the same restaurant and have another one of those pink shrimp omelets and buy his last pack of Elegantes, and then walk past Captain Bermúdez and ask him what the score of the game was the other night. And then, over the river—the Río Grande this time—to the U.S. side.

"Just a second, feller! What's your nationality?"

"I'm a citizen of the United States."

"Yeah? Where were you born?"

"In Los Angeles, California."

"Could be. Let's see your Selective Service card."

"I tore it up."

"What's your name?"

"Reyes, G., Number two-three-three-two-eight, dash, three-seven."

"Nice you remember it. Check on that, Joe. Let's have it again."

"I'll save you the bother. I was due to be inducted last Friday in Los Angeles. And for one reason or another, I didn't show up."

"You admit you're a deserter?"

"Not yet, chief. I'm still a civilian.I'd have to be *in* the army and missing for fifteen days before being a deserter."

"The guy's right, Bill. What do we do?"

"You can put me under arrest and the government pays my way to California, or you can let me get there on my own."

Korea, here I come! No two ways about it—there were *four* sides to this question. There was Eisen's side: You're only a half-assed American, a white Mexican at your best, with a lot of thick, black hair and a brown skin, and a name like Reyes; you're a Yankee Doodle Boy, No. 23328-37, when they want something from you—like your life, for instance.

Bishop was right, too. There were wars, and there were wars. Some were on the level, and some weren't. Bishop made the distinction, and if he—a bald, blond, ruddy Texan—couldn't, who could? If they had to sell it by shoveling it at you up to the ears, it stank.

The old gent was the rightest of all. He had the best case. Where Eisen and Bishop just scratched, he dug way down. About people. About countries. About governments; their flags, their languages, their laws—all different. People?—all the same, whichever way you look at it. Take a *world* census; ask *everybody*, and it will come out they all want the same things. At one point there, after supper, Don Solomón said something on this tack to the priest. It had to do with the Tower of Babel, and how the people, then, were all getting together so that there wouldn't be anything they couldn't do. And when God came around and saw this, He decided this wouldn't do. If the people all got together, they wouldn't need Him, and so He wiped out the whole project. "Occasionally," Don Solomón said, in that quiet way he has, "God remembers this as the worst blunder He ever made, and tries to repair it. He gave you Jesus, and later he sent Einstein."

All good, all solid arguments, he agreed. But from men who had the right to give them. Eisen making his pitch under his framed commission, ornamented with campaign ribbons. Bishop, with his Zippo lighter and that bayonet hanging up somewhere in his house. Don Solomón, who owed them nothing; whatever those countries called themselves or how often they changed their flags. *But he went!* And having gone, he could walk out and see if he liked it better somewhere else. They all went, once. Nobody was able to look at them as cowards.

There it is, he thought savagely. That's why I have to go—*once!*

The joint across the park, the pulquería, was really jumping. If they just let the guitar player finish something, it wouldn't sound so awful. But drunks—and it sounded as if there were a least ten of them—got started singing, and trailed off in screams and howls. . . . "Soy puro mexicano—" one started and was stopped by a bunch of them letting rip with a series of yelps, "Ay-y-y-y-Yay-Ya-a-a-yay—eeeeee!" That wolf-noise went for every kind of song, it seemed. Probably all of them in town for the market tomorrow. "Soy puro mexicano—mi tierra es bravía—"

He smiled in the dark, not at the singer—I'm a Mexican clear-through—my country is a wild one—but because he would see Inés before he left.

The boys in the Judge Not seemed to respect what he was thinking about and let the guitar strum by itself. Maybe they all got stiff at the same time . . . At this moment he had a very clear idea of what he was going to say to her. "Good morning, Inés. How are you this morning?" Snappy, huh! Anyway, if she called him primo—"Look, I'm not any cousin of yours, not even a second cousin. . . . And I think you're beautiful—yes, even when you look away from me like that. You'd be beautiful any place in the world, not only here. . . . If I wasn't going away, I'd tell you something. . . . But if it's worth enough for you to find out, Inés, you could ask Doña Elena. I think she knows. Maybe your mother also knows—the way she looked at me when I looked at you. . . . You mean you don't have to *ask?* . . . I'd like to carry a picture of you, here. This one? This is my mother. . . . Get a smiling picture made. It's for me, so I want to pay for it; so here's some—here's a hundred pesos. I'll write to you and tell you where to send it—and you write something on the back. . . . Oh, anything you want to say."

The music and noise of every kind stopped altogether. He turned to lie flat on his back so that, if by any chance he dreamed about Inés, he shouldn't be on top of her.

The fly screen on the barred window behind him, plucked by blind insects, vibrated harplike. . . .

> Firelight glowed on her cheek. Seated, crosslegged on the floor, resting her back against his legs. It was like looking at himself on television—he was wearing a velvet esmoquin and paratrooper boots. She said something which he didn't catch—she was talking into the fire. "Mande?" She spoke louder, "Tendremos que pensar en este asunto al fondo, Bruce." . . . Bruce? He checked with the heavy silver identification bracelet on his wrist and read: GAY-LORD McCRAE U.S.A. Bruce was close enough, though. "We're going to close the books," he said. . . . "No obstante—" . . . "It's essential the books got to be closed, Eye-nez." She stood up, rubbing one naked foot against the other, and set a big straw sleeping mat on the floor. Glancing at him, she unrolled it, quickly trying to make it cylindrical again, so he could not recognize who was hidden in it. It was either Paul Menéndez or the bashful young machetero

on the camión Gloria. Don Solomón was throwing handfuls of five-
peso Hidalgos, which landed with no sound, like discs of felt. Doña
Elena rocked a baby carriage back and forth. Sitting up in it was a
fat little guy, bawling like anything. She put a guitar in its hands . . .
"Here, Ramoncito—darling . . ." From crying, without changing
key, the kid tore into a chord and sang, "Soy puro mexicano—"
Bloink! Blam! Two strings went—

No guitar could have made the next two cracking sounds and two booming slams against metal. The cortina out front—stones . . . Stones—? Guns!
The profound bellow of a car engine brought him dazedly upright. Some
madman—lead-footed idiot—kill people that way. In the same eyeblink, a
fan of light swept the room and two punctures opened in the screen. He saw
them before he heard the explosions, no louder than toy balloons popping.
The engine snarl thinned in the distance. Running to the door, he trod on
jagged pieces of fallen plaster. He squirmed into his pants, and, while groping
for his shoes, the door opened.
"Gilberto—"
"Sí, señora."
"Don't show a light. Nothing happened—"
"Plaster is coming down," he said stupidly.
". . . to you; you are not hurt? ¡Gracias a Dios! Come out to the patio."
Her hand over the lens of a flashlight, she flicked it on, intermittently, and he
followed her to the kitchen side of the enclosure. "Right here; this is the safest
place." The two servants stood against the wall. He could not see them
clearly, but they radiated terror. "You two go back to sleep," Doña Elena said,
"Nothing has happened."
"Please, no, señora," Margarita begged.
"What am I standing here for?" Gilberto said, without bluster. "Where's
Don Solomón? He didn't go outside!"
Doña Elena pointed. "In the store, with Lorenzo; to see if—"
Both of them came out as Gilberto started for the entrance to the tienda.
Don Solomón held a revolver and a flashlight. Lorenzo carried a shotgun.
Any other time, to see a man with a nightshirt dangling below his robe, would
have struck Gilberto as funny.
"Put down that weapon, Lorenzo. Everybody is here, unhurt. Nobody
entered; the place is secure."
"They came for something, patrón," Lorenzo said.
"Drunkards! Brawlers!"
"Excuse me, patrón—they did not sing or shout. Not even '¡Arriba Ce-
dillo!' They simply shot. It must be—"
"Be quiet, Lorenzo!" The old man said it angrily. "Four bullets struck the
cortina. I heard two more."
"Over my head," Gilberto said. "Through the window. There are holes in
the screen, and the wall—"

Don Solomón looked quickly at his wife. Then he asked, "What hour is it, Gilberto?" It was a quarter after four. "It will be light in two hours."

"Are you going to call the police?" Gilberto asked. "I could fix the exact time—4:12. The car, I'd say, was a big, powerful job with some kind of hydraulic transmission—"

"There are three of the size you say, Don Gilberto," Lorenzo began. "All belonging to—"

"Lorenzo!" Don Solomón warned again. "We will talk about this later. Muchachas—Margarita—prepare coffee—and for yourselves. Serve us here."

"I better put on a shirt or something," Gilberto said.

As he turned, Don Solomón stepped in front of him and called to Josefina, "Bring my gray jacket for Don Gilberto, please. . . . Sit down, Gilberto; the coffee will be soon. . . . This is a fine despedida we have arranged for you. I am ashamed for my house."

"It's not your fault. Have you any idea—any reason somebody would have to do a thing like this?"

Before Don Solomón could say anything, Lorenzo intervened. "If it were the Dorados, like the last time, they would have been on horses—and Doña Julia among them—and she, shouting above the rest, '¡Viva Cristo Rey!' No?"

Don Solomón shut him up for the last time, and told him to go stay in the depósito until he was called. "And do not alarm the women with that nonsense."

"It is not nonsense, Sol," his wife said.

Calmly, but hurriedly, he stopped her from saying more. "Whatever it is, Elena, please allow me to manage it. It's lucky that our guest was not harmed."

"Lucky indeed!" she said coldly.

"I had better give my story to the authorities," Gilberto suggested. "I hate to think of this happening again, to you people."

"The authorities!" Doña Elena mocked. "Shall I tell you who the authorities are here?"

"I beg you, Elena, don't agitate yourself. Come with me, with your torch, and help me open the safe so that I can give Gilberto his money."

He sat smoking in the dark. It was clear to him that there was something about this shooting business that the old man was covering up. Maybe some kind of a feud—like in those expensive Westerns, starring Alan Ladd or Gary Cooper. Something the old man wasn't letting out to any stray cowpoke, who happened to take shelter overnight. Every time Lorenzo wanted to say something, he was choked off. The same, only politer, when Doña Elena beg n talking about it. Anyway, he just hoped it wasn't more than a carful of drunks, who might even come around later and shamefacedly offer to make good the damage.

Lorenzo shuffled back. "The señores?"

Gilberto pointed. "They went into the tienda for a minute."

"The sergeant, Don Vicente, is at the door." He repeated it to Don Solomón, who handed Gilberto a thick envelope.

"Count it later," he whispered. "Let the sergeant in, Lorenzo—and it is all right now to have some light."

Vicente said good evening and bowed to everybody in the patio. "I heard the discharge of firearms and I came directly," he said. He tried to salute and his hat fell off, and he almost fell on his face reaching for it. He was stinking drunk. "I was in the rear of the Judge Not, with Don Gumersindo, warming my hands. It is bitter cold out, if you don't know it."

"He wants a drink. There is mescal on the table in the sala; please bring it, and a glass, Lorenzo."

"Who was driving the car, Don Vicente?" Doña Elena asked him before he reached for the mescal.

Vicente waved his hand in a slow circle. "Twice around the Alameda, very slowly, until—" His voice died.

"Who was in it?" she asked.

"I saw no car, señora."

"Were you drinking with them, Vicente?"

"Please—" Don Solomón begged. "No more, Elena."

"I make my report," the drunken cop muttered. "Directly—at first shot, proceeded to—"

"Drink up, hombre," Don Solomón said. "See him to the street, Lorenzo."

Doña Elena's penned rage burst in one word, "¡Marranos!" Her husband took her arm, and they sat down as Margarita brought coffee.

"We will leave earlier, Gilberto. Let us say, about six," Don Solomón said casually. "In the truck."

"No, that's too much trouble," Gilberto protested. "Maybe I can rent a car."

"I find I have need to go. A report to the main district official of the postal service. A shipment of goods, also, for which I have invoices, on the truck line from Monterrey. I will be able to hire somebody to drive back. I assure you, Gilberto, it will be a favor to me. Lorenzo will come, too."

"Yes, there will be heavy boxes, the kegs of nails, the sheets of window glass," Doña Elena reminded him.

"In that case," Gilberto submitted, "I'll be glad to do it that way. Also, I could get the spare part for the ignition."

"Fine, fine. . . . What is it Lorenzo?"

"Don Vicente—he lies on his face in the callejón. The dogs will foul on him. And he mumbles. I cannot understand too clearly what he says. It seems, though, that I heard the name Vargas—"

"This is the truth, Lorenzo?" Don Solomón asked. "I know you and Vargas are not friends."

"As I stand here, Don Solomón! Vargas—" A pounding on the cortina at the front stopped him. "That is him again, having crept away. I shall tell him—" The pounding resumed, as a tattoo, with a club, and ended abruptly.

Gilberto followed Lorenzo and Don Solomón through the store, where they opened the inner door cautiously; then the smaller door cut into the iron shutter. Vicente stood rigidly framed in the metal square. Jerking his hand, he pointed to the ground beside him—"¡Mira!" and crumpled slowly to the walk.

Whatever bulked against the shutter looked like a mound of garbage until Don Solomón flicked on the fluorescent tube overhead. It sputtered and gasped before steadying to its sickly, blue glow. A rough jute sack and what had been spilled from it lay there—garbage. The tiny goat, its head not entirely severed, attached only by a strip of skin; its thin, black lips pursed as for a kiss.

"Ay, pobrecita . . . Qué depravación—" Lorenzo lifted it gently, and called it by the Mexican term for a dead baby—angelito.

The men could not look at each other as they proded the blood-soaked debris—the pudding of dry cereals, flakes, oatmeal, from packages hacked open. The candy, all pounded and pulverized; two new rebozos—in strips.

And all around, brutally shattered toys; pencils, broken in halves, thirds, eighths; and paper—not one piece larger than a playing card. Ink and blood and rice.

Gilberto stared stupidly at a curling strip from the cover of one of the three gutted books—0,000 LIGAS.

33

Don Solomón sounded as if he were apologizing for what happened, as if those pistoleros were Katzenjammer Kids who poured water in the guest's silk hat. Gilberto had been the kind of guest who merited that kind of treatment, something like a schoolmaster bringing gloom to a community happily at play. If he needed a clearer reason—clearer to himself—for going back, he had it here. It was clearer because it had to do with other people. It would be hard to tell—well, Dr. Eisen, for one, how, in thinking the whole business over, he had decided to come back, take what was coming to him and be clear in his conscience. No need to mention Don Perfecto, whose warning inspired that decision. Don Solomón and Doña Elena, yes, natural-ly. Anybody would understand that he would be putting them in danger by remaining in Zaragoza. The old man had been there twenty years, and nobody, no one person acting in his own interest, had a right to wipe out the safety he had earned.

This was probably the first time Don Solomón ever left his house with a gun in his pocket. Lorenzo sat on the bed of the truck, behind the cab, the shotgun across his knees.

"Compared to other places in the Republic," the old man was saying, "San Luis Potosí, you might say, is almost an enlightened region. Of its population of six hundred thousand, almost half know how to read and write."

Still harping on that, Gilberto thought; trying to convince him that some-body was actually eager to keep them from reading . . . *0,000 Ligas* . . . So eager, that they would kill somebody for bringing blank paper and colored crayons to a house that needed food. No, it was more than that. They were against corn flakes and goat's milk, and light—he remembered the shattered lamp in the rubble, the smell of blood and kerosene.

"To have almost a quarter of a million people who cannot tell you, when you ask them, what occupation they follow, that is a serious state of affairs."

More figures. He listened respectfully, but Gilberto found it easy to avoid comment. He had merely to gaze alertly at the road, as if driving called for his undivided caution. "No Distraiga al Chofer."

"They say, 'Command me. Is it to dig a grave? To carry a burden? I have a back. To plant *your* crop? To harvest *your* yield, yes, if you will lend me the implements. If not, I have hands.' Yes, he wins his daily bread, but is it enough to want only that?"

Gilberto felt he ought to say something. "Not if he's human."

"He is human. And sometimes he wakes up from his dream of only enough bread and a peaceful death. The history of Mexico is full of those instances."

"Revolution, that is."

"Claro. What else?"

Gilberto was pleased at having used the right word, plucking it out of the air. He repeated it. "Revolution—the government stands for it?"

"It must. No official, elected or otherwise, dares to say he is against revolution—*The* Revolution—or the very concept of revolution."

His saying that word wasn't guesswork at all, Gilberto commended himself. It was discernment—quite an advance in thinking over so short a period as ten days. "But not this force and violence stuff, like this Cedillo, that somebody mentioned."

"That, Gilberto, was counterrevolution. It was General Saturnino Cedillo who used force and violence against The Revolution."

He could pretend to stare out at the road, or say, yes, I see. But he didn't. Don Solomón had muddied up what was once clear. He heard him say, "I should have given you that book to take along. However, I can send it to you. It will explain more clearly than I can—who saw it—what kind of an adventure that rebellion was. In the capital they said his uprising was just childish petulance. But it was murderous for the time that it flared. He was defeated, killed and beheaded, as was predicted."

"That's what they do to traitors," Gilberto muttered as he slowed down for the bridge—the same bridge, but it looked much wider now, in the cool, clear morning.

"President Cárdenas did not call him that. When they brought him word, right to Ciudad del Maíz, where we are going, that Don Saturnino was dead and his rebels scattered, Don Lázaro said, 'He has forgotten his duty to the people.' You will find it in the book." As the truck thumped across the last plank, he said, "His planes dropped bombs in an attempt to destroy this very bridge."

"I look forward to reading that book," Gilberto said. "Is there anything in the way of books I could send you?"

"Just word of yourself," the old man smiled. "That you are well, you have not forgotten us, and that some day we may see you again."

"I promise you that, Don Solomón."

"If the time comes when you are able, and you hesitate because you doubt, then—remember you have seen the worst—"

"And the best!"

"Everything will be better. Caciquismo and those things which look upon a stranger with a book as an enemy will have died."

Ciudad del Maíz would be along pretty soon. He didn't want Don Solomón to stay on that note until the last minute of their parting. He didn't want him crying, like Doña Elena. It was better to keep him talking about things like the Cedillo rebellion—things that made him eloquently angry, rather than sentimental. "Caciquismo—I never heard that word before. What does it mean?"

"Well—let me see—more or less—let me think if I can find the same thing in English. Of course! You read in your history of feud—feudalismo."

"Oh, sure." He had read the word feudalism, or heard it somewhere. But its meaning was vague.

"Latifundists," Don Solomón added. "Those who own great amounts of land."

"Like this Coronel Carrasco in your neighborhood," Gilberto suggested.

"He is a good example, on a smaller scale, of a cacique. A military man. He actually participated in the putting down of Cedillo in 1938. Nobody can accuse him, to this day, of violating his soldier's oath. He knew that Cedillo was a fool; that Cárdenas would destroy him. And he had his eye on the rewards—the spoils. This is a shrewd fellow, this Carrasco."

Good, thought Gilberto, Don Solomón was hot again on politics, and so long as he was on this line, a show of attention would keep him on it. "This is very interesting, Don Solomón. I want to hear the rest of it." And, as he said it, he realized that he more than half meant it.

"Cedillo was a vain and pompous fool," Don Solomón continued. "He believed flattery. He believed the worst about the Mexican people and the best about himself. He believed that Mexico was another Spain; that the people were waiting for a liberator and that he was to be their Franco." He stopped and sighed. "Here we are, almost in the city, and I am trying to tell you crudely what you will be able to read so much better."

"Don't worry about it spoiling the book for me. . . . What was Cedillo supposed to liberate them from?"

"It was fantastic!" It was good to hear him laugh again. "The Asociación Española Anticomunista y Antijudía was telling forty thousand Potosinos who understood no Spanish, only the idiomas indígenas, that they would be liberated from Lázaro Cárdenas, the Tarascan Indian from Michoacán. The Falange de México, the Partido Nacionalista were going to liberate the peasant from his ejido and his tractor so that he could put the yoke back on his idle shoulders; save him the trouble of buying what he needs with money, when, after all, they know at the casa grande how much corn, soap, and cloth he has earned, and hand it to him directly.

"They promised the fanatically religious that the State of San Luis Potosí would become a Catholic enclave where only confessional schools would be permitted. The Centro Patronal—the employers—were going to free the Mexican worker from the oppression of a minimum five-peso daily wage, below which no man may be paid."

"How far did he expect to get with a program like that?" Gilberto asked.

"Cedillo himself, being a fool—all the way. But those for whom he played the fool expected no more than they got: a period of confusion, a break in the development of the Cárdenas program. Some say that it had begun too fast and that Cárdenas could not possibly hope to see the peasant of Mexico his own master in one administration of six years, or even in two administrations. And so it was. Some in the south, in Morelos, went even further than Zapata, their agrarian hero, dreamed. They have powerful ejidales and sugar and rice cooperatives. But here, in San Luis Potosí—well, I have heard many explanations, but none as clear as what I saw. Machinery idle in the sheds, crops—banana, coffee, mango—left on the trees one season. The failure of the banco ejidal and no credit the next. Peanuts, camote, melon, pineapple left on the ground; not because there was nobody to buy the crop—the cities were hungering for it—but because there was no gasoline for the trucks to take it to the railroad. The following season—no trucks.

"Then, Alemán ascended to office. A fine man. The first president of the Republic who had not been a general. A lawyer, he was; a man of commerce. Commerce and industry, he said, would make Mexico great among nations. Let there be great factories so that Mexicans can make the things it needs and even sell manufactured goods to other countries. Steel, glass, rubber, cotton cloth—by all means, cotton cloth! Millions of square meters were planted to cotton, which, as you know, is not very nourishing, except for the seed, out of which a fine grade of edible oil is expressed. But it is essentially a money crop. And there Licenciado Alemán was a true prophet. The factories hummed and the Banco de México bulged with money. Hordes of people abandoned the land and went to work for wages by the day. They made steel, brick, cement, and tile, but they continued to live in houses made of adobe and tar paper. They made glass—well, count the windows in the houses that you pass.

"Home then to his meal! The factory hand had given his wife a formidable amount of pesos—as much as eight for each day he had worked. What is there to eat, woman? Ah, menudo! Luxurious, but I have earned it. It has in it some tripe, a sheep's trotter, some pig's cheek, and some other slivers of meat. Very savory—and how much was expended on it? Ninety centavos. Including the onion, the chile, and the pinch of oregano? No, that came to twenty-five centavos more. An extravagance! However, the tortillas are cheap. Well, not as cheap as the day before yesterday, husband. There is a shortage of corn for the masa; I waited for two hours in a long queue at the molina de nixtamal, and then it was forty centavos the kilo. All right, woman, don't mourn. Where are the beans? There are no beans! With seventy-seven varieties of frijoles native to his country, of a color and a texture to please every taste, there are suddenly none to be had; not a handful! But there will be, soon, husband. It was in the newspaper which the man read to me. A shipload is coming from Africa, to be sold at a peso sixty the kilo—not more. ¡Válgame Dios! Beans from Africa! What has become of my poor country?"

It was funny, but he wasn't making fun of Mexicans, as they did in the States; as on that juke box record and on certain radio programs. The way Don Solomón imitated the confusion of the husband and the respectfully low voice of the wife was meant to amuse him. Although it was near the heart of the subject of Mexico generally, it was to keep Gilberto merry. He had mentioned the military, and from there, or from anywhere, he could have wedged in Gilberto's decision to return to California and present himself to the draft authorities. He had opposed Gilberto's going in his own way, and he was right on every moral count.

Once Gilberto heard a line—in a movie naturally, a comedy, where a politician says, "There is a time when a man must rise above principle." He didn't think it was too funny, but it got a big laugh. Now he understood it. There is a time when a fellow must rise above morality.

"The campesino who left the land to work in the factory," Don Solomón was saying, "returns to his tierra—let us say, this valley. He finds the fields cultivated again. Oxen, and not those terrifying machines, are again drawing the plows. Women and children are digging the sweet potatoes and hoeing the corn. Men are in the cane, *and there are beans!* Flowering hectares of beans. And who has brought about this mircacle? El Coronel Carrasco. Go see him at the casa grande, he is generous. And what a splendid hacienda—and a chapel! Work? Return in the morning before sunrise and the overseer will give him tools. Food? He will not go hungry if he is industrious, respectful, and obedient. Beans? Mountains of beans. Now he is to go to Doña Julia, the hacendado's sister—that pious bitch!—who will inscribe his name in a book and ask him many questions, mainly about the strength of his faith. If he has children, he is told it would be good if they helped him at his work. It would keep them out of mischief."

"She's the one who was supposed to have ridden with the Cedillo mob, yelling 'Long Live Christ the King!' Was she one of those Gold Shirts, or what?"

"An Acción Femenilista, also priest-led."

"Where do the priests fit in?"

Don Solomón looked at him and shook his head. "Gilberto, you have a curiosity about the ugliest phases—Ya? Here already? What a short ride!"

He stopped the truck in the plaza, opposite where he had taken Lucas's bus. He glanced behind to see if possibly the hearselike Sheik was where it had left him.

Ciudad del Maíz either had just risen, or it was its habit to go about its business at this dreamy pace. That was it—the cortinas of all the stores were rolled up and all the doors open. A rapid drumming of hoofs rattled out of the loudspeaker on a pillar of the bandstand—a commercial; a hoarse soprano singing, "Whoever drinks Don Quixote knows what he's drinking—¡olé!"

It may be a dismal burg again tonight, but this morning, the sun gilded all the corners that had been murky, and it was beautiful.

"My business takes me first to the Administration of Mails, only a few steps to the left, just to sign a document," Don Solomón said. "Then to purchase some revenue stamps for various bills of sale, and finally to the bank, where I hope I will not be detained."

"There's a garage," Gilberto suggested. "Instead of just waiting, I could be looking for that kit of points. Wait—wasn't there some stuff that had to go back?"

"Sí, señor," Lorenzo reminded him. "At the freight warehouse."

"Ah, yes." Don Solomón found three tissue-paper documents in his pocket. "A keg of nails, a wooden case of sheets of window glass, tiles—"

"Do you know the man who's going to drive you back?" Gilberto asked.

"I'll find him. . . . Here then—" He handed the papers to Gilberto. "The bills of lading. Lorenzo will guide you to the freight truck terminal—"

"And direct the retreat exactly flush with their loading platform." Lorenzo demonstrated by putting the edges of his hands together.

"Then you can recover me in front of the bank. We can go to the garage, obtain the accessories needed, and arrange there for a chauffeur."

Lorenzo got in beside him, wrapped his serape around the shotgun, and put it on the ledge behind the seats. "To the right, Don Gilberto; into the street where stands the boxing arena, and again to the right."

"What's the idea of the escopeta, Lorenzo—and Don Solomón with a revolver?"

"You are going by railroad or avión, from Valles?"

"By avión. . . . I asked you why you were lugging these weapons, Lorenzo."

"It is sensible when you are dealing with Carrasco's pistoleros—*and* their aduladores."

That word stopped him, and he asked frankly, "What is an adulador?"

"One who fawns on them, señor; who would like to be one—an aspirante."

Oh, a stooge—some punk kid, like in that George Raft picture; trigger-happy, wants to kill somebody and get to the notice of The Boss.

"The bodega, señor." Lorenzo pointed to a long, low shed near which two heavy trucks were parked. He made a wide left turn, and Lorenzo, standing on the running board, signaled him backward until he touched the platform.

"Like a kiss," Lorenzo beamed. "I will recover Don Solomón's goods. You will be required to sign papers, there in Don Antonio's office."

A tall, middle-aged man with black silk protectors drawn over his shirtsleeves stepped out of the office as Gilberto reached the platform. He glanced quickly at the truck, as if to make sure that it was the right one, and then stared at Gilberto.

"Don Antonio?"

"Su servidor," the man said rapidly. "Where is Don Solomón?"

"He has some business to take care of. I am to pick him up at the plaza, in front of the bank. But I have the bills of lading." He handed them to Don Antonio.

The man appeared nervous. "You drove very fast. I did not think you would be here so soon. They telephoned less than an hour ago."

"I don't understand. Who telephoned?"

"You are seeing Don Solomón directly, you say?"

"Yes," Gilberto said. "I told you. As soon as this stuff is loaded."

Don Antonio shouted to a man on the other end of the platform, "Hey, Andrés! Help with those packages for Zaragoza—hurry, man!" He snatched the papers from Gilberto. "The message is for him to get back as quickly as he can. There's been an accident."

"What kind? Not Doña Elena, I hope."

"No, not the señora-his-wife, assure him. But somebody called—a servant, on the señora's behalf. . . . Do they have a daughter—I don't remember—but look, boy, tell him any way you choose, but this is how I understood it. . . . Very soon after you left for here, this woman, Josefina—"

"The cook, she was hurt?"

Impatiently Don Antonio said, "No, no, please to listen. In response to a sound—a wounded dog, she thought—she went out to the callejón, and there was this girl, Inés—"

"Inés—" Gilberto made the sound of her name without moving his lips.

"Not a rag on her, they told me. But I didn't quite get who this Inés was, that's why I asked you—"

"She is not their daughter," Gilberto said, as if it were the most urgent thing in the world. He saw Lorenzo rolling a keg onto the truck, but hazily, as through pebbled glass.

"Whoever—from the excitement, I thought she may be a near relation," Don Antonio said. "Tell Don Solomón that she is in a very grave condition."

"Tell me what happened, señor."

"I am sorry I asked," Don Antonio answered slowly. "But I did—and the woman told me. The girl had been cruelly used—and beaten as well. And either was thrown, or fell, out of an automobile. A doctor was on his way, and—you need not tell this to Don Solomón yet—also the priest had been sent for."

His head numb, painless and senseless as under a tremendous dose of novocaine, Gilberto stared at Lorenzo and the warehouseman trundling a heavy packing case, inches from his toes or a mile away—he couldn't tell. He desperately wanted to make some kind of sound to end the booming in his skull. "This man who struck her—"

"Christ above us! Where the hell did Don Solomón pick up a clown like this? *Struck* the girl! Don't you know what happened to that poor girl? Didn't I make it clear? She was—Oh, good Jesus, did you ever see such innocence? The *man*, he asks! There were four or five of them."

They were tugging the last, the heaviest crate. Gilberto felt his arm gripped tightly. "I don't mean to be harsh, joven," Don Antonio said. "It is both a sadness and an anger that stirs me to hear of a woman, though she may be the daughter of a thousand whores—"

"I've got to go."

Don Antonio still held his arm. "With bad news, you ride a slow horse. . . . I have taken my share of God's bounty, but never like that. . . . Do you know what I would do to those reptiles—those dunghill machos . . . I would cut a small slit in their bellies—" A switch blade flashed in his hand. "Draw out only enough to nail to a tree—lash them with bullwhips and make them run. . . . And I am a mild man."

"Please, I must find Don Solomón."

"Okay." Don Antonio closed the blade. "You're loaded. Here, sign your name." He handed Gilberto the bills of lading and a stub of pencil.

He leaned the paper against the wall to write *Reyes, G. #233.* He was trying to remember the rest of it as Don Antonio spoke. "I was asked to be sure to tell Don Solomón that there was one name—Gilberto—the girl kept saying."

He dropped the papers and ran to the truck. The first time past, he didn't see Don Solomón in front of the bank. On his second turn around the plaza, he recognized him, coming forward slowly, not looking anywhere. He kept on, not knowing the sound of his own horn, but he looked up when Gilberto slammed on the brakes hard enough to warp the front wheels against the curb. Opening the door he called, "Don Solomón! Come on, get in."

"I was just on my way to the bank."

"Please, Don Solomón—there's no time. I'm going back with you."

34

The Surtidor was shuttered, and he thought, as he passed and swung into the alley, of a warm autumn day on Seventh Street, in Los Angeles; alive and crowded with shoppers—like the Alameda, now, on market day. And seeing placards on the windows of one store after another, some of the biggest, "Closed on Account of Yom Kippur."

There was a stain of blood and vomit in the yellow dust at their feet; both saw it, but neither looked at the other in mutual admission, as Josefina opened the sheet iron door to let them in. Seeing Gilberto, she slapped her hand to her mouth to stifle a scream, and it came out as a moan. "Señores, Doña Elena begs—you are not to go in."

"Where is the girl?" Don Solomón asked. Gilberto could say nothing.

But it was Gilberto the girl answered, "In your room, Don Gilberto. Shall I bring you something in the sala—the comedor?"

Don Solomón shook his head. "What doctor came?"

"The German one, who flies in the avioneta three times a week to La Corona. Doña Elena begged the Coronel to send him."

"In time?" The girl looked away. "Answer me, Josefina."

"He is still here, señor, calling for much cotton, and I am boiling many of his tools on the stove. Doña Elena is helping."

"And the priest, Don Perfecto?"

"That bastard!" Gilberto said it in English. Don Solomón touched his shoulder calmingly.

"Don Perfecto also; by the little table. He is begging Our Holy Mother—"

"Pelancha—has she been told?"

"A coche has been sent, sí."

The door of the room in the opposite corner of the patio—his room—opened narrowly and Doña Elena called, "Josefina—quickly."

He saw her clearly, and she had looked in his direction, but Gilberto wasn't sure that she had seen him.

"Did you see," Don Solomón whispered, "the expression on her face when she saw you; the happiness?"

"What about—"

"And when she tells Inés—"

"But why would they call the priest, unless—"

"He comes to see me, too; that doesn't mean—forgive me, son, I am talking like a fool."

The door opened again, wider, to admit Josefina with a boiling tray, and when she came out again, her arms were loaded with crumpled bed linen and she carried Margarita's wheel of keys. She tried to hurry past, but Gilberto got in front of her. "What is happening?"

"Permiso, señor, I am forbidden to tarry, to say nothing."

He begged, looking at the servant pathetically. "But you just *saw* her. Can't you tell me anything?"

In a rapid, disobedient whisper, Josefina said, "They have stopped the blood. I go for fresh linen," and hurried on.

Don Solomón looked at him. "Perhaps I am not such a fool, after all. That tells us we may hope. . . . Sit down, son; smoke, if it calms you."

He sat down in the same chair in which he sat at breakfast the day before. When, he thought, he knew from nothing; assumed this was some sort of a tourist-home, where they treat you like one of the family, nice and all, and that he would have to travel far to find another place like it. And what a hell of a difference 24 hours made, yet how slowly he had lived them; how they seemed to stretch out, to allow for all of these people to come into his life and, each of them to package their ideas for him to sort out and see which ones he'd buy. Well—he bought, and on an All Sales Final basis, too. Nobody said anything about 10 Days Free Trial.

"Ten days," he said aloud.

"What, son?"

The old man would understand. "I wanted to say how tough it feels, in the same ten days—to have two people—my mother first—and why should this hit me just as hard?"

Don Solomón waited for him to say more, and when after a moment Gilberto left it as a question, the man said, "It is clear now that my wife more than guessed what you have just told me, Gilberto. Elena knew your heart, and I know it. Now, if Inés could know—"

"I want to tell her." Gilberto got to his feet.

The metal door to the callejón shook. "Permiso—sit down for just a moment," Don Solomón said and went to open it.

Gilberto did not turn around and could not see the door beyond the angle of the kitchen wall. But he heard Don Solomón say, "Pelancha, come in."

"I have no hurry. I have prayed to God that she would be already dead." Her voice was utterly clear and even.

"¡Pelancha!" Don Solomón said. "¿Eres loca? She lives! Go see!"

"If it is so, that she lives, she will curse me with the last breath of her life for bringing this shame on her."

"She is your own child, Pelancha," Don Solomón argued gently. "You are her mother. What blame—what fault, is yours? Come—"

"The shame is mine. For my need of one, I took this man into my house. Fidel Vargas did this unforgivable thing."

When he heard that, Gilberto sensed the hum and shut his eyes against the flash of a bright steel disc that was whirling toward him with incredible speed. It touched his head and began slicing slowly through his brain. It was worse than when he first heard what happened to her. He wanted to go to the bathroom, but Pelancha and Don Solomón were coming toward him.

"Tía—Tía Esperanza—" Now is when she needed somebody to kiss *her* hand, but she drew it away from his reach. She looked beyond him, and when he stepped in front of her, holding his arms out, Don Solomón frowned, shook his head, and said in English, "Wait—till another time."

Don Solomón led her as far as the door of the room where Inés lay. There, on one side of it, where she would not impede anybody's going in or coming out, she sat down on the tiles and folded her rebozo—the old rebozo—to cover most of her face.

"Come, Gilberto," Don Solomón said, "let us go in the sala. It will be more respectful if Pelancha cannot see us."

The old man sat wearily down on the leather couch across which a thick shaft of sunlight slanted. It showed up the red stubble on his face. He tried to smile, but it ended in a tight-lipped grimace and he covered his eyes with his wrists.

"Lie down," Gilberto said, "stretch out," and going to the window, darkened the room.

"Ah, better," the old man sighed, and as he shut his eyes, Gilberto saw two big tears find their course in deep wrinkles he had not noticed before. "Sit, rest a little."

"No—later, maybe. Right now, where does Doña Elena keep those drops?"

"Don't trouble, Gilberto, she will—"

"Never mind. She's doing something else. In the cabinet here?" He spoke sharply, without meaning to. Don Solomón nodded, pointing behind him to the glass-fronted bookcase.

"How many drops?"

"Four in each eye," Don Solomón answered, leaning farther back and letting his hands fold naturally over his chest.

Gently, Gilberto mopped Don Solomón's eyes with a piece of tissue and held the lids open to apply the medicine.

"That's good," the old man said. Then, Gilberto laid the black silk cloth over his eyes and drew a chair toward the couch.

For a few minutes, they sat in silence. The curtains dulled the sounds outside to the soft murmur that hums in a sea shell.

Picking up a book from the ledge below the small table, Gilberto saw it was the same volume of Góngora's poems that had been in his room. What if they *were* over his head? He was not reading for his own benefit now.

> La más bella niña
> de nuestro lugar,
> hoy viuda y sola
> y ayer por casar
> viendo que sus ojos

> a la guerra van,
> a su madre dice
> que escucha su mal.
> Dejadme llorar
> orillas del mar.

The more he read, the more his own breath warmed the polished, precise verses:

> Dineros son calidad,
> ¡verdad!
> Más ama quien más suspira,
> ¡mentira!
>
> Cruzados hacen cruzados,
> escudos pintan escudos,
> y tahures muy desnudos
> con dados ganan condados;
> ducados dejan ducados,
> y coronas majestad,
> ¡verdad!

The door opened quietly and he looked up from the book. Doña Elena motioned him to remain seated, put her arms out, and looked at his face between her hands before she kissed him. "I can't speak a word, Gilberto. . . . You say something to me."

"Can you tell me anything yet? The way her mother talked—she doesn't mean it, does she? Tell me."

"I don't know what it is Pelancha said."

"I heard her," Don Solomón said, getting up. "You will forgive her that, eh, Gilberto?"

"If I do or I don't, what difference will it make if Inés doesn't live? Is all she can do—is all anybody can do around here, is be ashamed? What's being done about paying somebody back for this? Isn't there any law here?"

"They will live to regret what they have done," Don Solomón said.

"Probably made to be ashamed, also." He realized it was not these people who deserved this sarcasm. "They ought to die. What's being done? What about Vargas? I'm not going back till I know."

"Come," Doña Elena said, "let us wait for the doctor. He is very skillful."

"Be calm, son," Don Solomón said as they went out to the patio.

Esperanza had not moved from her place beside the door, but she lowered the rebozo and had seen them come out.

"Can't I say something to her?" Gilberto asked.

"What, what would you say?"

"I really don't know, Doña Elena. Will you tell her something, will you please?" he begged. Doña Elena thought for a moment and nodded. As she walked toward the door, it opened and Don Perfecto came out.

The priest's eyes were bright. His face was moist and had the purplish flush of men with intense black beards. He showed his gums in a quick smile to Doña Elena and curved to let her pass. But she did not enter the room, turning only, her back against a pillar, trembling at the sight of Gilberto moving forward slowly to meet the priest. Don Solomón saw only his back, but Don Perfecto saw his eyes. The flush left his face, but he did not look frightened and he raised his hands. "My son—"

Gilberto hit him with all his strength, flush on the mouth. He hit the wall as if he had been thrown bodily against it. Doña Elena gasped and Don Solomón ran forward to catch Gilberto's right arm, again in mid-swing. It struck hard and left the print of bloody knuckles on the priest's left cheek. His left fist swung again, below the right ear. Don Solomón caught his right arm, and Doña Elena got in front of him as the priest started sliding down the whitewashed wall. Only Esperanza did not move or make a sound.

Gilberto saw that they were trying to hold him, and sobbed as he shook them off, grabbed the priest, feeling the loose flesh of his breast through the clothes, and pushed him upright. Now the man's back flexed and he seemed to want to stand up straight. His broken lips dripped blood, which bubbled as he said, "My son—"

Gilberto slammed the rest of it back of his reddened teeth with a stinging slap. "Shut up!"

"Have pity!" Don Solomón begged, and Gilberto didn't stop to wonder why Don Perfecto waved weakly for Don Solomón to be silent.

He slapped him once more and the thud of the priest's head, cracking either the skull or the plaster, made Gilberto pull his next punch; but it didn't stop his hot tears. "Why don't you fight, so I can kill you, you dirty bastard!" he sobbed. "Why didn't you stop that—what happened? Don't tell me you didn't know. She's over twelve, so it shouldn't be any of my business! Huh!" The man started leaning forward, and Gilberto pushed him back. "Well, it is! See!" He drew his arm back.

"No!" Doña Elena called, grabbing his hand. "No more, I beg you." She pulled his head down on her shoulder, and he was aware for the first time that he was crying.

He felt his hand touched and held, and something hot and sticky brush it. It was the priest's kiss; he was on his knees. "I have prayed for that child's forgiveness—and I beg for yours, Don Gilberto." He dropped Gilberto's hand and pressed his own together against his brow. "And may our Good Shepherd, infinite in mercy, pity me, a poor one. In the name of The Father, The Son, and The Holy Ghost."

Esperanza moved, only to make the sign of the cross. Don Solomón helped the priest to his feet and supported him to the door.

"All right," Gilberto said. "After they get Vargas and the rest of them, they can come for me."

"Nobody will come for you. . . . Listen—you, too, Sol—don't let Don Perfecto be a stranger to this house."

"Good! You have seen him show contrition. You don't hate him now?"

"Only myself." She stood between the two men and looked at neither of them. "I could have spared him this—with Gilberto. I could have told you that inside, he knelt at Inés's feet."

"The doctor—"

He looked more like an engineer; tall, heavy set, and wearing light khaki pants and shirt. He put on a pair of sunglasses against the glare as he approached. Margarita, hurrying behind him, passed him, carrying a rolled up towel. Wrapped in it, Gilberto could see the ends of two braids of black hair, interwoven with bits of colored yarn.

"I will talk to you while I wash my hands," the doctor said, going directly to the bathroom. They followed and stood by the door while he filled the sink. "First of all, you understand, she is not to be moved." He spoke without looking at anybody, as if he were lecturing. His accent was foreign; he pronounced the j—the jota—gutterally, the way Don Solomón pronounced the last part of his name, when he said, "The room she is in, Dr. Zumbach, can she stay there?"

"Darken it and move the bed to the corner. The insensibility and the stertorous breathing will continue for ten, perhaps twelve hours, and is partially due to the morphine, but principally the concussion. There is no local or general paralysis, which is a good indication. But we must be conservative, and I rely on you, Señora Gulden—"

"We can get a nurse," Gilberto said.

Without looking up to see who interrupted him, the doctor went on. "Watch the ears and the nose for signs of edema of the brain. If there is the least trace of cerebrospinal fluid, inject one ampule, intravenously, of the hypertonic saline. Understood?"

"What about taking x-rays?" Gilberto said, louder.

The doctor looked at him. "Is that the novio?"

"Yes," Gilberto said sharply. "That's me."

Shaking the water off his hands and smiling, the doctor said, "And the engagement is not called off—?"

"What do you mean by that?" Gilberto said, trying to be calm, but the rest of it—"You fat son of a bitch!"—burst from him, in English.

"Was haben wir, Herr Gulden, ein Amerikanischer Kavalier?"

"Ja—aber das war nicht schön zu sagen, Herr Doktor," Don Solomón said coldly.

"Excuse me," the doctor said in English to Gilberto. "I mistaked you for Mexican."

"Never mind. How much do I owe you?" He put his hand in his wallet, but Don Solomón detained it.

"I am paid by the colonel—Carrasco. He send me." The doctor still spoke English.

Gilberto went back to Spanish. "I don't want anything from there. How much?"

"Wirklich, ein Kavalier! What can you pay?" Gilberto looked around, puzzled. It struck him that Esperanza was no longer at the door. "Ten pesos?" the German suggested.

Gilberto brought out his wallet. "Here's a hundred, and thanks for what you did."

The doctor put the money in his shirt pocket. "And now, gentlemen, if you will retire to the smoking room, I have some special instructions to give Señora Gulden."

"You have tied a nice Capeline bandage, señora; let me compliment you."

"Thank you, Doctor Zumbach. It is a pity that her hair had to be cut off."

"And you did that very artistically, too. It will grow back even more handsome. . . . Now, observe—this is not the first of such cases I have seen. There was a period, in my own country—however, well—we must be prepared for a syndrome—the nervous residue of this kind of shock."

"Must it be that way, doctor? Is there nothing we can do?"

"There are no drugs, if that is what you mean. But, unless the psychic trauma is too deep, you have the capacity to bring her out of it. . . . Is this too complicated?"

"No, doctor; I understand. It is like grief—and I know how that can strike; how hard."

"It is not the same, señora. Grief, as you speak of it, often brings on a melancholia. But it is benefitted by remembering, by mementos. And in time, and by happy chance, the condition is totally eliminated by contact with somebody who reminds them of the person for whom they grieve. This case is precisely the opposite. You see why. She will have a lapse of memory which may last for many days. Then, the shock of recollection will come."

"Gradually—suddenly?"

"It is immaterial—and unpredictable. You must be prepared for hysteria if it is sudden. The other is more grave; it may be a catalepsy, or, let me say, an inert state during which they *will* themselves to death. That, also, is suicide. . . . You must watch her. Except when she is normally asleep, she must not be alone. She must be spoken to, but calmly. And above all, no man is to enter that room; not until she is much, much better, and then only when she is told in advance who it is. Remember, it was men who have done this to her."

"How would you punish them, doctor?"

"I am not a penologist, señora," the German smiled. "Sometimes not even the doctor I should like to be. As now—much of what I am telling you may be unscientific. But this is not an institution, and you, señora, are not a ward nurse. But you are an intelligent, sympathetic woman. So, I need not make your work more involved."

"I want to do my best for her. . . . You had some specific instructions, I think."

"Ah, yes—the jaw fracture first; that will be reduced in less than a week, I am sure. We have disinfected the local tissue injuries—the lacerations on the legs and breasts—have we not?"

"Except—"

"There," he interrupted quickly, "you have the microscopic slides, and you know how to take a smear. And in due time we will make the other test—and deal with both, if we have to, eh, señora?"

"You are very gracious, Doctor Zumbach. . . . The fee, I know, is insignificant. Let me adjust it."

"I will perhaps let you. You may some day do me a professional turn, now that I know you have some skill with Mexico's favorite medical tool—the hypodermic syringe. I shall one of these days fail to come to La Corona to give Carrasco his injection. I shall telephone him and recommend you. It is nothing but five cubic centimeters of thiamin-chloride—a simple vitamin, as you know. He is under the illusion that he has syphilis and that this 'special medicine' has arrested it. He hasn't, of course, but I am terribly tired of his dull conversation, most of which is about himself as a hero of The Revolution."

"Whenever you command me, doctor. I will know when Coronel Carrasco sends for me—is that to be the arrangement?"

"Fine, let us leave it that way." He took the hundred pesos out of his pocket and placed the bills on the table. "This is for a present, for the bride—if the young man is as noble as he sounds, and she becomes one."

Gilberto sat at Don Solomón's desk and typed, at the merchant's dictation. ". . . by first class post to the address above," he read back.

"And now, 'Afectísimo, atento y su sirviente, Solomón Gulden.'"

"No," Gilberto said. "We don't write it that way in the States. Nobody is anybody's servant. We just say 'Yours truly.'" Without looking back for approval, he wrote 'Yours truly,' and under four spaces for the signature, he typed SOLOMON GULDEN. One final touch: four more spaces down on the left margin, he typed SG:GR and removed the letter with its carbon copy. While Don Solomón read the letter, he typed the envelope.

"And a copy to file away! So clear. I'm afraid my signature will not do justice to it." He signed. "And this little rubric in the corner with our initials—to show we have done it together."

"The boss and the secretary."

"The vice-president. . . . The motorcycle with the mail will not be here until Thursday, so we will send this by avión."

Still pitching, still trying to make me feel good, Gilberto thought, as he typed the envelope. He could say something to let the old man know that he appreciated it. "I wouldn't even call this a day's work for an office boy. Isn't there something else I can do around here?"

"You wish to be occupied . . . well, while you are seated there, why don't you write some letters of your own? I'm sure there are many people who would wish to hear from you."

"I think I will."

Now, who would actually *wish* to hear from him? First of all, the Romeros. All they knew is what he had told them the night he left; that he was "going away for a few days" before reporting for induction. Where? Oh, some beach, maybe Coronado, maybe Laguna. He would write to them in Spanish. It would please Mr. Romero—Oh-oh! It would also please the F.B.I. or whoever it was that threw the dragnet out for him. Certainly they had been interviewed by this time, probably accused of hiding him. Now, all they needed was to get a letter from him, from Mexico, and they'd really be up the creek; probably get deported. Nope—the Romeros were out. If he ever saw them again, it would be on his first furlough, whenever that would come—and he could explain that the whole thing was an error; here he was, uniform and all.

Verónica La Negra? Suicide! The first thing she'd do is give it to Yerno to read. And Yerno—he could just hear him: "Hey! Remember Elvira Reyes, the one got her start here? Well, her kid—big feller now—guess where—?"

Dr. Eisen would be the logical man to write to, he decided, rolling a sheet of paper in the machine, writing the date, and beginning: "Dear Doc. Eisen: As you can see—"

There he stopped. . . . What the hell am I doing? The same thing to him as to the Romeros? Maybe he's not as vulnerable as a Mexican family with only its First Papers; him being a former major in the U.S. Army and all, and a descendant of Alexander Hamilton's tailor. Just the same, they might check with him and ask him, just in a routine way, if he had any idea where this Reyes, G. might have gone. No? Then what's a letter with a Mexican stamp doing on your desk? That *could* embarrass him. Better if—

"As you can see—"

He turned away from the machine and stared at the slab of dead air between the door and shutter of the Surtidor. No use kidding myself or you, Doc, he thought. The reason I'm not writing to you is something else—not worry about whether you're being checked on. It's that secret we got between us. Don't make out you don't know what it is. You know damn well! All that hemming and hawing around about the shape of your nose and the color of my skin, and all the other differences between us and the regular gabachos. It got me steamed up, all right. In a certain way, I knew all those things. But you got it over to me that night that a Reyes is entitled to the same breaks, with his skin and all, as anybody named Devlin with the crispy blond hair. He's *owed* that! And if he doesn't get it, he's got a right to go look for it. But you stopped short, Doc. You didn't say, in so many words, "Beat it. Give yourself a break." And you could have! And that's why I didn't say, in so many words, "I'm going!" That's where our little secret comes in. . . . You were talking from strength, Doc, like a couple of other fellows I could tell you about. I can't blame you or them for having already done what they were asking me—in one way or another—*not* to do. But the kind of strength or smartness I need don't come secondhand. . . . One thing more, Doc—this business of being owed something. Maybe I'm getting smarter—or dumber; but my slant on it is that *I* owe something. To what or to who I owe it, I'm not sure. But the second pronoun (do you say who or whom?) being personal, kind of rings a bell. . . . Anyway, Doc, something happened while I was down here, and I'm hanging around to see what develops. And when it does, I'll get a clear signal; I'll know better who the who is that I'm talking about. . . . The whole point being, Doc, that one way or another, I'm going to square myself.

"As you can see—" Tearing the paper out of the machine, he carefully inserted a fresh sheet.

> Dear Bish:
>   You sure called the turn on relatives down here. No sooner do I hit this place when who do I run into but an Aunt of mine. I kind of detoured down here on my way· to Vera Cruz—

Here was another letter he knew he wasn't going to send, but he kept on writing:

> —checking on a prospect of a job along the lines I mentioned to you. Hope you got yours done O.K. in Matamoros on the beer pipes. Well, let me say you sure know your suds, that tip you gave me. Nothing but Orizaba beer for me from now on in. It sure is "tops." One thing I'm never going to forget is our ride from Laredo, and believe me, some of the pointers you gave me turned out just like you said: "the good with the bad." You got to admit there's plenty of both wherever you look, be it on either side of the border. And say, Bish, how did the Guadalupe medal work out? I sure would like to have seen the face of Miss Dolores, your fiancée, when you told her it was the Real McCoy and how you come by it. She had something there when she told you that those things work miracles. Only, she only told you the half of it. You can tell her for me, and I am not jesting, that it must work both ways. It worked for me in a way I never figured, like one of those "chain letters" they used to send around, if you remember. You being on the verge of getting married—in January, you said—might laugh this off, Bish, but with me the miracle turns out to be a young lady! Mexican, naturally, which kind of makes us kin, as they say. I won't go so far as to claim she's already my fiancée, on account of a little family opposition—well, you know how Mexican people are about their daughter's happiness. I guess you must have had the same problem to deal with. But when you know how you feel about a young lady, I guess there's no problem you can't handle. At least that's the way I feel, and boy!

she hit me. So I'm not leaving here till we have an "understanding" and no two ways about it. Her name is Inés. Nice name, isn't it? I regret to state that right now she is laid up due to an accident.

Doña Elena parted the door hanging behind him and called, "Gilberto, come—excuse me—"

"How is Inés, Doña Elena?"

"Sleeping. I have just now seen her. I came to call you to the table."

"Two more lines—"

Well, Bish, this being about all the news I got, I will close now, wishing you and the future Mrs. B. the best of luck and everything, and hoping you will drop me a line. Your friend, Gil ("The Thumb") Reyes

They ate in the comedor instead of in the patio. That was Doña Elena's suggestion, to lessen the risk of Inés hearing their voices, should she wake. Doña Elena ate scarcely anything, leaving her husband and Gilberto at Margarita's summons to the sickroom.

The two men sat in worried silence until she returned a few minutes later, smiling at their concern. "Everything is well. But I am glad Margarita is alert. There was no sign of what the doctor warned about; only perspiration from under the tight bandage. You men eat," she ordered and left again.

Josefina shook her head morosely as she carried away an entire breaded veal chop which Gilberto had been unable to eat. But that was fleeting; for most of the time, the woman wore the expression and carried herself with the pride of somebody who has had a share in a vital undertaking which turned out successfully.

"I know what I'll do this afternoon," Gilberto said. "I'll go over to her mother's and spend some time with her."

"Why, son?"

"Well, I know the way she feels. She thinks I'm the one who's been hurt the most. I want to get that idea out of her head."

"No, Gilberto, no. She can no longer have that feeling after seeing how you—uh—punished Don Perfecto. And I can tell you, he is there now, with Pelancha."

"I'm sorry now it all happened," Gilberto said, not looking at Don Solomón. "The reasons came all in a rush when I saw him come out of there this morning. First, it was the snide way he talked to you and not liking the way he came off second best."

"Thank you, thank you, my boy."

"Then the way he treated Doña Elena, and the remark he made about her to me."

Don Solomón chuckled, "A harlot, eh? A Babylonian whore?"

"An adulteress, that's what."

Smiling broadly, Don Solomón said, "His respect for her must be increasing. That is the mildest term he has applied to her."

"Well, I don't like it. . . . Then, when this happened to Inés, I couldn't see straight."

Don Solomón nodded slowly. "Your anger was formidable. It was not the kind of rage that comes from nothing. That he begged your forgiveness shows this."

"Do you want me to tell you, Don Solomón?"

The old man answered calmly, "We are men together."

"He knew this was going to happen. He as much as told me in advance."

"¡Hombre!"

"Listen—last night, when he told me my aunt wasn't married to Vargas— it didn't seem to bother him as much as Doña Elena being married to you— but he expected me to be shocked. All right, so I was—a little. But I wasn't going to let him see it. So I said it was strictly her business, she was over twelve. That was when he said she, Inés, was over twelve, too."

Reaching across the table, Don Solomón put his hand on Gilberto's. "I see, son. You took it as a threat. It could have been a warning."

"If he knew what Vargas was up to, why didn't he stop him?" Gilberto snatched his hand from beneath the man's and clenched it.

"I will not excuse him. He may have been able to; perhaps he tried and couldn't. He is a priest and had gone far in disclosing half the secret of the Confessional when he spoke to you last night."

"And he thought that was enough!" Gilberto said angrily. "Is that what a priest's job is; to wait till crimes get committed and then pass out—" He couldn't think of the word.

"Absolution," Don Solomón prompted. "But you saw, Gilberto; he assumed his share of the sin. He begged forgiveness. I saw his eyes—you didn't; they thanked you for the scourging. He kissed the hand that gave it, remember that."

"I don't want to think about it," Gilberto said. "But *he'll* remember it. He can report me to the Mexican Secret Service or whoever he likes. But they're going to have to come and get me. And they're going to have to carry me back." He saw Doña Elena enter, but he had to finish, speaking calmly and with force. "I'll be without a cent. I'm going to leave what money I've got with you, for Inés. If I don't have enough time till she comes out of this, and I can't tell her myself—" He turned to Doña Elena, who stood beside him at the table, "If I can't take her with me, you tell her, won't you, that I'm going to come back for her? Make her believe me!"

"Solomón, we must do something!"

"Now that Gilberto means not to run away—not today, not tomorrow—I will think of ways."

"How is she now, Doña Elena?"

"Asleep, still—and dreaming; possibly of you, Gilberto, because she smiled a little."

He smiled, too. "I hope she wakes up smiling. Can I see her?" Doña Elena shook her head. "Just from the door?"

"No, hijo, not yet; you will not like what you see." She saw his eyes and added, "Don't be frightened. She will be as beautiful as ever—more so. Her pretty teeth and wonderful eyes—"

"And her voice, señora. I never heard such a voice. Even before I saw her, I knew—How long do you think—how many days before I can—"

"A week, maybe longer," she said, sitting down between the two men. "Until then—until we are sure, even letting her see a mirror would not be the right thing."

"Naturally," Gilberto said, "the shock. I know what's likely to happen." He knew that from having seen it in the movies, but he didn't mention that.

"You are very understanding. You must allow time for preparing her to know that she will see you again. She must think you have gone away and you know nothing of what happened. The women and I will see to that."

"Then, maybe I'd better go to another town," Gilberto began as Josefina called from the door, "Excuse me, Don Solomón."

"What is it, Josefina?"

"Isidro Montes de Oca stands in the callejón." A frown crossed Don Solomón's face. "He wishes to see you."

"Tell him the hour when the Surtidor opens for the afternoon trade," the old man said curtly.

"He is not alone, señor. Three other cafeteros from Las Camelias are with him, and he asks that I say they do not wish to buy, but to sell."

Don Solomón smiled faintly and briefly. "They are to wait in the front if they choose, and if not, they may return to where they have sold before." As Josefina left, he turned to Doña Elena, tapping the side of his nose. "Something is stirring, Elena. Something is stirring in the conscience of a certain holy man."

"You are talking nonsense, Sol," she scoffed. To Gilberto she said, "I am having Felipe's room, the one nearest the gate, made ready for you. It is smaller, but in some ways more comfortable."

"Wait," Gilberto began, half rising to remonstrate, but she left, and he turned to Don Solomón. "What I want to say is that I can't just sit around here, doing nothing—just waiting. I don't feel right about it."

It made him almost sore to see Don Solomón still with that pleased smile on his face. "Come, perhaps we can find something for you to do."

When they raised the cortina, Don Solomón chuckled, "We shall see who is talking nonsense."

Outside, head to the curb, stood a line of eight burros, each laden with a large, well-sewn burlap sack of coffee beans. Four men in their white calzoncillos rolled to the knees, flat-crowned sombreros, and carrying woven bags on their shoulders, stood in front of the door.

"What an agreeable surprise to see you, Isidro, and this fine delegation from Las Camelias!" Don Solomón greeted the first man, who seemed to be their leader. He was short and lean, but with heavily muscled legs. Gilberto smiled a little, too; this greeting was too elaborate to be sincere. The cafeteros, each distinctly said his "Muy buenas tardes, Don Solomón."

"Please to step in, gentlemen, and tell me how I may serve you." They shuffled in, removing their sombreros and Don Solomón took his place behind the new calculating scale. "Some fine, new serapes oaxaqueños have just come in. Is it some tools that you need? Or possibly some finery for the ladies?" He winked at Gilberto, who stood also behind the counter, but to one side.

"Indeed, we shall want such things presently," Isidro said, "but did not the criada of your house inform you of why we came?"

"Oh," Don Solomón laughed, "she made some joke about your wishing to sell me something. . . . Let me show you this assortment of pocket knives, to be worn on a chain—"

"Excuse me, Don Solomón—"

"There is no immediacy about the payment, Isidro, as you know. After you have sold your coffee will do. Señor Reyes—please, that tray below the shelf, if you please."

Gilberto saw this was going to be fun; the old boy was in great form.

"Permit me, Don Solomón," Isidro said hastily. "It is about the coffee—you were not misinformed. David, Heriberto, Platón, and your servant,"—they nodded as their names were called—"we have come to receive your offer for the product of our cafetal." He waved to the burros outside. "Eight bags, each containing the usual sixty kilos."

"An offer? Do I understand you to say, Isidro, that I am to make an offer? To which you may respond, 'Too generous!' or 'Not enough!'"

"With all respect, Don Solomón."

"And do you reserve the same choice when you bring your coffee to the sheds at La Corona and Coronel Carrasco's sobrestante, Gordo, says, 'Three pesos!' . . . Tell me, Isidro."

Isidro's companions glared at him until he spoke up. "And what is your offer, Don Solomón?"

Don Solomón glanced at Gilberto, rather relishing his own performance. "Mira, Isidro—times have been when you have honored my store in search of a sombrero, a new machete, a hoe. And when you have chosen, do I ask you to make me an offer for it? No, hombre! It has a price!"

The trio behind Isidro exchanged nods. "The man has reason," Platón said. The others agreed, "Sí, tiene razón."

"Then, with all respect," Isidro said, "we are prepared to hear your price."

"Then listen well; I will state it only once."

"We hear. . . . We listen. . . . At your service," the cafeteros agreed.

"Four pesos and fifty centavos, señores!"

"Agreed! . . . A fair price. . . . Done!" But Isidro stared silently at the floor. David pushed him, "Say something, man!"

Stepping to the counter, Isidro put his hand out. "Done!"

"Done! Señor Reyes, will you please make the calculation." Gilberto put the adding machine on the counter. "Four hundred and eighty kilos at four fifty."

He punched the keys briskly, read out, "Dos mil ciento sesenta pesos, Don Solomón," and tried to keep from smiling as he handed the strip of paper ribbon to the old man.

Don Solomón repeated the amount and said, "And now, señor Reyes, have the goodness to strike off a receipt on the writing machine, as follows—"

He dictated the receipt and gave the names of the four associates: Isidro Montes de Oca, Heriberto Pimentel, David Lugo, and Platón Muñoz. When Gilberto handed it to him, he read it out formally and put it down on the counter, facing the men. Next to it, he placed an open ink pad. About to open the safe, he turned. "I forgot we had not been to the bank this morning. Will you please count out the sum due, señor Reyes."

"Sí, Don Solomón, con todo gusto."

Isidro watched the money counted out, and begging permission, counted it again before pressing his thumb on the ink pad and printing it next to his name on the receipt. In turn, the three others did the same.

"And now," Don Solomón said, "if you will lead your animals to the callejón, Lorenzo will help you unload into the camión."

"Platón, Heriberto—ándale," Isidro ordered and the pair named hurried out.

"And how," Don Solomón asked innocently, "did you find Don Perfecto?"

Isidro hesitated an instant before answering. "The párroco," he finally said, "appeared not well."

Don Solomón glanced at Gilberto, his eyes twinkling. "¡Qué lastima! Of what does he complain?"

"Of nothing, señor," Isidro said, "but there are some wounds on his face which make it appear that he had overturned on his motorcycle."

"Quite possible. I shall have to tell the good man that one cannot read his breviary and at the same time manage a motorcycle. . . . You met him then at—"

"At La Muela was where he overtook us. . . . I should like to ask, Don Solomón, if, at your convenience, you can come to Las Camelias and make an—a price for the bananas that grow between the cafetos to shade them. It is a splendid crop."

"If I have the occasion. . . . Señor Reyes—"

"Sí, Don Solomón—"

"Be so good as to make a note: Bananas—Las Camelias." Gilberto solemnly made a memorandum.

When Isidro left, neither Gilberto nor Don Solomón could keep a straight face. "So! This is the nonsense my wife thinks I have been uttering."

"She missed a wonderful performance."

"It was yours that I admired, my boy. . . . She will believe me when she sees the coffee, that these men came here at Don Perfecto's urging, but not that he did it out of his conscience."

"As a favor to you, though," Gilberto suggested.

"Less to me than to Isidro and his friends," Don Solomón said seriously. "What pleases me is that it has begun to make a difference to him—that there will be seven hundred and twenty more pesos in the pockets of his sheep."

Laughing, Gilberto said, "That's what he prayed for—so God would make him a better shepherd!"

When Doña Elena came in, they tried not to gloat. "Both of you," she said, "stop looking so smug. I saw the bags of coffee. Quite a shrewd fellow, aren't you, husband?"

"Tell her, Gilberto. A simple transaction of business, as in the past—and with others in prospect, such as bananas; and eventually tomatoes, melons, and various other produce."

"Which the priest diverted from La Corona, as you so wisely judged."

"Priest? Priest—what nonsense are you talking, my dear?"

She laughed. "You see, Gilberto, what it is to live with this man."

Lorenzo came in, showing a mound of green coffee in his cupped hands. "¡Mira! A beautiful bean, of the type of caracolillo."

"Explain that to Don Gilberto."

"Why to me?"

"You are going to sell it," Don Solomón explained. And he continued as Gilberto looked puzzled. "Tomorrow—at the coffee warehouse in Ciudad Valles, the Hermanos Pineda."

"The one on the calendar in the room?"

"Yes. It is some time since I have sold them anything, but our relations have been excellent," Don Solomón explained. "They will pay the market price and a premium, if, as Lorenzo says, the coffee is of such a high quality."

"But it is, señor. Feel it—taste it."

Don Solomón nibbled a bean and nodded. "Draw a canvas tightly over it, Lorenzo. And while there, Lorenzo, also show Don Gilberto the wholesale establishment. I wish for my account a sack of the roasted bean." He turned to Gilberto. "You have bought me out of that. And I will make a list of some other things needed."

"How far is Valles?" Gilberto asked.

"A matter of one hundred and sixty kilometers from Ciudad del Maíz."

"I think I'll need gasoline."

"Lorenzo will supply you from the steel barrel, and if it lacks, there is a Petróleos Mexicanos depósito where another barrel can be bought. Gilberto, please ask of the Pineda Brothers to pay cash instead of by the customary check. Or, better still, I will write them a note to that effect, which will also serve to introduce you. Also, while you are in Valles, you may find the accessories and whatever else you say the machine requires."

The clarity and directness with which Don Solomón covered these details impressed Gilberto. He knew his way about his own business far better than

Richardson managed his. Here was a whole day's program laid out for him. That was what he asked for, and he looked forward to its performance.

"I would enjoy going with you," Don Solomón said. "But in the absence of Felipe, and with my wife occupied with the Sleeping Beauty, I must give you Lorenzo as your adjutant."

Doña Elena beckoned him. "Come, let me show you the room. It is time that you rested."

"Look, Don Solomón—Doña Elena—do I have to wait until tomorrow? If it's all the same, I would much rather start out now."

Don Solomón said nothing to this, but Doña Elena protested. "After so little sleep last night; the going to Ciudad del Maíz and the return, and—and—No, you must not drive yourself like this."

"He may go," Don Solomón said, "but you would arrive too late to complete the business; that is my objection, Gilberto. The morning would be better; as early as you like."

"Then how about tonight?" Gilberto asked eagerly.

Before his wife could object, Don Solomón agreed. "¿Cómo no? But after a little rest. One must be alert on the highway. . . . And now, to the writing machine with you. That letter to the Brothers."

35

Not only did Don Solomón leave his "oxen" unmuzzled, but he housed them cleanly. Felipe's room, though smaller than the one in which Inés lay, was high-ceilinged. It had one window, but a slatted door allowed for good circulation of air.

Scott's *Kenilworth* had followed him here, and the poems of Góngora had been replaced by a leather-bound copy of *Obras* by Gustavo Adolfo Bécquer.

Gilberto smoked and read a month-old Mexico City magazine, all printed in rotogravure; but he was more alert to sounds in the patio. He could hear the brisk swishing of Margarita's broom and the pleasant rattle of water from a sprinkler striking the broad leaves of the tubbed plants. The corner of the Alameda which he could see from the window was already in twilight, but the glare from the whitewashed buildings on the east side of the square still glazed the trees.

The sound of Josefina pounding something in a tejolote—a bowl of volcanic stone—reached him through the kitchen wall. The pounding became rhythmic. She was whistling, and that was the best sound of all. Next to the voice of Inés saying anything—scolding her little brothers, saying "Adiós"— it was the best sound of all.

That cheerful thumping and fifing was as good as any hospital bulletin. It said the patient was recovering.

He stood by the window and thought of all the other pleasant sounds he had been hearing around here. At this moment, the birds, thick in the ahuehuete branches, their chirps modulated, respectful of falling night. Later on, there would be a convocation of dogs well away from the center of the village. It would sound very much like a legislative assembly. You could distinguish the chairman, a fellow with a gruff, deliberate bark. He would state the motion before the House and there would be discussion and argument, which the chairman would stop by a statement of arfs which clearly meant, "All those in favor, signify by saying 'Yipe.'"

But the best sounds of all came from the mouths of the people he had seen. Unlike English, the spoken Spanish was softer and more liquid. Those sounds that were not formed by the lips alone, came from no further back than their throats. None, as in English, started in the chest. Spanish was more a matter of breathing, he believed. His own name, for instance, the G was sounded like an H—just puffed out; while in the English way, it had to be bitten off.

"Gilberto—"

He turned and said, "Come in, señora."

"Is this *resting*?" Doña Elena said scoldingly as she came in. She looked at the narrow cot, at its undented coverlet, and shook her head.

"I wasn't sleepy. I feel kind of good thinking over that I can be of some use around here while I'm waiting. . . . Does the boss want anything?"

She smiled at "the boss." "*He* doesn't have to drive hundreds of kilometers, yet he is resting." She sat down in a chair and motioned Gilberto to seat himself on the bed.

"What's Felipe going to do if he comes back and finds me in his quarters?"

"I am afraid Felipe is not coming back to us."

"That's too bad," Gilberto said, secretly pleased. "Did anything happen to him while he was away?"

"He does not say. Another young man, his primo, came with a letter—asuntos familiares was the explanation—and recommending the bearer of the letter for the place."

"Did Don Solomón take him on?"

"No. He gave the young man his expenses back to León and explained that he has other plans," Doña Elena explained. "He would like to hear what you say about promoting Lorenzo. Do you approve?"

"Sure. But why ask me?"

"My husband values your opinion, Gilberto."

"Well, I didn't know this Felipe, but what I've seen of Lorenzo, I like very much."

"So do we," she said. "But I wonder how he will feel about taking up a new career, selling his mules."

"I'll teach him how to drive the truck," Gilberto suggested enthusiastically.

"Can you?"

"Easily. He's coming with me to Valles. I can explain to him what I'm doing, the theory; and then, when we get back, I'll start him behind the wheel." Doña Elena nodded approving. "He ought to like that better than mules. At least, when a truck isn't working, it doesn't eat."

"I'm glad to see you so cheerful, Gilberto."

"Well, señora, why not? In the first place, I'm *doing* something, finally."

"Does it give you great pleasure to teach somebody something—a skill that you know?"

The question surprised him. He had never thought about how it *would* feel to transfer an accomplishment of his own to the mind and the finger ends of another.

"The reason I think so," Doña Elena continued, "is because you were so disappointed when nobody wanted to learn from you how to handle the adding machine."

"I guess you're right, señora. If people didn't get pleasure out of teaching, there wouldn't be anybody to learn. . . . Gee, I'm beginning to sound like Don Solomón. . . . Did you see Inés?"

She smiled warmly. "Just a moment ago. I came to tell you, she is awake."

"And she's all right?"

"Still much bewildered. But she recognized me, and she seemed to understand when I told her that she was here, with me."

Eagerly he asked, "Nothing happened—nothing like what you were afraid of?"

"No; she was calm and not frightened, and that is a good sign. She touched the bandage on her head and it did not frighten her. Perhaps that means she remembered everything."

"Like a bad dream," Gilberto suggested.

"Let us hope it was not that way; that would not be good—to think it was a dream and then to find out that it was more. We cannot guess that the moment of truth had already come to her, or if there is yet to be the real awakening."

"Did she say anything?"

"Yes. She said, 'Where is my mother?'"

"The poor kid. Was she crying?"

"No. She seemed very calm. I asked her if she wanted to see her mother, and she said, 'No,' and shook her head."

"What do you think that means, señora?"

"It is hard to tell. We must wait to know."

Almost groaning, Gilberto said, "The last time you saw Inés, you told me you saw her smiling. Was she, really?"

"Yes, Gilberto, in her sleep," the woman said softly. "And I will tell you when she smiles again—awake and knowing why. It will be your doing, and so simple—if you will write her a letter—"

"Will I!" Gilberto burst out. "She's expecting one from me. As soon as I had a regular address. And she was going to answer and send me a picture of herself I could carry with me."

"How wonderful!" And cautiously, Doña Elena said, "And it won't have to be a different kind of letter, will it?"

"Naturally not. I see what you mean; it will be just as if I left before anything happened. She'll think I'm back in the States." He was elated. "And all the time I'll be almost where I can reach out and touch her. . . . About when do you think she ought to get it—about two or three days?"

"Not *too* soon. . . . But dear Gilberto, why didn't you tell me before that you and Inés had spoken about writing to each other?"

He looked away to give the blood time to drain away from his face, and he heard her ask, "When did you talk to her?"

It was hard to look at her, and harder not to. Her hand was on his sleeve, and he talked to that. "I didn't—I'm ashamed—I never said a word to her about a letter or a picture. I wanted to—I would have. I just *thought* about telling her, and just now, for a minute it was almost as if I *did* tell her. I—I wouldn't lie to you, señora."

"Stop it, Gilberto! What you say with your heart cannot be made into a lie. You meant it, did you not?"

"I don't know how to tell you, señora. I more than meant it! I meant everything I was going to write in those letters—just as much now as before anything happened."

Gilberto sat alone in the cab. It was Lorenzo's "duty" to guard the cargo, and he slept comfortably on the coffee sacks, wrapped in his serape. Don Solomón was right in warning that the night was going to turn chilly when he insisted that Gilberto take a sweater and a leather jacket. Lorenzo had wanted to take the shotgun, but Don Solomón said no; blood was dearer than coffee. However, Lorenzo slept with his machete, the thong around his wrist.

It was two o'clock, black and moonless when they entered Ciudad del Maíz and roused the Pemex gas station attendant. When Gilberto explained to him that he would service his own truck, the attendant thanked him for his consideration and dozed off again. Three more hours of easy running would bring them into Ciudad Valles—still too early. This, then, would be a good time to make a start at showing Lorenzo the ropes.

Lorenzo himself suggested siphoning the few liters of gasoline that remained in the drum into the tank. "Otherwise," he said, "we shall be buying it coming back."

That brought the gas level right up to full and a little more; enough to get them to Valles and back to Zaragoza.

"Now, Lorenzo, even more important than the gasoline is the oil which lubricates the engine. Should the gasoline fail, the machine would stop—nothing more."

"That one understands."

"But with oil, it is different. Unless there is enough oil in the sump here, it will end up entirely ruined. Now, I will show you how to measure if there is enough." He drew the dipstick out of its scabbard and showed him the three notches marked FULL, ADD, and EMPTY, the first words of Lorenzo's English vocabulary.

"Now the water."

"The water I understand, Don Gilberto. I have seen it poured many times into this hole here in front until it slops over."

"But you must also know *why* each thing is done," Gilberto said, "and I will explain while we are returning."

"Those little round windows, señor?"

"Yes; the largest one tells how fast we are marching and the others advise if the different parts of the machine are functioning well or badly. . . . Now, observe; this black box with the three knobs is the battery—the acumulador. This also requires water, but of the purest, distilled. Let us see if it has enough." He shone the flashlight into the cells; they were okay.

"It would be wise, would it not, Don Gilberto, to have a bottle of this special water in the camión?"

"Very good, Lorenzo. We will remember to buy a bottle in Valles." He was beginning to feel the satisfaction that came, not only from the possession of a craft, but from initiating an intelligent apprentice in its rudiments. "And now to the tires, Lorenzo."

The manufacturer's sticker, inside the lid of the glove compartment, gave the recommended tire pressure as 44–46 pounds. The gauge attached to the compressed air hose did not look reliable, and he made a mental note to buy one of the standard pocket-size gauges when they got to Valles.

"The tires are all equal now," Lorenzo said, rising from his knees at the left-front and coiling the air hose.

Gilberto smiled. Here was his chance, since he was a teacher, to pull his pupil up short. "All?"

Lorenzo totted off each corner of the truck. "Uno, dos, tres, cuatro. Sí, señor—all."

"Now think, Lorenzo. Only four? This is a camión, not a mule."

"I am sorry, Don Gilberto, for being so stupid," Lorenzo said and went to work on the spare tire. Gilberto realized that he had carried his sarcasm to the point of insult and regretted it.

Together, they cleaned the windshield and the lenses of the headlights. Before starting, Gilberto gave the attendant a peso.

Lorenzo climbed nimbly into the rear of the truck and slapped the side of it twice, the signal, everywhere in Mexico, to go forward.

The Route of The Sheik. It looked different, naturally, at his hour and from behind a steering wheel, than the last time he had traversed it. He saw things he had not known were there before; clusters of huts with conical roofs which deepened the sense of tropicality of the great slope toward the sea. Warm draughts entered the cab, each in its own time and with its own dominant aroma: soapy, like fungus; the smell of living wood, scorched all day, and now cooling; jasmine and carrion.

"My Dear Inés," "Dear Cousin Inés," "My Darling," "Dearest Inés"— Any of these would be all right if he were going to write the letter in English. But this was going to be in Spanish, and translated, they were all blah.

He was going to have to begin, "Muy cariñosa Inesita." Cariñosa could mean adorable or precious; on the other hand, something as tame as My Jolly Little Inés—depending on how you meant it or what the other person wanted to read into it.

The rest of the letter was no mystery to him. He knew every word that was going to be in it—unchanged, word-for-word, the one that formed itself so easily in his mind last night. This wasn't going to be a play-by-play account of where he was and what he was doing. It was to let her know how he felt about her. Hence, the place of origin of the letter—the envelope, rather—was a technical detail that had nothing to do with what was inside.

A match flare reflected itself on the windshield. Gilberto glanced around and saw Lorenzo sitting up. He tapped on the glass, beckoning for him to come into the cab, and prepared to slow down. Lorenzo shook his head, pointed down to the sacks, and then ahead.

There were the lights of a substantial town. Passing through it slowly, he identified it: Nuevo Morelos. This meant 18 kilometers more to Antiguo Morelos and 72 more, due south, on the principal highway, to Ciudad Valles.

Knowing it wasn't yet time for it, he looked intermittently at the sky for signs of dawn—or for that false dawn that he had read about, but had never seen. And there was still no horizon except the quivering line of deep blue at the limit of the headlights' throw.

The needle was at 60—kilometers, so he wasn't racing to overtake daylight. Easing his foot on the gas pedal, he held it at 50. Better this way—let the day catch him.

This, he convinced himself, the thing he was doing, paid off every foot of the way. First, there was the going there and the contemplation of the things to do: the presentation of himself and the letter, the disposal of the coffee, the purchase of crates and boxes and bales of goods at the wholesaler's, the *carte blanche* in the matter of automotive parts and supplies, the getting and the giving of receipts. And none of this patronizing "now-be-careful," and "do-this-right-for-once" that Richardson used to dish out every time he sent him around the corner.

Yes, the going, the doing, and best of all, the coming back.

He wouldn't mind running into Bishop—just like this; leather jacket open, elbow on the sill, sobrecargo sitting in the back, guarding the load.

". . . Oh, just a shipment of some high-grade coffee I'm taking into Valles and bringing some stuff back. . . . And by the way, Bish, how do you like this little boiler? Look at it inside, open its mouth . . . Yup, seven years old and clean as if it came off the line yesterday. And go? Like a striped-assed ape. Of course it ain't one of those Pullman jobs you showed me back in Texas, but she'll do what she's licensed for—and more. Oh, yeah—put a gauge on every one of those tires, *including* the spare, and I bet they won't vary so much as an ounce. . . . Oh, up there? . . . I'm going to have it painted on tomorrow— bright red letters with a border of blue flowers—INESITA."

36

In a papelería—Artículos Escolares, open early to catch the schoolboy trade—Gilberto bought a small memorandum book, a block of letter paper, and envelopes. Before they were wrapped, he added a typewriter ribbon and an eraser. The cost of these he entered in the notebook, under the heading "Personal." Later, on the page headed "Receipts," he set down:

496 k. Coffee, dlv'd to Pineda Bros., at 6.15 per k.————————P. 3,050.40.

Don Solomón must have written something very nice in that letter, from the way the Pinedas—all three of them—treated him. They asked about the old man and the señora-his-wife, and said they were gratified, after so long a time, to again be doing business with such a fine and fair man. "And please assure him that we are his attentive servants."

After weighing the coffee and praising its quality, calling him Don Gilberto all the while, the middle Pineda walked with him to the bank and handed him the efectivo, mostly in 50s and 100s. He begged Gilberto to stay for lunch and share a bottle of Manzanilla with them. When he pleaded that he had other matters to attend to at the wholesale house, at the dispensary of petroleum products, he was given the bottle to take back to Don Solomón with their saludos.

At the wholesale house he needed no letter; Don Solomón's written order was enough. When everything had been checked aboard the truck, Gilberto signed the invoice and was given a carbon copy. . . . Nothing here to enter in the book. But on the page facing "Receipts," with its one item, he had "Disbursements"—plenty of them—and for each item he had a receipt; from the 500-litre drum of Mexolina at 42 centavos a litre, down to 80 centavos for a half-gallon of distilled water.

A lot of these he would have to explain to Don Solomón: the necessity for the spare set of ignition points; two extra spark plugs, properly gapped, for emergencies; the tire gauge; the hand-sprayer to lubricate the springs; and all the other stuff. There was a case of a dozen tins of Mexolub 30—always handy. And the reason he bought the two kinds of grease—the special stuff for the rear end and the ordinary, as well as some No. 90 for the transmission— was because there was a good hand gun with fittings in the depósito. He would, he knew, have to show Lorenzo only once how to thoroughly lubricate the truck.

Anyway, what he *would* do, as soon as he got back, is type out a neat statement of the operations for the day and hand it to the boss, along with the balance of the money. Then, if there were any questions, he would go over them, item by item.

"Tell me what I am doing now, Lorenzo."

"You are raising the force to the third point, señor."

"Use the language of the automobile."

"Excuse me—you are going into high."

"And why am I doing that just now?"

"Because, as one can see, the road is again level and the motor does not need to work so hard. It marches faster with less labor."

"Very good, Lorenzo. Can you tell me again why that is so?"

"The teeth—excuse me—the gears inside the box of transmissions; the smaller, the faster it will turn. It is as you have shown me with the two coins."

"And which, then, is the *strongest* gear?"

"The low—there, at the left leg of the H."

There was a kick in teaching these things to Lorenzo. He thought of letting him take the wheel on a good, flat stretch of highway, then decided that would be rushing things. If he was going to be a teacher, be a good one. Tomorrow, let him grease the car and learn not to miss a single nipple. Next day, wash it and learn how to flush out the radiator until the water out of it was clean enough to drink. Then show him how to clean the battery terminals, smear them with Vaseline, and put them back on, good and tight. And one more apprentice chore: switching the tires to get even wear—x'ing them—right-rear to left-front, right-front to left-rear. These were all the things *he* had to perform up in work camp before they would let him near the cab of the old "cee-ment mixer."

But so far, Lorenzo was doing fine. He could now read three words: OIL, GAS, and AMPS.

"How many amps are we charging, Lorenzo?"

"Exactly none, señor."

Gilberto smiled, thinking how he could confuse him by switching on the lights. But the old boy had too much dignity to have gags played on him.

"Tell me, Lorenzo, if around the next bend the road should suddenly become very steep, what is to do?"

"Steep rising or descending?"

"Descending."

"As you have shown me, Don Gilberto: Instantly return to the gear of second speed—at the right arm of the H."

"Correct! The next such hill we come to, observe carefully and you will understand why that is done."

"I shall be very attentive, señor."

A while later, Gilberto said, "Now, in case Don Solomón should ask you, what are the three English words pertaining to the camión that you have learned?"

"There are six, señor."

"Six?"

"Oil, gas, and amps—also empty, add, and full."

In genuine admiration, Gilberto said, "Lorenzo, you're going to be all right."

He must have, happily, used the word that pleased Lorenzo most—diestro, a man of skill. Lorenzo flashed one of his rare smiles and brushed both wings of his bigotes zapatistas with a delicate fingertip.

Lorenzo began unloading as soon as Gilberto backed into the depósito. His legs wobbled, and he admitted to himself that *this* time—no kidding—he was really pooped.

"Did everything go well?" Doña Elena asked.

"Fine. How about here? I feel like I have been away for days." His dry lips split painfully as he talked.

"She is better by the hour." She took his arm when he tried to say something, and steered him to his room. "But I will tell you nothing now."

"Where's Don Solomón?"

"He will not listen to you until you have rested." She pushed open the door. "Josefina will bring you something."

"Just a bottle of beer, please. Nothing to eat." He sat down on the bed. Good, they had brought the typewriter in here, on the small table by the window. A little old nap and he'd make out that report.

As he took off his shoes, each as hot as a Bessemer, Josefina came in with the beer and said good afternoon. All he could do was yawn up at her. He drank straight from the bottle while undressing, leaving the money and the papers on a chair and leaving his clothes where he peeled them off. Naked, he slid under the covers and took the last swallow of beer. I'm drugged, he thought, and it felt, not unpleasantly, as if the back of his neck was being pounded with a nylon bag full of ashes.

He woke up in pitch darkness and listened to the parliament of the dogs until a member moved for adjournment. The loud approval lasted another minute. Again, dead silence, until the compressor of the refrigerator in the kitchen gave a mechanical sigh, followed by the hum-thump-hum of its motor.

Reaching up, he switched on the light. Again he had forgotten to wind his goddam watch! It had given out at a quarter past six.

Then it came to him, as he looked slowly around, that his clothes were gone—pants, shorts, shirt, socks. The money, the receipts, and his notebook were where he left them. What could he expect, he grumbled to himself, with no lock on the door? Well, it was their lookout if they come barging in on a guy who sleeps raw.

Darkening the room again, he crept to the curtained niche which served as a closet and slipped into his extra pair of trousers and a shirt.

Doña Elena was in the hammock and Don Solomón in a bamboo chair beside her, and he signaled for Gilberto to be quiet as he approached. They entered the comedor. The gift bottle of manzanilla and three wineglasses were on the table. When Gilberto saw that, he was disappointed because Lorenzo must have already delivered an account of their day. However, the accounting was more important.

"Congratulations, Gilberto," Don Solomón said, filling the glasses. "You should be proud of your first day as a comerciante. It is something to celebrate. Drink."

"I think we did all right. I'll type out everything later and we can go over the figures."

"Not a word about business tonight," Don Solomón insisted. "We have other news for you, but even that must wait until you have had something."

"Margarita has prepared a fine soup of beef and peppers—"

"With which," Don Solomón added, "this manzanilla goes very well."

"Wonderful!" The Spanish wine was pale, dry, and very smooth; not a drink for a lush. "What time is it, anyhow?"

Margarita answered, "Twenty three hours," as she put the bowl of soup in front of Gilberto.

"Little matter," Doña Elena said. "Pelancha was here today—with Inés, for a little time."

"Was that good, Doña Elena? Her mother knows I am still here, and if she told Inés—"

"No, everything is the same, except that the girl grows better. I spoke to Pelancha first and warned her."

"That's good."

"It can only help."

"Do you think it is all right for me to go and see her—Tía Pelancha, I mean—now; say, tomorrow?"

Doña Elena glanced at her husband and he looked doubtful. But it seemed to tell her what she wanted to know. "I think perhaps it would be better to wait. We have told her nothing of why you came back and *why* you are waiting still. She suffers under a great shame."

"That's why I want to see her, señora—to tell her."

Doña Elena was more firm. "No! No, Gilberto. With her it is this way: That the fault has been hers and that it has been done to you. And she cannot, like the priest, simply beg forgiveness. She must win it . . . from you, Gilberto."

"Why from me? Doesn't Inés count here?"

"Of course, hijo, but you count more. . . . Am I not right, Solomón?"

"It gives me no joy to say it," Don Solomón agreed, "but my wife is right in the case of a Mexican mother—and a proud one—of Pelancha's class. I wish it were not so, so relentless."

"Wait," said Doña Elena. "Pelancha will come to you." She got up. "I am going to look in on the child. Dr. Zumbach may be coming tomorrow. Good night."

"Good night, Doña Elena."

"Gilberto and I will have another glass and talk business."

"This wine is *something*." Gilberto sipped from his second glass. "I'll wind up an alcoholic."

"No fear, son; no man becomes a drunkard for love of good wine—or for love of anything. Hate is the great driver-to-drink."

"There's all kinds of hatred," Gilberto said, feeling the same mood, the same *ambiente* as once before, when he and the old man sat with a bottle between them. And that was almost forty-eight hours ago. The old man talked then, just as he was talking now. He remembered how he had been semi-drunkenly impressed, saying that those remarks should be put into a book, chief, and "You got something there, pal."

It was not that the forty-eight hours seemed long or short. They were just what the clock ticked off—two days. So time alone is no way to measure what happens to a man—in here and up there.

Mentally, he touched his heart and his head, and knew that there could not be any more encounters such as on that first night with Don Solomón—not with anybody. Talk could no longer be mere patter, not so long as there was such a vastness of understanding still to be redeemed.

"Yes, all kinds of hatred," Don Solomón said, "and that which is to *be* hated. When a man knows its name, it is no longer the Indomitable against which he had been breaking his chained hands."

That Which is to Be Hated—it sounded Kiplingesque to Gilberto. He did not know its name, but he had seen its face.

Only a disc of topaz shimmered in the bottle. It was past midnight.

What Doña Elena had told him about Pelancha's visit to Inés was the best of the news. The balance of the day's events was less pleasant. She had left that for Don Solomón to communicate.

"Vicente identified the three men with Fidel in the car, only after they had identified themselves—by flight. To give you their names would be useless. To try to punish them, well, vain. But I don't think they will ever come back to this valley; they have been, let us say, banished by Carrasco, very likely to a silver mine he owns in the State of Hidalgo. He may not have done this either, if it were not for Don Perfecto."

"What about Fidel Vargas? Is he under the Coronel's protection, too? That's the guy I'd like to get my hands on."

"Vargas," Don Solomón said, "is too contemptible a louse, even for Carrasco's gunmen to consort with. They would probably kill him. He is now a lone jackal, and Vicente says that Vargas had long ago meant to wet his back by crossing into Texas. The priest believes that is what Fidel would do."

"I'd like to know something about him," Gilberto said. "Some kind of a description. . . . I might run into him some day."

"It is better that you do not ever see him."

Gilberto rolled his head confusedly. "Here we were talking about hating, and I've got somebody real to hate that nobody else can do for me."

"There is something more real than Fidel Vargas which you hate more, and which will not disappear even if this one man, or those four, are hanged as high as Haman. It is that which breeds the Fidel Vargases of our times."

"You mean poverty," Gilberto said, aware of the utter ingenuousness of the remark, and trying to hide it, added, "Poverty is no disgrace," which made it worse. It was the opposite of what he said—or thought—when Lorenzo said that poverty was their brother.

Don Solomón smiled. "That saying was invented *for* the poor, not *by* them. Did you ever hear anybody say that ignorance was no disgrace?"

There was what he should have told Lorenzo, and he said it aloud: "The only brother poverty has got is ignorance."

"You have said that very well, Gilberto. It pleases me."

"I've got to tell that to Lorenzo. Incidentally, Don Solomón, I think he's going to turn out great."

"Yes," Don Solomón agreed. Then he said, in a calm, intense way, "But not only because he is Lorenzo. It is because he is not one of those, who, when asked, 'What do you know? What useful thing can you do?' need not spread his hands and bend his back to show that this is all he possesses."

Gilberto could hear him breathing fast. It was time to talk about something else. "First thing tomorrow, we're going to grease the truck, and gradually, Lorenzo will be able to do everything necessary."

"You are doing a wonderful thing for him, Gilberto, and for me, as well. And yet you were worried that you would be idle. . . . And if you are going to clamber about under the camión, you cannot do it in those clothes. Fit yourself a pair of work pants and a shirt from the shelf."

"That's a good idea."

He sat alone after Don Solomón had gone to bed, and relished a cigarette in the delicious air of the patio. Once, from his place in the hammock, he caught a streak of light under Inés's door. It stayed on for, he estimated, long enough for somebody—Josefina or the señora—to pour a teaspoon of medicine or administer a pill.

The chain of the hammock creaked, too faintly for him to hear it, but loud enough for Margarita. She appeared silently, almost invisibly.

"I come to ask if I may bring you something, Don Gilberto."

"No, thank you, Margarita. Don't disturb yourself."

"But you are wakeful. A cup of warm milk sprinkled with cinnamon?" He couldn't think of anything he detested more than warm milk. "It will only take a minute."

"Very well, Margarita." She made no light in the kitchen except what glowed from the stove burner. What he meant to do, it occurred to him, may be something that is just not done in Mexican households. Maybe it would look impish, but he had started on it and he had to finish it.

When Margarita brought him the milk, he said, "Now you sit right down there and drink it."

"I, señor?"

"And I'm going to sit right here and watch you."

"Sí, señor." She sat down on the bamboo chair and sipped, at first timidly, and then she smiled.

This is it again, he thought—that glow.

37

Lorenzo had begun washing the truck when Gilberto looked into the depósito at seven o'clock. He said, "Muy buenos días, maestro," and stood away, so that Gilberto could see the clean, yellow side of the body.

"Perfect, Lorenzo." This had all the earmarks of a custom wash-job. Lorenzo was using laundry soap, a bucket, and a brush, not just sluicing it down with a hose. "Only let's roll it out in the alley. We're going to have to lie on this floor later, when we start the greasing."

Going back to the room, he changed the typewriter ribbon and spent the next hour copying the accounts from the memorandum book:

496 k. dlv'd to Pineda Bros.,

at 6.15 per k.. $3,050.40

DISBURSEMENTS (As

per receipts herewith):

Mexolina Gasoline, 500 liters at

.42 per lit. 211.00

1 container Hypoid axle grease 88.00

1 case (12 cans) No. 30 Mexolub 27.00

6 liters No. 90 oil for transmission 20.50

5 kilos bearing grease 40.00

1 hand spray for oiling springs, etc. 25.00

1 bott. Agua destilada, incl.

deposit on bottle 1.00

1 set ignition points for distrib. 30.00

2 spark plugs (spare) 13.20

TOTAL DISBURSEMENTS $455.70

About to write, "Advanced by G. Reyes: $2,160," he changed his mind and put down:

Balance, as per cash .... $2,594.75.

He put the money in an envelope as a knock sounded on the door. It was Josefina. He laughed. In the dead of night they'll creep in and lift his clothes; and now, when he was fully awake, they'll knock and formally ask permission to enter. She handed him a pair of twill army-type trousers and a shirt of the same material. "Don Solomón asks to know if these will suit."

"I'll try them on, Josefina. Meanwhile, please give him this envelope and paper."

The clothes were a good fit, especially the shirt; ample as work clothes ought to be, and plenty of pockets.

Backing the truck in again from the callejón, he started Lorenzo on the greasing routine. He showed him how to unplug the rear-end housing and the transmission, and how to test the level of lubricant with the little finger.

He remembered seeing furniture casters in the Surtidor stock and told Lorenzo how they would build a creeper with three casters and some light boards. They had gotten as far as the king-pin bushings when Don Solomón peered down and told them to stop for breakfast.

They all admired him in the fresh and shiny cotton, and he, too, rather liked what he saw earlier in the mirror: Lieutenant Flash Reyes washing up before going into the Briefing Room.

Doña Elena told him that Inés had eaten some rice with milk, an egg, and a cup of chocolate. "She winced when I touched her head. But that may be due to the tightness of the bandage. When the doctor comes, he may order me to make a looser one."

"Did she sleep all right?"

"Yes; so well, and she looked so rested this morning that I decided to take the risk of telling her—I said it casually, 'The doctor is coming again today to see you.'"

"And what was her reaction?" Gilberto asked eagerly. "Did it do anything that we were afraid about?"

"I think no. I could not tell from her expression, because of her bruised eyes and swollen lips. But I am sure she was not startled. She spoke. She said, 'The doctor?' and the first thing that came to me to answer was, 'Yes, Inés, don't you remember?' . . . Now I think that all I did was confuse her."

"No, señora, I think you did the right thing."

"And if I am any specialist at all," Don Solomón added, "that is exactly what I would have advised."

"What else did she say, señora?"

"Nothing more. A little while later, Josefina called me in to see. She was asleep and smiling."

"Having a nice dream, I hope," Gilberto said.

"Cuidado," Don Solomón pointed his finger. "When a woman smiles in her sleep, she is either not sleeping or she is plotting. I warn you, my boy."

Doña Elena tilted her chin at him. "My specialist! Pay no attention to him, Gilberto."

Gilberto put the envelope back on Don Solomón's desk. "All I have coming is twenty-one hundred and sixty. Is there something wrong in my figures?"

"Your figures are exact to the centavo, and that money is yours. I have been doing a little calculating, too, and when I have given you forty-six pesos and fifty centavos more, we will have made an equal amount on our coffee transaction."

It was no use arguing with the old man once he had said, "If you didn't read the letter I sent to the Pineda Brothers, you should have. It identified you as my socio—in English, my partner. We have each gained three hundred and sixty-two pesos, seventy-five centavos."

When Gilberto said, "But it was your truck," the old man answered that Gilberto's work was easily the equivalent of the services of the machine.

"Technically," Don Solomón pointed out, "I am profiting shamelessly. Most of what Isidro and his friends received for their coffee will be spent here in my store. Already, they have ordered four hundred pesos worth of chemicals for spraying."

Don Solomón's figures were so accurate that Gilberto suspected that he had been secretly using the adding machine. He had even put aside the 72 pesos for the additional sixteen pounds of coffee. "When Isidro comes—tomorow, or the next day—I shall give him that money."

Gilberto was about to say something, but caught himself, and when Don Solomón urged him to speak, he said, "What I was going to suggest was, rather than wait for them to come—I don't want to sound like I'm really your partner—but wouldn't it be better if we brought them the money. Lorenzo could show me where their place is." The old man looked thoughtful. "Unless you need him around here."

"No, Gilberto, he is your ayudante. Good! Take him with you to Las Camelias. Let him stay by you while Isidro shows you the bananas and whatever else they are cultivating. You have your notebook? . . . They are good farmers in that colony, and unless something puts the fear of Carrasco into them again, they should prosper. I will show you how we can pay them a better price for their plátanos, their piña, and their jitomates, and still earn a reasonable profit for ourselves."

Ourselves. More bait, Gilberto thought; lining a nest for me. Every other appeal failed, and now, he suspected, the old man hadn't pressed too hard on any of them because he had this ace-in-the-hole—a kind of ready-made fortune.

Easiest thing in the world—to take this break as it came; forget that he was ever on his way back, and hope that everybody else would forget it. And it looked as if Don Perfecto had forgotten it, or was willing to.

But it was not fear of the priest or of any enemy, active or apparent, either here or on the other side of the Río Bravo, that had worked upon him. He knew deeply that coming or going—in flight or in turning back—nothing that he had felt could be equated with cowardice.

Yet, he realized that for most of his life, he had feared; and he recognized it—a spectre. He had feared the judgment of a caste, a distant lineage, not which held itself more noble, but which held him less. It was a tolerant order, and could be indulgent, if he behaved as he was told and gave it no trouble.

The end of that fear had come—not at any one point that could be marked with an X, but gradually, as it had been acquired.

If he should try to tell Don Solomón now, how would he put it? That by turning around and going back he was proving his courage, his manhood, or whatever they wanted to call it? It was worth trying, but the chances were that he would botch it up. This kind of resolution could not be declaimed offhand. It could be *thought out*, and only in exceptional cases written down— as he had written it down for Dr. Eisen. There, he thought, he'd made himself pretty clear—until he remembered that all he had put on paper was "As you know—"

The rest of it was still in his head, and he was quite satisfied to let it stay there. He had sold himself and he wasn't out crusading.

The men of Las Camelias had seen first the dust of the truck, rising in yellow plumes from the serpentine track winding around the low hills.

To Gilberto, the little farm settlement, which once rejoiced in the name Ingenio Las Camelias, looked less inhabited than it proved to be when they approached the first hut. He recognized Isidro Montes de Oca at the head of a reception committee of eight or ten farmers who stood in a semicircle, and a more informal group of women and children near a long shed roofed with leaves.

Deliberately, he made a wide turn and drove between two mouldering columns of stone joined by an eroded arch. They seemed to expect visitors to enter this way.

"Muy buenas tardes, Señor Reyes. . . . Muy buenas tardes, Lorenzo."

"Muy buenas tardes, señores," Gilberto answered and nodded also toward the distant group of women and children.

Surprised at being included in the greeting, they answered in rough chorus. Isidro reminded Gilberto of a headman in an African village, the kind you see in every movie about White Hunters, the way he gestured for the women to get busy about their work, and the way they obeyed.

Gilberto enjoyed this; more because he felt he was dressed for the part. When Isidro sent one of the men for the jug, Gilberto declined. "I have come for only one thing—on behalf of Don Solomón—in order to correct the account of yesterday. You are due this seventy-two pesos for the overweight of sixteen kilos."

He handed Isidro the money, but the farmer did not pocket it. "But our romana—"he pointed to a steelyard dangling from a beam of the shed.

"Don Gilberto watched the weighing very carefully at the warehouse," Lorenzo said.

"Yes," said Gilberto. "Your apparatus is light by two kilos in sixty. . . . Don Solomón requires no writing for the sum I am returning."

"We shall respect that," Isidro answered. "Don Solomón is a man with whom one can do business with a nod of the head."

Gilberto took out his notebook and made a mark in it. "I see a reminder here concerning plátanos."

"Yes, Señor Reyes, if you will have the goodness to recall you made the note the other day." Isidro bustled. "Allow me to show you."

The cafetal, two upward-sloping acres of coffee trees, was almost obscured by the banana plants which outnumbered them. He had seen banana plants before—even in the yards of poor homes in Los Angeles. Trees, they called them, but they were actually stiff bundles of tightly wrapped leaves from the top of which dangled, rather obscenely, a lumpy purple bract. But the best those California plants yielded were shriveled clusters of fruit about the size of his little finger.

Isidro and Lorenzo waited respectfully as he made a note of no consequence, but simply because he relished the effect. He wrote in English: "Bananas—8' to 10' high. Very nice. Grow upside down. Worth at least a quarter a bunch at A&P."

He was seeing coffee trees for the first time, and they fascinated him. They were evergreens, he knew, because the floor of the orchard was free of dead leaves. The slender, whiplike trunks looked strong enough to withstand high winds, and each tree appeared to be as carefully tended as a pet household plant and kept at a height of about six feet. The blossoms were creamy white, like the finest tuberoses, and their aroma was exquisite. Nipping off a berry, the size of a marble, he broke it open and saw the two beans bedded in pulp. Quite unconsciously, he nodded, a gesture which Isidro took to be knowledgeable approval. "True," said Isidro, smiling, "that arbolito is one of our best. She will yield us fifteen kilos when we have taken her third crop."

Gilberto smelled the crushed berry and nodded again, looking, apparently, more expert than ever. "I can see." Even Lorenzo looked impressed.

"But you are here with regard to plátanos," Isidro said, striding forward. "Mira—" Walking, he pointed up to the banana stalks, each heavy with green fruit and round as a barrel. "As a judge of fine fruit, Don Gilberto, look at this racimo of guineos—" He stopped and laid his hand on a stalk of plump, medium-sized fruit. "You will agree that here is something fit for the finest tables in the capital. Let me cut you a hand of these, so that Don Solomón may taste and judge for himself."

They crossed to another row of plants, and again Isidro invited him to admire. "Guineos morados, señor, such as you will not find between here and Orizaba."

These were smaller than the ordinary guineos, and they would be a glowing red when ripe. "Handsome," Gilberto said, and Isidro neatly separated some from the stalk.

"Now have the goodness to look at *these*, gentlemen!" Isidro gloated, pointing to a cluster of the most gigantic bananas Gilberto had ever seen. The individual bananas were at least twelve inches long. Gilberto wondered what this type was called.

"Machos," said Isidro. "Feel them, señor." They were hard as stone. "In five days they will be ready for the frying pan. . . . The good name of Las Camelias stands upon the flavor of this fruit—with a dash of lime juice." As he cut a handful from the stalk, he said, grimacing painfully, "What had hurt me deeply was to see Coronel Carrasco's people cart all this to Tampico, to be put into ships and taken God knows where."

What hurt him even more deeply, Gilberto mused, was the price Carrasco had been paying, if the price of the coffee was an example.

Back at the truck, Gilberto took out his notebook again. He jotted down figures as Isidro spoke. "There were only eighty-six plátanos when Don Solomón last saw them. There are now one hundred and two."

"How many of each?"

"Of the guineos, sixty-six; of machos, twenty-two; and of the guineos morados, fourteen."

There were other things Gilberto wanted to know, and hoped Lorenzo would be able to tell him. A question now, such as when the stalks would be ready for cutting, might destroy his reputation as an expert founded on silence and non-commital grunts.

The siesta was not compulsory in Mexico, but Gilberto wished it were. The cab was hot; as hot with the windows and ventilators open as before. Anything that cast a shadow—a scrub cypress, a dusty bush—sheltered a living thing, animals or their tenders. The road ahead was as bright as the field of a microscope with everything on it visible; bright green beetles, hairy spiders, and many lizards, running comically on the tips of their claws for a space ahead of the truck, kicking up little tendrils of dust before disappearing like genii.

Now was the time, Gilberto thought, to pull over to the side where there was some grass, and creep under the car for a nap. Not forgetting, of course, to slap a couple of big, juicy rocks under the wheels.

Lorenzo's eyes remained calm, bright, and always on the road ahead. Once, he lowered the window on his side and craned out to study something.

"What is it, Lorenzo?"

"Nothing, señor—not what I thought."

Gilberto was too sleepy to ask him what he was watching for so intently the last few kilometers. So far, Lorenzo had answered every question politely, and Gilberto had many more. But Gilberto's mind was too sluggish with the heat to care much what the replies were.

Five kilometers onward, they entered a canyon, or it might be a river bed, over which trees arched and cool air whistled through the wind wings. From here, Gilberto remembered, it wasn't much longer to the old ejidal road. He felt like talking again. "This time we'll back right in, so you can have your nap in the camión instead of under it."

"As you like, Don Gilberto, thank you."

"Inside, then. It would not look proper for one of Don Solomón's staff to be sleeping in the street."

"You have reason, señor. And, though the bed of the camión is itself

comfortable, I shall be sleeping elsewhere if Don Solomón retains me after
the month."

"Why shouldn't he, hombre!"

"The salary, señor—semejante a un príncipe."

Gilberto assumed that to mean princely. "How princely?"

"One hundred and eighty-five pesos."

Less than twenty dollars a month, Gilberto calcalated. Not much, but he
was getting his meals.

"One hundred and eighty-five pesos a month," Lorenzo said again, awed.
"The same as he had been paying Felipe." He sighed. "It will be long before I
can earn it."

A little over four dollars a week, and the man was afraid he was being
overpaid!

"And I am paying nothing for being taught the handling of this machine,"
Lorenzo said. "But I will serve him well, I promise you. In time, I will learn
the prices of all the articles in the Surtidor."

"They're all marked, aren't they?"

Lorenzo answered sadly. "Secretly, señor, with a cipher. Each letter of the
alphabet stands for a number—and I know only numbers."

"Then you will have to learn the alphabet."

"I am afraid, señor—"

"Nonsense. Felipe learned them, and Don Solomón did not say he was
intelligent. He said he was honest. . . . Mira—how many numbers do you
know?"

"Hundreds, Don Gilberto—thousands."

"And do you know how many letters there are in the alphabet, Lorenzo?"

"No, señor, but to print those thick newspapers and books—it is hard for
me to imagine."

"Well, I'll tell you: twenty-six."

"¡Increíble!"

"That's right."

"But there are big and little letters."

"I'll write them all down for you. I'll find out what code is used, and
before you know it—I'll give you enough time—it will be as if you knew it all
your life."

"I shall give my mind to it, as you order, Don Gilberto."

"Meanwhile, since you know how to figure, I'll show you how to work the
adding machine."

"I wish to believe that you are not making a joke with me, señor."

Lorenzo sounded almost tearful, and Gilberto felt deeply sorry for him.
"Honestly not, Lorenzo. The only joke will be on Don Solomón. We'll say
nothing to him about it until you are perfect, and then—okay?"

He gave his hand to Lorenzo and felt it clasped. He was looking ahead
and did not see his hand raised. But as he realized that Lorenzo was bringing

it to his lips, he yanked it roughly away. Angrily and in English he said, "Lay off, God damn it! No more of this!"

"Excuse me, Don Gilberto; it is that I am thankful."

Flushed, ashamed, not for himself, but for all the servility that he had seen, he said, "All right—all *right!*" Less violently, to save Lorenzo offense, he finished, "People shouldn't—they shouldn't have to do that."

They came out into the sun and heat again and rode in silence. Finally, Gilberto motioned for Lorenzo to steady the wheel while he lit a cigarette. He thought of how enthusiastically he had offered this program of education to Lorenzo—perhaps too eagerly, without thinking that it might take weeks. You can't just let a man memorize the letters of the alphabet and throw him over. But that's the way it would have to be. . . . On the other hand, he wasn't doing this for Lorenzo alone; it would be helping Don Solomón just as much to have somebody who could wait on people. Naturally, nobody could be as *good* as the old man in handling people who came to buy or sell; he had demonstrated that. Yet, somehow, it didn't fit in with the characters of Don Solomón or Doña Elena to, well, fish out a refresco of the right temperature from the ice chest, uncap it for the customer, ring up 30 centavos on the register and bring back the change, thank him, wait for him to finish, and finally stow away the empty bottle. . . . Yes, things ought to be made easier for those people. . . . If he could stay around for a while . . . How long a while? . . . Long enough to break Lorenzo in—

With something near to physical force, he wrenched his thoughts out of that channel. He had been in the Pipe Dream Department long enough, he decided. Time to give himself a pep talk . . . Let's call this one *Like* To and *Have* To. For 'specially lucky guys, the two could mean the same thing. Rare. So the thing to do is quit concentrating on what you like to do—particularly when you're *doing* it—or, the next thing you know, the thing you *have* to do starts fading further and further away. Lying in bed and thinking, thinking how nice it is, when you have to be at the foundry—that's a good example. That doesn't mean you have to go to the opposite extreme and beat yourself on the head worrying over what you *have* to do. Just forget it. The important thing is to be ready to do it when the gong strikes—when the bell tolls for you, as the saying goes.

Well, it'll toll soon enough for me, Gilberto admitted to himself. No fixed time. Amber signal, as in those flying pictures—stand by, alert. Meanwhile—

"Oye, Lorenzo—you think you're going to be able to save any money out of that princely salary?"

"Little, if any, Don Gilberto. I am thinking of taking a woman."

He glanced at the man, believing he would see him smile and willing to share his amusement. But Lorenzo looked quite serious. "Do you have anybody in mind?"

"Sí, señor," Lorenzo answered, intently watching the roadside, craning as though trying to see around trees.

Thirst and the hot wind granulated the edges of his lips. He looked sourly at the reflection in the rear view mirror, of the three bunches of green bananas on the ledge behind him.

"Why couldn't Isidro have sent back some oranges?"

"There is a naranjal at Las Camelias," Lorenzo said. "But the fruit is not attractive as to skin. It is good only for juice."

"Only for juice," Gilberto repeated. "That's just too bad."

He made up his mind that on future trips he would take along a few bottles of—beer? No—beer, unless you were sitting quietly in the shade, is more of a soporific. Soda—too sweet altogether. Water, or some of that Agua Tehuacán was the most sensible, or, better still, a crock of that wonderful, tart jamaica, the kind Inés poured out for him under the tamarind.

A knot formed in his throat, and it unravelled as he asked, "Lorenzo, tell me something about Fidel Vargas."

"I do not like to talk about him, señor."

"I know, I know; you told me he was no friend of yours. But, let's say, how old would you make him?"

"He has fewer years than I."

"Is he thirty-five, forty?"

"Más o menos."

"Is he a big man?"

"He would stand taller than you, Don Gilberto."

"How is he dressed?"

"Commonly."

"Look, Lorenzo, I'm trying to form a picture of this son of a bitch in my mind. Can't you tell me *something?* Does he—" He halted. It was useless to ask what color a Mexican's eyes or hair were. They were the same color as his own, as the average Mexican. "Was he wearing a mustache—bigotes?"

"No sé, señor. If he had, he has removed them; and if not—"

Gilberto punched the wheel with impatience. "What are you holding back for? Treating me like an outsider. Don't you think I have a right to know?"

Lorenzo stared forward and said nothing. A chachalaca, dun-colored and the size of a small rooster, flew across the road at windshield height ahead of them, and Lorenzo turned to study the clump of brush from where it launched itself.

"The reason I'm asking, Lorenzo, is that I may run into him some day. I'll be going through Texas, Arizona, California, and those wetbacks travel around."

"You will not see him in any of those places, señor. Vargas is not the man to go to the United States of the North; no, señor."

"Where else? Sergeant Vicente says that's where he'd be headed for."

"Vicente is mistaken."

"He'll be safe there, won't he?"

"Predatorios are nowhere safe, señor. The coyote, the chacal—they skulk by night."

Where could he hide?"

"¿Quién sabe?" Lorenzo said, much too rapidly. It sounded, to Gilberto, too much like, "Don't *you* look!" And he understood why Lorenzo probed every clump of chaparral behind which something moved, stared at every man they passed, and why he rode with a machete across his legs.

38

Doña Elena de Gulden darkened the room and returned to her husband's side. Her finger on the switch of the shaded lamp, she said, "The newspapers arrived today, four of *La Universal*. Would you like to hear the news from the capital?"

"No, Elena; I have something to tell you about which I will ask your opinion. . . . The two children of Pelancha, Pompeyo and the small one, are here."

"In Zaragoza?"

"They were here, in the store, earlier, to buy a meter's length of jerga for the old Berta, with whom Pelancha has left them."

"And Pelancha?"

"She has gone back home, to Tres Cenotes. I spoke to the older boy, and he gave me curious answers, as if he had been told what to say. . . . I do not like this, Elena. This is not Pelancha's way. Do you think—"

"Perhaps the priest advised her," Doña Elena suggested.

"I think not. Don Perfecto stopped also, to say adiós. He has gone to Guanajuato to make a novena. . . . But this business of Pelancha going back alone to the jacal—this can mean—if we can prevent it . . ."

"You are to do nothing, Sol," she said in a low, commanding voice. "Whatever is to be *prevented*, Pelancha has already done. . . . And you are to say nothing to Gilberto."

"But if he sees the children and asks?"

"Then he will be told no more than what they have told you. But he will know less, and it will not cause him to worry."

Don Solomón fidgeted. "Woman, take this rag off my eyes," he demanded.

"Don't you touch it!"

"I want to see if this is my wife or the Witch of Endor. They say she was beautiful as well."

"Solomón Gulden, you are an old clown. . . . What is Gilberto doing?"

"Resting, I hope, since I do not hear the writing machine. . . . And the girl?"

Doña Elena answered slowly. "I tell Gilberto that she becomes more cheerful. But the truth is that she weeps much, silently. She is remembering."

He made a gesture, deprecating her solemnity. "Eh! She will forget when the boy shows her that he has forgotten."

"You are so certain that he is coming back?"

"Seguro que sí, woman!" He sounded impatient with her. "When he goes, he will take with him only enough money to reach the border. The balance—a considerable sum—he will leave with me. We have an arrangement, Gilberto and I, about giving a certain amount every month—that is, putting it aside for Inés and her brothers."

"If you did not have the small soul of a comerciante, Solomón Gulden, you would know that is proof of only one thing: generosity. And not always. . . . Has he said when he was leaving?"

Don Solomón yawned. "Ahhh, I could sleep now. . . . Gilberto? As the other time, he wants to go while it is still dark." He flexed his shoulders.

"And you sleep!" his wife said, rising abruptly and leaving him.

She saw the clothes which her servants had washed on the cot before she saw Gilberto, at the little table by the window.

"You were packing—you were going to leave before morning, and you said nothing to me."

He was puzzled. "Leave? Oh! You mean San Luis Potosí. We want to get to Las Camelias by seven o'clock and have the men cut and load the bananas by ten."

"Plátanos, by ten," she said, relieved.

"But I'm not going to try to make it back the same night. Don Solomón has given me a list of shippers to see, so that means I may have to stay over. . . . Inés?"

"Sleeping, I think. I will look later. . . . Everybody is asleep except you, Gilberto."

"And Lorenzo. He's using up his siesta time learning the alphabet. . . . I—I've been writing a letter. I didn't use the machine because you could hear it across the patio." The letter, in ink, lay open on the table. "I'm putting it inside of an envelope, separate from the one that's supposed to be addressed to you. How should I mark it: 'By Courtesty of—' or, 'By the Hand of Doña Elena'?"

"Just write, 'For Inés.'"

"I wish you'd read it, señora."

She wanted to, eagerly. But she said, "Inés should be the first to see it."

"But you will have to read it to her anyhow—and write the answer, if there is going to be one. Here, please." He handed her the single sheet of note paper and made her sit, with her back to the light.

The letter began simply, "Dear Inés:" and Doña Elena read on, in a calm, slow voice: "Believe me I was awfully disappointed not seeing you before having to go back, and I guess Doña Elena or Don Solomón must have told you that I just had to leave before you showed up in town. Just the same, I am thinking right now of how you must have made the other girls jealous in your new rebozo. I've been trying to tell friends of mine about what a stunning girl you turned out to be, after me forgetting how much of a difference three years can make in a person's appearance. But I can't get to first base with my description on account of having no picture of you. So, I am enclosing enough, I hope, for you to get a picture taken, whenever you get around to it,

and write something on it. It does not have to be 'Your Cousin Inés,' because
I had it explained to me that we are not *really* cousins, not even second
cousins, for that matter. I hope you don't mind that I am writing you c/o
Doña Elena because I know how much trouble it is to travel all the way in
from Tres Cenotes for your mail. And so long as I don't have a permanent
address yet, that should not keep you from answering soon. Just give your
reply to her or Don S. to forward. In closing, I want to say what a big thrill it
was to meet you, Inés, and how I am looking forward to seeing you again, and
it won't be any three years either that I will be away. If you should think of
me once in a while during that time, who knows but it won't bring me back to
see you sooner. Also, give my love to your mother and to Pompeyo and José
and to the little goat. As always, Gilberto."

Doña Elena had to talk suddenly, to keep from crying. "This is a beautiful
letter, Gilberto."

"I don't know, señora. It's not what I want to say to her. What I want her
to know is—you understand—I know everything that's happened and it
doesn't make any difference to me in the way I feel about her."

"This will help her face it—when the time comes. This is good."

"How is she going to know that I *already* faced it? There isn't anything I
say here to show her that."

"There does not have to be. Not yet."

He folded two 50-peso notes into the letter and put it into the envelope.
"When are you going to give it to her?"

"I hope soon."

"Not before I leave, though?" He expected to hear her answer while he
wrote 'Para Inés,' but she said nothing.

When she took the letter, she turned his wrist to see the time. "It is time to
open. Please come help me with the cortina—or, no, I will call Lorenzo."

"I'll go. Lorenzo is doing his lessons."

Doña Elena left him alone in the store, and he watched, from behind the
rear counter, as Zaragoza stirred for the second, post-siesta, half of its day. A
shadow crossed the door; an old man with a lidless fruit jar asked for a liter of
kerosene. Gilberto decanted it from a dipper and accepted 25 centavos in
large copper coins. He was behind the cash register, putting the money on the
ledge, when Pelancha walked in. He leaned forward and put out his hand,
"Tía Esperanza—"

She raised her old black rebozo to her eyes and looked behind him and to
each side of the Surtidor; everywhere but at him. "Please, Tía—I want to
speak to you."

She turned and walked out quickly.

At supper he said nothing about Pelancha having come in and run out.
He refrained because it was a cheerful meal and the conversation was mainly
about the city of San Luis Potosí. He would like that city, they assured him
and they urged that he take all the time he needed to see everything that

interested him. And not to worry about Lorenzo; Lorenzo would, for choice, sleep in the truck and find his own meals. There were movie theaters in San Luis, and Gilberto thought he would enjoy seeing a picture or two.

Lorenzo came in twice during the meal; once to ask the price of a brick of pressed quince marmalade. "Are you ready for a test of what you are learning," Don Solomón asked, "or is it too soon?"

"I believe I am ready, Don Solomón."

"Very well. Then the price of this membrillo is EJ."

As they watched, Lorenzo half shut his eyes and answered, "The fifth and tenth letters. That signifies fifty centavos. But not for the entire piece."

"For one hundred grams," Don Solomón said.

"Which makes it five pesos the kilo," Lorenzo said.

"Bravo, Lorenzo!"

His eyes gleaming with the praise, Lorenzo went back into the store. A few minutes later, they heard the bell of the register and the clink of coins falling into the drawer.

At ten o'clock, Doña Elena went to give Inés some medicine, saying she would remain with her for an hour. "You should be asleep then, Gilberto, so good night—until tomorrow."

"Or the next day, señora. Good night."

In the next fifteen minutes, Gilberto and Don Solomón heard two more transactions being rung up, and they smiled to each other. "Let us give him another thirty minutes," Don Solomón said, "then close up."

"You look tired, Don Solomón. Why don't you go to bed? I'll go out there with Lorenzo for a while and the two of us can close up. I know where the locks are."

"Very good, son; thank you. But call me if anything—"

"No need to disturb yourself any more tonight. We'll be leaving at five."

Gilberto sat at Don Solomón's desk and watched silently as Lorenzo picked up object after object and studied the code markings.

A few minutes before eleven, Sergeant Vicente came in, heavy-footed and swinging his club. "¡Hola, Lorenzo! I see it is true that you are Don Solomón's mozo-of-confidence."

"As you see, Vicente; I am learning."

"¡Qué bueno! A real merchant we've become. What's happened to the gringo?"

Gilberto was about to get up from the darkened corner by the desk, but he remained there when Lorenzo spoke: "Do you wish to buy anything? I have no time to waste."

"Big man now, aren't you?" the policeman mocked. "I have a little news that may shorten you to your former size."

Gilberto came forward. "Anything we can do for you, sergeant?"

"A packet of cigarettes—Delicados."

Lorenzo gave him the cigarettes and his change from a peso and thanked him.

When the man strolled out, Gilberto said, "I don't like that son of a bitch; not since the other night."

"You have reason, Don Gilberto."

"How did he find out I was a gringo?"

"It is known, señor, that you are a norteamericano. He learned it from—" He stopped short, then finished with a shrug, "—God knows from what source."

"The hell with him. . . . Oh, I just thought of something, Lorenzo. While I'm closing up—"

"Sí, señor."

"There's a copper oil can with a spout on the bench inside. . . . You saw it? Good. Fill it with some of that Number Thirty oil from the open tin. . . . And I showed you the generator. . . . Well, on top of it is a little hole with a spring lid. Put a few drops of oil in there then put the oil can in with the rest of the tools under the seat. Okay?"

"Sí señor, en seguida," Lorenzo said, and left.

Gilberto lit a cigarette, leaned on the counter with his elbows, and decided that right at eleven he would start putting out the lights.

As he extinguished the bulb in the rear corner by the shoes, he ground out his cigarette and crossed to the opposite side and stood there, studying the panel of four switches. Somebody entered, and he turned. It was Pelancha, who took a sudden step backward when he faced her. "¡Tía! ¿Qué pasó?"

"Excuse me, señor. I thought it was Lorenzo."

"What is this 'señor' business? I want to talk to you. I don't want to leave here with you thinking—"

"I wish to buy some things," she said coldly.

"Wait, I'll call Don Solomón. Sit down."

"Please not to call anybody. Please sell me what I need and let me go. . . . I beg you."

"Why are you acting like this to me? I want to talk to you about Inés. I want you to know—"

She looked directly at him and said, "I have no time to talk, señor. Two bottles of aguardiente." She pointed to the shelf behind him where the bottles were stacked. All right, he thought, humor her; don't press. He read the labels on the bottles: Tequila Mono, Tequila Añejo, Habañero—

"Whichever is the strongest," she said.

The Tequila Mono was the cheapest, four pesos a bottle. He told her the price. She nodded and said, "And now—" turning, she pointed to the farming tools. Gilberto came around the counter to her side.

"A machete," she said.

He forced a laugh. "For yourself, Tía?"

She lifted one from its display hook, raised it, and felt the sharp edge of its 30-inch blade. He tried again: "Careful—don't cut yourself."

She put it down and picked up another machete, one with a broader and thicker blade, more like a cleaver. "This," she said. "Can you tell me the price?"

The letters AG were chalked on the blade—17 pesos. "Seventeen, I think. . . . But wait, I will ask, to be sure."

Pelancha gripped his arm. "No! If it is more, I will pay what lacks another time. Here—" She opened her hand in which there was a rosette of paper money. She drew one five-peso note out of it and handed him what remained.

He did not count the money until she had picked up the two bottles and tucked them, with the machete, under her rebozo and left.

There were exactly 25 pesos, in ones and fives, some of them torn and repaired with strips of adhesive paper.

He looked at the money and then at Pelancha, a hurrying shadow, weaving through the trees in the Alameda.

Lorenzo heard the tapping of the policeman's stick on the door of the depósito and meant to ignore it. But Vicente took to pounding harder, and, afraid that he may next beat on the sheet metal gate, Lorenzo suspended his work on the motor and opened the door to the alley.

"I ask you not to disturb the people of this house, Vicente," he said, preparing to go inside again. But Vicente detained him. "Go to the pulquería if it is drink you want; there is no more here for you."

"I would not touch it from the hand of a slave to Jews and gringos," the policeman snarled.

"You are not fit to lick up their spittle," Lorenzo said evenly.

"¡Cabrón!"

"Say that to me when you are not wearing your pistol and I will tear out your throat with my teeth, you pimp."

Vicente's hand went to his gun. "I could shoot your eyes out right here," he growled.

"I am waiting."

"You are mistaken if you think that time won't come. . . . But right now, I want it known that I came to warn your gringo master that it is no longer safe for him in this valley. Fidel Vargas is still in the locality."

Lorenzo said, "And those two things mean the same?"

"Pues, sí."

"And you give this warning because—"

"Because," Vicente interrupted, "Narciso the goat herder has already reported to a corporal of the Rurales that he saw Vargas in the basalt rocks on the Cerro de las Reinas; and so the word came officially. Otherwise, it is nothing to me."

"I shall inform all who ask that you have done your duty," Lorenzo said and closed the door. He returned to the store just as Gilberto turned off the last light.

"Who were you talking to out there, Lorenzo?"

Lorenzo answered, "A passerby. . . . Had anyone entered in the meanwhile?"

"No—nobody. . . . You will be sure to wake me?"

"Sí, señor, at five."

The patio was dark except for the streak of light under one door, Inés's.
Gilberto turned on the light in his room and saw instantly that something had
been done to it in his absence. Every time he turned his back—this time they
had come in to clean the ash tray in which there had been one miserable butt.
And they had left some newspapers. He glanced at them: copies of *La Universal* for the dates of October 23, 24, 25, and 26. He meant to read one; not as
thoroughly as he read the newspaper in the hotel room in Victoria, but skim
through it, anyway.

First, he laid out the socks and shorts he was going to wear the next day.
Propping the pillow behind him, he took the bottom newspaper and laid it
across his knees. The main headline was something about the new President
of Mexico, Ruiz Cortines "pledging an administration of morality." That was
a good thing. Turning the paper completely over, the last page announced a
contest for new subscribers to the newspaper; first prize, a 240,000-peso
house in the "refined and salubrious" Polanco section of Mexico City, "complete with every article of household utility" and ready for occupancy by the
winner. Nice break for somebody, he thought, if the contest wasn't fixed.

Funny if somebody like Esperanza won it. She could rent it out. . . . He
wondered if he ought to tell Don Solomón about her purchase. The machete
he could understand; Vargas must have carried off the one at the house. But
the tequila—that puzzled him. If she used the stuff at all, she would have
offered him a drink at her place. In any case, it was obvious that if she wanted
Don Solomón to know, she would not have run away.

He turned a page or two toward the front of the newspaper and saw with
lack of interest that Necaxa had beaten Guadalajara 2-0 at fútbol; the peso
was 8.56 to the dollar. On three columns at the top of Page 6, there was a
photograph of a squad of soldiers digging with spades, an officer nearby, and
a crowd of people in the background watching. A firing squad, he imagined;
this is the way he had seen it done in the movies. First the grave is dug, then
the condemned is given his last cigarette on this earth, then—might as well
read the caption. "Labor Intensiva de Reforestación." It couldn't be a mistake, displaced from somewhere else in the paper. He read the rest of it: "Con
gran interés ha sido vista la labor de reforestación que vienen realizando
conjuntamente las Secretarías de la Defensa y Agricultura. La foto muestra
soldados bajo la dirección de técnicos en forestación en el momento de abrir
una cepa para nuevos retoños de árboles. . . . Vigor y entusiasmo de los
militares para tareas de la paz."

There were six more paragraphs under the picture and he read them
slowly, eating every word, gulping unfamiliar, official phrases. He stopped
and steadied himself, to begin once more. "Una intensa y loable labor de
forestación de los bosques de la República está siendo realizada por elemen-

tos del Ejército Nacional en combinación con los del Departamento de Fomento, Reforestación y Viveros." . . . An intense and laudable work of reforestation of the wooded lands of Mexico is being fulfilled by elements of the Army working together with those of the Department of Development, Reforestation and Nurseries. . . . It couldn't be clearer. The type in the paper which said that was gray and faint. But in Gilberto's brain, it glowed.

Furling the newspaper, he put on his shoes and went to the door of Don Solomón's bedroom.

"Who is it?"

"Me, Gilberto. I must talk to you."

"Come in."

The old man was alone, struggling into his dressing gown. "This is private, Don Solomón. Where could we talk?"

"Go in the sala; we will not be disturbed there."

He switched on the lamp above the couch and walked twice to the window and back to the door, feeling electrically tense and awake. The moment Don Solomón entered, the pulse in his throat subsided and he felt calm.

"Now, what is this crisis, son?" He tried to sound, though not successfully, as if Gilberto roused him for nothing serious. "An alacrán in your bed, or a bad dream?"

"I just saw something in the paper," Gilberto said hastily. "You can tell me what it means. I'll read it to you." He shuffled the newspaper.

"Is it something bad?"

"It *can't* be bad."

"Then why such alarm, Gilberto?"

"You'll see. . . . I don't know. I read it twice already and I can't get over the feeling that I'm—my whole life is tied up in there. . . . Listen—"

And he read from the beginning, almost breathlessly: "'. . . consists of planting trees in all zones where the greedy and pitiless axe has fallen, destroying not only the wooded beauty, but the nearby soil as well.'"

"Yes, yes," Don Solomón nodded. "A little more slowly."

"Excuse me . . . 'This work of conservation is in conformity with a Presidential order of August 5, setting out that the obligations of the military are the same as those of the civil agencies, calling upon them to cooperate constantly and with method, pooling their corresponding abilities. Hundreds of thousands of seedlings will be put out, scientifically, according to the calendar of rainfall in the different parts of the Republic. Magnificent results are expected for the well-being of all the people from this joint action of the Army and the Conservation authorities.' . . . That's the end."

Don Solomón nodded slowly and said, "That is noble work."

"It's true, then? This is happening?"

"I believe so." The old man fought to transmute a sense of mystification in the boy's behavior to something of fact. "It seems to me that I read of such a Presidential order. My wife will remember. I will ask her."

"Wait! Before you say anything to Doña Elena—I don't want to be mistaken again. I want to tell you—you first, Don Solomón—out loud, what's in my mind, so if I have to change it back again, only you should know about it."

"Only I shall know," Don Solomón consented. "Sit down; talk to me calmly."

"Later—if this doesn't go through—after I'm gone, you can tell her that I really *wanted* to stay, but—" he faltered.

"But certain forces intervened," Don Solomón suggested.

"That's right. . . . Listen, when I read this thing in the paper it was as if it was meant for me, personally—Attention Gilberto Reyes—This is my work! This is something I understand. . . ."

He took Don Solomón back to Ventura County, California. As with Bishop, he called it Fillmore, not work camp. The squad leadership. The citation from the State Forestry people. The cutting of almost perpendicular firebreaks. Everything.

Once, Doña Elena knocked and looked in, but Don Solomón went to the door and told her they were having an important conference.

Don Solomón said nothing, only nodding and clasping and unclasping his hands all during the time Gilberto talked. And when he was finally silent, he asked only two questions: "You know, then, that this is what you want to do; in your mind and in your heart?"

"Yes, Don Solomón."

"What was your mother's name?"

"Martínez."

"Martínez," the old man repeated. "It is past one o'clock in the morning. The plátanos can wait another day."

"Do you need me here for anything; anybody you would want me to see?"

"No. I shall need the day to think over the best means; a *secure* way, a precedent, perhaps."

"Then I'll leave for Las Camelias with Lorenzo, on schedule."

39

Lorenzo slid against him as he swung around a sharp turn, and something hard pressed for an instant against his arm. "You might as well take that shotgun out from under your serape, Lorenzo. If it goes off in this cab, it'll kill us both."

"I am careful with it, señor."

"Why did you bring it in the first place? You know how Don Solomón feels about that."

"My duty is to see that you are not robbed. He may scold me, also, when we return, but—"

Gilberto laughed. "I'm not scolding you, only everybody is hiding weapons."

"¿Mande?" Lorenzo said, more as if he had not heard clearly than if requesting an explanation.

"Acting nervous, like my aunt last night—"

"Pelancha?"

"Yes—with her machete; hiding it under her rebozo, the way you were concealing that escopeta." Why, Gilberto thought suddenly, why didn't he tell him this last night, when Lorenzo, having obviously heard the cash register ring, asked him if somebody had been in? Not saying anything to Don Solomón was another matter: the concealment of her purchase of the tequila. Soon afterward, nothing was as important as what he had seen in the newspaper.

"So, Pelancha, the Widow of Reyes, bought a machete," Lorenzo said quietly.

"The price was AG, which is—?"

"Seventeen pesos."

"Correct. . . . That did not bother me so much as—Look, Lorenzo, you know her better than I do. Does she drink? You can tell *me*."

"I don't understand, señor."

"On the sly, I mean. . . . You see, she also picked up a couple of bottles of tequila."

That added up, Lorenzo thought. Pelancha had borrowed 25 pesos from him earlier in the evening.

"That's why," Gilberto continued, "I didn't want to mention anything to Don Solomón about her having been in."

"May I ask a favor, Don Gilberto?"

"Certainly, Lorenzo."

"That it remain between us—you and me, su servidor. It is not good for others to know."

"I agree with you. This is a small community, and a respectable woman with kids spending money on liquor—"

Fidel Vargas held the bottle toward the faint orange ray given off by the last, dying piece of charcoal in the brazier. He drank what was left and pitched the bottle noiselessly into a corner of the jacal. Groping for the basin of cooked beans, he stained his fingers with them and growled, "It's dark."

"We don't have a lamp any more," Pelancha said.

Vargas licked his fingers. He had been hungry, but he gagged when he tried to swallow anything. The first drink of tequila stopped the pain in his stomach. Each one after that quieted the ravening nerves whenever they rayed out and clamored in his guts. He swept the beans aside and said, "Is this all?"

Pelancha knelt close enough to him to see his handsome face, and there was still enough light from the brazier to discern a livid triple scratch that ran from his left eye across his thin nose to the corner of his mouth. "The other day we had a kid," she said.

He was tired and his mouth hung open slackly. For a time his lips formed words, first without sound, then, ". . . friends—*good* friends, eh! Take care of me good, they will. . . . Fine fellows—wait for them in La Quemada." Abruptly he became quiet and appeared almost sober. His voice was brisker. "Proves it, doesn't it; they stopped by here and left the liquor. Token of friendship, till we meet." Cocking his head, he added. "Two bottles you said—where are they?"

Pelancha said, fearing Vargas's clearer speech meant he was recovering a second wind of sobriety, "You drank one. I will bring you the other."

As she tried to get up, he clawed her arm. "Tried to hide it from me, eh!" Twisting free, she secured the bottle from behind the brazier. She had put it there to warm, to make the liquor stronger.

Uncorking it with his teeth, Vargas took a deep drink and shuddered. Rising, first to his knees, he stood, weaving. "I can't stay here," he said. "Give me money."

"I have none."

Vargas began to show fright. "You want me taken! It will be getting light soon and they'll see me. You want me taken!"

"No."

"Then—"

"I do not have the money in the house, Fidel."

"Hidden it, eh! Like my bottles—fetch it! I know, it's that gringo cabrón's money. Give it to me."

"I'll go for it," Pelancha said. "I hid it in a tin, under a rock."

"Where?"

"Not far; by the fosa."

"That's on my way. Start then," he ordered, "but I'm not letting you out of my sight."

He lurched after her out of the hut, hugging the bottle of tequila under his arm. The hazy moonlight was fading and the few stars struggled to stay alight. She had little time, but she could not hurry. Vargas took three eccentric steps to each one she took over the flint-littered slope. If she took his arm—no, she couldn't touch him. At the top of the colina he stopped. "Where?" She pointed downward toward a black line of treetops marking a deep ravine—a barranca, once the course of a torrent. Once it had been bridged—in Cortés's time—by an aqueduct. Now, only a crumbling tower of soft brick remained in the middle of the barranca, and on this end, a scattering of the same pumice-like material.

Where the downhill path began, Vargas stopped, put the bottle to his mouth, lurched, and made a braying sound—the beginning of a song. Pelancha walked back to him. "¡Callarte! Do you wish a Rurales patrol to hear you?"

Grinning, he put his hand over his mouth and followed her another hundred meters, to one side of the heap of ancient brick. Vargas made as if for his own bed, lurching toward a patch of lupin, and squatted down. Pelancha went toward the brick rubble.

"No tricks," he called to her. "I got—got my eye on you."

Pelancha scrabbled among the debris, waking faint echoes, the hasty scratchings of lizards. Glancing backward, she saw that Vargas had stretched out on the ground, his back against a fallen tree. The thin wedge of moon that remained gleamed on his moist neck, where the last of the tequila had dribbled.

She stood quietly, watching the even rise and fall of his chest, listening to the heavy, sighing breath. Closer, then directly above him, she could see the twitching of muscles in his neck and a tiny black ant scouting the cavern of his nostrils. Then she touched his face—with her foot. He shuddered slightly, and the cadence of his breathing became slower; each aspiration, a grating snore.

Slowly, she undraped the tattered rebozo which she had worn crossed on her chest and let it fall to the ground. Then, half turning, she lifted her dress to her hips. The machete hung from a string around her waist, at her right thigh. Unknotting it, she set the blade down on top of her rebozo and again approached Vargas. Kneeling at his left side, she got her arms under him and rolled him over. The log moved a little as she tugged; it was light and spongy, its fibers eaten out by generations of insects.

Vargas lay with his right arm on the log, pillowing his right cheek. Pelancha took the wrist and withdrew it, so that he rested, spread-eagled, still snoring and bubbling.

There was nothing beneath her dress, a shapeless cotton print with four buttons from neck to knee. She took it off and draped it on the spears of a maguey plant.

Pressing both palms in the dirt and rubbing it in with a washing motion, she picked up the machete and, straddling the log, stood at Vargas's head. Raising the blade with both hands to the height of her head, she struck. The second blow was too low, across the root of the neck. The third splashed into the brimming redness, severing the head. The blade stuck in the wood. As she drew it out, Vargas's knees drummed for several seconds on the ground.

Pelancha's breasts and belly were splotched with blood. Walking back to where she had left her dress, she stuck the machete up to the hilt in the dirt around the maguey and pulled it out again, clean. Returning to the log, she dragged the body off it by the ankles and to the edge of the barranca. And with a simple twist that reversed her wrists, it turned over and rolled down. She waited until the rustle and creak of disturbed foliage quieted, then a minute longer until tiny animal squeaks told her that the zarigüeyas, the coatí, and all the little carnivores of the arroyo had scented blood.

Her skin began to contract and itch, and she knew his blood had dried upon her. She went back for the head. When she picked it up, ants were already swarming on it, seeking a way into the eyes under the closed lids. Holding it by the ears, she spat in its mouth and flung it into the ravine.

Dusting her hands, she picked up the machete, rebozo, and dress, and, because it was getting light, she ran to the jacal.

There was a streak of pink in the sky when she poured water from a pitcher into a basin and washed herself carefully. She flung the water out, put on her dress, and lay down to sleep on her petate. She awoke three hours later, made a handful of fire in the brazier, warmed up the beans, and ate them. She missed her children, feeling uncomfortably idle without having to prepare food for them. But she would be seeing them soon, and she must remember to make her greeting casual; not as if she had been away on a long and lonely journey.

Meanwhile, there was work to do; the sweeping of the patio, the drawing of a bota of water from the cenote, the mending of José's little pink shirt. Then, she reflected, there may be visitors—brew some more jamaica, set it to cool.

Visitors came, in the afternoon, while she was busy chipping lengths of fat pine boughs into pencil-size slivers: ten for five centavos. This was a splendid machete, she thought; it still had the factory edge on it.

Three horsemen dismounted at the cactus fence and waited until she approached and asked them to enter. They were Rurales, federal constabulary. Each had a long sugar knife and a carbine slung on opposite sides of their saddles. The leader presented himself, Sargento Villanueva and Troopers Duret and García.

"My house is yours, caballeros. It is the hour of comida, can I offer you something?"

"Thank you, señora, we are provisioned for the field. The horses, however—"

"There is a spring, a hundred steps—there."

"And pasturage, I see." The sergeant gave an order and García led the horses away.

Pelancha warmed the soldiers' tortillas and made a few for them from her own masa, and there was enough coffee to brew each of them a half cup.

There was no talk of why the Rurales were in the neighborhood until the two troopers had gone to the horses and the sergeant and Pelancha sat alone, smoking. "It is not a liberty I have taken, señora," the sergeant explained, "but in line with my orders, I am inquiring of all in this barrio if they had seen these men. Three of them, possibly four. . . . Ah, I must explain—you have perhaps not heard. One car of the train to Tomasopo, which had become disordered while running, was loosened and derailed at a point between Kilómetro Seventy-two and -three, in charge of a watchman. These vandals of whom I speak, last night crept upon the watchman, killed him, and looted the car. This region is where they would hide until they believed it was safe enough to sell their plunder in Zaragoza. . . . You heard nothing last night, señora?"

Pelancha answered, "I cannot say that what I heard were true sounds or just my fears. I cannot ask my younger children, since I sent them to Zaragoza, to be safe."

"We know of your trouble, señora. And if this man Vargas should be one of the band we are hunting—"

"And if he is not?"

"He may be harder to find if he is not with a pack. But, if he shows himself—"

"If he shows himself—"

"I will call upon him once to halt. Often, they do not hear."

When the soldiers rode off, Pelancha went back to cutting pine chips. It would take many, many little bundles of them to pay Lorenzo the money she borrowed. But it was a useful investment, she considered. This was a splendid machete. The only waste had been in the purchase of the tequila.

She looked north, toward the barranca where the buzzards were wheeling in descending spirals. Wonderful fowl, those zopilotes. She had seen them at meat, plunging their horned beaks through hide—how easy for them through thin cloth—tearing, gulping, pausing to vomit, and going back to gorge.

If Fidel Vargas were to be found, she thought, they had better begin searching soon, or there would be little of him to be recovered.

That, for a change, looks like a city, Gilberto thought, as San Luis Potosí flung the colored domes of its churches into the violet air. He counted four, five, eight, ten, twelve hemispheres of colored tile capping an equal number of saffron blockhouses.

Lorenzo had not been in the capital for fifteen years, but he did not think it had changed much. The bull ring was here, where it always had been, and

there was the railroad station. And remembering that one kept the Alame-
da—it was called that here, too—on the right, he guided Gilberto up the
Calle de la Alfalfa and past the largest church, that of Nuestra Señora del
Carmen.

Their destination was the big covered market, ordained byPorfirio Díaz,
on the Calle de Acequia. It was a huge, steel and glass pavilion, reeking, even
as Gilberto sat outside in the truck, and noisy with the yells of a hundred
vendors trying to outshout the loudspeaker mounted on a truck near the
entrance. "Three bars for a single peso, señoras! But at that price, only for a
short time to introduce the Jabón San Antón to the women of this capital.
This soap, ladies, compounded from a secret formula of one of the mistresses
of Alfonso the Thirteenth, is obtainable for the first time by women of the
humbler classes. While the supply lasts . . ."

Lorenzo returned from the interior of the market with Don Alejandro
Carrasquedo, who sold fruits inside at his puesto at retail, and at wholesale,
to other merchants. He looked at the piled stalks under the canvas and
admitted it was "a fair fruit, and if the price is equally fair—"

"The price is seventy-five centavos the kilo," Gilberto said, "as fixed by
Don Solomón, and the weight of each stalk is marked at the butt."

Don Alejandro looked horrified and said that he could obtain bananas at
fifty centavos. Lorenzo moved in and said, "At the dockside in Tampico—for
the dross that is left after that which is fit for a Christian has sailed away."

"I have not known Don Solomón to drive such hard bargains, señores."

"Nor I," Lorenzo answered. "But if he had seen, as I did, that you were
selling them at one peso ten centavos, he would be less generous."

"How much is in the camión?"

"Something under two thousand kilos of the three sorts," Gilberto said.

"Well then, without haggling, let us commence the unloading," Don Alejandro decided.

"With much regret," Gilberto said, "I am ordered to offer half the load
to—" He consulted is notebook. "To Señor Javier Lima in the market near the
Church of San Miguelito."

It was two hours before Don Alejandro, Lorenzo, and a helper from inside
the market selected and carried in forty-three stalks to the weight of 970 kilos.
Then, while Lorenzo remained in the truck, Gilberto went inside and completed the transaction. "And," Don Alejandro said in parting, "should this
other merchant, for reason of bankruptcy or any other, fail to take the balance
of the plátanos, by all means bring them back here. And, let us say, an
additional five cents a kilo for your own pocket, eh?"

"I have no separate pockets, señor. I am Don Solomón's partner," Gilberto said cooly and with pride.

It was another hour and dark when they reached the smaller, more
modern market fronting the Plaza de San Miguelito. It had been closed for
the past thirty minutes, a watchman explained. But, if the señores had urgent

business with Don Javier, he made his residence on the Calle del Llano, only a few squares distant.

No, the business could wait until mañana en la mañana, Gilberto said, and would it be kindly explained to Don Javier that los representantes of Don Solomón of Zaragoza will call again at ten o'clock en punto. He gave the watchman a tostón "for his kindness."

"Let us have a bite of supper," Gilberto suggested as they were driving back toward the Alameda. "There seem to be plenty of places to eat."

Por gusto Lorenzo preferred to take his enchilada and his bottle of luke-warm soda outdoors.

"All right, but don't you want to wash up?"

"There is a fountain on one corner."

"My idea was to park ourselves and the truck and take it easy until morning."

"With your permission, Don Gilberto, I stay with the camión and the cargo."

They found a hotel—El Virreal, The Vice-Regal—on the Calle de Espe-ranza, around the corner from the Alameda, and Lorenzo waited in the truck until Gilberto came out, washed and with his hair combed. "There's a theatre practically around the corner. I will sit there in the front of the hotel and wait till you come back. Then I can go."

"Thank you, señor, but I do not care to go again."

"Again?"

"Sí, señor, some years ago I saw one of these films, at the cost of two pesos. The women were thin and ugly and the men appeared to be lovers of their own kind, if you will forgive me. They spoke a crude language and I was not able to read the labels under the pictures. . . . I was tricked, señor; I thought it would be a film about the herding of cattle or an intelligent dog." Gilberto smiled. "But, Don Gilberto, if you will have the kindness to wait here for one moment, I have a small errand."

"Con todo gusto."

Lorenzo trotted off around the corner and returned before Gilberto fin-ished his cigarette. He approached at a slower, dignified pace than the muleteer's trot with which he departed. There was pride and a trace of complacency in the man's expression. And Gilberto understood why that was when he glanced up and saw, in Lorenzo's shirt pocket, a memorandum book like his own and the gleaming brass head of a new mechanical pencil.

Before he reached the corner, Gilberto glanced back. Lorenzo was sitting in the chair that he had vacated in front of the hotel. His sombrero was tilted back, the notebook was open on his knee, and the pencil busy.

In a blue-tiled lunchroom he had two hamburguesas on split, white rolls called medianoches, midnights; and a vanilla-flavored leche malteada.

The night was chilly, and he felt a bit light-headed as he took the long way, around the Alameda, to the movie house. He recalled the long climb from a place called Laguna Seca and the way the carburetor behaved in the thinning atmosphere. Then, he remembered the road marker—Altura 270 Metros, easily 6,200 feet.

The picture was in the Spanish language, but made in Argentina, and it was one Lorenzo would have liked—about gauchos and cattle. But the story was corny: daughter of proud ranch owner falls in love with guy she thinks is common gaucho after he saves her life by stopping runaway horse; old man gives boy terrible lacing with bullwhip and drives him off the estate; girl wants to enter nunnery; on way there, boy and gang of pals hold up carriage and kidnap girl; old man relents and gives blessing after finding out that boy is son of old partner he rooked out of ranch and which had been on his conscience for many years.

The newsreel showed something of Mexico City; enough, perhaps, to prove to somebody who had been in both places that it looked like Paris, or it didn't. *Final Stages in the Construction of the Mexico City-Cuernavaca Speedway* also showed an aerial view of the newly built Ciudad Universitaria. There was the Archbishop of Mexico blessing the doors of a shoe factory and later sitting around with the officials and their wives, with a highball in his fist.

It was still early, not yet ten o'clock, when he left the theatre. A band was playing on the stand in the Alameda, a real military band of soldiers. The leader was an officer, with one gold star on his shoulder straps. The men wore dark green, well-used and well-washed uniforms with the number 12 in brass clips on their collars.

The benches were nearly all occupied, almost entirely by older people. The young promenaded around and around the band cupola, girls going one way and boys, the other. If he had a companion, he felt, he would enjoy promenading, too. Still, it was pleasant to sit for a while and watch.

When he stopped later at the truck, he looked in and Lorenzo was lying on the seat, face downward. At Gilberto's first tap on the window, he was up on his elbows, the shotgun ready.

"It's all right, Lorenzo, stay where you are. I'm going inside, Room Number Four, in case you need me."

"I was dreaming," Lorenzo said, smiling. "I was at the wheel of this coach and just approaching the pass at Santo Domingo. Ay, ¡qué suave!"

"Okay. Dream some more. Good night."

There was one dream that was going to come true, Gilberto decided. Sooner than Lorenzo thought. . . . See what happens, first thing in the morning—hand him the keys and say, "You take over, Lorenzo; back to Don Javier's place. You know the way."

In the tiny vestibule of the hotel, the owner, a Spaniard, handed Gilberto his key. There was a telephone on the narrow counter. He *could* call Don Solomón—make a routine report, like an agent to the home office. And maybe Doña Elena would answer, and he could ask about Inés. He had a hunch it would be good. . . . "And please, tell Don Solomón that what we

talked about last night—no, it isn't a secret any more—not from you, señora. . . . Yeah, the more I think about it, the bigger the glow I get from the
idea. . . . I hope Don Solomón can swing it for me. . . . Lorenzo is a great
help. . . . We ought to be getting back—back *home* late in the afternoon. . . ."

The Spaniard touched his arm and said, "Excuse me, señor, do you wish
to telephone?"

"No, thanks, no. I was just thinking—"

40

Within the first fifty kilometers on his own, Lorenzo demonstrated that he was not one of those clutch-riding, wheel-fighting drivers. At first, sharp turns, S curves, and dips caught him by surprise, until he learned to read "VADO," "CURVA PELIGROSA," "DESPACIO," and a few other highway signs. There was one— "CUIDADO CON EL GANADO," Watch Out for Cattle—that gave him trouble, but his eyesight was good enough to spot them well ahead; besides, he knew their habits. "If their heads are toward the ground," he explained to Gilberto, "they will remain so until you have passed. But, if their heads are up, they are pondering mischief."

At Santo Domingo, the place of his dream, he was sailing along at a good 70 k.p.h. Gilberto would be going faster, but for Lorenzo, this was doing fine.

The bridge over the Río Arenal, where Gilberto had his adventure, would be the acid test of Lorenzo's nerves. They were coming toward it—"PUENTE ANGOSTO"—when Lorenzo braked to a dead stop. He had seen something Gilberto did not see: two boys and four loaded burros a quarter of the way across from the other end.

Both kids thanked him politely for waiting, and he moved onto the bridge, tightening his lips. Gilberto instructed him calmly. "Loosen up—just enough to steady the wheel. Like that. . . . Good!"

Soon, the tops of the ahuehuetes of the Alameda showed. "Keep going," Gilberto said, "right up to the door."

Headed for the square, Lorenzo put his elbow on the window sill, as he had seen Gilberto do, and sounded the horn for an ambling pig. Not a soul was abroad to see him, Lorenzo cursed. Let him be astern of a lame mule and *everybody* would be out to mock him!

But there—and his heart leapt—coming out of El Surtidor were Don Solomón, Doña Elena, *and* Coronel Carrasco, who waved to them and entered his cream-colored Cadillac. When it pulled away, Lorenzo moved into its space under power and stopped. When he climbed out, he carried the shotgun in plain sight. Don Solomón could scold him, but it would be some time before he got around to it.

Doña Elena's kiss and Don Solomón's hug were as cordial as if Gilberto had been away for twenty-four days instead of that many hours. Margarita and Josefina, standing just within the patio entrance, squirmed with pleasure as he called to them, "¡Hola, muchachas!"

"Come with me—into the comedor, Gilberto," Don Solomón urged. "Margarita—beer into the comedor! Several bottles. . . . I have some news—"

Doña Elena cut him off. "This cannot wait! Into the sala. . . . Josefina! Coffee for Don Gilberto—and for me."

"Very well then," Don Solomón pouted. "But as soon as you have heard what she has to tell you—whatever it is, it cannot be—"

Doña Elena clung to his arm until they had entered the living room and she had closed the door. When she looked at him, her eyes shone. Some of the brightness was tears. "If you could have seen!"

There was no mystery about it; that what she had to say was about Inés. "The doctor was here—he said she was well?"

"No, no, no! He did not come. But she—she read your letter!"

"You read it to her."

"But sitting beside her, so that she could see every word as I pointed to it."

"How did she—?"

"Wait! Then she asked me to read it again—and now, I think she remembers every line. . . . Oh, Gilberto, you should have seen her face!"

"What did she say, señora?"

"Nothing. . . . But the way she looked—her eyes—when I gave it to her . . . And she folded it and put it under her pillow—and pressed her face against it, as if the letter was you."

"I wish I could tell you how really good that makes me feel. . . . You know, I almost called up last night from San Luis, on the chance, well, just to let you know that everything was fine, and hoping it was the same here."

"And we were thinking of you," she said, as Josefina came in with a tray. Doña Elena made him sit and drink a cup. "I wanted to call," she told him. "The telefonista could have tried every hotel in the city."

"I was at the Virreal."

"My husband said no; he worried that you would be disappointed that he could give you no news."

"But he has it now?"

She smiled. "Yes. Go and hear it, but don't let him play with you. . . . That man! Sometimes he behaves like a child."

"Yes, my boy, that was himself, Coronel Carrasco, whom you saw, and looking less like an ogre for the first time in years," Don Solomón said. "My wife had given him an injection, and he declared that he scarcely felt it. Dr. Zumbach was not able to come and he telephoned the coronel that in such emergencies, the Señora Gulden would attend to him; that she has the equipment and the supplies. He was furious when he called here, demanding that she go to Las Coronas; and completely enraged when I told him that he must come here."

"But he came, all right."

"And departed, as you saw, vowing that the German doctor was a butcher; that my wife was an angel and that hereafter he will expose his flanks, alternately, on Mondays, Wednesdays, and Fridays, only to her."

All very funny, Gilberto thought, even as he laughed. But the old man was doing just what Doña Elena warned him about: playing with him. What did all this have to do with the news he was supposed to impart? He asked, "Was that all he came for, to get an injection?"

"That's what he *thought*," Don Solomón answered. "He was not quite prepared for what I had to tell him. . . . We were together for two hours, the coronel and I. In your room, Gilberto."

Now it was coming; the bantering tone was gone from the old man's voice. "We borrowed a sheet of your writing paper, or didn't you notice?"

"No," Gilberto said. "I haven't been in there yet."

"Well, then," Don Solomón said, rising, "Let us go in, together."

He was still playing his little game, but it was nearing the finish. There was still smoke eddying slowly in the narrow room when they entered, and the fat butt of a cigar lay dead in the ash tray.

Gilberto walked directly to the small table by the window and found an envelope propped against a book. Don Solomón sat on the bed and watched as he picked it up. The writing on it, in a neat and angular hand, read, "Gral. de Brigada HECTOR VALDEZ, 'Quinta Carolina,' San Luis Potosí, S.L.P.

Gilberto read it: "*Gral* de Brigada?"

"General," Don Solomón said. "Brigadier General Valdez is retired, but Carrasco has sense enough not to remind him of it."

"The letter is open."

"Purposely, so that you may read what it says."

Gilberto glanced at the salutation: "Muy señor mío, estimado jefe y amigo."

"Do you know what's in it, Don Solomón?"

The old man laughed. He had one more fillip to his little game. "I have a sort of notion. You see, I dictated it to him. Here—I will read it for you. Sit down beside me." He put on his glasses and read:

> With this letter, which also carries my deepest respects, I wish to commend to your kindness the bearer, Gilberto Reyes M., of this place. Your superb memory, my dear friend, will instantly attach the name of Gilberto Reyes to another, who, like myself, has had the honor of serving under you during the Glorious Revolution. This youth before you is the legitimate grandson of that same valorous Maderista who shed his own and the enemy's blood at your heroic example.

"Is that really my grandfather you're talking about? I had no idea he was anybody."

"Everybody was somebody in those days. . . . He was a guerrilla, and without men like him, there would never have been a revolution." He read on:

> Today, representing his own generation, Gilberto Reyes M. returns to serve his people. With a superior education obtained in the

United States of the North, where he has lived since infancy (for family reasons), he brings back with him many skills. Notable among these is a mastery of forestation, silviculture, and crafts related to the noble work of conservation which the Citizen President of the Republic has decreed.

Naturally, the young Reyes dominates the English tongue, both spoken and written, and is dexterous with machines of commerce, like the typewriter and mechanical calculator.

This, then, is the youth who puts himself and his talents to the disposal of yourself, and such duty as the National Army may order him to perform.

I solicit you, my esteemed chief, that young Reyes be not embarrassed or delayed in his recruitment by lack of formal certificates pertaining to date and place of birth. For, in this regard, we of the military owe him that consideration.

"At this point," Don Solomón said, looking up from the letter, "Carrasco insisted on making his own explanation. This is what he says:"

You will surely recall, my general, that on the 20th May, 1938, when the main force of the traitor, Cedillo, moved upon your headquarters at Carmona, I deployed my cavalry, turning his flank. This maneuver cost us the temporary occupation of Zaragoza by a strong force of Cedillistas under Melitón Luna. Before my Fifth Battalion routed them, they had burned the Palacio Municipal and all the vital records of the population.

"Is that really what happened?" Gilberto asked.

"Yes, but not as Carrasco tells it. Here is the rest of it."

"Excuse me, Don Solomón; does this mean I could claim to be born here?"

"You claim nothing, Gilberto. The fact is, the parish priests keep separate records of the baptized and the dead. But since you are neither—well, listen—"

Although well and favorably known on his own account, I am, however, annexing attests to the good character of Gilberto Reyes M., subscribed by others, whose reputations should amply commend him to your distinguished patronage.

With nothing more to impart, and wishing you good health, I close, declaring myself affectionately, attentively, your servant and subordinate—Rodolfo Carrasco B., Colonel, Retired.

"That's the end," said Don Solomón, putting the letter back in the envelope.

"Who are the two letters of recommendation from?"

"Myself and—though it may surprise my wife—Don Perfecto. He will sign himself in full: Reverendo Perfecto Arellano, Society of Jesus. And I should not be afraid of what he will say. . . . When do you wish to go, Gilberto?"

It seemed strange to hear Don Solomón sound eager and even impatient; as if he were ready to hoist his bags, anxious to see him finally off.

"Back to San Luis Potosí—?" It wasn't easy to talk to the point or to say anything at a moment like this, which was the summing-up of all the factors of his existence.

The old man was not a simple onlooker to a man in the throes of decision. He touched the boy comfortingly. "Let me tell you, son, Carrasco is quite proud of what is written in that letter. He wants me to tell him how the letter was received—and about yourself."

"I guess he's entitled to know. . . . Starting back again today, that would bring me in too late, wouldn't it?"

"Unthinkable! Let us plan to have you in Monday, but not too early. . . . Shall I go with you?"

Gilberto thought a moment. "No, Don Solomón. I'll make it all right. Might as well start in being the person in that letter."

There was an entire weekend to get his affairs in order. Affairs—that sounded like a lot of important paperwork, when it was really nothing of the sort. Commitments, that's what they were. There was a commitment about Inés—and that was taken care of. Lorenzo—an intensive coaching tomorrow and the next day; and how good he would be eventually depended on how diligently he practiced.

It took ten minutes to draw up the account of the banana transaction: "Gross Sales 712.70. Expenses (Gas, Food, Hotel) 37.00. Net 675.70. Amount herewith."

But something was going to happen to him on Monday—if it happened at all—which, he imagined, called for some kind of "ringing document." A valedictory of some kind, or a letter of resignation which people would read and ponder and discuss, and say, "Reyes *had* something there! You can see he gave this thing some thought."

He tried to think of precisely what he was "resigning" from. Suppose a man working for one company resigns and goes to work for another outfit. They may not like it, but they accept his explanation that he wants to "better himself" and give him a testimonial dinner and a gold watch. Even so, he may be taking some of his former company's "secrets" to deliver to their rival.

Gilberto Reyes was delivering no secret data from the U.S. to Mexico. And since when was Mexico an enemy, or even a rival? The U.S. was so far ahead you couldn't even calculate. Okay, so he was taking a knowledge of trees—forestry—which he had acquired in work camp. What if he had been sent to San Quentin and learned how to make jute bags!

People have been resigning from countries as well as firms ever since—he thought back to the history he had learned—"Plymouth Rock, 1620, teacher." Earlier, in fact. All over the world there are bronze monuments, scratches on rocks, plaques and shrines with the dates when these resignations went into effect. For different reasons; shortages in some places, and too much of something else in others. Not enough potatoes in Ireland or spaghetti in Sicily. Too much misery in Poland and too little rye bread.

When people resign in mobs, they have each other to lean on and sing songs together while the CARE packages are being handed out to them. But it's lonely work when a fellow is doing the same thing solo.

He was tempted to compare himself to that regenerated monster in the schoolroom classic, *The Man Without a Country.* But it didn't hold. Gilberto had never wiped himself on the Stars and Stripes; for that matter, the last one he saw, he saluted. There was another difference: that fellow's name was Philip, not *Heel*-berto, and Nolan, not Reyes. And according to the Technicolor two-reeler they had shown in the McVeigh High auditorium, he was not a moreno like Reyes, but a rubio.

Whether he would miss them or not, Gilberto wasn't sure; but in this outfit he was going to join in San Luis Potosí, there weren't going to be any rubios. No "Whiteys," no "Swedes" or "Dutches" or "Limeys," and no Shapiros, either.

He almost shook Philip Nolan out of his mind, but he came back with a strong and sudden idea: When they kicked him out of the country, what did they do? Did they banish him to a foreign land? No! What they did was put him on board a ship that wouldn't touch land anyplace. They didn't even ask him where he thought he might be happier. The only guarantee that a man would be really without a country is to keep him from putting his foot into one. If once they put him ashore—anywhere in the world where there were people—the story of Philip Nolan would have an entirely different ending.

Margarita walked into the room as usual, without knocking. "If you are not occupied, Don Gilberto—"

"No, I have just finished. Does Don Solomón wish to see me?"

"No, señor. Pelancha sent me to inquire if she can see you for one little moment."

"Where is she?"

"In the patio. She will come in here, if she may."

He walked out, past Margarita. Pelancha stood in the shade, in the corner of the patio opposite Inés's room. The welcome that he first saw in her eyes was there again.

"Tía—"

She held him at arm's length, her hands on his shoulders, suddenly leaning toward him and kissing his face.

"I'm pleased that you know me again. What had I done that you acted so strange to me before?" he said. She shook her head in a way that meant she did not wish to be reminded of that. Gilberto understood this and asked, "Are you going in to see Inés—is she well enough?"

"I saw her; she is." But as she said it, her voice broke and tears began.

"Then why do you cry, Tía?"

"Because I cannot contain the great pride I have in you, Gilberto."

"I am going away, Tía. I wanted to say goodbye to you—in place of Inés, and for yourself as well. She thinks I have already gone." The woman nodded, and he continued. "But I am coming back."

"I know, Gilberto."

"Then, tell Inés. . . . It's a promise."

"She already knows."

"Then tell her again—keep saying it. Don't tell her you saw me; just say you *know* it."

She was about to say something, her lips for a moment parted. But she only nodded and turned to go by the iron door. "Where are you going now?" he asked.

"Home, where you found us."

"But Vargas—what if he—"

She began laughing, stopped long enough to say, calmly, "Vargas is not to be feared," and continued laughing as she stepped out into the callejón.

Gilberto went back to his room to change out of the cotton work clothes. He had meant to, but forgot to ask her about Inés, and more—why she had acted so peculiarly about shopping for a couple of bottles of tequila. It was no crime.

Church bells had been ringing since early in the morning, tinnily, like cracked kettles. Back in L.A. there was a set of bells on top of the church that Doheny, the oil man, built that you could hear almost to Compton. Gilberto, as he was shaving, thought how little he missed them. Giant firecrackers went off intermittently. Somebody was celebrating his saint's day.

As he was finishing and putting on his shirt, Lorenzo came to the bathroom door. "You have a visitor, Don Gilberto. Lucas Quintero begs a moment and waits in the store."

"Quintero?"

"Sí, señor, Lucas Quintero, operator of the Pegaso, the camión from Ciudad del Maíz. He says you will remember."

"I remember well enough," Gilberto said. "Tell him I'll be right out." He decided that if the guy was reasonable, he would be liberal with him. If he was nasty, he could—

Lorenzo handed him two fat, black cigars. "From Don Solomón." He put them absently in his shirt pocket.

The old man was puttering over by the small hardware and remained there as Gilberto walked toward the front of the Surtidor where Lucas waited. He looked utterly different, shaved and wearing a clean, white guayabera. In his left hand he held a small, wide-mouthed pottery jar. Offering his right to Gilberto, he said, "Your servant, Señor Reyes. I present my compliments."

"Okay. You have them back. What's on your mind?"

Lucas took off his hat and laid it across his breast. "I have come, señor, to offer my deep regrets for the way in which I carried myself on the evening when you were my passenger on Pegaso."

So—this wasn't what Gilberto expected the man's attitude to be. Or maybe it was just a buildup for something else. "There have been lies told about what happened on that trip," Gilberto challenged.

"I know, señor, and I wish to retract them, here, in the presence of Don Solomón."

"What—what?" The old man, pretending to have heard only his name, came forward.

"Lucas admits the accounts of what happened were false," Gilberto explained.

"Sí, señores, and I beg Don Gilberto to pardon me for my grossness and my conduct."

"I don't see how I could do anything else," Gilberto said. "Do you, Don Solomón?"

"I agree," the old man said. "Lucas, I know, is sincere."

"Muy bien, Don Lucas," Gilberto smiled and took the man's hand, pressing it hard.

"I thank you, Don Gilberto, and will you do me the honor of trying this small jar of dark honey? It is from my own hive."

"With great pleasure," Gilberto said and knew then what the cigars were for which Lorenzo had given him. "And will you please enjoy these?"

"Con todo gusto." Lucas took the cigars, smelled them, exclaiming, "¡Qué rico!" and laid them reverently in his sombrero. Smiling, he slipped a business card out of the brim of the hat and put it on the counter.

Gilberto read it aloud: "The Silver Arrow Line—Ciudad del Maíz-San Luis Potosí. Service of the First Class, Second Class, and Mixed Service, also Deluxe Tourist Coaches. Lucas Quintero C., Pilot." Lucas's name was written in.

"A sus órdenes." Lucas bowed. "We will be proud of your patronage, señores."

"Wonderful," said Don Solomón. "Don Gilberto will have occasion to use your service tomorrow."

"I begin my employment next week," Lucas said, "with a promise that I will be discharged the very first time I touch drink on the job."

"Good," Gilberto said. "I mean," he added quickly, "you will have much success. . . . What happened to your bus?"

"I have sold my machine."

"So Pegasus has run his course," Don Solomón said. "Did you obtain a good price?"

"Six hundred pesos, señor. Enough to post a finance bond and a hundred over. It has toiled fifteen years."

"Then I say it owes you nothing," Gilberto commented. "Oh, excuse me a minute—" Going behind the counter, he selected and tested a 20-peso flashlight. He handed it to Lucas. "For you, Don Lucas, and good luck."

"Oh, señor! Such a fine one! I do not merit it."

When Lucas left, Gilberto went to the cash register, rang up the amount, and deposited the money. Don Solomón watched him and said, "I am not vain enough to ask for a share in what you have just done, but I envy it."

Doña Elena called him in. It was time for his eye treatment. He went instantly, because he had this to tell her.

Lorenzo came in to report that he had X'd the tires and to ask for further instructions. Gilberto gave them: "Start the truck and park it in front of the Surtidor"—that simple.

"Do we depart on a mission?"

"Not that I know of. But you need the practice in getting in and out of the callejón."

Sergeant Vicente, walking rapidly toward the store, stopped and stared when he saw that it was Lorenzo indeed who had brought the truck up, stopped it flush with the curb, cut the engine, and stepped nonchalantly down. He passed Vicente with only a nod, but the policeman followed him into the store.

Lorenzo said nothing until he got behind the counter, at Gilberto's side. Then, "What can I do for you, sergeant?"

"I hoped to find Señora Esperanza de Vargas. I have information of an official sort for her."

"She has been here," Gilberto said. "Earlier, but has returned to her house. What is it about?"

"In what way are you concerned, señor?" Vicente asked huffily, taking out a frayed notebook. "Just the same, how well did you know Fidel Vargas? Appropriate sections of the law compel you to answer."

"I never saw him in my life."

"And you?" Vicente demanded, turning to Lorenzo.

"I hope I never know him better."

"I see," Vicente made a note. "And what is your occupation?"

"Confidential clerk in the tienda El Surtidor and chauffeur for the same."

"Formerly—?"

"Formerly muleteer," Lorenzo answered calmly.

Vicente, seeing that he had impressed nobody with his note taking, Lorenzo least of all, put his pencil away, lit a cigarette, and said, "Well, Formerly Muleteer, you have your wish. Only God will know Fidel Vargas better—if it is indeed and for certain he, whose remains they found in the barranca, by the old aqueduct. I have said it was Vargas, but the Rurales wish him identified by another. That is why I seek Pelancha."

"I am at your service, sergeant. Show me the body," Lorenzo said.

"Only the head. We have it in a basin of ice at the police casita."

"With your permission, Don Gilberto," Lorenzo said, "the casita is not far," and prepared to leave.

"There is no hurry," Vicente said. "It is not a cherub, simply a head, and it will not fly away. . . . And, Lorenzo, if you wish to avenge him on behalf of Pelancha, that has already been done."

"They know who killed him?" Gilberto asked.

"Beyond a guess," the policeman said. "Sergeant Villanueva of the Rurales reconstructs it this way, and I concur. Listen—" He stopped, swallowed hard, and licked his lips. "This dust—"

"Lorenzo, please bring the sergeant a beer."

"Warm, if you please, Lorenzo. A man must guard his lungs against fever." He swallowed some beer and continued. "Had Villanueva moved against those three shameless ones earlier, Fidel Vargas need not have died, you see."

"From the begining, Vicente," Lorenzo said. "What three?"

"Ah, you haven't heard. Naturally not—a police matter," Vicente resumed. "But earlier, these three—scum from the Serrano, beyond Ovejas, it is supposed—gave death to a railroad guard and stole all the brass fitments off a carriage. They were afoot and could not have gotten beyond the east edge of Los Basaltos, where Vargas may have been hiding and where they undoubtedly encountered him, as events proved. Now to the scene!" He drank the rest of the beer and gestured for another, which Lorenzo promptly brought him.

"The scene, Vicente—"

"But only as we police *suppose* it to have happened," Vicente warned. "At first, Vargas, being himself a fugitive and of the district, hence, knowing that the best place to hide was at the head of the old aqueduct, was taken as an ally. Evidently, they began to drink. Not what you might call a parranda, with only two bottles to be shared by four, but enough to loosen tongues. My belief is that Vargas boasted he had money."

"The source of which," Lorenzo said, "one is free to guess."

Vicente shrugged, drank, and went on. "However, they hacked Vargas's head off and cast him into the barranca."

Lorenzo said, "One may suppose also that he simply told him what *he* had done and thereby sealed his doom."

"In any event, señores, he was dispatched without a struggle and, mind you, by his own machete. Poor Fidel's blood still stained it when Villanueva and his men caught the assassins. They denied it, but their guilt was plain."

"Are they bringing them in?" Gilberto asked.

"No, señor, they were left lying where they fell. . . . What else could the Rurales do? Mira—Sergeant Villanueva and his troopers turn their backs to do an act of nature—"

"All at the same time?"

"And why not? . . . And so these fools from the hills commence to run, and—" Vicente pantomimed the raising of a carbine and clucked his tongue three times.

Gilberto did not look away from a spot on the opposite wall until Lorenzo left with the policeman, and until he became aware that he was staring at the bare place on the display board on which had hung a broad-bladed, 17-peso machete. Slowly, calculatingly, he crossed the store and hung another blade in its place.

Lorenzo had been gone only a few minutes. They looked squarely into each other's eyes, and Lorenzo spoke first. "Sí, señor, it was Fidel Vargas."

"I think I ought to inform Don Solomón, don't you?"

"By all means, señor."

Doña Elena watched Gilberto's face during all the time he spoke, telling it almost exactly in the language of Vicente's report. She did not look frightened, only grave. Don Solomón, lying there, with his eyes covered, listened quietly also, but wagged his head from time to time.

Up to the end, Gilberto had refrained from mentioning the weapon—let it be assumed, he thought. But the compulsion to make certain that they would not ask made him say finally, "They killed him with his own machete; there was blood on it."

It was quiet in the room for a long minute, for two, until Don Solomón spoke hollowly, like a man in his sleep.

Gilberto heard: ". . . atonement and two—one for blood and one into the wilderness—for Azazel . . ." but its meaning was sealed to him.

Gilberto and Don Solomón stood away, observing Lorenzo politely and efficiently selling three meters of manta, unbleached cotton cloth. When he looked their way, Don Solomón pretended to have his attention elsewhere. "Later, Gilberto, you might find Lucas and arrange with him to drive our truck back from Ciudad del Maíz tomorrow."

"I could, if you think that's the best way. But I think Lorenzo can handle it all right—with Lucas along, just the same."

"Very well. And since you are going first to present yourself to General Valdez instead of to the Comandancia Militar, you need not arrive in San Luis before the afternoon."

It was not so strong when he himself remembered that he was leaving. But when, as now, somebody else brought it up, he felt chilly and hot by turns, and his heart pounded.

Lorenzo was concluding his sale. "Manta, of the quality of two-eighty a meter; three meters, eight-forty." He rolled the cloth into a neat cylinder. "Ten pesos—" He rang it up and carefully counted out her change. "Para servirle, señora, y gracias."

Another customer, a man, came in and moved hesitantly toward the farm hardware and Lorenzo promptly offered his services. The man was interested in a zapapico. Gilberto had never heard that word and wondered what it was. Lorenzo probed in one of the bins and found it—a mattock.

"He is getting to know the stock," Don Solomón said, pleased.

"I was thinking he could use my civilian clothes and things," Gilberto said.

"In time, Gilberto; when you return, on leave, after your enlistment. How long after? Immediately—as soon as you have been examined and inscribed on the army rolls, you are given some days in which to settle your civilian and family affairs. At least I know that has been done for some boys in this region."

Lorenzo's customer did not buy the zapapico, "But," Lorenzo explained, "I have put one aside—AB.EJ, twelve-fifty—and he will return on Thursday with his brother to examine it. . . . And, señores, may I ask a great favor?"

"Is it money—do you wish an advance?" Don Solomón asked.

"No, señor. I have enough; both to hire of Miguel Fuentes his magnificent horse, El Sultán, and for that handsome box of chocolates there in the showcase."

"I begin to see," Don Solomón said pleasantly. "With the finest animal in the valley and the richest box of candy, what a man lacks is time."

"That is the favor I request," Lorenzo said, and continued in a perfectly even, serious tone. "I wish to undertake the courtship of Doña Esperanza, with your permission, señores." He included, quite deliberately, Gilberto in his bow.

"I wish you luck in your suit," Don Solomón said, and Gilberto added, "So do I." And Don Solomón finished, "But don't you think it is too soon after—after what happened?"

Lorenzo agreed. "Sí, señor. I am waiting until the afternoon."

Don Solomón roared at him, "Then why are you standing here? ¡Córrele! Go shave, see to the horse—and some pretty flowers!" Watching him go, he said to Gilberto, "Pelancha and Lorenzo—they will be good for each other. . . . I'm thinking—that hand-breadth of land opposite, in the callejón—if they want to put up a little house . . ."

"I like him," said Gilberto.

41

The proprietor of the Hotel Virreal greeted Gilberto like an old and honored guest and gave him the same room. "You will stay longer this visit, I hope, Señor Reyes?"

"I cannot say until I have—First, can one telephone the Quinta Carolina?"

"The estate of General Valdez—to be sure. Allow me." He gave no number, simply asking for the Quinta Carolina, and handed the telephone to Gilberto.

A woman answered the ring, and he asked politely, "May I speak to somebody regarding an appointment to see General Valdez?"

"The general is sick."

"I am sorry to hear that."

"Of his gall bladder."

"When do you think he will be better?" Gilberto inquired.

"At four o'clock, not sooner. Who speaks?"

"My name is Gilberto Reyes M., of Zaragoza, with the compliments of Coronel Carrasco and a letter from the same."

"Very well, coronel, I shall tell his man, Silvestre."

The woman hung up before he could correct her.

"You go to see the general with a petition?" the hotel owner asked.

"Just a letter of introduction."

"Then let me advise you, señor; if you wish him to read it, a gratuity for his flunky would be well spent. It is in his power to thwart you."

"Good idea," Gilberto said. "About how much should I slip him?"

"I would not try less than a peso; two, if you can afford it."

A three-peso ride in a coche libre left him on a hilly road, a stretch on which substantially built homes alternated with huts, jerry-built and askew on the edges of bean fields. The Quinta Carolina was a medium-sized monstrosity of green cement and gray stone, with small crenellated towers in imitation of a Norman castle. But it had a broad lawn of Bermuda grass with big, old shade trees and a brick walk from the gate to the front door.

"Do you want me to wait for you?" the cab driver asked. Gilberto did not know how long he would be. How much was waiting time? "I'll give you an hour, free; after that, three pesos," the driver suggested, and Gilberto agreed. When the gardener unlocked the gate for him and nodded toward the house, it was as if he had been expected.

But at the door, he waited a long time after ringing until it was opened, by a woman, probably the one who answered the telephone.

"I am Señor Reyes."

"Yes, the coronel."

"No, the coronel sends a letter by me."

Indifferently, she left him standing in the sky-lighted hall from which three flights of stairs radiated to the scrambled upper reaches, and five doors. He had time to fold a five-peso note between his fingers before one of the doors opened and Silvestre appeared. Tall, thin and wrinkled, but with luxuriant black hair, Silvestre wore a light tan military jacket over a pair of blue serge zoot pants. His first words were, "The general sees nobody. Tell your business to me."

"I present the compliments of Coronel Rodolfo Carrasco and this letter," Gilberto said, handing over the letter and the five pesos together. Silvestre skewered a look at the bill and palmed it, then making the finger sign for "one moment, please," he left.

Gilberto waited five, ten, fifteen minutes in the chairless hall. He wanted to smoke, but there were no ashtrays or even a window out of which to flick a butt. At last Silvestre opened one of the five doors. "Follow me, please."

A gloomy passage, lined with case upon case of soda water, led to a wide, stone terrace and a beautiful garden. The general sat under a plum tree, in a footbath of newspapers. He had a Foxy Grandpa beard that looked more like feathers than hair and wore a bathrobe, the really old-fashioned kind that tied with a string at the neck and ballooned out from there. He was old—more than 80—and seemed to be asleep, with Carrasco's letter in his lap.

"The young man, my general," Silvestre said, partially rousing him. "From Carrasco."

"Carrasco—?"

"Yes, my general, of the Fourth Regiment."

That information brought the general fully awake. "Oh, *that* manure-headed payaso!" he squeaked. "What does he say in this dispatch—" he fumbled with the letter. "*My* headquarters at Carmona! *His* Fifth Battalion! Melitón Luna's flank! Why, Luna had *invested* Zaragoza and would have torn Carrasco's flabby ass off if I hadn't sent artillery, Batteries E and B, to lay down covering fire. And that baboon declares here that *my* headquarters was being moved on. ¡Fijarte!"

"Exactly so," Silvestre agreed.

"You there!" the general pointed to Gilberto, "Sit down," and stabbed at the lawn. "I'll show you what I mean. . . . This letter says you have been given a superior education."

"I make no pretensions, my general," Gilberto said.

"Anyway, you remember the Battle of Stone River—"

"I am sorry, general—"

"Good! My headquarters at Cumbres de Carmona were situated in the same relation to Zaragoza as Johnson's to Murfreesboro. And let us say that the Confederate Breckenridge is Cedillo and Hardee is Melitón Luna. McCook, then, would be my Carrasco. Understand?"

"Yes, my general."

"Good. . . . Where was I, Silvestre?"

"McCook, my general. . . . I think you should rest."

The general ignored his batman and fixed his sharp and very blue eyes on Gilberto. "I read that you are something of a woodsman, joven. A fine thing to know. Anderson showed Meade on the first day of the Battle of Chancellorsville a style of forest offensive that . . ." The rest of it was unintelligible mumbling.

Gilberto looked up at Silvestre, who motioned for him to get up and wait in the entrance hall.

This time he smoked, hiding the burnt match and the ashes in his pants cuff. There were still 25 minutes of the hour left; then only 20, and 15. At ten minutes, Silvestre reappeared with the letter in his hand, and at the same instant Gilberto heard the engine of the cab start. Opening the door, he hissed for the driver's attention and signaled him to wait.

"Well, what does he say?"

Silvestre simply took the letter out of the envelope, uncreased it, and handed it over, his thumb indicating a line scrawled in pencil on the bottom of the paper. "Show this to Major Cabañas, first floor front, at the Comandancia."

"Major Cabañas—now?"

"Pues, sí."

In the cab, Gilberto read the General's quavery notation: "V⁰ B⁰—¡Un buen mozo! H. Valdez B., Gral. de Brigada." It meant Visto Bueno, the same as O.K. A good boy!

Soon, he felt, he would know the terms in military language for all that he saw around him; for the men who passed back and forth from the corridor where he waited to a railed area. It resembled a busy insurance agency, with soldiers instead of female employees at desks, typing, filing, telephoning.

He had been treated politely from the moment the sentries admitted him through the gates of the headquarters, 12th Military Zone. It confused him to be saluted a few times on his way across the court to the administration building of the headquarters, and again by the solider who took his letter into an office marked: Major CABANAS, Ayudante. In English, that meant adjutant, which meant assistant—same thing; but to whom? What did that braided cord running through the soldier's epaulette signify? How do you tell a top-sergeant? Those were the guys who, when they said, "Jump!" you jumped. . . . That John Wayne picture with him breaking the heart of that frightened kid, until the payoff, and then—

A buzzer rasped. "Go in, please."

Major Cabañas had the letter open on the desk and was frowning over it. A big-chested man, the top buttons of his jacket were open, showing that he was wearing a gold Guadalupe medal. He glanced up at Gilberto, and, although there was a chair, he did not ask him to sit.

"Gilberto Reyes, eh?"

"A sus órdenes."

"The M?"

"Martínez, señ—mayor."

"Have you known Coronel Carrasco, retired, for long?"

"No, mayor," Gilberto fumbled. "But my friends—I have here letters. From Don Solomón, from the Reverend Don Perfecto—"

"Just the first one. Never mind the priest." Major Cabañas took the letter and, without stopping to read it, stapled it to the one which General Valdez had endorsed. Looking more keenly at him, he said, "You're sure you want to come in?"

What Gilberto wanted to answer was, "Certainly, that's why I'm here." But he remembered that the best answers were the briefest. "Yes, sir."

"You have passed your eighteenth year?"

"Yes, sir, my nineteenth also."

"How is it you didn't answer conscription call for your year?"

Confused, Gilberto swallowed and pointed to the letter. "That—er—I thought—"

"Never mind; it's explained here. You were in the States, studying." The major pressed a button on the wall. It brought in a short, pale fellow who wore thick eyeglasses and carried a notebook, opening it on his knee as he sat opposite the major.

"Ready, sergeant? . . . Make out the proper enlistment forms. Name, Gilberto Reyes Martínez." He pointed to identify him to the sergeant. "Date of birth?"

"Twelfth March," Gilberto answered and gave the year in the Mexican fashion, "One thousand nine hundred and thirty-three."

"Name of father?"

"Fernando Reyes."

"Mother?"

"Elvira Martínez de Reyes."

"Okay," the major said, "attend to the rest of it outside, sergeant. I've got a lot of work here. Observe the pertinent material in this letter, countersigned by General Valdez, and attach to enlistee's file. One more thing: make note of the man's special qualifications—languages, crafts, and so forth—and copy them on Form 811, to the attention of all company commanders. That's all. . . . Go with the sergeant, Reyes."

Even the sergeant made him stand while he jotted things in his notebook, occasionally consulting the letter.

"I see there's a space there for my height and weight. Don't you want to know that?"

"You will be weighed and measured, and your teeth counted," the sergeant said, without looking up.

"When is that?" He got no answer and a minute later ventured, "I didn't get your name, sergeant—"

"'Sergeant' will do whenever you have occasion to speak to me, until you are a non-commissioned officer yourself, which seems unlikely."

Wise guy! Just because he happens to be the secretary to the adjutant—

"Sign here, Reyes." The sergeant offered his pen. Gilberto declined it and took out his own. "Let's see that pen, Reyes. . . . Huh, it's not a Parker."

"No," said Gilberto, "it's better."

"How much did it cost?"

"Six fifty."

"I'll buy if from you. I'll give you ten."

"Dollars," Gilberto said, "not pesos, is what I meant. Anyway, it's not for sale."

"You know, I could do you a lot of favors, Reyes."

"I'll think about it. What do I do now?"

"Wait," the sergeant said, "I'll give you this slip. Then you can go home. But report back here, Gate Five, in twenty-four hours for your physical. That means seven o'clock in the morning."

"Tomorrow?"

"Well—make it Wednesday," the sergeant said. "I'll date your papers as of tomorrow. . . . You see, I'm doing you a favor already."

"Well, thanks, Sergeant—"

"Espinoza—Tiberio Espinoza C. . . . I must have your address."

"I live in Zaragoza, but I'm staying here at the Hotel Virreal. Is there a cab stand around here?"

"Hey! What the hell is this! Living in a swank hotel, riding coches to and from the post, fancy fountain pens! Damn! If you weren't sponsored by the Old Chief, I'd swear you were a spy."

Gilberto laughed; they laughed together and the sergeant punched him on the shoulder. "No kidding, Reyes—this set of threads you're wearing; how about lending it to me some night?"

"Sorry, kid, I already promised them to my chauffeur."

He found out when he returned to the hotel, from Uruarte, the owner, the source of General Valdez's immense influence. The old gent was the father-in-law of three commanders of military zones and one cabinet officer.

"Is the military band playing tonight in the plaza, Señor Uruarte?"

"They should," the man answered. "They need the practice!" And he howled. Everybody was funny today, Gilberto noticed.

"I'll be checking out day after tomorrow, Wednesday, very early in the morning."

"And your business with the general, it is completed successfully?"

"It's getting along, thanks." He didn't know why he had to be so cozy about it. It was no secret, and he was brimming to talk to Don Solomón.

Later, after he himself calmed down to where he could report just the facts. Nobody could tell; a hitch may develop somewhere along the line. Not until he had a uniform on his back, he decided, could he safely say that he was in.

They must be anxious. If there was a telephone in his room, he would call them now. But the only one was on the counter in the tiny lobby. Later, then. He would ask Uruarte for the boon of a little privacy and put the call in.

In the room, he filled the wash basin, stripped off his shirt, and had begun to lather his chest when he paused. . . . A minute ago, it seemed the right thing to do—to dude up, go out on the town; see people, faces; pack in the best meal in town with maybe a glass or two of that wonderful Manzanilla. Now, suddenly, in the midst of preparing for it, that feeling vanished. For no reason at all, or for plenty of good reasons, the beat slowed. There was nothing morbid about it; no more than if a fellow getting all set to go out to a movie suddenly changes his mind and decides that instead, he'll stay in and read a book. It's purely a private decision either way, and no reasons have to be given to anybody. But if he were pinned down for one, such as being asked, "What's the matter; you sick or something?" it wasn't hard to make one up.

Drying his face, Gilberto furnished himself with an easy explanation of his change of mood: Bad business to eat heavy before a medical examination. Rich foods form gas. Liquor shows up in the glass of specimen. Excitement— you know, the gash department—works on the blood pressure and you get a bad heart-reading.

So, the thing to do was relax, eat light and put in plenty of sack time. He smiled, wondering if the Mexican doctor would prod him like a side of beef and say, "Pretty good specimen—for a gringo."

He felt in his pocket for a cigarette. It was the last in the package, and he sat down to smoke it. He would get a fresh pack on the way to supper. . . . This was an evening pretty much like his first in Mexico, in Ciudad Victoria, when he lay there, giving himself arguments—pro and con—about going out. The trouble there was that he was loaded, thousands of pesos. All he had on him now was a couple of hundred; small risk there.

It all began coming back to him; the band, the measured shuffle of the dancers in the plaza, Mauricio-at-your-service. . . . "I will ask the galopina, señor." And Rafaela, as she offered to mend for him. Then "Ay, Sandunga" and his mother's voice. The machos, dead and alive, and all the people of the newspaper mixed up with those of the vibrant streets.

And again Rafaela; her thighs and breasts yellow and burnt gold. . . . *Why don't I wish it hadn't happened with her, huh? Because I'm glad it did, that's why. Just as I'm glad now that it never came off with that needle-nosed bitch, Carolyn. For the monkeys! . . . But why didn't Rafaela take money? I offered it to her, and that would have been the end of it. Ah, but that's just why she turned it down. Get smart, boy. What's worth more to a woman—a few lousy pesos or that she'll never be forgotten? "So that you won't need to be ashamed with a woman," was what she said. Not me any more, Rafaela; it's somebody else I've got to help over being ashamed.*

With much buzzing of the lines and hammering, the connection was made in twelve minutes—he timed it. "Listo, San Luis—Zaragoza is ready, señor. Commence to speak."

"Can you hear me all right, Don Solomón?"

"Yes, yes, my boy, keep talking. Tell me all that has happened."

"So far everything is fine," Gilberto said. "I just hope it keeps on like this. Yes, it all happened one, two, three. I'll save the details for when I see you. Very funny; the old general is a sketch, but he certainly swings a lot of weight. Tomorrow—Wednesday, I mean—I'm all mixed up—I get my physical."

"We are all excited, too," Don Solomón said. "Then you can come home tomorrow."

"Come home" sounded warm and wonderful, with a special glow of its own that he could renew whenever he wanted to warm his heart. "I couldn't," he said. "I have to be at the place early in the morning and that would be cutting it too fine."

"Yes, you have reason, Gilberto."

"What I'll do is spend the day taking it easy, like a boxer in front of a big fight. Incidentally, Don Solomón, your letter was the only one the major paid any attention to. Didn't want the priest's, but thank him just the same."

"Do you need anything, Gilberto? Have you enough money?"

"Plenty to carry me till pay day. You see, I'm talking like a soldier already. Anyway, the next time you see me, I'll be in a uniform—on this furlough I'm getting."

"¡Qué bueno! Now another wishes to speak to you."

"It is so good to hear you again, Berto."

"And you, too, Doña Elena." He wanted to tell her that there was only one other voice that he would like to hear with as much pleasure. "Are you all well—at home?" It occurred to him that he had been away a little more than twelve hours.

She must have been thinking the same thing; she said, "Already we miss you; the house is sadder. But here is something to make you all the happier: a letter from Inés."

"I can't believe it! Not till you read it to me."

"Oh, not yet; we are still writing it. But it will be waiting here for you, when you come home."

How natural that sounded— "... come home." "... Solomón says it may be Thursday."

"I'm not sure, Doña Elena; but as soon as they let me, I won't waste any time."

His resolution to eat lightly quavered when he sat down in a small restaurant, which he chose because he could sit facing the plaza. There was no menu card, as he learned when a waitress set in front of him a sherbet glass brimming with diced alligator pear and a gravy dish of high-test salsa mexicana. It looked appetizing enough, and when he asked the girl what else there was, she said, "As usual, the comida corrida. With chicken, twenty-five centavos extra; with *breast* of chicken, fifty; with duck, sixty." Without the premium, the main dish, she said, was biftec con cebollas y papas fritas, con una surtida de verduras.

Before that, there was a thick soup with a veal knuckle in it and a piece of fried fish which tasted as if it were whittled from the same bone—but not bad.

The biftec, he hoped, would be a tibón. Instead, it was a piece of pan-fried rump with a heap of singed onions on one side of it and the potatoes on the other. The assortment of "greens," which turned out to be three distinct varieties of squash, came in plastic side dishes. As he hacked at the meat, the waitress took the knife out of his hand, stropped it on the edge of the stone table top, and handed it back to him.

She gave him the names of the assorted bottled soda, which came with the dinner—"Or coffee and beer, which is again extra." For dessert there was a medallion of flan, a terribly oversweet custard.

With the beer and the tip, the bill was five pesos. Half this much food would cost twice as much, even in a place like the Café Orizaba back—he almost said, home—in Los Angeles.

While paying, he asked her, "Is there going to be a band concert tonight?"

"No, señor; Thursday."

"Too bad. I was going to ask you to sit out a couple of numbers with me." As soon as he said it, he realized that he sounded—to himself, if not to the waitress—like the typical wisecracker. Feeling good was no excuse for acting like a crumb.

But the woman said, quite seriously, "A fine time I'd have, with my man keeping one eye on his music and the other on me! My Plutarco blows upon a pífano." She imitated a fife. "And the Holy Mother guard my ribs if, on band nights, I'm not out there with the kids. . . . But thanks just the same, señor."

Her taking it that way gave him back his esteem. Leaving the restaurant, he made directly for the picture theatre on the opposite side of the square. There were two features, and he was not sure that he had not already seen them, since they now had titles in Spanish. But the names of the stars stayed the same: Esther Williams, Montgomery Clift, Caesar Romero.

Standing away, he studied the lithographs for a hint as to the kind of films they were, since all were ticketed in the language of the trailers as "comedy," "action," "Western," "super-Western," and "society-melodrama."

Movie going, for Gilberto, had never been a matter of killing an hour, but of making one live. Some guys do that with a bottle and some, with a marijuana cigarette. This was cheaper and less wear and tear on the nerves.

For the next hour or longer he could be either or both of those two splendid fellows; living their lives and loving their loves. That is, he could, if he had no life and no love of his own and wasn't happy with being who he was.

The more he thought about it, the less enthusiasm he had for being—even for fifteen minutes—either Caesar Romero or Montgomery Clift, or any of the

Hollywood pantheon. Satisfied with being Gilberto Reyes M., he walked away. If he felt like it, he could come back tomorrow. And if they changed the bill, the new people would be just as attractive. But right now, he didn't need them.

Uruarte, at the hotel, was disappointed that Gilberto had already eaten. Had he waited until the civilized hour of ten, he could have been served here. "More wholesomely, and at less cost."

"By ten, I expect to be in bed," Gilberto said. "How about breakfast?"

"Good! You will have something to open the eyes. Then, a good, rich and savory gazpacho; a slice or two, as thin as cigarette paper, of jamón de serrano; an egg beaten into a little sherry to clear the throat; a tender chop, or, if you have not tasted it for a while, bacalao a la vizcaína—as I served it in my fonda, Las Mandarinas, in Bilbao."

Gilberto was a corn flakes and oatmeal man himself. But that sounded good. He had no idea that a gazpacho was a thick soup with a base of dried bread, impregnated with garlic and vinegar. But he had eaten bacalao, dried codfish, in the imitation Biscayan style, and liked it. "I know I shall enjoy it all," he said. "But soon I will not be able to afford such splendid meals. But I shall recommend your place, certainly."

"I thank you, Señor Reyes, since I can hope for only refined clients like yourself, among Mexicans. Most do not like to patronize a Spaniard, so I must be content with the overflow from the other hotels."

"What kind of prejudice *is* this? If they get good treatment and their money's worth—"

"They regard me—I mean the ignorant people—as a gachupín; sometimes as venomously as they look upon norteamericanos—gringos. But I owe them much. I have been ordained a citizen of Mexico, with full rights, by their president, Don Lázaro Cárdenas, when I escaped those bloody foulers of their fathers' beds, Sanjurjo and Franco."

"Don't you ever miss your own country?" Gilberto asked.

"Why? Who mourns for dry and stingy soil, hombre! When I weep, I weep for España, as symbolized by the Spaniards who died there."

"You ever expect to see the old country again?"

"Not in this life, joven! My countrymen have made their own Spain here: the Panteón Español."

The cemetery. The guy had it right, Gilberto agreed. When the day comes, it doesn't matter whether they plant you in Spain, Mexico, Jerusalem, or the Forest Lawn Burial Park, where he didn't think they sold space to Mexicans anyhow. Why, there were pet cemeteries in California where they wouldn't take a Mexican's dog!

It was so quiet in the room and throughout the little hotel that he was sure he was the only guest. He would see, though, in the morning, when he sat down to that noble breakfast. He hoped there would be others, for Uruarte's sake. Won't *he* be surprised to see him coming back Wednesday in a uniform with a pair of brass 12s on the collar tabs!

Stuffing his wadded shirt into the bottom of the bag, he felt the edge of a piece of folded letter paper and drew it out.

> Well, Bish, this being about all the news I got, I will close now . . . and everything and hoping . . . a line. Your friend, Gil ("The Thumb") Reyes.

He smoothed the letter, took out his fountain pen, and wrote:

> P.S.: About that forestry job above. It looks like I nailed it all right. Pulled some wires, generals and stuff, and tomorrow I'm signing the contract. Government work, out of San Luis Potosí. Will let you know permanent address in my next. The best. Gil.
>
> P.P.S.: Glad to say Inés (see above) getting along O.K. Family all on my side now, but no date set yet. Will let you know. G.R.

He got Bishop's business card out of his wallet and addressed an envelope.

42

The sun showed every vein in the wall when he woke up. What time was it . . . ? Ten after nine . . . *What* a snooze! Ten hours by the clock. And he felt something had wakened him or he'd have been sleeping yet. Naked, he left the bed and started across the room to the washstand; there was no bathroom nearer than the hall outside. There was a sharp rap on the door.

"Who knocks?"

A key turned, Gilberto sprang to the bed, but the door opened before he got there. A boy entered with a water tumbler half full of some liquid in his hand.

"Who are you?"

"Gonzalo, señor; the mozo here, at your service." Extending the glass, he explained, "The patrón sends you this, and begs it will be to your taste."

"What is it?"

"It is what he himself takes each morning for his health. . . . He asks to know when you will descend to your breakfast."

"Fifteen minutes."

When the boy left, Gilberto smelled the stuff in the glass. It was almost odorless and pale yellow. He tried a sip. . . . Manzanilla! Then, sip by sip, he finished the wine by the time he was dressed.

His breakfast was served in the comedor, at the only table in it—a large one which could seat eight. And it was a fact; he was the only guest. None of the tasties that Uruarte had promised him, not one, appeared on the table. But he had explanations for everything: For failure of some vital ingredient, the gazpacho would not "blend"; the tenderloin chop, which he had seen with his own eyes in the ice chest, had been "alienated"—vandals; the bacalao—he had tasted a pinch himself—could not be served without damage to the reputation of his house until it had lain soaking for another four hours in rich milk.

But Gilberto was famished—the Manzanilla had done that—and he relished the substitutes. It was the first time he had eaten pink-fleshed grapefruit, hot, glazed with honey, and broiled. Then an omelet of onions, peas, bits of potato and mild peppers, with a steaming heap of chorizo came on. The coffee was strong and black.

Gilberto was luxuriating in his second cup when Uruarte rushed in, pale. "Soldiers, Señor Reyes! They are stopping here! For you?"

"I guess so."

The tiny call-bell outside on the counter was being pounded insistently. Uruarte wrung his hands. "What shall I tell them, señor; what shall I do?"

"Nothing. If they're looking for me, tell them I'm here."

The poor guy was really shaking, Gilberto sympathized; probably still terrified by that Franco. Lighting a cigarette, he saw that his own hand was twitching.

A solider, dark-skinned and so broad of shoulder that he almost filled the doorway, entered the comedor ahead of Uruarte, advanced to Gilberto, and saluted. "Señor Reyes Martínez?"

"Yes—"

The soldier saluted again, holding his hand to his cap while he said, "Subteniente Gaytán Zamora, a sus órdenes, compliments of First Captain Jiménez," and putting a slip of paper in front of Gilberto.

It was headed: XII REGION MILITAR (S.L.P.), and the rest of it was a few lines of typing: "The recluta—recruit—Gilberto Reyes Martínez, domiciled at the Hotel Virreal, City, to report immediately to the undersigned, under escort; vehicle to be provided." Under "Compañía A—7° Regimiento de Caballería," was the name Arturo Jiménez V., Capitán 1°, Comandante, and the signature.

"I'll go with you directly, lieutenant," Gilberto said, rising.

"My bill, señor—" Uruarte wailed.

"Here is twenty pesos on account," Gilberto said. "My clothes are still here. And there is a letter on the commode, if you will be good enough to purchase a stamp and post it."

"Sí, señor."

"And if there are any inquiries for me by telephone, please say that I shall return later."

Uruarte watched him leave. . . . Yes, he would post that letter this instant; a farewell message to loved ones. In his day, when the Requetes—those bringers of their sisters to shame—seized people in Las Mandarinas, he would be stuck for hundreds of pesetas. Here, he was already at least six pesos to the good, and inside there was a bag of clothing.

The vehicle provided was a snappy Jeepster, with the top down. The lieutenant drove, and beside him sat a private, or possibly a non-com. Gilberto didn't know the insignia yet.

Alone, in the rear seat, it was hard to make conversation—if you could call it that. Gilberto felt as if he were doing all the talking.

"You know, I wasn't due till tomorrow till tomorrow morning for my physical, so I can't figure what this is all about. I'm not complaining, but I *would* like to know." But he got no help from the lieutenant. Maybe, if he tried a direct question, military habit would fetch an answer. "Who is Captain Jiménez?"

"My commander, señor."

"And what about Major Cabañas?"

"The adjutant, señor."

"Then whose orders go here?"

The lieutenant hesitated for only a few seconds. "Anybody's, who is of superior rank." Ambiguous, but the lieutenant seemed quite pleased at having stated it.

They entered the post through the main gates, Gilberto enjoying the way the sentries alertly presented arms, and the salutes given and returned. The Jeepster pulled up at the steps of a large frame building painted yellow, and the soldier opened the car door while Gilberto was still fumbling with the latch.

The lieutenant gave an order, "Conduct the señor directly to the captain. He is waiting." He saluted once more and drove off.

Gilberto followed the soldier to the rear of the long building's lower floor and saw that the back of it opened on a dusty field in which a hundred or more horses were corralled. The soldier knocked on the last door in the corridor, and a strong, clear voice inside said, "Enter."

The soldier saluted a man at the desk in a tiny, almost bare office, and put the typed order in a wire basket. The officer glanced at the paper and at Gilberto. "Reyes Martínez?"

"Su servidor, capitán."

The captain dismissed the soldier, and as soon as the door closed, his face brightened. He stood up and shook Gilberto's hand. "I'm glad you're here. . . . You can still sit down. Pull up that box."

First Captain Jiménez was not as tall as he appeared while seated, and his appearance was decidedly not Mexican. His eyes were blue and his hair was light brown, wavy, and thinning. Only from the waist down could one see he was a cavalryman; his boots were worn to a working softness and sheen, and his legs were fantastically thin. "Have a smoke," he said. "Here, try one of mine," he offered and lit it for Gilberto. "Relax and let's find out something about each other."

"At your orders, mi capitán."

"You can suspend with the formality, Reyes; you're still officially a civilian. How's your English?"

"Same as ever, captain."

"Mine's getting rusty."

"Like my Castellano," Gilberto offered.

"Well, anyway, Reyes, let *me* talk English. I need the practice. I have to give a class for eight officers who are going up to the States in a few months to play polo." From there, he swung into English. "So you're from California?"

"Yes, sir. But it's a long way behind me. . . . Nothing the matter with your accent, captain, if that's what you're worried about."

"No, it's the grammar and construction mostly. . . . How do you like it back in the native country?"

"So far, fine."

"Your file says both your fathers are dead. . . . You see! There I go, calling your parents both fathers, as they do in Spanish."

"And I make the mistake the other way around. I say parientes—relatives—when I mean parents."

"Do you have any parientes up there in Zaragoza?"

"Just some distant cousin of my mother."

"You probably have more than you know," the captain said affably. Then, more seriously, "All your schooling been up there in Los Angeles?"

Calmly and confidently Gilberto answered, "Up to high school, and then Fillmore, up in Ventura County."

"What's that, a private school?"

"No, sir. It's run by the state. Vocational school, where I picked up my specialty—you know, forestry."

"Yeah, yeah," Jiménez nodded rapidly. "I want to come to that later. That's what caused all the excitement around here yesterday when that information came through."

This puzzled but did not alarm Gilberto. He said, "I never figured I'd be able to do anything with it in Mexico while I was studying the subject."

"At least you learned something in your time in the States," Jiménez said. "Me, sure I went to high school for a couple of years in San Diego. But most of what I learned I got working down at the Bel Mar race track as an exercise boy." He told more about himself than Gilberto felt he would tell another Mexican, except an intimate, of his own rank. . . . His family had a ranch in the State of Coahuila. It was a tradition with them to send all the boys up to the States, on their own, for a few years. He stayed longer—to his twenty-first year. "Then the pressure got kind of heavy. I could have been the youngest trainer, at good money, with offers from some first-class stables. But I was a Mexican. They said to forget I ever was Arturo Jiménez, and call myself Artie James and say I'm a Texan. That would have looked fine to my family! But apart from family, there was myself. I could have made the decision—and, well I made it. You know how it is, Reyes; you were in the same spot, I guess."

"Pretty much, I guess," Gilberto said, "counting out the family. When my mother died a couple of weeks ago, I didn't have anything to keep me. And I couldn't be Ray Gilbert, or Gil Raymond, or anything except who I was."

"Didn't they want to grab you for the Army?"

"Sure, but I figured if I was going into *any* army, it might as well be this one right here. And when I saw that you people—I mean the Mexican Army—was going in for forest conservation on a big scale, I said to myself—"

"That," Jiménez interrupted, "is where I'm afraid I got some bad news for you."

"I was afraid of this," Gilberto said, feeling sick.

"Does it mean that much to you?"

"Being turned down—sure."

"Are *you* nuts!" Jiménez shouted. "Who the hell said anything about turning you down! You're in this goddam army now! While you're sitting there!"

"But my physical—"

"All right! You insist on a physical, I'll give you one right now. . . . Private Reyes, do you suffer from piles? Yes or no."

"Huh—piles?"

"This is a cavalry division. Do you suffer from piles?"

"I never rode horses much, captain."

"Never mind that; answer my question, Reyes."

"No, sir. I never had anything like that."

"Passed! Tomorrow morning is just a formality," Jiménez said, laughing. "Didn't your ears burn last night? . . . Well, they should have. All the company commanders got a slip on you, listing what you can do if they needed anybody for special service—clerical, administrative work, things like that. Three of them wanted you, including Major Cabañas. And so did I. And I got you! I might as well tell you why—it's no secret: General Valdez is my grandfather—my little old abuelito."

That's it! Gilberto remembered where he had seen those blue eyes and that fair skin.

"Look," Jiménez said, "instead of waiting till tomorrow morning, I'll get your medical record filled out before noon. Then over to the Quartermaster Depot for your uniform and equipment—"

A bugle sounded outside, followed by the stamping of feet, human and equine, neighs and snorts. Captain Jiménez got up, went to the window in an alcove to the rear of the room, stood for a moment, and beckoned Gilberto to approach.

The horses he had seen before now stood, flank to flank, in squads, shining and saddled. Their riders, about a hundred men, with bright spurs and polished puttees, and each with a carbine slung on his back, were ready to mount. Lieutenant Zamora, mounted, with a sabre in his hand and facing the ranks, barely moved the sword, and the bugler translated the order into brazen sound. The hundred soldiers mounted as one.

Another gesture of the sword, another call on the bugle, and the troop wheeled by the right and rode out of the gate in a low fog that was golden and sang.

"That's your company, Reyes."

"Jeez—that's wonderful!"

"Yes, Reyes, a good body of men, fine troopers. . . . I think we could do something with them."

A medical orderly took his blood pressure and told him, "Running all the way over here to work up a good high systolic. I know every trick in the book, joven, so just relax." Another non-com took his medical history. No, he had never had any serious illness; no surgery of any kind, never been in a hospital.

The only information that made the man look at Gilberto sharply was his answers as to the age of his mother and father when they died. "Father, at age thirty-one; cause, pneumonia. Mother, thirty-six, t.b."

"They didn't give you a good start, eh, chamaco?"

"They did all right," Gilberto answered coldly.

The man said contritely, "I didn't mean anything."

The last operation was by an officer who scarcely looked at Gilberto's face. He had his rubber glove on when he told him to assume the angle, and went at the examination mercilessly. He left Gilberto tingling as he ran down the chart slowly, made a mark or two, and signed it.

It was a relief to put his shorts on again. But he wasn't through. The orderlies took over again, laying out a tray of five hypodermic syringes—one giant-size.

"All for you, trooper."

"What are they for?"

"Mostly tetanus," the younger non-com said. "You die horribly if you don't get this. Your muscles turn into springs and you vault right up to the beams."

"But *with* this serum," the other one promised, "you die in bed—providing you're strapped in."

"Do I have to get them all at once?"

"No, José and I don't work that way. Only two at a time. Lay down there."

"What's that great big one?" Gilberto asked.

José shrugged. "We're only the help around here."

"But what's it for?"

"Who knows? Ask the veterinary surgeon. . . . On your belly, son. . . . Ready, José! Uno, dos, ¡ZAS!"

The battery fired another salvo. Gilberto lay, his teeth clenched, both cruppers fluttering and flinching in an agony of dread. It never came. "On your feet, trooper!" Just one of those barracks gags. "Get on your pants. The seamstress and milliner are waiting for you. End of this building, cross the company street, and turn right."

The regimental supply sergeant and his two aides stared sourly over their counter at Gilberto.

"Reyes Martínez, A Company, huh," the sergeant growled. "Imagine, men! Special orders on this guy. Everything's got to fit this manikin and pass personal inspection of the captain."

"Why the hell doesn't he send him to his tailor in the capital?" a corporal echoed, and the other chimed, "*Got* to fit! What the hell do you think you're joining up with—the Guardia Presidencial or a lousy, horsepiss-smelling cavalry regiment? . . . *Got* to fit!"

"Take it or leave it, fellows," Gilberto said. "*I* didn't give those orders."

"Okay, okay," the sergeant grumbled. "Get to work on him, men. And don't forget the eau de cologne."

There was no mirror in the place, and Gilberto, an hour later, had no idea how he looked when he tottered out carrying a laden barracks bag with his own clothes on top of the army clothes that had been stuffed into it. The green cotton uniform was new and felt stiff. The shoes and the leggings were broken-in and comfortable.

At the military stores depot he signed for a carbine, bandolier and cartridge pouches, and, as he walked to the Company A headquarters, he shielded his face in the barracks bag. Somehow, he suspected, they were laughing at him. There was a water spigot at the head of the company street and he gasped for thirst. But he was afraid that if he put all his gear on the ground, he would never be able to gather it up again. But he had to risk it. As he bent to drink, the slung carbine almost broke his back and he had to shift that.

A voice beside him said, "Come on, boy; the captain's waiting. He sent me to look for you." Gilberto smiled thankfully to a broad-nosed soldier who reached to help him. "All right," the man urged. "Leave your equipment here. I'll have a man take it up for you. You're in Number 9, Barrack Room C, upstairs."

"Thanks very much—"

"I'm your first-sergeant. My name is Meneses."

"Glad to know you, sergeant," Gilberto said, saluting awkwardly.

"This is how we salute, Reyes, and he demonstrated. And when Gilberto tried it, "That's the idea. Practice that on the way up and show the captain you're learning something. ¡Andale!"

He knocked firmly, and when he was told to enter, he stopped just inside and saluted. Jiménez returned the salute and smiled. "Very good, Reyes. Uniform looks all right; how does it feel to be in it? Salute was regulation, too."

"Thank you, captain. The top-sergeant helped me out."

"Meneses—wonderful soldier. Pure Yaqui Indian. Fought against my father and then served under him. You go to Meneses when you got any problem."

They continued to speak mostly in English, but lapsing now and then into Spanish. "Now that you're in uniform, it's improper for you to sit in the presence of an officer, in his office or quarters. But it's all right now. If anybody knocks, stand up and pretend to be at attention. I'm sorry you can't smoke. Anyway, I'm going to give you the whole pitch. You want to make some notes?"

"My pen and paper are in my stuff, Number 9, Barrack Room C, if the captain will give me permission—"

"No; here, write on this. First off, I want to fill you in on why I fought to get you. You see, I'm the educational officer of our regiment, with the responsibility on me of seeing that every man in it is alphabetized—that is, knows how to read and write simple Spanish. Every time I catch up on that work, bang! we get a bunch of transfers—analfabetos—that pull the record down again. Forty last week, and where do you think they're assigned? Most of them, twenty-eight, to my own company."

A clarity, like a warming light, shed itself as Jiménez related more of the problem. Gilberto began to feel that he was being urged, as a person of unique skill, to accept employment with a sincere boss who understood what results he wanted, as well as the problems entailed in getting them. Fifteen of these forty analfabetos were not only illiterate, but spoke no Spanish. They knew only an idioma indígena, having come from parts of the Huasteca Potosino, the Bajío, and other "pockets" where, after 400 years, castellano is still not heard. "They know the Spanish for horse, but not for saddle or stirrup. . . . You see the kind of problem it is, don't you, Reyes?"

"Yes, sir, but—"

"Wait a minute. . . . These Indians, after they serve their enlistment, they go back to their rock villages and they know *something*—fairly good Spanish. But take these men from the farms and even the cities. If after three years in the army they still sign their thumb prints and can't even read a No Smoking sign, then I think it's we, supposedly intelligent people—officers and enlisted men both—who have messed up."

So far, Gilberto had no need to make notes. It was all too clear and easy to remember. But soon, he would have to make memoranda; Jiménez was not going to leave this just up in the air.

"You see, Reyes, we professional army people, we can hold still for it when generals and zone commanders chew our ass for not carrying out government directives. But when the whole country—the people—say of what the hell use is the army when we discharge *one* illiterate, then—"

Time for notes. . . . A new alfabetización class, 40 men to start December 1, under one teacher—"You, Reyes." . . . Textbooks available, specially designed for adult instruction. . . . Show simple, approved calligraphy. . . . Classroom, blackboard, teachers' syllabus and plan; individual pupils' supplies all available on proper requisition form. . . . Examination on progress made, June 1, to be prepared by ed. officer representing Zone Headquarters and State Director of Education (civil).

"How does that sound, Reyes?"

"It sounds great, captain. But I don't know if I can—"

"I didn't pick you so you could give me that crap. I'm here to help you. You're going to have to put in some time—a whole month, to get yourself familiar with the job. You'll find a complete teacher's kit on top of your locker when you report to your quarters."

"Yes, sir."

"Sergeant Meneses has been given a set of orders about relieving you from certain jobs. I don't expect you to bone up on your own time altogether. On the other hand, you've got a trade to learn here, too."

"I understand that, sir."

"Very good, Reyes. You're relieved for the rest of the day. Get busy on those textbooks and come to me, let's see, Friday, after Retreat, and we'll go over them for a couple of hours. I live off the post. The sergeant will tell you where."

Gilberto stood up. "With the captain's permission . . . Will the captain excuse me . . . a question—"

"What is it?"

"I understood, sir—I was told—on enlistment—" He gathered his nerve. "A man gets a furlough. A few days, to go home. They're expecting me in Zaragoza."

"That's out!" Jiménez snapped angrily.

"Yes, sir."

"Maybe I didn't make myself clear. That's why I asked if you had any questions. Not that kind, though!" The captain was still angry.

"I understand, sir. I'm sorry. Permission to go?"

"Just one minute, Reyes." Jiménez's voice lost its crackle. "Better take a smoke. . . . You saw those men out there, riding to drill? . . . You don't know which of those you're going to have to teach. But you're going to, and they're going to know you. Some of them are your own age; some ten, fifteen, some twenty years older than you. They won't learn from you if they don't respect you—as a soldier, first. No private is going to be able to stand up there in front of them and call them numbskulls if they don't do their lessons. In one month you've got to make corporal—and in six months, sergeant. And you've got to earn the ratings. Understand?"

"Yes, mi capitán."

"You're on the company roster as a private soldier, Reyes, and you're going to have to do a private soldier's work *in addition* to what I'm asking of you. You're going to buck like hell for those stripes—and you may find plenty of competition."

"I'll do my best, sir."

Captain Jiménez put out his hand. "I think you will. . . . Wait—" He took a pad of pass blanks out of his desk and filled one in, then signed it. "Here's a twenty-hour pass. Good till diana—that's reveille. You can telegraph your people about the delayed furlough. I can't promise you one for a long time."

"I won't need more than a couple of hours, captain. I'll talk to them on the telephone."

"Whichever way you like. Show the pass when you leave; turn it in when you come back and report to the sergeant of your platoon. Dismiss! . . . Here—put out that cigarette first."

Gilberto saluted, turned briskly, and left.

Uruarte got his shock. "You tell me, Señor Reyes, that you did this in perfect sanity of mind; that you were not *impressed,* seized and *forced* to join?"

Gilberto laughed. "Do I *look* seized? Do I *sound* forced?"

"And *I* thought, all the time," Uruarte groaned, "that you were seeking a contract to provision the army!"

"No, just the other way around. . . . Señor Uruarte, I am going back to the post as soon as I have settled my account with you."

"Such eagerness, señor! You disappoint your friends—I heard the promise you made them—the señorita-your-novia."

"I know," Gilberto said. "I will explain to them. . . . With your permission—?" He touched the telephone.

The long distance lines were ocupado; they were being "worked," the operator said, and she would inform him as soon as the connection to Zaragoza could be made. Meanwhile, he could gather up his things in the room. The clothes he wore when he left were folded in the newspaper-wrapped bundle he brought back with him, and they could go into his bag, just as they were.

The first thing he did in the room was look at himself in the foot-square mirror over the sink. The face was not the same; his own, but different—older. Darker, too. The moss green of the blouse absorbed whatever neutral tint there was in his skin, leaving only the complementary brown.

A Mexican, he thought; I look like a Mexican.

Leaving the door open, he gathered up his razor, toothbrush, and comb, fitting them into the looped, imitation leather toilet kit. This is all he would take back to the post with him. Stowing the paper bundle back into the bag, he felt a piece of thicker paper folded and took it out. "Dear Doc. Eisen: As you can see—"

Now, he thought; right now was the time to finish that letter. "As you can see" was fine just the way it stood, because he had something to show.

As he uncapped his fountain pen, the telephone rang. Uruarte was there. "Sí, sí, señorita—correcto. De parte del Señor Reyes, sí. ¿Quién habla?"

Gilberto reached for the telephone. The line hummed briefly, then he heard the voice of Doña Elena. "Gilberto—!"

"Privado raso Reyes Martínez, Compañía A. Séptimo Regimiento de Caballería, a sus órdenes, señora. I am saluting, but you cannot see me."

"What has happened, Berto?"

"I will write you everything. . . . I cannot come when I said." He heard her gasp and Don Solomón's voice distantly saying, "Elena! What is it?" He repeated the question to Gilberto.

Rapidly, he gave Don Solomón a report of what happened. "I am standing in my uniform, Don Solomón. . . . Please explain to Doña Elena why I can't come. You've been a soldier—you've been under orders. . . . I will call you often; every opportunity I have. Meanwhile, I will write—everything. I expect letters, too—one that Doña Elena has promised I would get. . . . Here, to the Hotel Virreal for the time. . . . My clothes are for Lorenzo. They will be here, with the proprietor, Señor Uruarte. . . . Yes, the Hotel Virreal, until I have a permanent address."

He had to strain to catch what the old man said. "I had hoped—we did, that you would—that this would be—" His voice became stronger. "This is your house, Gilberto."

"Sure, sure, Don Solomón. I'll always think of it that way."

"Wait, son. . . . One word more. I will let my wife say it. Not that I feel it less, but it comes easier for a woman. . . . Here, Elena—"

"Señora—"

"Gilberto, hear me for all of us—Solomón, I, Inés—*all*! You have made us love you. And until we see you—"

"It is the same—" he began, and realized that he had spoken into a blank humming wire. He signaled. "Señorita, por favor—"

"The Zaragoza connection has retired, señor. Do you wish to make another conference?"

"No, señorita, gracias. Simply to know the charges."

That's all right. Doña Elena knew what he meant to say. She would tell them.

He called Uruarte and asked for his bill. "And for this conference, included. And then, I wish to ask a favor."

"Con todo gusto. . . . Have you been given bad news, señor? I hope no."

"Thanks. It was good news."

"¡Qué bueno! One is affected by tears in either case."

Tears? Gilberto wasn't aware. Crisply he said, "This favor, Señor Uruarte—I have taken the liberty of asking that letters be sent to me here, to your hotel, for a time."

"I am honored, señor," and he smiled. "From your novia, no doubt."

"And others," Gilberto nodded. He liked the word novia. It meant sweetheart and more: bride. "And my clothes, they will be called for by one who will identify himself—Señor Lucas Quintero, chofer of the Silver Arrow."

The innkeeper made a note and said, "I have enjoyed your company, Señor Reyes. I wish I could dispense with the bill, but, as you see—"

"It is a pleasure to pay this small account. Here is ten pesos additional for this call on the telephone."

"But it is less," Uruarte protested.

"The remainder to your cook and the mozo."

"Thanks—for them. . . . And you will recommend my house to your many and loyal friends, Señor Reyes?"

"Without hesitation, Señor Uruarte. . . . So—adiós."

"Adiós, and good luck."

Gilberto walked to the sun lit plaza, feeling relieved physically and every other way. Before he reached it, he admitted to himself that this was not an aimless stroll. It had a purpose: to be seen, to be looked upon as a stranger no more. He wanted to be asked his name and to give it.

A blue-uniformed policeman stood chatting on the corner with a girl, and Gilberto wondered if he should salute him. The policeman, however, saluted first, and he felt that their eyes were following him when he passed. Perhaps they were saying something about him. Good! Let them take careful note. He would walk past here again, a month from now, and he'd give them something to comment on. "Remember that soldier? Looks different, doesn't he, with his stripes."

A sudden eagerness to be at the post overcame him; to report himself present and ready for duty; to see Sergeant Meneses; to watch and imitate him.

Hurrying toward the first in a line of coches at their sitio, he stopped short before stepping off the curb. It was wiser, now that he was in uniform, to arrive like everybody else. To be seen stepping out of a cab would make him a still odder fish among those—those veterans.

He began walking until a bus to the Comandancia overtook him.

43

An old, weary, and unneat criada led Gilberto through the estancia of Captain Jiménez's house; a room half the size of Don Solomón's sala, but containing twice as much furniture and a massive chandelier fit for a ballroom. He stepped around a tricycle, a doll carriage, and a baby's playpen. He continued through the dining room, in which the electric refrigerator occupied one corner, and into a glassed-in back porch, where Jiménez sat over some books.

"Good, you're here, Reyes. I called the post, cancelling this session; one of my kids is sick—the youngest—but her fever is down now. They told me you'd already left. In a taxicab. Is that right?"

"Yes, captain. But I had to wait for my pass and I didn't want to be late."

"Well, don't overdo it, Reyes. On your pay you'll do a lot of walking—and running. . . . By the way, there's talk about you that you're stinking with money; that you're disappointed in love, and instead of joining the French Foreign Legion, you decided to give the Mexican army a break."

"Horsesh—I mean, sir, it's not true, sir."

The captain laughed. "It better not be. If you want to die romantically, you won't do it with us. You might as well make up your mind that if you're itching to fight the Reds, you'll have to do it with boxing gloves in the post gymnasium. We've got a lot of them in the regiment—including officers. . . . Let's see your pass. . . . Off duty till midnight. Well, I won't keep you long. Sit down. Want some coffee or a drink?"

"No, sir; thank you, sir."

"And listen, Reyes, if you've got money, don't keep it under your mattress, or even pinned to your skin. There are specialists here that could steal your socks without unlacing your shoes."

"I carry only a couple of hundred pesos with me," Gilberto explained.

"*Only* a couple of hundred! You couldn't shake out that much money if you turned everybody in A Company upside down. Including me. Did somebody leave you a fortune?"

"Well, no, sir. I came down with about 3,000 pesos from the States—"

"And with a stake like that you joined the army!" Jiménez said, amazed. "You didn't go into business?"

"Well, captain, you see, I got it invested up in Zaragoza, if it's not against regulations. I want to get married some day to a girl up there."

"What's not against regulations? Investing, or getting married? Why, with that much money, Reyes, you could *keep* a woman—a casa chica, too."

"I don't think I'd want to, captain," Gilberto said quite plainly.

Jiménez roared. "Jesus, Reyes, you're a simple son of a bitch!" That was in good-humored English, and the captain continued in the same language. "I swear, if you didn't begin to smell a little like a cavalryman, I'd be suspicious of you."

"Thank you, sir. I like the work."

"Fine, and this is one of the reasons I'm glad you're here: I've gotten three reports on you; from First Lieutenant Robles, Lieutenant Zepeda, your platoon leader, and Sergeant Meneses. Meneses's is the only one I asked for. . . . Relax—they're good; about what I expected, maybe a little better."

"I'm certainly glad to hear that, captain." Almost garrulously from relief, he went on: "I had no idea the horse was such a complicated animal. Why—why—you can talk to him."

"Okay," Jiménez grinned. "Let's hear what you say to him after your first sixty-kilometer march on his back. That'll be Monday at sunrise. . . . This is no order, Reyes, just advice: Take all of Sunday on your cot, with those textbooks. It'll help a little in the way you feel Tuesday."

"I'll remember that, captain. . . . Is it all right to tell the men?"

"Why not? But don't mention I said so. Just say you heard. You can figure out the reason for that, can't you?"

"They'll think I've got the inside track. Is that it, captain?"

"In a way, yes. But the psychology of it goes a little deeper. . . . Let me ask you, Reyes, after seventy-two hours, how many men of the Company do you know?"

"By name? My whole squad, and most of the platoon, and I'd say—"

"Good, good. Now, what I'm going to show you now is private, and you'll see why," Jiménez said seriously, reaching for a sheet of paper on which something was typed. "Here's a list of the men in A Company who are analfabetos. Copy them, now, in your own book and give it back to me."

Jiménez busied himself at going over some other papers while Gilberto copied the names of those who were illiterate. Among those he already knew, he was not surprised at some: Velilla, Mariscal, Fragoso. But he was amazed at others: Sierra, Treviño, Flores—especially Treviño, who had a superior intelligence. He finished and put the list of 32 names aside.

"Okay. Got them all? . . . Those are the men you've got to know well, Reyes. I don't mean suck up to them, but observe them so you'll have *that* advantage when your class starts. *They'll* be surprised, but you won't. . . . Any questions?"

"On this point, no, sir. Permission to go."

"You in a hurry, Reyes? Your pass is till midnight."

"I beg your pardon. I thought the captain was finished."

"I guess so; that's pretty much all I wanted to bring up with you at this stage," Jiménez said. "But we'll talk again." He stood up and Gilberto came to attention. "It looks like we're stuck with each other, Reyes. At least, you're what I bought. Anyway, you do your job right, and I'll keep my end of the bargain—the stripes. Dismissed."

Gilberto saluted, about-faced, and went out through the littered estancia. As he reached the door, a baby began wailing somewhere in the house.

Until midnight. With more than three hours, he moved as rapidly as if he had merely minutes. He could have walked to the Hotel Virreal in about twenty, but a coche libre got him there in six.

"¡Qué milagro!" Uruarte greeted him. It's always a miracle when one Latin encounters another, after a parting of anywhere from two hours to two days. "Your driver came and I have given him the valise."

"There should be a letter. Was there a letter?"

"Sí, there is a letter," Uruarte answered, without moving from his place at the counter. "And let me say, Señor Reyes, the señorita-your-novia writes a most cultivated hand. One can see—"

"May I have it, please?"

"I will fetch it directly, having put it aside, with reverence." Uruarte went to his cubbyhole of a despacho, and until he brought the letter, Gilberto's fingers did not stop drumming.

He ripped open the flap of the thick envelope and impolitely, without a word to the Spaniard, removed the contents. There was a sealed, folded envelope as well as two half sheets of letter paper. He read:

> It will hurt you, dear Gilberto, to read what is in the letter from Inés.

Hurt me—? His eyes skipped to the signature: E. M. de G.—Doña Elena.

> It is not the letter about which I told you—that *we* were writing—and for which, forgive me, I was making the words. In the midst of them, she begged me to tear the paper apart, and that I have done in front of her eyes. Then, this which is here, is what Inés herself says to you, in her own words, and will have no other. Please, dear Gilberto, be kind to her.

Fear stabbed him in every region where he could feel pain beyond the skin. It dried his throat and made insensitive hooks of his fingers as he plucked open the second envelope. The handwriting was the same, but tighter and with a blotch here and there, where a word had been scratched out.

"Muy señor amable y estimado primo:" This Dear Sir and Esteemed Cousin—there was a chill in it. He read lurching, like a broken field runner, with the phrases as his guide, and their meaning his goal.

I will keep your dear letter to me always for that you will not send me another again never. I send you this word in place of the photograph of me because I do not look any more as you saw me with your eyes that one time. I have spied myself in the glass and I say that for truth.

(The words "The sweet" partly obliterated) Doña Elena talked much with me that I should not make this known to you. But I prayed her with my soul to write down my words to you as I say them, each after the other, for I have not the alphabet.

It makes a week that I am not allowed to rise from bed from a sickness of a thing which was done to me by some men. Of them I knew one, whose name I cannot speak for that it makes me to tremble even though they say he is already extinct, being the same one who killed our little golden kid and the beautiful new rebozo from you.

For many days I also wished not to live because of this thing which happened, which, although Doña Elena says not, is a disgrace of the worst, and shameful. All know of it. And now I tell you, esteemed cousin, so that you shall forget me without fail. But I ask, in the name of my santa patrona, Sta. Inés, that you not forget Doña Elena and Don Solomón, in whose house I lie and who love you as of their own blood. And I, your servant, have the same temper of the heart, and a great sadness of it for the loss of your respect.—Inés María Reyes

Gilberto began reading it again, from the beginning, as, behind him, Uruarte said, "If it is urgent to answer—"

"Paper—do you have paper?"

"Seguro que sí, and pen and ink. Go sit in your own room, Don Gilberto, and write at your leisure."

As he read Inés's own words—"each after the other"—he remembered the third enclosure.

At first glance, the sharp, Gothic writing looked utterly foreign. But it was English, and read:

My Sir: As doktor of this jung Woman I inform you she is in two days of complete physikal health; and in her Mind and Spirit even better and stronger as before. The prove of this stands in her Letter which I examine, excuse me. To say strongly: fools are born with Luck, and you, my Sir, are most lucky. But, also the biggest Fool if you do not take this Girl for you and become happy with her.—K. Zumbach

Propaganda! The doctor joining up with Doña Elena to promote him into the right kind of feeling for Inés. Doña Elena—a woman in there pitching for another woman, he thought. Why couldn't she have told her right out that I know everything and it doesn't make a damn bit of difference. . . . But not so fast, boy! There's a reason Doña Elena didn't. And a reason, too, for letting Inés write that letter. Sure—the doctor put his finger on it. It was a sort of a mental test. And Inés passed it. Now it's my cue! The poor kid as much as says she's in love with me and thinks she's lost me. Well! And Doña Elena acting and making the doctor believe that I took a powder.

Only the old man was hep. Gilberto began to feel about him not merely that they understood each other, but a sense of having been through a lot together. He could just hear Don Solomón say, "Why are you knocking yourself out, wife? I know my boy Gilberto. Everything will be all right, I tell you." . . . I'll *make* it all right, Gilberto told himself and beamed a message to him: You're darn tootin', Don Solomón—Chief—Pop!

He could telephone; there was plenty of time. Talk to him, or Doña Elena? Have her give Inés the message, "Gilberto says—" No good. This wasn't a thing where you had to beat the clock. Minutes, hours, or even days—two days—didn't matter when there were years and Inés involved. There would be a message all right—like hers, "word after word"—only it would be the other side of the coin. And the first word would be Mi, and the second, querida—and they would mean My Darling—My Dearest—My Beloved:

First of all, I ask you, as a special favor, do not keep the letter I sent you before, just as I am destroying into little pieces the one I have from you. In place of that one, keep this one, and the many others which will follow, as my duties permit. I will explain to you why, and do not blame Doña Elena, because we thought it was for the best. When I wrote it, I was not gone, but still in Zaragoza, and so close to you I could have put it under your pillow and kissed your dear face if they would let me. So, you will understand that I knew, before your letter, all that you write. And I mean *all*!!! For truth, I had left that morning to go back to the U.S., but, as I said in my first letter (to be destroyed), meaning to return on my first opportunity. But when I heard of what happened, I turned right around from C. del Maíz and was under the same roof with you at all times, but without you knowing, till I finally left for San Luis Potosí, where I am permanently. And who I am, I will leave Don S. and Doña E. to tell you, since I have other things to impart of my emotion. Darling Inés, with all my heart, do not have remembrances of anything except the most joyful, which are to come, and of me, surely, if you will permit me your affection. Allow me the honor to think of you, Dearest Inés, as my novia, as I hoped with a great impulse of the heart when I first looked at you at the house of your Mother. To me, you are now as you were then and will be always.— Your novio-who-aspires, Gilberto

Rusty Spanish and all, he did not want to read it over. That was what he wanted to say, and it was said. If he were face to face with her, he wouldn't say, "Correction. Back there where I said 'destroying,' I meant to say 'tearing.'"

It took him nearly as much time to write a note of eight lines to Don Solomón and Doña Elena.

This was a night to walk back to the post. There was a sickle moon out, with the horns pointing up; the kind he liked. The kind he hated was the big, round, yellow bastard that once inspired him to plug over a poem—eleven stanzas and a *l'envoi:*

> The moon that shines o'er Malibu so mild,
> I see reflected in yon Car'lyn's eyes.
> Oh, why have you me roused to passion wild,
> Then left me fly into uncharted skies?

Oh, of course she denied up and down that she showed it to anybody, even when it came back to him in the form of a parody. It still made him sick to think of it:

> Reyes in the cockpit, his joy-stick in his hand,
> The sand was hot on Malibu and he felt it in his gland.
> So, he zoomed aloft to the sky blue yonder,
> Giving himself no time to ponder.
> Then to the laughter and the mirth,
> He spun on down and crashed to earth—
> > I theenk!

Screw that! Here was one White Mexican who turned brown and was giving them all the finger. You can all kiss my ass! Not so fast—my horse's first. Why, sure I've got a horse—capado bayo, Número 361. But I call him Nikko.

Two more blocks, then up a short hill to the barracks. Brother, this was good! Smells and all—of everything that exists *outside* of a man. But not that micro-thin whiff given off by the decaying nerves of men who fear and can't help it; each alone, frightened of his innate courage.

It was good even to hear the sentry's challenge: "¡Alto! ¡Avance a mostrar su pase!"

Sergeant Meneses checked him in. "You're an hour ahead of time, Reyes; just the same, no stomping around. The men are asleep."

And they might have been, until Gilberto stowed his money and everything but his clothes in his locker and began undressing.

"How was it, gringo?" Vega, on one side of him, began. The way the men in his squad called him The Gringo did not displease Gilberto. He realized he was in for a spell of kidding until Meneses came down with his flashlight and warned that he would take a couple of names down.

"How was what, Vega?"

"You know, that Retreat to midnight Special Clerical Duty you were posted for."

"It isn't midnight yet," Gilberto answered. "I'll let you know."

"I'll tell you what it was," Borbón, the trooper in the cot on the left, said. "Counting the hairs. Quijano saw him going into a hotel downtown. Who you got hidden there, gringo? Don't tell me the major's niece, or I'll cut my throat."

From Mariscal, across the aisle came a loud, kissing sound, and, "How I'd like to get my saddle on that yegua! The haunch on her! ¡Caray!"

"Hey, look!" Borbón suggested. "How about it for Monday night? All us country-boys, let's find out if these centros de vicio are what they say. Let's get some of that vice."

Right here, Gilberto decided, was a good time to—"Monday night you machos won't be able to peel the underpants off your raw rumps. Sixty-kilometer march coming up Monday. Full complement."

"He's kidding," Borbón warned. "How does he know? He hasn't even been to the latrine yet!"

"Sixty kilometers!" Mariscal mocked. "Why, more than half A Company don't even know how to sit a horse!"

"They'll know before the day is over," Gilberto said. "But don't take my word for it. Just step up Monday morning and call me a liar."

Meneses's flashlight wavered down the barracks and there was instant silence. Gilberto pulled the rough blanket up to his eyes and slid gently down a deep, velvet-lined tunnel, to sleep.

He dreamed of horses, one horse in particular: Nikko. *This* one, not the old Nikko of his childhood. He was standing in his stall and a long line of people were forming up behind him, past the stable door, alongside the cement trench, frothing with the contents of every equine bladder in the regiment. He recognized a lot of them—Richardson, The Dutchman, Dickie Collins, Morrissey—completely naked, except for a brass key-tag hanging over their privates. Gilberto wondered what they were doing so far from L.A. until he saw a Tanner Livery Bus marked "SPECIAL," and on the side of which was painted in whitewash: "SINK THE SHEENIES!" "ON TO FAIRFAX," "THE JEWVILLE LTD.," "FREE SALAMI!!!" And under that, the score: MCVEIGH-16, FAIRFAX-44.

That puzzled him. . . . That bus—he remembered it. And that game with all the slugging and body fouls that went on. . . . But it was so long ago. . . .

44

The very first day, he had given every one of the 32 men a three- by five-inch card with his name written on it. "Those are *your* names, as they appear on the roster, but the handwriting is *mine*," he announced. "But that's the way the separate letters are formed. In time, you'll develop your own handwriting. No two will be alike, as any banker can tell you. And the next thing you know, you'll all have your individual firmas with all kinds of fancy rúbricas."

The men liked this, or it seemed to him that they did. There was no doubt that they all enjoyed the idea of having firmas of their own some day; being able to seize a pencil and confidently knocking it off. . . . "Now beginning today, you will write your name forty-eight times a day. Twice, on each line of the first page of your copybooks, which have twenty-four lines. I see nobody has a name long enough so that it won't fit twice on one line, except maybe Dagoberto Henríquez y Bobadilla C. So, as a special favor to you, Henríquez, you can write yours sixty times."

The whole bunch of them laughed. It was a good way to start, having them like him. And if liking was too much to ask, the men could at least see that a newly-minted corporal—a three-week wonder—didn't have to be a sourpuss. . . . "And a week from today, after you have *copied* your names three hundred and thirty-six times, you are going to be called on, at random, to write your name on the blackboard from memory."

A week wasn't long enough. But in ten days, all of them could write their names and a majority of them knew the names of the letters which formed them. They knew the figures from 1 to 10 and, like Lorenzo, were amazed that the mighty wheel of mathematics had so few spokes.

Now, two weeks after the class had begun, Captain Jiménez wanted a report. It was four o'clock, and he was to have been finished with his English lesson for the polo-playing officers. But it was still going on, and Gilberto heard snatches of it through the transom of the officers' library in the Headquarters Building.

"Now, Lieutenant Salcedo, you are at this reception on Long Island, and I am your hostess—"

Whistles and hoots interrupted Jiménez.

"All right," he continued. "But she may not be as pretty as I am. . . . She asks you"—the question followed in English—"'Lieutenant, will you have a dry martini?' . . . What is your answer?"

In English, too, Salcedo said, "Plain whisky, please. I am still in the train."

"Major Cervera, what's wrong with Salcedo's answer?"

"The whisky?"

"No. He's not on the train. He's *in training*."

They seemed to be in no hurry to break it up inside, and Gilberto wondered if Jiménez had forgotten about his being out here, in the antesala. He had his records and attendance roll in a new portfolio on his lap and hoped he would not be asked for an individual report on each man. Some were dull and some were very bright. But they were all learning. . . . *Everybody* was learning: the officers inside; and even at home, in Zaragoza. Inés had herself signed the last letter, a little unsure and spidery, but very clear—Inés María Reyes.

And Doña Elena had written: "Little José is of course too young, but Pompeyo and eight other boys are going every morning to the parroquia where Don Perfecto is teaching them to read and write. Lorenzo fears that the priest is also enforcing the Catechism upon the children, but agrees that this is the price one must pay. My husband, as you know, dislikes to write and will put aside all his correspondence until he can dictate the replies to you, that much you have spoiled him. But he bids me to tell you that he has made a treaty with Coronel Carrasco and . . ."

The letters from home were making quite a file in his locker. They had to do in place of phone calls, because he had not been able to leave the reservation in three weeks.

"Busy . . . busy . . . busy . . ." he had written. "Foot drill, mounted drill, weapons instruction, farrier's class, topography, to say nothing of my special duty. And then of course the never-ending stable duty, so long as horses eat. Anyhow, Nikko is the best-looking animal in the outfit. Yesterday, on inspection, the Major asked Lieut. Bermejo if I wasn't riding an officer's mount, and I swear Nikko understood what he was saying. And listen, Lorenzo, if I have much more to do with caballos, you are going to have to teach *me* all over again what makes an automobile tick. . . ."

The day he became a corporal, he couldn't get out to telephone. But Sergeant Espinoza, the adjutant's clerk, took a telegram out for him. And that brought him his first letter addressed to the post: Cabo G. Reyes M., Cia A, 7° Rgmto. de Caballería, 12a Zona Militar, San Luis Potosí, S.L.P. ". . . So worried were we when they could tell us nothing, or would not, at the Hotel V, that Solomón was about to go to S.L.P. to learn what had happened. Then your telegram and the wonderful news! We could not sleep, and Inés is sure that you will soon be a Gral. de Brigada. Her pride is something wonderful to see—but you can read that between the lines of her own letter. . . . When *will* you get this furlough, so that we may all embrace you? . . ."

But it wasn't Inés's pride he wanted to read about. All this—the promotion to cabo—did was to give her excuses *not* to say those things in her letters which a fellow wanted to hear from his girl. Why, he grumbled, didn't Doña

Elena, who was doing the actual pen work for her—temporarily, of course—
tell her that a man doesn't want to hear household gossip. Well, most likely it
was natural for a girl to want to say those things at first hand—not that Doña
Elena was one of those public scribes who writes letters for people in the
plaza.

There was one piece of news that Doña Elena let Inés tell first, although
she could have written it in her part of the letter. ". . . and yesterday Don
Lorenzo and my mother became man and wife before the priest, who asked
no money for the misa nupcial, though Don Solomón gave him many artículos escolares in your name, Gilberto, for the children whom he is teaching,
Pompeyo included, who is very quick. I copy from his lesson book every day,
and I am also helped by Doña Elena. Don Lorenzo is much in the tienda, and
Don Solomón says that he has become a real brujo with the different machines of calculation, also with the camión. Although the house of him and
my mother and brothers lacks yet two walls, which will soon be fitted, they
find it already commodious to sleep and eat. But I rest here, already doing
what the señora asks of me, such as the ironing of her thin and fine robes of
the interior with an electric smoother, which I have learned; also the shirts of
Don Solomón, who says the tortillas which I make are the best in the Republic. But I beg you not to expose this to Josefina, who is to me like a sister. . . ."

The door opened suddenly. "Reyes!"

He saluted Captain Jiménez and came to attention. Inside, at least ten
officers were facing the open door, silent and appearing to wait for him to
enter. "This man can settle the argument, gentlemen," Jiménez told the
officers, as he closed the door. "Cabo Reyes, of A Company." Gilberto saluted
the group of officers, including Colonel Galindo, commander of the regiment
and third in command of the military zone. He remained standing, looking
hopelessly at Captain Jiménez, who gave him a quick, assuring nod and
spoke to the officers again. "First, does anybody want to ask the corporal any
questions, to assure himself of this man's fitness to give an answer? . . . No?
. . . All right, then, Major Ponce, go ahead."

Ponce, the captain of the polo team, a big man, faced Gilberto. "Corporal,
who was the last president of the United States, before Eisenhower, who was
a general?"

He answered instantly, meaning to sigh with relief later, "General
Grant—Ulysses S. Grant, sir."

Ponce's face fell, and another officer, Captain Arvizu, beamed. "What did
I tell you, Ponce!"

The loser challenged Gilberto. "What about Roosevelt? Not the last one; I
mean the one who beat the Spaniards!"

Gilberto said, "He was a colonel, sir, of a volunteer regiment. He was
elected vice-president and took over the chair when McKinley was assassi-
nated." Then he wondered how he ever came to remember that! Just one of
those things.

"Thanks, corporal. Wait outside, we'll be through here in a little while."
Jiménez gave him a light tap on the shoulder at the door.

Gilberto didn't know on whose side of that argument his captain had
been, but it was plain that he was proud to have a man in his company who
could settle it. And the odd thing about it was that this fact did not come up
during any of his history classes in McVeigh. Miss Halsey—Berenice Halsey,
who taught a thing called You and the Government—brought it out. She was
a bit on the frumpy side in appearance and a sucker for being jostled off the
subject—but not entirely off it—when some fellow or girl asked a question.
And that's how this information about Theodore Roosevelt came out; by
somebody asking how he and F.D.R. were related. She not only explained
that, but went back to President McKinley and used up the rest of the hour
talking about something called The Dawn of American Imperialism: how
McKinley told the country that he asked God for advice on what to do, and
while on his knees, God told him it was America's Manifest Destiny that we
should take over Hawaii, the Philippines, Puerto Rico, and a few other
spots—which we did, and established something she called hegemony.

And one fine day, she was called down to the principal's office, and that
was the last that was ever seen of Miss Berenice Halsey in *that* school. A male
substitute took over for the rest of the term. The Dutchman introduced him to
the class. "Mr. Ormsbee will do well enough if he can purge your minds of the
dangerous subversion that so-called former teacher of yours put into them.
We have been watching her for a long time—ever since we found out what
sort of magazines she was subscribing to." And so on, yackety-yack for about
twenty minutes. If there ever was a windbag . . .

One of the officers—it sounded like Major Linares—said loudly, "Sí, sí—
my faith is the Christian faith and my politics are Christian!"

"Early Christian, maybe," somebody answered.

"In some respects, yes, Leal," Linares said. "Anyway, I cannot defend, or,
for that matter, fail to see the complete nonsense of the North American
doctrine of equating Chrisianity and capitalism. That is, if you are one, you
must be the other. It does not follow."

"The norteamericanos don't mean us," another officer remarked. "That is
exclusively for Protestants."

"No, no!" Linares protested quickly. "They include us, too, into the
partnership. Furthermore—"

The gruff rumble of Colonel Galindo himself interrupted. "Despite the
fact that there are twelve million Catholics as good as ourselves in Italy, who
are Communists? Explain that, Linares."

"You cut it too fine, my colonel. They want everybody in! The Jews—they
want them in the capitalist syndicate, reminding them our faith is Judaeo-
Christian. And do they stop there, having at least a slender historical thread?
No! On the basis of the norteamericano crusade, the Turks are in all but
name Mohamedo-Christians, baptized by the dollar; the Nationalist Chinese
are Tao-Christians, and their leader, pure Baptist. Who says there is no

Shinto-Christianity and Buddho-Christianity, or that if the Devil worshippers hang back they won't be told they are really Satano-Christians."

Lieutenant Ponce called out, "What about me? I don't believe in any religion, only in capitalism."

"Atheo-Christian!"

There was a big laugh. Officers could talk about things like this, but it was different with enlisted men, Gilberto recognized. Nobody stopped them; they stopped themselves. Particularly the analfabetos in his class. They were much more touchy on such subjects as the established order in the Church and the relation between the clases humildes and those who were "placed above them." This did not mean only their officers; they went further, as far upward as the eye could see, in accepting superiors.

It was different with those men who could read and write. Their humildad ended at the gates of the army post. When they dealt with a shopkeeper in the town, he was simply patrón, not mi patrón.

Gilberto observed that off-duty, the analfabetos stood for as much blasphemy as the barracks-room iconoclasts could dish out. They showed their displeasure, but never argued, seeming to shield themselves in meekness and warning silence. But in the more formal atmosphere of the schoolroom, they fought back. Something happened the other morning which showed that: As usual, Gilberto had tacked up, on the frame of the blackboard, the front page of a newspaper for the men to browse over a few minutes before the class came to order. It had turned out to be a useful idea; repetition in the headlines of words like Corea, paz, mundo, China, guerra, México, and even longer ones like braceros and presidente made them recognizable to many of the men. One of them, Chagoya, handed Gilberto a crudely printed handbill, saying, "This came to me from my brother, who works in a tile factory in Jalisco. It is probably small news of my village, but may I hear what it says?"

"Why not? Let's all hear it," Gilberto said. "It can't be too confidential." He asked for attention and began, "Mexicans! Brothers! Jalisqueños! Already the devout are passing through our village, as pilgrims to make the verbena at the Sanctuary of Our Lady the Virgin Queen of Heaven in Guadalajara. And what do they meet here in place of the Charity and Openness of Heart, which the man who calls himself our Pastor has preached? They meet exploitation of their weariness, their hunger, and their thirst at the hands of the mother and the brother of this same priest—and we say, with his connivance! Extorters of the copper in the pockets of the worshippers, the false ones demand money for the—"

One of the men, Santillán, interrupted. "Permission to leave, corporal." Six others stood up with him.

"Why? What's the matter?"

"So as not to hear those insults," Santillán said boldly. "Our faith—"

"Look, men, there's no disrespect here to The Virgin. It's only a protest by the people. Here—"

"It offends, corporal."

"Very well," Gilberto agreed. "I'll read this to you alone, Chagoya, later."

Chagoya, who had not risen with the others, then stood up and said, "Gracias, cabo, but I do not wish to hear it."

That's the way they felt about it, and he wasn't going to quarrel with them. His job was to teach them to read—a skill that would open their eyes in more ways than one. At present, they could refuse to *hear* what they didn't like. But when people know how to read, it's a lot harder to *quit* reading, no matter how little of what they read appeals to them—or their prejudices.

The officers were leaving, and one of them said, "Captain's waiting for you inside, corporal." When Gilberto entered, Captain Jiménez, conversing with Colonel Galindo, excused himself and motioned for Gilberto to sit down at a library table by the window. The colonel remained in his former place, sipping a beer.

Jiménez was thorough. Before asking any questions, he went carefully through the attendance record and the weekly grades. "Ochoa, absent Thursday, absent Friday; why?"

"Orders of medical officer, sir. Confined due to injury. But he made up the work, sir."

As part of the general report, Jiménez asked if the class was abreast of the official instruction plan. "Are you skipping anything, Reyes? Do you find you have to go back anywhere?"

"No, sir. We are at balance with the schedule, captain. Several men have asked permission to advance, and—"

"Their names?"

"Lamadrid and Ruvalcaba, sir."

"What are you doing about them, Reyes?"

"With your permission, captain, instead of giving those two advanced work, I have appointed them, unofficially, as my assistants. They are helping the slower men." Gilberto felt uncomfortable seated, with Colonel Galindo sitting not ten feet away, glancing in his direction and certainly able to hear everything he said.

"That's approved," Jiménez said. His questions became less rigid. "How are you getting along with the men, outside of the schoolroom?"

"No trouble, sir. That's where I learn from them."

"Good. . . . I'll take these papers and go over them more carefully and return them to you. Any questions?"

Yes, he felt like saying, what about that goddam furlough? Here it is almost Christmas, and I want to go home with packages in my arms and put them down—and put them around somebody. . . . "No, sir."

"Dismiss."

Almost at the door, Colonel Galindo called, "One moment, corporal."

Gilberto about-faced, saluted. "A sus órdenes, mi coronel."

"What are you doing to educate yourself, corporal?"

"I read, sir."

"Books? Periodicals? Reviews?"

"Mostly books, sir, in the orderly room."

The colonel smiled. "Probably the same ones that were lying there when I was a non-com: An 1876 *Cavalry Manual; The Four Horsemen of the Apocalypse;* and *The Anatomy of the Horse*, by that pork butcher—what's his name?"

"Doctor Horacio Romero, sir."

"*That's* the fellow!" He swept the shelves in the room with his arm. "Somebody should be reading these books, since my officers won't. You, corporal, you have permission to borrow in any quantity from this collection. . . . Captain Jiménez will inscribe an order to that effect. I will countersign."

"I thank the colonel." Before he about-faced, Jiménez nodded and made the Stateside sign for O.K., with a circled thumb and forefinger.

That meant, "You're doing all right!" in any man's language today, and at that moment he didn't need anybody to tell him that. He knew it of himself, with confidence and certainty.

There was a great deal to read, and little time in which to do it. There were a dozen different *Histories of México* by as many different authors, but only one Bernal Díaz del Castillo and his *Verdadera Historia de la Conquista*. It kept him up, by the faint light in the orderly room, for a week of nights. The experience, even physically, was beyond and deeper than merely the reading of history. It was engulfing. He fired his musket into the feathered shields of the Aztecs and struck with his Spanish axe at the gold helmets of his ancestors. . . . Malinche—the traitress, but what a woman! . . . Gonzalo de Sandoval, Pedro de Alvarado, Francisco de Morla, Velásquez de León—what men, those conquistadores! Pride and shame alternated when he remembered that he came of them, the golden-bearded hellions; but of the conquered, too, whose blood torrent over the centuries washed the yellow out of the hair and the blue out of the ice-cruel eyes of the conquerors.

He brought himself back to today with the Latin American editions of *Life* and *Reader's Digest*. The first was full of Eisenhower and advertising; all and everything about him and his wife and his grandchildren, and how he liked to put on a chef's hat and barbecue steaks with his own special sauce.

The Mexican magazines, of which he appropriated those a week or two old, had names such as *Hoy, Mañana, Jueves*—Today, Tomorrow, Thursday. They treated Ruiz Cortines, the new president of Mexico, to less photography and somewhat more dignity. Naturally, they discussed and made comparisons between the two new executives. The Mexican people were happy for Ruiz Cortines. Here was a man who had been a civil servant most of his life, and now they had raised him up to the presidency. The U.S. weeklies, on the other hand, gave the impression that Eisenhower, the general, had consented to step down to the civilian job; that he was giving the people a break.

Here was that word hegemony—hegemonía—popping up in one of the Mexican reviews. A frozen echo of Miss Halsey's "You and the Government" lectures and the discussion among the officers. "Northern hegemony stops at the Río Bravo's edge," he read. "This is not Taft dealing with Díaz, or Wilson with Huerta, or yet Truman with Alemán, from which encounters two generations of Mexicans have learned lessons—many upon their backs—in popular sovereignty and independence. This, good neighbors of the North, is Citizen Adolfo Ruiz Cortines, in whose being is crystalized the aspirations of the Mexican people."

In one block of type that looked too ponderous to read all the way through, Gilberto glimpsed a recurring phrase: imperialismo yanqui. It came up as often as the word Communism in the American periodicals; repetition for the purpose of exhortation and warning. He went back and read a paragraph: "And speaking of cotton, the market for which no longer exists now that peace is in prospect, why the alarm in commercial circles? Is it the Law of Medes and the Persians that a Mexican must wear an 80-peso U.S. shirt or none at all? Why not one Made-in-México for 16 pesos, or even ten! Will the Colossus of the North which offered México an outright gift of 8 billion pesos for the establishment of an élite military corps in this country *lend* us that sum now, at a handsome rate of interest, so that we may build more cotton mills, more shirt factories? More employment for our working people, more happiness in their homes? And since the Mexican masses do not possess deepfreezers or televisions, a little more meat in the pot and, perhaps, a book?"

Practically the entire balance of the magazine was taken up with articles and pictures of the Virgin of Guadalupe. December 12 was her day, so it was not by accident that the political news, the new presidents, and tributes to the Virgen Morena were juxtaposed in the same issues.

There was a smaller magazine, pocket-size, almost lost among the big ones. It was called *Paz* and was supposed to be a monthly, but this issue covered two months, a tip-off that it was up against it financially. Sure enough, there it was, on the back cover: "*PAZ* Needs Your Help. We Appeal to Your Generosity. Every Peso Counts." And a coupon.

In thumbing back and forth, although there were no pictures of Stalin, and his quick eye did not catch the word Communism, which was sprinkled on every page of the U.S. publications, Gilberto knew it had to be there. Altogether, he decided, this little book was what you'd call subversive. Then—something held him—what was a Mexican general doing in its pages? "If others have the force of arms, we have the force of reason. The deceived must be shown the truth. The elimination of the lie is the primary advance in the campaign for peace.—General Jeriberto Jara."

A few pages onward, another: "Dijo el General Gabaldón: '¡Nuestros hijos no irán a Corea!'"

Scads of pictures; woodcuts that seemed to stand out from the cheap, gray paper of men who looked like Lorenzo and the fellows at Las Camelias, and women like Tía Esperanza. And the names of the artists who chipped them out were Zalce, Chávez-Morado, Leopoldo Méndez, and Pablo O'Higgins. He had never heard of any of them, but he had of Diego Rivera. Who hadn't? And here he was: "Diego Rivera. Después de su visita a las obras de Breughel del Museo de Viena, dice—" Maybe this had something to do with peace also, he thought, and possibly Rivera was claiming that the ilustre maestro flamenco was in favor of it. And spang in the middle of the book, here was another general—the last of Mexico's general-presidents. "Millions of men and women of all faiths and nations must carry on the moral aim to enforce peaceful convictions among the responsible leaders of the nations now in conflict, and to eliminate violence as a solution to international problems.—Lázaro Cárdenas."

Suddenly a batch of poetry; page after page of it, all about and by a man named José Martí, a Cuban fellow, it looked like. This one—it didn't rhyme, but it spoke softly—about a yoke and a star, and a mother telling her baby which he should choose:

> ¡ . . . La estrella como un manto en luz lo envuelve,
> Se enciende, como a fiesta, el aire claro,
> Y el vivo que a vivir no tuvo miedo,
> Se oye que un paso más sube en la sombra!
>
> —Dame el yugo, oh mi madre, de manera
> Que puesto en él de pie, luzca en mi frente
> Mejor la estrella que ilumina y mata.

A hand grasped his shoulder and shook it. Meneses. "Oye, chamaco, wake up and go to sleep. Diana in less than three hours."

45

They were coming today. They had started early and they would be here by noon—or sooner, depending on what they meant by early. Here, in the army, there was no such thing as early or late. Everything had its time, en punto: rising, eating, drilling, the furling and the unfurling of the flag. All done with bugles. A man got so accustomed to them that he could measure the lag between the time the notes came out of the bell of the horn and when they reached his ear. Even the horse, a far less intelligent beast than he was cracked up to be, reacted to the several llamadas de corneta which disturbed his ease. At first, when Nikko blew himself up by sucking air when the call sounded to saddle up, Gilberto thought it was pretty cute. But Sergeant Meneses explained that it was a sign of lower-than-average equine mentality. The really smart mounts were a step ahead; they spared themselves the shock of the rider's knee under the ribs, making them expel the air from every orifice. "Your mount will learn, Reyes, if you give him one, sudden-like, in the brisket. It's better than having him loosen the cincha at will."

And this was a day for bugle calls; all kinds and from all parts of the reservation. From diana, with only a fifteen minute break for beans, the whole regiment drilled in a purgatory of broiling sun, galling gnats that found the men's sweaty eyes, and the goading of the non-coms. The mechanized units had it no easier. In a haze of blue exhaust gas, they backed and filled and wheeled their jeeps, hub to hub. These and the command cars would be leading the parade, and the noisy half-tracks would be bringing up the rear. A good thing, Gilberto thought, that the Headquarters Company would be absorbing the automotive stench; then the regimental band, and behind it, Company A, his own. They were to ride with stripped saddle, meaning only carbine, cartridge belt, and water bottle. But that carbine—along about eleven o'clock it was no jackstraw across his back.

Finally, the regiment formed up to hear the special Order of the Day. It was not simply read, but orated over the P.A. system by Colonel Galindo on behalf of the commander of the military zone. He began too loudly, and part of what he said was lost in the metallic echoes beyond the target butts. "Officers and men of the *boom boom boom* . . . Brothers in *boom* . . . defense of the *squeeee* . . . Mexicanos!" But as soon as he stopped bellowing, the words came clearly. "Thirty-six years ago today, on the glorious Fifth of February, in the year One Thousand Nine Hundred and Seventeen, there was promulgated and delivered into the hands of the Mexican people that greatest of social and political documents—that Magna Carta—the Constitution which governs us today!"

"¡Viva la Constitución!" the men shouted.

"Bought dearly—written in the blood of heroes, it bases itself upon this principle: All power derives from the people! *All* power! Not one manifestation of authority without the explicit consent of the Mexican people."

"¡Viva el pueblo mexicano!"

This sounded more like civilian talk, and Gilberto had a feeling that Galindo was editing the order as he went along.

"Yes, the people!" Galindo repeated. "Whose servants we of the National Army have the honor to call ourselves—"

"¡Viva el ejército nacional!"

". . . end of sixty years of porfirista dictatorship, during which liberty was denied, the people's heritage torn from them and made into an instrument of their own oppression. The hand of tyranny was struck off in the glorious Revolution of One Thousand Nine Hundred and Ten—"

"¡Viva la Revolución!" the men roared, and even the horses nodded.

"And ten years later, on a day such as this, the Constitution was given and human dignity revindicated. So, again we march out in a demonstration of fealty to the people—honor a quien honor merece—and the land we have sworn to protect!"

"¡Viva México!"

"Attention!" Galindo drew his sabre and a hundred others rasped and flashed in the sun to the officers' shoulders.

"Forward!"

Bugles shrilled, and the regiment rode out through the gates of the post.

They should be here now, in town. And she would be with them. Doña Elena's postal card did not say so; merely that Lorenzo and Esperanza would be in San Luis Potosí on Thursday the 5th on a matter for Don Solomón, and they would "rejoice to see him if he was not compromised with the military." They would "headquarter" at the Hotel Virreal.

That she did not mention Inés at all was all Gilberto needed to convince himself that Inés was coming with them. He would watch for her. Not here, on the highway over which they trotted, although scattered family groups sat on the road banks and waved to the column. Not there, by a rural school where all the children had lined up, waving their little green-white-red flags and singing. But later, when they reached the populous streets on their way to the Plaza de Armas.

The sidewalks were crowded, three-deep and more, from the curb to the building line. Gilberto could see only to his right; Cabo Pinedo, carrying the guidon, was a step too far forward on the left of the column. Trying to distinguish one face in that rank of smiling brown people was tantalizing and hopeless. Perhaps Inés looked different now; even so, she could not have failed to see him, and called out or waved. Many girls were doing that—yelling to their Pacos, their Nachos; and calling to others whom they did not know, "¡Hola, guapo!"

For the rest of the way, up to the cleared side of the Plaza de Armas upon which the State house fronted, he kept looking for Lorenzo and Pelancha in the crowd.

As the column firmed for the ride past the group of officials on the balcony of the Palacio del Estado, Gilberto saw two narrow strips of sidewalk, on either side of the entrance to the Palacio, crowded with people; early comers, who had brought boxes to sit on. If they were not here, among these last couple of hundred people—well, it was possible that they had seen him further back along the line of march. But being seen is not like *seeing*.

"Eyes right!"

Gilberto flicked his glance to the draped balcony, and in the same instant, a hand flew up from the crowd on the last strip of curb. Palm outward, it waved rapidly, and Gilberto knew it was for him. It kept waving until he rode abreast and put all his heart into a long look at Tía Esperanza and Lorenzo—and Inés between them. He looked at her face as long as he dared, until Matabuena beside him elbowed a warning.

He could not tell what she wore, but he carried, as sharply as if it were an electroplate, the rose oval of Inés's face, the white line where her hair was parted, and other things observed normally by long, intense looks: the pale half-moons at the roots of her fingernails as she held them across her mouth and the ivory of her lids to which the flush of blood did not reach.

The column swung around three right angles of the Plaza and halted, in single file, facing the Edificio del Estado. But Gilberto's platoon was strung out, beyond the limits of the square. He strained to see Inés, off to his left, in the clear intervals between the passage of different elements in the parade. There came labor unions, each with their drum-and-bugle corps; men in dazzling white calzones and jackets from the various ejidales; sindicatos of miners, wearing their helmets and lamps; government employees with banners reading, "¡SUFRAGIO EFECTIVO! ¡NO REELECCION!" More miners, more peasants, more factory hands. The Frente Zapatista, led by a bunch of old fellows with tremendous sombreros and mustaches to match, riding tough little ponies, and by the leg of each man hung a sugar knife, a yard long and curved like a scimitar. And flags. One after the other, tiring out the buglers, who clanged the call to salute. Girls in white uniforms distributed halves of lemons to the soliders, and a brigade of schoolboys brought up buckets to water the horses.

Then, the last bandera nacional dipped, the regimental band, augmented by the State and Municipal aggregations, sent the first notes of the himno nacional crashing, and the multitude sang: "Mexicanos al grito de guerra . . ." At the cry of war, they'd be ready; and to Gilberto, they looked it. Not alone the soldiers, but these men of the sindicatos, the farmers, the zapatistas and their sons—*and* their daughters. But the cry to war would have to be something more than a whine on the radio from some distant chancellery. It would have to come from the watch towers on their own soil to find its echo in the hearts of the people. The Mexican lucky enough to own a wind-up phonograph is not going across wide seas to preserve his yanqui brother's fine 21-inch television.

The governor of the state made a speech which would have been the right length if some busybody politician could have been restrained from calling for vivas every time His Excellency paused for breath. He ordered cheers for most of the Mexican presidents from Carranza to the present day; for a new irrigation dam in Papaloapan; the firmness of the peso in the world financial market; the National Army, and, of course, the doughty Seventh Regiment. There was one also for the marina nacional "for heroically dispersing Northern shrimp pirates from Mexican waters."

When the governor finished, he introduced the dignitaries on the platform. The state director of education spoke very briefly about the people's cultural gains and, in turn, introduced a young man, whose name Gilberto didn't catch; the winner of a hard-fought, nation-wide oratorical contest. The cheers for him blasted the birds out of the trees in the plaza, and he apparently deserved them. He ignored the microphone, but everybody in the square could hear him as he began, "I rise to give you my thoughts upon the Word and the Weapon. Of ink which is stronger than iron. Of blood which weighs greater than lead. Of bread and stones and things by which people live."

Surely it was about the Constitution into which this fellow—and Gilberto—were born. And men and women were listening who helped give it birth and blew breath into it.

Gilberto wished he could take it down. The words were so simple that he was sure that, in a week or two, the soldier students of his class would be able to read it. Like music, although it engrossed him so that he did not miss a phrase, he could still think of Inés and the others who had touched his life in this old land that was scarred with so many new wounds.

There were no vivas except the last, quietly spoken by the young orator as he finished: "Long live our Constitution! Up with democratic constitutions in all the countries of the world! Viva the compact of Man with himself!" That speech, a raucous announcement said, marked the end of the patriotic exercises.

Gilberto rose in the stirrups to look toward Pelancha, who was taller than either Lorenzo or Inés, and in the flurry, as many people detached themselves from the crowd, he saw them. They were trying to come toward him, a passage that would have been easier if they each made their own path through cross currents and whirlpools of people. But they both held Inés's arms, and no swath wide enough for three people abreast opened for them. He beckoned—another twenty feet and she would be directly opposite him— if they would only hurry into that clear space ahead. Hurry! Look how close! Pelancha was already waving and pointing to Inés in a way that said, "Look who I've got here!" He desperately wanted to shout her name, even against the sudden clatter of nervous hoofs drumfiring on the pavement and Lieutenant Zepeda's shrill order, right at his ear, for the platoon to form fours, a maneuver which caught Gilberto with three riders between him and the opposite curb.

"At a walk. Forward!"

He looked back an instant before the column turned out of the plaza. But he saw nothing, only a thousand people massed.

The bus from the post went no further than the Alameda. Nikko would never forgive him for the hurried stabling and sloppy rubdown to which he was subjected. . . . "Let it go this time, 'mano. Look at *me*! No shower, smelling like a goat, and *I'll* catch it from Meneses, not you."

With his own comb and the bus window for a mirror, he curried his hair, which had become as brittle as a mane. He'd have given any amount for a palmful of vaseline hair tonic just then.

When the bus pulled up at the northwest corner of the broad Alameda and the men poured out, Gilberto lagged. It occurred to him that Inés, her mother, and Lorenzo might be here, waiting for him. That would be too soon and too sudden. He needed time; the time it would take for a slow walk from this point to the Virreal. A man has to adjust his walking pace, compose himself so that he wears the right kind of expression. Is it better to have that military look, or should he forget the uniform and the stripes?

As he walked, he thought of what he would say when he had covered the distance from his first sight of them to beside them. Or don't you say *anything*—just gasp out people's names, as they do in the movies? There was nothing strained or unnatural when he saw them first, in front of their hut in Tres Cenotes, but this was different. Though they were still the same people, the balance of relations had shifted.

Waiting to cross the street, he looked down at a washtub full of flowers: gladioli, most of them yellow, and some deep red, and others the color of tallow. "How much are these?" he asked the woman kneeling by the tub.

"Six little pesos."

He didn't know whether that was a fair price or not. He had never bought flowers in his life. "For a dozen?" he asked.

"For all of them, my little captain. But I see you only want the red. Take them for two pesos."

"It just happens I like the gold ones."

"Yellow for your grandmother, red for your sweetheart. Take both, for four pesos."

There was nothing to wrap them in, and as the woman shook the water from the stems, he said he would buy a newspaper.

The woman looked pained. "Why do you wish to hide them? Aren't they beautiful? And what is more wonderful to see than a soldier—a *live* soldier—with his arms full of flowers! Take them for nothing!"

He laughed and gave her five pesos. She was right. In the next three blocks, not a person who saw him failed to smile; the free kind of smile to which the only response was one of his own, repeated so often that it stayed there when he saw Lorenzo up the street, buffing the fenders of the truck with a chamois.

"Lorenzo!"

They hurried toward each other. "¡Qué milagro!"

"¡Qué milagro!"

"Lorenzo, my old friend!"

"Don Gilberto, my master! How we waited!" He unclasped his arms from Gilberto's shoulders and wiped his eyes with his sleeve. "But now—let me see you clearly—"

The old fool is actually crying, Gilberto said to himself, and he'd better cut it out, or he'll have me— "I caught sight of you at the plaza; you and Tía—and—"

"I burned my eyes out looking for you, Don Gilberto."

"Drop the don, Lorenzo. From now on, just forget it, as a favor to me."

"I know the face of every man in the regiment. But to see yours again— Ay, ¡qué milagro!"

"Tell me, how are they at home? Doña Elena?"

"Well, and sends you many kisses by Pelancha and—"

"Don Solomón, does he still suffer of his eyes?"

"Less now and swears that when he lays them on you, Gilberto— But hear from the women; they are inside, faint with eagerness," Lorenzo said, drawing him into the hotel. At the counter, he stopped, laid his hand on the open ledger that served as a register of guests, and said, "We inscribed ourselves, as you see."

Gilberto saw: "*L. Aguilar y Esquivel, y esposa, de Zaragoza S.L.P.*"

"Wonderful, Lorenzo! A firma like a banker."

Twisting his head modestly, he pointed to the line below: "Inés María Reyes, idem." "By her own hand, also. Neat, is it not, Gilberto?"

"Perfect."

"And that Pompeyo! He writes like a regular clerk. . . . Don Perfecto sends his greetings."

Señor Uruarte called an effusive, "¡Qué sorpresa agradable, mi cabo! The ladies are in the comedor; the beautiful señorita-your-novia—" and with a bow in Lorenzo's direction—"with the simpática señora-her-mother. I run to get a vase for the flowers."

Lorenzo pushed open the door of the dining room and stepped behind Gilberto. Both women were standing; Inés, her eyes down, her fingers twined in the fringe of her mother's rebozo. As with a small, timid child, Pelancha wheedled, "Look, niña; look who is here!"

Still without raising her eyes, Inés put her hand forward to be shaken; proof that she had not seen him since he entered the room, or she would have known that he held flowers in his arms.

"I brought these, Inés, thinking—"

She looked at them first, and then at him, then back at the flaming stalks, as Pelancha took them out of his hands. "I am so happy that you came, Inés," Gilberto said, and turning to Pelancha, "and that you brought her, Tía."

As if to emit the warmth of both welcomes by her own embrace, Pelancha drew him into her strong arms and kissed his cheeks.

"And *you* stand there!" Lorenzo chided the girl. "For what did we come leagues and leagues? Embrace the man!" But it was Gilberto whom he pushed toward her.

Holding her rebozo across her shoulders with her left hand, she gave him the other. He held it and touched her clipped hair, letting the cut end touch his finger tips. "I like it better this way," he said.

"There, child!" Pelancha said, "What did I tell you!"

"Certainly," Gilberto agreed. "It goes with your face." And, as she smiled up at him and said, "Gracias," he put his finger very lightly on her temple, tracing the line of a healing abrasion. Forgetfully he asked, "What happened here; were you hurt?"

Her eyes opened wide in sudden incomprehension. He felt her attempt to draw her hand out of his, and he held it tighter.

"Mamá!" she begged and began to cry.

"Inés, I'm sorry. I didn't mean—I *know*! I shouldn't have brought it up. What I meant was—" He couldn't tell her what he meant, and if he let her go to her mother now—

Pelancha understood what he wanted of her and turned her back. And Inés seemed to understand, in her turn, that here was a stronger bastion between her and nameless fear. She was within it as Gilberto's arms went around her and her burrowing face found the heart of a man loving in his strength.

And though her weeping was still loud, Pelancha looked and smiled because she knew that the deepening sobs were the end of tears.

Uruarte burst in, a clay jar in his arms. "¿Qué pasa? In my inn, do I hear weeping? Do my ears—"

"Never mind your ears," Lorenzo said. "Where are your eyes, hombre? Don't you see here is a meeting of lovers? Have Spaniards no soul?"

"Haven't they, though!" Uruarte thumped the jar on the table and thrust the flowers into it. Then, louder, obviously for Gilberto to hear, "Or the delicacy to leave lovers to weep alone—to kiss, and sigh, and kiss again. . . . Come, drink a glass of wine with me."

"Wait," Gilberto said, still holding Inés. "Bring a bottle—several, of the Manzanilla, patrón. And drink with us."

"Thank you," said Uruarte, and with a slow grace continued, "Señores, I have been bidden to drink with dukes, and for an answer, I have spit on their carpets. But on this occasion, and to the health of such novios as these, *with all pleasure.*"

Inés had taken less than half a glass of the wine, and that only at Pelancha's urging, but it brightened her eyes and set a tiny smile to playing around her mouth. Uruarte was saying amusing things in the pure accent of Spain, at which most Mexicans smile indulgently. But Inés's was neither of amusement or politeness; its source was a secret, even from herself.

She sat between Gilberto and her mother, upright, yet without looking rigid. Her arms, smaller replicas of her body's angle, were lax; the hands, palm down, on her thighs. He put his fingers around her wrist and it quivered; he felt two pulses, hers and his own, at his fingertips. She moved then, only slightly, inclining toward Pelancha, so that their hair mingled. Gilberto understood; his head was just as near, but Pelancha was his surrogate, receiving acknowledgment, in his place, of an act of wanted tenderness.

He whispered to her, "You must be hungry." She nodded. They were all hungry. How could they help it, with Uruarte sounding off on the wonderful food he used to put out when he was the owner of the Fonda las Mandarinas in Spain. "Had I known then," he declaimed, "what I knew a year later, I tell you my friends, I could have saved my country at the cost of two pinches of arsenic blended into the paella which I cooked for the fascist pig Queipo de Llano and that stinking viper, General Mola. And once, earlier, none other than that mother-fu—your pardon, ladies, but you understand that I mean Franco himself—sat his well-used buttocks down to a duck stewed with plums, into which I could easily have stirred—"

They were saved from more of this by the bell which rattled on the counter outside.

Pelancha and Lorenzo walked arm-in-arm ahead of Gilberto and Inés toward the restaurant on the Alameda where the waitress had a husband who played the pífano in the banda municipal. Two blocks from the Virreal, Lorenzo stopped suddenly and turned. "The letter," he said. "I forgot to give you the letter, Gilberto."

"From home, from Don—"

"No, one that came to Zaragoza for you, by the mail. I will run back to the camión for it. Don't wait, I will catch up with you."

Gilberto, walking slowly between Inés and Pelancha, wondered aloud where and from whom he could be getting mail. "Did you see it, Tía, Inés? Was it a letter from—was it a foreign letter?"

Neither had seen the envelope. They knew, though, that Lorenzo had brought it; he had mentioned it to them. "So," Pelancha said, "it is as much my fault that it was not given to you."

"Mine as well," Inés said.

"It is probably of no importance." But it bothered him. "When did it arrive?"

Inés answered. "Yesterday, by the motorcycle of the mail, with some others. But your name I could read the best."

A half block onward, Lorenzo, trotting, overtook them and gave Gilberto the letter. "Forgive me for the delay."

It had a Mexican 25-centavo stamp, and the envelope was Mexican, with lines of green and red printed on the edges and the words Correo Aéreo. The address was typed in smaller than ordinary letters—elite. "Señor Gilberto Reyes, Lista de Correos, Zaragoza, San Luis Potosí, México."

Nodding, as if he knew all about it, he put it in his pocket and took Inés's arm. His last glance had been at the postmark, but it was too scuffed to read.

When he led them into the restaurant, he hoped that in the bustle of being seated, he could glance at the inside of the envelope. But all six of the tables in the place were occupied, and they were told that very soon one would be free. This was a día de fiesta, and every other restaurant was just as busy.

Somebody in the rear of the place hissed, "pssst!" The dart of sound was for Gilberto, and he turned to see Captain Jiménez, seated with his wife and three children, beckoning to him. He saluted and approached.

"We're almost finished here, corporal, so you can have this table. . . . Oh, this is my wife." Señora Jiménez was a short, pale woman. The three children—the eldest about four years old, the middle one and the baby, less than a year old—were all blondes. "Are those your people?" he asked, nodding toward them.

"Yes, sir, some of them."

"You mean there are more?"

"In Zaragoza, yes, sir; two people. They're kind of what you'd call—well, I don't know how to say it in Spanish—not exactly padrinos, but—"

"Padres adoptivos—something like that?"

"That's exactly it; thank you, sir."

A couple at the adjoining table bustled up. "Take that one," Jiménez suggested.

Gilberto introduced them. "Captain Jiménez, my commanding officer, and the señora-his-wife; the señora-my-aunt and her husband, Don Lorenzo Aguilar y Esquivel, and Señorita Inés María Reyes—"

"Don't tell me you're married already, corporal!"

Gilberto blushed furiously. "No, sir, it just happens the name is the same. We're about fifth cousins."

Jiménez laughed and said in English, "Don't apologize. She's a knockout."

The waitress, on her own, pushed both tables together, and Gilberto was about to tell her to leave them apart, as they were, when Jiménez said, "That's fine. Let's have some beer." He called past Gilberto to Pelancha, "Do you know what I said to this boy in English?"

"No, señor capitán."

"That your daughter was very beautiful—you can listen, too, señorita— and I don't blame him for wanting to get married as soon as he gets out of the service."

Inés's face took fire, and Gilberto came near to actually hating Jiménez;

Lorenzo, too, for grinning that way. "And now that I see the novia," Jiménez continued, "I don't see how he can wait that long. . . . What is your opinion, señora?"

"With the captain's permission—" Gilberto blurted. The bastard! Where the hell does he get off butting in like this! The regulations don't give him any authority to—

"I was speaking to the señora, corporal."

"If they know their minds," she said calmly. "If his duties under the captian permit—"

"Ah! So you've made me the villain, eh, Reyes?" the captain said. "Well, I'll fix that. Any time after June the First, with getting married as his purpose, I'll see that he gets a ten-day furlough. . . . How do you like that, Reyes?"

"I thank the captain," Gilberto scowled, and under his breath he said, "Son of a bitch!"

Jiménez roared. "I heard that, corporal," he said in English. "But I don't think you meant it." He made it worse by remarking, "It seems that I am embarrassing my corporal; something I wouldn't do if I didn't like him." Although he said that directly to Inés, Pelancha and her husband beamed with pleasure.

"Don Solomón will ask," Lorenzo said, "and he will be told of this."

"That's the padre adoptivo of the corporal, eh?"

"You may say of all of us, captain," Lorenzo answered.

The beer came to the table and Gilberto began drinking his quickly, afraid that Jiménez might start a round of toasts.

Charitably, Jiménez changed the subject. He knew something of the Zaragoza valley; he had hunted jabalí, wild pig, there with some officers. Their host on the hunt had been Colonel Carrasco.

The faces of Mexicans have a way of going stony, but at the same time, their eyes take on a fire which belies that calm. "You know him, I see," Jiménez said. "Well, we won't talk about him. His kind are on the way out."

"Ojalá," Lorenzo said.

"If I ever retire, that's the country I'd like to settle down in." Jiménez looked at his wife. "¿Eh, vida? A few hectares of grassland to raise colts on. . . . Oh, well, it's nice to think about."

Señora Jiménez leaned toward Pelancha. "He dreams. But we are both from army families." She looked lovingly at her youngest child. "I am happy to have only daughters."

The captain got his check and began the bustle of herding his family out. It was then that Gilberto became aware that the officer had had a lot to drink; the way he swallowed two bottles of beer to drown a thirst brought on by some stronger stuff, his swaying as he stood up, and the careless way he wadded his change into his pocket were signs of that. His wife bowed politely to everybody and started out with the youngsters. The captain, however, made his goodbye more elaborate, shaking hands with everybody except

Gilberto. Then he began staring at Inés fixedly and without smiling. Somewhat frightened for her, Gilberto took her hand. It was cold, and it amazed him that she kept her head up and her eyes directly on Jiménez as he spoke. "Maybe you know this lad better than I do, guapa, but I think you're going to do all right with him, just as he's doing for me. And you might as well know— it's as good as official—that your man's going to make sergeant in a few months. And if he doesn't get his commission a year after that, I swear I'll break him to the rear ranks." He hiccuped, said "Excuse me," and looked from one face to the other, slowly, in turn. He seemed to have lost the thread of what he was saying, but only for a moment. "Oh, yes—" he resumed. "After his hitch, he wants to go to college at the government's expense—the Instituto Tecnológico—and get to be, of all things, an ingeniero agrónomo."

"An engineer of *what?*" Lorenzo interrupted.

"Never mind! If he picked it, it's good. . . . That boy—" his finger weaved and found Gilberto, "is going places! And you, chula," he tapped her shoulder, "you're too pretty to get left behind."

Gilberto thought she would cringe when Jiménez touched her, but not a quiver. With a curt, "¿Permiso?" the captain turned and strode out. The clink of the loose change in his pockets sounded like spurs. Just the right kind of sound effect for that payaso—that clown—Gilberto cursed silently. . . . *My* captain! Going and spilling his guts like this in front of people. It wasn't the drinks alone; he'd seen him a lot drunker and more on his dignity. . . . Having a guy over to his house a couple of nights a week; taking an hour going over his reports, then spending two more pumping him, fanning the breeze about life and things like that. He never was interested in anything that happened in the past; not five years ago, or even a year, or yesterday, for that matter. And he knew what was going to happen tomorrow—that was all scheduled. What Jiménez kept coming back to in all of those talks was always: when a man gets to be 30 years old, what's the best kind of life he could pick out for himself; something he'd be happy in and wouldn't want to change when he got to be 35, 40, 60?

His whole motive was pretty simple now. No mystery. Jiménez was 29, and to quote his wife, "He dreams. We are both from army families. I am happy to have only daughters." . . . Nothing could be clearer: Jiménez wanted out! Like most men around his age do, and *should*. Maybe even old-timers like Colonel Galindo—who can tell? Sergeant Meneses? No. With him, the army was a job at which he was better than any man on the post, major officers included. No illusions. He used to say, "There's the Art of War," and point to a pile of manure you couldn't see over. "The Art of War is what they worked out in the Roman times when they were always crossing Rubicons and stuff. We, we're not crossing anything." But suppose *they* invade *us?* "Let 'em come. It'll be the same as with the Spanish Conquest. They kill till they're tired and leave just a few of us alive. And that's where they make their mistake. Look around and what do you see? Mexicans! More of them every time you turn around. At least I'm doing my best."

What had been foaming anger at Jiménez, now simmered as irritation; resentment for the way he took the whole play away from him. It wasn't bad enough blabbing out the things Don Solomón and the others should rightly be hearing from Gilberto himself, first; things like bucking for sergeant, the prospect of a commission, and a government scholarship to the Instituto Tecnológico. It was possible that Tía and Lorenzo and Inés didn't understand some of the army terms like "making sergeant," "hitch," and being "broken." But it was pretty clear when he talked about Inés—laid his whole proposal on the line; practically telling her in so many words what a big mistake she'd be making if she didn't grab this prize-package. Saying right out in front of her and everybody those things that a man looks forward to saying himself, in person, at the right time and the right place.

The man's whole behavior puzzled Gilberto, and he groaned, "How do you like *that* for a commanding officer!" It was a mocking complaint, and he expected no answer. But Pelancha said instantly, "Is he so proud of all his men as he is of you, Gilberto?"

"Huh?" This was a new slant on the thing. Maybe Tía Pelancha was right. After all, Jiménez had gone out of his way to pick him to run the literacy show, and he had come through so far, that is. "Did it seem that way to you, Inés?"

She faced him and said, "Yes, Gilberto; he is your good friend."

"And no enemy to you, either, Inesita," Lorenzo smiled.

The fife player's wife almost cheerfully brought them the news that there was scarecely anything left to eat. "The comida corrida has been eaten. Nothing left but some scraps; chicken wings, salad, a dish of guacamole which the idiot in the kitchen overlooked—things like that. I can make you a sandwich if there is bread. Not a drop of soup, and the cat has been into the fish."

"Well—" Gilberto muttered.

"Or," the waitress suggested, "I can run across to the stand on the corner and bring you back some tacos of young pork."

"No, no, no," Gilberto blurted. "Maybe we had better—"

"Look, Gilberto," Pelancha said. "It is already late, and the señor patrón of the hotel wishes eagerly that we shall relish the supper he will serve us at ten tonight."

"You have reason, vida," Lorenzo said. "If that fish tastes as he described it—and the other things—I wish to do them honor. You, too. Inesita."

"I do not have hunger, Don Lorenzo, thank you."

"You see! Speak to her, Gilberto. Doña Elena *orders* that she eat!"

"Sí, hija," her mother chided quietly and explained to Gilberto. "All this child has had since this morning was a chop and a knuckle of venison, which we brought from home."

The knuckle of a deer sounded like a substantial hunk of meat to Gilberto, but he touched her arm, and smiling, though trying to look stern, he said, "You'll have to do better than that."

He ordered tortillas and guacamole, a piquant spread of mashed avocado; sandwiches, when the waitress remembered that a ham lay in the ice box; and coffee.

There was a large bowl of green chile sauce, and when the sandwiches came, Pelancha and Inés ate theirs, but Lorenzo removed the meat and rolled it into elaborate tacos, laced with the fiery sauce. "Simply as an aperitivo, children," he said, between bites. "What a sadness, Gilberto, that you cannot sit with us to that fish."

"Yes—thank my captain that I'm Non-Commissioned Officer in Charge of Quarters tonight, and I have to be back at nine. Everybody else has until midnight. *That's* how proud he is of me." He scowled, but not without humor.

The women consulted whisperingly with the waitress and left the table. Lorenzo leaned eagerly toward him, saying, "You must make the most of the little time you have; you will take the girl walking—to the cine, if you like."

"It's proper to ask her mother if I may, no?"   .

"Sí," said Lorenzo slowly. "That is the custom. But I courted Pelancha alone."

Gilberto smiled. "I remember. Still, I think she would like to come to the cine with us."

Lorenzo glanced hurriedly behind him and said rather plaintively, for him, "As among men, Gilberto, listen to me. This voyage here, of us from Zaragoza, has more than one function—"

"A commission for Don Solomón."

"Nothing—the simple delivery of a few papers to the post office and the recovery of another." Lorenzo faltered slightly. "It is also for us—for Pelancha and me—in the nature of a luna de miel, as the thing is spoken of. . . . The children are always about, and Pelancha being a woman of great reticencia—"

"I see what you mean, Lorenzo. You wish—"

Lorenzo looked relieved, volubly delighted that Gilberto understood him. "I told you Spaniards have no soul! Putting me in one room, and my wife and her daughter together in a matrimonio as soft as moss. Now if it had been you—"

"Okay, okay," Gilberto said curtly.

"But your time will come."

"I said forget it!"

Inés did not ask where they were going, and Gilberto deliberately did not tell her. But when they reached the photographer's studio, she slowed beside him. They stopped between the display cases of pictures in the narrow entrance. "What's the matter, Inés?"

"Must I, now?"

"When is a better time?"

"When I do not look like this."

He smiled and said, "And how do you *think* you look?" She looked away and her finger touched the faint scar near her eye. "That's nothing," he said. "A little powder and it won't show."

Her eyes roamed the case of photos, most of them of girls. "Can I be made to look as pretty as these?"

"*Made* to look? You're prettier than any of them. . . . You're beautiful." He said that slowly and softly, and while looking at her until she smiled.

The stairs were narrow, and she walked up ahead of him. Her back was straight, and she did not touch the treads with her heels. The backs of her shoes were slightly scuffed; they were Doña Elena's. So was the dress of soft, gray jersey with the white collar of ribbed linen. She had no stockings on, and her legs were brown satin that shimmered as the long muscles of the calves tightened.

Upstairs, in the studio, he gave her his own comb to fix her hair, and the woman who assisted the photographer told her to put on some lip rouge. Inés looked helplessly at Gilberto and said, "Lipstick? I do not have any. I have never—"

"One can see that," the woman said. "The true blood is more beautiful, chula, but shows pale on a photograph. Here, let me fix you."

The crimson glistened and looked moist as she sat down on a piano stool under the photographer's lights. "Bend slightly forward, señorita; look past me, and—"

Gilberto smiled to her from behind the camera and her teeth gleamed for an instant. "¡Encantado!" the photographer said. "Step down, please."

"I hope you got that, maestro."

The man looked scornfully at Gilberto as he snapped a new plate into the back of the camera and said, "And one of you, sir?"

"Certainly. And when will they be ready?"

"In one hour," the man said and left to deliver the exposed plate to the darkroom.

"Then," Gilberto said to Inés, "we'll take one together. If I have only yours, the men—people—they will not believe that you are—, that you and I—, that you're my novia."

"If you believe it, Gilberto," she said quietly, "must other men know?"

"Just me, then. I want to be able to see us together; to have a picture of what it will be like when we are together for truth."

"I have that for a dream." She wanted to say more. Her quick breathing expanded the space between the smooth mounds of her breasts. To lay his cheek there—

"Gilberto—"

"Okay, corporal, let's take both of you together. You sit here, señorita, like this. And you, señor, stand next to her, slightly to one side; one hand touching each of the young lady's shoulders, as though you were helping her on with her coat. Or better still, as if you were about to give her a sweet kiss."

46

Twilight, dusk. Nice words; the lips alone can form them and they can be heard. And in soft castellano, in the hour when gray velvet spreads taut from swollen dome to dome of San Luis Potosí's churches, the words can be felt upon the eyes. Nochecita, little night; entre dos luces, between two lights: the light of day and the light of night.

They had walked by themselves, but not alone, in a country where lovers walk all the time, with their eyes on the stars and their arms around each other. When they grow tired, they stand on the street as if in a glade shimmering with flowers, the loved one between the lover's knees; veiled by unguessable dreams, tasting the sweetness of each other.

It must be, Gilberto thought, these potosino kids were too broke to take their girls to the movies. Well, he had the dough, so why didn't he take Inés? Maybe the answer was the same for these fellows and girls as for him: he didn't *need* the movies. Why buy three lousy pesos' worth of fantasy when you've got the real thing in your hands?

When he stopped earlier to buy Inés a silver ring set with an opal, he hurriedly picked the biggest—22 pesos—so that the halt would be briefer. They were walking again when he put it on her finger. It would have pleased him quite as much to have bought the ring while strolling, the way he bought the ice cream cones, with the vendor trotting beside him.

The opal wasn't her birthstone; she was seventeen in January—garnet. October was opal, or was it? Once, and it wasn't so long ago, he could reel that right off; the same with the top ten batting averages of the National, American, and Coast Leagues. All of that was just information, facts. And, he realized, information alone was useless until you're asked for it. *Knowing* was something else, not merely pat answers to direct questions. Knowing wasn't all in the head; it meant *feeling*, too, and the thinking-out of things that never get to a final definition. Something like the woodchuck-could-chuck-wood jingle ran through his mind: Knowing is knowing what you want to know, knowing you can't know it for sure.

But nothing, he recognized, was frozen in positive sureness. Not even me. I'm 20 now and I'm not the same guy I was when I was 19. The package looks the same, but what's in it has shifted. You don't feel it, but you know there's been a rearrangement of the stock. Then it seems like the one thing you *can* be sure of is that the same thing—that rearrangement—is happening to everybody else. To Inés.

Four times in their walk they circled the area between the two plazas, although there were other places to go; there were "sights," fireworks a half mile back from the big cathedral. But like children who had just moved into a new neighborhood, they remained in sight of the Edificio del Estado.

Their arms touched from the shoulder to the fingers, and sometimes, by timid design, their legs along the thighs. Random street lights sprang on, and Gilberto guided Inés across a busy avenue to a stone bench in front of the Carmen Church. In the Plaza de Armas, behind them, there had been frenzied putting-to-bed of the bird colony. Here, the pigeons, drumming their way home, entered their apartments in the carvings high above the church doors and settled down.

Inés kept turning the ring on her finger and he remembered what made him pick the opal. It had the same oily gleam as that unreflected yellow dividing the blue and green tiles on the dome of the church. He pointed this out to her, and she said, "Yes, Gilberto," without looking away from his lips.

"I can always see this church, at least the roof, from the barracks," he said. "And you can look at the ring and remember how we sat here, and the lights going on."

"I shall wear it on a blue ribbon I have."

"Is it too loose on your hand?"

"Not for that. Until you come back home, Gilberto, the ring is only for me to see. . . . When?"

"June, the middle of June, when my class graduates."

Her fingers curled secretly in reckoning. "So many, many days that is."

"Count it by months, that way it is shorter."

"For Don Solomón and Doña Elena, for—" Gilberto waited for her to say, "For me." Instead, she finished, "For all of us, they will be long months."

He meant then to say to her that they are working him very hard in the Company, but that he is not griping. It was all going to pay off—everything that Captain Jiménez said already and said better, right from the feed box. He groped for something that Jiménez may have left out. . . . Well, not much. The only thing he didn't *quite* say for him was, "Inés, I love you."

That was something he would have to say for himself. But *when?* Why should it be so hard to turn it into words? It wasn't that they were stuck in his throat; it was deep down and locked up in one leaden box after another and then in a capsule, like U-235—that's how precious it was. And that's how he meant it. Why had he been able to say, "I love you," over and over again to Carolyn Muller and *without* meaning it? Looking back over the time, how *could* he have meant it?

"I know," he said suddenly. "I'll make it seem shorter. I'll write twice, three times a week. . . . Your picture—"

He put her portrait and his fountain pen on the wide cement arm of the bench. "Then I will write something on my picture for you" he said and smiled. "If you still want it—?"

"Más que nada." More than nothing. But that is how they say more than anything in castellano, and the idea amused Gilberto.

"Please," he said, uncapping the fountain pen for her.

"I beg you not to look," Inés said, and turning aside, wrote for some minutes. He looked, meanwhile, at the people who were passing. When she finished, she turned the photograph face down and handed him the fountain pen.

"When I write what I wish to say, we will look at the pictures together. All right with you, Inés?"

She looked frightened and doubtful, then nodded. He wrote rapidly and neatly across the bottom of the photograph, where it was lightest: "A Inés, mi querida novia, con todo mi cariño. 5 de febrero de 1953." That much—To Inés, my darling bride, sweetheart, girl, or any way anybody wants to read it, with all my love—he knew he was going to write, even before he touched the pen to paper. Then, after writing the date, he made a dash and added, "y siempre—and always—, Gilberto." This touch pleased him. He waved it to dry the ink, and handing it to Inés, reached for hers. She held it tightly, but he slid it out of her fingers.

The handwriting was better, clearer than the newly literate scrawl he was prepared to see, and he read: "Gilberto, por siempre jamás en mi corazón. Inés María Reyes." He repeated it to himself, in English: Gilberto, for always never—that being the way they say forever in Spanish—in my heart. He sensed there was something finer in this simple sentence than in what he had written, *with* its trick ending. He read it again and saw why. That she had not written *To* Gilberto, as he had *To* Inés, made hers more than a personal pledge; it was a declaration to the world—to everybody in it and his brother.

"I am happy with what you have written, Inés."

"When I read what you say to me," she said, "I feel ashamed for what I put down."

"But you mean it, as I do."

"You wrote of yourself, Gilberto." She touched his picture, then pointed to her own. "And that is what I have practiced over and over to write."

"I would not want anything else. . . . Don't you see, we wrote practically the same thing, but yours *means* more."

Night came on a gentle breeze which retired as soon as it tucked the dark around them. Then a light directly above their bench shattered the opaque blue shell. It parted, also, the complete but frangible silence which they had built around themselves. Now they could hear the band music which everybody else in San Luis Potosí, the capital, had been hearing for almost a half-hour.

They walked to the plaza, trippingly, to the music of "The Hunter and His Dog." Tu-*weet* tu whu-whu tu *wheep*-tu-whee—and Gilberto wondered if the waitress's fifer was playing that whistling obbligato.

They sat down, facing the band. They were novios. They did not have to walk, boys and girls separately, around and around, in separate circles, clock-

and counter-clockwise. The music, although it did not make the promenaders change their pace, sublimated this to a sort of courtship-dance. Gilberto remembered his movies: *In Darkest San Lewis Patoosi, the native men, called* hombrays, *pick their future mates among the tribal beauties, known as* m'chachers, *in this dance, rarely seen by the white man. . . .*

"Something makes you grave, Gilberto?"

"I was thinking."

"Is one permitted to know—of me?"

The music was extremely loud, but he knew what she asked him because her lips stayed parted and her expression of frank anxiety. "Not of you, Inés—not then—" It was hard to hear. Her frown showed, but she did not move closer, and kept on turning the opal on her finger. Less gently than he meant to do, he stopped her play. "But now I am thinking of you, Inés; thinking of how I'm in love with you."

She heard him—over the brass and the blare his voice sounded thunderous in his own skull—and she looked up when he felt fire rush from her hand into his. She said, "I also, Gilberto, with you—if I may."

The dial of his watch leapt at him. A quarter after eight! It was a 25 minute haul in the bus back to the post, a ten minute sprint back to the Virreal. No margin— "I must talk to your mother before I go. . . ."

They filled the little antesala of the hotel when they came in, and Lorenzo and Pelancha sprang from their places on the bamboo settee.

"Qué mi—" Lorenzo began.

"Excuse me," Gilberto broke in. "I have very little time. I must say something to you, Tía."

The woman's eyes widened, but for an instant only. They were half-lidded when she turned coolly to Inés and said, "Say goodbye to Don Gilberto and go to your room."

"Sí, mamacita." She put out her hand to Gilberto and the opal glowed on it. "Adiós, Gilberto."

He took it, and holding it, he leaned forward and kissed her quickly on the lips. It was long enough only to know that their thinness and coolness would not always be that way.

She left without looking back.

"Tía Esperanza, I wish to—, I have the honor—"

"We know—" Lorenzo began in the face of his wife's glare.

"You, too, Lorenzo. Andale." Beat it, she meant.

He turned, and in the doorway leered back and called, "Adiós—yerno."

"Now, tell me, hijo—"

"I—, I wish— he fumbled. "I shouldn't have—, I need more time—"

"I am here." Her voice was thick.

He was calmer. "It is not fair to tell you in the few minutes that I have left before—"

"Then in the name of God, say it quickly!" she flung at him, white and shaking.

All right, he decided; he'd miss this bus and put on as good an act as he could by roaring up in a cab—overdue, but eager.

"Then, Tía Esperanza, this is what I wish to ask of you." No need to hurtle along now, he told himself as he paused; take it easy and say all you want to say, but say it nice. "You do not know me for such a long time, or as much about me as a girl's mother is entitled to. I don't have any family, as you know, but from the day I got here—I mean, in Zaragoza—I never once felt alone."

Pelancha's head dropped, and it seemed to him that she was crying. Anything I said? he wondered. "It's still the same, only more. How should I say it? The thing is, Tía, well, in addition to me *belonging*—being taken care of by people all along the way—I want somebody that belongs to *me*, whom I can take care of. And that somebody happens to be Inés. . . . You just saw— well, we're novios, Inés and I." He paused again. His chest and temples were running sweat. "And Tía, I came—, I want to ask your permission to marry her. I don't mean right away; I know she's too young yet. What I mean is when my hitch is over—my military discharge, or *whenever*." He heard himself shouting the rest of it: "And if not, I want to know what objections you have!"

That was how he meant it, too; straight and challenging. But pity subdued him as he saw her, bent over the counter, the rebozo over her face, and sobbing. He touched her gently on the shoulder. "Did I say anything? I'm sorry. . . . I don't want you to feel this way. . . . If you're worried—"

"You, who brought light into our house—"

He barely heard her. "I promise you, Tía, I'll be as good to her—"

She straightened up so suddenly that he stopped, and when she turned slowly to face him, the tears were still there, but her eyes were clear. She put her arms out, and the rebozo draped around them made a little tent over him.

"She is yours, Gilberto, when you want her. She has been yours from the first day—none other's. Know that!"

He nodded in the warm dark of her arms. "Sure, I know it."

"Now go to your work!" She pushed him almost roughly away from her.

Except for two sleepers—Lozano, enfermo, and Cuevas, confinado—the barrack room was empty.

"I'm leaving," Sergeant Navarro said. "I'm in that domino tournament over in the armorer's shack. Castro relieves you at midnight, but he'll probably roll in stinking and you'll have to stay on the job. . . . How was the parade downtown?"

"Great—I loved it," Gilberto answered.

"You would!" Navarro pointed to the wire basket on the desk. "Stuff to be posted, and some mail for the rack outside."

Mail! Gilberto slapped his pocket for that letter Lorenzo gave him hours ago. But he withdrew, instead, the picture of Inés. The letter could wait. "How do you like this, Navarro?"

"Hmm—like a mango," the sergeant judged, and read the inscription in a falsetto. "Gilberto, forever in my heart, Inés María Reyes.". . . Why don't you make it *de* Reyes while you're about it?"

"I'm going to. She's my novia."

"Yah, yah, I know," Navarro mocked. "You buy those pictures for a tostón apiece and write in your own name."

"You think so? Have a look at this." He showed the picture of the two of them together. "And it's not posed, either, that's her natural smile."

"It looks like you've got something there, boy. . . . See you in the morning. So long."

Now for that letter. He studied the blurred postmark under the desk light and made out only the letters, widely spaced, N E A, and the date, 26 Ene 53. . . . Now who in Christ's name—Bishop! That's who it must be! Old Bish, the only one he had written to who *could* answer from this side of the border.

He tore across the edge of the envelope and took out two sheets of thin paper, closely typed, with the same small letters as on the envelope. There was still some hardened glue on the top edges, where they had been torn from a pad. In the top-right corner, he read, "Ensenada, Baja Calif., México, Jan. 25, 1953." He jumped from there to the signature: Sam Eisen.

How did this come to happen? He had never written to Dr. Eisen. He had *meant* to, sure. It was all framed, practically word for word, in his head. He remembered how it began: "Dear Dr. Eisen: As you can see—"

But after that, what? There was not a single sentence of it that he could bring back, but he knew that he was sore about something Doc did. Or maybe it was something he *didn't* do. . . . Ensenada—less than 200 miles from the center of Los Angeles—full of tourists and getting to be more like Tijuana all the time. No reason why Doc Eisen shouldn't be in that mob. No problem getting across there. Not for a guy who was just going down for a shot of tequila and coming right back again to 2663 Wilshire Boulevard, Suite 516, L.A. 36, Cal.

The paper rattled in his fingers and he put the sheets face down on the table. A cigarette. His lips felt like blubber around it, and it took two matches to light; the first broke in his fingers. He asked himself: What's the smartest thing to do; burn it, or read it? What do you mean *smartest!* What you really want to know actually is what's the least chicken. You saw that it began, "Dear Gil," and not, "Dear Sir," or "My Dear Mr. Reyes." Anyway—burn it! And who'll know that for one minute you went gutless so that for the rest of your life you won't be raked over, which this letter is liable to do? What could Eisen want anyway, besides showing how cute he was by remembering the name of a town in the State of S.L.P.? So burn it, you schmuck! And see the last bridge between the Here and the There, and the Now and the Then, turn into black ashes. So he was a white gringo—one simpático norteamericano! So what?

He lit another match, watching it arch upward like an aspiring penis, fading to the orange-red glow that burns in the heart of an opal—and die. He turned the letter over and read:

> The day you walked out of my office about four months ago, I figured the chances of my ever hearing from you again at 100 to 1. A couple of weeks later, something happened that brought it down to 10 to 1. That something was the FBI, who came to ask me a lot of questions about you. It seems you've got plenty of company, lad— 66,000 since the start of the Korean business. I would have guessed less, but I'm giving you the official War Dep't. figures, plus about 50,000 more (also official) who changed their minds after they were in uniform.

Gilberto pulled his eyes away from the paper. If that was Eisen's whole purpose, to heckle him, what was the use of going any further? It was like getting a notice from one of those collection agencies. "Regarding your bill of So-and-so dollars and 32 cents, blah-blah—" It hits you at a time you can't pay it; and if you could, you wouldn't want to. So you read only that far. But—

> Having had some experience with these jerks, I got more information out of him than he got from me. For one thing, that you skipped across the border at Laredo without tourist papers. They're sure that after a time the Mexican authorities are going to catch up with you and you will flop back in their arms; especially so, since I told them you were broke. Incidentally, how is that $400 holding out? If it's gone, I hope you put it to good use, such as getting yourself fixed up with some kind of papers. But if you need funds, let me know immediately c/o Hotel Príncipe, Ensenada, B.C. I'm here every weekend. A better idea would be to wire me collect.

This was no credit agency letter! This was somebody who already settled his account, telling him, "Look, you may be on their books, but you don't owe them a thing. They won't write it off, so you just forget it."

> The fact is, I had been hoping to hear from you before this, but it is just as well. I have known the mail carrier in my building for 15 years, but there are many people whom I have known longer—well, you get what I mean. But to go back to the way the odds fell, here's the story: There was a doctor I knew in Europe, even worked with for a time in Spain, who once talked about going to San Luis Potosí—city or state—where he had a married sister. I couldn't recall his name, but found it finally in a batch of notes I had made for a book that I had been intending to write. Finding the name,

Kurt Zumbach, refreshed the whole character and personality of the man. At this point, you're probably well ahead of my story, but let me tell it my way. I need the practice for when I start writing my book. I got Zumbach right on the telephone beside me in this room. I simply said, "I wish to speak with Dr. Kurt Zumbach in San Luis Potosí." And in less than 10 minutes I had him. Like myself, he was weak on names. But "Zaragoza" was the key, and he described you perfectly. Between his bad English and my worse Spanish, I made out something about a rape, and I thought for a minute that you'd turned sex fiend on me.

Very funny! Not Dr. Eisen; he didn't know. But that fat bastard making jokes about—

However, he set me straight and said that the whole story would have to come from you—a matter of ethics. By the way, Gil, this Zumbach is quite a character. Used to be a Lutheran minister, but he gave it up because, to quote him, "he now believes in Christ." You ought to look him up if he's anywhere near and make friends with him. You can talk about me as a common subject. Ask him what he thinks of antibiotics now—he was strictly a sulfathiazole man himself in dealing with staphyloccal infections. Make that read "staphylococcal."

Sure, look him up. I owe him an apology, too, Gilberto admitted to himself, for the way I flew off the handle that day. He must be all right if Doc Eisen says so.

That's a natural error for a doctor whose practice is leaking away, little by little, principally because I want to retire, an aim in which I am being helped along by a couple of hospital boards who won't let me set foot in their lazar houses until I sign a loyalty oath. I told them to carve it on a pineapple and shove it. I realize at this point that I'm just rambling on, but you'll have to forgive me, Gil. I'm getting so I like to write, and there are fewer and fewer people to whom I *can* write. It's begun to replace talking with me, and frankly, I used to be quite a talker—not a conversationalist, just a talker. But it's getting hard to find a listener. And as for people answering back, there just aren't any. I tell you, lad, something has them scared shitless. They know what it is, too, but they don't want to talk about it. And when you mention it, you find yourself suddenly alone.

That's right; that's what Bishop said, too. Ask a question and you get, "Leave me out of it." Try to give them *your* opinion, and it's, "Excuse me, I got a date." It was certainly true, as he thought, back there in Matamoros, that Doc and Bish would get along fine.

My wife and her mother have gone to Europe, early enough to get good seats for the Coronation, and I started coming down here on weekends. Lately, I've stretched those from Thursday-to-Monday, occasionally Tuesday. This is as far as I can go without a passport, which document I can't get. Maybe it's because I talk too much. And now I'm writing too much, at least in this instance, where the chances are still 2 to 1 that this doesn't catch up with you. Anyway, I should be asking you how you are, what you are doing, and are you safe, and reminding you, incidentally, that if you're in any trouble that money can get you out of, a wire collect is the quickest way. You may not want to answer any of those things; still, I would appreciate knowing if you got this. A postal card will do, simply saying, "Nice to hear from you, wish you were here, etc." Anything.

Don't kid yourself, Doc—you'll hear. Not anything, as you put it, but *everything*.

I almost forgot—an item that ought to interest you: The name of Reyes has gotten a lot of prominence in your old home town. It started at that new housing development put up by an insurance company out by Baldwin Hills. One morning the whole side of the main apartment building was painted "REYES WAS HERE!" It took them a week to paint it out. Pretty soon it began to pop up on new apartment houses all over town. I should have stuck in a clipping about it, with a picture showing "REYES WAS HERE!" in the wet cement completely around one of these places. Big mystery! Who's Reyes?! When all it means is that the Reyeses built these places, they can work in them as sweepers, now why can't they live in them? Let's hear from you pronto. As ever, Sam Eisen.

¡Pronto y prontísimo! Ahora mismo and right this minute! Gilberto took the dust cover off the typewriter and went to his locker for the paper and envelope. He rolled a sheet into the machine. Regulations or no regulations, this was the paper he was going to use. Jiménez didn't count the sheets when he told him to keep it handy for any reports that may be needed. What a start old Doc Eisen'll get when he's handed the envelope with the army insignia on it and "Cuartel General, 12a Zona Militar." And it will rock him back on his heels when he opens it.

In the blanks for the filing data, the first line required a number, *Expediente Nº*. Without hesitation, he typed in #23328-37 and wondered if he had gotten it right. Anyway, right or wrong, it was somewhere along the road to Ciudad del Maíz in tiny pieces.

Date. He wrote it Mexican-style: 5 de febrero de 1953. *From.* The works! Cabo (Corporal) Gilberto Reyes M., Compañía A, 7° Regimiento de Caballería. *To.* Dr. S. Eisen. *Subject.* Personal.

"*Dear Doc Eisen:*" . . . Now what? He lit a cigarette, and staring at the solitary line, he thought, I've got plenty to say; my skull is busting with things to tell him—him or anybody else, interested or not—just for the pleasure of putting them down in words. But how do you begin? . . . What's the matter with:

As you can see from the above, it gives the answer to the main question as to what I'm doing and how I'm doing—

Should he go on and tell how he made cabo in less than six weeks, asking no favors? No; no bragging.—*and I hope you're not disappointed that I wound up wearing a uniform after all, which now, after thinking it over, you tried like anything to talk me out of.*

Wrong. True, but this isn't quite the way to start off a letter to somebody who, the first thing in his own letter, wants to know how you are fixed for money, with the idea of sending you some. Mention that, but come back to the other thing about that last day in his office.

The $400 you are so kind to ask about I can tell you is not only holding out, but it has built up to where I will have quite a bundle by the time I'm out of the army.

Tell him how? How Don Solomón is giving me a share of all the business he does with the growers, and even giving *them* a better break than they had with Carrasco? That would mean starting from the beginning when he walked through the iron door into the Surtidor.

It's invested. But going back to what I started out to say re being in uniform, a couple of times I started to write you a letter, but now I'm glad I didn't, not only for the reason you state, i.e., they might be checking your mail. The thing is, the day after my mother died and we had that talk, I stood there hoping and praying that you would TELL *me what to do. You* NEVER DID, *or maybe I was just too dumb to catch on. When I left, I didn't know where I was going or what to do, except that I was not answering that induction call. I still didn't know when I got here to México (by way of Brownsville, not Laredo; they're all wet). Only after I'd been here, I came out of the fog and some of the* REASONS *for what I was doing began to shape up. Here and there they matched up with the things you told me, such as what Rights a man had, etc. But more things got added as I went along. Mainly, that this idea of Man becomes* MEN *(and I don't mean only machos*

He didn't like the way the word sounded, even on paper. Certainly it means male, just as hembra means female, but Doc knew some Spanish and he didn't want him to get the wrong idea. He x'd out macho.

males). And Men becomes People, and that seems to count down here as I think it should every place. I don't know, Doc, if I'm getting this across clear enough. I may be able to explain it better after I've read more, but you learn as much from the people around you as out of books and magazines. People write those, too, but sometimes it doesn't sound like it.

Nor does this, he thought, sound like anything I might have written a year ago—or four months ago, for that matter. And I'm glad I didn't try! I'd have got off a letter full of cry-baby alibis about "nobody-loves-me" and "from here on in I'm strictly on my own. See?"

As you can see, Doc., I'm in this man's army and it was my idea strictly, with my eyes open. Why and how is another story, which will have to hold. To bring you up to date: Since making corporal, I've been assistant to the Capt.-in-charge of the Regimental Alfabetización (literacy) Program and teaching my own class of 32 enlisted men. Not that we expect to put all those public escribientes out of work with one fell swoop, but the men are doing great.

Tell him about the sergeantcy coming up? The conditional enrollment in the Instituto Tecnológico? No, save that. Don't tell everything in one single letter. If Eisen likes to write as he says—and he's got something there—save something for later. It was getting late, anyhow. The men were rolling in, and if he didn't finish pretty soon, the typing would disturb their sleep. Cuevas, confined-to-quarters, had been the only man so far to make a complaint. But he excused himself when he saw the printed top of the paper. "I'm sorry, cabo, I didn't know it was official."

"What did you think?"

"Oh, I thought it was a love letter. I heard you were engaged."

"Where did you get that?"

"Oh, it's all over the post," Cuevas said. "I hear you got something quite appetizing. You going to tack her up so the boys can—"

"Get out of here before I tack you up—with a bayonet!"

It may sound funny to you, Doc, but personally I get a great kick out of seeing men who, not so long back, didn't know an A from a Z now beginning to read and write, and it was me who taught them how.

"Me who taught them—" That wasn't right. It should be, "I who taught them." Maybe I ought to go back for a few lessons myself. . . .

I feel myself that I could write a book if I went back to scratch and put in all the things in the last few months, which seems like longer, since you saw me. It would have to run into pages because it's not only about me and what I did, but scads of people. Not only those I personally had to do with, but in a general way, if you get what I mean. All kinds of types that you see only a flash of, but who you can't get out of your mind because some way or the other they mixed themselves up in your life without their even knowing it. Take for instance one very old gent coming on board a bus with a bunch of flowers in his hands. What I mean is, when I think about that time, I swear the smell of them comes back to me just as real.

A fellow could keep on like this, and before you know it, he *would* have a book with all those characters strung out in an endless chain, all the way back and hooked up with other characters across the border. Skip Bishop—he's a book all by himself. . . . The head of Fidel Vargas in a basin of ice. Were the eyes open? Was it stuck in upright, lying on its face, or displayed like a cabeza de puerco in a delicatessen window? Anyhow, it's what brought him there that mattered. It was savage ignorance; his hatred of a book and a lamp to read it by. That's what did it for Vargas. The—, the *thing* against Inés was his way of showing it. . . . Better to forget Vargas altogether, and if any more of them show their hand, teach them, or— No! Teach them, no matter how much it hurts.

He did not know that Sergeant Meneses had come in until he bulked over the typewriter. If Meneses was drunk, he didn't show it. "What passes, kid?" he asked.

"What time is it?"

"It's twenty-three hours. . . . What *is* this, double duty? In-Charge-of-Quarters and making out a report at the same time?"

Meneses was okay; you could tell him the truth. "Frankly, sergeant, it's not anything official, but I'd like to finish it. Will it bother you?"

"No. Go ahead. I got a slight amount of mescal to sleep off; not enough to make me mean-tempered." Meneses smiled and lay down on his cot.

That's only one, and if you should ask me why him in particular, I'd be stuck for an answer. And the same goes for the rest of the above mentioned.

He turned to see if Meneses was frowning or anything at the sound of the machine. The sergeant was asleep, his lips in a pout, like a baby's. . . . Yeah, what I just wrote about an old man goes for babies, too. The country was just brimming with them—and the women likewise. Come to think of it, didn't Tía, sitting back there in the restaurant, have that comfortable cow-look of a woman that knows she's going to pop one? It's possible Lorenzo wants to hang up a record as good as that of the old guy with the trash cart in Matamoros. . . . The way you jump from old men to babies and back again. . . . That brown butterball on the way to Ciudad del Maíz, sucking titty and looking at him with its big eyes, as if knowing what It was all about. He wondered, did my mother ever lug me around like that, wiggling me around, showing me off, hungry for somebody to smile and say, "Ain't he cute!"

Being a doctor, Doc Eisen might be interested in hearing about Concha— maybe some other time, but not now. And if he did, later, he'd talk about her the way they wrote up cases in his own medical journals: "Miss C., age 14 (?), victim of—" or something like that. . . . Alvarez, with no starch and a jelly backbone; and you could see why. Once sweat got into his eyes in the cane field, and when he opened them, he had seen all the pain one man wants to see in a lifetime. How he must have loved that kid of his! And didn't Concha's mother; calling her every kind of tart in front of people, and then, when she thought nobody was around, hugging and crooning to her. "All kinds of types" he called them, as he looked back over what he had written. It was a mistake to do that. Nobody is a "type" really, except in pictures, regardless of whether they're in the *National Geographic* magazine or in the moving pictures. Once they step out of the page or off the screen and laugh, yawn, belch, wink, eat, say good morning, or scratch, they're no more than you or I, my boy. Certainly not to each other—or to me!

The way I look at it, Doc, a fellow like Vicente the local cop and Lorenzo, or The Sheik and Don Lucas, compared are not one less important than the other, only different in the way they affected me.

He changed "affected" to "effected" and, reading the sentence over, wondered if Eisen would know what he meant; or, did he himself know? The way to make it absolutely clear would be to say, "These people, whose names I took out of a hat, are mentioned to you, Dr. Eisen, as being of *some* importance to you in relation to what I, if anything, mean to you." But that was getting in deep.

But kindly leave that aside, as I am again talking in a general way. I could be more specific and tell you about Don Solomón (who happens to be an israelita, which is the way, including the small "i" they say a Jew here) and Doña Elena, his wife, but can't at present as there is too much to say in one letter about these people. Having the facilities here, namely typewriter, and depending on your reply, you will get a much fuller run-down on the afore-said.

The last few words on the line were wobbly, at the bottom of the sheet of paper. He resumed on a fresh one, after a glance at the slumbering Meneses.

Well, Doc, it seems like every time I start a new paragraph, I'm dragged back to trying to explain what I intend to do down here, not just for the time of my enlistment, that's pretty much settled, but after that. When I'm 30 instead of 20, and even past that. So as not to go around in a circle, I'll make this the last one for the time being and say that one of the things I'm going to do is get married—believe it or not!!! Remember the Inés that was mentioned in that letter by my aunt so-called? Well, sir, when the time comes, she will write her name Sra. Inés María R. de Reyes! By a coincidence, we got engaged this very afternoon; no function or anything like that, but official, just the same. But I'm due a furlough along about 2 June, at which time I am sure the folks in Zaragoza will want to "go to town" with a party and make it formal. Honest, Doc Eisen, I wish you could see her. Next to one other person—and I don't have to tell you who that is, my mother—

Sergeant Meneses's hand struck him lightly on the back of the neck. "Hey! It's midnight. The men are pouring in. Where's Castro?"

"He didn't report, sergeant. I'll check the men if you want."

Meneses frowned and pointed. "All done with this?"

"Just a few more lines."

"Go ahead and finish it. Give me the roster."

"Thanks, sergeant."

—who I want to wish me luck, knowing if you do, I can't miss. Please write soon. This being all, I remain Your True Friend who won't forget.

Now, four spaces for the signature and the address. Still plenty of room on the page to say more, *if* there was more to say, after reading the whole thing over.

Meneses was shouting, "You tiptoe past Corporal Reyes! You hear me, you oxen! You tiptoe, or I'll personally—"

P.S.: This is a lot more than the postal card you bargained for, eh, Doc? But the "wish you were here" part goes double, and I am serious about this. If you could see your way to make it down here on an honest to God PROFESSIONAL VISIT, *it is worth $4,225 (pesos) which I will send you by wire, in advance. This is a case of eye trouble dating back to the 1st W. War, not the last, and you, having been an army doctor, would know a great deal about. If the money isn't enough, I will go in hock for any amount you say, which is*